Nightlord:
Phoebe's Tale

From His

Shadow

By
Garon Whited

Thanks and appreciation to:

Channa

Other Books by Garon Whited:
Dragonhunters
LUNA
Nightlord, Book One: Sunset
Nightlord, Book Two: Shadows
Nightlord, Book Three: Orb
Nightlord, Book Four: Knightfall
Nightlord, Book Five: VOID
Nightlord, Book Six: Mobius
Nightlord, Book Seven: Fugue
Nightlord, Book Eight: Penumbra

Short Stories:
An Arabian Night: Nazin's Dream
Clockwork
Dragonhunt
Ship's Log: Vacuum Cleaver
The Power
The Ways of Cats

Copyright © 2022 by Garon Whited.
Cover Art: "Phoenix Rising" by Rachel C. Beaconsfield
ISBN: 978-0-578-28918-2

This is a work of fiction. Names, characters, places and incidents either are the product of the author's imagination or are used fictitiously, and any resemblance to any actual persons, living or dead, events, or locales is probably coincidental.

Secrets.

My whole life has been about secrets. Pop's enormous, world-shaking secrets. Our family's scary, peasant-angering secrets. My own secrets, as a little girl, as a young lady, as a grown woman—secrets on a more personal scale, but no less important to *me*. Even in a house full of psychics, no one has complete and total knowledge of another. We are all ourselves, not each other, and we have to be. Without our boundaries, we would not be individuals. Some boundaries are more extensive, some are more definite, and some are more open, but we all have boundaries of some sort to define our selves.

Sometimes I wonder if Pop ever pried into my secrets. When I was little, I'm sure he did. I was entirely his responsibility, so he had to know things. It goes with being a parent, I think—for a while. When he started to respect my judgment... no, when I started having good judgment, I had judgment he could respect, he stopped prying. He settled for asking. He started taking "No" for an answer instead of an opportunity to further my education.

Maybe that's how you know you're a grown-up. You have secrets nobody gets to know. Or maybe that's how you know someone loves you. You have secrets they let you keep. And if you love someone, you know which of your secrets to share and which secrets to bury.

My whole life has been about secrets. Knowing them, keeping them, ignoring them, and forgiving them.

How Does This Journal Thing Work?

I came home to say goodbye to Pop.

My house is in a 2060's New York, across the street from Riverside Park. This worked out really well for Gus and sometimes for Rusty. Gus is half Golden Retriever, half German Shepherd. He's a huge dog, made bigger by all the fluff. He has tags on his collar, a friendly demeanor, and an intelligence entirely too big to fit inside a doggie skull.

I would say I blame Pop for that last, but I have a hard time blaming him for anything.

Having a house across from the park meant Gus didn't have to stay at Pop's house—the one in 1950's Iowa—to play outside. It also meant Rusty had someplace convenient to go after the full moon went down. Originally, I had hoped to stealthily change from my Madison Building residence to the new place. I wanted to keep the watchers from knowing where I lived, but I don't think I did it sneakily enough. There are now mind-controlled homeless people watching both places. Someone also parked a flying camera drone on a building across 80th. It's been there for at least a week.

What bothers me about the drone is I don't know whose it is. Reverend Adam Alden is the psychic whosiwhatsis controlling the mindless horde of homeless, but he doesn't have a lot of experience with technology beyond the 1950s. Why would he have an up-to-date, 2060's version of a camera drone watching me? How would he even know to use one? And, if he has a psychic connection to his mindless minions, why would he bother? It makes me think there's someone else watching my house and I don't know who or why.

I don't like it. I kind of understand some of Alden's motives. I know he wants power, which means he wants Pop, which means he wants to use me to get to Pop. Who else would want to watch me? A peeping tom? None of the windows on that side of the house are bedrooms or bathrooms, and the drone's view is from much higher than the house. What does this leave? Someone interested in my rooftop? If I sunbathed up there, maybe. Or is there interest in my comings and goings, because I'm a hobbyist superheroine? Maybe.

The last thing I need is an unknown person sticking their nose into my personal business. I suppose I could shoot it, but then someone would be aware I'm aware of their surveillance and they'd try to be sneakier about it. Better to have one camera I know about than six I don't.

Hang on. Am I starting in the wrong place? I mean, I started to say how I came home and said goodbye to Pop. Should I start there and go on? It's so hard to tell with a journal. I mean, if this is to make sense, I have to pretend I'm telling someone who doesn't know how I got to this point, but there's one *hell* of a lot to go over before anything makes sense. Assuming it ever does. Life can be like that.

All right, I'll assume. This isn't for you; it's for me. If you don't understand, I apologize. Sometimes I don't, either, but that's why I'm writing a journal. You're not the only one who's going to have trouble keeping up. I'm trying to make sense of my life and you're coming along for the ride!

Okay, so, where does this leave me? Let me think.

Yesterday, I guess, or maybe all the way back to before I was born.

I'm probably on the high side of twenty-one years old. My age is a little indefinite because we kept switching calendars when we switched timelines. Regardless of my chronological uncertainty, I'm a grown woman, on my own, living in New York, with friends, allies, enemies, hobbies, and a project. Technically, I even have a job, if you count being a self-employed vigilante superhero witch.

I'm still ironing out the wrinkles, but it's a cool job description.

When I moved out of Pop's house and into this version of New York, Pop supported me. New York is a place for people with rich parents. He provided money, a car, my false identity, and my laptop. I didn't start out to be a vigilante superhero, but when it sort of just happened, Pop even went out and found me a sidekick.

Pop was always supportive whenever I wanted to try things. How many other kids have a rock collection from every planet in the Solar System? I even got to make faces at a Mars rover. A working one. Pop didn't scold me, either. He helped me make signs! "Go humans!" "We believe in you!" "Upward and outward!" "We love your TV shows!"

Looking back, I would pay good money to have been a fly on the wall in mission control. I was six at the time, so I didn't think of it.

Now I'm on my own. I don't know exactly what Pop needs to do, but I know he's been... not exactly putting his life on hold for me, but close. I've been holding him back. He's been a responsible parent and, from my point of view, a *fantastic* one. Thing is, he has more important things to do than play Papa to a grown daughter. He may not think so—he hates the idea of leaving me on my own—but *I* know he *has* to do the things only he can do. So I made a bit of a fuss about it, insisted I was a big girl, and kind of turned him loose.

If I'm being honest, it's also kind of thrilling to know I'm on my own. Not totally on my own, obviously. I have Gus, my Uncle Dusty, my teddy bear, and—if everything goes entirely wrong—a way to interrupt Pop and whatever he's doing. But I'm out from under Pop's roof, doing my own thing my own way, and I feel so independent and free! Everything is up to *me*, now. I'm the one making all the decisions and taking all the consequences. I'm a responsible adult out on my own! Woo-hoo!

Pop always told me to try and rein in my unbridled optimism, but what's the worst that could happen?

Okay, I followed the rabbit trail long enough. This journaling thing is *hard!*

I came home, said farewell to Pop, and saw him off. He stepped through the magic mirror in my workroom and disappeared into yet another reality, this time a place called Tauta. The Tassarian Empire is having a religious schism and it's causing political issues. Pop's kind of in the middle of it, so he's going to be gone for a while, sorting it out. I told him not to worry about anything going on here. I know about Adam Alden, Pop! He's a psychic priest with plans to telepathically dominate the planet. I can deal with him. Everything will work out. Trust me, Pop!

And, since he does, he did.

What I did not tell him was how worried I was. Pop was all set to kill Alden outright, because Pop's idea of subtlety is evisceration. I didn't like the idea because the collateral damage was likely to be measured in casualties, blast radius, and fallout patterns. It wasn't easy to talk him into letting me punish Alden for being a bad person. Pop agreed, reluctantly, because he trusts me when I say I'm up to a challenge, and because he's always tried to help me be a better person than he is. He left for Tauta at my insistence. I'm a big girl and he has his own things to do.

Now I have to figure out how to do *my* things, which I'm not sure how to do. How do I spank this guy? I think he's trying to do mental surgery on enough people in power so he can rule the world, but maybe he only wants to own New York. Either way, he deserves a spanking. A metaphorical one, probably; I don't go in for that sort of thing, myself. But how? Deliver a beating? Shoot him without killing him? Whatever I do, I need to make sure he understands why. If he doesn't, there's no real point to a punishment. First, though, I need to find a sensitive spot I can poke, and keep poking until he decides to be a better person.

Or, let's be honest, until I'm convinced he never will.

Yes, I'm hopelessly optimistic. I'm weird and I know it. I don't really have a choice. On the other hand, I'm pretty pleased to be exactly who I am. I'm told most children grow up with the idea they need to impress their parents, or take over the family business, or "fill their shoes" in an arcane and mysterious way. I don't have this problem. Pop has always been impressed with me. He's immortal, so I'll never have to take over the family business. Besides, filling his metaphorical shoes involves a shoe size like a phone number.

It helps to know Pop loves me and is proud of me. I get the impression other people don't always get that from their parents. I did. I do. I don't even have to ask because it would never occur to me as anything to question! I don't need him to tell me every morning at breakfast or as he kisses my forehead when he tucks me into bed. While I was growing up, our household consisted of four telepathic beings—a sword, our cars, my Pop, and me. So *I know*. It's not even an article of faith. It's a *fact*.

For now, though, I've kissed Pop goodbye, sent him on his way, and I'm not going to see him again for quite a long time. He's going to be busy, so I'm not going to call him. *He's* got empires and religions to deal with. *I've* got a dipshit psychic priest with delusions of grandeur.

For the first time in my life, I'm really on my own. It's a glorious, independent feeling, and utterly terrifying.

It's late, I'm tired, and I'm already missing my Pop. I'm going to bed.

Journal Entry #2

I cried for a while. I think I'm allowed.

Mister Stuffins, my attack teddy bear, crawled across the bed and hugged me. He's done it before, but not since I was a little girl. Now I know it's part of his programming. I still appreciated it, mostly because Mister Stuffins is really good at being absorbent. This is not a bonus when it involves bloodshed, but it's first-rate for weeping. Part of why I appreciated it was because Pop did the programming, so it reminded me Pop thought I might need a hug when he wasn't right there. He anticipated he might not always be in arm's reach. He might even have anticipated I would miss him when I grew up. I wouldn't put it past him to think so far ahead.

And that made me cry harder. It went on for a while.

Once I had the waterworks out of my system, I lay there and stared at the ceiling for a while. It obliged by pretending it wasn't at all concerned about my gimlet gaze. It probably wasn't. My gaze isn't at all intimidating and the ceiling is an inanimate object. Pop could have intimidated a hole in the ceiling, the upper floor, and the roof. The clouds above would have taken a detour so as not to attract his attention. Rain would have fallen around the hole. Hailstones would turn around and go back up to wait. Hurricanes would dodge, or, if he looked up through the eye, hold very, very still. Pop is the only person I know for sure can tell a tornado to *stay!*… and it does.

Fair warning: you're going to get sick of me talking about Pop. I'll try to keep it to a minimum, but he's always been an enormous part of my life. It would be fair to say he's been the center of my life. I'm an only child and have always been Daddy's little girl. So, when I ramble on about Pop—or when I compare everything to Pop, my life with Pop, or how Pop did things—please remember he's the yardstick I have. Try to bear with me, okay?

Eventually, after much thinking about everything, I noticed I was asleep. This is usually a good thing. If I manage to get to sleep when my mind is racing, I do a lot of my best thinking.

Next morning, I dragged myself out of bed and slouched into a warm shower. Pop always said I tried to shrink myself, but he's got thermodynamic problems with his mass and metabolism. I don't think my showers are particularly hot. The rest of the world is cold, that's the problem.

I wear my hair shorter, these days, a real fuzzy duck, to fit under a helmet. Drying it was quick. I pulled on a fluffy Fourth Doctor bathrobe and watered Mabel, Charlie, and Petunia—my bonsai, my cactus, and potted petunia. Technically, I don't water Mabel. She has a mechanical misting unit. I did check the water level.

I headed to the kitchen to make breakfast. Bacon hit the pan and, right on cue, Rusty and Gus came in. Gus spends a lot of time at Pop's place in a 1950's Iowa. It's another timeline of Earth, effectively an alternate universe. How he knows I'm cooking in *this* one remains a mystery. It's likely to remain one indefinitely.

Rusty is a werewolf. His real name is "Wesley," but his hair and fur have a reddish-brown color, hence the nickname. Gus doesn't like Rusty. I think it has to do with a pack mentality. Gus won't accept Rusty as higher up the pecking order, and Rusty, being a werewolf and inherently superior to a dog, can't bring himself to give Gus signals that would reassure him, even as a politeness.

So far, it's been a tense détente. When I cook, Rusty gets a chair and a plate. Gus gets a bowl of his own. Rusty sits at the table. Gus stays in the kitchen. They don't have to look at each other, which cuts down on the low growls and the curled lips.

I had intended to have a quiet breakfast by myself, but unexpected guests aren't a problem. I learned to cook with Pop. Pop's daylight metabolism makes him eat like three football players. "Portion control" meant getting control of my portion before Pop ate everything on the table. He wasn't unwilling to share, but "Are you going to eat that?" encouraged me to eat quickly. Gus and Rusty have similar manners, but theirs are more about keeping what they get than looking at yours expectantly.

Pop used to drop in unexpectedly, too. My pantry looks like I'm prepared for the apocalypse. I stay ready to feed several guests disguised as my father.

I slid breakfast onto the table. In the kitchen, Gus got three cans of dog chow. And a few tidbits. And ear-scratching. And maybe some fur ruffling. Little things to let him know I love him. He's not as psychic as the rest of my family, so he needs little reminders.

After breakfast, I told Gus to go elsewhere. He's a smart dog. He has no problem with me being friends with a werewolf. He has his own ways of relating to one, that's all. Besides, he has Pop's place in Iowa to roam around. He'd use the upstairs doggie door. It goes into the local teleportation closet, which goes to the cross-universe teleportation closet in my old place in the Madison Building. From there, Gus can shift to the closet in Iowa. It's a peculiar arrangement of magical transfer booths, but Pop is the only one who really understands them. Gus and I—and Bronze—just use them.

Sometimes I wonder if he's ever built a wardrobe. Or a police box. Either one would suit his sense of humor. Please note: I am not questioning whether he could. I'm wondering if he ever took it into his head, on whim, to actually do it.

Rusty, meanwhile, polished off the remains of breakfast and was nice enough not to eat from my plate. We're still working out rules of polite behavior. Werewolves aren't uncivilized, but they sometimes have to remember to suppress non-human instincts. I get the impression some are better at it than others, rather than it being a generic trait. Rusty might be slightly on the wolf side of the bell curve. On the other hand, maybe he feels comfortable around me and doesn't try to wear "company manners" as much as he should. I'm trying to take it as a compliment.

"Delicious," he told me, sitting back. "I should drop by in the mornings more often."

"For the record, I am not always happy about uninvited guests. Not unwelcome, you understand, but uninvited. Or unexpected."

"You usually invite me in. You let me keep clothes here. You even gave me the code for the back door. And didn't you put in the animal door for me? And program the whatsit—the thumbprint sensor thing."

"Yes. It has your wolf-form nose-print on file so it will unlock and disarm the security devices, mostly because I'm a nice person. But," I added, sweetly, needling him, "it's a convenience for Gus. *He* lives here, but you can use his doggie door. I let *you* transform here when you need to. It's not an invitation to breakfast every morning. Do I have to mark my territory?"

"No," he muttered. "I thought... No."

"I'm glad we have that sorted."

"Uh, right. —and thank you for breakfast."

"You're welcome. Next time, call ahead."

"I will. I'll try to remember," he added. I took it with a grain of salt. He would try, but he's not good at those sorts of things. Plus, he keeps misplacing his phone. I know because I've found it in a pile of his clothes. Someday, when it rings and says "Mom" on the caller ID, I'm going to answer it and see how it goes.

"Good. Now, how are you feeling? You were shot several times on the yacht."

"Nobody was using silver. It hurt, but even the East River can't kill a werewolf."

"I was worried about you drowning."

"I can swim."

I *desperately* wanted to make a joke about dog-paddling, but it would have hurt his feelings. My sense of humor I got from Pop, in much the same way as one gets leprosy: Close proximity and long exposure.

"Does drowning kill a werewolf?" I asked, curious.

"It can. Takes a while, but it can," he admitted, then went on with, "Have you figured out where we're going next?"

"JFK International Airport, I think. I need to do more spying."

"Suits me. We bringing Jason along?

"Probably."

"What's he got against me, anyway?" Rusty asked. "I get it how Mark made a bad first impression, but is that any reason to be snippy with me?"

"If you don't mind standing in the hall while I change, I'll try to explain."

"I've got good ears."

I went to my bedroom and dressed for running. Rusty stood out in the hall and I raised my voice for clarity.

"Jason," I told him, "is a Perfectly Normal Human."

"I thought you said your dad did something to him?"

I checked my gym clothes where they hung from the shower rod. My cleaning spell was working. Rather than wash a running outfit every day, I hang them on the magic rod. By morning, the gunk has migrated down to the bathtub drain and the clothes are fresh and clean. The closet has something similar. I wear an outfit, hang it back up, and it's ready to go again the next day. In the closet, though, there is no drain. I have to change the collection bucket, but I don't do laundry.

Being a witch has awesome perks.

"Yes, but nothing extensive. Some fix-it stuff. Jason's main issue, I think, has to do with you being something other than human. All his life, he's been sure the human race owns the planet. Then he encounters something to blow all his preconceptions out of the water."

"My idiot brother gets high right before a full moon and shapeshifts in front of him."

"The shock baton might have had something to do with his transformation, too."

"I'm sure it did, but he's still an idiot," Rusty insisted. "I'm his brother. I can say that."

"Oh, I don't disagree! Please remember, Jason's first encounter with anything so world-shattering was in a high-stress situation. And the encounter was dramatic. It wasn't a little fairy thing sitting on top of a Christmas tree, pretending to be an angel or a star or whatever. It was a seven-foot, hairy half-man, half-wolf with huge teeth going into convulsions in the middle of a firefight."

"Yeah? And? What's this got to do with me?"

I pulled on running shoes while I reflected on how so very many men in my life are handsome, adorable, and dense.

"Maybe it's because he knows at any time you could become a seven-foot-tall hairy half-man half-wolf with huge teeth?"

Rusty didn't have an immediate answer. I strapped on my wrist and ankle weights and put on my wraparound augmented reality visor. It's a high-end visor, as far as this version of Earth is concerned. It ties into my smartphone, which ties in to Zeno, my computer, through the mobile network. He maintains the encrypted communications, watches everything, records it all, and analyzes it as I jog along. He also alerts me to incoming threats I might not be able to see, plots my routes, and highlights hazards. Most important, he also manages my playlist.

"Well?" I asked, stepping into the hall.

"Maybe you have a point."

"I was hoping you would be nice to my vanity."

He whistled appreciatively. I sighed and shook my head.

"It doesn't count if I have to ask for it."

"It doesn't?"

"Spontaneous displays of appreciation are more highly valued, but I thank you for the attempt."

"I thought you were raised by a single father? Very tomboy and all that?"

"I was, but he didn't try to raise me as a son."

"I'll try to find the right social balance. Could take a while."

"I'm surprisingly forgiving."

"Thanks. Jogging through the park?"

"Yeah. You want to come along? Or do I bring Gus?"

"I'll pass today, thanks. There's a demonstration going on. Angry mobs make me itch. Besides, I promised Mom I'd help set up for the drum circle tonight."

"I've never been to a werewolf drum circle."

"And you're not likely to," he admitted. "You're not a relative. If you can't regenerate, it wouldn't be entirely safe."

"Ah, it's like that. Sorry."

"It's okay. But is it safe for you to be out and about at all?"

"How do you mean?" I asked, cocking my head adorably. I've practiced in the mirror and I've seen the way men react, so I *know* it's adorable.

"Never mind the risks of a woman—a *hot* woman," he amended, and I smiled at his compliment, "—out jogging near a political protest. I'm thinking about this Alden guy. Doesn't he have a bunch of mind-controlled homeless people spying on you? On us, I mean? I'm sure you mentioned how your father told you about it...? Or am I eating too many sardines and pepperoni before bed?"

"If it's a nightmare, it's a real one. It happened. And yes, Alden's got hundreds, at least."

"And you're still not worried about getting mugged in the park?"

"Nope."

"I know why *I'm* not worried," he observed, "but I'm fuzzy on why you aren't."

"You can be fuzzy, which is why you're not worried," I corrected. "You're not clear on why I'm not worried."

"You're hilarious."

"Yes, I am, but in different circles from Pop. I have three reasons. First off, Gus is enormous and extremely off-putting for anyone who thinks about getting grabby.

"Second, Alden is using the homeless drones as spies. He wants to keep track of me. He doesn't seem to want to *do* anything to me, just keep tabs on me. I'm not sure why he's so interested, but at the same time so reserved. I suspect it has something to do with not making Pop angry, but I can't be certain.

"Anyway, I let him think he's getting away with spying on me. He gets to know where I am, for the most part, if not what I'm actually doing. This makes him happy and gives him a feeling of security, which means he won't escalate without a good reason. As long as he gets reports of a trip to the coffee shop and gossip with the girls, he'll think all is well as far as Phoebe is concerned. He's got other things, I'm sure, to demand his attention and time.

"Third, if worse comes to worst and a hundred homeless people start closing in on me, I'll notice. I'm aware of them and I'm alert for them. They don't understand—Alden doesn't understand—what he's dealing with. I'm human, but I'm an *exceptional* human. I can outfight any three of them, outrun all of them, and I will bet my life I'm better at parkour than any of them."

"There are a lot of them, though," Rusty pointed out. "Numbers count. Trust me. Pack hunting is kinda my thing."

"I trust you," I agreed. "Alden doesn't want me dead. I don't know all his goals and motivations, but I do know he wants something from Pop. Inconveniencing me will get Pop mad at him, and I'm pretty sure Alden knows that's what professionals call a Really Bad Idea. I don't think Alden's ready to face that. I'm still studying Alden, but I know he doesn't want to precipitate anything before he's ready.

"On the other hand, it's barely possible he might be interested enough and curious enough to send little challenges in my direction. Tests. How fast can I run? How well do I fight? Can I beat up a mugger? Two muggers? What sort of weapons do I carry, besides the obvious ones for a woman out for a run? Little things that don't implicate him, but could be attributed to life in the big city.

"Once he does something of the sort, it changes the situation. It will warn me about escalation. It'll say he's planning something regarding me and he wants more information to work with. I'll have to decide what my response should be. Until then, I'm not giving away anything he doesn't already know, and I have more time to prepare for the escalation."

Rusty stared at me as though I grew a third eye.

"What?" I asked.

"You're not like other women I know. Not even the werewolves."

"How do you mean?"

"On second thought, never mind. I'll... uh, I gotta go. You'll let me know when we've got us another job?"

"If you ever answer your phone."

Sheepishly, rather than wolfishly, he collected his phone.

My run through Riverside Park was uneventful. Gus loped along next to me, enjoying the outdoors. He wears a collar, but no leash. I'm sure there are leash laws, but anyone giving me grief about Gus being able to roam is welcome to chase after us and complain. Good luck with that.

The protest, whatever it was about, had a lot of people there, taking turns yelling through a megaphone and probably streaming the proceedings live. The physical crowd was only a couple hundred or so, but my visor supplied the virtual avatars of thousands more. Nobody bothered me, so I didn't bother them. Zeno charted a slightly longer route around the shouting for me.

I mostly do cardio and yoga in public. I enrolled in Columbia for a semester, mostly to have access to student services and learn more about the social norms, slang, and expectations on this version of Earth. It's important to sling the lingo of the locals if I don't want to be called out as a stranger from a strange land. Language aside, though, one of the first things I learned was not to do any strength training in the student gym.

I'm not entirely sure about the nuts-and-bolts details of what Pop did to me while I was growing up, but my mother was from the hereditary warrior caste. That's a really good start. I look like an athlete and I'm much stronger than I look. And faster. And—well, Pop did his best to make me the best I could be, physically, and *his* best is disturbingly good. We're not talking about a spell to encourage my body to heal or grow muscles or whatever. We're talking about a systematic, thorough approach from infancy to adulthood to make me as perfect a human specimen as possible. Perfect by Pop's standards, anyway, and Pop was always a fan of Fred Rogers and his cousin Steve.

I never got injections, but there was a lot of vitality thrown around the house.

These days, I have exercise machines at home so people don't gather around to watch and stare. When I'm out for a run, people still look, but for completely different reasons. I mostly don't mind. I look good and if people enjoy looking, I take it as a compliment. Let 'em stare, and thank you for your accolades, ladies and gentlemen.

The few who are bold enough to try and chat me up also have to *keep* up. So far, nobody's managed it, not even with me wearing the wrist and ankle weights. When I put the hammer down, I can pass extremely surprised *cyclists*. Gus has a lot of modifications and enhancements, too—and he's got four legs. Even I can't keep up with him.

Whenever we go for a run, I try to count how many homeless people I pass, then compare notes with Zeno. I spot most of them, but Zeno is a computer. He sees everything. The number has steadied to about twenty-three. They're spaced pretty evenly along my usual route, keeping track of my movements through their psychic connection to each other and Alden. They lost me for a while during the detour, but I felt confident their report would include the protest, so it would be unremarkable, understandable, rather than an alert about me spotting them and trying to do something sneaky.

Alden definitely knows my routine. I don't think he knows what goes on inside my house, though. This suits me. I want him confident and feeling secure. I like it when other people underestimate me. Partly for that reason, I carry the usual stuff for a woman jogging: a pepper-spray cannister in one hand, a mini-taser in the other, and a panic-button bracelet. And, of course, the visor, recording everything. Nobody likes to commit a crime on camera. All this makes me look like a normal New York girl out for a run and like less of a target. The self-defense gadgets—unlike Gus—are mostly for show, as deterrents to the more mundane menaces. I don't want to show off where Alden's spies can see.

We got home, cleaned up, and I did basic maintenance around the house. Gus slobbered up a lot of water and went through the closet to play in Iowa. Due to the time differential and the weather, it was much cooler there.

About the time I finished unnecessarily wiping down the dining-room table, I realized I was procrastinating. Is it still procrastinating if you're working hard at something else to avoid doing the thing you should? Anyway, that's what I was doing. I was putting off a visit to a sick friend, partly because I didn't want to see him when he was sick, but partly because it made me sick to think it was at least partly my fault.

I dressed for a day out in the late 1950s. Circle dress, hat, handbag, even the white gloves.

There are many worlds, many Earths, and Pop can go to any of them, find anything he pleases among them. I know, because he took me to quite a few. While it's hard to do, I can go to most of them through my magic mirror, too.

Today, I was going back to Shasta, California, to visit Cameron at the Fields of Lilac Sanitarium.

Cameron was my first serious boyfriend. I had a couple of kiddie-boyfriend-crushes when I was younger, but Cameron was the one I had at seventeen. I was convinced he was husband material and wanted desperately to find out if he was *my* husband material.

He wasn't, but that's another story.

I walked into the common area and he looked up from his jigsaw puzzle. I smiled at him and he smiled at me. He stood up as I approached his table. He was still in slippers and the hospital-issue pajamas. It was a mental hospital, after all.

"How are you?" he asked, hardly stammering at all. He gestured for me to sit. I took the chair across from him and we both seated ourselves. I ignored the rest of the common room and focused on Cameron. If I tried, I could hear his thoughts, faintly. His mind was far from normal, but it was mostly recovery weakness. Probably.

We used to be able to press foreheads together, stare into each other's eyes, and hold a purely telepathic conversation. Not now.

"I'm fine," I replied, slightly stressing the first word. He missed the emphasis and nodded.

"Good. I'm glad. Do you like puzzles?"

"Some puzzles," I agreed. "What is this?"

"I think it's a puppy. The box has a puppy on it. And a big flower."

We chatted for a while. He definitely recognized me, remembered me. He had enough presence of mind to rise and to be polite. He could carry on a conversation and work puzzles. Okay. Pop said Alden damaged Cameron's mind, but didn't think it was beyond recovery. Fine. Dandy. He was definitely doing better than when Alden pried his brain open to find answers.

I still blame myself. And I blame Alden, yeah, but mostly I blame me. For one thing, I taught Cameron to be sensitive to psychic operations. If he hadn't resisted—that is, if he hadn't been able to feel and recognize the mental invasion for what it was—Alden's mental probing wouldn't have hurt him much. And I blame myself for having a magical gateway connecting my big mirror to Cameron's closet doorway, which is what first got Alden's attention and got Cameron probed.

Nobody told me having a boyfriend was going to be so difficult. Nobody told me I was going to feel guilty about no longer wanting him to be my boyfriend, either. I mean, Cameron is a nice, well-meaning, generous young man, but he's also patriarchal, provincial, and ignorant. I like him. I'm fond of him. He was my first real and intimate boyfriend. I love him, but the word covers so much ground it's almost not worth using. He's wonderful, but he's not someone I can see myself with on a permanent basis.

How did I not see it before? Or did I not *want* to see it? I was younger then—a year, I think? Were the changes in me as profound as the ones in him?

I know what the problem is. Pop pointed something out to me, once, but I wasn't in a state to apply all its ramifications.

"Phoebe," he told me, "you're going to face a rather serious problem, and I apologize for it."

"Why?"

"I'm the one who gave you the problem."

"What's the problem, Pop?"

"You're exceptional. Even more exceptional than most people would believe. I did this to avoid and minimize other, more acute problems, but this will be a chronic condition you may have forever."

"How is being awesome a problem?"

"You are about as perfect as a human being can physically be, and your education and powers are also beyond the norm. You will live among people who are average. You think this isn't going to be a problem?"

"I don't see why."

Pop shook his head and dropped the subject. Maybe he thought I wasn't old enough to understand. Or maybe he realized I would have to learn it for myself.

Cameron is a fine young man and I'm glad I had him. We had good times at my house, playing games, talking, listening to records, and dancing. We also had good times when I practiced things I'd learned about from various professional ladies. Intellectual understanding is important, but Cameron helped me develop skill. He was quite happy to help, and I was quite happy for his help. He learned more than a little, too. No doubt there will come a day when his future wife learns a lot from him! I hope it doesn't raise awkward questions.

The thing is, in the larger, more general sense... I don't want to say he can't keep up. It sounds egotistical and hurtful, and I don't want to hurt him. I wish I could blame it on some sort of political requirement—the Princess can't marry the stable-boy, no matter how handsome and charming he is!—but I have to admit it. I'm the problem. Me and him. We don't match up. I would be the brilliant scientist by day and the superheroine by night, and he'd be the house-husband. It would eviscerate his male ego and leave him humiliated, neither of which I want to do. I've already made enough mistakes to get him badly hurt. I don't need to make more and kill his spirit, nor him.

Now he's in a mental institution because he was the gatekeeper when a nasty man came looking for me and my Pop. How do I tell him we can't have the same relationship we used to? This is hardly a good time!

Or is it the perfect time? Or is it heartless, cruel, and just plain mean? I've accepted I'm going to be regarded as a bitch, on occasion, because I don't always grasp the subtleties of any culture I happen to be in. I don't like the idea of being a bitch to Cameron.

How do I explain all this to the guy with psychic stitches holding his wounded mind together? I suppose I could take this as an opportunity to try to drain away some of his attachment to me. I could try to diminish the intensity of the glow around all the memories of me, make me fade in his mind as though the memories were years, even decades old. It would take away most of the pain, I think, but I don't know how it would affect his recovery.

Maybe I'll put it off until he's stronger. He's been hurt enough.

At least the visit went well. He's recovering steadily, which pleases me. Regardless of how we feel about each other—or how differently we feel about each other—I'll always hope for the best for him.

"Phoebe?" he asked, as I stood up to leave.

"What is it?"

"Is this all my fault?"

"Is what your fault?"

"All of it," he said, looking troubled. He was trying to formulate a complex thought in words and had difficulty with it. "You're mad at someone. And my head isn't right. And I keep having dreams about how I'm on a tiny little island and there's nobody on it, but I can see other islands and wave to people, each on their own island, and we can't talk because we're too far away, so all we can do is wave?"

"No, Cameron," I told him, fighting to keep my voice steady. "It's not your fault." And, as I said it, and thought it at him, hard. *It's not your fault.*

"Oh," he said, smiling. "Good."

I kissed his cheek and let him get back to his puzzle.

What Alden did to Cameron was worse than what he did to Pop, but he owes me something for both. A *lot.* I don't know how I'm going to punish him, or even if it's going to be punishment, necessarily. I do want him punished rather than killed out of hand, which is why I lobbied Pop to let me do it. But where Pop would turn him into fried holy wafers, I want him to suffer. Maybe the word I want is "vengeance." I would like to think my goals are more noble, so I'll call it "justice" and try to believe it.

Hello, my name is Payback. You hurt my father. I can be a bitch.

While I was in Shasta, I bought a new hat. It was a box hat and had a bit of a veil. My plan was to poke around in Shasta and see what I could find out about Alden on this end. Pop and I built a tracking system to find him in my Manhattan, but I wanted to know more about him, not simply his location.

Shasta, though, had people who might recognize me. How much of a problem was it likely to be? Some of them were of the opinion I was a witch—true—and should be burned at the stake—less true. What was the likelihood I would be recognized? I left when I was probably a little short of eighteen. Now I was probably about as far on the other side of twenty-one. I had different hair, different makeup, a hat with a veil, and plausible lies. I was confident I could visit without any major risk of being burned as a witch.

I also had pepper spray and a high-capacity .22-caliber automatic in my handbag. Pop was never a Boy Scout—not that I know of—but he taught me an awful lot about being prepared.

So, where to start? Logically, I should start at the Church of the Pentecostal Fire, where Alden established his local base of operations. Emotionally, I wanted to go to our old house. Pragmatically, I called a cab.

The cab delivered me, for a first stop, to what was left of our old house. I handed the driver a five and asked him to wait. In 1950's money, it was enough to be certain I wouldn't have to walk.

The old homestead was surprisingly clean. I'm not sure what I expected, so of course I was surprised. The house itself was nothing more than the basement hole, a pair of pillars opposite the brickwork porch, across a piece of the circle driveway. A length of charred beam still connected the pillars. The yard was badly overgrown, almost wild. I couldn't find the spot where the idiots had erected and burned a cross. The fence was still intact, but the mechanism to slide the gate open was broken. In this world, how much time had passed? A year? Two? Or was it only a matter of months?

My flowerbeds were the only spots of color. They grew wild, now, but the grass was taking over. It made me sad. I worked hard to get those flowerbeds just so. It's not as easy as you'd think with a life-sucking monster living in the house. On the plus side, the claymore mines Pop planted against the house, behind my flowers, didn't sprout, grow, and bear pineapple fruit.

There's another thing I wouldn't put past Pop. His sense of humor is skewed in ways even I don't always understand. At least he never had to detonate the things and destroy my flowerbeds. We had crazy people bother us, but never the angry mobs of crazy people he prepared for. Pop used det cord, not carnivorous grass, to make the lawn deadly, but I have no doubt he could have found some. It would have made Rodney's job as our weekend groundskeeper much more challenging, though.

Now the flowerbed mines were destroyed. They burned in the house fire, so they probably weren't dangerous anymore. Another year and the casings would be invisible under a green net of runners. Someday, when someone bought the property to build something here, they'd still be lurking patiently to give the construction crew heart attacks.

The batting cage survived, of course. It was entirely made of metal pipe. The netting burned, but the cage was fine. The barn burned down, ruining the vehicles in it, but the burning wasn't complete. Most of the rear wall was still standing, which I thought was odd. If there was anything still standing, it was because Pop wanted it to.

I had a bad moment when I saw Pop's horse-sculpture poking out of the barn's ruins. Of course, it wasn't Bronze. It wasn't even large enough to be Bronze. It was more nearly horse-sized.

I took a little walk around the house's basement hole, poked a bit at the burned ruins of the barn, and wondered. Why was I here? When I was little, we moved a lot. Why was this place worthy of my nostalgia and sentiment? Was there a reason? I wasn't sure. Maybe it was the house I knew when I developed the ability to come back to it. The others were gone, taken away, but this one I chose to leave. And now I chose to return for some obscure reason of my own.

An owl perched on the remains of the barn's back wall, watching me. I waved to it. I've always liked owls. Before I found Gus, I must have made a hundred refrigerator-art pieces about them. Crayons and construction paper, scissors and glue, even a couple of attempts at paper owl models to hang from the ceiling. I wonder whatever happened to them all? Lost in one move or another, I suppose.

I kicked over a bit of old, charred wood. I took off my white gloves and tugged away the remains of a couple of charred timbers, skipping back to avoid flurries of dust. It hadn't rained in quite a while. Metal and rust looked at me with gears for eyes. The clockwork sculpture Pop started would never be mistaken for an actual horse, but I have to hand it to him. He did a bang-up job, considering he never got to finish it.

Maybe that's why I'm here. There are things to finish. Things left undone. Things abandoned. Unfinished things we left behind. Pop has to be able to let them go, I suppose. He's immortal. If he never let anything go, he'd have an eternity of accumulated anxiety and angst. He's been forced to learn how. I haven't learned to do it nearly so well. Maybe in a thousand years, if I live so long.

I considered the partial horse as it stood there, somewhat obscured by fallen boards and other burned debris. It was far too big to move, but I might be able to define a shift-space around it. Not today, but someday. I'll think about it tomorrow.

Still thinking, I returned to the cab and had the driver take me to church.

The church was in much better shape. I expected it would be, since Pop didn't try to burn it down. When Pop and Firebrand decide to burn something, the Devil prays for rain.

There's a reason some less technologically-advanced cultures mistake Pop for a God of Fire.

My Uncle Dusty is the demigod, not Pop.

The church was open, so I went inside. A man scrubbed at the woodwork with a rag and polish. I looked around the sanctuary area and determined we were alone. He didn't notice me until I changed my walk and made my heels clack on the hardwood floor. He glanced my way, wiped his hands, rolled down his sleeves, and ran a hand through his hair. Once he turned, I spotted the crucifix tie-clip. He looked young for a preacher, but he might be an assistant to Reverend Culson.

"Ma'am," he said, by way of greeting. "I'm Reverend Howard. How may I be of service?"

"A pleasure to meet you. I would like to speak to the Reverend Culson."

"I'm sorry, he's not here anymore. He's been moved."

"Moved? I don't understand."

"Are you one of his churchgoers?"

"No, I'm afraid not. I'm visiting and I had hoped to speak with him. What do you mean by 'moved?' Has he been reassigned?"

"I suppose you might say so. He's in a hospital. The doctors say something… happened. To his head. Some sort of injury, maybe from a fall or something. I've taken over his duties here, if I can be of any help?"

Poor boy. I shouldn't have dressed pretty. He was doing a good job of keeping his eyes on my face, or what he could see of it through my veil, but he seemed a little awkward. I wondered if his particular sect had vows of chastity.

"I'm not sure," I admitted. "I'm in town on a sort of visitation. I recently found out my eldest brother and my niece died in a house fire. I hoped to ask Reverend Culson about them. About my niece, at least. Knowing my brother, I doubt he ever set foot in here."

"Oh, you must mean the Kent family," he decided. His mood changed from awkward to worried. A subtle distinction, I admit, but his eyes told me everything.

All right, I'm lying. His eyes were a clue, but I'm psychic. I sensed the change in his mood. I also took a moment to examine his mind a little. He didn't have any peculiarities in his psyche. Since he was a normal human, Alden was probably a one-off weirdo, not the result of a theological secret society's magical experimentation. Probably. I might be wrong. It pays to be a little paranoid.

"Yes, that would be them," I agreed.

"I'm sorry. All I know is what I heard. There was a fire. I only arrived a couple of weeks after, so everything I know is from what I've heard. Rumor and gossip."

"I see. Thank you for your time."

"No trouble, Miss…?"

"Clark. Martha Clark. Kent was my maiden name," I told him, lying shamelessly. "I don't suppose you know what hospital Reverend Culson went to?"

"I think it was the Lilac Hospital, or something like that."

"Perhaps I'll drop in and see if he's taking visitors."

"I'm sure he'd like that very much."

"Funny, though… I seem to remember my niece mentioning someone else in her letters. Was there another preacher here? A Reverend… oh, what was his name?" I paused for thought and Reverend Howard failed to supply me with a name. He didn't even think of one. "Alden? Does that sound right? Or Adam? It was definitely an 'A' word."

"I'm afraid it doesn't ring a bell," he answered, and I could see he was telling the truth. Perhaps he was assigned to this little church once someone realized it didn't have a preacher in it. It made me wonder whether Alden was a legitimate religious figure or not.

"Oh, well. Perhaps I'm confusing the preacher for her boyfriend. She never was very good at holding to a thought in her letters. Thank you so much for your time, Reverend."

"My pleasure, Mrs. Clark."

I didn't go straight back. I did more investigating, checking up on people who tried to get us burned as witches—victims of Alden's mind-control. Mostly Chuck, the Chuckleheads, and Deacon Foss, but there were a few others. I managed to get near several of them, spoke with a few others, and took a good, hard look at the thinking of everyone I could find. There were signs of tampering in quite a few, but I wasn't in a position to do a real analysis of their embedded programming. They went on living their lives relatively normally, but I wondered how they were changed.

Was it worthwhile to kidnap someone, strap him down, and go for a swim through his thoughts?

No. At least, not yet. The fact I could tell they were altered was a good start. Alden's psyche is a powerful one, and his work has a characteristic... fingerprint? Style? Impression? It's hard to describe. As a psychic, I can recognize psychic effects. With lots of examples to study—at a distance, to be sure—I now feel I can recognize not only Alden's personal signature, but also some of his alterations. Mind-controlled zombies are obvious. An aversion to witches is more subtle. It's something one does not normally notice, but it leaves an impression in the aura and can be detected, given time and opportunity.

Can I fix what Alden does? Maybe. It depends on what he's done. If he's ripped out chunks and replaced them with his own instructions, no. I can't put back bits if they're no longer there. But if all he's done is insert extra instructions—"All witches must be burned." "This particular person is a witch."—and turned them loose, I can alter or erase the instructions.

Is that what I should be doing? Wandering around, meeting people he's met, and undoing anything he's done to them? If I did it in New York, it would certainly frustrate him. Trouble is, it takes me a fair amount of effort to search for changes, then a lot of time to find the exact nature of an alteration, and even more time to remove it. It's not quick or easy. I can't quickly glance at someone, sip my coffee, and repair his mind from across the café. And Alden has quite a head start...

While it's a worthy goal and definitely a good deed, even if I could do it, I'm not sure it counts as a way to punish Alden. Annoy, yes. Frustrate, yes. But it doesn't have enough of a revenge factor compared to the effort it costs. It also doesn't encourage him to use his powers more responsibly. It would encourage him to work faster, which is kind of the opposite of what I want.

I still haven't found the sensitive spot to stick a knife in. I'll think about it.

Did I learn anything about Alden's past? Where he came from? What he wanted in Shasta? No, I can't say I did. I did ask, but nobody knew much about him prior to his arrival in town. It wasn't a wasted trip, though. I did learn things about how he used his powers. Maybe next time.

It was a long day and a busy one. The cab driver, Quentin, didn't complain. I smiled at him whenever I got in or out of the cab, and I kept giving him more money. I suspect he would have driven across the country if I'd asked, stopping for food and fuel along the way.

Eventually, I came full circle, right back to where I started: the Fields of Lilac Sanitarium.

The hospital was divided into two basic sections: Maximum security on one side and "please don't wander off," on the other. The minimum-security side was a little more firm about it than a polite request, naturally, but the inmates… no, no, no. The *patients* weren't going anywhere without rational thought, a little planning, or convincing paperwork. The *inmates* on the maximum-security side were going to need rational thought, extensive planning, and a cutting torch.

Cameron was on the nice side, where the funny farm included garden patios and sunshine. Culson was on the not-nice side, where the doors were padded steel. Given the way he kept getting in Pop's face, I was surprised he was still alive. Although if he had a mental breakdown bad enough to require a trip to the laughing academy, that could be Pop's doing, too. I meant to find out.

Getting in to see the Reverend wasn't hard. I told a couple of whopping big lies and gently nudged the minds of those who heard them. Since they didn't have any evidence to contradict me, they simply took me at face value and allowed "his sister's daughter" to visit her "dear old uncle."

I see why Pop loves the 1950s. Everything is so much more personal, much less computerized. It lacks a ton of conveniences, but it's much more accommodating to us oddities. Human error is much easier to generate.

If Culson had been raving, things might have been different. His particular brand of crazy tended to sit quietly. When he was off his meds, he tended to claw at the windows and doors, trying to get out, whimpering about being lost in the dark, and occasionally attacking anyone who tried to restrain him. With his meds, he didn't seem to mind so much. Since he was having a Haldol of a day, he was allowed visitors.

A large, broad-shouldered man in an off-white uniform unlocked the Reverend's door and stepped inside, asking how he was feeling this evening. The Reverend mumbled something incomprehensible. The tone implied he was feeling comfortably numb.

"Mrs. Clark? You can come in, now."

I stepped through the door and regarded the minister. He wasn't in restraints, although the bed had several built in. He needed a haircut and a shave, but was otherwise in reasonably good condition.

His eyes flicked to me, locked on, and blazed. He made an inarticulate noise, halfway between a gasp and a sob, and threw himself on the floor. The orderly moved quickly toward me to intercept the Reverend, but it was unnecessary. The madman was on his face, hands clasped and outstretched to touch one of my feet, while he babbled about light and dark and salvation.

I'm used to male attention, but *this* was new.

While the orderly stood over us, I went to one knee and touched Culson's clasped hands. He continued to mumble. He either wouldn't or couldn't say anything coherent. I wasn't sure if this was because of what Alden did to him, the medication, or a combination of the two.

On the other hand, I was touching him and, psychically, I'm very well-endowed.

For me, reading someone's mind is often a full-sensory experience. It's not like their thoughts pop up in word balloons or pictures. Sometimes I hear them as overlapping voices, some thoughts being louder, some thoughts quieter. This is what usually happens when I'm listening and someone thinks at me. There's one main "voice" with mutters and whispers of other things in the background. Most of the time I'm not trying to delve into someone's mind and find out what's going on in there.

When I am trying to get inside someone's head, it's like swimming through a sea of brains.

Okay, maybe that's not the best image, but it's hard to describe. I went inside Reverend Culson's head, sort of like stepping into someone else's headspace. Pop and I did it often enough. The major difference is most people haven't built a mental metaphor of an internal, personal thinking place. In a headspace, the conscious thinking goes on in the metaphorical construct and everything else happens outside, beyond the walls. That's why you don't mess with anything outside the study area. You're meddling with your own mind. The headspace is where you can consciously think and exercise control over the thoughts most people recognize as "thinking." What happens outside is all the stuff normal people aren't conscious of—the "thinking" that happens below the conscious level.

Like most people, the Reverend didn't have any walls around a central island of thought. Most people don't have a mental construct in their heads where they can go to think! I stepped into a fairly typical mess of random concepts. All his thoughts were there, jumbled together, flowing and shifting, back and forth, some mounting higher to swamp others, some drowning in the sea of other thoughts, some coming together to change color and direction, others dividing into fragments and scattering.

I swam through this mess like a shark. His mind was worse than a normal person's. Normal people—those not under enormous stress, anyway—have a relatively straightforward division in their thinking. Layers, if you like. Culson's mind was a mishmash of incoherent nonsense. Everything was loose and drifting, with nothing to center around. He lived in a mental darkness, directionless, with no guiding star, no purpose or reason for anything. He had a lot of memories and his brain kept firing thoughts around, but there was no plan, no coordination. His mind wasn't walking from point to point, following along semi-reasonable paths. It was flailing randomly, like a blinded swimmer in the deep end. It was total confusion, completely uncoordinated.

In his immediate memory, I saw what happened. Out in the physical world, when I came into the room, the wild flailing changed. What he saw—because I saw it in his mind—was a figure of light. I'm guessing his oversensitive mind detected my psychic energies and latched on to me. Why? Because everything done to him by Alden was to make him compliant, obedient, and easy to manipulate. Anyone with a dram of psychic power could have told the Reverend to go climb a rope and he would have shinnied up a hangman's noose. I have more psychic wattage than anyone I've ever met—barring Alden and Pop—so, to him, I was a burning star from heaven in the shape of a woman. For him, it was like seeing an angel descend from on high, wreathed in celestial brilliance.

I remained on one knee next to the Reverend, mouthing words for the orderly's benefit. "There, there." "It's all right." "You'll be fine." That sort of thing. It gave me time to do my brief examination inside the Reverend's skull. The orderly was on his toes, ready to subdue a maniac, but Culson lay there quietly, mumbling his thanks.

Definitely Alden's work. Fixing the Reverend was beyond my skill, but maybe mitigating the damage wasn't. He was completely without self-guidance, constantly waiting for orders, but if I could short around a few of the damaged areas, he could be waiting for orders from anyone, not just Alden… and, with a little fine tuning, orders from people perceived to be authorities—doctors, orderlies, police, his superiors in the church, those sorts of things.

Was it possible have him also do things on his own while waiting for orders? Yes, but not much. His initiative was badly damaged. He wasn't apathetic. Nothing worthwhile motivated him. He didn't have a quest, or even a goal, and couldn't find it in himself to generate his own. Give him one and he'll obsess over it, but...

It's not a cure, but it's an improvement. It might get him out of the rubber room and into the sunshine, at least.

When I finished, I stood up and nodded to the orderly. The orderly gently urged Culson toward the bed. He went willingly enough. Good. I made my exit.

In Quentin's cab, I sat and thought. Did this teach me anything about Alden? Yes and no. Clearly, he was capable of pounding someone's brain into jelly and turning them into a slave. According to Pop, Alden did this to a whole slew of homeless people, only to an even greater degree, reducing them to near-mindless automatons. Culson, on the other hand, was still in there, still a person, but he had no personal motivations. He needed to be told what to do, but he still had most of his personal abilities. Give him an order and all his faculties focused on it.

Why the difference?

Did the Reverend need—did Alden need the Reverend—to keep up appearances among uncontrolled people? By contrast, Alden's homeless army didn't need to be overly social to eat, sleep, beg for loose change, and spy. It confirms again that Alden can make alterations along a whole spectrum of possibilities, from mindless automaton to... what? Someone has no choice but to like him? What's at the other end from mindless automaton? A perfectly normal person with one aberrant "fact" in their head?

Which is worse? Having your sense of personal identity erased, or leaving it intact except for free will? If you no longer have a sense of self, do you care? If you have a sense of self, but you can't think about the fact you're enslaved, does it count? If you don't even know you don't have free will, does it matter? And if it doesn't matter to you, should it matter to others?

I finished my visit and headed back across the worlds. I had a coffee date with Susan in the afternoon and, if the criminal element cooperated, an appointment in the evening.

Journal Entry #3

The coffee date went well. Susan and Jamie and I met up in the late afternoon, after all their classes were over, and had a lovely time. We swapped gossip—Stacey (formerly Steve) had moved in with Brian, Tim was now dating Orishi, Janice was upset with Oscar again, and Pam was moving across the continent to Hollywood. I had questions about Pam relocating, as well as concerns. She was moving in with a guy named Harrison ("Call me 'Harry.'") she had never actually met. "Harry" was an agent, supposedly, and thought Pam had talent.

We all agreed we should keep alert for a sudden disappearing act or a shout for help. Jamie tried to talk Pam out of going, but Pam's chasing The Dream. Susan supported Pam going out and making the attempt, but was also going on the road trip with her, to get her moved and settled before leaving her there. She also planned to find out more about Harry, where they were living, and so forth. I suggested she also take his picture, at least, and get him on video. I did not mention I would need these things if I was going to send out a tracer spell to locate him. After a bad experience in another world, I generally don't advertise my witchery.

Since Susan would be out of town for a few days, she recruited us both to help with her psych project. It wasn't a big deal. We were to hand out flyers and ask people to take a survey. Part of the study was to see if there was a difference in response rate between the hand-delivered flyers and a digital request. She needed people to actually do the handing out, and she tapped us for it.

I met a lot of people during my semester at Columbia. It was kind of the point, really. Back then, Susan asked a lot of people—one of them me—to help with a campus crusade for improved security. I'm usually against ubiquitous surveillance, but I'm also against robbery and assault. Well… on regular people. Assaulting and robbing criminals is fine. I'm not required to be consistent. A foolish consistency is the hobgoblin of little minds, or so I'm told.

While we chatted, I discovered I was paying more attention to my friends. It felt strange to be so… so… so on my own, I guess. No doubt Pop was still in my corner, but more remotely so—not paying such sharp attention, not as easily available, now that I'd sent him off to live his life while I lived mine.

No, not "on my own." Alone. I spent all my life moving from one place to another, abandoning friends, then abandoning acquaintances, then abandoning people. Did I forget how to be friends with anyone? Friendly, yes; I could do that. But I think, maybe, this could be the one way Pop let me down. He never taught me how to… what? I don't know how to describe it.

As I watched Susan and Jamie chatting—yes, yes; I chatted just as much, but… well… I felt I was more watching than participating. I felt partly outside, somehow. Distant. One step removed. I was the witch. I was the alien. This place, this world, this time—none of it was mine. This was *their* home. They belonged here. All I did was keep a local address.

It was weird to feel this way. It used to be I lived wherever Pop lived. Home was wherever Pop was. Now it was… not here. Pop was elsewhere. I had a place here, but I didn't belong here, if that makes any sense. I'm not sure it does.

I didn't like the feeling.

It was getting dark by the time we finished up. I drove home after the coffee date, having made a note with Zeno to remind me of my appointment to hand out flyers. He added it to my calendar.

When I say I drove, I mean I drove my car, a high-speed, gas-powered, four-wheel-drive hatchback with a rally-car attitude and a fantastic sound. Bronze picked it and wore it for a while, so it's more than it seems, as a car.

I did *not* take—and do not particularly like—the robotic electric taxis running all around the Five Boroughs. Bronze hates wearing them and I'm with Bronze on this. They creep me out. Partly, it's because they *remember* things, like who you are and where you went and who you were with. Partly, it's because I'm used to Bronze's driving and I trust her. I don't know these cabs. By contrast, they seem impersonal. They have no personality. They aren't drivers. They're things. I feel trapped inside a high-speed zombie without so much as a steering wheel. Oh, I'll use them—they do have their uses—but toilet brushes have their uses, too. I don't have to like them.

To be fair, Zeno can wipe anything they can record, or take control of it and do anything I tell him with it. My dislike of the robocabs is irrational. I know it. It's an emotional response, not a logical one, so it isn't required to be rational.

Jason was already there when I arrived. He loves to be early. He let himself in through the roof access door, away from most of the cameras. Those tend to watch at street level, not along rooftops.

Dang. There's a camera drone watching from across the street. I don't know if it's watching the roof or the street level or both. I'll have to warn him.

Jason's a very manly sort, one of those hardbody types with a jaw like an extra fist, deep-set eyes, and an indefinable something implying he's made of sterner stuff than normal mortals. Not aggressiveness, but an unrelenting quality. He gives the impression the quickest way to piss him off is to shoot him. He's a professional mercenary, which leads me to my main gripe about him: He has no qualms about murdering people out of hand.

To be fair, we've been facing drug dealers who are more than willing to kill us, so I guess he's not unjustified in his attitude. He's a lot more hair-trigger than I am. I prefer to go in with our metaphorical phasers on "stun" and switch to "kill" only if we have to.

Sadly, our phasers are entirely metaphorical. What we do have is *massively* enchanted, high-tech armor. It started out as a practice project for me, placing enchantments on armor appropriate to worlds where such things are fashionable, but the design and capabilities have grown over time. I didn't intend to kick off the manufacture of super-suits, nor for them to get this complex and complicated, but I must admit, they are fun.

We've been practicing with these new suits for a while, but being proficient isn't the same as being expert. Pop helped me with a lot of the spell designs, so *of course* they work, but making them user-friendly is one hell of a lot more difficult than I ever thought.

When I say it's "user-friendly" I mean it isn't actually "user-hostile." Mundane people like Jason can use it, but it's only intuitive if you think like Pop, meaning it isn't.

Jason's suit isn't quite up to speed with mine. He has most of the functions, but he's not sensitive to magic. It's kind of like being trained in a classroom to be a pilot, but without setting foot in a plane. He can operate the controls, but he doesn't have an intuitive grasp of how to use it. That's mostly where the "user-friendly" part comes in.

I have an advantage. I'm a magic-sensitive person. In my suit, I concentrate on the spell's effect and it does what I want it to. Jason has to use the controls to adjust the variables. I'm still testing and experimenting, though. When I add a new spell to my suit,

I'll practice with it, get it integrated and perfected, then I'll add it to his. Assuming. We're still getting used to the things under field conditions.

On the other hand, they're designed to be idiot-proof. Why? Because Pop doesn't place much faith in people to be anything other than idiots. He says he's being realistic. I think he's being cynical. What bothers me is we may both be right.

I gave Rusty a call and was gratified to find he actually had his phone on him. He and Jason joined me in the media room. I called up and projected maps recorded from my magic mirror observations.

"Last time," I began, "we hit one of the couriers for cash shipments. We recovered a lot of cash from Kaswell's yacht and burned the rest. I made sure we got his computers, so we got the information we wanted while making it look like a robbery."

I didn't actually get his computers. I connected them to the Internet and let Zeno do his thing. Even if someone did a forensic analysis of the machines, they wouldn't detect the fact Zeno read all their files.

"Another courier is Pendleton. He's one of those pond-hopping sorts who bounces back and forth between Zurich and New York every week in his private jet. He can't carry as much cash, for obvious reasons, and he never carries drugs. Not through the security at an international airport."

"He parks the jet at a public airport?" Jason asked.

"Yes. Private hangar, though. According to my sources, he rents it from a shell corporation that nominally owns it. Technically, he rents the jet, too. But, for all practical purposes, he's the owner. For *legal* purposes, he's some poor guy who had no idea what the owners were doing with it."

"Ah. And the so-called owners?"

"According to the records, they live in Bolivia."

"Good luck with extradition."

"No doubt that was a factor. So, here's the layout." I keyed the overhead projector and it shone down on the table.

"Big building," Rusty observed. "Long sight lines inside and lots of illumination."

"It's a hangar," Jason sighed. "They put airplanes in them."

"I know."

"I'm glad."

"Now," I interrupted, "with the yacht burned to the waterline and the cash no longer in play, financially speaking things have become a bit unbalanced. Esterhauser will need more money, and soon, to keep things running smoothly. Since Pendleton came back to America well ahead of his usual schedule, there should be an outgoing shipment in the near future. Normally, Kaswell would sail his yacht down to the Cayman Islands and enjoy a little time in the tropics, but now he can't. Pendleton should be able to take up part of the slack by a couple of turnaround trips to Zurich, but it's more of a risk. It ties more of their network together in an investigative sense, but if nothing else goes wrong, it should handle the pothole they just hit."

"So we're going to stop Pendleton," Rusty grinned.

"Obviously," Jason replied.

"What we're going to do," I continued, steamrollering over yet another beginning argument, "is a little more involved than our usual breaking, entering, and breaking."

I had their attention. I hoped I had their cooperation.

In this world, JFK International Airport is strictly for airplanes. Dirigibles can dock in the cradles atop the Twin Towers for passengers and light freight, but mostly they moor at La Guardia. I think this is to keep dirigibles from clogging up the air traffic where planes are trying to land. If you want a pleasant cruise, you take a dirigible. Thing is, most people want to get there quickly, not enjoy the ride, so dirigibles are usually the heavy haulers of the sky.

As for us, we didn't want to go anywhere. All we wanted was to conduct a terrorist attack on a major international airport. At least, that's what people would think. Planning ahead, Jason and I started our midnight escapade with a partial charge in the spells storing momentum.

Our armor is some of the most complex thaumaturgical engineering since Victor von Doom decided to upgrade his underwear. We have two things to keep track of. One is the magical charge. That's kind of the big deal. It's the power supply. The other thing is the momentum. The spells store momentum from potentially any impact. We can use this momentum in a variety of ways.

Getting onto the field wasn't hard. We simply expended some of the momentum charge and leaped a tall fence at a single bound. Landing was even less of a concern. We hit the ground inside and absorbed the impact back into the suits. It costs magical charge to do it, but we started with full batteries.

Rusty had a harder time of it. He had to go around until he could find his own way in. I offered to pick him up and jump the fence, but he declined.

We regrouped at the designated hangar. Rusty did his I'm-just-a-dog routine and padded around the place, returning to report the presence of over a dozen people, mostly men, in the hangar.

Oops. Well, there went Plan A.

Given the sensitive nature of Pendleton's money-hauling, I had intended to make this a stealth run, planting evidence and escaping. If the authorities found drugs and money on the plane, it would cause even more problems for the organization. Now, though…

Oh, well. I should have done a last-minute scrying survey. I thought we had at least a day before they would be headed back to Zurich. I didn't realize they'd be doing an immediate turnaround.

"What do you think?" Jason asked.

"No plan survives contact with the enemy?"

"You're not wrong," he agreed. "Do we want to abort?"

"I don't see why."

"If you say so."

"Rusty? You want to catch anyone trying to escape?"

Rusty, in wolf form, peeled back his lips in what could technically be called a smile. When he has four legs, he loves to chase things. He reminds me of Gus, but I will *never* mention it to him. And I will never ask him if he wants to play Fetch. Not unless it involves retrieving someone who is fleeing.

"Okay. Jason? Front door or back door?"

"How about I hit the roof and start picking them off from above?"

"We're not trying to kill people," I reminded him.

"Yes, so you've said. Well, if you insist. Since the aircraft door isn't open, I'll take the front. I can handle the attention while you come up behind them."

"Let's go."

He went around the hangar and came up to one of the front corners. I twiddled the lock on a human-sized side door, made sure to bridge the connection on the fire alarm, and slipped inside.

Inside the hangar was the private jet, which I expected. There were half a dozen cars, as well. Most of them were transport for guards and luggage. Pendleton wasn't in sight, but he could be in the plane or in the hangar's office space. Everyone else was either standing around with a submachine gun or loading the plane. There was a lot of luggage. From the way they hefted it, I guessed it was cash.

Electronic credit transfers are faster, but they're also more traceable. There are a lot of good points to old-fashioned cash. There are bad points, too. Flammability is one.

I worked my way toward the offices. I didn't know who or what was in there. My armor's helmet looks a lot like a motorcycle helmet, all smooth on the outside, so it wasn't a big deal to press mine to one wall and amplify the vibrations.

A radio was listening to the control tower. Nobody was talking. I couldn't hear breathing, but the sound filter wasn't great. There were a lot of ambient noises in the hangar. The office window, though, was normal glass with a set of blinds on the inside.

"I'm ready," I said. My helmet radio crackled, "Roger."

Jason came around the corner of the hangar and approached the two cars out front. Nobody noticed him for three paces, four, five, six... then someone pointed a gun and shouted at him. He didn't change his pace at all. He was a dark figure walking toward them in the dim lights around the hangar. They hesitated. He waved as he approached and they hesitated a little longer. Someone waves at you on a big, public chunk of tarmac. This makes firing a submachine gun hard to justify. Given the situation, whoever started a firefight when he didn't need to would be explaining himself to his boss. Possibly while suspended upside-down over a piranha tank.

They shouted for him to stop, to identify himself. Jason kept walking at a moderate pace. He made no sudden movements, but he stopped waving and casually brought his shotgun down from behind his back, sliding the strap around as he did so, leaving the gun at hip level, pointed forward. They opened fire on him then, which grabbed the attention of everyone in the hangar.

While bullets spattered around him and, on occasion, glanced off him, the people in the hangar turned from their tasks and readied weapons. They headed for the front door. I waited while they moved. Someone hit the switch to open the hangar door.

The door was a sliding thing, in several parts. It wasn't telescoping, exactly, but it worked in a similar manner. It provided a wide front through which they could move, rather than a single, man-sized door as a choke point, but it took time to open it.

As it cranked slowly aside, Jason continued to close on the exterior guards. He opened fire.

I don't like killing people indiscriminately, but I will admit there are times when it is called for. Therefore, in general, Jason uses beanbag rounds in deference to my preferences. They aren't non-lethal, exactly, but they are *less* lethal. Hit someone in the head with one and they may well go down for good. I'm told it's like being hit with a sledgehammer.

About the time the main door started to slide open, I pulled out a pair of flash-bang grenades. I pulled the pins, carefully. I punched through the window of the office, shattering the glass, and dropped the first grenade inside. You don't throw a grenade at a window in case it's shatterproof. Having a grenade bounce off plate glass and land at your feet is embarrassing. The other flash-band I sent skating along the concrete toward the cluster of gunmen. I called a warning through my helmet radio as I let it go.

There was a profound light and a pair of overlapping thunderclaps. I took a second to confirm the office wasn't a threat—it wasn't; nobody was actually in it. Oh, well. Better safe than sorry. Then I charged into the stunned and reeling gunmen.

Jason likes his shotgun. I don't blame him. He's a normal human being, albeit one with a lot of training. He's had practice with the armor, but he doesn't use it like I do. I'm not only an enhanced human, I'm a witch. I understand the magic involved and can switch between the functions, fine-tune the effects, with a proficiency he simply can't match.

For example, when I hit someone, I hit someone *hard*. My Kung Fu is strong. I can add stored momentum from the armor's reserves, if I want, with a variety of possible effects. I can send someone flying away from me—with or without broken bones!—or I can focus the effect to turn a punch into penetration.

Amid the stunned and reeling gunmen, I was the fox in a chicken coop. All I needed was big, technicolor word balloons of "Biff!" "Pow!" and "Socko!" to appear.

I admit, knocking out stunned gunmen by hitting their heads wasn't the safest thing in the world—for them, I mean. While it might not be immediately lethal, it was potentially life-threatening, especially if I did it wrong. I didn't particularly like it, but it came with the territory. Both for me and for them. We each chose our line of work. We knew the risks. At least I was trying to not kill them outright, unlike some people I know.

Jason, meanwhile, sprinted forward into a more comfortable range, went to one knee, and raised his shotgun to aim. As I worked my way down the line of reeling gunman as fast as a kid playing Whack-A-Mole, he covered anyone who looked like they might be able to raise a weapon. Two people might have managed it, so there were two shotgun blasts. Beanbags centerpunched them, knocking them down and reinforcing the fact they were supposed to be out of the fight. Neither of them argued with the beanbags.

Behind me, there was a whirring, ratcheting noise. I couldn't turn at the exact moment as I was still turning stunned people into unconscious people. I wasn't worried about the noise overmuch. The material of my armor will shrug off anything short of a high-caliber round and the magical defenses will absorb even bigger threats. I elected to finish with the gunmen rather than have them recover while I was dealing with something else.

Jason and I regrouped by the edge of the doorway. Almost everyone who was outside the plane had hurried to defend the hangar. After Jason and I were through, they were all in a line, lying there in various states of unconscious.

Now that we could pay attention to other things, we knew what the noise was. Someone had started the engines on the plane. I didn't think they could turn a key and start them. I thought jets needed an external starter machine. Well, it was a high-end aircraft. Maybe they anticipated needing to land and take off from an obscure little airstrip.

I picked up a submachine gun.

"Left?" I asked, over the helmet radio. Jason nodded and moved left, to the other side of the plane. He loaded a pair of flechette shells into his shotgun as he did so. I thumbed my own weapon off safe and moved to take aim.

The pilot wasn't a complete fool. People pointed guns at his plane. He ducked. It didn't help. We weren't after the pilot.

Jason's first round went right down the throat of the starboard engine, banging through the blades of the intake fan. The second one followed a moment later. His rounds were penetrators, designed to punch holes in body armor. Jet engines didn't appreciate them.

I unfolded the stock, clicked the selector to semi-auto, took aim, and emptied the magazine into the intake fan of the port engine as quickly as I could squeeze the trigger.

The pilot was no fool. He shut down the engines before they caught fire.

We unlocked and opened the airplane door. Jason persuaded the pilot to stay in the cockpit and keep quiet. I went aft and found Pendleton. He was a big, healthy man, but he carried a couple of extra pounds. It made him look soft. He wasn't. His bodyguard was a smaller man and came straight at me. He didn't try shooting me. Maybe because we were on a plane? I don't know. The plane wasn't going anywhere, so why not use a gun?

Still, he came at me, shouting in proper martial-arts style. He was good, too. The plane wasn't over-large, so we had cramped quarters for a fight. It's hard to do a spinning leap for your roundhouse kick when you can barely stand up straight.

He tried to punch me. I blocked several times, absorbing the force of his blows, and gave him a palm strike to the center of the chest, along with all the force he'd directed at me. He went backward with broken ribs and lay there, coughing blood.

"Pendleton?" I asked.

"Yes," he replied, and raised a big damn pistol. Bright, shiny, probably chrome-plated, with a massive slide and grooves for the porting. Clearly, he had no qualms about guns on a plane. Fifty caliber? Probably. It was one of those weapons you never see anyone really use. Maybe you use it as a close-in weapon for finishing big game. It's an intimidation tactic, not a practical combat weapon. He held it in both hands like he knew what he was doing, though. He fired it, braced for the recoil, and kept firing it until the magazine was empty.

I stood there and looked down at the floor. I knelt, scooped up several slugs, and tossed them at him, one by one. They were still hot.

"You done?"

"Yes," he said, in a completely different tone.

"Tell Esterhauser you couldn't do anything about it," I advised.

"About what?"

Four minutes and a lot of jet fuel later, Pendleton was in the back of a car, zip-tied to the seat, along with a bunch of weapons, several bags of cash, and with a ring of hired muscle lying piled around the car. Everybody conscious watched the plane burn while the airport security and fire vehicles closed in.

Rusty didn't have anything to do in this fight, poor guy. He was the free safety, roaming around the edges to watch for incoming surprises and outgoing escapees. Neither of these was an issue. All he did was to run across a bit of tarmac—as a wolf, or a big dog, but who can tell at that speed in the middle of the night? The incoming emergency vehicles had a bit of a delay when the driver of the lead car stood on the brakes to avoid him.

Rusty simply wandered off. He's a wolf. He can do that. Jason and I separated, sprinting for the border of the field. I hopped the five-meter fence without slowing, landed lightly on the far side, and sprinted for a bit again. When I could, I leaped to the rooftops. There are fewer cameras and even fewer witnesses on rooftops.

Much farther away, north of Rockaway Boulevard, I came down in a quiet little spot and changed from "armored ninja warrior" to "citizen headed home." Unlike Pop's heavy plate armor, my ninja suit folds and fits together into a surprisingly compact bundle. I unfolded my little wheeled travel bag, stowed everything, and calmly hailed a robocab. I'm a lady with a big shoulder bag and a smallish piece of luggage. I could be anyone on a weekend trip.

I slid my prepaid card through the robocab's door-slot, it opened, and Zeno's voice welcomed me. My laptop doesn't come from this century. Pop found it for me. It doesn't own the local internet, but it has an awful lot of digital penetration. The records of the robocabs wouldn't show anything about me, so my movements wouldn't be correlated with any incidents.

Jason made his own way back to the rendezvous at my house, but Zeno kept an eye on him. Anything Zeno could find relating to Jason, Zeno altered or deleted. I'm pretty sure Zeno is the only reason we can get away with this sort of thing. It makes me wonder how comic book superheroes manage to avoid having the FBI show up every other episode.

Back at my place, I transferred the stolen money from my shoulder bag to a backpack. Rusty, delighted beyond words, took it and said he knew what to do with it. I believed him. He didn't care for Zeno's money laundering or digital shenanigans, but nobody arrested him, either. If anyone can keep his mouth shut about where the money came from, it's Rusty. I trust him.

Jason, meanwhile, accepted a cup of iced coffee and put his helmet on the table.

"These things are marvelous," Jason told me, flexing his gloved hands and rubbing fingertips together.

"It's impressive," I admitted, proud of Pop. "Sometimes I'm startled, too."

"I can hardly believe the sophistication of the technology used here. It's like alien artifacts, or magic."

"Well, Pop always said the only way of discovering the limits of the possible is to venture a little way past them into the impossible."

"Did he develop all the technologies in these suits?"

"I understand he did a lot of the theoretical work, but for the realization of the designs, he had help."

"I don't doubt it. Do you know how it all works?"

"Only the theory. I don't think I could duplicate most of it. The engineering is Pop's. He's the genius of the family."

"I'll take whatever you're allowed to tell me."

"You know almost as much as I do. The suits store momentum. We smack into a wall, we come to a stop, and the suit stores the force. We use the stored energy by transferring it to ourselves—we can jump really hard—or to other objects, as if we hit them really hard. If you're asking about the theoretical physics, I don't understand the math."

The last part almost wasn't a lie. *Pop* understands the math. He understands all the math. He knows enough math to define an inter-universal wormhole and maybe even do taxes. He really is a genius. Me, I've been trained in some higher math, but I'm more comfortable with things I can see and feel. I'll calculate your hyperspace jump if you insist, but I'm more comfortable threading the needle down the canyon run to the exhaust port.

"I suppose I would be just as lost," he admitted. "I do have a complaint, though."

"What is it?"

"There are two things I need to keep track of. One is the battery charge. The other is the force charge. Yes?"

"Yes," I agreed. Technically, it was the magical charge and the momentum charge, but he was close enough. "The battery is how much power you have left. The force charge is how much momentum you have stored up for immediate use."

"Right. So, if I fall off a building, I hit the ground, and the force charge increases. There's a sudden blip as my battery charge goes down a little, but the battery charge is constantly going down. The more force I store, the faster it drains the battery. Yes?"

"Yes. Think of it as using a force field as a scuba tank. The more air you compress inside, the more pressure the field has to hold, so the stronger the field has to be. If the battery gets low enough, it'll start bleeding out the force charge—letting the air out—so you don't suffer a catastrophic failure."

"I understand. My problem is the ergonomics. I need a better way to see where I'm at for each. The ghostly dials on my visor are okay for measurements, but they take up too much visual field. A vertical bar on the right to show how close I am to a maximum force charge would be better. A bar on the left can show my diminishing battery charge. A timer on that one wouldn't go amiss. A better thought, if both start out green at the top and slide down to red at the bottom, I see at a glance whether I can keep going or need to retreat."

"That would be better," I agreed. "I'll make a recommendation for the next-generation helmet."

"Thanks. On a less theoretical note, do you know what we're hitting next?"

"No. I have a lot of research to do, chasing up the chain. Both Kaswell and Pendleton reported to Esterhauser. Now Esterhauser has serious issues and will probably have to consult with his other clients and/or his bosses. When he does, I hope to find out who they are."

"I understand. Another concern of mine is we got away with a lot of cash, but what about marked bills or recorded serial numbers? I know you usually handle the money laundering, but are we sure no one's going to track the money?"

"Trust me on this," I told him. "Rather, trust the people in charge of it. I don't know how to launder money, but an army of forensic accountants can't track your pay back to Kaswell or Pendleton."

"I was thinking of Kaswell or his bosses tracking *their* money to *me*."

"Same difference. By the time the money reaches you again, it will go through so many laundry transfers Lincoln's beard will be white."

"I only wanted to bring it to your attention."

"And I'm glad you think about these things."

"Thinking about how things can go wrong is part of my job." He then asked, diffidently, "Will you always be bringing the werewolf along?"

"You mean my friend, Rusty?"

"Yes."

"Probably."

"I wish you wouldn't," Jason sighed.

"Why not?"

"It seems wrong."

"Look, I understand you don't feel comfortable with werewolves and other creatures—"

"Monsters."

I was silent for a moment while I considered how to address that.

"Jason."

"Yes?"

I didn't answer. I looked at him and waited.

"Yes, Ma'am?" he corrected.

"I'm going to tell you something you probably don't want to know. Pop never actually explained it to me, but I picked up on it."

"Am I cleared for this? Or am I going to get my throat cut for knowing?"

"I was never officially told, so it's only hearsay. Assume you aren't cleared for it, but it's gossip—not official. How's that?"

"I've heard things around the scuttlebutt before. Go ahead."

"The things you call 'monsters' are, quite often, trying to get by in a human world. The werewolves aren't rampaging through the streets. If someone gets eaten by a pack of werewolves, he was probably hunting *them*—and got what he had coming. Overall, they aren't trying to make trouble."

"Yeah," he agreed, rubbing one shoulder. Mark bit him during our initial meeting with Rusty. It took a couple of full moons before he was convinced their lycanthropy wasn't the contagious sort. It's a species thing, not a disease.

Yikes. *Theirs* is. How many worlds have cursed werewolves? I know there are lots of different species of vampires, but how many different types of lycanthropes are there? And how many different animals? Werewolves, yes. Were-cats? Were-lions? Were-bears? What's the lexicon of things people can turn into? Or the animals that can turn into people?

"Now, some creatures—like humans—may be predatory monsters."

"Hold on… a…" he trailed off.

"You were about to say something about how humans aren't predatory monsters? There are no evil human beings bent on murder, rape, pillage, and so forth?"

"Go on," he replied, grimly.

"There are bad people. There are bad monsters. Take vampires, for example. There's more than one species. One type is a black-hearted pile of walking evil, deserving only of being put down—those are your predatory monsters. Another species I know of is… well, they're like regular people, motivated by all the usual motivations, but with special dietary requirements."

"They drink blood."

"Yes, but do they have to drink *human* blood? If they can get by on blood from the meat-packing industry, is their diet fundamentally different from a human's?"

"How do you tell the difference?" he asked, ducking the question.

"I'm not sure. My point about monster-hunting is this: Fangs or fur doesn't make it a monster. There are a lot of humans who are more monstrous than the 'monsters' are. Okay?"

Jason nodded, probably remembering particularly unpleasant people he had known. I couldn't hear his thoughts, though. I made sure to include psychic shielding spells. The last thing I wanted was to give Alden a free shot at someone wearing a super-suit.

"I'm going to ask something, and I recognize it may be above my pay grade," Jason told me.

"Shoot."

"Your father hired me to be your sidekick. What he meant was he wanted a bodyguard for someone doing dangerous stuff."

"Isn't that what a sidekick is?"

"Not exactly, but we won't stress the point. At the time, you were on a drug-dealer kick, raiding and ruining their business."

"Still am."

"Yes, but we're not focusing on the traps or the crackhouses anymore. We're moving up through the organized crime tax bracket. It's also not my point. Now we know about—I know about—creatures. Some of them are monsters, whether they're human or not."

"So?"

"Given some of the things I've seen," he said, rubbing his fingertips together again, then flexing his gloved hand, "lead me to believe there's something more going on than a rich kid using her father's resources to go out to play superhero. No offense."

"None taken. What are you asking?"

"Are you practicing on drug dealers? Field testing equipment, for example? Or as a way to get experience before going after bigger fish? Monster hunting, maybe? Is this the family business?"

"What? No! It's definitely not the family business."

"So? Why are you being trained to hunt monsters?"

I bit back a quick response and considered my answer.

"I'm not," I told him, slowly. "I've been trained because… no, that assumes things. Let me start again.

"Pop believes I should be able to make my own way in the world. I'm not going to get into what the fundamental duties of parenting are, but Pop did everything he could with the resources at his command. He spent most of my life helping me develop every skill, from cooking to killing, so I could have a decent chance of being equipped to do whatever I want to with my life." I quirked a smile at him.

"Being a badass is an unavoidable side effect. He didn't think I'd enjoy beating people up—and, truth to tell, I don't, or not much—but he didn't want me to be afraid of anyone or anything. So here I am, taking names in preparation for kicking criminal ass, thanks to Pop, at least in part."

"And maybe the general ass-kicking is what I'm asking about. Does he, ah, deal with monsters on a regular basis?"

"Oh. I see what you mean. Yeah, you could say that."

"On what scale?"

"I don't understand the question."

Jason leaned his chair back a bit and looked up at the ceiling, thinking.

"What bothers me is the way you take monsters in stride, like they're part of the same bestiary with wild dogs, feral cats, or Manhattan sewer rats. How widespread are these… things? All the things, not just the ones I've seen. Is there a hidden war going on? Is there a struggle between humanity and everything else? Or is it more on the order of keeping the cockroach population down?"

"First off, 'cockroach population' implies—"

"I'm sorry. It's a metaphor," he said, sitting straight again. "Not a polite one, and one I won't use in anyone else's presence. You know what I mean."

"Hmm. All right. So far as I know, there's a substantial presence of Things in the world, although not a… how to put it? Not enough to threaten the dominance of mankind. If anyone is the cockroaches in this metaphor, it's the humans. Carnivorous, intolerant, heavily armed, paranoid cockroaches have taken over the planet, so everyone else is in survival mode."

"Hmm," he said, lips pursed in thought. "All right. But, for example, is what we're doing leading up to something? Or part of an existing… group, cabal, or conspiracy to… to… to make sure the werewolves don't take over Australia, breed an army of millions, and take over the world?"

"I don't think Australia is the place for them to try and take over."

"You know what I mean."

"No, because there's no need for such an organization."

"Permit me to doubt."

"I'm serious," I insisted. "If it came down to cases, there aren't enough werewolves to go to war. Bullets have a hard time killing them, but fire and explosives work perfectly well. All the savagery in the world won't help against cruise missiles and carpet-bombing. Then, when you get them down to manageable numbers, you have to worry about them infiltrating. Fine, so you poke them with a steel needle and a silver one to see which one bleeds. If one does and the other doesn't, one less werewolf.

"In a similar vein, vampires have even more problems. They have more powers than snarl-and-slash, obviously, but half the time they're lying there, helpless. Their diet is also an issue. Maybe they can drink animal blood, but how obvious is it going to be when there are so many hungry undead they buy slaughterhouses to refrigerate tanks of the stuff? All it takes is for someone to get suspicious and start looking into the matter. It's hard to hide ongoing shipments of two-hundred-liter barrels of raw blood!

"And if they need *human* blood, it's way, way worse. The ratio of humans to vampires has to be low or people start to notice. One in every hundred thousand? One in every ten thousand? What's the practical maximum for staying mythological? You need millions, as you noted, to have an army. This could happen with vampires pretty quickly, I admit, but even if they win, what would they eat? They have to police their own population and prevent undead population explosions from causing more literal explosions."

"And if they don't?"

"If it turns out Transylvania is ruled by vampires amassing an army of the undead, feeding them by claiming they need lots of blood from the Red Cross, yeah, we probably need to do something about it. But how stupid would they have to be to alert their flamethrower-equipped food supply to the danger?"

"So we do hunt monsters," he simplified. "Human ones, for now."

"Yes. And," I added, as realization hit me, "I've got one in particular I'm working on. How comfortable are you with taking on a powerful, evil man who practically owns large chunks of the city authorities?"

"Depends. Do I get to use a rifle?"

"I'd rather see him punished for his deeds rather than killed out of hand."

"'Punished'?" he echoed. "Punished how?"

It was a good question and one I wished I had an answer to. For the moment, though...

"It's not so much "punishment" as he needs to learn he can't simply do anything he pleases. He needs to learn there are consequences."

"You want him to suffer for his sins."

"In essence."

"I'm up for it," Jason agreed, interested. "Do you have any consequences in mind?"

"I have a preliminary idea of imprisoning him. Maybe."

"You sound uncertain. Is he going to be hard to capture or hard to contain?"

"A bit of both."

Jason muttered something. I didn't catch it, but I could make a good guess.

"It's what I'm being paid for," he added. "Let me know what you decide. We'll pick it apart until we can't find flaws."

"Good. Because Rusty is probably going to help actually do it."

"I still don't like having a... having a werewolf..."

"It takes getting used to," I sympathized. "Rusty isn't a bad person. Mark is the dipshit. Has he apologized?"

"Rusty made him apologize," Jason said, voice so neutral it needed a Swiss accent.

"Yeah, doesn't count," I agreed. "Maybe you and Rusty should hang out a bit, get to know each other."

"I'd rather not."

"Are you sure?"

"Positive. But thank you for the suggestion."

"Meaning I should butt out and let you work it out on your own," I translated.

"Not to put too fine a point on it, but yes."

"You two sort yourselves out however you like," I decided. "I'd rather not have to choose between you, okay? As long as you can work together, I don't care how you get along in your off hours."

"I can do that. Make sure you tell the hairy one."

"I'll phrase it differently for him, but it'll all get sorted."

Journal Entry #4

I've been using my witchcraft to track and trace a drug syndicate. I'm living in a late 21st-century Earth timeline, so they don't even believe in magic for the most part. They have technological jamming devices and drone trackers and a bunch of other electronic precautions, but I'm not using technology. Using a magic mirror to watch from a continent away is something they don't, they *can't* plan for.

My problem is the same, but from the other end. Given that I can look pretty much anywhere in the world I want to, where *should* I look? I have to have an idea of what I'm looking for—or who. I can't tell the mirror, mirror, on the wall to find me the worst drug kingpin of them all. So I have to watch a known associate, listen in on the conversations, and gradually make the connections to someone closer to being in charge.

The organization chart of a syndicate is more complicated than one might think.

At first blush, one might think there's a mastermind, somewhere, who runs a whole organization. Under him are various lieutenants, possibly in charge of different geographic areas, or maybe in charge of different corporate departments—distribution, production, refinement, quality control, and so on. This is not the case.

Oh, there are organizations like that. They're run like corporations, or close to it. They're sort of the middle ground between someone cooking meth in her kitchen and one of the major cartels. When you get into the big leagues, it's more like a bunch of interlocking nations, with alliances, trade deals, diplomacy, bribes, and maybe a couple of territorial skirmishes now and then.

How would you draw an organizational chart for that? I mean, really. By the time you're done, it's no longer valid! It's like trying to keep up with the interlocking associations of nations, but *worse*! Nations usually try to have propaganda, if nothing else. What they want you to see can tell you a lot about what they *don't* want you to see.

Pop brought my laptop—Zeno—from a much more advanced timeline. Zeno has a number of communications channels into this Earth's cyberspace and can correlate anything I ask him to. He can do this with nations and keep it up-to-date nearly in real time. My problem—our problem—is when dealing with criminal organizations, things are a bit trickier. They don't want to let anyone know *anything*—not who owns what, where it is, what they want it for—they don't even release propaganda! They're criminal organizations, so they try to stay not merely out of sight, but invisible.

I realize Pop would say "officially criminal organizations," but he thinks of politicians as successful con men who lie, cheat, and steal from their fellow citizens under the guise of governing. I think he's a cynic. Doesn't mean I'm sure he's wrong, necessarily, but he's still a cynic. I remember he once said something about how he missed Diogenes. I get the impression they were friends. I wouldn't be surprised if Pop has a favorite alias when he's visiting a timeline in ancient Greece.

Zeno can use his intelligence analysis capabilities to give me ideas on where to look for my spying targets. I supply him with non-public information about who reports to whom, what's shipped where, and so on. With these as facts, he can firm up his probability analyses and make better predictions.

Eventually, I'm going to find someone in the top layer of the drug-dealing scum. Knocking over retail centers and couriers is rewarding, but I feel like I'm not accomplishing anything in the larger sense. I mean, I'm not going to single-handedly bring down the entirety of the drug trade. Eager volunteers will spring up faster than I can quash them. I can't even spot them as fast as they appear!

Now, though, I'm hunting for the more high-ranking targets by following the money. Anyone involved in the major money movements is a power to be reckoned with. If I keep following the money, tracking where it goes and how it gets there, I should be able to figure out the rest.

Hang on. I had a thought.

Okay, it didn't pan out.

Here's the thing. There's a camera drone across the street, parked on a building. My first thought was Alden, but only because he's my latest project. Then it occurred to me someone might have managed to track me back from a raid on a trap house—

As an aside, a trap house is a place where they actually process raw materials into street drugs. Depending on the neighborhood, they may also have facilities for the end users, either attached or nearby.

Anyway, people involved in drug trafficking would be more likely to be using the local technology than a priest from the 1950's.

Zeno, on the other hand, is *future* technology. He runs on the wall current like any other laptop, but he runs a personality simulation and several expert systems on hardware that would, in local terms, take up a major skyscraper.

Using several of the nearby phones—most of them in neighboring buildings, rather than my own phone—and the various supposedly-private wifi devices in the neighborhood, he found the signal used by the drone. It's encrypted, of course, but we don't care so much about what it's seeing. We care about who's watching it. Sadly, it's a broadcast signal. The signal is piggybacking on the local wifi and streaming live video to the whole world. Anybody with the proper decryption key can watch the feed.

On the other hand, I have a magic mirror and pretty delicate fine control. I got Zeno good images of the make, model, and serial number. He scoured the Internet and more than a few secure networks to identify the purchaser: Michael Finnegan.

Mr. Finnegan is a nonagenarian gentleman, a long-retired entrepreneur in the elderly-care hospitality industry. He has a nice house upstate, a small river running along his property, and a collection of rods, reels, and fishing waders. Zeno has looked into his affairs and can find precisely two connections to the drugs trade. Two of his six grandchildren are "recreational" cocaine users. Neither of them live in New York. I haven't caused them any problems with my hobby. Neither was ever in any of the places I busted, nor did they do business with any of the dealers working there. As far as I can tell, he doesn't have any reason in the world to know about me, much less care about me.

I'm stumped. Maybe he's working for Alden as a non-mindless minion. If he's able to think for himself, he can use his familiarity with this century, which might result in a camera drone keeping an eye on me. Zeno can't find any records of him ever meeting Alden, but we didn't track Alden's movements perfectly from the moment he got here. It's unlikely they know each other, but not impossible.

If not, Mr. Finnegan might be interested in tracking down the low-profile superhero stuff I'm doing—I try not to make the news, if at all possible—but I can't find any connections to law enforcement, either. Maybe he's curious? Or is someone using his credit card and he doesn't know it?

Short of going there and asking him, I don't know how to find out. I don't want to go there, either. Blowing away the drone says I know it's there. Confronting the guy who might have been tricked into buying it reveals more about me than I'm liable to learn about *them*. Him. Whoever is responsible for the drone.

Anyway, yes, it's tough to figure out what criminal organizations are doing, much less get an organizational chart put together. As tough as this is, it's nothing compared to figuring out what Alden is doing. Drugs are for sale. The sellers want money. This isn't a hard motivation to grasp. But Alden? I know he wants power, sure, but is it all he wants? If power is what makes him tick, what makes him tock? Does he want power for its own sake, or does he have a goal requiring power to achieve? He appears to be working his way up to world domination. If so, is this a case of the end justifying the means? Does he think he can do good by uniting the world under his rule? Or is it because he wants it? Does he even want to rule the world, or am I on entirely the wrong track?

At least finding Alden is easy. Pop and I set up a three-coordinate system of psychically-sensitive theodolite…

You know what? Skip the details. Zeno can track him. We have a hard time directly watching him, for technical reasons, but his dot on the map is definite.

While Zeno incorporated my latest scrying information into his syndicate patterns, I replayed Alden's movements on another screen. He was all over the map, from city hall to ivory tower to cathedral Mass to corporate headquarters to police plaza. His day was a busy one. It exposed a lot of people to his influence, which I expected.

He's building up a following. I get it. I'm not sure how dedicated a following it is, though. If I'm any judge of psychic powers, the farther away you are, the harder it is to do anything. Modifying someone's memories or mental processes requires effort. I know, because I can do it.

Alden is stronger than me. A lot stronger. How much can he change in someone's head without *obviously* doing anything? Can he do it while sitting in the same room, sipping his tea and looking innocent? Does he need to have a conversation to tell them what they should think? Or can he carry on an unrelated conversation while doing psychic surgery? What are his limits?

As I regarded the map of his travels, I noticed something I should have noticed before. Alden, being a preacher, usually hides out in the evenings by going to a church. It doesn't seem to matter which one, although he has his favorites. He does something I don't understand—something Pop doesn't understand, either, which scares me a little—with the holy ground of the church. It throws up a static field, making it impossible to see anything through a scrying spell. It may not be intentional. It may be a side effect of something else, but it *acts* like a jamming signal and it persists even after he leaves.

I hadn't given it much thought. If Pop couldn't unscramble it, I certainly wasn't going to. He got around it by using a small gate and opening a physical hole into the area, like looking through a tiny window. I'm sure I can do it, but it'll take me a while to set up and there's no guarantee I'll get it right on the first try. Pop does gates like he's making paper airplanes. I can do gates, but for me it's more like prepping a real airplane for takeoff. I go through a checklist and I do *not* do it from memory.

I suppose I could use the micro-gate inside the phone Alden stole from Pop, but I don't want to draw any more attention to it than I already have. No, on second thought, it wouldn't work anyway. It's inside the phone. I can't see anything through it without a scrying spell, and the static would foul the image.

On another note, Alden is pretty much immune to traditional magical location spells. He stole some of Pop's less-lethal gear and it includes magical cloaking spells. When he's not on holy ground, he can still be seen through a scrying spell, no problem, but magically locating him ranks up there with six other impossible things before breakfast. This is why

Pop and I put together the triple-axis psychic triangulator to track his location. We're using his own overdeveloped psychic power against him.

Anyway, Alden hides out in churches and cathedrals. The map had his movements time-stamped, so I should have seen it earlier. I called up an almanac and started making comparisons.

Alden was usually on holy ground by sunset. When he went in for the night, he didn't come out until dawn. True, there were a couple of exceptions on when he went in, but the majority of his evenings took place inside a church.

I started hunting down the exceptions by date, time, and location. Was there a pattern? Yes, there was. Every one of them was something public. Drastically public. A party, a reception, a dinner, something of the sort, with a guest list of at least a hundred and, in every case, some form of official media coverage, not just people livestreaming from their AR headgear. The reasons for the events didn't have anything in common beyond something charitable or do-goodery, but the guest list did. They were all events with the great and the good—or the wealthy, which often amounts to the same thing in their own eyes.

I sat back and thought about these things.

Alden and Pop remind me, in some ways, of two tigers in the same forest. Or two gunslingers in the same small town. They're both powerful figures and they don't like each other. Pop is currently out of town on his own business, but I don't think Alden is aware. I also doubt Alden knows I'm planning to bring to his attention how his behavior will have consequences. If he knows, he isn't taking me seriously. Once I start making it obvious, it'll force his hand, so I need to think things through.

Now, Alden—according to everything I've heard—believes Pop is a time-traveler. This is incorrect. Pop's gates can reach alternate realities, including those which seem to be more or less advanced in their timeline progress. Want to see a world where the Axis won World War Two? How about one where it achieved victory last week? How about one fourteen years later, when Japan starts its invasion of India? Or would you prefer to get an up-close and personal look at a dinosaur? If so, bring your running shoes. If you pick the right alternates, it looks a lot like time travel, but it's really travel between different worlds.

Another thing Alden doesn't know—probably doesn't know—is the fact Pop is a vampire. I don't *think* he does, but it would explain his tendency to be in a church after nightfall. From what Pop has gathered from conversations with Alden, Alden believes he and Pop are *related*, somehow. Alden believes he and Pop are the same type of creature— Alden's type of creature, or a close variation. Alden's let drop hints about not being human, so his actual species is still up for grabs. I keep thinking of him as a mutant with psychic powers.

Could he be part alien? I mean, if there were Ancient Aliens, could they have interbred with humans? If so, it would explain why he thinks he and Pop are related and why he has powers beyond the human norm.

Regardless, Alden isn't a vampire, ergo, he probably isn't thinking Pop is one, either. I will admit Pop does a remarkable job of looking and acting human most of the time. Around other people, anyway.

Alden also knows some magic, or has a basic sensitivity to it, but he wants more. Specifically, he wants to get it from Pop. To time travel? Maybe. But it begs the question of what his motives are. Is magic more versatile than the powers he already has? Or does he want magic for a specific purpose—say, to go back in time and have a conversation with his alien father? Or a fistfight? To get special training with his powers? Alter history to suit himself? Or hitch a ride off this planet?

I hate not knowing what he wants. I know what drug dealers want. But Alden?

It's tempting to phone him up and ask him. He has Pop's old phone, after all. It's one of a pair, linked together with ultra-small gates inside, except the one I have doesn't have a gate anymore. Pop took it out and used it as part of a setup to pump radioactive oxygen through it. It's slowly poisoning Alden with radiation—assuming he's a creature vulnerable to radiation. Whenever the phones engage, they now produce a bit of static, too, to conceal the more-rapid rush of pressurized, radioactive gas. If Alden has it near his face, it's the perfect time to gas him, not so?

Pop has a temper, immense powers, and a shortage of qualms. I think trying to slowly poison Alden with radiation shows great restraint, all things considered.

Part of the reason I doubt the effectiveness of this ongoing murder attempt is those aforementioned magical doodads, mostly one ring and the amulet. The other ring provides handy focus points for micro-gates, so it's really a tool rather than a defense. But in the amulet and the other ring, there are a variety of magical properties involved. More than one function heals the wearer. Whether Alden is vulnerable to chronic radiation poisoning or not, whatever healing magic Pop has in those widgets…

Hang on. Do those even engage for radiation poisoning? They're usually for trauma, so they might not activate unless he's actually bleeding. I don't know all the conditions. I don't even know all the spells; Pop includes shielding in his stuff to prevent other wizards from casually analyzing it or screwing around with it. I'm not even sure if Alden is enough of a wizard to figure out how to manually activate things off Pop's ring or amulet. Maybe Pop really is slowly killing him.

They say a bullet can have your name on it. A grenade is more "To whom it may concern." Pop can be precise when he wants to, but he has a tendency to go "Dear Latitude and Longitude…" Irradiating Alden to death is pretty subtle for him—and immensely less destructive than I feared.

Anyway. Can I call Alden up on a regular phone? Yeah, probably, but it might make him wonder why I didn't use the super-duper dedicated phone.

No, I won't call him. I will spy on him a lot, though, whenever he's not on holy ground.

I'll set it up so Zeno can observe him through a magic mirror. If the scrying spell is the visual sort—it creates an actual image on the "mirror screen," rather than giving the user a psychic vision—I can get a webcam to see it. It still won't help when he's in a church, but the rest of the time he should be visible.

This is a brilliant idea. Maybe I don't have to personally watch everything in pursuing information on drug syndicates—or Alden, for that matter. It's power-intensive to produce an image instead of a psychic vision, but if it means Zeno can do the spying directly…

Journal Entry #5

The webcam idea worked as I expected. I was a little concerned about the power requirement, since I built several, but it was a silly concern. I have converters to turn electricity into magical energy. I can practically plug a magic mirror into the wall.

This solution led me to all-new problems. Locking the mirrors onto various drug dealers is simple enough, so I put eight spells down and got Zeno a hub for the multiplicity of webcams. Normal humans are easy.

Alden, however, was more of a problem. He's moderately sensitive to magical operations. Normally, one component of a scrying spell locks on to a specific person and automatically follows him or her around. Alden is a low-grade wizard and would be likely to notice a targeting lock if we could get one—but we can't. The same spells keeping us from locating him with magic keep us from locking a scrying sensor on to him to follow him around.

Thanks bunches, Pop, for getting your stuff stolen. –All right, all right. I'll take some of the blame. I'm the one who created a gate and didn't tell you. And I didn't have internal alarms at my old place to warn of intruders. Mea culpa.

Alden's sensitivity to magical operations means he can recognize a magical object when he sees it, although I'm not sure how easy it is for him to notice. He's stolen a few geode-sized power crystals from my place and powerfully-enchanted objects from Pop. At least he didn't try to make off with any of my plants. I can enchant a power crystal, but losing Mabel, my little bonsai tree, would be heartbreaking.

Hang on.

Alden is wearing powerful objects and surrounded by powerful spells. He's not as proficient a wizard as I am, and he's so far from Pop's league they're not even playing the same sport.

When you've got the music turned up, you might not hear the siren of the cop pulling you over. Would Alden be able to detect minor magical effects while he's wearing all the other magical stuff? We still can't get a spell to lock on to him or the magical gear he's wearing, but we can manually pilot a sensor near him.

If it's close enough to him, yes, he probably can. How close is too close?

Let's find out.

Okay, if I stick a scrying sensor in his face, he notices. He doesn't seem to be able to identify it, but he starts looking puzzled and begins to search for whatever is disturbing him. I have no doubt he can deliberately try to look for one farther away, but as long as I put it ten or fifteen feet distant, it's outside his casual detection radius.

With that solved, all that's left is getting it to follow him.

This is the hard part. We could, I suppose, keep pecking away at the cloaking fields surrounding Alden. In a low-magic world like this, his stolen devices have to be recharged periodically. He didn't steal any of my electromagical transformers, but if he simply turns the spells off while he's sleeping on holy ground, safe inside his static effect, they can recharge. If I keep pecking away at them, forcing them to expend energy, they'll eventually run down.

Thing is, there are small power crystals tied into the amulet. I know that much about it. They're meant as emergency power supplies for all the amulet spells. I'd have to expend everything the amulet has and I don't know how much it holds.

The two problems with this are the effort and the obviousness. It'll take time and energy to force the amulet to expend all its charge, and there is no way to make it subtle. Alden will notice and, if he has any sense at all, will head for a safe house. If I can't see the target, it'll be even more difficult. I won't be able to shoot it; I'll have to throw grenades. The power expenditure on my end will be enormous

All right, it's not a good solution.

There is one obvious way to follow him around with a scrying sensor. I can manually pilot the thing, rather than lock it on to him, but we're back to the problem of me having to do all the spying.

I'm adopted, but I still got my laziness from Pop.

Zeno and I have a set of psychic-frequency theodolites constantly aimed at Alden's emanations. Each one is carefully monitored for its exact orientation, enabling us to triangulate his position. This is great for determining his GPS coordinates, but I haven't got a clue how to tie the system into a scrying sensor.

If I treat a scrying sensor like a flying camera, there are certain axes of motion involved. It needs to move up and down, left and right, forward and back. It also needs to pitch and yaw, possibly even roll.

I may not understand how to tie a psychic triangulation system into a scrying spell, but I can have a scrying spell key off a video game controller. Or... no, that won't work for Zeno. I need the opposite. I need something Zeno can use to create a physical movement. The physical movement can be tied into crystal controls at this end of the spell to pilot the sensor.

Is Radio Hut a thing in this world? I checked online and no, there isn't, but there's an ElectroShack. Same-day delivery? Yes, but I'll still go to the store to shop. I can browse through the parts and see what leaps out at me. Besides, the trip will give the homeless network something to mutter about.

Journal Entry #6

I spent several days working out a system to let electronic impulses operate manual controls to operate magical controls. Zeno can send signals to electric motors, turning them precisely. These have crystals on the rotors, tied into a scrying spell on a mirror. Each rotary widget controls the movement of the scrying sensor in one aspect.

That's it. That's the gizmo. I'm immensely glad Pop already set up the movement functions in a mobile scrying sensor. I don't think I could develop one from scratch. I only wish I had access to Pop's material resources. I'd love to build my electro-spell-interface device using orichalcum wiring, rather than with attuned crystals on mundane copper coils. Pop had all the orichalcum in the world. I don't. And I'm starting to realize what it means to be on a budget. I don't think I ever understood how wealthy we were, not in any sense of the word.

I'm working with what I have, and man, I am beat. This spellcasting stuff isn't physically demanding, but the finicky bits of soldering components and tying them into spells—it's draining, that's what it is, especially with non-magic-friendly materials!

It's dark outside. I think it's time to go to bed.

Journal Entry #7

I let Zeno gather information for a few days. With his ability to tie every fact on the Internet together with every other fact, he doesn't need much extra input to analyze and synthesize new information. Now he has multiple mirrors following new sources of information.

I caught up on episodes of my favorite podcast, *Dark Desires*, made sure Mabel, Charlie, and Petunia were doing okay, trimmed Mabel, and did the grocery shopping. There are several devices at Pop's place to keep Gus cleaned and groomed, so I helped him get wet and muddy down by the river—in Iowa; I wouldn't risk the Hudson or East River. We had a great time, splashing about and chasing things.

I also spent a day on campus smiling at people and handing out hyperlink cards to help with Susan's psychology project. Janice and I went for coffee a couple of times to talk about her brother and how his rehab was going. She didn't bring up Oscar and I didn't ask, having been warned about their troubles.

In the coffeeshop on the corner, I played a little chess with Sacha, an elderly Russian gentleman who immigrated only a few years ago. I try to drop by at least once week to get absolutely thrashed at chess, but I brought it on myself. I told him whoever loses buys the coffee next time. He's nice, though, and he loves helping me practice my Russian. I think he doesn't like having to learn English. Most of his family are fluent in English and insist on full-time practice at home.

We became instant friends when I placed a coffee order. I gave the name "Spartacus." When they called it out, I stood up and said, "I'm Spartacus!" Sacha unhesitatingly turned in his seat, waved his cane, and shouted in that thick accent of his, "No! *I* am Spartacus!"

We were the only people in the whole damn shop who got the joke. Sometimes I wonder about modern education.

I also played in the park with Gus and any of the children who chose to play with him. He collects playmates the way I used to collect rocks. They gravitate to the big, fluffy dog and he licks their faces until they laugh. He didn't get to come when I played tennis with Sandra—she arranged to have Theo and Martin join us for mixed doubles, followed by lunch and drinks. I know for a fact Sandra is serious about her relationship with Tina, so I wonder if she's trying to get me a date. She keeps telling me I need to get out more.

Now I know how Pop must have felt when I kept trying to set *him* up with a date.

I also took a night off to attend the final performance of *La Sylphide* at the Met. I like ballet. I like dancing. I would have been a ballerina, except for everything about my body type. I'm too tall, too solidly built, and a bit too top-heavy. Most companies wouldn't have me. Ah, well.

I do like *La Sylphide*, though. I still say Madge is more than a bit of a bitch. Typical evil witch stuff, but still, an unworthy use of her powers. I always feel bad for the sylph.

The one time Pop and I went to the Met together, he pointed out the vampires in the audience. This time, I took a look during the intermission, concentrating on the crowd. My ability to see auras isn't the same as Pop's, and it certainly isn't as easy. I saw a few odd flashes, here and there. I'd guess a half-dozen undead were in the crowd this time.

Do all vampires have a predisposition to opera and ballet, or just the ones who remember the Good Old Days? Or is it a good place to rub elbows with influential people? Or is it an opportunity to be social after dark? Maybe I'll ask one, someday.

While I caught up on my social life, Zeno field-tested the new controls by keeping track of Alden and recording everything. He sometimes had issues when Alden used any form of transportation. A car can outrun the sensor, at present, and I haven't figured out how to speed it up. When Zeno loses sight of him, he starts homing in using the tracking system, driving the floating, invisible sensor straight at the new location as fast as it will go. Cars take streets and have traffic regulations. Zeno flies the invisible, intangible magical sensor in straight lines.

I wish I could add a function where Zeno can turn it off and turn it back on, aimed at the new location, but if I knew how to do it, I would be able to tie it into the tracking system directly.

I want to bother Pop, but I won't. I asked for this. These are my problems. Doesn't stop me from missing him something awful, though. Besides, he has his own problems. If he needs me, he'll tell me.

No, I take it back. Bronze will tell me. And if she can't, Uncle Dusty will.

Zeno also kept track of Esterhauser, him being the next up the syndicate chain of command. Zeno now wants to follow a guy named Nikolaev. The other pocket mirrors were in a similar situation. Zeno was fairly sure the subjects were even lower down than Esterhauser or Nikolaev. He learned who they all report to, so now we need to follow the next level up. I re-targeted the Esterhauser mirror by using the image and voice recordings Zeno provided, and repeated the process for the others.

With all my catch-up boxes ticked, I did my strength training in the home gym, assaulted the heavy bag repeatedly, and fenced with my shadow a bit.

Someday, I'm going to work out a spell to let me actually do what it says on the tin. Pop has an animated shadow. Why can't I?

By the time I rinsed off and dressed, Zeno had a report for me.

"Oh? What have you got?"

"Excellent news! Nikolaev reports to a man named Schumann on several different transportation businesses, including drugs."

Zeno is such a cheerful computer. He always sounds so improbably happy.

"Nikolaev is likely the man in charge of transportation, in general, for this Schumann person?"

"Probability in excess of eighty-six percent. Nikolaev controls, directly or indirectly, a wide variety of transportation services. The probability he also provides transportation for other illegal goods is beyond a six-sigma limit."

"And is Schumann the head of this chain?"

"Probability in excess of sixty-two percent."

"That's a lot of leeway," I decided. "Let's switch tracks to Schumann and find out more."

"Up or down?" Zeno asked.

"What do you mean?"

"With each new observation, the default tracking direction is to determine who is higher up the chain of command. One of my presets is to re-confirm the default option periodically. Do you wish to continue up the chain of command or begin tracking down the chain of command?"

I thought about it for a minute. Every time you make a new opening in a criminal organization, someone comes along to fill it. Better to remove the whole organization. If it has to start from scratch, maybe the legal authorities can stay on top of it.

"Now you mention it, we should probably keep track of as much as possible. If the head guy goes down, someone else will step up. We should assemble as complete an organizational chart of the criminal network as is practical and possible."

"Query. You say 'criminal network.' Is the interest solely in the drug trade, or are the other criminal enterprises also to be tracked?"

"What other criminal enterprises are involved?"

"At this level, drug traffic, human traffic, antiquities traffic, weapons traffic, and exotic wildlife traffic."

"Exotic wildlife?"

"Endangered, rare, or otherwise valuable plants and animals, or products from such endangered, rare, or otherwise valuable plants and animals. For example, rhinoceros horn is illegal to own or sell. Despite cloning efforts of the past two decades, they are still on the endangered species list. Smuggling this substance would be considered trafficking in exotic wildlife."

"I'll take your word for it. These people trade in drugs, weapons, people, and animals?"

"The discussion between Nikolaev and Schumann indicates it, yes, Ma'am!"

"I'll switch the mirrors to whoever you want to track. Find out what you can and we'll track everyone back down the chain again. Or up," I added, "if Schumann's not the top."

"Right away!"

I replayed the recordings of the Schumann guy and changed the mirror's scrying spell to lock on him. He didn't look like a smuggling kingpin. He looked like a kindly grandfather sitting in an old-world banking office. I wasn't fooled. I don't look like a witch and Pop doesn't look like a nuclear power. I re-tasked the other mirrors and left Zeno to it.

As for me, I got comfortable in my witchy workroom, where I keep the tools of the magical trade.

While Zeno did the legwork, gathering information on smuggling operations and on Alden, I continued working on a personal project. Pop gave me his early-generation magical rings and whatnot, sort of sorcerous hand-me-downs. I've been working on them, a little at a time, to update them. For example, the healing spell in one of the sapphires was extremely old-fashioned and incredibly basic. Better to have it than not, but I'd rather pull the old spell out of its sapphire chip and put an updated, more efficient, later-generation version back in.

Again, it's an example, not a list. The rings do a lot of things, and more of them now that I've been working on improvements.

He gave them to me because they were useful, true, but also because he knew I'd get a lot of practical experience taking them apart and putting them back together. And, damn it, the clever bastard was right.

He's my Pop. I can affectionately call him names. Don't you try.

I finished putting a spell in a sapphire chip and started the process of sinking it into the gold band of the ring. It would vanish inside, making the ring a plain gold band, and the metal would help protect the gem. I sighed, sat back, rubbed my eyes—

"Whatcha doin'?" Rusty asked, right behind me.

—and I almost hit the ceiling. I spun around on my stool and glared at him. He noticed my reaction and smirked. He more than startled me. He scared me. If he'd interrupted while I was working with my spells, here in the house's high-intensity magical environment, things could have gone extremely badly. I have a deep and abiding respect for magical foul-ups.

I stood up, still glaring, still making strong eye contact, and growled. His eyes widened and he back up a half-step.

"All I did was ask—"

"No. You came into my house. You came into my workroom. You snuck up on me while I was busy with something. You did it deliberately!"

"Huh? Yeah, but I didn't—"

"'But' nothing! What you did isn't as important as what you didn't do. You didn't respect my boundaries. You didn't respect my territory. You didn't respect me."

"Look, I'm sorr—"

"You've said that before, but you do it anyway. You don't mean it. Out!"

"Ex*cuse* m—"

"Out! Get out of my house and out of my territory. If there's no other way to make you understand, I'll whack your nose with a rolled-up newspaper and piss in the corners! GET OUT!"

Rusty looked, by turns, shocked, insulted, and afraid.

"I didn't reali—"

"No talking! No puppy eyes! No argument! Get going!"

"But it's rain—"

"If you don't get moving, you'll find out how I'm armed!"

He lowered his eyes and backed up another half-step. He didn't say anything for several seconds.

"Human?"

I wasn't sure what to make of the query. He didn't sound accusatory, nor derogatory. It wasn't a derisive, "you're only a human" tone. Technically, it could be a form of address, as I was the only human in the room.

"No," I replied, less forcefully. "Not right now. Maybe later. Right now I'm the most dangerous thing in the room." He didn't argue the point.

"Can I come back?" he asked, rather plaintively.

"You can try. Ring the doorbell. Ask permission. Tomorrow, or the day after. Right now, don't say *anything*; you'll only make it worse. Go. Now!"

Rusty sighed. He sounded… sad? Disappointed? I'm not sure. He slunk out, removing clothes as he did so. I waited a minute, getting my temper under control, before I followed. I collected the trail of clothes leading to the doggie door and put them away. As he indicated, it was raining. It wasn't much, but thunder grumbled overhead. Good.

There are a lot of things about Rusty I don't understand. One minute, he's a canine, the next he's a human being. His behavior swings back and forth like a saloon door. I've tried to track it against the phase of the moon, but it doesn't seem to relate, aside from being an involuntary wolf during the full and an involuntary human at the new.

As a wolf, I love him. As a human, I'm not too sure. All I know for sure is we're friends. We haven't explored any romantic possibilities. If he can't learn basic human social conventions, we never will.

Damn it! I'm being narrow-minded! Is he *being* polite—from a wolf perspective? Or from a werewolf perspective, at least? Am I the one being unreasonable? I did program the fingerprint scanner on the doggie door to acknowledge his nose-print. Am I being too territorial about not wanting him to casually stroll in unannounced?

No. No, I'm not. It's my house. Most importantly, it's my workroom. A major error can cause major consequences and none of them good. I'm reasonable about having certain friends over with or without an invitation, but some spaces are *private* spaces, damn it all!

Even so, maybe I should make more of an effort to learn what's polite in his subculture so I can understand better when he seems to be a total cootie factory.

Only after I calmed down did I get around to wondering what he wanted. I didn't feel like calling him to find out.

That night, when I went to bed, Gus pinned my feet down and slept on them. I didn't mind.

Journal Entry #8

Over the next three days, I drew up a digital floor plan of a trap house in Queens. Jason and Rusty would enjoy knocking it over. I enjoy the planning more, I think, but I would enjoy the fight, too. I hoped Rusty and I could work out better boundaries, though. How complicated are human relationships? Adding a bit of wild animal into the mix can't make things simpler!

While I planned in the small-scale, Zeno made great strides in the large scale. He identified people in charge of different sorts of smuggling, as well as amassing details for who took what where, to whom, and for how much. A surprising amount of cargo went by dirigible. Giant ships plied the oceans with their cargo containers, but dirigibles roamed the skies. They carried goods directly to every major city, not just to seaports. No doubt they all had import and export security, but how tight was it? How *do* smugglers smuggle despite everyone trying to stop them? High-tech concealment? Or is it mostly bribes?

That's not what Zeno was told to find out, so he didn't. "How" wasn't our major concern. "Who" was all I was after.

I also spent time thinking about the bigger problem.

Alden is a psychic who is—as far as I can tell—bent on world domination. Originally, I was thinking about ways to deal out consequences, a sort of automatic spank response when he was naughty. In order to smack him for mental meddling, I need a way to make the meddling trigger something unpleasant for him. Like, if he tried to stick his fingers in someone's mind it gave him a nasty shock. Simply reading their thoughts would be okay, I suppose.

I'm sure I can develop a spell for that, but there's no reasonable way to cast it on him. The other alternative is worse: cast it on everyone in the world? *How?* Pop might be able to do it, but I can't!

Until I develop a way to link a negative consequence to his psychic actions, I don't have a way to spank him. I don't have a soft spot to go for. And I'm not sure I *can* do anything like that.

What does that leave? Killing him? It would be simplest, sure, but maybe we don't have to go quite so far. Can I capture him? Imprison him? Lock him away for a year or ten before letting him out with a warning not to do it again?

Hang on. Alden is grabbing lots of minds. He's not focusing on only the powerful and influential, he's grabbing even the homeless. The homeless are getting their brains mostly wiped and reprogrammed. Take it from me, this requires power. What it does not require is finesse.

They make good troops, but they aren't really allies. If he wants to build up a following—on the order of what he did to the Reverend Culson, for example—he has to be more delicate. He wants the person intact, but willing to do what he wants. Setting this up in someone's mind without causing insanity-inducing internal conflicts requires not only finesse but skill. The last thing you want is your new servant at City Hall being removed from his position because he's suffered a mental breakdown.

What would happen if I removed the mental blocks on some of them? Not all of them, just the ones who occupy the highest positions of power and authority? If Alden expects help from the Chief of Police, the Mayor, the Governor and he doesn't get it, can I use this to send a message? The message he shouldn't be meddling in people's minds?

What if I remove his tampering and leave his victims with the knowledge of what he did? They may not be able to do anything—how do you prove someone is a psychic mind manipulator in the courts?—but they can stay away from him and make his life difficult. The more people in authority he affects, the more difficult life becomes when they turn against him!

I thought about the problem while doing repetitive things against resistance. Gus lay nearby, watching me. He doesn't understand "exercise," but he keeps trying to see the point. If you're not having fun, why do it?

At the sound of the front doorbell, he perked up. He made a noise halfway between a woof and a bark and scrambled downstairs to investigate. I put a towel around my neck and followed more slowly. I found him facing the vestibule doors and growling a little.

The inner doors of the vestibule have high-tech glass as part of their decorative appearance. All my window glass is bulletproof, of course, but the inner doors' glass is also a video display. It's relayed from the outer doors. From the inside, it looks as though the inner door windows are actually the outer door windows.

Rusty does show up on video, not that I needed to see him. Gus already told me who it was.

I opened both sets of doors and Rusty stood there, fidgeting on the stoop.

"Hi," he offered, awkwardly, brushing his rust-colored hair back, out of his eyes.

"Hi."

"Uh… How you been?"

"Good, thanks. How are you?"

"I'm fine." He fidgeted for another moment and I let him. I wondered if his awkwardness was from my exercise clothes or from not being sure he was welcome. It was a tough call. His eyes kept coming back to me, then veering away. He settled it when he spoke.

"Am I allowed in?"

"Since you asked, yes."

He came inside, paused, turned around and went back to shut the outer doors, then came inside and shut the inner doors. He was working hard to be as polite as possible. I approved, but I also wondered why.

Nothing ventured…

"Rusty?"

"Yo?"

"You're trying really hard to be polite. Why?"

"You said—" he began, and reconsidered. "Aren't I supposed to?"

Holy crap. I'm the alpha. I didn't say anything while I tried my best to keep my features from showing it. Can a female be the alpha in a wolf pack? How about a werewolf pack? Do they even have formal packs? How does their social structure work?

Dammit, Pop! Why didn't you teach me *useful* stuff?

Then again, I've seen the same look on human faces, too, generally on the faces of boys who don't know how to talk to a girl. Maybe it's not his wolf side giving him fits about how to behave. For all I know, wolves and werewolves don't have this problem. I'm human, so his human side may be confusing his wolf instincts. Or my human reactions are. Or maybe I don't react the way he expects a human woman to react. I was raised by a single father, a machine-possessing spirit, and a psychic sword in a variety of different cultures. I admit I have some social handicaps.

"Yes," I told him, gently, "you are supposed to try to be polite. As I understand it, when you're in someone's territory, you should try to follow their rules. You don't have to be perfect, usually. Show a willingness. Most of the time, you can work out what really matters to your host and what will be annoying but acceptable."

"Okay." He fidgeted for a bit, trying to think of what to say next. I gestured him to a cushy chair—the non-cushy chair is for Pop—while I headed for my couch. We both sat down and he cleared his throat.

"Okay," he repeated. "I'm... I'm not good at being... see, I grew up as a city wolf, you know? I've had to deal with humans all my life. I grew up around them, but humans were always *them*, not us. They just... I guess they always thought I was one more asshole in a city full of them. See?"

"Not yet," I admitted, "but I would like to. You and I get along pretty well, for the most part."

"Yeah, but you know what I am, and you're not exactly standard, yourself."

"Being a witch?"

"Yeah. I know a couple of witches, real witches. At least I know 'em a little. They ain't exactly friends, if you take my meaning, but we know each other enough to nod. Mom doesn't like it, but Dad says it's good to know a guy who knows a guy."

"Got it."

"They're not like you," he went on. "They mutter their spells and wave their hands and draw things on the floor and the walls, throw stuff into fire, pour out water or kill a chicken, stuff little bags with weird herbs, all that stuff."

"I do it, too," I told him, "when the situation calls for it."

"Yeah, see, you don't need to do it all the time. They do. And they're old folks, gotta be in their forties and fifties, not like you."

"Is all this leading up to something?" I asked, trying to get him back on track.

"I'm trying to say I'm sorry. I'm not used to anyone being my friend who isn't a werewolf. Humans are..." he trailed off, groping for a word. "They're difficult. Complicated. They don't act like us—werewolves, I mean. And you're human. I think I'm driving hard to be polite and you still get mad. It's like I get no credit for being super tolerant and I get smacked down for not being perfect."

"You know, I was thinking about that," I told him. "Your ways aren't all human ways. Your social cues aren't the same. It's like monkeys and wolves. Monkey tribes evolved into human tribes, basing their social order off simians. Werewolf social order presumably evolved from wolves, based off canid behaviors. Neither of them is pure monkey or pure wolf because we developed self-awareness and intelligence."

"It's not a complimentary thing to say."

"About evolving from wolves?"

"Yes."

"In this metaphor, I also said humans evolved from monkeys."

"Okay, fair. I guess. Insulting me while insulting yourself in the same way... Still, we didn't evolve. We were humans, a long time ago, and became werewolves. The evolution thing doesn't sit well with us. I'm not sure my father would take it well, so don't ever mention it to him, okay?"

"Surely. And, before I go any further, let me add I do appreciate your patience. I appreciate it even more when you tell me why something I did offends you. You're good at concealing it when you're angry."

I didn't mention I could see his aura, if I tried, and he should never, ever try to lie to me.

"I should tell you when you do something?" he asked, cocking his head. Gus, sitting on the floor at the end of my couch and watching him, cocked his head in the same manner. I skritched his ears.

"Please. And I'll do the same. Eventually, we'll learn to not annoy each other so badly. We'll develop thicker skin to things we may not be able to avoid."

"Huh." He thought about it for a long moment, working through a few internal scenarios. "I can see how it might work."

"Good."

Rusty relaxed a little, settling back into his chair. Gus lay down on the rug but continued to watch him.

"We're going to be friends, right?" Rusty pressed.

"We are friends," I corrected. "You have some habits that are annoying as hell—but you tell me I have some that annoy the hell out of you, so it works both ways. I'd like to think we're working out ways to minimize how badly we annoy each other. Oh, we could have blown this all out of proportion and had a major falling out, but we're not idiots. We may have communications issues from our drastically different backgrounds and upbringing, but I'm sure you've had practice at overcoming that problem with humans, just as I have. We'll work it out because we'll talk to each other.

"And," I added, "I want to add something else."

"Go ahead."

"I'm sorry. I yelled at you. I snapped at you. I made derogatory remarks—one might call them racist remarks. I apologize for my behavior."

"I provoked you, and you're apologizing?"

"Motive counts. At least, it should. See, you didn't realize you were provoking me. I should have told you so. Actually, that's not quite right. I did tell you, back when you were poking around the house and I came downstairs in my robe. Remember?"

"Yeah. Sorry."

"Forget it. What I'm getting at is I should have told you firmly enough the first time to make you understand. And, if you're not perfect—"

"—which I'm not."

"—I should have been less angry… No, I should have *sounded* less angry and more firm. Then I could have reminded you about how I felt without shouting."

Rusty drummed his fingers on the arm of the chair and put his chin in his other hand.

"Now, see, I don't… I don't know how to respond to that."

"Why not?"

"It's a human thing. It's not how we would do it."

"By all means, tell me how you would do it."

"We love a good fight. Werewolves, I mean. If we have a disagreement, we have a fistfight to beat it out of each other, then go have a drink. We don't apologize."

"And if it was a serious disagreement?"

"We'd have a wolf-fight. In really serious cases, a hybrid-form fight. A wolf-fight can cost you an eye or cause serious damage. A hybrid fight is to the death."

"When you say 'hybrid,' you mean the half-man, half-wolf form you go through on the way to man or wolf?"

"Yeah."

"Can you stop anywhere along the way, between man and wolf?"

"Sure, with a little effort. Most of us start the change during puberty. We can't help but go to one extreme or the other. With practice, you learn to pause—ha, paws—halfway.

We eventually learn to stop anywhere along the way. Most of us can, I mean. It's not as easy as going to either end. I can get bigger and hairier, but still human, or I can be an exceptionally large and toothy wolf, or anywhere along the spectrum between man and wolf.

"As for the hybrid form, it's the midpoint of the transformation. It has its advantages. Your hands have claws, but they're still hands. You're bigger and stronger and regenerate faster. You're not as fast as a wolf, you can't run as far without tiring, and you're not acceptable in human company. It's like getting into your riot gear and strapping on all your guns."

"I can see why someone dies. All right. Humans sometimes get into a fistfight to settle their differences, too. Want to go find a bar and see who gets chucked through the window?"

"Uh? No. No, thank you. I, uh… no."

"Don't feel you have to take it easy on me because I'm human. If it's a human-form fight you want, I'm always up for one."

"If it's all the same to you," he said, carefully, "I would much rather accept your apology."

"Are you trying to accept a human solution in order to make nice?"

"Yes. Yes, that's it," he agreed, quickly. "That's absolutely it."

He was lying through his teeth. I can't be completely sure, but I think it had something to do with seeing me fight my way through a crowd of drug-fueled maniacs during a crackhouse raid. Maybe I flatter myself, but I think I look damned impressive. It's the armored ninja suit that really sells it.

"Well done. I'm proud of you, Rusty. But don't feel you have to. I'll try and meet you halfway. You've been a good friend and I don't want to jeopardize it."

"You won't. I think. We're both going to work on it, right?"

"Right."

"Great. So, uh… I don't suppose you were planning to make lunch?"

"On one condition."

"Sure."

"You've never really gotten to know Gus."

"Oh, *hell*," Rusty responded. Gus sat up and looked back and forth between the two of us. He's a smart dog and he's very sensitive to my thoughts. He picked up a little of what I was intending and wasn't a fan of it, either.

"I'm not asking for anything extreme. I want you to go with him to the park. I know, it's beneath you. He's only a dog. But I want you to play with him—not as a wolf and a dog, if you don't want to. You can think of him as a pet, if you like. You can teach him, as a pet, how to behave around wolves. He's very smart. Or you might want to wolf out and run around with him, showing him more of the neighborhood—or Manhattan—from a four-legged perspective."

Rusty chewed on his lower lip for a bit, eyebrows down and drawn together. He wanted to say something and was trying hard to come up with something *else* to say. Gus wasn't too sure he wanted to play Frisbee with a semi-wolf person, or follow a semi-human wolf around the city.

"I don't want to seem as though I'm offering a bribe," I added, to both of them, "but I did pick up some semi-exotic meats when I was down at the market."

"Semi-exotic?" he asked, curious. I had Gus' attention, too.

"Venison. Buffalo. Elk."

"You expected me to come back," he accused.

"I hoped," I corrected.

"I guess I can show your idiot kid brother around the neighborhood. Sort of. Yeah, your *dog*, but I'm trying not to think of it—him—that way, all right? I can... babysit, or have a playdate, or whatever. We don't get on well with dogs. Dogs are domesticated. You would call them 'civilized,' but we don't. I'm not sure Gus will want to get along with me, ever, even if I can think of him as a... whatever."

"I'll tell Gus to be on his best behavior," I promised, and did so. Gus whined in protest but agreed. To both of them I asked, "What do you want to eat?"

"You said there was buffalo?" Rusty asked. Gus' front paws danced. He didn't care what we started with.

"Yes," I agreed.

"I've never had buffalo. We've taken down deer, moose, and elk, but I've never had an actual buffalo."

"I can fix that."

Rusty went to the trouble of changing into his wolf form. I warmed some raw meat to living temperature and divided it between the two of them. While they still eyed each other as they chomped into their appetizers, they didn't have any arguments about who got how much.

Meanwhile, I prepared a red wine-braised buffalo tongue for the appetizer, then pan-seared buffalo steak with a white wine chimichurri sauce.

I really do like Rusty, despite the occasions when he pisses me off.

Once Rusty dressed for a human dinner, he continued to be nicer than ever to Gus. Every third or fourth bite, he flicked one over the dining counter and into the kitchen. Gus wasn't willing to sit by the table and wait for Rusty to give him snacks, but he had no objection to food magically appearing in the kitchen. I didn't say a word.

Peace offerings. I think it's a good sign.

After dinner, Rusty pushed his chair back from the table and sighed contentedly. His table manners aren't the best, but at least he doesn't belch, unbutton his pants, and pick his teeth at the table. At least, not that I've seen. I appreciated he was using "company manners" even at a private meal.

"Rusty?"

"Thank you," he said.

"You're welcome, but it wasn't a prompt."

"Oh. Yes?"

"Thank you for being so nice to Gus."

"You made it clear it was important to you," he replied, uncomfortably.

"Thank you for listening, then," I said. He chuckled.

"Hit me with a rolled-up newspaper when you want to make an impression."

"Ouch. I'm going to hear about that one for a long time."

"Maybe. I'll remember it for a long time, because you wouldn't have said it if you weren't well and truly mad at me. Can you tell me exactly what I did to piss you off? Was it startling you?"

"No—or not entirely. I don't like being snuck up on. I sometimes react faster than I think and it could get you hurt. No, what bothered me most was I was doing my witchery. If I'd been in the middle of something delicate and powerful, it could have blown up and turned us into carnivorous shoes."

Rusty blinked at me for several seconds, probably trying to decide if I was joking. I wasn't. He nodded, slowly.

"I'll try not to startle you while you're working. If I startle you some other time and don't duck fast enough, it'll be my own fault."

"That's fair. Come on. I want to bring you up to speed on what we know."

"Sure."

Rusty and I moved to my computer room to talk to Zeno. Gus, after a few moments, followed me. He lay down on the opposite side of my chair from Rusty.

I can hear Gus thinking. He's been my dog since I was... four, I think. Five? Somewhere in there. A long time. Gus doesn't particularly like Rusty, but Rusty is trying to be nice to me and to him, and Gus knows I want the two of them to get along. In some ways, it's harder for Gus. His intellect isn't as highly developed as Rusty's, so his instincts are harder to ignore. He's trying, and that's all I can ask from anyone.

"Okay, Zeno, what's the scoop on Alden?"

"I have his movements plotted, Ma'am!" Zeno reported, enthusiastically.

Rusty gritted his teeth. I glanced at him.

"Something wrong?"

"No, no. Nothing. Go right ahead."

"How well do you get along with computers, Rusty?"

"Fine. Fine. Absolutely fine. Nothing to see here. Continue."

"Okay. Zeno, what's Alden been up to?"

"I'm sorry, Ma'am! Did you want a full analysis and projection?"

"Of course. It's the same sort of thing as the smugglers and whatnot."

"You didn't specify, Ma'am, and I apologize. I can run the correlations now, if you like."

"Please do."

Zeno was quiet for several seconds. I waited for what seemed a long time. Zeno doesn't usually take any time at all to answer my questions, but I suppose he does a lot of his correlating and extrapolating before I ask. I've got to remember to specifically ask him to do things. He's not a "real person" AI. He's a bunch of programs, each of which does something fairly specific. He doesn't actually *think*. He only does what he's told. The user interface program is upbeat and friendly, though, so that's nice.

"Zeno?"

"Yes, Ma'am?"

"Anything?"

"My report is incomplete," he told me, still cheerful. I'm not sure if it's a limitation of his personality simulation software, or if the software is sophisticated enough to use a cheerful tone to imply, "Quit bothering me." Kind of like someone asking, "Is it much farther?" and the cheerful-tone answer, "Not far now."

Am I making my computer angry? I hope not. I wouldn't like it when it's angry. It's wired into most of the planet in one way or another.

"Give me something," I suggested.

"There is a correlation between some of his movements and an increase in automotive accidents."

"What sort of movements? What sort of accidents?"

"Since active monitoring began, Alden has visited the Manhattan Bridge, the Brooklyn Bridge, and the Carey Tunnel. He has paused at the midpoints of the structures in question, remained three to six minutes at each, and departed.

"Within twelve hours of his visits, each of these structures has had at least one car fire, with or without occupants."

"How can there be a car fire without an occupant?"

"In one case, no body was found. Police reports indicate the fires started in the passenger area of each vehicle, regardless of the number of bodies, or lack thereof."

"Were these self-driving cars?" Rusty asked.

"Just one! The car with no occupant was the only self-driving vehicle," Zeno reported.

"The other cars—they had bodies, right?"

"You guessed it!"

"I'm also guessing at least one of those bodies was behind the wheel?"

"You're on a roll!"

"Did all these car fires take place after dark?"

"Every single one, Rusty!" Rusty looked startled at the use of his nickname, but I knew Zeno wouldn't call him "sir." It's a user access authorization thing.

"What are you thinking?" I asked. Rusty smiled a big, toothy grin.

"Vampires."

"Vampires?"

"Vampires."

"Why vampires?"

"Because vampires can't cross running water," he said, positively. "Everybody knows that."

I didn't know it. I resolved not to tell Pop. He might suddenly realize he couldn't cross running water, which would annoy him. Then again, he swims like a brick, so he might walk across the bottom. He's not a fan of bathtubs, much less any water deeper than his nose.

"The East River counts as 'running water'?" I asked.

"I'm sure it does. Almost certainly. Probably. I think so."

"Okay, you're going to have to explain the vampire thing. I'm not seeing how it has anything to do with car fires."

"Vampires can't go on holy ground, right?"

"Sure."

"This Alden guy—he's a priest, right?"

"Yep."

"If he does something to a bridge to make it holy ground, vampires get scorched when they enter it, right?"

"Seems logical," I agreed, thinking of Pop's stories and a bunch of legends.

"If they attempt to drive over a blessed bridge, they catch fire!"

"Huh." I considered it. "All right, I can see it. They don't actually have to set foot on it. Put another way, if wearing platform shoes doesn't protect them, a car might not, either. Maybe the consecration effect radiates upward, or it's an area, not a surface. How does this relate to vampires not crossing running water?"

"Vampires can't move themselves over or under or through running water. Not on their own power, anyway. A self-driving car will carry one wherever he wants to go, though. And a mortal servant can carry one, too. So if you want to fry a vampire, you hit him when he's vulnerable. The bottlenecks of the bridges and tunnels are good places.

"I don't know the details," he admitted, "or what their limitations are when they're in the process of crossing water, but they might not be able to immediately scream for the car to turn around. Even if they do, the traffic sure as hell won't let them. If they don't stop, the car may get them out of the tunnel or whatever, but by then the whole thing will be on fire. If they stop, it's worse. The vampire would keep burning as long as it's on holy ground. So if the car catches fire and does an emergency stop, there's nothing left of the vampire. See?"

"Zeno?" I asked, turning back to the artificial face on the screen.

"The conclusion is valid," he agreed, happily, "although the probability assessment is incomplete."

"Is that a complicated way of saying he might be right?"

"Yes, Ma'am!"

"Noted. Continue with your analysis. —No, one more thing. How many other bridges and tunnels have had similar accidents since Alden arrived?"

"The total number is eighteen. Should I include ferry ports?"

"Have there been any incidents on ferries?"

"Not on ferries, but there have been eleven unexplained fires on ferry docking stations."

"Assume Rusty is right and a vampire gets into a car and tells it to get him off the island. What are the odds of the vampire not bursting into flames?"

Zeno projected a map of Manhattan and put a red dot on fire incidents.

"One in four-point-six-two, although the automatic vehicles are weighted to take roads rather than ferries. This assumes a random distribution. The odds improve to near-unity if a human driver is instructed to avoid bridges, tunnels, and ferry ports known to be incendiary."

I looked at Rusty. Rusty looked at me.

"He's killing vampires," Rusty observed, sounding pleased.

"No," I argued. "Or, yes, but only incidentally."

"Incendiarily," Rusty grinned.

"That, too. Look at the map. See how these points are distributed? Zeno, put a blue line along any road or access to Manhattan that hasn't had a car fire." He did so. There weren't many. "See what's going on? He's isolating Manhattan. Once they can't come and go, my guess is he'll start hunting them and clean them off the island."

"More power to him," Rusty decided.

"It doesn't make sense," I argued. "If they can't cross running water on their own and can't take a bridge, they get a servant to fly them out in a helicopter or something. Or a private yacht. Or buy a dirigible ticket. Hell, a vampire could be boxed for transport and shipped via cargo container!"

"Maybe he's trying to convince them all to leave?" he suggested. "If it's inconvenient and dangerous, they'll go away, won't they?"

"Maybe. I don't know why he would want to make Manhattan an anti-vampire island. I only know some of his goals, not his motives. "

"Oh? What do you know he wants?"

"Power. I'm not sure how this relates, though. If it does."

"Got me. Maybe he doesn't like blood-suckers?"

"I'm cautious about most of them, myself," I admitted, and an idea hit me. "On the upside, I do know something Alden is making."

"What's that?"

"Enemies."

Rusty gave me a look mixed of equal parts *Well, duh,* and *That's crazy.*

"No, hear me out. Vampires—most vampires—aren't necessarily evil. More often than humans, maybe, but it's not actually a requirement for most of them. They may have to drink blood and they've acquired interesting powers, but they're humans who adapted to extremely difficult changes."

"They're monsters," Rusty stated, positively.

"Some types are," I corrected.

"Vampires eat people. They drink their blood."

"How many humans have you eaten?" I countered.

"Huh?"

"As a werewolf. You turn into a seven-foot hairy thing with claws and teeth. Eaten anyone? Crushed their heads in your jaws? Clawed someone open until their entrails became outtrails? Anything like that?"

"Uhm," Rusty said. He tried not to look guilty. "I haven't actually *eaten*—"

"You monster."

"That's different."

"How?"

"I... uh... Well, when I'm defending myself from—"

"—humans who want to drive a stake in your heart? Oh, no, wait. I meant, 'shoot you with silver.' Sorry."

"At least I don't have to *eat* people!"

"True. You're a seven-foot hairy thing with claws and teeth and eating people is optional. They're humans with an infection *forcing* them to drink blood. You were saying?"

Rusty looked unhappy.

"Look, Rusty. You're a good person, or mostly. I know you, but from a human perspective, both vampires and werewolves are monsters. Not only are you something other than human—both, from a human perspective—you're dangerous to humans. As a werewolf, you're heavily armed, but you don't have to eat them. Vampires aren't as heavily armed, but are required to have a predator/prey relationship with humans. It kind of balances out."

"I don't agree, but I understand what you're trying to say."

"I'm sorry. If it helps, I don't think of either as monsters. Just different."

"Then I guess I can't call you a racist. Ignorant, maybe."

"That stings," I admitted, "but I'll also acknowledge you may be correct. There's always something more to learn. Bear with me while I do. And I will bear with you while you learn, too. Have you dealt with vampires a lot? Personally?"

"Hmm. Personally?"

"Yes. How much of what you know is from firsthand experience?"

"I don't like you throwing doubt over everything I know on the subject. I mean, I know what I've been told, but I haven't had a lot of personal... hmm."

"Maybe we should get some information directly."

"All right," he decided. "What do you have in mind?"

"First off, I have to tell you there are two major types of vampires."

"Good and evil?"

"No, evil and maybe-evil."

"Oh, well, that's a relief."

"Is it?"

"It's mostly sarcasm."

"Ah. Maybe you should stick to blunt truth."

"Noted. Go on."

"Okay. The majority are the maybe-evil. Kind of like normal people, really, like I said. The other type, the really evil ones, aren't really people anymore."

"What are they, then?"

"They started as humans, then got sort of possessed. They've become a kind of extension of a dark and powerful entity reaching into this universe to drain life energies out of it."

"So, they're demon vampires feeding on the living universe to pipeline it back to some arch-demon?"

"Excuse me?"

"I watch a lot of anime," he confessed. "This sounds like one of the plots."

"I haven't seen much anime, so I couldn't say."

"Oh, it's awesome stuff. There's—"

"Maybe later," I interrupted. "My point is, these creatures aren't human anymore. Their sole concern is to suck up everything they can, so everything they do is geared toward improving their sucking efficiency, either in the short-term or the long-term."

"There's an ex-wife joke in there, but I'm not going after it."

"Probably wise," I agreed.

"So, if the always-evil ones want to gulp down the universe, what do the not-necessarily-evil ones want?"

"What does anyone want?" I shrugged. "Food, security, friends, validation, leisure time, all that good stuff. My point is, good, bad or indifferent, I have no doubt all the undead are getting pretty fed up, not to mention scared. Random vampires are going *foof* when they drive in or out of Manhattan."

"I'd think the sound is more of a—"

"Skip it. They're bursting into flames and dying, and it's happening on more and more of the island's accesses. They may not know why. I hope they haven't figured it out. It'll be more valuable to them when I give them the information."

"You want them in your debt?"

"At the moment, they either don't know I exist or don't know enough about me to care. If I make them notice me, I'd rather they felt grateful for my help. I'll settle for them owing me a favor."

"If they have to pay attention to you, I guess that's a good way to do it. And the goal, here? The reason you're going to rat out Alden to a bunch of bloodsuckers?"

"They don't usually care for such derogatory language, fleabait."

"Not me. Special shampoo. What's the reason you're going to rat out Alden to a bunch of undead?"

"They may or may not kill Alden for it, but they're certain to make his life miserable, and that's one of my goals in life. He needs to learn there are consequences to exercising his powers indiscriminately. If someone else is helping, whether they know it or not, I'm okay with it."

"Is that the reason? Or is it because he hit your father in the face with a frying pan?"

"Yes. No. Mostly."

"I love the way you can be so precise."

"Shut up and help me figure out how to detect a vampire."

"I thought you were the expert?"

"Strangely enough, I never had to go looking for one."

"If it helps, I can smell them."

"You can?" I asked.

"They're dead. They don't smell the same as living humans."

"I suppose they don't. All right, where do I find one? If I'm going to give them help to beat the snot out of Alden, I have to at least know where they are. So, where do I find one?"

"Beats me. I don't hang out with vampires."

Sometimes, Rusty reminds me of my Pop. Not in a good way.

"Either we hang out at the Met in the evenings," I decided, "or I'm going to be in the workshop for a while."

"Huh?"

"I'll explain later. Right now, I should take a look at a bridge."

"Whuffor?"

"Because this is all speculation and deduction. I want to see for myself what's going on at these locations and get more information. I don't see a way to confirm anything, short of kidnapping a vampire and conducting an experiment, but maybe I can look at a site Alden was at and find evidence of what he did. Assuming, of course, he did anything. We've been guessing. Good guesses, sure, but we don't *know*. Zeno!"

"Yes, Ma'am!"

"You have the coordinates where Alden paused on each of the bridges?"

"Yes, Ma'am!"

Rusty elected not to come along. Obviously, there would be no vampires on a blessed bridge in the middle of the day. Instead, he decided to consult with his family about vampires—their habits, hangouts, and how they might be made efficiently dead. Deader. Destroyed.

I selected the Brooklyn Bridge for examination. Zeno compared my GPS coordinates to Alden's recorded location and guided me. I drove right past it the first time, circled around, and came back. There was definitely something mystical going on, centered near the midpoint of the river, but I kept breezing right past it. There was nowhere to stop. Literally, nowhere. No shoulder, no breakdown lane, nothing. You were either zipping across or you were blocking traffic. Since I didn't feel like getting hitting the emergency stop in a robocab and getting a ticket, I thought about other ways to get there.

According to Zeno, Alden was in the middle of the bridge for several minutes. Since Zeno confirmed there was no report of a traffic problem at the time, he must have been on the pedestrian walkway. It runs down the center of the bridge and is elevated above the level of the traffic. I took a scenic afternoon walk.

You'd think a supercomputer would have told me he went down the pedestrian walkway. Sometimes Zeno's limitations are a pain in the neck.

I had Zeno play back the scrying observation from when Alden made his trip. I should have done that in the first place. I'm not used to having video surveillance. Zeno confirmed my guesses about the pedestrian walkway. The image faded into static while Alden was sitting on a bench, however. I wasn't surprised. It lent a lot of weight to the "holy ground" theory. I had him play back the original recording through my augmented reality visor to guide me.

Yep. Found it. Near the middle of the river, the bridge has seven antique lamp-posts for the pedestrian walkway. At the base of one, there was a peculiar energy effect. I spotted it because I knew something like it had to be there and I was looking for it. It registered as light—not normal light—radiating through the wood and metal, running along it like paint, clinging to it, layering itself on everything. It spread several hundred feet along the bridge in both directions, slowly fading in intensity.

It took a little searching, but the video playback guided me to the center of the effect. I could see something bright, shining behind a big piece of metal. By kneeling on a bench, leaning over the rail, and reaching over and around an I-beam, I found what I was looking for. Feeling for, I mean. Stuck underneath the sheltering overhang of the I-beam was a hard little nugget. Touching it told me this was the source of all this celestial radiance.

It didn't want to come loose, but I can be persuasive. It cracked into pieces before it came free, though, so I didn't get to analyze it the way I wanted to. As I snapped it off the beam, I reflected that, at the very least, I identified his technique—the incendiary area— and I gained a sample of whatever it was Alden used to energize a piece of bridge.

When it broke, the power broke, as well. The brightness in my hand flicked out like a candle. Poof. Gone. It would take a while before the charge on the bridge wore off, but now it would eventually dissipate. Even with the widget, it might have had a limit on how long it would last; but by removing the focus, the effect couldn't be self-perpetuating.

The object, whatever it was, I put in a pocket of my purse and took home.

Journal Entry #9

I don't know how Pop can spend so much time in his workshop. Is it a guy thing? They love to spend time in the garage or the shed or whatever it is, building things, taking them apart, and doing stuff like that. I'll work on a project, but I won't live in the workshop.

I spent more time than I liked dissecting the broken bits of a hard little lump.

Most of it was a greyish substance. It was a putty epoxy, originally stuck to the steel and determined to stay there come hell, high water, or toxic waste.

The inside was considerably more interesting. When I broke it free, the lump cracked. Within it, a glass bead also cracked. More properly, it split in two under the force involved. The broken surfaces were bright and shiny.

After testing my epoxy theory by applying chemistry, I rinsed away sludge and was left with a broken bead of glass, dark brown bordering on black. When I pressed the pieces together, I got a natural-looking, uncut piece of glass. It was a semi-ovoid shape with what appeared to be parallel grooves running around it. It looked like a piece of obsidian.

Why would Alden use volcanic glass to—for lack of a better term—consecrate an area? Did volcanic glass have special significance? Purified by fire, maybe?

I had Zeno give me a rundown on obsidian. Unsurprisingly, it was a fairly detailed lecture, but I wanted those details. How do I tell if a piece of black glass is obsidian? Turns out there's an easy way. Heat it. Apply a clear, blue flame to it. Obsidian is formed from lava flows, usually under a layer of pumice. There are lots of gases trapped inside obsidian, so when you re-heat it, the gas comes bubbling out, turning the obsidian glass into froth, which cools into pumice.

Half my glass rock went under a pencil-torch and heated nicely to a white-hot glow. It didn't melt. It didn't froth. It sat there and took it like a champ, which told me one thing for certain: It wasn't obsidian.

"Zeno?"

"Yes, Ma'am!"

I described what my sample was doing under the flame test and asked if there was anything else it could be.

This got me a lecture on tektites.

If you don't know what a tektite is, don't feel bad. I'd heard the term, but the definition didn't stick. Tektites are glass bits formed in some meteor impact craters, where the ground is melted by the heat and pressure. Bits of molten goo are blasted out when the meteor hits. These bits cool in mid-flight and rain down on the surrounding area. Some of these bits, if the impact ground is made of the right minerals, form beads of meteoric glass as they cool. These are tektites.

Yay! Now I know what Alden is using!

Boo! I don't know why!

Lacking anything better in the way of leads, at least I could try and find out where he got them. I put Zeno on the project, checking to see if there was a lot of tektite buying and selling going on. One wholesaler in precious and semi-precious stones was doing a brisk business in tektites, mostly back and forth to other wholesalers, and mostly at a minor loss. Hundreds if not thousands of the things were going through his shop every week, and pretty much all of them lost the company a few cents on the dollar.

But they sold a very few, usually one or two at a time, at a weekly meeting with a private buyer. Zeno didn't get a name, but he did confirm it was the same customer account.

Was this company willing to lose money so one person can have his pick of the crop? Why would they do such a thing? Or was someone willing to pay so much for those few he liked as to make it worth their while?

Zeno checked the business ownership and correlated scheduling. He confirmed a meeting between Alden and Mr. Calumet. The company records said this all started before we began to physically track Alden, but Alden still went to a weekly meeting with him quite regularly, almost religiously.

The man likes his tektites, but he's incredibly choosy about them. He only wants a few. A fraction of one percent. A small fraction. This small fraction can apparently be used in conjunction with his powers, somehow, and act as a… what? Transceiver of celestial forces?

I wish I had an intact one to examine. Then again, if he's glued them to bridges and tunnels, I should be able to get one. Since I also know what he's using to fix them in place, I should be able to get it loose without breaking it.

I refilled my spare plant-misting spray bottle. Zeno gave me coordinates in the Lincoln Tunnel.

It helps when you know what you're looking for. It also helps to have a sort of pedestrian walkway alongside the traffic lanes. Periodically, there are doors and hatches, along with cable runs, traffic cameras, lights, and a whole slew of other things that come in handy when you want to conceal a hardened lump of goo the size of a thumb. Or an actual thumb, if you're into that sort of thing, I suppose, but I didn't find any.

There's nowhere to park in the Lincoln Tunnel, so I dressed for a run and went jogging along the pedestrian walkway. I got funny looks from drivers and passengers, but nobody had an accident. Over eighty percent of the cars in the greater New York area are now electric and/or self-driving, and the tunnels are all restricted to autopilot-only. Manually trying to drive your car in a tunnel earns a pretty hefty fine. It's cut down on accidents and closures, so I can't really fault them.

I jogged to the coordinates, put on my surgical gloves, spritzed the solvent, scraped fizzy goo out of a gap in the tiles, wiped off most of the more oozy parts, and peeled off a glove to turn it inside-out and effectively bag my prize. It went into a plastic bag, then into a pocket, and I was off, headed back the way I came.

Nobody tried to stop me, which told me something. It's possible Alden didn't have a real-time link to his energy-center locations. He might not know one of them was already running down. It's also possible he did know, but he didn't manage to redirect his homeless network in time to monitor all the other ones.

Of course, he might also have some peculiar power allowing him to watch over them, and now he would see me stealing a second one. I'd know more about it if and when he reacted to the losses.

I made it home without so much as a harsh word. I'm still not sure if he noticed.

Yep. It's a tektite. This one was intact and doing its thing, radiating celestial energies. I was a bit concerned about it being a beacon for unknown powers. Was it spreading a slow field of vampire-incinerating energies? It was trying to. Would it spread out as much as it did in the tunnel? Did it have a pre-defined shape or border, if not size? Did it require Alden's help to reach full size so quickly? Or would it spread slowly until it reached some sort of innate limit? Would it wear out over time, like a battery? Or was it generating power on its own?

If Pop showed up unexpectedly one evening, would it set him on fire?

Lacking any immediate answers, I put it in a small, iron box and drew containment wards on all six sides. It wasn't magical force, but magic can be used to affect other forces. Fortunately, this wasn't a particularly powerful source, so it only took a little fiddling before I figured out how to block it.

It pays to be careful. I might not be the only person who could detect these sorts of energies. Or was I? There were several of these things around town and there were no news reports of ethereal glowing auras along certain sections of tunnels. Nonetheless, Alden might be annoyed at having to re-do two of his... spells? What do I call these things?

It might be best to call them spells. The tektite was a power source. It somehow resonated with a celestial energy plane, allowing the higher energy level to seep down through the tektite and power the... the Holy Ground spell? It wasn't a magical effect—magic is a whole different sort of energy—but maybe celestial powers can be used in similar ways. Celestial magic instead of mortal magic, maybe. Miracles do happen.

So the celestial spell of Holy Ground gets cast on a bridge or tunnel and the tektite, as a power focus, keeps it supplied with energy to maintain itself. This isn't much energy in the celestial being sense. It's merely the background radiation of a celestial plane, insignificant in the greater scheme of things. Focused through a tektite in whatever fashion, it seemed to me it was specially tuned to fry vampires.

I've encountered Uncle Dusty on several occasions and the... what's the word? Aura? The power surrounding his presence was more generalized. If Uncle Dusty gave off a white light, the tektite was giving off light in a very narrow band of color. What little energy it allowed through underwent a sort of... not exactly a lensing effect, but maybe a frequency redistribution. If it was white light on the far side, the tektite shone with a purely red light, for example.

I'm not sure I'm explaining it very well.

After examining it—and locking it in a box—I think the Holy Ground spell can be overloaded and broken. There's a *very* limited amount of energy you can drag through such a conduit. Every vampire you fry will use up part of the energy and shrink the size of the area, draining more and more away. Over time, more can ooze out through the specially-tuned tektite. But if you shove enough vampires through the area, it will probably break the spell.

How many will be incinerated in the process? Is it more than two or three? Or are the dangerous areas a bluff? If five vampires go in there, one by one, do the last two come through fine? Or the last four? Or will one charged-up area fry a hundred before it runs out of charge? Does it matter what type they are, or how old and powerful they are?

So many variables!

I checked the other examples of Alden's vampire-frying work by trying to scry on them. Sure enough, I got interference. Zeno mentioned it when he watched me close in on the bridge tektite. It wasn't anywhere near as bad as a church or any holy ground structure Alden spends the night in, but it was enough. Zeno might not be able to see through it, but he has a hard enough time running controls on a scrying spell. When I do it, I can fight with it and get a grainy, snowy image. I can force it, but it's like looking through gauze curtains with an intermittent strobe light.

Would it be worse if Alden was present? Or was the effect based only on the amount of power involved? Or, since the energies produced by the tektites were specifically tuned to vampire-cooking, were they less effective at scrying interference? Was a church more steeped in celestial energies, and therefore more difficult to see? Or was it a combination of the two—Alden's presence and holy ground intensity? I think it's the two, taken together. I can scry into a church if Alden has never been in it, and, after a little experimentation, I determined the effect gradually wears off once he leaves, so it's not a permanent thing.

All right, what did this tell me? Rusty was right? Yes, by and large. It was bad for vampires and other unholy manifestations adversely affected by celestial energies.

Why?

There's the rub.

At a temporary dead end in my tektite investigations, I turned my attention to other matters. I'd work on something else while letting my subconscious gnaw the tektite problem. I had plenty of other things to do!

If I can explain to the local vampires what Alden is doing, they'll make his life miserable and possibly short, but I'm betting on misery. He seems able to protect himself. He'll probably be miserable for quite a long while, which I'm perfectly willing to see happen. Even better, his apparent plans for world domination will suffer serious delays, which gives me more time to figure out what to do about them and him.

Damn it, I still don't know what to do. Oh, I'm sure the vampires will come up with something. I don't know what *I* want to do, me, personally. I can't think of anything besides incarceration. What I really want is something like a shock collar to zap him whenever he's bad. What I have is a lack of ideas.

Why can't I think of anything? I always thought I was brilliantly creative. Pop always thought so, too. Not only did he say so, but I saw the look on his face. More than once, I offered a thought on one of his existing spells or techniques and he had a combination of amazed, sheepish, and proud on his features.

Then again, maybe it was Pop who made me creative. No, that's badly phrased. Maybe it was the both of us, bouncing ideas back and forth.

This being on my own thing might not be as much fun as I thought.

So, given vampires exist—and boy, do I know it!—how does one go about finding them? Spray blood on a wall and see who comes to lick it up?

Believe it or not, with certain kinds of vampire, this works. You do *not* want it to, but it does. Trust me. I've seen things I don't want to see again.

The local vampires are a more sophisticated breed. I've seen them at the opera. They pass for human with relative ease. I tend to lump vampires into two types: the Evil Baddies with the dark-souled nastiness, and regular people with a dental condition. While there may be subdivisions under the second type, they all started as humans and, presumably, got selected for vampirism by someone who had a reason.

How do I find a vampire in Manhattan? A real one, with teeth and everything, not a metaphorical one.

There are a number of ways. First off, I can see auras. This has good points and bad points. It's not an automatic thing. I don't go around seeing a rainbow nimbus surrounding every living thing all the time. It would get old, fast. So much radiant energy would cloud my vision to the point of uselessness. I wouldn't be able to walk through a crowd, drive a car, or even deal with walking down the street. Get me close to someone specific and I'll tell you if he's healthy or happy or undead, no problem, but I'm not going to go on a long-distance LSD trip if I can avoid it.

The other problem is the effort. I have to *try*. Imagine deliberately crossing your eyes and holding them there. How long can you do it? How long until the headache starts? And how many things do you run into?

A better option, from a headache perspective, is to get leads from Zeno. He's been happily infiltrating every computer network he can find, including little things, like the various police departments of the Greater New York Area. He can do a correlation to analyze trends and give me a good idea where someone might have a hunting ground. This narrows the search. He can also look into ownership of butcher shops, records of blood banks and hospitals, and a variety of other sources. Again, more leads.

Hmm. The reported information may not be the true information. He'll have to cross-reference what gets reported with other sources and look for discrepancies. But he knows his business. His intelligence analysis capabilities are stunning. The trick is, I have to tell him what I want to know. It's hard to remember he's not a person.

Still, leads aren't vampires. They're places to start looking. If I had a dozen people to do the legwork, no doubt a few of them would make contact with a vampire and get eaten. This would narrow the search, but would be a bit too expensive for my taste. Rusty promised to ask his family about vampires, so maybe they'll know where vampires hang out—as places to avoid, if nothing else! I doubt they can tell me where one keeps a residence, but you never know. Even so, a vampire hangout is likely to be loaded with humans. Depending on the hangout, there might be a lot of humans dressed in vampire-esque outfits.

And so, my third option. Pop gave me a werewolf detector. It's a lovely mechanical wristwatch with a magical complication. The enchantment built into it is... You know, I'm not sure if it's one of Pop's more complex spells or if it's a "messy bits" spell, as he calls them. Among his more complex creations are things *I'd* have to do with goat blood and raven guts. But he built it, so it will last forever. As long as I don't break it, I won't have to try to make one on my own.

What it does is send out a low-power locator pulse, like radar, which only bounces off werewolves. If it detects anything, it tingles my wrist. Getting it to do all that mystifies me and I'm not even sure where I'd start. How do you tell a human from a werewolf when they both look human? Silver? Moonlight? Pop managed it, which I find unsurprising, but he gave it to me as a gift, not as a lesson.

Vampires, on the other hand—the local ones, I mean—are dead. D-E-A-D, dead. They don't breathe unless they remember. They don't have a heartbeat. They cool to room temperature if they don't have a way to artificially warm themselves. These are characteristics they can't shake off like a werewolf shaking water out of his fur all over the bathroom.

Don't ask. I've put a sort of squeegee spell on the doggie door since then.

Still, I could start with the scanner Pop built. I could add a spell—not an enchantment—and connect it as a bypass around part of the enchantment's functions. The spell would substitute vampire search criteria instead of the built-in werewolf search pattern. Then, when I'm reasonably close to a vampire, I'll know it. Hopefully, I'll know it before they know I'm close to them. Best of all, I don't have to be *too* precise in the pattern definition. I can look for a corpse and I should get hits. I might also want to set it up so I can switch between the two, or have it detect both at once... how do I tell the difference, though, if I'm running them in parallel? Tingles are tingles. Maybe a color change? I don't think an actual glow is a good idea, but maybe if the watch changes color? Silver for werewolves and dark red for vampires? I get a tingle, which tells me to check and see which sort is present? Yes, that should work.

So I did. I locked the door to my workshop, though, to keep Rusty from interrupting my witchery. Good intentions notwithstanding, having an interruption in my experiments could be detrimental to his continued health. It might be bad for me, too. It's seldom good to have an experimental spell go wrong, especially in a highly-charged magical environment! It would be even worse if I got distracted during the work and broke Pop's (irreplaceable!) enchantment. Worse for Rusty, I mean.

Of course, once I had a workaround in the enchantment, I had to test it. And I planned to, right after I took a day off from all the witchery!

Before I went off to do dangerous things involving corpses that didn't want to lie down, I paid Cameron a visit. He's doing better, but not a lot better. He was glad to see me and did remember my previous visit, so there's that. I sat with him by the pond and held his hand. He was content to sit, so I took the opportunity to look in on his mind, make sure the stitches were holding, and to massage the psychic scars.

I may not love Cameron in the way he wants me to, but I do love him.

After the visit, I took a cab out to the old house. The place was exactly as I left it. This time, being dressed less Suzie Homemaker and more Pioneer Woman, I cleared debris from around the clockwork-themed partial statue. I did a little preliminary work, preparing it for a teleport into the basement of my house. It's good to have something at both ends. It saves a lot of headache and power.

An owl—I think it was the same owl as the last time—sat on the sculpture's not-quite-head and watched me work. I grinned up at it as I considered its unusual behavior, given how owls are nocturnal.

Hang on. Are all owls nocturnal? Or is it a common belief? Are there owls that prefer daytime?

"Everything all right?" I asked, on the off chance it would reply. It blinked at me, which I did not consider an answer. I listened with my inner ear and didn't get an answer that way, either. Oh, well. Maybe owls are allowed to be curious. So was I. I checked my purse, found a packet of beef jerky, ate a little, and offered the rest to the owl. It was a brave owl. It fluttered down to the incomplete shoulder of the statue and solemnly took the strip of meat in one claw. It nibbled on it. I finished clearing the area and used a handy chunk of debris to carve deep lines in the dirt around the semi-statue.

Wait just a cotton-pickin' minute, I thought. *I didn't hear **anything** from the owl.*

I looked around for it, but it had flown off. This bothered me. I should have heard some sort of thoughts from the thing. I should have been able to read something. Anything! Curiosity, concern, hunger—something!

It bothers me when my powers fail me. Either I have a problem, or something I don't understand is going on, which means I have a different sort of problem. Sadly, in this case I had nothing I could do about it. I kept a little attention reserved for spotting the owl if it came back, but I went ahead with my transport preparations.

Back at my house, the basement is a parking garage. I had a contractor do a lot of work to strengthen the place and get me a ramp down from the curb. Bronze parked her spare vehicle down there next to my car. This still left me with plenty of room to park a horse or four. A clockwork-themed partial sculpture of one would be easy. I went through a fair amount of my magical reserve to summon it from Shasta, but I have a space-frame setup already in place for moving car-sized things from world to world. Pop did the major work on it, so of course it works flawlessly.

The sculpture and I appeared without fuss, along with a small cloud of dust and old ashes.

I resolved three things immediately.

First, get a bigger vacuum cleaner. I have a spell on the house to keep it clean, but it's mostly for light dusting and fur control. This mess would take days to remove.

Second, expand my crystal battery array. A large-sized interuniversal teleport is *expensive!*

Third, get welding gear. If I'm going to work on a clockwork-sculpture horse, I'm not doing it with my bare hands and spells.

You'd be amazed what you can order online. The vacuum cleaner and large quartz crystals? I expected those. But welding gear? I found that surprising. Turns out the equipment is easy. Getting gas bottles is a little more involved.

Journal Entry #10

I called Rusty and we arranged to meet. I wanted to bring him up to speed on my latest wristwatch complication. Since I was going jogging—the weather report said it would rain, later, and I didn't feel like changing it—he decided to meet me between Mount Tom and the River Run Playground. It would look like a happy accident rather than a deliberate meeting. I didn't think much of it, one way or the other, but I'm trying to humor him. He doesn't like Alden's mind-wiped zombie spies; they don't smell any different. They make him nervous. Wolves are pack hunters, so maybe he doesn't like the idea of humans doing it better.

When we spotted each other, I waved and veered toward him. We walked together past a couple of street vendors, picked up lunch, and found a bench.

"So, let me get this straight," Rusty said, leaning back. He handed me my falafel. "You have a vampire detector which might or might not work, and you want me and your pal, Jason, to cover you while you see if you can identify undead?"

"Yup. Are you in?"

"I'll bite anything you want," he volunteered, "but I prefer abusing drug dealers and other criminals. It's profitable."

"I sympathize. Are you in this for the money? Or for the feeling of righteousness in pursuing a good cause?"

"Mostly it's fun," he decided, "but money helps. It sure makes my Dad happy to see me earning a living, even if he doesn't approve of how much exposure I could be getting."

"Fathers can be so protective. Would it help to make more money?"

"How much can I have?"

"You want it in cash or in securities? Or a trust fund? How much a month?"

"I was thinking in terms of a share of the loot, not a paycheck."

"Either way works for me. I don't need the money."

"You're serious?"

"Money is not a problem. My connections have turned our ill-gotten gains into capital gains. Ten million in a Swiss account? Or do you prefer the Cayman Islands?"

"Uh... I'll get back to you."

"Anytime. So, it is mostly about the money?"

"Nah," he said, waving a hot dog carelessly. "It's the getting it. You know, taking it from people who, like, deserve to lose it. I like getting to rip into people who deserve a ripping. Or something. Maybe it's not about having their money so much as taking it away from them."

"I promise we'll steal a pile of it—or burn it. I have plans in the works for the next hit."

"I'm okay with that. I'm less okay with your Jason."

"I know, I know! You don't like him. Look, just because he shot your brother—"

"—with silver."

"With silver," I agreed. "Remember, Mark bit him first. It was an impressive bite, too. Don't say it wasn't. If it wasn't for the armor, Jason would be missing an arm *at least*. I can fix a lot of things, but I'd have to work fast to keep him from bleeding to death right there, on the spot."

"Well, yeah. Mark was high, but not so high he wasn't surprised when Jason shot back."

"Let's settle for saying they attacked each other. Is that fair?"

"I guess I can go for it. Mark won't."

"Pride? Or stubbornness?"

"More like general dipshittery."

"Jason's still salty about it too, but I've talked to him. He's going to try to be professional about it even if he can't let it go. Still, this doesn't make either of them a bad person. You freely admit Mark is an idiot."

"Well, yeah, but he's my brother. *I* get to say that. Doesn't mean I'm okay with any pipsqueak gung-ho human with a nine-mil popping rounds into him."

"I understand the feeling. And I also understand Jason's point of view. Thing is, I'm going out to test a gadget for hunting human-eating creatures. I want backup."

"Why not have him do the experiment?"

"Because he can't operate the prototype."

"How about I do it for you? I can smell them."

"If I'm using the detector and something chases you, you can run while I still do the test. Do they recognize werewolves when they see one?"

"Um. Sometimes. I'm not sure how they know, or why some of them do and some of them don't. We tend to avoid each other."

"Really? Why? I've always heard legends about vampires and wolves getting along."

"Wolves, maybe," he snorted. "They don't understand when they're being used. Werewolves don't appreciate being used by anybody and, as I understand it, vampires don't appreciate being chewed to ribbons."

"That's reasonable."

"Speaking of reasonable, why not drive around during the day? Your gadget can detect the things at a distance, right? It's not like you have to shake hands or slap one on the back, do you?"

"No, it works at range."

"So cruise around in a robocab and do your mapping. Put pins in a map wherever you get a beep or whatever. I talked to Mom and Dad. They called around and got suggestions on where to look."

"I can and I might, later. This is the testing phase. I have to confirm it actually works before I start getting a ton of false positives to cloud my results. It's *supposed* to detect undead people, but it might go *ping* for recently-deceased corpses, too. Who knows how many corpses are lurking anywhere?"

Rusty chomped into his hot dog to give himself time to think. I devoted more attention to my own food. Randall is my falafel connection whenever I jog along the Hudson River Greenway. He makes the best.

Watching Rusty demolish a hot dog, I wondered how hard it was to be a werewolf in the big city. Admittedly, the guys in animal control weren't going to be a major issue, but keeping a low profile as a rogue wolf might be important.

What *is* the wolf population of Central Park? Or of Long Island? And what's the *werewolf* population like? He mentioned his mother and father calling around to ask friends. Is it a large community? I wanted to ask, but I didn't. I have restraint.

"You're the one who wants to find vampires," he shrugged, finally. "I'm not sure that's a totally sane idea in the first place. They don't like being found. I talked to Dad about these things. They have human servants, but not a whole lot of them. Letting living people know they exist, even to make them a servant, can be grounds for getting the vampire drunk."

"Vampires can get drunk?"

"Drank? Gulped down? Eaten by his own kind."

"Oh, *drunk.* Got it. And there's another reason I don't want to put Jason out front. I want to find them so I can talk to them. He has too much of a murder agenda. I think and hope I can arrange to have a civilized discussion with them."

"Maybe, but I agree with him on the vampires."

"At last. Common ground."

"Yeah, I guess."

"You don't want to find common ground with him?"

"I don't like him."

"Your privilege. What it all boils down to is this: He's going to help me with the vampire hunting test. Are you?"

Rusty curled his lip at me before wolfing down the rest of his hot dog. I took it as an affirmative.

I dressed like someone out for a good night on the town. I went with the Little Black Dress in velvet and ballistic fiber. The idea was to be in the mid-zone of dressiness where I would be acceptable in almost any venue. With the accessories and makeup in my purse, I felt sure I could make adequate changes. True, I might stand out a little as someone who misjudged the dress code, but I wouldn't be glaringly inappropriate. An evening gown at a techno dance club would stand out, just as sequined short-shorts and halter would stand out at Rockefeller Center. Middle of the road, that's the ticket, until I decided which side of the street to walk.

I made sure my more routine magical gear was armed and ready. I wasn't wearing my super-suit, of course. It's hard to blend in with a suit of high-tech ninja armor. You might think that makes it easier to remain unseen. After all, ninjas do it. Pop never got around to sending me to ninja school, though. The stealth functions are good, but they aren't the same thing as being invisible.

Hmm. Invisibility. Something to work on. It's a tough spell to do well, but I'm starting to wonder if I should invest the time and effort.

Jason, on the other hand, wore his suit. He followed me around by leaping tall buildings in a single bound, or at least leaping from rooftop to rooftop. I made sure not to lose him.

Rusty also followed me around, although he used different methods. It took him a while to adjust to the idea of wearing a collar as a wolf, but he managed it. I think it helped when I pointed out he was using human civilization against itself, tricking them with their own rules. A wolf wearing a collar and tags is effectively *disguised* as a dog. To save his paws, he rode with me in a cab for a while.

At Rusty's suggestion, I told the autocab to head for *The Night Crawler*, a two-storey club in a four-storey building. It shared a block with other structures, but while it joined others on the sides, a narrow alley ran behind it, dividing the block. The club had lots of blue and purple on the outside, which kind of set the tone for the place.

I opened the car door facing away from the club and let Rusty out. He padded off between two parked cars and took his station. I stayed in, closed the door, checked with Jason through my phone, and gave him a few moments to find a good spot. Jason worked his way around the club, on the rooftops, while I switched over to my earpiece. I climbed out of the cab, held out my phone in proper selfie-taking style, and turned in a circle.

The tingling sensation came only from the club. I couldn't tell how many were in there, but it was a broad arc. There might be two or three, or it could be the Secret Vampire

Cabal Headquarters. Either way, it was open to the public and casual murder would get the place noticed in ways nobody wanted. Going in, looking around, doing a quick vampire count, and leaving should be safe enough. I put my phone in my purse, leaving the call connected to Jason.

Fortunately, it was not a private club of the sort I'm used to. This wasn't a place where you had to apply for membership, have an interview, maybe get voted on, and so forth. This was a party house with an entry fee. I could probably have skipped the line if I cared to change into something less "little black dress" and more "rave on." It was more important to avoid complications, though, so I waited, altered my makeup while in line, paid the fee, and made it past the velvet rope.

Pop would *loathe* the place. I wasn't immensely fond of it, either. The lighting was dim, mostly black lights or deep purple. Fans of red laser light accented the blues and purples. The music was loud. Two or three mini-spotlights pulsed white lines of light overhead, in time with the music, sometimes crisscrossing or slashing narrowly through the dark. The people were a crowd, not individuals, and moving through it reminded me uncomfortably of rush hour on the subway, only with less purpose.

Structurally, the place occupied most of two floors. A thick central pillar dominated the room and a circular bar surrounded it. The pillar concealed stairs, at least; it had a door, probably for supplying the bar during business hours. I didn't immediately see anywhere along the bar where it would open up. A mezzanine ran along all four sides of the room, with spiral stairs in the corners and a smaller bar in the center of each wall. A raised area opposite the main door was probably for live entertainment, but it was presently occupied by a DJ and a collection of DJ-related electronics. The tables were mostly on the mezzanine level, but a couple dozen small, put-your-drink-down tables were scattered along the ground-floor walls.

I wished for Pop's darkvision so I could ignore the shadows. Then I thought how much worse this place would be if there wasn't any darkness. Or would it? The contrast wouldn't be so bad, but there would be so much visual activity it would still be a pain. I decided to work my way along the walls, checking for doors and exits before anything else.

Exit signs? Yes. Illuminated? No. Obviously, this place had a few health and safety violations. At least I found the toilets without much trouble. I also found several unmarked doors along the sides, but didn't try to open them. Two exits were on the wall opposite the entry door. The mezzanine level became overhanging balcony along the front and back. To the sides, it was recessed. I concluded the public area didn't occupy all of the first floor.

"Anything?" Jason asked. My earphone volume was turned up as high as it would go, but I still barely made out what he said. I tried to respond verbally, but noise-canceling microphones can only do so much. After a bit of texting, we settled on the usual one-for-yes, two-for-no code. I tapped fingernails on the casing of the ear unit.

At least my wristwatch worked. I went across the floor, up a spiral staircase to the mezzanine level, and back down again, triangulating.

The crowd had two hits. The mezzanine level had four more. The upper floors had another two.

Below the ground floor, there were dozens.

I was less comfortable with my plan. While it was possible the underground corpses were nothing but corpses, out here in public they almost had to be walking-around corpses. Discounting those, there were still a lot of undead.

I wanted one vampire, not *eight*. Eight above ground, I mean. I had no desire to meet twenty or thirty at once. I felt I could handle one at a time. Two would be a bit much. All I wanted to do was get close enough to confirm my detector was actually registering what I wanted it to register. If I found a second one, great. I could double-check and make sure it was working properly.

Only then would I want to magically follow one around, find out who might be a good vampire to approach about ratting Alden out, and arrange a meeting. What I did *not* want was to walk into a whole nest of them!

On the other hand, following one around might have led me here, anyway. At least I had plenty to choose from. Smoothing out the detection criteria so it didn't register regular dead bodies would come later. Come to think of it, what was the process for these vampires to go from human to vampire? Were there preliminary stages that might also set off my detector? Good question, Phoebe! Pity about the lack of answers.

I decided to get Rusty some club-going clothes and bring him in. Then I thought, no, wait. Does he have to be in wolf form to smell them? He didn't specify and I didn't ask. Crap. Now I would have to give multiple people the big eyeball in less than ideal circumstances.

There are several different healing spells in my rings. Two of them would be able to help with the upcoming headache.

I spent the next hour drifting through the crowd, occasionally staring too hard at people. Part of the time, I rested my eyes from the exertion, but the time wasn't wasted. Between bouts of eyeballing, I practiced using my wristwatch scanner in a less-obvious fashion. I found I could hold my arm at my side, holding on to my purse strap, and use my forearm as the primary line of detection. This was less accurate, but helped narrow my field of focus when I got close, which cut down on my headache-inducing efforts.

Yep. Vampires. Rusty was right. *The Night Crawler* was a vampire hangout. I began to think Manhattan had a lot more undead than was good for it. Not that there aren't enough unpleasant people to feed Pop and a hundred more like him, but these guys weren't as picky. Or, no, maybe they were just as picky, but in their own ways. Come to that, they may not have the same feeding schedule as Pop. Do they need to kill a victim? Do they need to feed once a month, a week, or every night? Or does hunger drive them to eat whether they need to or not?

Their feeding techniques were pretty much identical, as far as I could see. The vampire emits a sort of aura of attraction, of fascination. People sensitive to these things—or more vulnerable to such influences—gravitate to the source. It looked straightforward to me. I could do something similar, no problem, but I get enough attention as it is. I never saw Pop do anything like it, though. He was much more straightforward about hunting prey. But the other psychic titan, Alden... did he do this sort of thing? Did it draw people to him, give him the illusion of charisma, and open them up to more direct and invasive influences?

Here and now, though, nobody was actually feeding on anyone where I could see. The unmarked doors to the sides, under the recessed mezzanine levels, led either to other rooms or to stairs or a combination. One of the vampires I identified led her upcoming brunch through one of these doors, so it wasn't unreasonable to assume there was privacy available. Upstairs, maybe? Surely the building has an elevator.

As an aside, the gender of the completely undead confuses me. I mean, they're not doing anything the living would do with it. They still seem to stick to traditional gender types, though. Maybe it makes hunting for a meal easier. It certainly takes the concept of necking to a whole new level.

I decided I'd gathered enough intelligence on the place. I'd personally seen eight vampires coming and going over the course of the evening, right down to their auras, and detected what could be even more in the building. With their physical parameters of the eight I observed, as well as their auric signatures to go on, I felt confident I could scry on at least a few of them without much trouble. Locking a scrying sensor onto them might take work, but it would be more tiring than complicated.

As I left the club, I received my forty-seventh or so invitation to dance, get a drink, or otherwise begin the preliminaries to more intimate social interaction.

I've never quite understood why a loud, dim, crowded room is considered a good place to meet people and socialize. Dance with random strangers? Sure. Catch six different kinds of a cold? Definitely. Swap spit in the shadowed corners? If that's your thing. Have too many drinks, pills, and morning-after regrets? No doubt. Get high, get stupid, and get a social disease? You bet.

Pop never taught me proper behavior for a nightclub. He did escort me to a couple so I wouldn't play Jane Hayseed if I walked into another one, but he hated them. Maybe that's why I never understood them. An Old West saloon? I'll take one of those any day. You can sit somewhere, have a drink, and—best of all—a conversation.

Anyway, as I started to decline the latest invitation, I waved a hand in his direction as part of the brush-off. My wrist tingled with a much sharper, more intense sensation than before. The young man trying to pick me up was hoping for a dinner date.

Make that *nine* vampires over the course of the evening.

As I've noted, it's hard to have a conversation inside a club. Anything more than a shout about what you'd like to drink is problematic. On the other hand, this guy had resources of his own. He ignored my wave-off, sidled up next to me, flashed a smile, and said something almost impossible to make out. I'm pretty sure he suggested we go somewhere quieter. Strongly suggested it, I should say.

I was not impressed.

My earrings are small studs with three little spell crystals, each, designed by my Pop and built by me. They registered the impact of a mind-affecting force. The outer defenses detected it and absorbed it. The inner shields were never even touched. Judging by the effect, I could have shrugged it off with my naked brain, but I have shields so I don't have to.

The outer shield is a soft thing, designed to give the impression of success when someone shoots a non-communication thought at me. It doesn't ricochet or reflect or anything. If someone tosses a thought my way, but isn't actively trying to read my mind, they don't get any feedback to tell them their attempt failed.

Think of it like gunfire. The outer layer is a thick wall of ballistics gel. You shoot it and the bullet goes in, as expected. The second layer is a layer of ballistic fiber inside ballistics gel. Bullets go in, but they come to a sudden halt. The third layer is the armor plate. No fooling around.

Pop is *paranoid* about mind control. Considering his abilities, I'm *glad* he is. Plus, it means I'm a lot safer mentally than in any other way, so that's a plus, too.

I had a vampire propositioning me. We were unlikely to have any sort of conversation in this environment, but could we find somewhere quieter to talk? If so, I would save myself a lot of work in tracking down someone to explain Alden to. The thing of it was, though, I did *not* want to go into a back room in the vampire frat house. This did not seem wise. But if he was willing to follow my lead, he might be the right person to open negotiations.

I took his hand and promptly headed for an exit. He didn't seem to mind leaving the building. My guess was his psychic suggestion was to go somewhere quieter without specifying where. Private room, upstairs boudoir, back alley—they all meant more privacy than a dance floor, so he didn't care too much.

We made it outside, into the cooler, damp darkness. It was raining slightly, one of those rains too heavy to be a mist but too light to be real rain. The weather had cooled markedly and, combined with the humid air, my breath fogged. His didn't. The door swung shut and we held it closed, him with one hand, me with my back. He moved in to kiss me as a starter, but I held up a hand and covered his mouth. I pressed a finger to my lips. He cocked his head, puzzled. His eyes were quite striking. The irises were thin rings of blue around enormous black pupils. The whites of his eyes were stark, featureless white.

"Shh. Listen for a second," I suggested, lowering my hand.

"Relax," he countered. The impulse his mind sent out was considerably stronger, but it didn't have a prayer of getting through. "Just go with it," he added.

"No, I don't think so. If you're feeding in back alleys, you're probably not the person I should talk to. I'd like to speak to someone with more authority, please."

His entire demeanor shifted. A romantic dinner was now off the table. A field-stripped dinner after a violent, bloody hunt might not be.

"Who are you?" he demanded. He raised one hand, presumably to hold me by the throat, but I surprised him. He didn't expect me to move so fast. I may not be faster than every vampire, but I'm faster than many and much faster than they expect. I don't lack for power, but speed and skill are where I excel.

I have never been afraid of Pop's hands. When I was little, they were the most powerful things I could imagine. I deeply respect his hands, but fear them? Never.

Other vampires' hands, though, are a whole different box of crackers. I am afraid of those. Not a quivering, terrified, helpless fear, but a rational and understandable fear. They are dangerous. They are weapons. A vampire is armed even when he's naked. Never assume otherwise, because you will be wrong and then you will be dead.

With a human being, I would have gone for a simple lock. With a hand turned in an improper way, most humans will happily cease hostilities in the hope you won't do anything worse. Vampires, on the other taloned member, are different. They're stronger, they regenerate, and their reflexes are generally predatory, geared to attack, not wince in pain.

I twisted his hand to the outside, out of the way, punched him in the throat, ducked under the inward sweep of his other hand, kicked his knee hard enough to pop it completely out of place, stepped and turned, caught him as he topple-turned toward the now-useless leg, and whirled him up and over and down the three steps to the pavement. I didn't hold back at all. Broken bones take longer to regenerate than soft tissue injuries. He made a lovely *whump!* sort of sound, along with meaty cracking noises.

I came down from the doorway—I don't like being backed into a corner—and moved off a couple of paces down the alley. I stepped out of my shoes. Heels don't usually go well with a brawl. He lay there, looking up into the misty rain, blinking. I think he was also letting his vampire regeneration take care of the worst pains before he moved again.

"I don't want to fight," I told him. "I want to talk. There's a guy named Adam Alden and he's a bigger problem for you than you realize. If you can speak for the vampires of New York, great. If not, I'd like to speak with someone who can."

As I spoke, he made a growling sort of noise and turned over onto his belly.

"Are you going to be reasonable?" I asked. "You tried to grab me and I resisted—that's all. I didn't follow up. And you regenerate, so there's no lasting harm done. I'd like to think we can have a civilized discussion."

The reddish gleam in his eyes made me fairly certain he wasn't going to be civilized. The lengthening fingernails and the fangs were also clues. Either he was a particularly short-tempered individual, or this particular breed of vampire had predatory instinct problems. Maybe it was fragile male ego problems. I *did* defend myself a little more forcefully than was strictly necessary, but Pop never complained when I dislocated anything on him.

"This is not how I wanted this to go," I added.

He shook his head, clearing damp hair from his face, and leaped for my face, propelling himself toward me with hands and feet, springing like a jungle cat despite the damage to one leg. Even if he'd had both in perfect working order, it was a bad move. You don't get to make course changes in mid-air.

I dropped and rolled forward along the damp pavement, ignoring the stray bits of paper and other alley garbage. His snarl of rage turned to a snarl of dismay. I was on my feet and facing him by the time he landed. He rolled to his feet a trifle awkwardly. His knee was still giving him trouble, but his shoes also skidded slightly on the slick surface. No doubt the knee pained him as well, but the structural issue was correcting itself.

"You don't want to do this," I cautioned. "You don't know what you're getting into."

He paused long enough to let his knee make a wet, popping noise as it clicked back into place. His eyes still glinted red.

"Tell me who you are," he rasped. His throat wasn't in great shape, either.

"No. I'm only here to help before I go on my way."

He blinked, startled. No doubt he expected his influential powers to reduce me to compliant goo. They hadn't worked before, but he tried again, anyway. Obviously, he wasn't the quickest bat in the cavern.

"You have only a few options," I went on. "You can talk to me, put me in touch with someone who can talk to me, you can walk away, or we can get into a short, vicious, probably fatal fight. I *want* to behave in a civilized and non-lethal fashion, but it's really your call. What's it to be?"

"I will be repaid for this indignity by the terror in your eyes when I squeeze the last breath from your body."

"Not bad," I admitted, sighing. "Did you memorize it?"

He snarled and crouched and Jason landed on him.

For the record, the suit enchantments normally absorb all the energy of a landing. This means whatever we land on doesn't go *squish*. If you land on a car roof, you come to an instant halt and you're suddenly standing on a car roof. If it's a ragtop, your feet still might rip through the material, but only because you're standing on a ragtop!

On the other hand, sometimes you want to hurt something. Normally, the suit stores momentum so you can use it later on something else—even yourself, for leaping tall buildings at a single bound. If you don't want to keep it for later, it's perfectly reasonable to—as a random example—transfer the momentum from an eight-storey fall directly into whatever you land on. In this particular hypothetical example, let's say it's an undead person.

It's kind of like a trick shot on a pool table. One ball hits another exactly so. The first one comes to a halt and the other one shoots away. With the armor, this means Jason came to a stop mid-air as he touched the vampire's head or shoulder or whatever. The vampire, however, now had all the momentum. It was the same effect as if the vampire was the one who fell eight storeys.

Vampires make crunchy noises when their bones snap. These almost drown out the squishy ones. Jason dropped the final five feet or so and landed on the crunched vampire.

I decided it was time to go. This first-contact interview did not go well. Whoever this vampire was, he would either report the incident or he would try not to let anyone know how he was humiliated—but he would probably hold a grudge. There was at least a decent chance he would keep his mouth shut. If not, then someone farther up the food chain might be interested in hearing what I had to say.

Jason, having done his Superhero Landing, punched his victim through the back of the head. Yes, I said, "through." Super suit, remember? His fist went through the head and made a melon-popping sound as it scattered a large percentage of a vampire's head around the alley. He also made a small crater in the pavement. At least he had the presence of mind to angle the blow so undead bits didn't splatter in my direction.

The remains instantly crackled and shriveled, visibly mummifying as it died. A pale vapor hissed out of the tissues and dispersed in the air while the flesh and bones shrank inward and crumbled slowly into a light grey powder.

Note to self: Celestial energy causes fires. Normal killing causes crumbling.

Well, at least he wouldn't be telling anyone what happened. Kind of an upside. On the other hand, other vampires might wonder what became of him.

"Nice going," I told Jason as I approached. I dumped as much sarcasm into those two words as I could, which was a lot. I studied under a master. Of course, Jason ignored it.

"At least I didn't need a wooden stake."

"It's good to know beheading works," I agreed. "Pity I can't ask him anything. It would really help if I could have gotten, you know, information. Plus, I'm *positive* murdering one out of hand will help convince the rest of them to be helpful."

"He was attacking you."

"And I was in danger, yes. I agree. Not a lot of danger, though. I didn't feel overmatched. Lucky for me, you came to my rescue and crunched him up like a brittle accordion."

"It's my job. It's what I'm paid for."

"At this moment, no one is more acutely aware of this than I. I am also aware you did not have to smoosh his head." I toed the dampening dust. It would be several minutes before the thin rain started washing it away.

"Can we talk about this somewhere else?"

"Probably best," I agreed, icily. I had the presence of mind to collect some of the dead vampire's dust before recovering my shoes and stalking off down the alley. I felt Jason staring after me for several seconds. Finally, he leaped to rooftop level again.

Rusty waited at the mouth of the alley. He came out of the shadows and joined me in an autocab. We used it to make distance before he walked with me into the subway. I made a note for the future: carry a coiled leash in my purse for emergencies. As a wolf—a canine creature with a collar and tags—he attracted attention, but not much. If he changed, he would have an inventory issue in the menswear department, which would attract more attention. This kept our conversation to a minimum as we took a circuitous route to shake off tails or spies, as well as confuse video surveillance.

The irony is, Zeno makes use of those same Internet-connected video cameras to check for people following me. Then he overwrites and edits the footage so I don't appear in it. I have a surprisingly small digital footprint, and I am incredibly glad my Pop thinks of these things. It means I have a chance to learn about them, myself. I can't be his little girl forever. I have to learn to survive in the multiverse on my own.

I'm really starting to appreciate the technology of the 1950s.

Back at my place, Rusty trotted off to change. I went to the bathroom to wipe the rest of the club atmosphere off. I removed makeup and changed clothes, but mostly I wanted to get rid of the glitter.

Glitter. I don't even know where it came from. I didn't think the club was the sort to encourage glitter. I don't know how it can get everywhere, but it does. It's like it spontaneously generates. It's worse than sand.

The roof access chimed. I checked the security monitor before buzzing Jason in. I know it sounds silly to have a security door on the roof while having a doggie door big enough for Gus, but it's more than a simple flap. It's an armored door with a biometric fingerprint scanner, for one thing. There are other things which I will not discuss.

The garage door isn't as hard to get through as the doggie door, but I wouldn't try ramming a car through it.

With Rusty wearing his human form and clothes, we sat down in the media room, around the table. Usually, we have a map layout and holographic reproduction of where we're going to go, but Zeno was working on larger issues in the smuggling world and I had vampires on my mind.

Rusty started us off.

"You had to kill it, didn't you?"

"I had to try," Jason replied, flatly.

"Couldn't wait to crunch something?"

"It's important to know the weaknesses of anything I plan to kill. Now I know crushing the head does it. Wooden stakes are not required, which is something of a silver lining."

"Silver?"

"Oh, please. Don't read into it."

"Don't read into it? As in, I should ignore it? Or as in animals can't read?"

"I never said anything of the sort. You're reasonably intelligent, considering."

"Both of you!" I snapped. "Stop! This isn't happening now. You want to get into a fistfight later and match testosterone, fine. For now, cool it. I need professionals, not macho punks."

Rusty looked surly, but subsided. Jason sat up and adopted a stiff, military bearing.

"Yes, Ma'am."

"Now, yes, Jason did determine catastrophic damage to the head kills these things. We don't know if a stake through the heart does or not. Some types of vampire are merely paralyzed. Others stop regenerating as long as they have something sticking into the heart, but are otherwise unaffected. There may be another type who don't even notice or care. Beheading usually works, so it's a good follow-up move."

"If you'd have asked, I would have told you," Rusty pointed out.

"You know all the ways to kill vampires?" Jason countered.

"Not all of them."

"Then I'll keep testing new possibilities."

"Or you could learn from people who know more. Then you don't have to find out the hard way. Or are you wanting to screw up Phoebe's plans and need an excuse?"

"No," I leaped in, before Jason could answer, "we're not going to start throwing accusations around. It stops now and doesn't start. Both of you." I looked from one to the other and received nods.

"The situation tonight evolved into something other than the primary mission and Jason conducted a valid test. I wanted you two to be there only to rescue me if things went horribly wrong, but I didn't define 'horribly.' There were a number of things we didn't do—I didn't do—and I should have. That's part of this meeting. Another part is explaining my overall goal, not just the immediate mission objectives.

"To that end, let us begin with the goals. Since we know Alden is doing things to kill vampires, we can, as a working theory, assume they are not pleased about him. They may not know who he is, however.

"What I hope to do is communicate to the vampire community, however large or small it may be, how Alden is the one making the bridges and tunnels incendiary to the undead. This should get their attention focused on him. This serves several purposes. First, it interferes with his plans if they send minions to un-incendify things as fast as he makes them. Second, it will make his life difficult and unpleasant as they make their displeasure known. Third, it will keep his focus off me."

"Possibly permanently," Rusty added. Jason pressed his lips together and said nothing. I thought about what I wanted and how to phrase it.

"Yes, he might be killed," I agreed. "I prefer it if people don't die, but it's not an absolute priority."

"Yet," Jason pointed out, "you keep going into these situations where you know people are likely to… let us say, insist on not accepting the potential consequences."

"I would have even more regrets if I did nothing. I will not stand idly by and watch while people commit atrocities."

"Ah," he nodded. Rusty nodded with him, noticed they were both in agreement, and stopped.

"And you're okay with vampires potentially murdering this Alden guy out of hand?" Rusty asked.

"It's a risk, but I'm reasonably comfortable with the risk."

Jason raised an eyebrow. I could almost hear him thinking, *Wow, you **are** mad at this guy.*

"If I might ask," Jason began, "why do we need to involve vampires? They're anoth— they prey on humans," he corrected. "I get how Alden is a psychic with mind-control abilities, worming his way into the halls of power, but does he have anything to prevent me from punching his eyeballs out the back of his head? Or," he added, nodding toward Rusty, "anything to prevent his head from being eaten? Does he have the ability to recover from it?"

"We don't eat people," Rusty replied.

"You don't have to swallow."

"Look, if you're going to keep making comments—"

"To get back to the question," I interrupted, "no, I don't think he has anything to overcome a quasi-beheading. My thought was to let him and the vampires slug it out. If we can watch how they kill each other, we learn a lot about how each operates, their resources and tactics. If they kill him, I will regret it, but he's a priest and he spends his nights inside churches. It's clear he's taken steps to protect himself, so it's a risk I'm willing to take. I want him to understand he can't go around doing the things he's doing without consequences. Personally, I want to punish him, but I'm still working on how to do it. This is..."

"An expedient form of vengeance?" Jason suggested.

"Yes. I can't sit back and do nothing, but I also can't bring myself to assassinate him outright." *Because I am not Pop*, I didn't add. "This will give him serious problems while I work out problems of my own."

Jason nodded, smiling. Either he was proud of the way I'd learned practical lessons, or he was enjoying the idea of monsters killing monsters. Maybe both.

"All right," he agreed. "I made a mistake in killing our prisoner."

"You didn't take him prisoner," Rusty pointed out.

"I reduced him to the point where we could," Jason replied. "I should have taken him prisoner instead of killing him. Happy?"

"Nope."

"I didn't think you would be. Now that we all understand we're trying to get information out of the monsters, what next?"

"I'll take care of it," I told him. "I've seen several of them. I'll get my intelligence analysts on it and find out who they are, or at least who they claim to be."

Jason's lips twitched in an almost-smile. Pop recruited him, and Jason was still under the impression I was an adult child using my father's access to classified resources to play superhero. I never saw a reason to correct his notions—and plenty of reasons not to.

"Moving on, I know I made big mistakes on this one. I also know where I made them, and why. I was too eager. I usually plan our raids well in advance and in detail. This was a field test of a gadget, not a raid, so I didn't bother to plan ahead as I should have. I didn't scout out the location. I didn't observe the traffic. I didn't check anything with remote reconnaissance. I went in to do reconnaissance instead of conduct my test and get out with the results.

"Moreover, I didn't adhere to the mission objectives. It was supposed to be strictly a gadget test. I expanded on the test and moved on to an attempt at contact, which I should not have done. I won't make this mistake again."

Jason nodded his agreement. Rusty shrugged. Rusty is a whole lot more impulsive than Jason. Must be nice to be a regenerating creature.

"With this in mind," I continued, standing up. They stood when I did. "I'm going to get an information-gathering process in motion before I go to bed. And I remembered your technology request," I added, to Jason. "Hand over the old helmet and I'll switch it out for the new one."

I took it to my witchroom and worked on it. He and Rusty waited without trying to kill each other. I took it as a good sign as I handed him the updated helmet. It wasn't hard to fix; the spells remained the same. All I had to do was change their visuals on the inside of the visor.

"There you go. Now, thank you for your time, gentlemen. I'll keep you posted. That will be all."

Jason went up to the roof to leap tall buildings in a single bound. Rusty went downstairs to the kitchen.

He doesn't actually like dog treats when he's in human form. They're delicious when he's a wolf, sure, but his senses alter along with his shape. Nevertheless, when he first started hanging around, I had to remind him those crunchy things are for Gus, and to make a point of it. Rusty's instinct is to assert dominance. Gus has the same instinct. I'm trying to get both of them to get along.

Why is it all the males in my life are difficult? Almost all, I should say. Pop never gave me grief like these boys do. Someday, if I'm very lucky, I'll find a man like Pop and marry him. I hope Pop extended my lifespan. I'll need a lot of time or a lot of luck.

As for the information-gathering, I got out several mirrors and prepared to get Zeno on the job. Of course, I had to find vampires to scry on, but I had vampire dust, as well as several specific vampires I'd seen that evening. The dust was useful in refining my detector's vampire settings.

I got the mirrors working, then discovered I needed more cameras. I temporarily put mirrors side by side, so Zeno could watch two with each camera. He would watch and listen with inhuman attention, sorting out who said what, recording everything, and give me a report on who to watch next. I'd get cameras the next day.

Thank you, Pop, for Zeno.

It was a long night. I went to bed.

Dream Journal #1

I opened my eyes to a brilliant whiteness. Fog? Or a white emptiness? Hard to tell with nothing else around.

"Not nothing, exactly."

I spun around. Standing before me was a tall figure in a three-piece suit. His eyes were pits of blackness, but not empty. They were filled with a darkness as deep as wells, as thick as walls, as solid and real as stone. The suit was a deep, shifting grey, as though shadows flickered over it—possibly cast by something inside the suit, as his necktie looked like a necktie-shaped hole in his chest. This lead to a fiery center like a hollow tree, burning inside after a lightning strike. At one hip was a dragon-hilted sword. The outline of an infinitely dark and empty hole rippled behind him like a cloak in a nonexistent breeze. You'd think a cloak and sword wouldn't go with a suit and tie. You'd be right. He made it work by not giving a damn. Behind him, a shining, golden ghost implied something like a horse. It tossed its head and I felt I knew it.

My first impulse was to shout "Pop!" and hug the guy. I didn't. Given the strange meeting, I couldn't assume anything.

"You look an awful lot like my Pop," I said, instead.

"I ought to. I'm his energy-state twin, your Uncle Dusty. We haven't met here before, only on the Epiphany line."

"Oh! Is that what you usually look like?"

"What's wrong with how I look?"

"Nothing," I lied. "Why are we here?"

"To talk. You're dreaming. I can talk to your father pretty easily, but making contact with other minds is more difficult. It's easier when you're dreaming."

"How did you get past my shields?"

"It's a miraculous vision, not a psychic contact. Do you have any anti-angel defenses?"

"They're more Pop's problem than mine. I have a couple of spells I can activate if I have to hide or make an escape, but angels don't usually notice or care about me, so far as I know."

"Very good. When they're off, I can reach you like this."

"Glad to hear it. It's good to see you, Uncle."

"Likewise."

"Did you drop in for a visit? Or is there something I can do for you?"

"I wanted to chat. Mind if I generate something a little less empty?"

"Help yourself."

He gestured. The floor darkened to a greyish, stony color. It spread out around us, flowing into shapes, changing direction and apparent materials. Four firepits appeared in the floor, ignited themselves, and burned low. The walls went up, curved over from the sides, met in the middle, and formed an arched hall. The roof lightened to metallic gold, making the light from the fire seem even warmer, cozier. A balcony area formed. At one end, two great blocks of stone pivoted around, spinning in place to open and close like two massive doors. At the other, a dragon's head sculpture projected from the rock, over a dais. In the walls, wide veins of metal grew up from the floor, spreading, branching, developing gems like fruits, until the finely-divided branches met the golden, metallic ceiling.

"Nice trick," I observed. My voice echoed as if we were in a cavern. "I'd like to learn it."

"It's not hard. It's a case of imagination and will. This is your mind, dreaming. It's like the desktop in your headspace. You can do anything you want in here."

"I can?"

"Sure." He gestured again, making a small window, hovering in mid-air. It was dark outside. He lifted it open. "Listen."

"I hear breathing."

"That's you. You can't see out the window because your eyes are closed, but your ears work fine."

"Can I try?"

"Maybe we can save the lesson until the end. I do want to talk, and if you wake up, I'll have to wait until you're asleep again. Unless you want to really rev up the divinity dynamo and maybe pray, too. Long-distance calls are expensive."

"Oh. Okay. Please, sit down."

He banished the window as we arranged ourselves on the edge of a firepit. It felt perfectly real to me, right down to the warm air and the smell of smoke.

"I dropped in like this to see how you were doing."

"You don't know?"

"Actually, I do know a few things. I promised your father I'd keep an eye on how you're doing while he sorts out a few issues."

"Like an Empire coming apart, temple schisms, and stabilizing the succession of his House?"

"Yep."

"Keep an eye on him, will you?"

"I'm doing more than that," he assured me. "I can be in more than one place at a time, so I'm also watching over you."

"On one level, I'm pleased to have a guardian angel watching over me," I admitted. "On another, it's disturbing to be observed all the time."

"Guardian demigod, please. Angels are another species entirely. And I'm watching over you in a very broad sense, not sitting on your shoulder."

"Okay, guardian demigod. So what's the difference between 'watching over' and the other thing?"

"I'm keeping tabs on your well-being, not stalking you."

"Reassuring. Sort of."

"I hope so."

"I'll guess I can live with my funny uncle checking up on me. And I am glad Pop is still thinking about me, even if he is insanely busy."

"You're always on his mind."

"He loves me," I stated, simply. Uncle Dusty nodded.

"I also wanted to check in and ask what you're up to," he admitted.

"Up to?"

"What's on your plate?"

"How do you mean?"

"I know you started a campaign against the retail drug business, and I've been told you're moving up the food chain to bigger fish. You have a friend who happens to be a werewolf and a sidekick who dislikes all supernatural entities. And, of course, you have a psychic priest you've stolen from your father."

"I didn't steal him!"

"You adopted him as your project?"

"I... huh. Well..."

"Do you have any idea how much your father wanted to kill the guy?"

"Pretty bad?"

"You may be the only person who could have talked him out of it."

"But I didn't."

"No, you talked him into letting you do it. Not quite the same."

"I hadn't thought of it in that light."

"How's it going?"

"Pretty well, I think. He's been killing vampires, so I plan to tell them who he is. They'll keep him distracted while I find a better way of enacting *some* sort of justice on him for being a bad person."

"Correct me if I'm wrong, but you're out for vengeance? Is that it?"

"I'd like to think my motives aren't as base as that, but maybe I'm fooling myself. Yes, I'm still upset he treated Pop the way he did and made such a hash of our life in Shasta, but Alden is being a bad person in a more general sense! He's psychically dominating people. That's a bad thing, and he deserves to suffer for it. He needs some sort of... of..." I paused, trying to put into words what I'd been feeling about him.

"You know how everything in nature has limits?" I asked.

"Maybe. Elaborate."

"Rabbits don't reproduce until they carpet the world. They have predators. Even the predators have predators, even if it's competition from each other. The whole balance of nature may wobble back and forth, but it generally wobbles around a balance point. Yes?"

"I think I see what you're saying. Sure."

"Alden doesn't seem to have anything to balance against. It's like introducing an invasive species to a new continent. If it's got no natural predators, no natural checks and balances, it expands until it destroys."

"And Alden is the invasive species. I see."

He looked at me expectantly.

"Am I missing something?" I asked.

"I don't know, but I have an idea."

"Maybe a little hint would be in order?" I suggested.

"All right. What kept him in check back in Shasta?"

I opened my mouth and closed it. This process repeated a few times.

"I don't know," I finally admitted. "I did a little investigating, but only to get a better look at what he did to people."

"Could be worth it to find out why he didn't make a play for world domination back then. Back there. Back where he came from."

"I'm not sure there's anything to find, but I'll see what I can do."

"Good. Glad to help. And, speaking of help, could you give Me a hand?"

"The demigod wants help?"

"Gods only do the miracles. For everything else, we send prophets and heroes."

"Which am I?"

"Depends on how much help you are."

"What do you need?"

"Your father and I sorted out the avatar-making process for me, but there's a wee bit of a problem. While I can use magical devices—much like anyone else—I have issues when it comes to utilizing magical forces. My avatar-clone isn't much when it comes to wizardry. Turn on a gate? Sure. Operate a scrying mirror? Absolutely. Cast a spell on a match to waterproof it? Nope."

"So, being a god, you're incompetent as a wizard?"

He looked pained.

"I suppose you could put it that way, if you really wanted to."

"Sorry. I didn't mean to poke you in the ego."

"It sometimes needs a little deflating, I guess."

"Is this a fundamental issue between celestial beings and magic?" I asked. "Do all energy-state beings have problems with using magic?"

"Well, as energy-state beings, yes. That's a problem. Incarnated in a mortal form, I'm guessing the magical facility is somehow based in the flesh. I haven't done the analysis, but I think it's a case of who you possess—if that's the right word. If you use a wizard's body, you have whatever capacity his nervous system can handle. If you use the body of someone magically inept, you can know every spell by heart and still not light a candle. It's My working hypothesis."

"That seems odd to me."

"It doesn't make Me too happy, either."

"The body you have—whose was it?"

"It's a clone, not a person."

"Is it? So it never had a soul? Could that relate?"

"Got Me. There are any number of factors that may go into whether or not a person develops magical capacity, both genetic and environmental. I haven't done the research. I've been busy and I have more immediate problems."

"Oh! I'm sorry. You mentioned you wanted help. What can I do, Uncle?"

"Glad you asked. What I need from you is to take a little trip to one of My reactor worlds and help Me out. I need a wizard—or a witch, if you prefer—to do magical work. Do you mind?"

"I don't mind. Is it pressing? As in, drop everything and do it now? Or can I check my calendar?"

"By all means, sort your schedule out. It's things I need done, not damage control. I'd like your help as soon as possible, but I don't need it immediately."

"I'll get back to you."

"Thank you."

"You're welcome. Now, tell me how I fill up a white-space dream with the stuff I want."

"You've already had headspace lessons?" he confirmed.

"Of course."

"All right. Let's start by imagining something…"

Journal Entry #11

I did my checking on the spinning whirligig Pop and Uncle Dusty call a divinity dynamo. It's a cylinder, about a foot long, upright, and spins on the vertical axis. It has spells on it and it's plugged into the wall. It also glows, shining in a spectrum unlike anything else I usually see. Well, almost unlike. There's a resemblance to the energy aura around Alden's vampire-frying tektites, so I think it's a different flavor of the same stuff.

I have no idea how to make one.

Oh, the physical components, sure. All I need is a hefty electric motor and a lot of osmium. That covers the materials. I'll also need a lot of time. I could probably monkey-see-monkey-do a copy of the spells on it, but it's tuned to emit a complex… harmonic? Chord? A pattern of energies. I could probably copy it, tuning it off the existing dynamo, but I doubt I could build it from scratch. I'm hesitant to try. I run the risk of scrambling or erasing the pattern and I only have one.

On the other hand, it can spin a lot faster than it currently does. The electric motor can take quite a bit more power. The Ascension Sphere surrounding the arrangement is in equilibrium with the house's magical environment. I can increase the magical field intensity with an electromagical transformer inside the Sphere, no problem. I can even nest a couple of Ascension Spheres, further upping the field intensity. And, to keep the osmium cylinder from deforming, cracking, or coming apart under the ultra-high revolutions, I can coat it in a layer of super-hard polymer to keep it together.

Is this efficient? Nope! The ratio of kilowatt-hours to celestial wattage drops like a lead brick on Saturn, but the net output goes up. Instead of a highly-efficient car getting the best possible mileage, I'm souping the thing up to be a race car with terrible mileage but tons of power.

I understand why Pop and Uncle Dusty want the maximum bang for their buck. Uncle Dusty has nuclear reactors powering banks of dynamos, or so I'm told. The reactors have limits. Big limits, granted, but they still have a maximum safe output. Every watt they produce needs to be converted at the highest possible level of return. My situation is different. Why should I bother with maximum efficiency? I've only got one dynamo and I can tap a whole power grid. How fast can this thing spin? How intense a field can I put around it? Forget miles per gallon! Where's my horsepower?

There went my morning. At least I got to go for a run to various stores. I needed more webcams, anyway.

Now Uncle Dusty has a stronger link to my alternate Earth. The dynamo is running at a ridiculous RPM, which means it's now bolted to the table. It won't stay on otherwise. I should be able to ask him directly about what he thinks of it.

I sat down, adopted a meditative posture in front of the thing, centered my thoughts, and tested it.

"Hello?"

Interesting.

"Is it?"

I don't usually have a direct conversation with anyone but your father.

"Pop's a special case? I'm shocked. Shocked, I tell you."

You inherited his sarcasm.

"It's environmental, not genetic. So, you said something about needing my help with a reactor?"

It's a world where there are nuclear reactors powering banks of these dynamos.

"Pop's mentioned them. Do you have targeting coordinates?"

Yes. If you'll try to relax, I'll try to give you a proper idea of where to aim for with your micro-gate and mirror.

I relaxed, deliberately letting Uncle Dusty think into my head a bit more deeply. The perspective of the destination was a bit weird, not being centered in a single pair of eyes, but spread out over an entire complex of rooms, corridors, and equipment. I didn't see the place so much as I was part of the place, permeating it. One area in particular felt more highlighted and significant in this particular revelation.

Got it?

"I think so. I feel confident enough to give it a try."

Great. When can we try it?

"I was thinking I'll make a couple of calls, make sure my day is clear, and—hang on. Is there a time differential?"

Not with your world. Not a specific one I know of, he corrected. *There's the usual random skips, but no micro-gate ticking between them. Do you want one?*

"Yes, please."

Which way?

"I don't want the vampires and Alden to get away from me."

Good. That's easiest. Once we get it to link, set the micro-gate on your mirror's frame to ticking. You'll land in my slowest world and your gate will run it faster relative to yours. You can even take the shift-booths linking my reactor worlds to the one running fastest. I don't know what the ratio is, but it's pretty steep. We'll talk there.

"You have multiple shift-booths? To multiple worlds?"

They're all branches of the same timeline, so they're almost identical. The micro-gates of the shift-booths connect them in series to increase the differential by multiple steps.

"So, next to no time will go by here?"

Correct. But make sure your micro-gate ticks with the destination I gave you. We don't want to leave your world completely unconnected from my little constellation. It's statistically unlikely to have any large differential, but sometimes you hit the jackpot.

"On it. Let me get my calendar cleared for the day, just in case, and I'll be right with you."

I spoke to Zeno, made sure everything in his new monitoring hookup was working, checked to see if anything was looming on the intelligence analysis horizon, gave him messages in case I got calls and wasn't back, double-checked all the locks and alarms, and headed for my witchroom.

I'll say this for Uncle Dusty: He gives good directions. I had no trouble targeting his chosen world with my mirror's micro-gate. I scried through it for a minute or two, looking around the immediate area. My micro-gate had linked with a small ring mounted on the steel frame of a non-residential doorway. Judging by the magical setup, Pop had taken a mop closet and turned it into a powerfully-enchanted device for traveling between alternate realities.

Typical.

The door was open, so the open rectangle would be quite convenient as a portal frame. I carefully set a spell on my own micro-gate to start ticking after the main mirror-frame gate closed. It would keep linking with the micro-gate in Uncle Dusty's reactor world on a short basis—every few seconds—and keep my own world's timeline from running away down the time-track.

I shifted the connection to the mirror frame and the doorway. I stepped through quickly and found myself in a tiled hallway under ugly fluorescent lighting. I moved the connections back to the tiny gates and my witchroom disappeared from the doorway, leaving an empty mop closet.

A moment later, the micro-gate connection closed. I waited. A minute later, it clicked on again for an instant and closed again. Good. The one in my witchroom was cycling, provoking this world to "run fast" while my world ticked along more slowly. It did it again as I watched, confirming it was repeating.

"Everything all right?" asked an unfamiliar voice. I spun around. I didn't recognize him. He was tall, broad-shouldered, square-jawed, all that stuff. He looked like a decathlon medalist. He could have modeled for athletic fashions. He wore his hair long and tied back, but he was smooth-shaven and smiled with a mouthful of perfectly human teeth. I notice teeth.

"Who are you?"

"I'm your Uncle Dusty. Well, this is My physical avatar."

"This is what you look like? I thought you were supposed to look like Pop."

"A common misconception. We grew this body in a highly-charged celestial energy field so I could occupy it from the beginning and make it Mine."

"Is this a highly-charged area?" I asked. "It feels muggy."

"The weather here is a bit humid in the rainy season," he admitted. "All the celestial energy, though, is tuned specifically to me. There's an insignificant amount of celestial sideband stuff, but nothing should bother you."

"I'll wear a cooling spell. What's your cloned avatar body got to do with not looking like Pop?"

"In My celestial form, I bear him a strong resemblance. What face I wear on the outside isn't important. It's what's inside that counts. This is a skinsuit."

"And you decided not to look like him?"

"It wasn't a priority. It's not a clone of your father because there's no way to clone him, so far as I know. So we did a lot of gene splicing from several donors. In fact, I could have as easily worn a black body, or a female one, or even a gorilla. Possibly a gorilla," he corrected, frowning. "I'm pretty sure I could do it, if the clone went through the whole process."

"How about a dolphin?"

"Almost certainly, but I'd be concerned about being so far from the coast. The reactor is a good distance inland."

"Fair enough. Uh…"

"Hello, niece," he offered, and held out a hand. I took it. We shook hands. "Awkward?"

"A little," I admitted.

"It's weird, meeting a demigod," he sympathized. "You're family, so don't sweat it."

"I'll try. So… this is your place?"

"One of them. It's a material realm where My power production is carried out. All this is artificially-generated faith energy. Tauta, on the other hand, has organically-grown, all-natural faith. I'm not in a position to turn down either."

"Must be hard," I suggested, trying to empathize.

"It can be complicated. We gods are very food-motivated."

"Like Labradors?"

"In many ways," he agreed, amiably enough. "Some of us are about as friendly. Some of us are smarter. Want to look around?"

"If it's no trouble."

"Sure. But you've got time issues, so let's go through the shift-booths to the fastest branch. If you see one, you've seen them all."

"Oh. Right. Good idea."

He led me into the mop closet and ran a hand down the doorframe, from top to bottom, crossing over several scored lines and arcane runes in the metalwork. I recognized the craftsmanship and the handwriting. He opened the door again and we stepped out into a somewhat dustier copy of the same hallway.

"Multiple branches from the same timeline," I observed. "Right. Got it."

"Aren't you used to shift-booth transfers?"

"Yes, but not usually to copies of the same world."

"Oh. Well, I needed more than one reactor and My semi-avatar was in a hurry. Let's walk and I'll show you around."

We did and he did. The nuclear power plant produces electricity. This, in turn, powers an Imperial shit-ton of divinity dynamos. I don't know what that comes to in Metric. These, running in row upon row upon row, in rack after rack after rack, take up almost the entire electrical output of the reactor. Solar power conversion spells, drawing on sunlight and on the waste heat from the cooling towers, help keep the environment magically charged. It's all here to provide energy to an energy-state being and keep him fed enough to grow stronger.

There are *seven* such setups. Uncle Dusty is an atomic demigod.

He sounds like a rock band. Atomic Demigod. I wonder if he can play any instruments. Then again, I wouldn't want him to play the trumpet. He might bring the house down, or maybe the city walls.

"Setting this up took forever," I noted.

"Time streams, robot labor, and a lot of automated production," he answered, "but, at this end of things... yes. It took years."

"I'm impressed."

"Thank you, but I didn't do the initial setup. I'm here to handle glitches."

"Speaking of glitches, you say you've got a problem? Why not call Pop? He built all this, didn't he?"

"He salvaged the power plant and set up the automation," Uncle Dusty corrected. "I'd bother him if he wasn't busy. Right now, he's in Tauta. People need to see him. He needs to be... what's the word?"

"He's a figurehead?"

Uncle Dusty winced.

"I'm not sure that's the right word," he decided. "It implies he's not important. He *is* important. He's less of a figurehead and more of a symbol. He's the only person his people will listen to unconditionally."

"They listen to Leisel."

"Yes, but *he* is the source of her authority. You've got to understand the Tassarian Empire. He's the head of the House. She's his delegate, or viceroy, or whatever. If he died, she would be out of a job because there would be no House. He's the keystone." Uncle Dusty chuckled. "He doesn't like it."

"No, he wouldn't. But couldn't they spare him for an hour?"

"Probably, but he's got his own things to think about and work to do. I don't want to distract him from the war effort."

And, just like that, memory leaped out and ambushed me. I was lying in my bed, having been tucked in moments ago, and Pop sat on the edge of the bed next to me. It was a reinforced bed frame; Pop thinks of these things. He patted the covers over me and sang a lullaby.

I only remembered one verse and the name of the song escaped me, but the vision of where I was when Pop sang to me was as vivid as if I was three years old again.

> *Bye lo, baby, bye lo, baby.*
> *Bye lo, baby, bye-lo-baby-bye.*
> *Daddy still loves you. Daddy still loves you.*
> *Daddy still loves you, though he's gone to war.*

My heart thumped in my chest and my eyes were hot with tears. I got a grip on myself and refused to consider any of the reasons my subconscious might have chosen to throw that particular scrap of song at me. Uncle Dusty was still speaking.

"...and if we're going to win this, he'll have to stay focused on it."

"That's a terrifying thought," I observed, and was pleased to find my voice didn't break. "Pop giving something his total attention, I mean. Even when he's on your side, his undivided attention is a little scary."

"Isn't it, just?"

"All right. What do you need me to do?"

"How are you with solar-conversion spells?"

Uncle Dusty's main problem was reactor maintenance. The machines were all right—there were repair spells to keep them intact, cleaning spells to cut down on oil changes and other gunk, the works. The problem was the fuel.

Yes, the fuel in the reactor. Did you know they can run out?

A typical fission reactor runs for years on its fuel rods, but, as they emit their radiation, they burn up. It's like gasoline in a car or wood in a stove, aside from the fact it takes a lot longer and releases more energy. Thing is, when you're dealing with time dilation effects, a long time can go by in nothing flat.

So he was looking for more power sources. Things to last centuries instead of a few decades. Water power. Wind power. Tidal generators. All the renewable energy stuff. Which led to another complication.

In theory, he could find the same original timeline Pop did and branch off a new little universe where he would have a practically-new reactor. It would take a lot of repairs to get it fully on-line, then even more work to build—or relocate—the divinity dynamos, but it would be easier than building all-new power plants.

Why wasn't he thrilled with this idea? One reason is all the spells Pop has on and around the reactor. The dynamos work best in an intense magical field, hence the energy-conversion panels and the Ascension Sphere around the complex. Uncle Dusty has no way to duplicate them.

Another reason is the sheer quantity of dynamos. It doesn't matter how many power plants he's got, the energy has to go to the dynamos. Moving them is possible, of course, but it's like packing up all the trees in Colorado and moving them to Idaho. Sure, we can do it, but how long is this going to take?

"So, let me make sure I've got this," I said, looking down at the notes and doodles I'd done in my pocket notebook. "You need, A: the dynamos. B: A way to power them electrically. C: A high-intensity magical field around them. Yes? Those three things?"

"Yes."

"We can't move the dynamos—well, we can, but it's a last resort. There's no *practical* way to move them. On the other hand, we can run wire anywhere we want, since this world is uninhabited. This means we can—you can—build a power station anywhere you want, using whatever power source you want, and feed the electricity to the dynamo farm. Yes?"

"Yes, but I don't have heavy, industrial robots. I have small, automated forklifts with arms."

"But I don't need to move Pop's solar panels? The magical environment doesn't need to be around the power production, right? It only needs to be around the dynamo racks?"

"Correct. The dynamos require a high-intensity magical field to run properly. Although you may want to put panels over an electrical plant to run repair spells. I don't really know how many of the things he has over My reactors, but they supply all the power to the various spells and help charge up the field around the dynamos directly. The reactor output goes strictly into the generators, and those go into the dynamos."

"Gotcha. So, any new construction will be the problem. I don't understand how Pop can make spells self-replicate, so I have to build solar converters by hand. It shouldn't be a major problem, though, as long as I have a steady supply of magical energy. As for constructing a power plant… this is a post-apocalyptic world? Yes? Can we salvage existing stuff from the ruins?"

"I'm sure we can, but you'll need to be the one to cast repair spells on rusted equipment."

I sat back and thought about it.

"The major issue—the thing that changed everything—is the fact this reactor's output is dropping. Yes?"

"Yes. The maximum power setting isn't spinning all the dynamos properly, so I've had to shut down a rack of them. Then another rack. Soon, I may have to shut down even more of the electric motors so the others will spin at optimum speed."

"I see the problem. Exactly what type of reactor is this? It's not a fusion plant, obviously."

"No, of course not. If it was a fusion plant, I'd already have started deuterium extraction from seawater. This is a thorium fission reactor."

"Thorium fuel rods?"

"It's a molten material, not fuel rods."

"Dang it. I'll need to read up on how these work. I was hoping it would be a matter of taking out an expended fuel rod and sliding a new one in. Do you know how they usually refuel this sort of reactor?"

"There are technical manuals," he assured me, "but I haven't studied them like I should. I think they drain the molten mix and put new fuel in. I haven't seen an output pipe, so I assume they shut down to do it. From what I remember about thorium reactors, what they take out, they run through a recycler to remove byproducts. Some are disposed of, others are treated, still more are put through a neutron breeding cycle to produce different types of fuel—bunches of things. A few wind up back in the reactor again. The rest are either stored as waste or shipped elsewhere for other purposes."

"But, if we opened a hole at the bottom of the reactor while we opened a hole at the top, we could let old molten reaction material pour out the bottom while pouring fresh molten reaction material in through the top?"

"Two gates…" he mused. "That would refuel the reactor, certainly. It would deal with most of the waste materials, too, in a sense. We need spells to preferentially direct the waste isotopes into the waste gate, and we'll definitely need to protect the physical gates, the actual material they're made of, from neutron absorption…"

"I don't suppose you have iridium rings lying around?"

"No, I'm afraid I don't. But I will be delighted to make some for you, along with lunch."

"You can do that?"

"I do have robots—and meat suits need to eat, too. You think I let the living avatar of a demigod get His hands dirty?"

Uncle Dusty can operate magical devices in simple ways, such as turning gates on and off. That's not an issue. The issue was setting up the gates. We want to remove a lot of used radioactive crap from the reactor without removing the fuel. Fortunately, I now know how a thorium reactor works, in principle, thanks to the reference materials at the power plant. With an extremely small gate on either side of the fuel chamber—say, one millimeter in diameter?—we could afford to leave them open all the time. Just to be sure, I'd add several dozen more power panels to the overhead array. Another spell—a plain little cleaning spell!—would gently move waste isotopes to one opening and let them ooze out elsewhere. Luckily, the molten thorium in this reactor design wasn't under pressure. The water going through the heat exchanger was the high-pressure portion of the powerplant.

Where to dump the radioactive waste products was a bit of a question, but Uncle Dusty had some good ideas. There were functional thorium reactors in other worlds, actively in use by people who knew how to maintain them. We changed the plan. Instead of leaving the mini-gates open all the time, they would periodically target molten thorium. One of them would be the output gate, squirting thorium waste products into someone else's reactor. The other one would be the input gate, sucking fresh material in from yet another reactor. I planned to have them run on a three-second cycle, on and off, until the local reactor was back up to full power, then have it tick over only when the cleaning spell's detectors reached a critical point and triggered it. High concentrations of waste material go away, fresh fuel appears.

This may be a simple matter to Pop, but for me, there are issues. Figuring out the targeting was one. I can't stick my head inside the reactor and look at what I need to target. It involved scrying and study and forethought and a lot of trial and error with fish tanks and food coloring.

As for the neutron absorption issue, the iridium rings we used had to be protected from the environment inside the reactor. Uncle Dusty was adamant about not letting the gates have a structural failure, citing experience with a reactor prototype Pop built for his friend, Diogenes. He didn't explain.

I also had to consider how to get a cleaning spell to be precise on an atomic level, how to tie it into the gate activation protocols, include manual overrides accessible from *outside* the reactor, set up a monitor for the amount of fuel in the reaction chamber—you don't want it to run out, nor do you want to over-fill it—and all the attendant details.

They say God is in the details. They also say the Devil is in the details. Make either one of them angry and your nuclear power plant will rain radioactive fire on you.

It took us days to work out all the fiddly little bits. We kept going back and discussing how the current setup could go wrong, then adding a new safety measure or, once, completely redesigning things.

Finally, when I had the plans drawn up and every single part defined, I started work on the actual enchantment portion of the exercise. And these did need to be enchantments. Spells are fine and dandy for anything I might want to abandon, giving them a quick slap *en passant* to un-magic them as I departed, but Uncle Dusty needed things he could rely on.

Pop would have done it in a day. Maybe overnight. He might have done it all and gone off to play the Ghost of Christmas Yet to Come with all the time he had left over. Me, I took a week and a half, if you count my prototype, beta, and production versions.

I have never cast so many solar conversion panels in my life. I cheated, though, by drawing power from the existing array to cast the largest panels I could. As with so many things, size matters. Uncle Dusty had a minor drop in food output when the magical field intensity dipped a bit, but he didn't complain. The new panels were a long-term investment and he knew it.

Finally satisfied it was all looking good, Uncle Dusty then pointed out we needed to do all this six more times.

"There are seven reactor worlds. This one is running low and the others will too— eventually. Now that you've got the method perfected, shouldn't we get them sorted out?"

I groaned.

"Look, Unc, I don't mind doing a little R&D in the lab, working out new problems. Building all this stuff by hand the first time is taking the laboratory to field testing. Fine! But I'm not in a sweatshop! I'm not equipped to be… be… be industrialized production! Maybe it's okay for Pop, sitting on the dark side of the moon for hours or days on end, hyper-focused on hand-crafted bespoke magic, but he's not normal! *I* don't have that kind of concentration!"

"He doesn't have the patience," Uncle Dusty replied. "Why do you think he invented a self-replicating program for spells?"

"I'm aware of it, and I also know it's incredibly complicated!"

"He's an *intelligent* lazy man. He put in the effort so he could be lazy."

"Implying I haven't? Or he's a genius and I'm not?"

"Can you do the complicated thing to bypass the tedious work?"

"All right," I agreed, throwing up my hands, "I'll do it one damn thing at a time! But you *owe* me."

"I will be delighted to repay the favor. After all, the more of a power budget I have, the more easily I can repay it, not so?"

"I look forward to it," I muttered.

"Oh, and while we're on the subject…"

I groaned, but I didn't stop him.

"Could you, perchance, find me a Nobody-Left-Alive world with fusion technology?"

"You want a fusion reactor?"

"Yes, please."

"We went over all the problems with refurbishing a tide-powered generator, hydroelectric plants, and all the rest," I pointed out. "We set up your existing thorium plant so it would never run out of fuel. Now you want me to help build a *fusion plant?*"

"No, no! I want you to *find* one. Maybe you could add an eighth stop on the shift-booth setup. Put together one more set of time-tickers. I'll do all the legwork. It'll be my project. All *I* need is *access* to it." He looked sad. "I can open a gate, but I can only open them wherever they're targeted. I can't even steer them."

I sighed, thinking about how my life would be much easier if I had a supernatural patron who didn't actually want anything. Technically, I do. It's Pop. Uncle Dusty gets in free because of him, though. There are downsides to being a witch.

"You're going to need a wand," I told him.

"What for?"

"Repairs. You can't expect to replace parts, so you need a wand with a highly-advanced, anti-entropy-based repair spell. The highest-quality repair spell I know, in fact."

"Can't you cast a repair spell on the whole reactor?"

"Not if you want it to actually do anything. Size matters!"

"So I'm told," he agreed, mildly. "I would think a wand with a basic repair spell would be sufficient. You don't need to put yourself out on that, I think. I know a lot about technology."

"Yes, but you *suck* at using magic. You can't direct the spell and alter its parameters. All you can do it set it off. The spell in the wand for repairing delicate electronics has to be *sophisticated.* It has to function on an entropy level, reversing the effects of time and wear, which involves a lot more then slapping the target into the right shape. It has to suck in the correct elements, form complex molecules, precise crystals, the works! Worse, for you it has to be highly automated, purely point-and-shoot."

"Oh. Huh. You're probably right." He looked worried. "Am I asking for too much? At least, too much right now? Or could you come back on weekends and do a little bit at a time?"

"Finding you a world with a fusion plant shouldn't be a problem. I'll find you something before I start work on the other things you can't do. And while I'm ranting, why didn't Pop set you up with a fusion plant in the first place?"

"I'm not sure. I suspect he didn't think of it."

"Why not?"

"He sometimes avoids things, unconsciously, that have bad emotional associations for him. He's good at denial. And a fusion plant is, basically, a tiny sun..."

"Ah. The light begins to dawn."

"You might put it like that. Also, we didn't grow up with fusion power. He unconsciously thinks of nuclear plants as fission. He's familiar with those." Uncle Dusty chuckled. "Nowadays, I'm sure he could find all sorts of things he didn't used to—laser guns, force shields, all sort of high-tech goodies he never used to be familiar with. He doesn't think to try."

"Kind of like a puppy who can't jump the fence, so, as a grown dog, he still stays in his yard?"

"Something like that. I'm not sure, of course; we're not the same person. But that's how it seems to Me."

"Makes sense to me, too, once you point it out. I am going to need your help on this project, though."

"Sure. What wonders shall I perform in My mysterious way?"

"Start with dinner," I suggested. "I won't be ready to help out with a whole new world until I get something to eat." I paused and considered how I felt. "Plus, I am *knackered.*"

"Oh?" He laid a hand on my shoulder and the world brightened. Colors leaped into brilliant intensity. I felt taller, stronger, able to leap tall buildings in a single bound without anything as clunky as magic armor.

"What was *that?*" I demanded.

"You're in My place of power," he pointed out. "Getting energies to My other selves, on other planes of existence, involves a huge loss in the transfer. Here, though—this is where the energy *is*. Here I can work miracles. I'm saving most of it, at the moment, to help My former avatar. But helping you helps Me to help him, so I think we'll turn a profit."

"What did you do? It felt a lot like what Pop did, once."

"What did he do?"

"He hit me with a healing spell, then poured a bucketful of vital energy into my system."

"This was much the same thing, albeit a celestial-energy version. Still tired?"

"No!"

"There you go. You're welcome. Amen. Selah. Et cetera."

"You're not doing my demitheophobia any good, you know."

"I wasn't aware you had it. Or that it was a word," he added.

"I didn't! It wasn't. You're creating it."

"Sorry. How about I go get you something to eat? If I make you a sandwich, will it help?"

"Only if I get to eat one, rather than being turned into one."

"That's silly," he said, walking away.

"Glad to hear it!"

"I'd never turn you into a sandwich," he assured me, over his shoulder.

I muttered under my breath about crazy uncles and consulted my notes. We already did the research and development, so now it was a matter of production…

Journal Entry #12

The micro-gates connected to the shift-booths are also the time-tickers for keeping the time differentials between his collection of worlds running. He can rearrange the order of his worlds in the chain because Pop set it up to be easy. What he did not do was leave behind a selection of magical devices I could use to hunt down and enchant things.

I made a new magic mirror. If nothing else, it was nice to cast something besides power conversion panels.

While I was looking for high-tech worlds with no populations, Uncle Dusty watched, fascinated, at my magical operations.

"I'd love a fusion plant," he sighed, serving vegetable stew into a plastic bowl. It had, written on the side in magic marker, *Dhatri ka katora*. "I see problems with implementing it, though."

"Too big?" I tasted the stew. It needed salt, less tomato, and a lot of help. He tries, but he's definitely not the cook Pop is.

"Yes. I don't see how we could get any of the things from where they are to here."

"Eh? I thought you were going there to set up a new dynamo farm?"

"It was one option. I'm not entirely comfortable being spread out across multiple worlds like this. Concentrating things helps with the power intensity and celestial growth. It's a planar thing."

"I'll take your word for it."

"Did you try checking for starships?" he asked.

"Huh? No. Why?"

"Ships are easier to move. Hey! They might even run on antimatter," he enthused. "An antimatter reactor would be excellent."

"That's silly."

"Why is it silly?"

"Do you have an antimatter mine?" I asked, still spooning my way through stew.

"A mine? Like, an explosive device with an antimatter warhead? Or a hole in the ground where I dig it up?"

"The second. Where do you get antimatter?" I pressed.

"I don't," he replied, reasonably. "If I had to make antimatter, I'd make it somewhere in orbit, preferably solar orbit, far away from anything I cared about."

"There's a good reason not to use it," I agreed. "Any screwup will get you killed. Antimatter is stupid."

"I would think the power-to-weight ratio would be a factor."

"How much antimatter are you bringing? How big is the fuel tank? My hydrogen tank holds more fuel and it doesn't need powered containment. If it ruptures, there might be a fire, but it won't turn my ship into particles. How big is your antimatter mix chamber? How do you turn the heat and radiation into usable power? My fusion plant has all your containment stuff, too, and runs at about the same temperature. If I run out of gas, I scoop more from a gas giant. Even from a star. Or I grab a comet and crack water for a few days."

"I still think antimatter gives more bang for the buck," he insisted.

"If you want to blow something up? Absolutely! However, if you want a controllable source of steady energy—like you do here—it's entirely the wrong choice. Everybody is confused about antimatter and fusion. Both release energy, but it still has to be contained and converted into something you want, and most of the equipment is the same regardless of which fuel you use. Antimatter destroys your facility if *anything* goes wrong. Fusion might melt things, but once you lose pressure, the fire goes out. I've been on starships. I know what I'm talking about."

"So, maybe we get a starship?" he prompted, changing the subject.

"Moving a starship would be easier than a ground-based fusion plant. No worries about the foundations or slippage or sudden sinking. And I wouldn't have to kill myself trying to channel enough energy to break mechanical bonds, separating the foundation from the ground around it. Even Pop hates to do *that*."

"Great! Let's find a starship."

"There are different problems. Most starships aren't designed to land, for one thing. Even the ones that are, if they have a working reactor, they'll have a crew who don't want to be hijacked. And, worst of all, the ship will be even bigger than the reactor—and in another universe. Pop once swiped a whole interstellar battleship, but he came prepared with pre-drawn spell icons, a couple of big crystals, and Bronze. Plus, he picked a ship with a working reactor he could tap for additional power. He put so many conversion panels in the reaction chamber, it was safe to look inside! Even then, he only moved it in the same universe, not out of it. I'm not sure I could duplicate the feat, much less bring it across to this universe."

"This fusion thing is harder to get than a social disease."

"I wouldn't think those are hard to get."

"You weren't a nerd in high school."

"I had other problems."

"Still," he went on, avoiding the subject, "you don't necessarily have to move a fusion plant to Me," he reasoned. "If I find one in an NLA world, you could set Me up with another stop on the shift-booth circuit, couldn't you? I could handle the rest."

"How will you set up the Ascension Sphere?"

"Damn it, you're just like your father. Why must you always have a practical, well-reasoned argument about why My insatiable lust for power has to go unsatisfied?"

"Because Pop isn't here to do it. I also have both a family obligation and a sense of responsibility."

"And you are," he sighed. "You are very responsible and I thank you for it. Speaking of which, is there anything I can do for you?"

"Is it possible you can find me something dead or moving slowly enough to catch? I'm not hungry enough to eat the rest of this."

Journal Entry #13

I got home after a month. It was like taking on a temp job in another country, sorting out the whole organization, and going home. But, due to the time zones involved, I came home *on the same day I left.*

Holy shit. "The Spirits have done it all in one night!" and suchlike. I spent all that time getting Uncle Dusty's reactors refueled and enchanted and whatnot and was home in time for lunch! Ebenezer Scrooge must have had the same kind of temporal whiplash.

Mind you, it didn't feel like one night. It felt like two years, but part of it was how time goes *thud* when you're not having fun. You'd think I'd be used to it, what with all the field trips Pop took me on. Those usually had a decent time differential, too, but most of them were also less time-critical. I didn't have to be back the same day. We'd go somewhere for six weeks and come home after having been "on vacation" for a week or a weekend. It wasn't this extreme!

Or as boring. Figuring out how to do spells is a lot more interesting than actually casting them a hundred million times.

I did come home with souvenirs. I brought back half a dozen spare dynamos from Uncle Dusty's dynamo farms. He still has a production line, complete with shift-boxes, for building more dynamos. Taking a few home with me wasn't a problem. Three of them went in my house, as "kinetic sculpture," or conversation pieces or something. The other three went through the shift-closet to my condo in the Madison Building. Uncle Dusty now has a toehold in this Earth, so it's a lot easier for him to yell for me if he needs me, and vice versa.

I looked forward to lunch in my own home. Don't get me wrong. Uncle Dusty feeds his meat suit. There are animals all around his reactor-residences. He even has fruit trees and enough gardening to be called farming. It's all robot-tended, so the production isn't impressive, but there are seven worlds doing this and they all run at different time rates. It's far more than any one man needs to keep body and soul—if that's the right phrase— together.

I wonder if he eats like Pop does? It would explain the extensive gardens.

The trouble is, Uncle Dusty can't cook. Rather, he can, but in a very caveman sort of way. Proteins are exposed to heat. Things get boiled. Mostly, the microwave ovens in the breakrooms see a lot of use.

I wanted something *good.*

I made a real lunch. I took my time. It was a brief but successful love affair—exciting in the beginning, fun in the middle, and a happy memory afterward. I started with a cheddar-and-apple grilled sandwich for munching on while I prepared the tortellini caprese salad. They both went down very well, indeed. I moved on to the lamb in a red wine sauce while silently hoping to get through it without interruption.

Gus showed up. Rusty did not. Well, fifty percent is sometimes good enough. I shared a little of the meat and Gus got all the bones. I'm told it is not normal for a dog to crack open bones with one chomp. It's normal for Gus, so I don't care what other people think. He doesn't eat the bones, just splits them open and licks them clean.

The after-dinner chocolate, on the other hand, would be bad for him. I selflessly ate it all to spare him from any danger.

Pleasantly satisfied, I swirled wine in a glass, added a trifle more, corked the rest, and went to ask Zeno about the vampires.

Of the eight vampires under observation, seven were simple creatures. They went out for a nice evening, a bite of dinner, and home again for a quiet night in. These lived alone or with a human. Zeno was sure about the humans. The vampires retired for the day and the humans didn't.

Retiring for the day was more involved than I expected. Each of them had a peculiarity to set them apart from the others.

One of them threw a rope over a rafter and gently hung by the neck for the day. Another carefully stuck a knife in his own heart before going quietly to sleep. A third took razor blades and slid them into her wrists—not slicing into them, but planting them in the flesh. To keep the wounds open, maybe, rather than let them regenerate?

Those are examples, but all eight of them did something lethal to themselves before doing their day-sleeping thing.

Weird? Yes, I thought so. I don't know why they did it. Custom? Superstition? Or a generic weirdness regarding the way this vampire species works?

The exception was Vampire #8. Prior to daybreak, he did not mind his own business and go home. He was still inside *The Night Crawler* when I originally acquired him on the mirror. He spoke to a number of guests and employees around the club before going through an unmarked door, down a corridor, and into a private elevator. He used an old-fashioned metal key on the panel and pressed the fourth-floor button.

People addressed him as "sir," or "Dietrich"—no other name, yet—and he seemed to have quite a bit of authority around the place.

He didn't look like someone who would be inside, much less in charge of, a techno-rave nightclub. He was dark-haired with streaks of silver along the sides. He was a trifle taller than I, standing about five-eleven or so, and was built more like a keg than a barrel—same design, but not quite as hefty. He wore a three-piece tweed suit, dark gray, with subtle vertical stripes. He sported a maroon tie with a stickpin rather than a tie clip. He carried a walking-stick with an ornate silver handle and consistently faked using it. Was it a habit? Or commitment to making people think he needed it? Or was it more than a cane?

Upstairs, things were much quieter. He immediately moved to a security room and met with people who might as well have worn name tags saying "muscle." The room was full of monitors, all showing various angles on the floor of the club and at least two angles on each of the entrances and exits.

This Dietrich vampire observed a playback of my encounter in the alley. He was expressionless throughout the whole scene. Since the cameras were mounted elsewhere in the alley, looking down it and covering the whole thing, they didn't have a direct line on the door. They did have a wonderful view of what happened once my dance partner came whirling out the exit door's alcove.

Marvelous.

I don't look good on security camera footage. Well, yes, I do, but I don't look my best. At least I now knew for certain this sort of vampire does show up on camera as well as scrying devices. Whether they showed up in more mundane mirrors or not was another question. It varies quite a lot between species and sometimes between individuals. Pop once explained how video cameras aren't the same thing as film cameras, silver-backed mirrors aren't the same as chrome or aluminum-based ones...

It was all very technical and complicated and finicky. There are various levels of the phenomenon. I should have paid more attention.

The whole alley encounter played out. There was our altercation and our lip movements—no sound, thank goodness. Jason landed and the vampire took a powder. He leaped away and I gathered vampire dust.

Dietrich shook his head and mentioned he would have to "report this." He didn't get to it last night, but Zeno would keep one of his Argus eyes on him during the day and through tonight, at least. Whoever he was reporting to would be someone worthwhile, I felt certain.

On the other hand, if he had sufficient clout among vampires—and if they had sufficient internal organization—for him to report to someone in authority, could I skip the spying and make contact directly with Dietrich? I could explain the fight in the alley and apologize, possibly pleading self-defense, and go on to explain about Alden. He could report as much of it as he felt relevant to whoever was in nominal charge and they could respond at their leisure. If I dropped him a note this afternoon, he could have the message when he woke up…

No, bad form. If I sent him a note, I would be sending the wrong message. It would tell him I knew who he was and where he slept for the day. These are not things a vampire wants known, not even if you're trying to be helpful. If the tax-man shows up at your place of business to let you know one of your employees is skimming, it says a lot about the attention the tax-man gives your business!

Whether I spoke to Dietrich or not, it might be a good idea to know who his superior was, and if that guy also had a superior. How many levels are there in the vampire hierarchy? Is it a rigid social structure? Is there room for movement up and down? Is it based on age? On one's powers? Does one's level of influence and power over mortal affairs come into it, too? If I'm a relatively young vampire but have control of a multi-billion-dollar corporation, does it mean anything, or is it regarded as fleeting, temporary, a momentary fluctuation not worth considering?

When he checks in with his boss, we'll find out more. Then we'll spy on his boss and find out lots. I hope.

I decided I deserved the afternoon off. I'd spent weeks camping out in Uncle Dusty's Nuclear Motel and it's not exactly five-star accommodation. His physical, biological, mortal-flesh accommodations have a very make-do quality to them. He salvaged a lot from the ruins, but it was exactly that: salvage. Maybe it's all the same to the meat-suit puppet of a celestial entity, but after sleeping on a camping cot for so long, I deserved a holiday.

Unfortunately, it was a Thursday. I could never get the hang of Thursdays. I haven't held down many regular jobs, and none of them for long enough to truly get a grip on a "work week." Most of my knowledge about a five-day week comes from what other people tell me. Thursdays aren't the first day of the week, so you can't dread them like a Monday. They're not the midpoint, so it's hard to be glad you made it to halfway, like on a Wednesday. They're not a glorious, end-of-week Friday. They're kind of a "middle day," where the week is starting to wind down, but it's not close enough to the end to get excited.

On this particular Thursday, everybody I knew was busy. There's always something to do in the city, but I had hoped I could do it with friends. It kind of spoiled the idea of a holiday. I trimmed Mabel—a bonsai always needs a little trimming—and made sure Charlie and Petunia were okay. Charlie might need a bigger pot.

I like my plants, but they're poor conversationalists.

On the other hand, I could mix business with pleasure. I meant to check in on the store where Alden shopped for tektites. The shop usually handled fine gems and jewelry. I could pick up a few more pieces for my spell storage collection—a girl can never have too many spells in her rubies—while I shopped for tektites.

A woman shopping for jewelry doesn't need a reason. Shopping for tektites, though… why? They aren't even very pretty. I thought it over in the autocab.

I don't particularly like autocabs, but I have to agree with Bronze. Sometimes, they're amazingly convenient. Besides, I'm reluctant to go anywhere on the subway now that Alden has so many underground friends.

Calumet & Sons handled quite a lot of jewelry. Rather, they handled quite a lot of precious stones and had a sideline in jewelry. The shop displayed a lot of custom-made, hand-crafted stuff for the discerning buyer seeking something unique. The display cases were typical of the breed, although the sparkling-clean, gin-clear glass was thicker than my thumb.

The larger portion of the business resembled a bank, but handled sparkly rocks instead of cash. That side wasn't really a place for customers. If you wanted pretty rocks, you called ahead, they selected things from their inventory, and the rocks were delivered to the shop for you to view. Employees—mostly family members—came and went, but strangers were not allowed in the Big Box of Booty.

Pirate booty. Loot. Gems and jewels. Maybe I should have said "Baubles." Nevermind.

As a result, I was allowed to view a nice, velvet-covered tray full of tektites, from which I was encouraged to take my pick. I was not allowed into the back, through the triple-locked, armored door, to view all the racks of trays. If one of these does not meet with Madame's desires, we will be happy to select the choicest of our stock for Madame's perusal. May we fetch Madame a latte while one waits?

I did buy a few small pieces of jewelry. I like rubies, but emeralds also appeal to me. I think they look lovely with my skin tone. Sadly, I did not see any tektites I wanted.

What I wanted to do was examine the entire stock, up close and personal, to see if I could detect anything unusual about them. If I could identify the qualities of a tektite useful to Alden—that is, before he got to it and *did* things to it!—I might have a better idea of what he did to do what he did. So to speak. I wanted a "before" example to go with my "after."

Note to self: come back after they close.

Or… wait. If I charge up everything in the house, how long can I keep a small, eyeball-sized gate open? It'll have to be a one-ended gate, obviously, but instead of trying to get a scrying spell to see what I can see, I can get a naked-eye look directly at the inventory, or as much of it as I have time for.

Let's do the preliminary scrying on their vaults. Maybe I'll get an inspiration on how to detect weirdness through a scrying spell.

Either the tektites in stock are all horribly mundane or I can't tell the difference through a scrying spell. It's possible I won't be able to tell with a naked-eye look, either, but I'm going to give it a try instead of assume I can't do it.

I should have stopped at a crystal shop on the way home and got a couple more big crystals. They could be charging while I planned my viewings. Oh, well. I could start by looking at a few trays to see what sort of power consumption I was in for.

In the early evening, as the western sky was darkening, I shut down my gate observations, rubbed my eyes, and tried not to think about my headache. The gate spell was hard enough. The power expenditure was impressive, but the headache-inducing

Significant Stare was another limiting factor. I had to examine one tray of stones at a time, shut down the gate, and rest my eyes. This gave my crystals a chance to charge between viewings, at least.

It was an expensive evening. I thought I could afford to eyeball the whole inventory, but I was wrong. I didn't realize how much power my constantly-running arrays of scrying devices was costing! —not until I used a lot of power and saw how slowly things charged up again, anyway. It's like spending near my income. I don't get to put away much in the way of savings. I either need to build more solar conversion panels on the roof, or I need more electromagical transformers. Maybe I need a bigger power main, too.

How would I go about getting a higher-capacity power line to my building? Claim I'm turning one floor into a separate apartment, so it needs its own power line? Maybe I'll call Tesidon Consolidated in the morning. Or maybe I'll ask Zeno. It won't do me any good until I have enough—or a big enough—electromagical transformer to actually *use* so much power, though.

Man, my eyes are tired.

On the upside, I found one—yes, *one*—tektite with something odd about it. Physically, it's a rough glass bead. Mystically, there's a sort of signature. It's not any sort of innate power, as such. There's no charge of any sort in it I can detect. It's more like a fingerprint. If I were a psychic nuke and I melted dirt into glass during my detonation, some of the droplets might retain enough of an imprint to be like… like… like tuning forks. If you hit the right note, a tuning fork will vibrate without being struck. This could be the psychic equivalent.

Not all glass beads do this, obviously, just as not all forks are tuning forks. I wanted to know if this thing could be used by any psychic, as-is, or if it needed to be *tuned* to a specific psychic. If I grab Alden's rosary, can I make his beads sing for me? Or should I be more concerned about getting it away from him, or even destroying the beads?

Ooo! Is this a sensitive spot? Can I tell him not to be such a bad person and use his love of these things against him? That might actually be painful enough to work!

The rub, of course, is finding a way to reliably steal the things. He's not going to let me take one. Maybe if I break one? They're glass, after all, and they're rare. Replacing them has got to be a major pain. How would I go about remotely—and reliably—cracking a glass bead? I'll need a way to do it so he knows it's me, but also a way he can't stop. Figuring out how to do it will put a crimp in the old grey matter…

I put the tektite away and let one of my healing spells work on my headache. I stretched, popped my neck, rolled my shoulders, and went to brew up a nice cup of hot tea. With cup in saucer, I returned to my witchroom and frowned at my stolen tektite. No doubt someone at Calumet & Sons would notice it was gone, but, more to the point, I had one to examine.

I already examined it. At the moment, I wasn't going to get any further with it. I went to a lot of effort to find it and grab it and my tektite-hunting brain cells were empty. Despite this, I wasn't sleepy. What else did I need to do? Scrying on a place where we could swipe massive amounts of illegally-gained cash was nice, but there was something I intended to do, if I could recall it. I should make a list. Superhero stuff, I think. Helmet for Jason? Done. Picking a new target, just for funsies? Got it. Already have things in place for laundering the money, no problem. Entering the place where they keep the money, got it. Getting it out again, got it.

Ah. Now I remember.

Being a part-time superhero is *not* the bed of roses I thought it would be. Once you get past a certain technological era, you either have a public identity—*a la* "I am Iron Man"—or you bloody well need to teleport away from the scene. Keeping out of sight in a major city, or at least leaving no trail, is *hard!*

Leaping tall buildings is fine, but eventually you want to change out of your super-suit without giving yourself away. A phone booth might have worked a century ago in this reality, but nowadays there are entirely too many security, traffic, and handheld phone cameras floating around. It does no good to be seen entering a robocab on 9th Avenue as a ninja warrior and emerging from it as a civilian on 80th. You may not be seen changing, but the investigation is going to be *quick.* Using prepaid cards with no ID tags means the cab doesn't know who you are, but it remembers where it went. After that, everyone else's surveillance becomes an issue.

Preventing this unfortunate turn of events is most of what Zeno does. He tries to counteract this sort of tracing and tracking. I have no doubt he makes it difficult, but even he might have trouble erasing or altering video records in *every* phone, *every* bodega door-camera, *every* home security system, *every* dashcam, and so on. This is why I try to leave as little as possible in the way of evidence.

Come to think of it, is anyone trying to stop Zeno? If not, how much trouble might he actually have? The natives of this world would say he's from the future. If the devices are connected to the Internet, they're effectively defenseless to him. I'm almost afraid to ask how much of the Internet belongs to Zeno.

Rusty assures me he has his own ways of avoiding detection and tracing. Animal Control hasn't shown up to take him in, so I believe him.

To be safe, I really should enchant something with an invisibility spell. Casting the spell is time-consuming and power-hungry, not to mention technically sophisticated. It's not for amateurs. It's not even something experts particularly like. Once you cast it, it takes a fair amount of attention simply to keep it working correctly.

To keep the illusion of empty space while holding still is a little challenging, but moving requires an enormous number of real-time changes in the illusion. It results in a blurry, distorted area rather than true invisibility even when you're controlling it yourself. *You* know how you're moving because you're the one doing it. The best I can do is to disappear into a sort of heat-shimmer effect wherever I'm standing.

An enchanted item has a much harder time. An object has neither judgment nor intelligence, so it does an even worse job of following along. I'm guessing an item will have to work on an area, producing a volume of space with a level of distortion to it. I'm not sure this is adequate as far as invisibility is concerned—the blur will be obvious and be relatively easy to track—but it's much harder to pin down who it belonged to. It could be good to have.

This still leaves me the problem of what to do when I'm trying to do something with my bare face on. If I'm not wearing my super-suit, I still might have to do the Kung-Fu Hula to save my own life. I'd rather not be mistaken for a member of the Danny Rand Dojo. How do I hide my identity from a security camera without being obvious about it? Go to ninja school? Good idea, but how does one *find* a ninja school? Ask a ninja? That has the same problem!

I didn't have a good answer, so I spent the rest of my time doing research on digital camera technology. You've got to know your enemy.

By the time I realized I missed dinner, I had a few tentative ideas for how to foil video surveillance. Cameras don't work in quite the same way eyes do.

I microwaved a snack and started cooking dinner. Gus came downstairs with me and sat at the entrance to the kitchen, waiting patiently. I don't mind tossing him the occasional treat, but Pop spoils him *rotten*. He's learned bad habits. Maybe this would be a good opportunity to teach him not to expect to clean the dishes after every meal.

With that thought, the lack of Pop's presence snuck into my kitchen and hit me. Hard. I had a bad moment of missing Pop. I mean a really bad moment. It felt as though something inside me cracked. All of a sudden, the world fell to pieces and scattered. There was no center to anything and I was alone in the middle of the ruins. I had to put down the spatula and lean on the counter.

Will I ever see Pop again? He's off doing things *he* thinks are dangerous! How can I possibly know? I'm not even sure what they all are! There's an empire and a religion and a whole bunch of irate people, angels, gods, and for all I know, demons. There's stuff he couldn't, wouldn't do when I was little, so he put it all on hold until I was old enough to be on my own—because *he* thought it was too risky! Now he's got all this dangerous stuff that's been sitting and maybe getting worse.

When I was... two? I think? ...I remember Pop sitting next to my bed to tell me bedtime stories. It started out as little shadow-puppet shows. He'd set up a night-light so he could move his hands in the light and throw shadows on the wall. Looking back, he was okay at it when it was just his hands.

Then he started making the shadows do things you can't do with hands. Now I know it was his shadow doing it, but it was the most glorious magic in the universe at the time. Castles rose, unicorns ran, the Sun and Moon revolved in the starry sky, dragons flew and flamed, knights rode giant horses—all horses *had* to be giant ones!—ships with billowing sails plied the oceans of the world, ships with the hearts of suns plied the oceans of space, pirates attacked both sorts, and everything was filled with wonder, including me.

Now I'm all grown up and no longer living under his roof, eating his food, existing in his shadow. Yes, it's time for me to step out of the comfort and safety of his shadow, but sometimes I miss it terribly.

Will I ever see Pop again?

I hate that question.

I turned down the stove, gave Gus a sharp warning, and went up to my workroom. The divinity dynamo in the corner was still whirring away on overdrive, ablaze with celestial energies. I sat down in front of it, cleared my mind, and focused on my Uncle Dusty.

I heard his voice in my head.

You know, most worshippers don't get the privilege of a direct line to their god.

"I'm special."

Isn't vanity one of the big sins?

"Depends on your religion."

Ha. Good point. All right. You've got My attention. What's on your mind?

"Tell me how Pop is doing."

He's fine. A bit antsy, though.

"Is he?"

Yes. I'm doing most of the work. I've got him doing a little busywork, mostly to keep him occupied. I'm not letting him do anything dangerous with Me around!

"So, you really are watching over him?"

You bet I am! I'm watching over you in the sense I'm keeping an eye and ear devoted to your world in case you, I don't know, do something like you're presently doing, id est, praying to get My attention. I also check in periodically to make sure you're breathing and so forth.

*By contrast, he's in a world where there's an active population of worshippers, not just a so-so believer and a few dynamos. I've been shoving power into My aspect in his world for a while. If anyone comes for him, they're going to have to get through **Me**. I may not have your Pop's stamina, but I punch in ways they don't understand. They won't expect a bolt of lightning from a clear sky and they won't expect the earth to open up, chew them to bits, and swallow them. So stop worrying about him. He's as safe as it's possible to be.*

I sighed, relieved.

"Thank you."

By the way, do you recall anything in your studies about the household gods? They were all the rage during part of the Roman era.

"Yes. I recall them. It wasn't unique to the Romans. There were a number of cultures with spirits devoted to the family or to one household. Sometimes they were ancestor spirits, while other had spirits of a particular place—a *genius loci*, if you will—"

A simple "yes" would suffice!

"Oh. Sorry. Yes."

With this thought in mind, I am the household god of your family. I'll be looking after you for the rest of your life, because the originator of your family line created Me in his image—and I look after him, too, because he needs all the help he can get. Got it?

"Got it. And thank you again. Pop sometimes needs a keeper."

No, he's usually got personal survival pretty much covered. What he needs is a compass.

"I've never known him to be lost."

A moral compass. He's seldom geographically uncertain, but he sometimes needs guidance in other ways.

"Oh. Yeah, you have a point. He mentioned it once to me. He knows."

I did not add that he considered me to be his moral compass. It was a big responsibility and one I did not—*do not*—feel comfortable having. Even now, I'm not sure it's a job I'd willingly take. But who else would I trust with it? "Here's the Armageddon button. Hang on to it, would you?" Who would you trust to hold it?

No, that's not fair. There's a lot more to Pop than the end of the world. He's more like a genie. He's a well-meaning genie, but he's so far from human he doesn't always understand your wish. He's not malicious—not usually. He's trying. You state your wish and he does his best, but between your own foolishness and his lack of comprehension, it doesn't end well.

This may explain a few of my own peculiarities. My therapist would be right to say a lot of things are my parent's fault. I'm not sure how I feel about it.

Anything else I can do for you? Uncle Dusty asked.

"I'll let you know."

And vice-versa, to be sure.

I felt his presence diminish and I finished cooking dinner.

Gus was a good dog and didn't demand any of the ravioli. He also didn't eat any from the stove while I was upstairs, which is more than one can expect from any normal dog. I curled up on my favorite couch and turned on the video wall. Gus curled up on the floor and waited. He can be very patient—especially so when there's meat sauce involved.

I scrolled through possibilities and settled on old *Addams Family* episodes. Why do I enjoy the show? I'll let someone else figure it out. John Astin looks nothing like Pop, but there's still something about him that reminds me of Pop. Come to think of it, he does have the same merry twinkle in his eye. It comes more readily to Gomez, though. Or maybe it's the lighthearted swordplay. Pop can be amazingly fun when he's in a good mood!

I hope I'm more of a Morticia than a Wednesday, but I suspect there's a lot of Grandmama.

With dinner devoured and Gus delighted with the sauce left over—yes, I was still thinking a bit about Pop, and Gus was perfectly behaved, so I gave Gus the bowl—I decided to check in with Zeno before going to bed.

This was a mistake. Never check your messages before bed if you're expecting news. You check your messages, read something important or disturbing, then either have to do stuff or lie awake thinking about it. This is not how you get ready to sleep.

It seemed innocent enough at the time.

"Zeno. What's new?"

"Plenty, Ma'am!" he announced, all enthusiasm, as usual. "Where would you like to start?"

"How are we doing on the smuggling operations?"

"I have been monitoring communications among high-level executives in the organizational chart. This leads me to believe I need to redirect the monitor mirrors."

"Do we have a listing of top-level executives?"

"Yes, Ma'am, although they are probabilities, not confirmed."

"Okay. I'll re-target the mirrors and you keep me posted. Still tracking Alden?"

"Yes, Ma'am! His route is time-stamped and on the screen!"

I looked it over. As usual, he spent a lot of time in big buildings. City Hall, Police Plaza, convention centers, skyscrapers…

"Hmm. He's obviously the head of his mind-controlled network, so tracking him is probably giving you a lot of information on who he's got hooks into, yes?"

"Yes, Ma'am!" Zeno agreed, and threw up a bundle of data. Lots of columns, lots of names, oodles of probability figures. It was chaos, not knowledge. Rather, it was neat, orderly information I couldn't process fast enough to make sense of, much less use. I did note each person had a "transcript/replay" option next to them, and an "elapsed time" figure.

"Bear in mind he doesn't necessarily need to be talking to someone," I pointed out. "He has telepathic powers."

"Shall I begin correlations based on his proximity to persons of influence?"

"You haven't been?"

"No, Ma'am! I was not instructed to do so."

"Damn it." I had to remind myself Zeno's personality simulation is a really good simulation, but it's not an actual intelligence. He's a collection of programs, not an entity.

"Okay. Build me a chart. Build several charts. Build all the charts. I'm going to need visuals, not just reports. This is getting painfully complicated and I'm definitely going to need visual aids to understand how it all relates. Tell me if Alden is involved in anything. No, center on Alden. Find out what he's involved in, connected to, controlling, influencing, the works."

"Working!"

"Good. And tell me what mirrors I need to readjust."

I did so, targeting people Zeno thought were most likely to provide maximum information. I didn't recognize any of the new people he wanted to watch, but I didn't have to. He gave me names, pictures, voices, and even locations, and I tracked them down in the mirrors. Sometimes I wonder who works for whom, me or Zeno.

Zeno, on his own, is a laptop. A shockingly powerful one, true, but he's hardly a combat robot screaming "Exterminate!" On his own, he can't even close his own cover, much less move around on the desk. Connected to a high-technology society with a pervasive Internet, though, he becomes much more frightening. He has access to robotic capabilities and a whole world of digital information.

Come to think of it, he could probably take over a robotic factory and start producing stuff, but robotic factories rely on the deliveries of specific parts for the things they build. He might be able to cobble together something different out of the parts, but a robotic press producing car door panels only does one thing—it produces door panels for cars. There are very few true "robots" on an assembly line. They are usually machines designed so each one does a specific task.

I wonder. I know they make metal-based three-dee printers. Feed in wire and it produces a metal object. They also make computer-controlled milling machines capable of creating quite complicated parts. They're not usually used for mass production. The wire-construct parts are slightly more fragile, for example, and the computer-milled parts could usually be made in bulk in cheaper ways. But if Zeno had one robot like the ones Uncle Dusty uses at his power farms and, say, a dozen of each of the part-producing gadgets…

Nah. Still not too worrisome. He'd need an entire supply chain full of automation before he could start replicating his own parts-making stuff, much less build his own power plants. Impractical.

But becoming a robotic overlord is the least of his technological terrors.

You want to go on a secret little trip, a private getaway for two? Okay. Your phone has your location and the network knows it. Turned off the location function? It still has to access the network towers, so you're still trackable, if not as precisely. And are you logging into the hotel wifi?

Okay, never mind the phone. Turn it off. Take out the battery. Wrap the phone in metal foil. You bought fuel for your vehicle, right? Did you use a credit card or pay cash? And did the security camera at the gas station get your face? No? How about your highly-visible license plate? You better be using an old-fashioned, fuel-powered vehicle, because if you're driving a modern electric car, your car's transponder will automatically log your usage whenever it's on the electric lane of the road—the one with the induction strip. And you need to be on the induction strip if you expect to get very far. A car only goes a hundred miles or so on the internal batteries.

Back to the subject of money. Did you book your hotel on-line, or did you show up and hope they had a vacancy? You did pay cash for the room, right? Including a huge deposit, since you didn't use a credit card? By the way, did they ask for ID at the desk? Yes? Aw, too bad. Larger hotels are like that.

How about we go low-rent, so they're less concerned? Maybe you can find a room at a sleazy motel where they don't much care who you are because they're not as concerned about damages. Unless we're camping out, we better try it, because you're not getting away with that sort of thing at any hotel with more than a two-star rating.

Now, about all those traffic cameras and speed cameras along your route. I know you paid close attention to traffic regulations so as not to draw attention, but they don't record only while the light is red or when they detect speeding. They're always on! True, it may be impractical for most people to search through all of it to look for your license plate or your face, but computers don't mind zipping through the digital recordings at ridiculous speed. This narrows down the possibilities to something humans can go through manually.

Do I need to mention all the personal security cameras, phone cameras, and the like? Every passerby is a potential electronic spy, depending on whether they have their AR visor on or even if they merely have their phone out.

Welcome to the digital world, all connected, all the time. There's no such thing as privacy anymore. If it weren't for Zeno, acting as my digital fingerprint remover, I'd have been identified and put on wanted posters after my second vigilante outing.

I'm beginning to see why Pop always liked it in the 1950s. It had a lot of the conveniences without being nearly as invasive. "Connected" meant having a radio, a television, and a phone with a long cord—maybe even more than one phone in the house. When I was a teenager in the 1950s, Pop made sure I had my own phone up in my room. Later, he made sure I had a mobile phone capable of calling his, even across universal boundaries—at least, until Alden stole Pop's phone. I wish Pop had remembered to replace it before he went off to wherever he went. I miss him.

I also miss our house in Shasta. I adore my house on Riverside Drive, but I miss the old place. I felt safe there, and not only because Pop fortified it. Now it's burned down into ashes in the basement, and that hurts a little.

Still, if I want something so quiet it's practically dead, there's always his house in Iowa. It's still in the 1950s. At least the date is. The countryside in Iowa makes me think it's the 1880s.

While I sorted out Zeno's human spying connections, I paid attention to the vampire spying connections, too. Zeno didn't have any level-ups for most of the vampires. They simply didn't report to superiors. I think it's because the criminals have business to conduct. Most vampires are connected socially, as a minority group, not as business partners keeping in close contact.

Or, usually not as business partners. Their society has business to conduct, and it definitely has a kind of hierarchy. Dietrich was up and around as soon as there were stars in the eastern sky. He went immediately to a meeting with another vampire, apparently one higher up the food chain. Since there were several people—all vampires—taking turns seeing this higher-up, we concluded he was important.

I re-tasked one of the other vampire-following mirrors to monitor the important guy. The other six I aimed at vampires in the waiting room on the theory that if they were important enough to get an audience, they were worth watching, at least for a while. Dietrich's mirror I left on him.

If I'm lucky, we just identified the whole vampire ruling council or whatever for New York. If the head guy reports to anyone, maybe he'll show us the whole global vampire conspiracy, assuming there is one. They might not have anything more than regional organization, or they might have individual tribes constantly fighting for feeding turf. Does the one guy act as a councilman for Manhattan, or is he the Vampire King of New York? Does he govern with an iron fist, or is his job more like a troubleshooter? Finding out is one reason to watch them.

"Okay, Zeno. I think I've got everyone on the list. Do I? I'm tired and I want you to double-check me."

"Yes, Ma'am! I've got sight and sound on everybody!"

"Thank at least a couple of gods."

You're welcome.

My Uncle Dusty will go to great lengths for a well-timed one-liner. He and Pop are definitely related.

"Anything else for me before I sack out?" I continued, to Zeno.

"Do you want a report on Dietrich's meeting, or do you want a playback?"

"Is it important?"

"I'm so sorry, Ma'am! I can't tell!"

"Why not?"

"I do not have adequate criteria for defining what is important. I lack human initiative and intuition, Ma'am!"

"I'm sorry, Zeno. I keep reminding myself because I keep forgetting. It's also late and I'm little punchy. All right. How long was his meeting?"

"Thirty-seven minutes, eleven-point-six seconds."

"How about we approximate?"

"Yes, Ma'am! Thirty-seven minutes, give or take."

"Thank you. I can spare thirty-seven minutes. I'll take it on the main screen in the media room."

"Right away, Ma'am!"

I tromped into the media room and flumphed down in the deep, cushioned seat. Then I struggled up and switched to one of the tall stools by the built-in mini-bar. If I got too comfortable, I'd fall asleep.

"Okay, Zeno. Hit it."

The playback of the meeting told me a few things. Zeno didn't get the name of the HVAC—Head Vampire At Court—because it was never mentioned. Dietrich was addressed by name, of course.

And I didn't have a clue what they were saying.

"Zeno? Any idea what language this is?"

"One moment!" No doubt Zeno accessed everything there was to know on languages and did a lot of comparisons. It took several seconds.

"The language has no good matches," he reported.

"How about bad matches?"

"There would seem to be loanwords or roots from the protoliterate period, and possibly from the proto-elamite language. Research into these languages is incomplete and the probability of accurate analysis is low. More research exists on the written forms. If a sample of the written language can be obtained, a much more comprehensive analysis can be conducted!"

"Good to know. Any idea what they're saying?"

"Not a clue, Ma'am!"

"Yeah, I didn't think so. How old would you say this language is?"

"Five or six thousand years, Ma'am!"

Five thousand years. Sheesh. I immediately thought about finding a world where people were barely starting to grow crops in the Fertile Crescent. I could live there for a while and learn their language. It was a very brief thought.

The meeting did not seem to be one Dietrich enjoyed. He wasn't reprimanded, but I think he was threatened. I might not understand the language—I can't use a translation spell on a recording!—but I can read body language and tone. The HVAC dismissed

Dietrich, who promptly bowed and backed up three paces before turning. He got out through an exit door, rather than leave through the way he came in, and he departed in an extra-long, human-driven sedan.

With the playback finished, I sat quietly, thinking. Some of the words didn't have ancient counterparts. "Cocaine," for example, wasn't a substance back at the dawn of civilization, so they used the modern word for it. They also used occasional proper names. *The Night Crawler* was mentioned.

I didn't like how closely the two words followed each other in the conversation. It implied the incident at the club and the subject of drugs were interrelated. Which implied...

Okay. Okay. This isn't a complete disaster. Unpleasant, yes, but not a disaster.

The vampires had heard about my midnight hobby. Well, of course they had. It made the news. There were no pictures, of course, thanks to Zeno, but we did leave a lot of witnesses. Now the vampires were interested. Why?

Well, Jason did show up on security footage behind *The Night Crawler*. The outfit would be recognized from any descriptions. Were the vampires more concerned about a vigilante superhero hunting them, resulting in suspicions about pyrotechnic death on various bridges, or were they more upset about the interruption in the smooth operation of drug trafficking, in which they might have business interests? Come to think of it, would they have fingers in the drugs business? They might. Yet, Zeno hadn't reported any vampire cross-connections in his analysis of—

Dammit. I need to be specific.

"Zeno!"

"Yes, *Ma'am!*"

"Have you found any connections between the drugs traffic and the vampire subculture-society-thing?"

"No, Ma'am. I was not instructed to conduct such an analysis. I was tasked to define the chain of command in two separate organizations. My latest instructions are to see what Alden's organization is and to correlate it with the criminal trafficking business."

"Fine," I agreed, because it was exactly what I did tell him to do. I felt my headache coming back. "Add this. I need to know what the vampires know about me."

"Very little," Zeno replied, happily.

As an aside, when I was growing up, I read stories where someone suddenly felt a cold sensation when they got bad news, or something frightening happened, or similar nonsense. At least, I thought it was nonsense. Bad news is cause for higher heart rate, maybe. A tensing of the muscles. But a feeling of coldness? That's stupid. It doesn't make sense.

Suddenly, I felt a cold sensation. Well, what do you know? It does happen.

"Zeno, how do you know?"

"Their searches for information on you keep turning up only the falsified data I planted. It's my prime function. Relevant information update: The drone across the street is spying on the house for Dietrich."

"How do you know he's responsible for the spy drone?"

"He contacted the man responsible for spying on you. They suspect you are involved with the 'ninja vigilantes'. This is reinforced by the observed interaction in the alley behind *The Night Crawler*, as well as the coming and going of Jason through the roof access door. They know there are at least two persons involved. They are not certain whether or not you are one of them or a member of the logistics and support team."

"They think I might be playing Alfred to Jason's 'Batman'?"

"It is one possibility. They are not discounting the possibility you are one of the direct participants. Eyewitness reports do indicate at least two people, one probably female."

I sighed.

"This is not helping me get to bed," I observed.

"Is it something I should prioritize?"

"No, I'll manage." I rubbed my eyes and tried to think. "Is there anything out of the ordinary—anything at all—to imply there is any sort of unusual security problem tonight? Anyone planning a raid, people sneaking up on the doggie door, anything?"

"No, Ma'am!"

"Then I think I'm going to bed, anyway. Hold the fort."

"Yes, Ma'am!"

I went upstairs to bed. Strangely enough, knowing vampires were specifically and suspiciously watching me was not an inducement to restful slumber. Pop watching me? Pop watches *over* me! Other vampires? Not so much.

Eventually, I grabbed my teddy bear, Mister Stuffins. We went through the shift-closet to the Madison Building apartment, then used the shift-closet to go to Iowa. Pop keeps a bedroom there for me. I would not be surprised to find Pop, wherever he lives, always keeps a spare bedroom on hand in case I drop in. He's like that.

With Gus curled up on one side and Mister Stuffins tucked in on the other, I had no problem sleeping there.

Journal Entry #14

There's something about waking up to a dog licking your face you either love or hate. Gus loves to wake me up with kisses. He's in my list of top four favorite creatures. It's hard to be more precise, what with Pop and Bronze on the list.

He stood on the bed, nose-down, licking me awake. I grabbed him and rolled, playing with him. He weighs almost as much as I do, and I'm no bird-boned runway model. We squirmed around, me skritching him everywhere and him writhing on the bed, play-pushing me away with all his feet, swishing his tail back and forth like a feather duster on speed.

You may or may not be a dog person, but for me, this is a good morning.

Pop keeps his house stocked. I made coffee and checked the dog feeder. The hopper still had food in it, but it was running low. Pop hadn't been here for a while.

He always said Gus was my dog and I had to take care of him. I tried to be a good dog-mom, but I was five. Sometimes I forgot things. Pop never let Gus go hungry, though.

I worry about Pop. No, I take it back. I worry *for* him. The only thing keeping me from being too worried is the fact he's never alone. He has Bronze, Firebrand, Uncle Dusty, Velina, Leisel, and a whole bunch of really enthusiastic warriors whose cultural values remind me of the samurai. They all want him alive and unharmed and are prepared to sacrifice everyone else's life to get their way.

I worry, but I'm grateful to everyone helping me to not worry as much.

I refilled Gus's food dispenser and checked the time in my world. It worked out I was slightly ahead, here, this time. At my house, it was still only about four in the morning. I zipped home, set my mirror's micro-gate to dialing Pop's house in Iowa, and came back to finish a leisurely breakfast. There was no pressing need to do anything else. I had Zeno working on finding out things and I didn't have anything I absolutely needed to be doing.

Dang it, no. There was something I needed to do.

Translation spells mostly rely on a peculiarity of speech. People try to talk to you in whatever language they use. This activates parts of the brain not used when someone is only thinking internally. This is a much more precise and focused form of thought. A translation spell detects this, runs it through your own speech centers to turn the thoughts into your words, and you "hear" what they meant to say in your language.

It doesn't work with recordings, which is frustrating. I'm pretty sure Pop has a specialized version sensitive enough to pick up the meaning from impressions placed in hand-written documents, but I never bothered to learn it. Maybe I need to spend more time in an Ascension Sphere. Maybe I need to study harder. Maybe I need to accept Pop is a legendary, if not mythic-level wizard and he can do things no one else will ever manage to duplicate—not even if he personally trains them from birth.

As for the present translation problem, I might have an idea. I can build a recording spell into a crystal—build several, I mean. One for each mirror. If I can tie it into the psychic impression version of a scrying spell… no, it won't work. Or will it? I might have to raise the sensitivity on the scrying spell to get the proper inputs. Yes, that might do it. If I can amplify the scrying spells, the recording spells should be able to hold on to the imprint of all the conversations. Then, when I want to play them back, I can route the psychic emissions through a translation spell in tandem with the normal playback and, poof! Instant foreign-language dubbing!

Bloody vampire elders. It never occurred to me they might have an ancient language they still used. Is it a cultural thing? "We started out speaking Linear A and, dammit, all you newbie youngsters are going to learn it as the Tongue of the Undead!" I can see advantages to having a Secret Language™ for your undead legions, but it seems like a lot of trouble. Maybe you don't get to learn it until you've been dead for a couple of centuries. Maybe language lessons are a thing you have to do to prove you're worthy of being a blood relation.

I finished breakfast, cleaned up in case Pop came home, and took a trip to the store to pick up a few things. More than one store, actually, since I needed a lot of crystals. Once I came back to Pop's house, I locked everything up, put a brand-new can of chili-with-beans on the kitchen counter, stuck a note to it ("I love you, Pop!"), and borrowed his workroom.

He doesn't use this workroom much. I can tell. Well, he's been busy elsewhere. I made good use of it—and the time differential—to sort out the modifications to the standard-issue psychic scrying spell, make sure it worked in tandem with my recording spell, and put the new combination into crystals for each of my existing scrying mirrors.

I had a time differential in my favor. I took frequent breaks. Gus plays with a kid who uses the shed as a personal clubhouse, but Gus would rather play Frisbee with me. He's got to treat normal people gently, like they're puppies. Me and Pop, not so much.

Of course, then we had to wash him down. Cleaning spells are great, but he loves a bath—and to shake. There's a reason Pop has a lawn sprinkler and dog-grooming brushes. Gus was in heaven.

With Gus happy and all my spells in order, we went through the shift-closet relay to my house. I suppose I could alter the closet in Pop's house to have an alternate setting directly to my house, rather than the Madison Building condo. Maybe I will. It seems like a lot of effort to eliminate a two-second delay in the transit time, though.

Once I had the new translation setup installed, I planned to be down in my basement parking level with a welding torch. Gus planned to nap before galumphing off to play in the park with other people. He likes the park, but he also likes my couch. Nap first, play next, nap again, that was the plan.

He's a big dog, but he's adorably fluffy and knows how to make a good impression. How he knows who the dog people are, I'm not sure, but I've seen him playing Frisbee and Fetch with children in the park. More importantly, with children I've never seen before. Maybe he goes up to the parents and acts like a perfectly-behaved dog, sitting, rolling over, and whatever else on command. Maybe he finds a stick, walks up to a kid, and plunks the stick down at his feet while wagging his tail. He's good at making friends.

Down in the garage, I looked over the incomplete clockwork sculpture. Pop started with a central framework, kind of like a skeleton, and did preliminary work to flesh—or iron, copper, and brass?—it out. Was I going to continue the way he was going, or was I going to do it my way?

I got out a pad and pencils to do preliminary sketching. The sketches were basic, but they gave me ideas of how it would look if I continued in Pop's style. Then I did more sketching, this time to see what I thought might look good. The two styles were more than a little different. The man raised me to be *me*, not him, and I'm still working out the differences. I'm still living in his shadow, really, trying to find out who I am, what I want to be, where I want to live, what kind of life I want—maybe what kind of life I can have.

On the other hand, in certain ways, *everyone* lives in Pop's shadow. He comes and goes as he pleases, can wreak total havoc on entire universes, and the only thing keeping him from doing it is his personal self-restraint.

No, I would not want to be Pop. Being me is hard enough.

As for the artwork, Pop went for a spare-parts motif. The gearing included parts from automobile transmissions, rear axles, and universal joints. The "musculature" was, so far, a collection of automotive shock absorbers. None of it could move, being welded solid, but I have no doubt Bronze would have given it full mobility in five minutes.

The whole design was seriously industrial. While I liked it, I thought it could be prettier. The industrial parts could be concealed by an outer skin. For the outer layers, how about a lot of interlocking cogwheels? Some large, some small, and all interlocking. They didn't all need to turn, so they could be artistic instead of mechanical. The largest ones could be the size of—or maybe could actually be—circle saw blades. Smaller ones might actually be from clocks.

How small did I want to go? Pocketwatch gears? No, probably not. At least, not on the body. Around the head, perhaps. Maybe centering on the eyes, nose, and ears? That seemed reasonable. How would I handle the tail? A pendulum? Wire? Uncoiled clock springs?

With a start, I realized I was considering this statue as a potential mount. Was I going to animate it?

Maybe. Bronze might want to try it on, but as far as making it a personal enchanted item, I wasn't sure. There are practical considerations when making a golem horse. It would be nice to have, but it also wouldn't fit in where I was living. Possibly useful in a low-tech universe, though, where the roads or lack thereof contraindicated a car…

I finished sketching and took them upstairs, placing them around the second-floor living room. The first floor is mostly for company. All the private stuff happens higher up. I'd look the sketches over as I went about my day, letting their impressions sink in. Eventually, I'd know what I wanted.

The doorbell rang. I checked the video monitor through my phone. Janice stood outside, looking miserable and knotting her fingers together. She does the finger thing when she's upset. I was surprised to see she had her hair tucked up under her hat. She's inordinately proud of her hair and always wears it down. From that and the lack of makeup, I guessed she hadn't had much time in the bathroom this morning. Come to think of it, I was pretty sure she should be in a class at this hour.

I went into the vestibule to let her in and paused to collect the mail. The mailbox next to the door has a letter-slot to the outside, but I'm uncomfortable with unguarded holes into my house, so there's a collection box with a lid. I let Janice in.

She took one look at me and burst into tears. I put an arm around her and patted her back and let her cry.

Yes, I could have listened to her mind and found out what was wrong, but it's impolite. Even so, I could hardly avoid hearing her projected thoughts. By design, low-power psychic energies go right through my shields. It's like wearing hearing protection. I can have a conversation, no problem. Higher-powered impulses get blocked. You can't forcibly change my mind, but you can offer up arguments all you want.

Janice projected her breakup. It wasn't a detailed report, merely a general sense of what was wrong. I wasn't aware she was having this degree of problems with Oscar. Then again, I hadn't seen the two of them together in a while. We don't go to school together anymore, so we don't hang out nearly as much. I spend more time on rooftops, these days. Nights. That is, I spend more time planning and preparing for clandestine activities than I spend on friends. I wonder what this says about me.

I got her into the house, into the living room, and finally onto the couch. She sank into it while I fetched her a wet cloth and a dry one. She would want both.

Her story came out in fits and starts, and only pieces of it. She didn't go into detail about what happened, only that she was moving out, immediately, right then, without delay—and needed help. Packing a bag and abandoning their shared apartment was one thing. Abandoning all her stuff was something else.

"But I remembered you have a car," she said, now mostly calmed down. "I need help, and I can't get everything out of the place before noon."

"Why noon?"

"Because he'll come back after his Poli Sci class and it gets out at eleven-forty-five."

"All right. Where are you going?"

"I… well, I thought I would apply for a room in the dorms, but it takes a few days to process."

"Uh-huh. So, you've got a hotel?" I asked, not very hopefully.

"No. I… I need to call around and see if, if, if I have a friend with a… a spare bedroom. Or a couch. Or something. Until the paperwork goes through."

I nodded, recognizing the hint for what it was.

"All right. Let me change clothes and we'll move you out. Are you on the lease?"

"No."

"Even better. Help yourself to the bathroom. I'll get myself together."

I brought my car up the ramp and out onto the street. There was an autocab outside, waiting patiently, meter running, still holding the things she grabbed while leaving. I brought the stuff inside and sent the cab on its way.

Getting her moved out wasn't any great trick. It was a lot of back-and-forth between car and apartment, but there was no one home. She and Oscar lived in one bedroom of the two-bedroom apartment. Stacey and Brian occupied the other bedroom and Mike had his couch in the living area. The bedrooms were originally one bedroom, but the landlord added a wall to divide it and call it a "two-bedroom" apartment. The living room was much the same. The other half of the living room was now part of a different apartment—presumably the other half of what used to be a *real* two-bedroom apartment.

Their side had one bathroom, standing room only, which made me wonder if they had a strict shower schedule. They'd have to. Wouldn't they?

There were a lot of stairs, but Janice did most of the packing, stacking, and stuffing. I did the climbing and carrying. I had to. Even with a minor spell to make my car unnoticeable, I wasn't happy leaving it unguarded.

Hey, I got my workout. And on real stairs, not my stair-climber machine.

With everything loaded, I drove my little hatchback home while Janice took a cab. There was only room for me in my car when we finished loading. I blame her clothes and books. She had more physical books than anybody else I knew in this world. Everyone else uses their personal data unit—that is, their "cell phone." The things evolved from mobile phones and I still think of them in those terms. A lot of them don't even have screens, anymore. They connect to an augmented reality visor and you use that. They even make AR visors to your eyeglasses' prescription!

Unloading would have been quick, but I nixed it. We only unloaded the stuff she brought in the autocab. I made sure she packed her personal, day-to-day stuff with her. That way, why unpack my car when she's going to a dorm room as quickly as possible? Unloading would have implied a long stay. Leaving all her stuff crammed in the car and inaccessible emphasized it was a temporary arrangement.

Very temporary, if I had my way. There's a lot going on I would rather she didn't know about! Worse, it might actually be slightly risky for her to bunk here. Alden and vampires—at least the Dietrich one—were keeping an eye on the house. But how do I tell her I can't let her crash here when I have about one and a fraction floors more than I actively use? "Sorry, but I'm expecting a vampire infestation and my buddy the werewolf is a bit casual about his nudity" doesn't work, does it? Sure, it would prevent her from staying, but only because you don't sleep near crazy people.

When I had a private moment, I told Zeno to expedite her application for a dorm room. He promised to accelerate her paperwork in every way, aside from any hardcopy stuff.

Janice settled in as much as she could. We got her into her bedroom, sorted her bathroom stuff out, and I left her alone. She didn't want to talk right then. Later, yes. Now? Now was the time for curling up in a darkened bedroom and crying until she was finished. I've done it myself.

Okay, I have a guest. Let's see. Make something she can eat, put it in a container, put her name on it, and leave it in the fridge? Yes. Hang a towel in her bathroom? Done. Leave the coffee out on the counter, next to the machine? Definitely yes. Wrap a strip of tape around the lid of one of the ice cream jars and write "Help yourself" on it? Reluctantly, yes. I guess I can get more…

Lock doors? Definitely. Lock all the doors, inside and out. Outside doors lock automatically. Inside doors are another matter. They all have locks, so use them. It's a very firm way of saying "private," at least, and probably more polite than sticking "Keep Out" signs everywhere.

Do I need to do anything with Oscar? No, for two reasons. First, it's not—strictly speaking—my business. Janice is merely crashing here for a while, not asking for help with her relationship. Second, even if it was my business, all I have is coffee-shop gossip. I don't know if this is all a huge misunderstanding, irreconcilable differences, or if he asked for a threesome and she's overreacting. Until—and *unless*—Janice says anything about it, I'm forbidden to interfere.

Okay, I'm not *forbidden* forbidden. I was raised to mind my own business. Maybe it didn't completely take, but it *is* how I was raised! Pop broke his own rules when he felt the need, but there had to be good reasons. Rules are not there to be broken, but you *can*… after much thought and careful consideration! Even though I don't live under his roof anymore, I still don't break Pop's rules. There were very good reasons for them. Although… Okay, I *usually* don't break Pop's rules. There have been exceptions.

I should install doors on the stairs. I could lock whole floors off. Note to self. I did take a few minutes to add soundproofing spells to her bedroom and to Zeno's computer room.

Dang. Jason and Rusty. I called Jason and let him know I had a houseguest. He promised to be circumspect. Rusty was more problematic. I cleaned up his clothes—he tends to leave them scattered around—and tried to call him.

I heard ringing in my laundry hamper. I don't use it, but Rusty sometimes throws clothes at it. The werewolf is a bit hit-or-miss about carrying his phone. Since he can't take much with him as a wolf, he tends not to put much in his pockets. This isn't the first time he's left his phone here. I decided I would simply have to hope he noticed Janice before turning into a naked human or after he managed to dress. If they ran into each other unexpectedly, Rusty was about to be promoted to my boyfriend in a hurry. At least, it's what we would tell Janice.

Were there any other potential unexpected guests? Pop was unlikely, but still possible. Just in case, I put a note on the inside of my witchroom door. He might step through either the closet or the mirror. The last thing Janice needed was to surprise Pop in my house.

The last time it happened, it ended badly for Pop. Next time someone surprises Pop, it might end *very* badly, indeed—but not for him.

Houseguests. *Pff!* I've never had to worry about anything incriminating lying around the house before. We packed up and moved whenever we were found out to be "odd." I never liked moving and I didn't like cleaning up evidence, either. At least Pop was good about not murdering anyone in the house. Usually.

Which reminded me to have a word with Mister Stuffins. No killing the houseguest!

I should have offered to put her up in a hotel. It would have been less trouble. Then again, being a houseguest is different from accepting money, somehow. I'm not sure why or how, but it does seem to be a thing. I never learned why.

Late in the afternoon, my phone rang. Not my usual phone. My Alden-phone.

The tiny gate allowing those two phones to communicate is supposed to be inside the phone casing. Currently, my end of the dedicated gate connection is part of an elaborate setup in my old apartment. It still acts as a communications link to the electronics, but those electronics forward the call to my current phone. From the perspective of a typical user, it's nothing more than a phone.

It also means radioactive oxygen can be piped through the open gate without coming anywhere near me. I don't have either end of the gate connection on me. Alden has one, so every breath he takes is putting at least a little unstable oxygen into his lungs, his bloodstream, and pretty much all the tissues in his body.

Pop has a mean streak and, sometimes, he displays outright genius along with an amazing amount of bloodthirsty patience.

When Alden called I decided to take it in the media room. Zeno could give me a video feed during the conversation.

"Hello?"

"Good evening, Miss Kent. I trust you are well?"

"Yes, Reverend Alden. And how are you?"

"I've been better, but everyone has their little difficulties, now don't they?"

I sat down as Zeno echoed the scrying image onto the wall-screen. Alden was in a small, well-appointed office. There were quite a number of religious icons on the walls and shelves. A younger man sat in one of the visitor seats. His expression was completely blank, but his forehead still had round pressure marks on it—fingertips, perhaps? Probably. Physical contact makes the psychic connection much easier. My perspective was from a corner, near the ceiling, as far away from Alden as the space permitted.

"So I'm told," I agreed. "To what do I owe the pleasure of your call?"

"I've been reviewing reports from my subordinates—" Alden-speak for *mind controlled drones* "—and I've noticed a peculiarity."

"Oh?"

"Yes. It would seem there was a bit of a misunderstanding about a particular piece of property."

"Go on."

"I'm told you may have mistakenly removed an object of mine from a bridge?"

"Oh. Oh! Was it yours?"

"Indeed."

"I apologize. I noticed it in passing. I wasn't aware it belonged to you. I should also add I found another one in a tunnel…"

"Yes. I was about to bring it up."

"I do apologize. I'm investigating them. Rather, I *was* investigating. It didn't occur to me you might be involved. I'm afraid I broke the one on the bridge in getting it loose, but I could return the other one. Or would you rather I put it back where I found it in the tunnel?"

Alden grimaced, but his voice stayed serene. I looked at him more closely. He seemed bigger than I recalled. Not taller, but heavier. Was he gaining weight? It was hard to tell through the cassock. I was sure his shoulders were thicker, broader. Maybe he was working out after the way Pop manhandled him.

"No, but thank you for the offer. I called to discuss the issue and I'm pleased it was merely ignorance on your part. It did not occur to me to inform you. Now that we've established their presence, I trust you will not interfere with the others."

It was a statement, not a question. It bordered on an order.

"I'm sorry, but the static is particularly bad, today. Are you on holy ground?"

"Yes. Does it matter?"

"Pop said high-intensity holy ground might be more difficult to get a signal through," I lied. The hiss was of gas through a tiny opening. During active phone calls, the pressure went up to maximize the amount of gas near his face. The rest of the time, it was a quiet leak. "It's sometimes hard to hear you. You were saying something about interfering with others? What others?"

"If you detect any other such items," he said, slowly and distinctly, "I trust you will understand they are mine and are not to be touched. May I count on you to be less free with my personal property?"

"I'll certainly try. Are you sure all of them are yours? Should I call to ask if it's yours if I encounter another one?"

"There are many more. You may safely assume they are mine and there for good purpose."

"I can assume they're yours, certainly. I can't assume they're there for a good purpose without knowing more about what they are and what they do."

"I doubt you are capable of understanding the complexities of the situation."

"I'm pretty bright. And I'm capable of finding these things, ripping them off walls, and taking them home to study. Of course, this would only go on until my curiosity is satisfied. I'm *sure* I'll finish my studies of the things long before I run out of examples. If not, well, when I run out of examples, I suppose I'll have to come to you again and ask for help in understanding the things."

"Hmm."

I waited. He thought it over, clearly seething. His expression was one of frustrated authority. He was used to giving orders and having them obeyed.

While he considered what to do and say, many things had to be going through his mind. Was it worth it to tell me what they were for? Was it more or less trouble than having to replace them as I broke them? How difficult would it be to guard them? Was it worth trying to force me to stop investigating them? What were the long-range costs? Was this particular hill one he was willing to die on?

He sighed and ran a hand over his face.

"You are aware there are dark forces in the world, yes?"

"You better believe it."

"They must not be permitted to gain control of humanity. They have terrible plans. These devices are the beginning moves in a long campaign to restrict their movements, hunt them down, and bring the world out of darkness."

"Oh."

Now it was my turn to think. He's setting fire to vampires. No, it's more than that. He thinks he's saving the world from vampires. He's starting a conflict with some of the most powerful, dangerous, cunning creatures in the world—or he's escalating the conflict, depending.

Pop always talked about the difference between intelligence and wisdom. Intelligence is using logic and science to determine exactly how much water it will take to put out the fire. Wisdom is pouring water on the fire before it spreads. I think Alden isn't nearly as wise as he is smart. The time to stop the spread of vampires is when there aren't many of them. Once you have a whole subset of human society with a thirst for blood, it's too late to talk about extermination. It's time to think about negotiation. Maybe Alden was making fast, bold moves because he saw how much control the vampires already established.

"I wish you luck," I added.

"Thank you. I trust we will have no further difficulties along these lines?"

"Not from me, certainly. I plan to leave these... beads?"

"You may think of them as beads, yes."

"I plan to leave these bead-things alone." It suited me to play the part of ignorance. If I didn't even know they were tektites, it would help him feel confident and paint me as even less of a potential problem.

"Capital," he said, smiling. "Good evening."

"Good-bye."

He hung up and turned his attention to the young man in the chair. Alden pressed fingertips to the fellow's head and concentrated. I wished I knew what he was doing. No, that's badly phrased. I knew what he was doing. He used the guy as a focus and a sort of antenna for accessing information from his homeless network. I wished I knew more about how he did it.

As for the vampire issue, I wondered if he had any idea what he was getting himself into. *I* had no idea what he was getting himself into. The only vampire I really know well is my Pop. He's so far from average even he can't see it from there.

On the other hand, if the vampires of this world have "terrible plans," what are they? Are they planning to quietly run the place from behind the scenes? Do they already run the place? Or are they planning to change the balance of power? Will it be a sudden change in the politics of the world, or a gradual change in the way society works? How much influence do they have? Have they been secretly building their own influence and networking for centuries, or are they desperate to avoid attention because they'll be swamped under modern weaponry?

I have this terrible idea. What if both the world wars were power struggles among vampire factions? I might as well worry about the Illuminati while I'm at it—assuming they aren't the same thing.

Is Alden seeking to undermine their influence in the only way he knows how—namely, by taking it for himself? Has he grabbed the minds of people under vampire influences—mind control, blood magic, or blackmail—and turned them to his cause? If so, are they wondering why their mortal servants have suddenly switched allegiances? Or has he broken the hold of the vampires over key people and told his new allies to lay low, keep up the pretense until he's ready?

Ready... for what?

And what is Alden trying to do? What's his goal? Kill all the vampires? He keeps wearing religious outfits, so I wouldn't be surprised. But more short-term, what does he want right now? Own New York and clean out the undead? It sounds like it. It might be a stepping-stone on the way to owning national capitols and seats of government.

Or is he after metropolitan centers? If the local vampires need to feed regularly, it's easier to do in a major city. If Alden manages to control Manhattan, can he drive out the vampires and force them to relocate to other cities? Can he repeat the process with other metropolitan sectors and force them out of their prime hunting grounds?

What then? Reveal the reality of vampires to the public and call for purges? Or conduct a shadow war with secret police and intelligence agencies? Or a combination of the two? Or something I can't even guess at?

There are a billion possible moves in such a game and I don't want to play. In point of fact, I don't want him to play, either. This world seems pretty decent, as Earths go. I like it here! I don't see the problem with letting a secret cabal of vampires pull strings as long as they don't let the place go to pieces in the process.

I have an unusual attitude to vampires, I admit. It comes with the territory.

That was my intellectual consideration. Emotionally, I had other issues.

First off, Alden is doing things I find morally objectionable. Rule the world? Fine! Go right ahead, if you can manage it. Grab people by the forebrain and force them to love you? No. Not fine. Maybe I get my aversion to slavery from Pop's attitudes, but does it matter where it comes from? I don't like the idea and I will continue to not like it until Alden forcibly removes it!

The other thing isn't something I got from Pop. It's all mine.

During the phone call, Alden took it for granted I'd simply shut up, sit down, and stay out of his way. I didn't like it. I never have. Do not pat me on the head and tell me to run along. Pop never patronized me that way, but plenty of other people tried. I sometimes wonder if Pop kept us in the 1950's for that reason. It taught me to endure a lot of patriarchal nonsense without redefining foot-ball.

Maybe I'm merely an apprentice to the Big Bad Wizard who Alden views as his proper nemesis. He never really seemed interested in me, only in Pop. Or maybe he thinks of me as "the young woman." What can a woman do? "I'm dealing with matters involving the fate of nations, woman! Get back in the kitchen!"

Clearly, he's forgotten the gods of Greece. Nemesis was a goddess who enacted retribution against those who demonstrated foolish pride and arrogance. I am not Pop and Alden should be grateful for the fact. He's too ignorant to understand how grateful he should be.

And, because I am not Pop, I want to teach him a lesson. If ignorance is bliss, I want him to suffer. I've been wondering about imprisoning him. Now I'm *thinking* about it!

"Zeno!"

"Yes, *Ma'am!*"

"How much does a private island cost?"

As it turns out, isolated islands in the middle of nowhere are hard to come by. Want something near a coast? That's easy. Lots to choose from. Something far away from shipping lanes and large populations? That's tough. There are islands out there, but they aren't listed for sale.

Makes me wonder who owns them and why. Governments? Supervillains? Eccentric billionaires with secret space programs?

It doesn't help that I don't know how far Alden can send a mental impulse. Can he call a brain-drained drone from the other side of the world? Can he communicate in dreams from here to Mars? I can solve a lot of this problem with a psychic shielding enchantment on his cell, but he's also sensitive to magic. He may not be a great wizard, but even a wimpy wizard can eventually scratch away at the mortar and tunnel his way to freedom. Psychic freedom, in this case.

This can be troublesome. I know because I sat down with a pad and pencil and started making lists. What do we need for an Alden-containing cell?

Psychic shielding was a must. All of it has to be enchanted into objects, too. A spell can be manipulated fairly easily. An enchantment, once set, is reinforced by the physical structure of the object, making it much more difficult to alter.

Hmm. Shielding for the enchantments, too. I don't know if *Alden* is capable of it, but *I* can fiddle with Pop's werewolf detector and jump around the search pattern, substituting vampire parameters. Of course, Alden won't be able to actually lay hands on the enchanted devices, nor do I think he has the skills, but, just in case...

Physical restrictions also have to be in place. How strong was he? Pop mentioned Alden was tougher than a normal man. Last I looked, he was bigger, more muscled. I guess a box made of steel and concrete might be in order. A bank vault? Maybe something custom-built?

Which leads me to ask about his other powers. Can he look through a wall and move things with his mind? *I* can! He might be able to unlock things. How do we stop him? Can I reverse an Ascension Sphere and drain all the magic out of an area? Sure. I don't see why it wouldn't work. But what if he has a non-magical telekinesis? I can cut off his access to magical forces by removing them from the area. Can I do something similar to drain away any psychic emissions? Or project a psychic static to scramble anything he tries to do?

So, bank vault. Reversed Ascension Sphere around it. A containment diagram around everything to stop psychic calls for help. Emitters to pump psychic scrambling static into the cell.

It would take a while and a lot of personal work, but it could be done.

Now, where do I put it? An island is probably a good bet, but I want something Muffy and Biff won't park their yacht alongside while the butler sets up the picnic on the beach.

"Oh, I say, Muffy; there appears to be a giant metal box here."

"What do you suppose is in it, Biff?"

"I've no idea, Muffy, dearest. Have Jeeves fetch a box of dynamite, would you? That's a good girl."

"Do we even have dynamite, Biff?'

"We had best have some available or I shall sack him on the spot."

No, an easy-to-reach island wasn't my first choice. I wanted something much more difficult, more out of the way.

Could I put this on the moon? It would be easiest to build it here, on the ground, but then I would have to shift the whole thing in one shot, as a unit.

Ouch. Maybe not.

Could I build it in place? Maybe. I'd have to build a dedicated shift-closet, probably by enchanting something from IKEA. I'll also need a space suit.

Once on the moon, I could shuttle back and forth with parts. I would probably have to build it in stages and bolt it all together. Does IKEA make space station modules?

It would be immense trouble, but there are advantages. Who's going to mess with it on the surface of the moon?

Damn. Space programs. I'll have to bury it. If someone sees it from a satellite or spacecraft, they'll spare no expense to go mess with it.

I'm not kidding. Imagine it making the news, wherever you may happen to be. If everyone agrees there's a structure on the moon and nobody knows how it got there, how fast would there be a new lunar launch to investigate? How many telescopes would be permanently aimed at it? How many tight-beam radio antennae would be trying to pick up—or send!—all possible signals? Intelligence agencies would be falling over themselves to determine whose it was. Scientific types would be going nuts with the possibility of evidence of alien life.

Hmm. Technically, I'm not from this planet. Does that make me an alien life-form? It's a technicality, sure, but still...?

Anyway, a buried lunar vault. At last! The perfect prison—

—provided I want him to suffocate or starve to death. It's not like I can hire guards for this. First, the whole project is illegal imprisonment. Second, guards need to have shifts, take breaks, and have time off. Third, if anything goes wrong, Alden will pretty much own them and have a neat little lunar base of his own. Admittedly, the only way up or down will be my hypothetical shift-booth, so I can put it in a semi-secure location, but if the guards can shuttle back and forth to work, how do I keep mind-controlled guards from bringing Alden back to Earth safely? Build a lunar city where the guards live, full-time?

This is getting out of hand.

The imprisonment idea needs more work. So far, it's still my best idea. Never mind how I stick him in his custom-built Bad Boy Corner—that's an entirely different operation! First I have to have somewhere to put him, then I have to figure out how to keep him alive in there, and *then* I can worry about how to get him there!

Am I going to lock him away? Is that what I've decided on?

Looking at the scribblings and doodles of my prototype lunar vault, I think maybe I have.

Wait.

Am I missing a bet?

There's something. I don't know what it is, but there's an idea I should be having and I'm not. Something about imprisoning Alden. The principle is sound, but the method... There's something about the prison. I'm not sure what, but there's something about the prison I should do better.

What is it?

I know there's something. There's something I know and it's relevant to this, but I can't quite make the connection. I've had this happen before and it annoys me something fierce. What am I missing?

Journal Entry #15

Janice went out to talk to Oscar and hopefully work the kinks out of their relationship. Or maybe work more acceptable kinks into their relationship, if it would help. I offered to go with her, but she felt it was better to have a private chat. Besides, Stacey and Brian would be home.

"If I'm back late, is that all right?" she asked.

"Sure. Ring the doorbell. I'll let you in. I don't have a spare key lying around."

"You sure? I hate to wake you."

"It'll be fine! Or call me when you're on your way back, if it's really late. The doorbell might not wake me. I'll go right back to sleep, no problem. You go sort out your boyfriend."

"Thanks, Phoebe. You're the best!"

"'*C'est moi, c'est moi,* 'tis I.' Do your thing, Jan."

She went. I stayed. I also stayed up late, thinking about designs and qualities of a jail. I went down to the parking garage level. I like to work with my hands while my brain does more esoteric things. The inner framework structure of the horse was complete and I was starting to add cogs and gears as external decoration.

While the welding flame hissed, I worked out the process for putting a psychic-containing jail on the moon. All things considered, it wasn't unreasonable. Not all that unreasonable. Not *totally* unreasonable. All right, it was difficult and dangerous and would require immense effort, but it might be worth it.

Keeping him alive while he's in there would be easier than I thought. I can include all the stuff for life support and give him the manuals. Staying alive then becomes his problem. I do need to leave out anything that could reasonably be used for communications from the far side of the moon. And leave out any space suits. I can leave out airlocks, for that matter. All the occult containment can be placed outside, comfortably out of reach of the prisoner. It's hard to interfere with a spell when you can't even see it, and even harder to interfere with an enchantment. I'd probably have to enchant a lot of items to keep him penned in. I did not relish the idea of so much work.

Or did I? If I make it clear he's on the moon and doesn't have a space suit, is he going to try and break out? There won't be an airlock, so he would have to literally break out. Or would it be better to let him think he's somewhere people could rescue him? He could waste his time and effort trying to call for help.

Making this a totally closed system could be tricky, though. Without airlocks, how do I supply him with vital life-support materials? A one-way shift-booth, maybe, about the size of a mailbox? Something for sending and receiving letters and emergency supplies— without any magic of its own! Up there, it's a box to target. Down here, I have a power grid to draw on. I can afford something smallish, like a mailbox, on at least a weekly basis. Maybe even a daily one, depending.

Can I shift things across the surface of a reversed Ascension Sphere? I don't see why not. There's no magic inside it? Fine. I'm supplying all the magic from down here and throwing it up there. It might cost even more to send something, but in a low-magic environment, the reversed Ascension Sphere won't be pumping out the area with any great force.

I can't quite shake the feeling I'm still missing something. Something fundamental. Damn it, I hate this feeling!

Hang on. Why not Mars? Interspatial shifts don't get much more expensive as they get farther away. You can go across the universe cheaper than you can leave it. So, Mars? Or, since they have rovers roving on Mars, how about Ganymede? Titan? Or how about we dump him on Pluto?

No, if I move him too far out, I'll need to include a power source. I'm planning to use solar power conversion to keep the magical gadgets running and maybe supply life support. Pluto is a bad choice. The Earth's moon has two weeks of darkness, but I can charge crystals during the two weeks of sunshine.

Damn it! No matter what, I'll have to provide power for the mechanical life support and suchlike! I'm not designing a prison, I'm designing a damn *space station!*

Hang on a minute.

Why not use an actual space station? There are universes where nobody's alive to argue about it. Do any of them have loose space stations floating around? Maybe, but it's unlikely. If the world suffers nuclear holocaust, biowarfare attacks, or a zombie apocalypse, the space stations are probably okay. Then again, how long do the residents survive on them? The ones I'd want would have self-sufficient life support, so the survivors would survive until the equipment wore out...

Hang on *another* damn minute!

Why am I worrying about a space station? Why not penal colony the guy? I can use a whole world! If there's nobody alive but the zombies and the carnivorous plants, do I care where he goes or what he does? Let him dodge whippy, thorny vines that want to drink his blood. Let him mind-control the mindless hordes of brain-eating zombies. It would serve him right for making so many zombies out of people!

I don't need to build a prison! I need to send him to a *world* so awful he'll wish he was in a nice, clean prison cell. Maybe I can even drop in supplies every so often with a note about how the people he's mentally mutilated are being gradually restored!

Hot damn! I have a plan! Okay, I have the beginnings of a plan. Okay, I have an idea. An idea that might actually work! I call it progress!

The doorbell rang. I hurriedly spoke to Zeno—he's got remotes throughout the house. I explained my idea quickly. I didn't want to lose the idea like Coleridge getting Porlocked. As I did so, I shut off the welding, put the mask aside, and didn't bother to take off the apron or gloves. I went upstairs and checked the inner glass as someone rang the bell again and held it for several seconds.

Some guy was on my front porch. I'd never seen him before.

He looked about twenty-five. He might have been six feet tall, but he was one of those long, lanky sorts that give the impression of height. His clothes were glossy and his shirt too tight, same as the waist and hips of his pants. The shirt was frothy at the throat with silvery, metallic lace and his pant legs flared like skirts, starting at the knee. Very fashionable in certain circles, but I didn't generally move in those orbits. He wore his hair swept back and his eyes were surrounded by an elaborately striped pattern of eyeshadow. I thought it gave him the impression of wearing a rainbow-colored domino mask, but my tastes aren't quite in synch with the locals. It was well-done, though, which made me think of a personal valet or a salon job.

His car was parked on the street. It was a large, well-appointed thing, very new, very expensive, and parked exactly where I would park if I didn't have a garage. I was pretty sure there was a driver still in the car. I pressed the intercom button.

"May I help you?"

"Is this the home of a Miss Phoebe Kent?" he asked, smiling at the intercom's camera. I'm sure he meant it to be a charming, engaging smile. His tone was smooth and warmly intimate.

"It is. May I ask who is calling?"

"My name is Alonzo, and I've come to deliver a letter." He produced a piece of paper, folded into itself to form its own envelope, and sealed shut with a wax stamp.

"Please place it in the mail slot," I directed.

"I'm so sorry, but I've been instructed to deliver it personally. From my hand to yours, so to speak."

I gave it more thought. What would Pop do?

I shivered. No, on second thought, what should *I* do?

"All right. I'll buzz you in and be right down," I lied. I buzzed the outer doors and he stepped inside. He tried the inner doors as the outer doors closed.

"Hey! These doors won't open!" I didn't answer. I was busy getting out of an awkward apron and welding gloves. Let's see… my jogging defense devices should be understandable insofar as I was a female answering the door late at night. However, carrying a lethal weapon inside my own home wasn't against the law. Caution being something Pop tried to train into me, I thought it wise to have a gun. Not in hand, of course. Just in case.

Meanwhile, Alonzo became a bit frantic at being trapped, then settled down into what I can only describe as a sullen silence. When I finally opened the inner doors, he stomped inside.

"Took you long enough!"

"The letter," I said, coolly.

"Here!" he snapped, and thrust it in my face. I took a half-step back and accepted the letter.

"Thank you. You may go."

"You haven't read it."

"And I'm not going to until after you leave."

"That's not how this works."

Maybe it was my earlier conversation with Alden. I'm not usually so quirky about being dictated to. I like to think I'm more patient and even-tempered. I didn't snap at him, but I did speak rather coldly.

"First of all, if you are not privy to the contents of the letter, I have no intention of permitting you the opportunity to learn them. Second, I see no reason to explain anything to you, a messenger boy, when you are rude to someone your employer wishes to impress." I waved the wax-stamped envelope. "Third, you are no longer invited into my home. Neither you nor anyone you work for may set foot in my domicile. You are banished and forbidden. Leave now."

He stared at me in surprise and wonder.

"You can't expect—"

I crossed his palm with his shoulderblade, pushed the button to buzz the outer doors open, and introduced him to the world. I didn't hurt anything but his pride and maybe his shirt as I released him on the porch. He continued to squawk the whole way. I closed the outer doors by hand as he staggered and regained his balance.

I'm pretty sure I heard someone laughing in the car.

Inside, I examined the note with considerable care. It was sealed with a monogram of "J" and "D" pressed into a dark red wax. I carefully cut the paper underneath, leaving the seal intact. The note was a lovely, handwritten thing. Someone used a fountain pen, but I suppose it's hard to find a reliable quill supplier, these days. It was an invitation to meet, with the location and terms negotiable. It included a telephone number.

"Zeno?" I called. He was upstairs in the computer room, of course, but the house is wired. Note that: wired. Not wireless. Security is an issue.

"Yes, Ma'am?"

"Did you spot that Dietrich guy writing a note?"

"Yes, Ma'am!"

"This it?"

"It certainly looks like it, Ma'am!"

"Thanks."

I called the number. A lady answered the phone.

"Dietrich and Associates. How may I direct your call?"

I glanced at the clock to see how late it was. Clearly, it was a twenty-four-hour call center.

"I'm calling about a meeting request."

"Of course. I will be happy to put you on the schedule. May I ask your name?"

"Phoebe. And you are?"

"My name is Alicia."

"Alicia *Marchbank*?"

"Why, yes. Have we met?"

"No, but I'm pretty sure you—ah, you met my—my grandfather."

If I recalled correctly, Pop was wearing a disguise spell at the time. I always thought of it as his Silver Fox disguise. Silver hair, a thread-fine network of wrinkles, all the little things to say a man is getting on in years, while doing nothing to conceal what a handsome man he is. He came home from a charity event with Alicia Marchbank's personal phone number written on his palm. I didn't blame her a bit.

"I meet so many people," she agreed. "May one ask who your grandfather is?"

I thought fast. What alias was Pop using in my world? Dammit!

I hit the mute button and consulted Zeno before answering.

"Pop—that is, my grandfather—is Jerry Dandrige. I think he made a donation to... a police fund? For body armor, or something?"

"Indeed he did," Alicia agreed, almost purred. "It was quite a generous donation. He's your grandfather, you say?"

"Yeah, but he raised me. I could call him 'Grandfather,' but he's always been 'Pop' to me."

"You are most fortunate. So, you need an appointment with Mr. Dietrich, I believe. When would work best for you?"

"Actually, I don't really need an appointment. If he's interested in contacting me, he's obviously the person I've been trying to reach. We've sort of been two ships passing in the night. All I really need to do is give him an information packet. Is there someone who could pick up a small package? I don't want to send anything via email, and there's a lot of information."

Alicia was silent for a moment. Possibly she was considering the reasons why I wouldn't want to send something through the Internet. It's also possible she was perfectly at home to the idea of classified communications being sent by courier and was simply trying to figure out who was available.

"I believe we can have someone knocking on your door in moments."

"Not that twerp Alonzo, please. I'd hate for him to miss all the steps on his way back out and hurt himself on the curb."

The line went silent for a moment. I recognized the effect of the mute button until she spoke again.

"I believe an alternative can be arranged."

"Wonderful! I'll leave the package in my vestibule."

"Even better. Say, five minutes?"

"Make it fifteen. I want to make sure I've got everything up to date."

"Fifteen minutes, then."

"Thank you."

"And thank *you.*"

We hung up and I got busy with Zeno. In less than a minute, we had Alden's tracking records, meeting appointments, proximity notes, and, more recently, audio, video, and transcripts of everything he did while not on holy ground. We included maps with the known holy ground areas marked, as well as blessed bridges, tunnels, and ferry ports, plus the coordinates of the tektite focus maintaining each.

I didn't put Alden on a plate for them, but I did make it very clear he was a problem. It would keep him as busy as a one-armed paper-hanger while I picked out a prison for his penance.

Fifteen minutes later, there was a small box with a data module in my vestibule.

The car out front was still there. Alicia got out of it, leaving a sulky-looking Alonzo behind. She gracefully ascended the steps, rang the doorbell, and calmly stepped inside when the doors buzzed open. She looked around the vestibule for a moment, performed a curtsey-like movement to pick up the small box, and breezed right back out again.

No muss, no fuss, no problem. I liked her a lot more than I liked Alonzo.

All right. Vampires: Notified. I'd still have Zeno keep track of Dietrich and any other vampires, though. At least one of them is interested in me and it would be wise to keep tabs on them. Zeno would also continue correlating information on the criminal underworld and—

Hmm. Maybe I should do much the same thing with the criminal underworld as I did with Alden. In his case, the vampires are pissed, but now they have someone to be pissed *at.* It should give him no end of headaches and slow him down a lot.

As for the crooks, the vampires either won't care or will *be* the crooks. But once we have a detailed power structure for organized crime, does it remain my adopted problem? I can go beat up a dozen of the top men, sure, but is taking down the entire power structure of a criminal underworld the job for one witch, a professional mercenary, and a werewolf?

On the other hand, we can anonymously hand over a complete dossier on everyone involved. Even a well-bribed national justice system would have trouble avoiding convictions when all the *other* national justice systems have the same evidence. If the justice systems of a hundred and ninety-seven nations all get the same files, it's going to be hard to sweep it under the rug no matter how many people are bribed.

What if they all suddenly develop outstanding warrants, already in the systems? Or tax investigations? Or outright audits of them and their companies? Or if the evidence on all of these crooks is distributed to the press, worldwide, with confirmation documentation and sources pre-loaded for easy access?

Definitely something to think about.

What else do I have on my plate? Janice. I'm glad she wasn't home to get caught in the potential crossfire, here. Clearly, my "secret identity" is a bit compromised, at least as far as the undead are concerned. Will they out me to the public? If it's in their best interests to do so, absolutely! But if they think it's something they can hold over my head later, when they need to influence me, they'll keep quiet. People are tools, resources. I'm not sure if they regard me as a dangerous resource or a problem to be solved, but if they think the risk is worth it, I should encourage them to keep thinking it.

Nevertheless, if I'm likely to have vampires or their couriers hanging on the front-door bell, houseguests aren't a good idea. I'll have to get her moved out even quicker than I expected.

Other things… The statue in the basement? It's a structure, now. I can pay attention to the exterior and how it's going to look, rather than making it stand up.

Invisibility? Darn it, I still haven't even *started* on an invisibility enchantment. And, really, what I need is something more complicated in principle, perhaps, than in execution. I want something to hide me from technological observation—a camera-fuzzer, or something like the way some vampires don't show up. It's not the witness I mind so much. It's the recording. Witnesses can say whatever they want, but photographic analyses will stand up in court.

I really need to get on that.

What I *want* to do is poke a scrying hole through the universes and peek at Pop. I'm not going to, though. First, because he'll notice it, and he might not know it's me. Second, because when he notices, he might react first and apologize later. I've heard him grump about being spied on and I don't want him being grumpy if I'm anywhere near the line of fire. And, third, I have a better way.

"Hey, Uncle Dusty?"

Yeeeeeees?

"How's my Pop?"

He's okay. Antsy, maybe a little angry, annoyed at a number of things, but it's par for the course.

"I wish there was a good way—a safe way—to hurry him up so I'd know if he comes out of this all right."

Hmm.

"Hmm?"

I'm thinking.

"Hey! Couldn't I set a little gate to ticking Tauta along faster than my world?"

Um. Yes, in theory.

"In theory?"

He's actually got a gate speeding you up, in case you need him.

"Ah. But wouldn't it be better for him to finish what he's doing so he doesn't have to worry about being here and there at the same time?"

That's one argument. He's also got a couple of things that will take time—lots of time—and he's hoping your stuff stabilizes before he sets his phone to "Do Not Disturb" and goes off to build a laboratory or something.

"He still hasn't replaced the Dadphone Alden stole."

Has he not? Uncle Dusty hesitated for a moment. *You know, I don't think I'm going to remind him. Not right now. I will—eventually. He's a bit busy and really doesn't need to be nagged at this exact moment. If you need him, tell me. I'm used to being a divine messenger.*

"Doesn't that make you an angel?"

The distinction is a fine one, but also not relevant to the discussion. Is there a problem?

"Not one requiring a lightning rod."

Lightning rod?

"Nothing worth attracting his annoyed attention. It'll wait."

Ah, now I get it. Good one.

"Thanks. As for the time differential, my stuff is more indefinite than his. It could take years, even decades. If I catch Alden and stuff him somewhere, how long should he be in there? Ten years? Fifty? How long does an imprisonment last? How long does it take before his penance turns him into a penitent?"

Search me.

I thought about it for a bit longer.

"All right. Where's the time-ticker stuff?"

...why?

"I think Pop has it wrong. He and I should run on about the same time scale, not one sprinting faster than the other. All his other time-tickery trickery can stay, obviously. I'm only talking about him and me."

I'm not sure he'd approve.

"I'm not asking him to approve," I stated, trying to sound definite while my stomach did a flip-flop. It's not often I deliberately meddle in Pop's business, but I have to trust my own judgment, don't I? And it wasn't like I was interfering with one of his projects. It was my time differential, too.

Oh, it's like that, is it? All right. It's your responsibility. On a more personal note, am I going to get into trouble for this?

"How much do you do without consulting him?" I countered. "How much stuff would he like to know about and you conveniently don't mention?"

Your point is cogent, well-put, and cheeky bordering on insolent, but I see it. All right. Is your mirror charged up? If you want to reset a time-ticker, I'll show you where it is— but make sure you take the blame. I don't want him upset with me.

"If he wants to come visit to deliver a reprimand, I'll be glad to see him."

You're not too big to spank, Uncle Dusty cautioned.

"Yeah, but I'm old enough he'd feel weird and awkward if he tried, so I'm not worried. Show me."

Journal Entry #16

I woke up to Zeno spouting a verbal wake-up call.

"Tick-tock, seven o'clock, time to get up, time to get up, seven o'clock!"

The voice wasn't Zeno's, but I didn't immediately place it. It was a nice voice, though.

"Why," I asked, as reasonably as I possibly could, "do I have to get up at—what time is it?"

"Nine-twenty-six AM," he supplied, more normally.

"I thought you said it was seven?"

"That's the default wake-up sound your father set, Ma'am! It's a direct copy from *There Will Come Soft Rains,* by Ray Bradbury, read by Leonard Nimoy."

"I suppose there are worse ways to wake up," I grumped, "than to the sound of Spock. Why do I have to get up?"

"You wanted to be notified when Janice was coming back."

"Is she at the door?"

"No, but she has left her apartment and has given her autocab this destination."

"Oh, I see. Thank you for the warning."

"Always a pleasure to be of service, Ma'am!"

I rolled out of bed and into a bathrobe. My hair is usually well-behaved, even when it's this short. I ran fingers through it and it settled perfectly into place.

Yes, I have personal hygiene spells in my rings. Pop's idea of hygiene is "clean." While I agree with him about cleanliness, it's only a starting point.

I went downstairs to start breakfast. Gus and Rusty were already there. Rusty had rummaged through the fridge, cooked—that is, "exposed meat to high temperature"—and shared with Gus.

Yes, I was annoyed he went through my fridge. On the other hand, I was overjoyed he was finally getting the hang of getting along with Gus. And vice-versa. Gus wasn't growling at him. Gus wasn't taking commands, either, but he was waiting patiently to snap a snack out of the air when Rusty tossed one. I think Rusty was content to be the one controlling the food.

I call it a victory. Not a total victory, but an important one in the campaign.

"Morning!" Rusty offered, waving kitchen tongs. Gus put his paws on my shoulders and licked my face. I ruffled his neck-fur and put him back on the floor, silently thanking Pop again for putting an anti-dog-breath spell in Gus' collar.

"Good morning. I see you two are getting along."

"The food hasn't run out," Rusty observed.

"Fair point. When it does, I hope the two of you will work together to hunt down prey, rather than eat each other."

"Oh, I think we will. Probably. At first, anyway. Depends on what we can find."

"I guess that's not unreasonable, all things considered." I went through the cabinets as we spoke, poured myself a bowl of cornflakes, and settled at the kitchen counter to watch Rusty fry things.

He's not a cook. He can make raw things edible, but it's not the same.

Janice rang the bell halfway through my bowl. Gus disappeared to sniff at the front door. Rusty shot me a questioning look.

"Janice is staying with me for a day or two. Be circumspect."

"Ah, yes. Well, 'circumspect' is my middle name."

"'Wesley Circumspect Giancomo'? I thought your middle name was 'Flynn'?"

He stuck his tongue out at me and I chuckled.

"While I'm being circumspect—or pretending to be—who's Janice?"

"Mortal, human, female, mundane, short-term guest."

"Oh. Can do."

I let Janice in, introduced her to Gus again—he'd met her before, but it had been quite a while—and inquired about Oscar. Things were going well for her and Oscar, at least as well as could be expected at this point.

"Not staying over there?" I asked, while she assured Gus she remembered him.

"No. Oscar and I... we're talking. I need space while we do. I don't need the pressure."

"Any luck on the fundamental problems?"

"He's admitted he's been a jackass and promised to do better."

"Has he? How many times?"

"Excuse me?"

"How many times?" I repeated. "How many times has he promised to be less of a jackass?"

"What do you mean?"

"Not just last night," I clarified. "In the time you've known him, how many times has he promised to do better and not done it?"

"I don't think it's any of your business."

"You're right, and I don't want an answer. I want you to think about the answer. You won't, but you should."

"If I want relationship advice from you, I'll ask for it!"

"Yeah, and until then you'll fumble around on your own, not listening, even when you're asking for my help in other ways. Just because you're sleeping in my spare bedroom doesn't mean I get to make any observations about why. Right?"

She looked away uncomfortably.

"Right," she agreed. "Are you cooking?" she asked, trying to change the subject.

"Not yet. Come meet my friend."

I showed her into the breakfast nook adjacent to the kitchen.

"Rusty, this is Janice. Janice, this is Rusty."

Rusty waved the tongs before flipping a piece of sausage to Gus. Janice, on the other hand, stared at him. Her eyes narrowed as she looked him over, up and down, with a peculiar intensity to her gaze. Then, as suddenly as it came on, her overabundance of interest disappeared.

"Pleased to meet you," she offered, moving to the counter and sitting down. I resumed my seat on the neighboring stool and worked on my cornflakes. Rusty and Janice chatted.

I didn't like the way she'd stared so suddenly and so hard at Rusty. It was blatantly weird. Under normal circumstances, I'd notice it was weird and ignore it as a peculiarity of her state of mind and the pressure she was under. Thing is, I also detected something strange in her aura while it happened. There was a pulse of energy I didn't expect and didn't instantly recognize.

Alden? Maybe. Could he be using people I know in order to get a spy into my house? Was he using Janice to get the layout of the place while making plans to break in? Was he taking inventory and looking for grimoires? What was he after?

I sat at the counter, almost rubbing elbows with her, and put my cornflakes on autopilot. I had something else on which to concentrate.

Janice chatted with Rusty, mostly about Gus. I examined Janice's thoughts. Swimming through the surface layers, she was interested in who Rusty was, why he was here, whether or not he was my boyfriend, and if he was going to offer her any of the food. All of these were, to one degree or another, expected.

Farther down, in the unconscious currents of her thoughts, there were the usual rocks. Preconceived notions, beliefs, personal truths—all the things people have as blockages to their thinking, installed by themselves, by society, by education. These are also things I expect to find because everyone has them. What I only half-expected to find were the suspicious-looking barriers implanted by someone else. Nevertheless, find them I did.

I'm familiar with Alden's handiwork. I recognize it when I see it. This wasn't it. What I found in Janice's mind was less artful. Where Alden could stitch and sew and do needlepoint on a mind, this was a fist wrapped around a bunch of cloth. It wasn't a *change* as much as it was a *grip*.

And it wasn't alone. The metaphorical fist was attached to a wrist, the wrist to an arm, and the arm vanished into the distance. This wasn't a permanent change to her thinking. It was control, active control, enforced by a power elsewhere. Yet, there was something else, too. All through the fabric of her mind, dark threads spread through the pattern. It was subtle, pervasive, and strongest near the grip.

I wasn't sure how much control this grip had. It wasn't a method of mental connection I'd ever seen before.

So, yes, a spy. Probably not Alden's spy, but a spy. Unless he was using a new technique, specifically designed to disguise his involvement...

I came back to my cornflakes, finished the last couple of bites, slurped milk—Pop always shook his head at me, but he never stopped me—and I put the bowl in the sink.

"I'll be upstairs," I told the three of them—I count Gus—and headed for the stairs. Gus perked up his ears, Rusty nodded, and Janice waved. In the computer room, I checked in with Zeno.

"How goes the paperwork for getting Janice into a dorm?"

"I have processed the request through the university web access, but I require a human interaction."

"Oh? What's the trouble?"

"There is a confirmation dialogue requiring human input."

"Show me."

Zeno popped up the offending page. I scanned through all the data fields, trying to find the problem.

"Where's the problem, Zeno?"

"Here." The page zoomed in on the captcha box.

"You need me to click the box for 'I am not a robot'?"

"Yes, Ma'am!"

I sighed deeply enough to stretch my lungs. Zeno owns the internet the way a kid owns his sidewalk chalk, but he wasn't told to hack into the university. He was told to expedite the paperwork. I had to remind myself once again how Zeno isn't an actual Turing-level AI. He's a collection of expert systems and a personality simulation.

"Zeno. Two things."

"Yes, Ma'am!"

"First," I clicked the box, "finish with her dorm assignment paperwork, please."

"Right away!"

"Second, if you run into any more 'human interaction required' cases, I authorize you to pretend you're a human and just check the damn box."

"Yes, Ma'am!"

"Good. Now, how goes the paperwork?"

"Wonderfully, Ma'am! She has digital documents to sign in her email!"

"Good. Carry on."

"Yes, *Ma'am!*"

I went have my shower and dress for the day. No run this morning; I had a sudden need to be a witch.

Around lunchtime I had to admit I was stumped. You'd think backtracking a psychic link stretching from someone's brain off into the distance would be easy as the first nine digits of pi. You'd think so. I thought so. We thought wrong.

My biggest headache was Janice. I didn't want to knock her out, drag her into a charmed circle, and use her as a focus point. I mean, sure, I could. And if she was out cold, I doubted strongly anyone using her as a remote camera would get anything from her. But it didn't seem fair to Janice. She was already being used. I didn't want to add my using her to get to whoever was already using her.

On the other hand, I might not have a choice. Tracking down a rogue psychic channel running into the house was giving me fits.

On yet a third hand, while I couldn't track it back to its origin, I could do something about the connection, itself.

The house has a number of defensive spells on it. For example, there's a fairly complex spell keeping the magical output of my electromagical transformers from being lost to the environment—kind of like insulation, in a way. Your oven turns electricity to heat, but keeps it in the oven where it can be used. There are other spells, as well, for other purposes.

How difficult would it be to put a hard psychic shield around the house? Not a shield. A *wall*. Forget subtle. Forget reading minds through the front door. Brick up the mental barriers and cut off all psychic contact between the inside and the outside.

Would it break the contact for Janice? Yes, I'm pretty sure it would. Would the connection grab her again when she left the building? I have no idea. I haven't put her in a charmed circle and analyzed it!

Sometimes I envy my Pop. He'd have glanced at it, figured out what it did and how to break it, traced it back to whoever was responsible, scried on their location, found the address, and done it all while his mouth was full of cornflakes. He might have used a little milk to doodle on the countertop.

I can do this. It will take me longer, but I can do it.

All right, I decided, if someone's going to use my friends as spies, I'm going to tell them they can't. I drew my conjuring circle, sat in lotus and meditated, held a charged crystal in either hand, gathered power from all around the building, and prepared my shielding spell. It formed as a sphere around me before expanding. It moved outward until it touched the house's outer wall and the magical containment barrier. As it continued to try to expand, it molded itself into shape like a balloon inflating inside a box. When it filled all the corners, I smoothed it into place, locked it into position, and tied it into the house's magical power systems.

Damn it. Another drain on the house transformers. I really do need to build more of those.

I relaxed for a minute, resting from the spiritual fatigue that comes with a big spell. I broke my conjurer's circle, put the big crystals into little holders to recharge, and went downstairs for lunch.

Rusty crouched next to Janice, holding her hand and lightly slapping her face. She lay on the floor, twitching, with her eyes rolled back in her head.

"What happened?" I asked.

"She sort of fainted. She was sitting by the counter with her sandwich and we were talking. She fell down and started doing this whole jerk and shiver thing."

"Well, that's not good. Hold on."

I took her other hand and closed my eyes.

Inside her head, there was a lot going on. Metaphorically speaking, the fist holding on to her thought processes had disappeared, but only in the sense an ice sculpture disappears in the heat. Whatever made it up was still there, but it had no form, no direction. It rolled around inside her like ink in a jar of water, spreading out and coloring everything. The dark lines in the fabric of her mind pulsed with this... liquid? The dark lines thickened as they absorbed what little remained of the original energies gripping her mind.

I tried to gather it together, hoping to somehow pull it out, but it was even more like ink than I realized. I could swish through it, as though scooping it, but it rippled and flowed around my imaginary hands. There was nothing to grab on to, nothing I could feel. It gravitated toward the dark threads, like spreading ink filmed in reverse.

The threads, strangely, weren't actually black. They reminded me of photographic negatives. Back in the old days, photography used film. The film would be developed and prints would be taken from them, reversing the light and color values. As the threads continued to work their way through Janice's mind, they took on counter-colors, if that's a word.

I opened my eyes and frowned. Well, the psychic wall worked, at least. Now I had to figure out what was wrong with her. That was a whole different order of problem.

"Help me get her up to my workroom."

"Yes, Ma'am."

Janice is currently tied down on the bed in her room. She's not really violent, but she's having some sort of reaction.

Rusty was amused when I admitted I didn't have anything specific for tying someone down. He had me pegged as someone who would own leather straps and a riding crop. He's not wrong, necessarily; if there's a riding crop involved, *I* will be the one holding it! But, more generally, that sort of thing doesn't appeal to me. We had to improvise with rope, a couple of belts, zip ties, and duct tape.

What's wrong with Janice? I put her in a charmed circle—seems as though she was destined for it—and took a good look. The problem goes a little deeper than a psychic grabbing a fistful of brain. There's something in her system, like a drug or maybe a disease, coursing through her whole body. From what I can tell, it was somehow being kept in check by the psychic hand controlling her mind. The stuff inside her acted like a kind of antenna (for the scientifically minded) or a correspondence point (for the thaumaturgically minded) so the psychic grip could be maintained over great distances.

When I put up the new shield around the house, it cut off the psychic channel. Now she's going through... well, whatever it is the stuff inside her does when nobody's trying to control it.

I'm watching her carefully. I don't like what I'm seeing. She's pale, her breathing is rapid and shallow, she's only semi-conscious, she has a low-grade fever, and she keeps reflexively struggling against the restraints.

Her struggles are getting stronger. I'd expect them to get weaker as time goes on.

While monitoring her condition I'm also trying to figure out how to reverse it. At the moment, all I can do is keep her fever down and put fluids in. Technically, I can feed her, too—she'll bite anything near enough.

Oscar called, looking for Janice. I told him she was out. No, I don't know where; she didn't say. I'm not her keeper, just the couch she crashes on while filing for a dorm room. No, I don't know if she's really going to a dorm or not. No, we haven't talked about it; it's her business, Oscar.

He wanted to come over and wait, hoping to talk to her. My first impulse was to say no, and say it firmly. The last thing Janice would want is her possibly-ex-boyfriend to be waiting on her, semi-stalking her. On the other hand, Janice wasn't exactly going to know, and Oscar would believe she wasn't here. What was he going to do? Demand to search the place?

And if he did, what then? Whatever was wrong with Janice might also be wrong with Oscar. If someone wanted to get Janice into the house, why not mind-grab both of them, have a "real" fight for everyone to see, and also have Oscar available to check up on Janice if something went wrong?

On the other hand, it could as easily be Janice, alone. Then the sequence is the mental monkey wrench makes her a bit cuckoo, she picks a fight with Oscar, and off she goes to take shelter at my house. This would leave me with a concerned and confused boyfriend who could make trouble.

How hard would it be to install a locking door at the top of the first-floor stairs? No, at the bottom. The way the walls are set up, the bottom would be better… Dang it, I'll need a door! No time to go get one. I'll have to settle for an illusion of wall. If there are no stairs to be found, you can't go up them, right?

Let's have Oscar over and see if he's got the same condition. If he's a plain-vanilla boyfriend, he's not going to find anything. If he is also controlled, at least he won't be reporting back to whoever controlled him.

Oscar walked into the vestibule and collapsed.

Well, that answers that.

Unlike Janice, however, he got up again, looked wildly about, screamed inarticulate noise, and started beating on the inner doors, trying to get in. He sounded as though he was trying to say something in the midst of gargling pudding and screaming.

I wasn't worried. The inner doors were security doors, the same as the outer doors. There's no point to having a secure little airlock for questionable guests if they can kick their way in.

One particularly good blow cracked the inner glass.

Okay, now I was worried. Not about the damage; the house spells would repair it in a day, at the most. The fact Oscar could damage it at all implied he was A: stronger than he had any right to be or, B: had a zombie-like lack of regard for his personal well-being.

Most zombies aren't actually any stronger than a living human. They don't have the safeties that keep living humans from damaging themselves through over-exertion.

Rusty and I moved to either side of the inner doors. Gus stood in front, but back several paces. He half-crouched and made a low, rumbling sound, reminding me of a steamroller about to turn someone unpleasant into a floor. I buzzed open the inner doors.

Oscar came through about two steps, looked wildly about, ignored Gus, snarled at me— maybe because Rusty's bigger than I am—and headed in my direction, hands stretched out. Since he was courteous enough to offer me a free shot at his hands, I took one and used it for leverage. He described an arc somewhat reminiscent of a piece of the Golden Spiral and wound up lying on a perfectly good piece of hardwood floor. Gus landed on his chest and threatened him with bloody dismemberment.

Gus is heavy, but most people become extremely floor-like for reasons having nothing to do with his weight. I think they get distracted trying to count how many teeth Gus has incredibly close to their face.

Not Oscar. Oscar didn't care. Hardwood floor, high speed impact, gigantic hound from Baskerville, dog drool—none of it bothered him in the slightest. He struggled almost instantly, trying to get into a position where he could fight. One arm came up, bashing into the side of Gus's head. It would have knocked any other dog to the ground, whimpering. Gus's head snapped aside and came right back into line. This time, there was a gleam in his eye which I recognized. I shouted for him to back off, and he did—barely. Gus caught one of Oscar's ankles instead of his throat and *crunched*. Gus also pulled, making life difficult for Oscar.

All through this, I never let go of Oscar's hand. As he started to writhe around, preparatory to rising, I planted a foot between his neck and shoulder, twisted his arm, and persuaded him to thrash around ineffectually. Not my first choice of response, you understand, but I had help. With Gus helping to keep Oscar stretched out, Rusty took Gus' original position by landing on Oscar's chest with both feet. This knocked the breath out of him and cracked a few ribs. With the blow delivered, Rusty performed a controlled collapse into a sitting position, straddling Oscar's abdomen, allowing him to start bouncing Oscar's head against the floor like a basketball he didn't particularly like.

Oscar took it like a champ for about eight bounces before he finally gave up consciousness. I was impressed. Rusty's not superhumanly strong, but he's pretty butch for his size.

"He seems upset," Rusty observed, still prepared to bounce Oscar's head again.

"Quite." I hadn't let go, either. "You want to get the duct tape?"

"You two got this?"

Gus grunted an affirmative. He hadn't let go, either. Between us, we had Oscar stretched like a man only partially affixed to the rack.

While Rusty went for the duct tape, I sat Oscar up and undid his belt. It was long enough to go around his hips and forearms. He could struggle out of it, but he wouldn't suddenly spring up. There would be thrashing around for a few seconds, giving warning.

Rusty returned and we wrapped him in duct tape from shoulders to fingertips. I held Oscar's feet up while Rusty continued to wrap him down to the knees. Then we added a couple of turns of rope. Then more duct tape. With him moderately secured, I carried him up to Janice's bedroom. The way she was tied down to it there wasn't room for him, but it was a big bed with a heavy frame. I laid him on the floor next to it and we tied him to it by ankles, waist, and neck.

I never thought I'd wish Pop taught me about bondage. Knots, yes. Every Scout knows knots. But how do you secure a prisoner? That's a different skill! Leisel and Velina helped a lot with my education—there are places in Tauta where those sorts of professionals are available, either for use or for instruction—but I didn't think I'd need to know this sort of thing for *practical* reasons!

"What do we do with them now?" Rusty asked.

"Good question. I'm still not clear on what's wrong with them." I scratched Gus behind the ears. He stayed next to me every second.

"Can you tell me why's Oscar so much stronger?" Rusty continued.

"I'm not sure he is. Human bodies can exert a lot more force than you think. People won't usually go all-out enough to damage themselves. He may be in panic-mode overdrive."

"Yeah, but Janice?"

"She may not be in the same stage of… whatever this is. And, at the moment, her leverage is *awful*. I mean, I'm not sure *I* could break free in her position. But, if you'll excuse me, I need two syringes, blood samples, and time in my workroom. Can you sit on the children and keep them from being too difficult?"

"Sure. Gus and I make great watchdogs."

"That's not—"

"Hey," he interrupted. "I can make those jokes. With you. Not with Jason."

"Oh."

"You might want to check the guy, though."

"Oscar."

"Yeah, the guy. I'm not sure his skull is still in one piece."

I ran a couple of spells over Oscar, checking his physical integrity. He had a mild cut on one hand, from the cracked glass, and his ankle wasn't going to work correctly for weeks. Five of his ribs were unhappy, too, but not actually broken. The biggest problem was all the fractures in his skull, mostly in the back. The floor was a lot harder than the heel of Rusty's hand. He wasn't leaking brain fluid or bleeding into his brain, but he was definitely shaken and not about to stir.

I was about to tell Rusty not to worry when something caught my attention. I examined the skull fractures even more closely.

They were healing. It was slow, almost too slow to see, but a minute hand moves slowly, too. As I conducted my initial examination, they healed only a tiny bit, but enough to notice. Once I started watching for it, I confirmed it.

"He's getting better," I observed.

"Good. I'd hate to think I killed him accidentally."

"No, no. He's *getting better*. The skull fractures are visibly pulling themselves together. If he lies there, he should have his head together—physically—by midnight. Morning, at the latest." I checked the ankle Gus chomped. The puncture wounds had stopped bleeding, both externally and internally. The bones weren't pulling themselves together like Pop's regeneration would, but I didn't think the ankle would require even a bandage.

"If he stirs," Rusty pointed out, "I don't know how to knock someone out without hitting them in the head. Is it okay to bang his noggin again?"

"Try strangling," I suggested, still musing on the ankle.

"Takes a while."

"You regenerate."

"Yes, but he's going to be unreasonable about it."

"You're tough."

"Dang," he sighed. "I was hoping you didn't notice."

"It was obvious. Now I'll try to figure out what's going on with these two. Shout if you need me. I'll leave the doors open so the soundproofing doesn't block it."

"I'm on it."

I headed for my witchroom with Gus at my heel. I went to one knee and explained to him what a good dog he was, and how I needed him to keep an eye on the two in the bedroom. Rusty would need his help. At least, that's how I phrased it. Gus, for his part, confessed—to me—he didn't think Rusty needed any help. I pointed out there were two of them and only one Rusty.

Gus is a damn smart dog. He agreed to help Rusty.

There were other things I wanted to do today, but, darn it, people started foaming at the mouth in my living room and I got distracted.

Most of my work on What The Hell Is Going On gave me only minor progress. Whatever *it* was, it was not only in their minds but spreading all through their bodies. By the time I got to look at it, it had spread all through the flesh and was growing rapidly stronger. I couldn't find a definite source of infection, such as a wound, so perhaps it was inhaled or ingested. The idea it might be airborne concerned me greatly, but it didn't seem to be leaving their bodies at all. I was relieved—sort of—when I recalled Oscar's rapid healing. If there was a wound where it originally got in, it was long-gone by now.

As for the way it spread through their minds, it drove them to downtown Nutsville on the Wackado Express. On the way to the corner of Deranged and Demented, it gave someone a handy-dandy place to get a grip on their thinking parts.

I did my best to analyze the stuff. I had two examples, blood samples, and a home laboratory. I'm a professional witch. I conducted a lot of tests, made lots of observations and tested a couple of hypotheses.

I was pretty sure the source of the problem had to be a vampire, although this particular power wasn't one I'd seen before. I tried to manipulate the dark stuff and it simply didn't notice me. It was a psychic phenomenon, yes, but a tuned one, specific to an individual. Magically, I could slow the process, but only by about half. I might have done better if I started sooner. Smaller infections are easier to treat. As it was, this train was going to the station and I wasn't able to stop it.

My guess was someone bit Oscar and Janice, infected them, used their infection as a way to control them, and sent them to reconnoiter. I'd never encountered this before—Pop didn't do this sort of thing—so I wasn't sure if there was anything I could do to *un*do what was done.

For reference, Janice moved from shivering wreck to the same sort of screaming assailant as Oscar a few hours later. By then, Oscar was also feeling better and attempted to break free. Gus sat on Janice to help hold her down. Rusty improvised with more zip ties and rope. By restricting their breathing—zip ties, tight around the neck—they kept passing out from exertion, recovering consciousness, struggling briefly, and passing out again. There's more to that werewolf than claws and fur.

My own studies and experiments didn't get me much else, although I did get a sort of confirmation on my vampire guess. The sun went down and the blood samples in my containment-and-analysis diagrams got frisky. It didn't get up and try to crawl around, no, but the cellular activity multiplied tenfold.

Gee, what sort of thing suddenly gets really active after nightfall? Let me think, let me think. What could it be? It seems as though I should recognize what this might be. Oh, if only I could remember where I've heard of anything like this!

Yeah, vampires flapped to mind, like bats coming home to the belfry.

During the course of my education, Pop and I looked at our own blood under a microscope and through magical filters. I know what Pop's species of vampire looks like. He's a Nightlord. They have chaos-based effects in their blood—although he did caution me his might not be typical. He's eaten a lot of things normal vampires may not have heard of, never mind eaten!

The local vampires are not based on void-energy chaos phenomena. The samples are, fundamentally, magical in their essence, presumably caused by a wizard attempting something stupid, impractical, or impossible. Some vampires are deliberately created by wizards seeking immortality. Others are the result of spells gone awry—thaumaturgic accidents, usually involving blood magic. I wasn't sure what caused this sort, but they weren't chaos creatures.

I heard a loud, crunchy snap, suspiciously like an oak timber in a bedframe being broken. Immediately thereafter, I heard Rusty shout for me, along with a loud, deep, familiar barking. I hurried to Janice's bedroom and helped them subdue the half-vampire maniacs as they tried to break free.

They get worse after nightfall. Important safety tip for dealing with vampire minions who have a vampire-based infection. I mean, I could have guessed, given a few minutes more, but it was nice of Janice and Oscar to demonstrate.

Gus, Rusty, and I had the advantages of total freedom and coordinated efforts. Janice and Oscar had the advantage of superior strength—something I would not have predicted. Gus chomped hard enough to break bones and jerked them unpredictably, but Rusty is the one who really made the difference. He slid about a quarter of the way along his human-wolf spectrum, growing larger, heavier, hairier—and considerably uglier. It gave him more mass and strength, as well as fingernails like claws, but it did nothing for his compunctions. They weren't *his* friends.

When I came through the doorway, Rusty had already broken Oscar's back with satisfactory levels of paralysis to show for it. No apparent shock, but Oscar wasn't, at this point, entirely human anymore. Janice had finished yanking one arm loose, breaking it in the process. Since her ankles wouldn't reach the bedknobs on the footboard, we didn't tie her ankles to them directly, but ran a length of rope from each knob to each ankle. These she snapped with ease, leaving her with one wrist bound to a bedpost and a determination to rip it free. Gus had her broken arm in his teeth and was struggling with her, keeping her from getting leverage on the remaining arm.

I landed on Janice to drive the air out of her and in the same movement punched her squarely across the face. I got a snarl in response.

Note to self: people in the throes of being turned into vampires do, at some stage, stop caring about how much it hurts. It also becomes a lot harder to punch their lights out.

While I wrestled Janice, I sent Gus to help Rusty. Oscar was loose, even if he could only crawl; Janice was still limited to the near proximity of one bedpost. Gus grabbed an ankle and yanked Oscar back while Rusty took careful aim.

Oscar and Janice were both struggling furiously, ignoring the plastic straps that were supposed to restrict their breathing. It was dark out, so I guessed they didn't need to breathe anymore.

With Gus and Oscar in a tug-of-war about whether or not Oscar would leave the room—Oscar had the edge, being able to dig fingernails into my floor for better purchase—Rusty had a clear shot. He jumped into the air and came down hard with one foot, right below the bulge of the back of Oscar's head.

Breaking Oscar's back partially paralyzed him. Breaking his neck slowed him down a lot more. Oscar kept snarling and trying to bite, but he couldn't operate anything below the level of his jaw.

Meanwhile, I mixed my Jiu-jitsu and Aikido in getting Janice turned over. I let her chew on the bedspread instead of me. I wanted to get her free arm in a hammerlock, but when the forearm is already broken, what's the point? I sat on the back of one thigh, caught the associated foot, and settled down into a toehold.

She didn't care. It may even have motivated her to go ahead and dislocate her shoulder and break her other arm as she pried her wrist away from the bedpost. Rope and duct tape snapped and tore.

Well, crap.

At least I had her face-down on a mattress. This didn't help her leverage, especially with two broken arms, but it also meant anything I wanted to do involved her being on a padded surface. It wasn't the best of choices, but it was better than nothing. I had to do something; she was fighting me no matter how hard I twisted her foot.

I recalled how I saw slow regeneration in Oscar's skull. Maybe it would help with a broken back. Assuming anything would help them, given their current state.

With this thought in mind, I let go with one hand, turned slightly, and drove my elbow down hard in the middle of Janice's back once, twice, three—there we go. The wet, crunching pop took sixty percent of the fight out of her. With two broken arms, she had plenty of fight, but zero functioning hands. I managed to sit on her shoulders while Rusty sat on Oscar's shoulders and told Gus what a good dog he was.

Victory. In more than one battle.

"Looks like strangulation isn't helping anymore," he told me. I cursed under my breath. With all their exertions, they should have passed out. I checked Janice's neck for a pulse and couldn't find one. She might have been thrashing around too much, so I did it the hard way, using a spell to examine her vital signs.

No heartbeat. Okay, that's a problem. They didn't yet have real claws and I didn't yet see fangs, but they weren't completely human, either. How long had this been going on? How long did it take to reach this stage? And how long would it be before...?

"Can you keep them from being troublesome?" I asked.

"Now that I know what to expect?"

"I'm sorry. I didn't realize this would happen."

"Assuming nothing else goes weird, sure. Gus and I can manage from here."

I went inside Janice's thoughts and came right back out.

"Nevermind," I told him.

Janice's thoughts weren't. There was a heaving mess of hunger and rage. Somewhere in there was an undercurrent of pain, but what I saw was bestial and deadly and in no sense human. The negative-colored threads were a webwork all through her, pulsing and writhing like a wrestling match under a blanket.

Janice wasn't in there anymore. What I had pinned to the mattress was a monster.

It's hard to kill people. That is, I find it difficult to murder someone out of hand. If they're trying to kill me, okay. I was taught from an early age to do unto anyone who is trying to do unto me, but do it faster, harder, and without hesitation. I can do that. On the other hand, simply ending someone's life because it seems like the easiest thing to do? I'm not comfortable with that.

Even now, looking at the thing I was holding down, I could see Janice on the outside. I *knew* the thing driving the body wasn't Janice. Janice was dead already. Whatever was in there wasn't her.

Still looked like her, though, which made what I had to do much more difficult.

Ask Rusty? I could. He wouldn't have the same qualms. But Janice is—was—my friend.

Friends don't let friends turn into mindless killer zombie vampire creatures. It's not *comme il faut*.

So, that was settled. I was killing her. It. Not her. *It.* And to do that, I couldn't go at it in any half-hearted way. Being borderline undead—maybe all the way undead, lacking both heartbeat and breathing—it wasn't going to be as simple as sticking a knife in her.

I thought about it, walked through all the necessary movements, considered exactly how I was going to do this, and envisioned it clearly. When I moved, I moved with purpose and with determination.

Janice's head came completely around and her neck snapped.

She bared her teeth at me and tried to hiss. Dammit. No level of neck-breaking was good enough. It would have to be full-on beheading.

I considered what tools I had in the house. Then I considered how messy this might be. Would they bleed? When Pop's in night-mode, he doesn't. But these were another species of vampire entirely, plus they weren't fully converted or transformed or whatever the word is. A lack of heartbeat implied they might leak or ooze, but they shouldn't spurt or spray.

Rusty helped me move the semi-undead to a guest bathroom. With broken necks, they didn't have much to say about it as he held them over the edge of the bathtub. While he kept them from slithering off, I went down to the kitchen for the cleaver.

Their necks were already broken. Hacking through the meat was no great trick at all. One head, then the other, fell with a thud into the tub. They didn't bleed, either, or not much.

Rusty stood up and sighed down at the meat.

"Shame about that. I kind of liked Janice."

"She was my friend," I replied. I was feeling a lot of things and they were all fighting for room.

"You okay?"

"No."

"First time you killed someone?"

"No. Well…"

"I asked a bad question. I meant like this."

"It feels like murder."

"But it isn't," he pointed out.

"I know. I know. But Janice…"

"…was your friend. Right. I remember the first time I killed someone I knew. It's different for different people," he assured me, shrugging. "I grew up in a household that took death very seriously, but always had it as an option for problem-solving. I look at it differently than you do."

"Apparently."

"Good thing, too," he added. "Do you want to help me dispose of the remains? Or would you rather be alone? Or do you need a drink? Or what?"

"I'm not sure."

"Take your time."

"Thanks, Rusty."

He offered his hand and I took it, stepping carefully out of the tub. The spell on the house would clean it up once we got the bodies out. Another spell on the house would eventually repair the bedframe Oscar broke, too. It would help if I at least rinsed the tub, though, and jammed the broken ends of the bedframe together...

I kept telling myself I didn't murder my friend. It didn't change my memory of the surprised look on her face as her head fell off her neck.

Journal Entry #17

I felt nothing but tired when I laid down in my own room. No, that's not right. I felt a lot of things, but they were all trying to get in front of each other and I couldn't get a clear look at any of them. At least I could ignore them while they sorted out which was going first.

I'm not sure sleeping was a great idea. Janice kept bothering me. Oscar hung around, too, but I barely knew Oscar. Janice would look at me over the back of her chair and carry on a conversation like it was perfectly normal. She always looked surprised during our conversations, no matter what we talked about. She also kept complaining about her neck and asking if I had a coffin she could sleep in.

When I woke up, I lay there, sweating and tense and breathing hard, staring at the ceiling for minutes. I often have vivid dreams, but seldom do I have nightmares. This one was particularly vivid and, to judge by the way my heart was banging on my sternum, terrifying.

Somewhere, there was a vampire—possibly two vampires—who did awful things to my friend and her significant other. Oh, sure, they were sent to spy on me. Yes, that's unpleasant and something worth considering. But the big thing is the way someone used my *friends*. Bit them, bloodied them, whatever it is they did to them to control them, and turned them into slavering, flesh-and-blood-thirsty monsters! And, by direct concatenation from these events, forced me to kill Janice!

Raining down consequences on Alden is tricky. It's a challenge. It isn't something I feel confident in doing, exactly, but something I believe I can eventually manage. Having a serious discussion with a lesser vampire about why you Don't Do That wasn't in the same league. Someone was going to get things broken as an expression of my ire. Bones, possibly. Financial empires, likely. Hearts, certainly.

I wanted names.

I rolled out of bed and shouted for Rusty. Wouldn't you know it, he wasn't in the house. All right, if I couldn't find a werewolf, I could certainly find someone with knowledge of vampire society. I still had the phone number for Alicia Marchbank.

A minute later, it was ringing.

"Hello?" answered a sleepy voice. I figured it must be difficult to be up most of the night and get phone calls early in the morning.

"Good morning. Alicia Marchbank?"

"Speaking."

"This is Phoebe Kent. Remember me?"

"Oh, Miss Kent!" she replied, perking up. "Yes, I do recall. Thank you for being so helpful—"

"Save it. Someone sent a couple of involuntary personal servants—you know the sort I mean—over to my house under false pretenses, trying to spy on me and possibly more. I take umbrage at this. I am annoyed by this. I want names and it's possible I want to start a collection of *teeth*."

Alicia was silent for several seconds. I waited while she caught up to the conversation. I felt a little bad about waking her up and hitting her with so much before coffee, but if she wasn't ready for nasty shocks, she shouldn't answer the phone.

"I see," she said, finally.

"I hope you do. I'd like to speak to someone about this, please, before I invest in a dental display case."

"From what I can gather, you have every right to be upset. I assure you, I had no idea such a thing was being planned. I'm reasonably certain I would be aware of it if it involved my branch of the family business. Can you tell me more about the situation?"

So I told her about Janice and Oscar. I didn't hold back, either. Zeno was monitoring the call, so I wasn't worried about someone tapping the conversation, but Alicia had no way of knowing. I was talking about vampires! And about them turning people into angry zombies, controlling them with magical powers, and sending them into my house! On not any old phone line, but *her* phone line. It put her in a highly disturbed frame of mind.

"I'm sorry, but I don't know who could help you," she equivocated.

"Don't give me that. You work for Dietrich. He is responsible, knowledgeable, or capable of finding out."

"I do wish you wouldn't say such things."

"All right. How does this sound? Let me talk to your supervisor."

Alicia was silent again for a moment. I thought I heard the click of fingernails on a touch screen.

"I can arrange it, but I'm afraid I'm the senior member of the team today. It will be several hours before anyone else becomes available. Would you like someone to return your call?"

"I think I'd rather have a meeting."

"Oh? That's... something I can arrange. I'll have a car pick you up this evening, if you like. Will eleven o'clock be satisfactory?"

I didn't like the idea of going to an undisclosed location to meet with a vampire—possibly a senior vampire. On the other hand, I was more than a little miffed. I figured there were ways to minimize the risk.

"I should expect the car at eleven, rather than expect to make it to the meeting by eleven?"

"Yes. The car will arrive then."

"I'll be ready."

"Very good. Is there anything further I can do for you?"

"No. Or, one more thing. You remember my Pop?"

"Your grandfather? Jerry Dandrige? Yes, I do remember him."

"If he asks you to dinner, would you be willing to go?"

"I would be delighted," she agreed, and I could hear the smile in her voice. "Is he likely to?"

"I don't know. It depends on his schedule and whether or not I survive the appointment. No doubt he'll be in touch, either way, so you'd better be ready."

"Ah. I see."

"I'm not entirely sure you do, but I hope you don't have to."

I hung up and went back to my workroom. I had things to do to prepare for an evening out.

What does one wear to such an appointment? Besides fashionable body armor and a gun?

I got myself together, picking out what I'd want, and an entirely different question wandered into my head and asked for attention.

What did Rusty do with the bodies?

I spent a few hours reviewing the information Zeno compiled on criminal activities in his highly-illegal research. Zeno goes through this world's computer security in much the same way hypodermic needles go through rubber gloves. He was in the process of amassing an immense amount of evidence, from video recordings to dossiers. I switched all the mirrors to target fresh sources for him and let him continue with it.

There has got to be a way to let him pick a target and change the target lock. That's much simpler than trying to tie things into the Alden-detector. Sadly, now was not the time to figure it out.

I considered the whole structure of organized and interlocking crime, such as we had defined it. When I started my superhero adventures, I was knocking over drug dens. Why? Because it was fun? Because it was profitable? Because it was a good real-world testing ground for the super-suit? Because bad guys deserved to be done unto instead of doing? Yes, to all of it.

Now, though, the idea I could Make A Difference by kicking over individual, retail dealers seemed ludicrous. Handing over a detailed account of world-wide criminal activity to the authorities seemed a much more telling and brutal blow to organized crime. True, I was violating a lot of civil rights, but as an anonymous source of information, can't the police use it? It's not like *they* violated the law. I'm making an anonymous report of what I saw, or something like that.

Could I still make a difference through personal effort, though? I thought there might be a way.

One of the major issues for criminal businesses is the money. True, there are a lot of ways to legally move money to pay for illegal goods and services. Simply lying about what the money is for is the simplest. I buy a dozen women for my brothel and pay by money transfer, but the supplier and I agree to list something else for the receipt. Caviar and champagne? If someone investigates and wants to know where all the product went, point to a toilet.

On the retail side of things, there's cash. You don't buy a dime bag with a credit card. All this cash has to flow upward through the organization, concentrating as it goes. Eventually, someone has to take a truckload somewhere and turn it into digital money. You don't buy a yacht by plunking down a briefcase full of small-denomination bills. You can, yes, but it causes comment.

Kaswell's yacht was on the bottom of the East River. The fire got to the diesel fuel. There might have been a bit of a leak beforehand. Maybe the word I want is "rupture."

The point is, he was taking the money to Europe so Esterhauser could work his financial magic on it. How he dealt with the cash was anybody's guess, but I didn't much care. When Kaswell delivered money, it went in Esterhauser's vault, was washed, rinsed, dried, pressed, starched, counted, and bundled.

Money is still made of paper. It would be simplicity itself to put a couple of oxygen tanks—with the valves open—inside the vault, along with a few gallons of something volatile. Something similar happened on Kaswell's yacht. Why change a winning strategy?

Assume this happens. What effect does it have on the money?

Drat. The vault's fire-suppression systems would go off. Nevermind.

All right, it wouldn't be as easy, but it would still be pretty direct to look inside the vault, estimate a rectangular space, and switch that space with an empty spot in my basement. If a couple million dollars in cash simply disappears without a trace, it really hurts the business. No doubt Esterhauser's clients would be moderately discomfited, which would make Esterhauser extremely so.

A true blow for all things right and good? Maybe. I'd have to do it several times, preferably in close succession, before I'd make global criminal enterprises feel truly hurt. It was something to consider—and to plan for—when the authorities started using the information we were gathering. It's important to be able to pay your lawyers, and if your digital assets are frozen by court order, you depend on your cash reserves.

If we locate and target major private vaults, safety deposit boxes, and the like, we can charge up a whole array of crystals, have shift-boxes prepared, and steal everything at once. Boom! You're out of cash the same day the cops knock on your door.

On second thought, preparing so many shift-boxes sounds like a lot of work. Don't safety-deposit boxes have standard sizes? What if I make one for each size and work up a target list? Or, maybe… what's the largest box size? If I use one corner of it as a zero point, can I draw lines on the inside to define different spatial dimensions, then have the spell pick the optimum size? I might need only one box, one shifter spell, and one additional spell to sort by target size!

It'll require some R&D. Of course.

Wait. How many targets will I have to hit? A hundred? No problem. A thousand? It'll take time and effort. Ten thousand? A hundred thousand?

Maybe I need multiple boxes after all. And more crystals. And I definitely still need another electromagical transformer!

Timing. Everything requires timing. Zeno is working on the targeting, but I'm probably going to have to do a lot of things myself before we can pull this off.

Speaking of timing, I was preparing my lunch when Rusty put in an appearance. He rang the doorbell rather than strip down, go wolf, and use the doggie door. I told Zeno to unlock the door while I checked my weapons. When the door opened, it really was him. He came into the kitchen area and grinned at me.

"You look like you just caught your tail," I observed.

"Dog joke?"

"Meant with affection."

"Yep, I'm pretty pleased," he agreed, sliding onto a stool at the kitchen's counter. "What's for lunch?"

"I was grilling a steakburger, but I suppose I can throw on a couple more. What're you so pleased about?"

"No vegetables on mine," he suggested. "Oh, a little of this, a little of that. Two bodies went into the city's organic waste recycling plant late last night."

"I'm not familiar with it."

"Big grinder-shredder thing starts it all off before the shredded bits go through this computer-driven, bacteria-enhanced composting plant. Very eco-friendly and a loud talking point in city politics. All I care about is the grinder-shredder thing. Good for getting rid of evidence, if you need to. And if you know how to get to it without a lot of people knowing."

"No doubt. It's probably popular with a lot of different groups."

"Yep. Which is why there's so much security around it. Can you imagine a crime family having unrestricted access to the thing?"

"Easily. How do you get to it?"

"I have relatives who work there. It's a cottage industry for my extended family, sort of."

"Ah. That would do it."

"I also," he added, sounding exceptionally smug, "may have a unique opportunity for you."

"Oh?"

"Not *unique*, exactly," he hedged, "but rare."

"Oh, well, if it's not unique, then never mind." Rusty blew a raspberry at me and I chuckled. "All right, what's this not-unique-but-rare thing you've got?"

"My father wants to meet you."

"I thought it was a bad idea? You did say it was a bad idea."

"No, I said attending a drum circle was a bad idea. It's a werewolf party and things can get a bit lively, which means a bit bloody. Dad wants to meet you because you killed a fledgling vampire. With your bare hands, no less."

"And how did he find out?"

"I couldn't take credit for both of them," Rusty replied, looking shocked. "That would be wrong."

"Oh, of course. Naturally. I don't know what I was thinking."

"Dad wants to meet the mighty warrior who slew a fledgling with her bare hands."

"Why? I mean, surely he doesn't want to meet every slayer of vampires in the world?"

"No, but you and I hang out together. You're in the know, so to speak. Mom thinks you're a loony New Age crystal-vibration witch, but Dad is prepared to give you the benefit of the doubt. Killing a vampire, even one in the early stages of transformation, is no little thing."

I forced myself to relax my mouth. It drew into a tight, hard line at the comment about my witchery. I like to think I'm not too sensitive when it comes to people dishing out insults. I believe I have a certain amount of self-confidence and personal assurance. But sometimes I can be a bit... I don't know. A bit of a bitch, maybe? Push my buttons and I may push back.

"I see. And when does your father want to meet me?"

"At your convenience, of course. It's not like he's demanding it. He... uh... he extends his invitation to you."

"Hmm. Will your mother be there?"

"I dunno," he shrugged. "Could go either way. I'd suggest waiting until four days from now, though."

"Why? Oh, right. Full moon coming up."

"Yep."

The comment about the loony New Age witch still stung, so I'm blaming it for the sudden decision to impress his mother.

"Tell me something. When you have to change, does it only happen on the actual night of the full, or is it all day, or what?'

"When the moon is down, I can go back to human form. When it's visible and the sun is out, I can resist it, but the wolf is always close to the surface. Usually, it's two nights, but sometimes it's three, depending on the almanac or whatever. It's reversed for the human times. It's hard to turn into a wolf, even at night, during the dark of the moon, but during the day I simply can't."

"Okay. Got anything to do today?"

"Huh? Not especially. Why?"

"I need a favor. Just a few things from around town."

"Sure. What do you need?"

"Blood from a wolf, blood from a human, a wolf pelt, and a swatch of human skin. I'll fetch the difficult stuff."

Rusty looked at me with a peculiar expression.

"I have questions, but I'm choosing not to ask them."

"Think of it as a grocery run."

"Sometimes I wonder about your grocery shopping."

Journal Entry #18

I know I'm no Morgana le Fay, but I'm a damn competent witch! The idea someone might regard me as *in*competent really stings. I know I shouldn't let it bother me, but it does! The grown-up, mature thing to do would be to let it go. Let Rusty's mother have her silly opinion. Eventually, she would learn enough to change it, or we would move in such different circles it wouldn't matter.

Or I could accelerate her education. That is, I could show off.

I'm not as grown-up as I thought. It's a process, right?

So, if I'm going to demonstrate how I'm in the same league as Glinda—or maybe Baba Yaga—how do I do it? The idea had to be something werewolf-related, and my brain supplied a good one.

My rock collection isn't the largest rock collection, but it does have a few unique specimens. There are Martian rocks, Lunar rocks, one from Mercury, a few from around the world, and a couple of teeny-tiny asteroids.

The asteroids are chunks of space debris, pulled through a gate from the asteroid belt, but I put in a lot of work to figure out how to get them. You can't just open up a gate from Earth to the asteroid belt. Oh, technically you can, but it doesn't do you any good. You have to find the rock you want, first. It's not like in the movies. It's usually hundreds of miles to the next space-rock, not narrow gaps you can barely fit your space-fighter through. There's almost nothing there, even in the thick of the belt. You can't open a hole to the general area and expect to find an asteroid.

Even after you pick your floating space rock, there are other problems. If you open a gate on Earth, the first thing to happen is air rushes through into the vacuum. Since your gate is pointing at the rock you want, it gets blown into the distance, away from your gate, and you've wasted your effort.

The proper technique is to build a glove box. This is the funny-looking thing on old sci-fi shows where there's a box with gloves sticking through one side. You put the dangerous thing inside the box, seal it, and you do stuff with it by putting your hands in the gloves. In this case, we pump out all the air from the box so it's a vacuum, like in space. The gate is inside the box, so when we open it, nothing happens. You reach through and grab your space rock.

When I was younger, Pop did the gate work. He made *me* figure out the rest of the process, but he warned me to use tongs. I wasn't worried; we had jumbo-sized tongs in the tool rack. Pop thought ahead. He knew we would need them, so we had them. He didn't want me hurting my hands on super-cold rocks.

What I wanted today was somewhat closer to home, but I had to do the scry-targeting and gate workings myself. Blasting air through the gate wouldn't be disastrous, but it would make things much more difficult.

I cheated by going to Iowa, giving glove-box plans to a welder, coming home, ticking Iowa along faster, then going back to pick it up. I bolted it together in the condo in the Madison building—I didn't want it cluttering up my home workroom—and did my fetching there.

I didn't want an asteroid. I wanted dust. Dust from the Moon. The local moon, not a moon rock I picked up in another universe. I scooped dust up in eight places, around the lunar equator, just to make sure I had enough to confuse things.

Confuse things? Yes. These dusty places were certain to have different levels of sunlight. I would have gone for a dozen, but I had a power budget issue. Spatial gates aren't as expensive as universe gates, but they had to be big enough to reach through and I had to hold each one open long enough to get a scoop of dust.

Back at home, Rusty brought me blood—in recycled bottles for eyedrops—and swatches of skins. I deliberately failed to ask him where he got it all, but it was fresh. When he tries, he's a great assistant.

He's also a good sport. He held still for the experimentation with magical spells and lunar soil. I discovered it was possible to provoke a transformation using one sample, or to prevent one using another. One could act like a full moon and keep him in wolf form. Another could act like a new moon and keep him in human form.

He didn't like it, so I explained.

"Look," I began, "since rings, belts, and so on are kind of impractical, if you had a chain collar you could wear in human form—like a necklace?"

"Yeah?"

"You could then wear your personal camouflage—the tags—in human form, along with the decorative thingy I'm making."

"What decorative thingy?"

"I'm not sure what it will look like, yet, but I hope to have it override your dependence on lunar phases. Think of it as carrying around a much smaller moon. One you can set for one-quarter and leave there forever, so you don't have an obligatory form twice a month."

Rusty let out a low whistle.

"That would be... I dunno. It would be something."

"I'm not sure it'll work, yet. I'm pretty sure, but not totally sure. We'll have to test it Saturday night, once you change."

"What's the wolf fur and the human skin for? And the blood?"

"Messy bits."

"Huh?"

"There's a lot of symbolism involved. Wolf blood and human blood, each calling to those aspects of you, will help balance out your moon-swings. Ditto for the skins. Your wolf-skin and your human-skin will—when I'm done, and I hope—also keep trying to balance you in the middle. Then you can *pick* which way you go, rather than pointing whichever way the moonlight says."

"I *like* it!"

"If it works. I think it will. If it doesn't work perfectly, I'm guessing it will at least lessen the pull. Maybe you can still go human under a full moon, even if it takes a lot of effort. Something like that."

"Okay. Saturday, you say?"

"Yep."

"Do you need me until then?"

"Immediately, yes, but once I get the setup started, I should be okay. However, I would like your help with something else."

"Sure."

"I have an appointment with a vampire this evening. I don't think it'll be too awful—they should know they owe me for putting the finger on Alden—but they also have a burning curiosity about me. I think they want to know things while I want them to tell me things. I'm not sure how it'll turn out."

"Consider it done." Rusty paused and added, "Is Jason going to be around?"

"Yes. A car is coming to pick me up. I don't know where the meeting will be."

"Oh." Rusty looked thoughtful for a moment, planning how to chase a car, probably. "Yeah, I guess we need him."

"Let me finish this thing. Any idea when moonrise will be?"

"Six fifty-two PM."

"How do you know—? Oh. Of course. Nevermind. I'm hoping to get the amulet basics sorted out in the next couple of hours. You can stick around?"

"No problem."

"Great. Let me get a few pounds of plastic explosive and we'll get started."

"Have I mentioned your shopping trends disturb me?"

Journal Entry #19

The car pulled up right on schedule. I walked calmly and confidently out the front door. I chose to wear a semi-formal outfit, much like Alicia's, minus the flared lower leg. This provided me with good range of motion, ample places to conceal small objects, layers of protective materials, and very fashionable-looking designer boots. Boots, I might add, with low heels, suitable for sprinting.

I *detest* all those movies where the "heroine" apparently can't run ten steps without falling on her face. Sometimes I do wear high heels, but you can bet I know how to run in them! It might also be wise to assume they're the equivalent of spiked knuckles for my feet.

I didn't say it would be "safe" to assume. I said, "wise."

Thinking back on it, Pop looked pretty silly wearing heels, but, as with anything he wanted me to learn, he was going to learn it himself in order to teach me! He may be the only male vampire who can kick a high heel accurately up someone's nose. He may never need to use that skill, but if he ever does, I want to see the looks on the faces of everyone in eyeshot.

The car was a four-door sedan stretched to a six-door size. The driver got out, opened a rear door for me, and handed me in. I settled in the passenger cabin, put my handbag on my lap, and smiled at the gentleman across from me. Dietrich was seated on the passenger side, facing the rear. I was seated on the driver's side, facing forward. He had his fingers interlaced on the silver head of his cane.

"Good evening."

"And a good evening to you," I agreed. The driver pulled us gently away from the curb. "Where are we going?"

"Nowhere. Just for a drive. We'll have you back at your house at the end of it."

"Ah. Preventing eavesdropping?"

"Indeed. It pays to be cautious."

"And yet, you haven't bothered to confiscate anything from me. You haven't even waved anything over me to detect transmitters." I kept my mouth shut about Rusty following us in an autocab. Technically, Zeno was following us with the autocab and Rusty was along for the ride. Jason was doing his usual roof-level bouncing.

"Quite so. Partly because the car is shielded. You'll find your phone gets no signal. Partly because you would not benefit from revealing anything to the world at large. Mostly because I have no problem with the world finding incontrovertible proof of vampire existence."

"That's…" I hunted for a word. "…surprising."

"Oh, yes. It would be a somewhat surprising attitude to most of my colleagues, as well. There is, however, a rather large difference between actively seeking to reveal our presence and being prepared for the inevitability." Dietrich smiled, showing fangs. "I assure you, I have lived quite a long time and intend to continue doing so."

"I can understand that. And, for my part, I have no present objection to your continued survival. Nor to your present mode of existence, as far as being a vampire goes."

"Oh? Because you, yourself, operate below the level of societal awareness?"

"No, because I was raised by a vampire. I understand the ecology of the blood-drinking undead. I do wish you went to more effort finding people who *deserve* to be food, rather than taking whatever you can reach."

Dietrich's face gave nothing away, but he didn't answer immediately.

"I see," he finally said. "You do raise a good point about proper livestock management, but I lack the authority, at present, to impose more stringent measures. As for you being raised by a vampire, well, it's certainly an interesting claim."

"If true," I added. "That's what you were thinking."

"You can read my thoughts?"

"Nope. But you *were* thinking it," I added. He chuckled.

"Touché."

I smiled at him while he smiled at me. He wanted me to elaborate. I refused by simply keeping quiet. He nodded, very slightly, acknowledging it.

"Very well. To business?"

"Certainly. Shall I go first?"

"If you wish," he agreed.

"I don't have the patience for a lot of dancing around, so I'll come straight to the point. Adam Alden is a problem. He's a powerful psychic and working his way into a position of power over humanity. His control extends to an army of homeless in the subways, to political figures, and to people who can influence the financial markets. By this point, he may even be in a position to sway the military, with or without civilians, politicians, giving his orders. With me so far?"

"While the information you provided to Alicia has not all been verified, quite a lot of it has shed illumination on things of recent concern," he admitted. "I am prepared—provisionally—to accept your statement as truth."

"Subject to confirmation. I understand. Thank you. My point is, there's not much I can personally do to Alden. He's too powerful for me, alone, at the moment. I have a plan, but while I'm working on it he's worming his way into greater and greater power. I suggest this is a bad thing for you, as well. The longer he goes unchecked, the more dangerous he becomes—to you and your kind, and to me. Not so?"

Dietrich tapped one finger on the back of the other hand, thinking. I wondered what the tapping signified. Was it a sign of something, a tell? If so, of what? Intense thought? Worry? Discomfort? Or was it a bit of theater, signifying nothing?

"There are others who have made similar observations regarding humanity in general," he said, finally. "They argue the humans have advanced technologically to a point where they are more dangerous as prey than we are as predators. There is no consensus on this, but the arguments are there.

"The question I pose to you, Miss Kent, is this: Is Alden a human being?"

It was my turn to consider. Did Alden qualify? He possessed an uncanny level of affinity for celestial forces, as well as immense psychic ability. But he used tektites—some tektites—as amplifiers for at least some of his powers. Take those away and what do you have left? A powerful psychic priest? The tektites seemed to be useful to him not only as psychic resonators, but also as foci for celestial forces, somehow...

Interesting question. If I became a priestess of Uncle Dusty, could he and I duplicate the feats Alden already demonstrated? Possibly. Maybe I should get out my untreated tektite and do more work with it. Later.

"I believe he's human," I decided. "Not a normal human, obviously, but the same might be said of magic-workers and psychics. He can achieve what appear to be superhuman feats, though, and I'm not certain what the mechanism is. For example, he may be able to push his body to feats of strength a normal human can't, simply because he can ignore the self-preservation functions and damage himself through overexertion whenever he wants. Likewise, he may be able to concentrate on an injury and force his body to heal it quickly through psychic bio-control.

"Regardless," I went on, "he does seem to be a priest, and one of remarkable power."

"Yes. I was afraid of that. Very well, you tell me Alden is gathering power to himself in the form of political, financial, and military influence. He, personally, has access to religious and psychic powers."

"And magical powers," I added. "I know for a fact he's been hunting down magical devices and, as I understand it, using his psychic powers on magic-using humans to rip knowledge from them. He's not primarily a wizard, but he's not entirely ignorant of magical operations."

"Wonderful."

I had to respect Dietrich's self-control. There was only a trace of sarcasm. I'd have dumped enough in that one word to burst the doors off the back of the limo.

"Subject to further confirmation," he continued, "I am prepared to accept that Alden is a threat to our quality of life. Mine *and* yours. Everyone's. Something must be done about him. You say you have a plan for dealing with him?"

"I do, but it'll take time—time I do not believe we can afford—to flesh it out and develop. As a result, he's liable to complete his plans for… what's the word?"

"I believe the phrase you are looking for is 'world domination'," he suggested.

"Yes. Dominating the world in the iron grip of a psychic tyrant. Where you or I might gain control—or strong influence, let us say—over a small portion of human endeavors, we wouldn't try for global dominance. The attempt alone would draw too much attention and therefore too much opposition. Whoever runs the world holds too much power for their secret to be kept, even if they try to keep it a secret."

"I don't know if I entirely agree," Dietrich said, mildly.

"I mean *controlling* the world. Alden has the potential to mentally dominate every human being on the planet and control them as his personal meat puppets. Running things from behind the scenes, steering things, is a very different thing."

"Ah. Yes. Indeed it is. What do you suggest?"

"He believes he is, essentially, unopposed. Normal humans can't resist his power, so he has no reason to fear them. He needs to be more afraid to extend his reach—afraid of reaction, afraid of backlash, afraid of consequences."

"You're saying his activities need to be curbed. He needs to realize there are other powers in the world who will not sit idly by."

"Exactly. A new balance needs to be achieved. You have some influence on human society. So do I, although to a much more limited extent. Most of mine is in the form of being wealthy; I *buy* what I want. That's all the control I care about. I don't want to rule the world or even own it!

"Other creatures, other methods. Vampires have their needs and enough control over the larger society to feel reasonably secure about meeting those needs. Werewolves, witches, wizards, mummies, elementals, merfolk, the lot—each has their own way of coping.

"But nobody has, as you put it, dominance. Alden wants that dominance. He needs to run face-first into a mountain of consequences. It'll make him walk instead of run. If he hits it hard enough to bloody his nose, he might view it as a border and stop going that direction."

"If there is no resistance to his activities," Dietrich mused, "he will continue until he completes them. Of course, there is also the risk the mortals will discover what he is doing—not 'how,' but 'what'—and react in some fashion. It will act as a sort of limit to his expansion. A consequence, if you wish to call it that."

"Enough of a limit?" I asked. "One he will view as too dangerous to risk? Or will he think of the 'mere humans' as something he can control? And how do we prepare for either course? What happens if the news media breaks the story?"

"Alden will not permit witnesses. This is an established fact."

I didn't ask him how he knew. I had my suspicions.

"However," he went on, "wild theories can spread faster than a plague. Rumor travels around the world while a denial is still lacing up its boots. If enough humans take in enough rumors and conspiracy theories, they may react in a panic fashion. This is likely to have far-reaching ramifications. He has taken steps to prevent this."

"He's still running a risk."

"But an unofficial risk," Dietrich reminded me. "Rumor and gossip are not news—or should not be." He shook his head, sadly. "So many times have I observed innuendo and lack of information presented as evidence within the press."

"I blame social media."

"I blame the printing press."

Ouch. I had to remind myself I was dealing with someone a lot older than he looked.

"Answer me this, if you can. What would happen if mortals were to discover psychic powers do exist?" I asked. "I mean, if it were made generally known."

"It would lead them to question other things," Dietrich replied, frowning. "They would have a renewed interest in all manner of occult subjects. Does magic exist? Do legendary creatures? These are questions about which we wish them to be complacent. It would be a poor move on our part to lead them to regard such questions as anything but thoroughly settled. Moreso," he went on, "because psychic abilities may not be immediately dangerous."

"How do you mean?"

"Psychic abilities have at least a little pre-established validity within mortals' science-based structure. If it were advertised as a fact the humans are evolving to develop telepathy, for example, it would not be overwhelmingly surprising. The fact magic exists and people can learn spells? This would provoke a much greater change for human society." He smiled, showing fangs again. "It is a scientific age, young lady, where mortals are slow to believe in things they cannot prove—or are reactionary to things contradicting what they take on faith."

"A carefully-engineered state of affairs?"

"I would like to believe so, but I suspect it is more good fortune and opportunistic action than planning. But I say any such revelation would be a poor move. Science is a technological thing in the minds of most. You use a machine to do what you, personally, cannot. To reveal psychic energies as a fact would restart serious investigation into such powers, as well as prompt a 'fringe' reaction in other occult subjects. This would, in the long run, begin a series of events requiring extensive effort to suppress. Even in the best of cases, it would provide humanity with additional resources for information-gathering without a corresponding advantage on our part. No," he finished, "I do not think it wise to encourage humans to think more than they do."

"No offense intended."

"Indeed not."

"I guess we aren't going to out Alden as a mind-controlling priest, then."

"I should think not."

"Come to think of it, the situation would be further complicated, in the short term, by the backlash Alden would cause. If we out him as a psychic, would it force him to move faster or force him to retreat and retrench?"

"If he feels he can succeed in his aims," Dietrich began, and stopped. He pursed his lips and cocked his head, slightly. "It does raise the question of the extent of his influence at the present time. Is he too powerful to contain? Should we even try? Or should we strike quickly, remove the head from the serpent, and wait until the thrashing of the body settles down?"

"I admit I don't know," I told him. "I'm not a political analyst. I can track him down and get a good idea of who he's talked to—talked to in his oh-so-persuasive way—but I don't know the people, much less the details of what he's done to them, and I have no idea what the effects of removing Alden would be. They will continue to do what they are doing, but it's possible the trigger conditions for a particular course of action may never come. Or their attitudes and objectives won't change and they'll still support whatever agenda Alden told them to. And so on."

"I understand. It is a puzzle. Still, it may be best to eliminate him quickly and hope we have done so before a critical threshold has been reached."

"I'll leave it to you. I'm still working on a way to trap him and imprison him."

"Oh?"

"I don't like killing anyone who isn't actively trying to kill me. I'd rather imprison him to convince him he's not an unstoppable force. He needs to learn he can't do anything he pleases without provoking people of equal or greater power. Maybe I can establish with him the idea of being a supervillain is going to beget superheroes. Persuade him that his personal world domination is something nobody will stand for. Maybe he should shoot for being an idle billionaire, instead. Or a charity organizer. Or something."

"I feel certain killing him would be relatively simple."

"Probably, but it's a personal choice. If nothing else, being imprisoned means he's available for questioning. There are several very pointed questions I'd like to have answered before giving him a haircut down to his shoulders. What are his minions programmed or instructed to do? Who are they? What are his immediate, intermediate, and long-range goals? He might not want to answer, but between us, I'm sure we can work out a way to ask nicely."

"A worthy viewpoint," Dietrich agreed, "even if I find it somewhat naïve."

"Yeah, you and my Pop."

"I hope you have the chance to try it."

"Me, too. Which brings me to a couple of other points."

"I am all attention, dear lady."

"First off, I believe Alden is our common enemy. Or our common problem, at the very least."

"For the sake of this discussion, granted."

"This may not make us friends, but it makes us allies of a sort. Yes?"

"I can agree with that. I might even persuade others to this point of view."

"And, with this thought in mind, would it be unreasonable to say you can simply call me when you want to talk to me?"

"I have no problem with that."

"Excellent! Likewise, I hope I can be permitted to speak to you directly when I have something important to say?"

"Ready communication strikes me as eminently sensible."

"Good. So, who was it who decided to do unpleasant vampire things to my friend and her boyfriend in order to spy on me in my own home?"

Dietrich's expression never flickered. I had to admit, being dead had its perks. Without involuntary responses, like a blush reflex or adrenaline production, or even a heartbeat to suddenly go from *thump-thump* to *THUD-THUD,* I would hate to play poker with this guy. He answered smoothly.

"Allow me to assure you this will not be repeated."

I sat back, setting more comfortably in the seat. I watched his eyes for several seconds, waiting for him to add anything. He met my gaze, didn't try anything, and kept silent.

"Did I provide you with valuable information on Alden?" I asked.

"Yes, you did. For your own benefit."

"I might argue it was for the benefit of the world. Which, I should add, includes you."

"If you wish."

"Had I told you I possessed such information instead of providing it, would you have attempted to obtain it?"

"Probably."

"Then, by giving it to you, I think I would not be entirely incorrect in feeling you were indebted to me in a minor way."

"The information is useful in the sense it accelerates our own investigations. No doubt, whatever we choose to do will be the same as if you had not. Yet, I am willing to concede you have materially moved up our timeline and, potentially, assisted us in reaching a decision before Alden can achieve his ends. Is this what you mean?"

"Close enough. So, with this thought in mind—and bearing in mind we have this mutual interest—an interest where my support and assistance might be of further value— how unreasonable is it to ask who was involved in murdering my friends?"

"Were they murdered?" Dietrich inquired. "Strange. I don't believe they were treated in a such a manner. How, exactly, did they die?"

"They went berserk and had to be put down."

"Tsk-tsk-tsk. Such a shame. There are different procedures for turning a human into a vampire. One of these can cause a bloodthirsty rage in the early stages. If they are killed during this period, they rise again as a feral vampire. Eventually, they can recover, at least somewhat, from the mental distress. You may wish to observe their bodies to see if they reached a point where they can rise."

"What if their bodies are finely chopped?"

"Ah. No, I'm afraid that is a bit much," he admitted. "Typically, being shot or stabbed is typical for the modern era. Beheading is much less common than it used to be."

"Can a feral vampire survive it?"

"No, naturally not."

"Would you care to elaborate on the vampire creation process?"

"If you ever need to know, I will be certain to tell you."

"All right. But your point about the death of my friends?"

"The vampire responsible, I believe, did so only to make his or her mental grip on them strong enough to remain in effect even during the day-sleep. This is, I might add, a violation of our rules. One cannot go around creating—potentially—blood-crazed berserkers who rise from the dead. There is a process one goes through. Not merely a biological or transformational process, but a social one. There are interviews, tests, apprenticeships, and so on. Grooming a new vampire of the *archontiá* can take years. Decades, even."

"Like Alicia?"

"Indeed, yes. She is a prime candidate and would have been one of us by now if she could find an adequate replacement for her present duties. But your vampire—the one who offended you—is not responsible for the death of your friends. Whoever killed them is the one you want."

"I choose to view the biting as the instigating event," I told him, levelly.

"I can see your point, but I cannot agree. However," he added, as I opened my mouth to reply, "I can also assure you the individual responsible has violated *our* laws and customs. Seriously violated them, I should add. While this one does not face penalties for the death of your friends—in our society, killing a human, in and of itself, can hardly be considered a crime—this one does face a rather harsh punishment for the actions we *do* regard as crimes."

I thought about it. What did I want? Revenge or justice? Revenge is usually more personal. For example, I get to kick someone in the face. Justice is still punishment, but someone else does the kicking. One makes me feel better. The other addresses an imbalance in the karmic potential of the universe.

Which isn't to say you can't do both. But which was more important?

"What sort of punishment?" I asked.

"The usual penalty is a bit of alone time."

"That's it? Isolation? Solitary confinement?"

"Buried in a box," Dietrich added, "about six feet deep."

"For how long?"

"A year, perhaps."

"A year, locked in a box? That's it?"

"My dear young lady, no one feeds the condemned. A year of horrific hunger, with only one's own screams for company or for entertainment? It is surprisingly effective."

"Ah. Well, in that case, if the perpetrator is punished in this fashion, I waive privilege."

"Privilege?"

"It's my privilege to hunt down and punish those who hurt me or my friends. Whether you help me find them or not," I added.

"I see. Well, if it comes to a personal conflict—and it would be a *personal* conflict? Not a pogrom?"

"Oh, absolutely!"

"Then I see no cause for my involvement. Or anyone else's, I should add. I shall be delighted to inform you of the outcome of the adjudication, if you wish."

"I look forward to hearing all about it."

"Always a pleasure." He pursed his lips for a moment, considering his next words. "I do have another point I should like to address, unrelated to the incident."

"Which is?"

"I am sure you know we have intelligence regarding your occasional nocturnal activities."

"Such as?"

"You and two gentlemen—one of them a lycanthrope—seem to enjoy causing difficulties for certain criminal enterprises."

"And if this is true?"

"Some of these enterprises are quite lucrative, but the money, while not immaterial, is not the most important aspect. If you were to limit your assaults to retail establishments and cause difficulties to them, both from a financial and product-moving standpoint, I feel there would be no need of action on our part. Mortals agencies would, of course, take their own steps to deal with what is, to their minds, a mortal issue. But *we* would not, if you take my meaning?"

"I do."

"The trouble is, your pursuits have led to a bit of trepidation among the more wide-reaching elements of the businesses in question. The flow of goods often has ripples in it; turbulence is always to be expected in the supply chain. What bothers some of us is the way those ripples appear to be spreading and growing. They have not yet disrupted other flows, but there is legitimate concern they may begin to. Specifically, the traffic of livestock."

"Livestock?" I asked, thinking of rare and endangered species.

"Yes. While a vampire is capable of feeding on... shall we say 'lesser beasts'?... the human equivalent is like the consumption of water to assuage hunger. A vampire can survive on the blood of cows, but this does not cure the hunger he feels. It may grow no worse, but it also grows no less."

"Ah. You're talking about human trafficking."

"Indeed. You seem a reasonable sort. I feel it best to simply inform you, thus smoothing the way for future negotiations—and to warn you."

"Warn me? Is that a veiled threat?"

"Not at all. While we have a common enemy at the moment, which means you are useful to us and reasonably safe from organized opposition, perhaps you should be warned. There are those who are more concerned about their food supply. If all you want to do is reduce the level of drug traffic, by all means, go right ahead. It does no harm to anyone of consequence and gives you something to do. I applaud the sentiments.

"However, if you choose to interrupt the steady flow of vital commodities, there will be consequences."

"I see. What sort of consequences? Private individuals taking matters into their own hands? Or more systematic repercussions?"

"Under normal circumstances, no doubt there would be a council meeting. The gathered council would have the final say on the exact nature of any reprisal, but reprisals there would certainly be."

"You say 'under normal circumstances' as though these are not."

Dietrich looked, for an instant, pained. The expression was gone as quickly as a candle-flame when it's blown out, but he gave something away, or thought he did, and he kicked himself for it.

"There is a great deal of concern about Alden," he replied, smoothly. "Few of us have encountered powers of this sort, and the ability to create an area where we dare not go—and without an obvious sign, such as a church or other religious icon—is a threat we cannot ignore.

"Alden has caused consternation all through the elders of our kind. There are debates about what to do. I haven't seen so much argument since the night after poor Franz was shot."

"Franz?"

"Ferdinand. I rather liked the fellow. Met him in Australia when he was hunting for kangaroo trophies. Bit odd, really, his fascination for game trophies. It was almost an obsession. Still, he was an amazingly energetic, authentic, and sincere fellow. Unlike many nobles, you knew where you stood with Franz. I respected that. I was deeply saddened to hear of his assassination.

"And now, as then, this is a delicate time where precipitous action is very much on the table. In these circumstances of today, if you become more trouble than aid, you may push an already-tense situation beyond words into deeds." He shrugged. "I feel adequately prepared, either way, but I would be saddened if a young lady such as yourself were to come to grief."

"How drastic might this action be?"

"I am not a council member, so I cannot gauge their intentions, but the results will not be solely predicated on Alden's actions. There are other issues on the table which will alter their thinking and color their decisions." He shrugged. "Politics in vampire circles are seldom so very different from human politics."

"My condolences."

"Thank you."

"All right. I'll lay off the human trafficking to help keep things calm. You punish the person or persons responsible for my friends. We both eyeball Alden—I supply whatever information I can, and you can ask me to find out things I haven't thought to look into. If I can, I will. Between us, I hope we can minimize his influence and the aftereffects of his removal—whichever one of us effects his removal."

"We will probably kill him," Dietrich noted. "There was a suggestion we attempt to turn him, but with the powers of a priest on his side, it is somewhat problematic."

"He's also a powerful psychic," I added. "Once you bite him, you'll have your work cut out trying to control him."

"Which is another point in the argument," he agreed, "but you misunderstand. If we want him as an *archontiá*, rather than a mindless *periplanómenos*, we will have to feed him blood for a considerable time to prepare his system for a smooth transition. The bite, alone, brings madness and a crazed lust for blood. These are the animals of our kind, gradually evolving into something resembling a civilized being. To fully retain one's intellect and will, a subject must be prepared while yet living. Thus, to retain Alden's abilities and talents, he would have to be restrained and forced to drink—which would, during this process, make him even stronger, increasing the difficulty." Dietrich shrugged.

"When I was consulted, I counseled against such a plan, although not for that reason. I felt it was hardly in our best interests to turn him into a vampire when he clearly desired our destruction. Why make him immortal and able to carry on the fight for eternity?" He shook his head, lips drawn in a thin line. "Sometimes, I wonder if senility comes to even my kind, albeit much more slowly."

"I didn't know that about vampire creation. So, Janice was going to be a crazy vampire lady, no matter what?"

"If she was not adequately prepared? Yes."

"Are you sure one year in the grave is sufficient for whoever did it?" I asked. Dietrich chuckled.

"There is a question I will happily raise on your behalf. But, to return to our muttons. Your summation of our overall alliance is a good one. We will work separately on the problem of Alden, but with mutual communication. You will have vengeance for your friends, under our laws, and, *quid pro quo*, we will not need to devote energies to stop you from causing chaos in our lines of supply for the more vital goods."

"It sounds like we have an agreement."

"It certainly does. And may I say, this has been the most pleasant discussion I've ever had with a wizard or witch? Most of them are prideful, arrogant, and preemptory when they aren't paranoid, defensive, and threatening. You are a refreshing change from the norm."

"Thank you. You've been quite reasonable and polite, yourself—but that, at least, I expected."

"I hope I have exceeded your high standards," he chuckled.

"I would say so. I think my Pop would like you."

"I will take it as high praise."

"It is. Are we done?"

Dietrich pressed a button on the ceiling.

"Sir?" said the grille beside the button.

"To the lady's home, please."

"Certainly, Sir."

When we pulled up in front of my house, the driver opened the door for me and handed me out. Dietrich called from within and leaned forward to look at me.

"One more thing, Miss Kent?"

"Yes?"

"When you stepped into the car with me, you had to know what you were getting into."

"Yes."

"If it was not ignorance, what was it? Arrogance? Overconfidence?"

"Possibly a bit of each," I admitted. "I'm young and I know it. But I think, mostly, it was the preparation. You're immortal and probably quite attached to being immortal. Yes?"

"Yes. How does this work to your advantage?"

"My handbag has a hair trigger and five pounds of plastique in it. If I was about to die, I wasn't dying alone."

Dietrich smiled, a surprisingly genuine and pleased smile. He nodded approvingly.

"I am now even more delighted to have made your acquaintance, Miss Kent. Do have a pleasant evening."

"And you, sir."

Inside the house, I double-checked everything. Rusty came in—I made sure it was him. I buzzed Jason in on the roof—Yes, it was Jason. The house was empty, aside from us. Zeno said so and I made doubly sure. Anything missing? No? Anything present that shouldn't be? No? Anything tripping an alarm spell? No.

Okay. Maybe it was all good.

Pop warned me how ancient evils from the dawn of time can be subtle, clever, and treacherous. I figured caution was in order.

"Now that we've swept the premises," Jason suggested, "perhaps we might hear how things went?"

"Sure. Oh! Dang it, let me put this purse in the arms locker."

"What's in the purse?"

"The plastique."

"Plastique?" Jason echoed.

"She insisted," Rusty told him.

"If it was necessary," I told them, "I was going to point out how you don't try to feed on the person carrying a bomb with a deadman switch. Fortunately, the subject didn't really come up."

"Fortunately," Jason echoed.

I put the explosives away and briefed them on the meeting.

"The upshot of it all," I finished, "is the vampires, in general, agree Alden is a problem. Since they think of me as a nonstandard mortal, being engaged in clandestine activities, they assume I don't want publicity any more than they do."

"They should have publicity," Jason muttered. "People should know they exist."

"No, they shouldn't," Rusty countered.

"Oh? Because then they would believe in werewolves?"

"No, because then they would see vampires everywhere. They would riot in the streets. They would drag people who work nights out of their beds and stake them, accusing them of being vampires or working for them. There would be witch hunts and cleansings and enough nutcases to burn down half the world."

"He's got a point," I added. "If you tell people it's okay to hunt down evil things that look like people, they hunt down people they think are evil. Vampires would be just another excuse. We repeat the Salem witch-trials with the Manhattan vampire trials."

Jason subsided. He saw the point and hated it.

"So," I continued, "with the whole maintain-the-secrecy thing in mind, we're going to trade information on our mutual problem. As a long-term goal," I said, looking at Jason, "I hope to learn more about vampires in general and the really evil bastards in specific. Our *immediate* goal is containing Alden. I'm not ignoring later objectives. Okay?"

"Yes, Ma'am." His demeanor lightened as he replied. The idea there would be vampires to hunt cheered him right up. Wraithist. "I suppose this means we'll be putting other projects on hold?"

"Yes and no. I'll still be collecting intelligence for a major raid on a cash shipment, but routine raids will be suspended." I didn't mention the raids would be mostly for their benefit. I would enjoy it, too, but none of us would enjoy vanishing the cash from deposit boxes. No fight, no fuss, no fun.

"I suspected. I do have another question, though."

"Surely. Go ahead."

"Are you ever going to come clean?"

"I beg your pardon? About what?"

Jason shook his head and sighed.

"Ma'am. Phoebe. Can we agree I'm not an idiot?"

I shot Rusty a look sharp enough to cut. He swallowed what he was about to say.

"Yes, I think we're all in agreement." I answered Jason, but I spoke to Rusty. He kept his mouth shut, but it was such a perfect setup! It hurt him not to respond.

"Thank you." Jason glanced at Rusty. "And thank you for your restraint."

"Don't push me," Rusty advised. "Get to your point."

"I've had issues with werewolves—minor issues, all things considered, all right? Misunderstandings. Can you meet me halfway?"

"I guess. Understand I don't care for your attitude and no werewolf ever will. I'm at the very limit of tolerance. Everyone else will be *way* less understanding."

"You've made an effort for Phoebe. So have I. Rather than simply hate each other, can we at least agree, whether we like each other or not, we're willing to work together in the name of a larger cause?"

Rusty grumbled, but he didn't disagree. Jason went on.

"I know it sounds prejudiced to lump all werewolves into a category. I've been doing that. I apologize. I was wrong."

Rusty sat up, blinking in surprise. I don't want to say he was shocked, but I know *I* was surprised.

"I've been giving it a lot of thought and I've come to the conclusion werewolves—as a… as a community? You—they?—The were-creature community hasn't done anything intrinsically… bad. Evil. They exist and I'm… yes, I'm racist, I suppose. 'Speciesist' might be a better word. I have at least one example who proves werewolves aren't fundamentally monsters," he gestured at Rusty, who looked even more surprised, "but I won't go out of my way to act as though I like any of you.

"My point is I know you exist. I don't have to believe in you. I *know.* Your existence is an established fact. Vampires? Ditto. These mythological creatures from the ancient tales actually do walk the earth, wielding magical powers science is at a loss to explain.

"Which brings me to the existence of magic. As futuristic as it looks, the level of technology required for this armor I'm wearing is nothing short of… 'sufficiently advanced.' Do you get my drift? Or do I need to spell it out?"

Rusty and I traded looks. Rusty shrugged. I gritted my teeth. I should have anticipated this. It's not like a sidekick is on the outside, looking in. Robin knows Batman goes incognito as Bruce Wayne. Maybe it was time for Jason to be fully briefed. He should understand what we were dealing with, but I wondered how he would take knowing he was working for a witch.

Let's not even think about explaining Pop. Come to think of it, Pop didn't brief him on the whole story. Did Pop deliberately not tell him so I would someday have to deal with the explanation? Or is this one of those inevitable moments in the superhero life?

As I thought it over, I remembered some of Jason's comments. He kept dropping little hints, none of which I took as an opening for explanations. He's known, or at least suspected, for quite a while. He's been immensely patient, waiting for me to trust him with the truth. Despite this, he's been a hundred percent behind me all the way. Maybe the truth was overdue.

"Phoebe," he went on, "I understand you may not be comfortable with explaining everything to me. I'm the hired help. I'm aware of it. I'm comfortable with it. I don't need to understand the larger issues. I can be a good little weapon and wait patiently until you're ready to use me. I chose a career as a mercenary, and I chose to accept this contract. I've been paid in ways most people can't understand and I'm regularly and reliably paid more than the job's worth. If you can't tell me—because you don't want to, or you don't know, or if I'm not cleared for it—I'll continue to do my job and never ask again."

"No. No, you're cleared for it. I just cleared you for it. You probably have a need to know, as well. So, yes, I get your drift. And yes, I'll explain a lot of things in short order. Not right this instant—I'm not prepared to give a coherent briefing—but I'll put one together for you. All right?"

"I look forward to it. Will it include a more thorough briefing on this Alden person?"

"Yes, and I apologize for not bringing you up to speed sooner." I drummed my fingers on the dining-room table and rested my chin in my other hand. "There are a couple of time-sensitive things I have to do tonight, but I can get things together for tomorrow. Can you be back over here around noon?"

"Going where you tell me is literally in my job description."

"Oh. Right. Okay. Just so we're clear: vampires are temporarily being used to go after the psychic bastard Alden. Try not to piss them off until we don't need them, and then preferably not until we have adequate intelligence on them. Got it?"

"It's crystal clear."

"Good. You go. I'll sort out Rusty and get your briefing put together."

"I look forward to it," he repeated, sincerely, before heading upstairs to exit via the roof. Rusty shook his head and sighed.

"He's not going to like this."

"How not?"

"You're a witch, aren't you?"

"Yeah, but I'm planning to spin my witchery as something humans can do, provided they know how. Which, if I'm honest, isn't completely wrong. His problem with all this is he doesn't like monsters. He does like magic armor, though, so I think it'll fly. The idea, not the armor."

"Could you make flying armor?"

"Technically? Yes. But Earth doesn't have the magical field required to maintain it for long. Technology can make a jet pack but it can't carry enough fuel for more than a minute or so of flight time. A magical flying suit would be in a similar situation. Now, a large backpack with a crystalline matrix in it, to act as the power source for an extended flight..."

"I can see I've started you thinking again. Will you please stop?"

"Stop thinking? I don't think I can do that. It's not how I was raised."

"I mean, thinking about that in particular. Here, think about this. What do you mean by sorting me out, like you mentioned to Jason?"

"Oh. While the moon is up, I want to work with you to get this amulet finished—or, at least, figure out why it doesn't work so I can redesign it."

"Fantastic! When do we start?"

"Right now. Follow me."

A few hours later, the dawn started and my ritual spell was done. Technically, it was my third ritual spell, but I was pretty sure I nailed it the third time. Third time is the charm, after all. We finished up on the roof and took a breather.

Rusty had a man's chain necklace around his neck. It doubled as a dog collar, but it gave me more of a headache than the amulet did! If it fit his wolf-shape as a collar, it was too small for the intermediate stages of his transformation to human. Only in human and wolf forms was it just right. I had to get a special, memory-metal alloy from another world and use magic to trigger the changes in length.

Once I had the chain ready, it held what looked like military dogtags—and would act like dog tags while he was in wolf form. Good disguise. The chain also held a small, metal sphere containing a special, swirly glass marble. The glass was made from lunar dust. It reminded me of Bennington marbles, or the surface of the moon. Appropriate, I thought.

After the ritual, I cleared a path to the nearest bathroom before letting Rusty come down. He was still a bit gooey from the human and wolf blood. While he showered, I cleaned up the mess on the roof and erased the various lines of my diagrams.

As I did so, I wondered. Would Pop be proud of me? The spell was, I felt, workable. It would do the job. In that sense, yes, I was sure I would get the smile and the approving nod. It was also a kludged-together monstrosity. It wasn't just a "messy bits" spell. It was a "wish real hard" spell with extra focusing agents. I'd have to say it walked the line between a traditionally-designed spell and a wish.

Did it work? I was confident. Was it a lovely piece of thaumaturgical engineering? No. Not in the slightest.

Pop *would* be proud of me, I decided. Refined, slick spells are the end product. A functional prototype is only the first step.

I came down, making sure the roof door latched behind me. I checked in on Zeno on my way down. He had put together a presentation for Jason. I skimmed it and resolved to go over it in more detail, later. Meanwhile, Rusty was all the way down on the first floor, in the kitchen. At least he was clean and wearing his own clothes, not my bathrobe. He didn't even track wet footprints from the upstairs bathroom down the steps.

The bathroom was a mess, of course, but I didn't find out until later. I absolutely need to work on another electromagical transformer. And bigger cleaning spells for the bathrooms.

"Breakfast?" he asked.

"I'm famished. Then I need a nap. Then I need to get Jason's briefing in final order."

"I could use a snooze, myself. If this works all the time," he said, tapping his necklace through the shirt, "do you want to come visit on the night of the full? I ask because it'll make one hell of an impression."

"We'll save it for after. Let them talk about it, first. And if it works now, it should work forever. This is an enchantment, not a spell. How much does it help?"

"It feels... I dunno. Easier? I mean, there's no difference I can feel between going one way or the other. I went back and forth along the whole spectrum of transformation, fast and slow, like you saw up on the roof. It didn't feel any different to go either way."

"Can you go into your halfway-hybrid form thingy during the new or the full?"

"Yes, but it's hard. You have to push to get there, then you have to think about it to hold it. You start to drift toward the monthly end if you don't keep a grip. With this thing—" he tapped his shirt again, "—I didn't have any problem stopping at any stage I wanted and staying there. It was *easy*."

"Okay. Keep me posted."

"I will. Got anything else for me, today?"

"Not unless Gus wants to play."

"Haven't seen nor smelled him. I guess he's off to wherever the closet goes."

"Have I explained about the closet?"

"Nope. I smell things, though, so I assume there's a way to go somewhere else by using it."

"Magic closet. It goes to my old place in the Madison Building."

"Makes sense." He scooped a bunch of sausages from the pan onto a plate. As an afterthought, he put two on a smaller plate and gave it to me.

"Does it make sense?"

"No, but you're a witch. I'm guessing it makes sense to you."

"It does. See, the closet upstairs goes to the Madison Building. The closet there connects to my Pop's house in Iowa, back in 1952."

"Of course it does."

"You don't believe me?"

"I believe you. Is it like a magic wardrobe where you have to walk through the coats until you get to the other end?"

"No. It's like a Star Trek transporter. You disappear in this transporter and reappear in another one. The one upstairs only goes one place. The one in the Madison Building goes here or to Pop's place."

"So that's why Gus smells different. He didn't pick up those scents in the park."

"I'm sorry. I'm tired and not thinking clearly. Obviously, there's a lot I should have explained to you and to Jason. Especially now that I'm explaining a lot more to Jason." I sighed and munched on a sausage. "I spent most of my life being a private person. A very private person. I'm learning who to trust, but it takes a while."

"Sounds like you're learning there *are* people you can trust."

"Maybe," I allowed, and took another bite.

I wondered, as I chewed, about my upbringing. Pop raised me to keep secrets, and that's a valuable skill. Do I need to keep everything a secret? What's the difference between learning the lessons our parents teach us and living our lives the way *they* want us to? Or, maybe a better way to put it, where do we draw the line between lessons learned and living our own lives?

"I don't suppose I can sit in on the briefing?" Rusty asked.

"Hmm? Oh, sure. Of course you can."

"Confabulicious. I'll bring a bag of jerky if you provide the popcorn."

"I'll also bring drinks."

"I'm liking this more and more."

Journal Entry #20

Trust isn't something I do exceptionally well. Better than Pop, maybe, but it's not a high bar. There were, of course, things I didn't want to go into in any detail. As far as Jason was concerned, being in the employ of a vampire was one hundred percent out of the question. He could be counted on to assume it was all part of a sinister plot.

On the other hand, working for me and Pop when we're both human beings—albeit humans who had learned to harness magical forces—was considerably more acceptable.

Explaining how humans were capable of manipulating magical energies took a while. People can use magic. It's a fact. But the magical field of Earth makes it the province of people who have an enormous talent for it, or who live on top of a magically-significant spot.

Or, if I'm totally honest, who have the technology to turn other types of energy into magic. We didn't go into details. Magic exists, rare people are good at it, and without talent you can't do anything.

"The point of all this," I finished, "is the armor is, in fact, enchanted. It's cutting-edge stuff as far as the materials go, but also from a magical standpoint. It's experimental, using breakthrough theory, and built by people who have been working with magic for hundreds of years."

"Hold on. I plug it into a wall outlet to recharge. Seems like technology to me."

"It took quite a while to figure it out, but there are ways to turn one kind of energy into another. Electricity can be turned into a magnetic field or into light. It can also be turned into physical motion. The conversion process may be primitive or sophisticated, more or less efficient, have byproducts—lights also produce waste heat, for example. Finding a way to turn electricity into magic involved the wizard equivalent of Nikola Tesla."

"Don't you mean Edison?"

"Edison was a marketing genius, not a researcher. People working for him did the brainy parts. Edison's big talent was consistently turning a profit."

"If you say so. I plug in the suit and let it charge the magical batteries. That's the upshot of all this."

"Yes. But you knew that."

"I suspected. I can still think of it as charging the batteries, right? It doesn't matter if they're holding an electrical charge or a magical one, right?"

"Correct."

"How do I tell if the suit is doing something with science or magic?"

"You don't. Not if I've done it right. Not if it's sufficiently advanced, and we've been trying very hard to make it sufficiently advanced."

"Ah, I see. Okay. I think I'm up to speed on the armor. Now I have other questions. Who—or *what*—is this Alden guy? According to what I'm seeing, he's a priest and a bodybuilder, but you say he's also angling for evil psychic overlord. How is that possible?"

"Hold on. Bodybuilder?" I thought back to the map of Alden's movements. Was there a regular stop at a gym? Or did one of the churches where he spent the night have extensive exercise equipment? I doubted it.

"I did my basic observation with plain optics. He's big," Jason pointed out. "He's one of those naturally mesomorphic body types. He's got the muscle mass to be a problem even if he doesn't have much training."

"I don't recall him being especially massive. Although," I added, "I do seem to remember noticing he was bulking up a bit."

"Is this something he's doing with a built-in power, or is he evolving into a more powerful form, or what?"

"That's an excellent question," I agreed, and started in on what we knew about Alden. Mostly, he's above the norm at physical strength, toughness, and psychic power. He uses a specialized power to fry vampires—laudable, if a bit indiscriminate—but he is also psychically doing nasty things to people, destroying their free will, enslaving them to his cause, and working toward, apparently, world domination.

"I don't know how he manages to wield these powers, but that's not the foremost concern. What is concerning is he's willing to kill and torture to gain power," I finished. "He actually invaded my home, attacked my Pop, stole several magical devices, and made it to the top of the family shit list. He's lucky beyond belief."

Rusty raised a hand. Jason shot him a look, but I saw the way his face moved. He wanted to tell Rusty to keep quiet; the humans are talking. But Jason checked himself. Rusty wasn't interrupting. Rusty was going out of his way not to be a jerk. So, rather than be proven more of a jerk than Rusty, Jason kept quiet. I nodded at Rusty.

"How is he lucky?" Rusty asked. "I mean, being on your list is probably not a good thing." Rusty pointed at Jason. "He wears stuff you don't see outside a comic book. If you can build these things, you can do a lot of other things, too."

"Just what I was thinking," Jason agreed. Neither of them looked at each other. Agreeing with each other and admitting it was a step in the right direction, so I treated it as though it was only to be expected.

"Being on the list isn't the lucky part. It's the fact I'm handling it. I want him to learn the error of is ways, not simply vanish in a puff of high-intensity plasma."

"I don't understand. I don't think I understand," Jason admitted.

"Pop is easily the most powerful wizard the world has ever seen. Look at the capabilities of your suit. He can make it, and make it user-friendly. I can maintain and repair it, like a mechanic. I'm not the engineer who designed the equipment. Some other spells require expert handling beyond my level of skill. He can do things even I don't understand. Pop is the engineer."

"So, what's stopping him from using a plasma weapon or the equivalent?"

"Me. I think Alden deserves a chance to be a force for good—or, at the very least, not an active force for evil. I'm hoping he can be persuaded. If I'm wrong, he's a dead man."

I wondered if Pop would bother with a fancy weapon. He's usually content to wave around Firebrand and his Sword of Ludicrous Sharpness. On the other hand, Pop knows where to find all sorts of things. I've seen weapons ranging from stone axes to flintlocks to lasers to gravity beams. He's even let me zap asteroids and fire nukes.

My summer holidays got me in trouble. "What I Did On My Summer Vacation" essays got me yelled at for making stuff up. I told the truth and was punished for it. After that, I wrote about the most boring things I could think of. Ah, public school! I don't miss those days.

"I'm convinced," Jason admitted.

"Convinced he needs to be eliminated?"

"Alden? Provisionally, yes. Your father?" Jason shrugged. "He's been unfailingly fair to me, if not entirely honest. I don't think I can hold it against him. There are things I wouldn't have told me, either. I also note he's not—and can't, if I understand you correctly—mass-producing these suits for his personal army. He strikes me as the sort to be happily left alone to mind his own business, which will work out wonderfully for anyone who doesn't go out of their way to get into his business."

"You have no idea how right you are."

"Fantastic. We have agreement. Now, what else can you tell me about Alden? Are we sure he's human? I want to be clear in my bestiary."

"How do you mean?"

"Do I list him as a monster with psychic powers and mutant-level strength, or do I list him as a human mutant with multiple powers? And does he do the priest thing because he's actually a priest, or because he has powers that can do what *look* like miracles? Or is he actually a saint and we've got a severe moral dilemma?"

I had to think about it. What, *exactly*, was Alden? I had always treated him as a human with psychic powers and it seemed to fit. I had him pegged as a mutant: fundamentally a human being, but with extras. I mean, what else could he be?

A small parade of possibilities wandered by, shuffling their feet as though surprised to be summoned.

"Well, damn. Now I'll have to go find out. You two—talk amongst yourselves."

I did not find out that day. Jason went off to do Jason things. Rusty reminded me of his father's standing invitation. We scheduled it and I told Zeno to remind me. Rusty, pleased, took his leave.

I went to my witchroom and made nasty remarks about Alden. I spared a few for Pop's overdeveloped sense of paranoia. Sorry. "Caution." I meant "caution."

Between the stolen ring and amulet, I was stumped. Pop's defensive spells keep him off the radar. In order to examine Alden more thoroughly, I would have to do it the hard way. I needed to get up close and do a direct magical probe—which, of course, he would notice. Not a good way to start a lengthy scan and analysis!

I was still tired, and I knew it. My nap hadn't been enough, so I only fought with the problem for a couple of hours before I admitted it was going to take a breakthrough in my thinking. I went to bed and slept the rest of the afternoon and most of the night.

And dreamed a little dream.

Dream Journal #2

The place? A forest. I'd almost call it a jungle. The trees were set close and undergrowth was everywhere. Things chirped and trilled and chittered in the treetops, but nothing on the forest floor seemed to make any noise.

I stood in front of a low hill, but I wasn't fooled. It reminded me of a hobbit-house, being either underground or covered in sod. The door wasn't easy to find, but once you knew the face of a buried boulder didn't have an actual boulder to go with it, you could tilt it up easily. Counterweights, obviously.

Inside, it was indeed a pleasant little dwelling. Or it would be, if someone wasn't such a fan of early movie serials, like Flash Gordon and Buck Rogers. Electrical things sizzled and sparked. Gizmos whirled. Tall tubes of colored fluids bubbled and burbled. Lights flashed on consoles. Banks of dials spun and dozens of meters flickered.

The man at the center of all this looked familiar. He wasn't Pop, obviously, but he could have been his brother. There was more than a passing resemblance.

He watched me as I came in. He held a bulky contraption in his hands, reminiscent of a blunderbuss. The trigger mechanism was considerably larger than required for a gunpowder weapon. I suspected it might do more than throw things really hard.

"Phoebe?" he asked, surprised.

"That's me. Uncle Dusty?" He nodded as he put down the weapon.

"What are you doing here? *How* are you here?"

"I don't know. I'm asleep. I've had a long day and I'm frustrated as hell over a problem, so I have no idea why I'm dreaming about this."

"Ah. Maybe you're dreaming Me up so you can ask Me questions and let your subconscious work it out."

"Seems plausible."

"Fair enough. Pull up a stool and tell Me all about it."

"Can I ask why you have a mad scientist's hobbit-hole?"

"Melkor will never see Me coming."

"I don't get it."

"Yes, well, dreams can be like that. They're often like prophecies. You don't understand them until you look back on them."

"That's not useful," I complained.

"No. It isn't. I'm sorry."

"It's okay, Unc. You would be more helpful if you could."

"Always. Now, what's your problem?"

"It's Alden. I've been confronted with the fact I don't actually know for sure what he is."

"And it matters... why?"

"Because if I'm thinking of him as an Evil Mutant, I'm not thinking of him as... as... as a shapeshifting alien agent from the planet Yuck sent to take over the world?"

"Good, good. You've grasped the concept quite well."

"Thank you. So, can you help?"

"Let me see... you do have problems with identifying him, don't you?"

"Yes. Pop's got all sorts of don't-find-me spells in his ring and amulet, so I can't scan the guy. I mean, I know where he is, so a lot of it isn't an issue, but a straight-up scan won't work, either. I know those spells. They return results of 'perfectly normal human,' or they block the scan entirely, depending on how invasive the scan is. I have to break through them, and that's a major undertaking!"

"And I can't help, either. For Me to take a close look at Alden would require penetrating the anti-angel cloaking spells."

"Would it?"

"Wouldn't it?"

"As I understand it, angels can still see Pop in whatever way they do. He mutes his chaos aura or whatever so they don't see him as a glowing beacon, blinking 'Come Kill Me!' in fiery letters. Once they look at him, they see him fine. Or do they?"

"Are they looking at him with a generalized scan from the celestial plane? Or are they occupying a physical being and eyeballing him in frequencies associated with the material plane? It changes their perceptions."

"Damn. From what I've been told, they're generally occupying a human. Does this mean you can't see Pop when he's hiding?"

"Interesting question. Maybe you should ask Me when you wake up."

"I'll try to remember."

"In the meantime, how do you propose to get past the magical barriers around Alden?"

"I don't."

"No? Why?"

"Are you kidding? Those are *Pop*'s spells! I play the Last of the Red-Hot Swamis to his Merlin! His spells are like fortresses! Sure, I can dig through a castle wall with a spoon, but do you know how long it will take? And how many spoons?"

"I think you underestimate yourself. I think it's more like Tinúviel to his Aulë."

"You mean Miranda to his Prospero! I wouldn't know how to *begin* to take one of his defensive spells apart!"

"Would you not?" he asked, smiling. "Anything you know how to build…" he trailed off.

"But these were built by *Pop!*"

"Using the same principles *he* taught *you*. Think about it! Nothing is perfect. There are ways through or around. He's built the Maginot Line and you have a spoon. Obviously, you don't dig through it. Think!"

So I thought about it. If I'm not going to listen when my own subconscious is trying to tell me something, I may as well quit the whole witching business and take up beachcombing.

Come to think of it, spending a week or two on a sandy beach with nothing to do but walk in the surf, lounge in the sun, collect seashells, and drink margaritas does sound good.

Okay. To work. I have a block of steel and concrete and there's someone inside I'm trying to get to. I have a spoon. How do I go about this?

No, no, no. That's a terrible start. Let's think about this another way.

The defensive spells in question aren't physical objects. They're more like… like… like force fields? Yes, sort of. They draw in magical energy, run it through spell wiring, and generate a field of a certain type. Whether it's a force field or a cloaking device or whatever, it's an energy pattern around the wearer.

Does this help? Not yet, but let's keep working on it.

The fields do several things. Mostly, they contain or alter things. If the wearer radiates something detectable, the fields contain it. It's kind of like putting a bowl over a light bulb to hide it during a wartime air raid. Still, an old-fashioned filament bulb gives off not just light but heat. It will eventually warm the bowl. So the spells let through other things, such as the psychic energy Alden emits. That's how I can track him.

Does this help me identify what he is? No, but at least I know *where* he is.

Okay, let's come back to it later, maybe. The other thing the cloaking spells do is alter things. A sensor pulse, like radar, goes out from me, hits the target—Alden—and bounces off him, taking with it information about what it hit. With radar, it's things like size, shape, velocity, and so on. With a sensor spell, I can get far more information.

The problem is the alterations. The spells he's wearing will either lie to my sensor spell—"No, nothing unusual here. Just us perfectly normal humans!"—or, if the sensor pulse is up close, personal, and powerful, simply block it while alerting the wearer to the fact there's someone trying to scan them.

I explained all this to the Wise Old Mentor figure in my dream. He nodded thoughtfully, as Wise Old Mentors are prone to do.

"What did you say these enchantments run on?"

"Magic. They're not psychic resonations or anything. I'm not even sure you can make a psychic enchantment. Although," I added, "you might be able to put a specific psychic imprint in something, then power it with your own psychic force."

"What would be the point?"

"It would mean you don't have to teach someone how to do it. They could use whatever psychic power they possess to power the thing even if they don't have any skills. Normal people are perfectly capable of communicating psychically, but they can't focus their thoughts precisely enough in their underdeveloped psychic channels to send a thought. Even if they did, nobody else is trained in how to recognize the difference between a telepathic sending and one of their own random thoughts. People have the wattage, but they don't have the skill."

"So you could give someone an earring of telekinesis and they could wear their brains out controlling the flip of a coin?"

"Potentially. I haven't really looked into it, but it seems to match what I know."

"Could you use magical energies to produce psychic force? A converter, perhaps?"

"I'm sure it can be done, but I'm not sure how to go about it."

"How about the enchanted objects Alden stole? Alden can't power those with psychic force, can he?"

"No. Like I said, they're strictly magical. He'd have to find a way to convert his psychic energies into magical ones, and that's so esoteric I'm not even sure it can be done."

"Can he direct celestial energies into them and run them that way?"

"He has the same problem with those. Celestial energies are nothing like magical energies. It's like trying to charge a battery with gravity. Gravity and electricity are so far apart, it's hard to get them to even talk to each other."

"That must be quite a problem for a wizard. On Earth, I mean."

"Yeah. The magical background is *awful*. If I didn't have a bunch of transformers plugged in, most of the magical gadgetry and spells in my house would have run down—" I broke off, because an idea whacked me in the forebrain.

"Yes, I imagine it would cause problems," Uncle Dusty went on. "I take it you have several things all packed together in a small area? If they didn't have a transformer providing power, would they fight for a slice of the too-small pie? Would any of them function, either at a reduced level, or at all? Or would the biggest one—the one drawing the most power—be the only one to work? Or would the tiniest one be the one to function? Which is more important, the amount it tries to draw or the amount it needs to run?"

"I *really* need to remember this when I wake up," I complained.

"Then I'm sad to see you go, but I understand. Ready?"

"Uh, no? Ready for what?"

He gestured in my direction and everything shot away from me—or I shot backward, or something.

Journal Entry #21

I felt as though I crashed down into my bed and woke up, heart pounding, to stare at the ceiling and concentrate on what I learned.

I remembered, at least for the moment. I scrambled out of bed, down the hall to my witchroom, and wrote everything down. I spent considerable time on it, making sure I wasn't scribbling half-asleep notes I'd never decipher. When I was done, I sat back from my worktable and regarded the spinning cylinder in one corner of my witchroom.

Did Uncle Dusty help me out? Is that what guardian angels are like? Or household gods? Or friendly energy-state beings? Or did I dream about my problem and latch on to the handiest imagery?

Maybe I'll ask him, someday. Maybe he'll bring it up. For the moment, though, I went back to bed.

My idea was a simple one. The majority of the things Pop routinely wears are in sleep or standby mode. He doesn't like auto-activation things. There are always conditions he hasn't thought of. The majority of his always-on stuff is low-powered. Stealth, cloaking, and deception spells don't require a lot of power. Most of the time, the gear Alden is wearing shouldn't be drawing too heavily on the power storage, if at all.

But even the low-power stuff can be made to work harder. Certain other spells *do* have automatic activation, in case Pop is so hurt he can't consciously start them up. Others might be triggered manually—and remotely—but only because I know the design and function of those.

In a low-powered Earth world, I could keep pounding the magical devices until I ran down the batteries. They couldn't possibly recharge as quickly as I drained them! I would still need to go about it carefully and with adequate preparation.

First, I needed a way to target Alden in the long term. I might be able to use the psychic theodolites for that. They were always pointed directly at him, so firing a pulse of something along the line of their detection was going to hit him, no matter how far away he was.

What worried me about this idea was the fact it might lead him to investigate where these pulses were coming from, which would lead him to the theodolites, which would mean the tracking system would be toast.

It'll take more thought, but I'll come back to it.

Second, I needed to cost him power. Consistent, persistent "attacks" that Pop's defensive spells would "fight off" were the key. I had to force them to use more energy than they could possibly ever get from the local environment.

I did calculations based on what I knew. There were power crystals incorporated in the amulet, of course. Alden also stole three geodes from my house. If these were all spaced out so their power intake didn't interfere with each other, he could move from one storage crystal to another and recharge periodically from each. It wasn't a complicated process, so I was sure it was within his grasp. Anyone with even basic sensitivity could manage it.

I didn't like the level of attack I would have to maintain. It would be such a high-level series of effects that he was sure to notice.

Again, I don't have a good solution, so I'll come back to it.

So, assuming I can target him wherever he goes, and have the spells to constantly provoke various functions, it's only a matter of time before they start to fail from lack of power. Once they start to fail, Alden will be visible to scrying, not only to psychic tracking devices. Angels will be able to see him, too, although I'm not sure how or even if it will matter. On the other hand, Uncle Dusty will be able to see him, and I think it's a fantastic idea. He can take a close look at Alden and, hopefully, see how human he is.

In the meantime, I have to figure out how to make as many of the spells as possible on Pop's old devices run as long as possible.

Hang on. At least one healing spell is constantly running. Without physical trauma, most of the others don't fire, but the generalized healing spell should be trying to undo the radiation damage. I didn't account for that. It's running all the time and will likely continue using power for the foreseeable future. I did account for the anti-scrying and anti-angel cloaking spells, though. Those *never* shut off.

What about physical defenses? Pop hates having things activate spontaneously. We discussed it during our lessons on magical defenses. If I have something to make me inertialess and I don't have any control over it—if it turns on by itself—this can be surprisingly inconvenient. Very quickly, the file of triggering conditions, and the associated sensing spells, get so elaborate and complex they bog down the response time. The spell detects the incoming bullet, for example, runs through the lists of when to fire and when not to fire, and activates the appropriate defense as the bullet is creating an exit wound.

Pop usually prefers to have his first-aid healing magic set up to auto-fire, with most of the defensive magic activated manually. He's superhumanly tough and only has to survive until sunset before his regeneration takes care of most problems. Me, I'm the more vulnerable type. Compared to most humans, I'm made of brass and teak, but I'm fragile compared to Pop. I like the idea of having at least *some* defenses against sudden death.

I wonder if he's included anything new since Alden ambushed him? I would bet he has. Not only did it piss him off, it pointed out how vulnerable he was. It also gave him a wonderful opportunity for a total rebuild and update on all his gadgets.

I saw it as a wonderful opportunity. He did *not*.

At any rate, I don't think his old stuff has anything I can trigger simply by attacking. Well, not exactly. Shooting him is still on the table. It'll trigger more healing spells and the more power-expensive healing spells. It's something to think about.

On the other hand, I know a lot about these devices. Can I activate their other functions remotely? Can I trigger, say, a momentum-absorbing spell? Those are pretty expensive and not terribly obvious. Not unless someone throws something at Alden, or rams him with a car, or something. Could I activate the entire defensive suite of spells? Inertia, momentum, deflection… maybe even Pop's old Ring of Many Gates? Those things really eat up power! No, Alden doesn't seem to be wearing it. Besides, the little iridium rings aren't actually gate-enchanted. They're enhanced versions of a targeting point—and I can't target them inside the cloaking fields!

Wait a hotrod minute! The phone has a micro-gate inside it. The connection has been running forever! Why hasn't it discharged all the—no, back up. The gate on *my* end is in a high-magic zone and is being powered by electromagical transformers. My end powers the gate, not the one in Alden's phone.

Can I dial back the power on my end? Yes. I can force the other micro-gate to draw on the energies available to maintain the connection. In fact, since he usually has it on him…

Pardon me while I smack myself in the forehead.

Alden is walking around with an active micro-gate on his person. That's how Pop is poisoning him with radioactive oxygen. I've been ignoring this because I can't effectively use it to find him. But if I want to send things through the gate—such as hacking Pop's old gear with a false activation signal—who cares where the other end is? I don't have to send a spell screaming down the line defined by a theodolite. I can stuff it through the micro-gate and let it go off wherever the other end is!

This still leaves me with the problem of the stolen power crystals. I have to deal with those, first. Under ideal conditions, even with everything on him triggered and running, his power budget could almost break even. He would have to keep moving from crystal to crystal to recharge, but it could be done.

It won't be ideal conditions, though. I doubt he's much good as a wizard. He would have to recognize the attack for what it was and what it was trying to do, then rush from crystal to crystal. It would keep him busy, at least, and divert him from his plans for a while.

Only for a while. Possibly a short while. Once he catches on, suspect he'll ditch the phone. Why? Because he'll start paying close attention to everything he's wearing, trying to figure out what's costing all the power and why these spells keep activating. I would. Then he'll start manually turning them *off*.

If he does it wrong, he can turn things off he shouldn't. Automatic healing spells, for one thing. Anti-scrying spells, for another. No matter how you slice it, he'll have to do a lot of trial and error before he figures out all the functions, what they cost him, how long he can afford to run them, how much power he can get from the local environment, which ones he wants running, which ones can—and should—be set to automatically activate…

Okay, I have the beginnings of a plan. I have ideas for the spells I'll need. I'll also need to find where Alden keeps his spare batteries—my stolen power crystals! If he's going to have to fight to keep the gadgets running, I want his endurance chopped down to a stump!

I rubbed my hands together in glee. He loves having magical powers at his command. He tears wizards' mind apart to steal whatever magical knowledge he can salvage from the ruins. He's big on gathering all sorts of magic to himself for his personal use.

Oh, he was going to *hate* this!

First things first. Wiping out his power budget involves stealing my power crystals back. We'll see if he has the gall to complain.

Journal Entry #22

I did a lot more thinking. If I were a stolen power crystal, where would I be? Ideally, I'd want them on my person, but these were large, chunky geodes, the better to blend in with home décor. Next choice would be spread out a bit so they don't compete for the magic available in the local environment. Of course, if I can't have them on me, I'd want them somewhere safe, where a casual scrying scan won't find them.

And where on this planet can I *not* scan? Alden's holy ground areas.

A quick question to Zeno about Alden's churchgoing habits and I had my preliminary targets. Zeno downloaded floor plans, tourist guides, visitor pictures and videos, all those sorts of things in order to assemble an augmented-reality mockup. My visor provided image overlays so it would be like walking through the places before I ever set foot in them.

Pop spent a lot of time trying to teach me to think ahead. Now I'm learning *why*.

With the digital mockups ready for a little augmented reality jaunt, Jason and I spent the night in Letchworth. Letchworth Village is an abandoned... village? Sort of? It's a lot of buildings about a half-hour drive from my current place in Manhattan, if you let the traffic control computer do the driving.

Autocabs annoy me, but I will admit they are efficient at moving people. I ride in them a lot, but I am glad I have my own car, off the grid, under my personal control whenever I want it.

I miss Bronze.

Originally, Letchworth was meant as an isolation community for mental patients before it went out of business. Now it's a bunch of crumbling stone and brick structures with a lot of vegetation, graffiti, and mold. It makes a good place to go when we're practicing. There's usually nobody around. Anybody who is around is neither a credible witness nor someone interested in attracting the attention of the authorities.

It didn't have any mind-controlled Alden-drones. I *did* scan for them.

Our practice for tonight was pretending to search various cathedrals as projected on the visors. We gained familiarity with the layout and especially where the doors and windows were. I planned—note that: I *planned*—to go in during the day and do a quick look around while Alden was elsewhere, but Jason argued me out of it.

"Correct me where I'm wrong, but during the day, he can go anywhere he wants. You say he tends to stay indoors at night, presumably to avoid vampires, so that's when he's nailed down in one spot, right?"

"I wouldn't say he's nailed down," I corrected. "He tends not to leave once he's in a church. I'm sure he can. What I'm not sure about is how much of a risk he thinks he's taking."

"But if someone is on station, waiting for him to leave, and does something to discourage him..."

"You want to shoot him?"

"Not fatally, since you insist. Maybe one round through the liver. It should put him in the hospital, which should let you continue about your business. More long-term, it will make him less inclined to go out at night. Although," he added, thoughtfully, "if I put a silver bullet through him—don't tell Rusty, please—and he shrugs it off, that's important to know. If he retreats to cover but doesn't seek medical help, he's confident he'll recuperate. If he does go to hospital, we know he's vulnerable. See what I mean?"

"It might not be a bad idea. I know he recuperates awfully fast, but I don't know how fast. At the very least, it would cost him more and more of his power reserve as the spells activate to deal with the injury, but he probably doesn't know how effective they are. His initial reaction will reflect his native capabilities. But you're right. Even if he handily survives, it will make him even less likely to leave his sanctuary after nightfall. "

"There you go. While he's locking himself in every night, you can ninja your way around cathedral after cathedral, searching for your magic rocks."

I had to admit, his plan was better.

We didn't get to carry it out immediately, however. I wanted more practice in the virtual environments. I also had an appointment to meet Rusty's father.

Journal Entry #23

We met at an unassuming little bistro in northeastern Manhattan, a couple of blocks from Harlem River Drive, on 129th Street. It was one of those tiny, crowded little places that makes ends meet through delivery and pickup services because there isn't enough floor space to seat customers. It was almost painfully clean, but also older than me. Maybe as old as Harlem. It could use Pop's handyman touch to fix a dozen cracked floor tiles and touch up a thousand different places worn thin. But it didn't give the impression of a run-down place. It wasn't shabby at all. It had an antique, traditional, long-established air.

Rusty's father was waiting when we arrived. He was a stocky sort, much more so than Rusty. You couldn't spot him as a werewolf because he was hairy like an ape. Thick hair, and lots of it, as black as my own. Summers had to be brutal on him. There was a touch of silver salting in the dark, dark hair in front of his ears. Overall, I guessed he was in his fifties, but it was hard to say for sure.

He stood up and I realized he wasn't quite as tall as me. I regretted wearing a nice outfit, especially the heels. I offered my hand and he took it, bowed over it slightly, and shook it. I'm not sure he knew the proper protocol, so I made sure to give him a good, strong handshake. He looked startled, then grinned with a mouthful of white, white teeth.

"Phoebe Kent, may I present my father, Stefano Giancomo. Dad, this is Phoebe Kent."

"A pleasure to meet you, sir."

"*Una casa senza donna è come una lanterna senza lume.* Welcome! To you, I am Steve." His accent was hard to place. Definitely a New Yorker, but with a big scoop of Italy and a splash of something I couldn't pin it down. He nodded at one of the kitchen staff. The front door was locked and the sign flipped around to "Torno Subito."

"In that case, I'm Phoebe." He grinned at me even wider and gestured us to sit. One of the cooks—there were no waiters, not for only four tables—brought out a bottle of red wine, three glasses, and a deep-dish pizza pie with every meat known to man in it. Not the typically thin New York style I foolishly expected, but the high, crusty bucket of Chicago style.

Rusty and Steve grabbed big chunks and started shoveling it in their faces. Well, when in Rome—and I've been in more than one Rome—do as the Romans do. I dug in and was pleasantly surprised. It was much more savory than I expected. The tomato sauce was there only as a seasoning. The garlic wasn't nearly as strong as the restaurant décor implied. The cheeses were the glues holding it all together, and the aggregate in this block of food was the chopped, diced, and sliced meats.

Protein for the day? Check. Probably for the week. Although eating this pizza was not for the weak. Between the three of us, we—ha, ha—wolfed down the whole thing. We didn't talk while eating, which I could respect. Food first. Everybody happy. Then have the after-dinner conversation. Is that primitive or civilized? Either way, I approved.

I was glad when we reached the burping stage, where one sits back and sips at the wine. Rusty and Steve went through most of the bottle while I limited myself to two glasses. When we finished with the napkins—linen, I noticed, and oversized—Steve grinned at me again.

"You eat like a hero," he told me.

"You think I don't burn through calories?" I quipped. He laughed.

"It is good you do. My son has spoken highly of you."

"I'm glad. I'd hate to think a friend talked bad behind my back."

"I do not think he has ever had anything bad to say. He is a good boy. You are pretty, you carry yourself well, you eat like you killed it, and I'm told you have many skills."

I glanced around the empty restaurant. One of the cooks happened to be looking our way and caught my eye. He grinned and made a teeth-snapping movement.

"Family-owned restaurant?" I asked.

"Six generations. We were here when it was Italian Harlem. We stayed when it became Black Harlem. It is now all Asian, but for us. We remain, and when someone who knows anything about anything sends for a pie, they send someone here. We are the best," he finished, with an air of pride and certainty.

"I believe it."

"This is good. You should think about your future. Someday, all this will belong to Wesley."

Wesley visibly winced.

"I thought Mark was the elder brother?" I asked, dodging the suggestion. Steve's mouth drew into a thin line before one corner curled.

"He is."

"I've opened my mouth on a family issue," I observed. "I apologize. I didn't know."

"It is nothing. Not your business, but you saw. I like that. I take no offense."

"Thank you."

"So, you are going to marry Wesley and make an honest man of him?"

Wesley turned red and, clearly, wanted to hide under the table.

"I hadn't planned on it."

"Good. You cannot make him what he is not," Steven said, grinning.

"I wouldn't try. But, out of curiosity, if you don't mind?"

"If it is offensive, I forgive you in advance. Ask."

"Would it be… what's the word? Kosher? Acceptable?…for him to marry a human? I don't know how it works."

"Ah, that," he said, nodding sagely. "It can be done, but it is not often. Not that *I* have anything against humans, but some of us feel differently."

"Watering down the bloodlines?"

"So some see it. Not all the whelps turn out. Many say we must keep the strain pure to keep it at all, but I am more a romantic."

"You married Mom," Wesley pointed out.

"Your mother came across the ocean to marry. Your grandmother arranged it with her mother over a cup of coffee in the same kitchen where she is today. They were wise to bring in fresh blood and avoid inbreeding. As for a human," he nodded at me, "she is also a witch, and she is, as you say, a looker." He turned to address me.

"Apologies for talking about you," he added. "No offense meant."

"No offense taken. It was all complimentary."

"So it was, and so it is. I see why Wesley likes you. Not only are you pretty, you are powerful." He leaned forward, arms on the table, and his demeanor shifted, lightning-quick, from affable flirt to all business. "This amulet you gave him—how hard are they to make?"

"I did most of the research and development already. I can probably make one in a few hours."

"I know many people who would be interested in one. And, from what Wesley tells me—"

"If I may interrupt?"

"My guest may always speak."

"It bothers me to see Rusty wince every time you use his right name. Could you call him by his nickname for a while?"

Steve stared at me with a blank look for several seconds. Then he threw back his head, slapped the table, and laughed. He wiped the corners of his eyes while the laughter subsided into chuckles.

"Oh, she's a rare one, boy. Rare among the rare!"

"Yes, sir."

"Girl—your pardon again, please. I sometimes am too familiar. Phoebe, do you know why *Rusty* likes his nickname better?"

"No, I don't."

"You have never asked?"

"Nope. It's his name, his business."

"Tell her."

"Dad, I don't..." he began, and withered under the resulting glare. "Uh... My name is Wesley, after the... the... the dread pirate."

"You mean you're named after the farm boy in *The Princess Bride*?"

"Mom loves the story," he sighed. "She read it to me every bedtime until my first change."

"I would not let her name our firstborn," Steven said, "but she got her way with—with Rusty. He inherited more of her hair color, too, so she gave him not only his name but his nickname."

"I think he'd make a wonderful Dread Pirate Roberts," I suggested, loyally. I didn't really think Rusty would be great at it, but I was thinking how good he could get, not about his present skills.

"I will pass it on to Kathleen. It will tickle her. But I still have my questions, if you do not mind."

"Not at all."

"Rusty tells me you can heal wounds."

"Sure."

"Do you have something for burns?"

"Yes. And, if I were to guess at your next question, yes, I have healing spells that should work on silver injuries, too. You do heal silver wounds, but slowly, right?"

"I told you she was smart," Rusty said. Steve nodded.

"You can let us change even when *la Luna* is against us and you can heal our injuries of fire and silver. Lady, you can name your price. What would you ask? I might offer my firstborn, but you have met him and I would feel bad to cheat you. You may have Rusty, if you wish."

"Hey!"

"Down, boy. It is my little joke and you know it. I need you to take over the restaurant."

"Hold on," I said. "I didn't make Rusty's amulet as an advertisement. And I certainly don't think I can cope with a full-time furball at my house. There's hair enough as it is!"

"Hey!" Rusty repeated.

"Kidding, furball."

Steve looked as though his suppressed laughter was going to rupture something. The snickering from the kitchen area was clearly audible. Sharp ears on the staff, regardless of the phase of the moon.

"All right," Steve said, finally. "All right. Ah, it's good to laugh."

"No doubt," Rusty muttered.

"Oh, take a joke, boy," Steve told him.

"You're not the one being laughed *at*."

"Do I stop you from making jokes about Mark?"

"...no."

"When you stop making jokes about your brother, I will stop laughing at jokes about my sons."

Rusty didn't exactly sulk, but he did shut up.

"Back to our talk," Steve continued. "I am interested in all these things. Fire mostly, because clumsy people are easily burned." He leaned back and raised his voice, directing his comment at the kitchen area. "Is it not so?" A ragged and reluctant chorus of "Si, signore" came back.

"Burns we have enough of. There are very few silver bullets."

"Either way, there isn't much difference. Not to me," I corrected. "The spells to do the healing will work on any wound. It will be faster than a human's healing rate, but the best part is it will be reasonably complete. You won't have a bunch of scarring."

"Will it get rid of old scars?"

"It shouldn't."

"Can you take it off before it is finished, so you can leave a scar?"

"Certainly," I agreed, puzzled.

"Then I am still interested. It is one thing to do the healing, another to change the phase of the moon. Two different things? Yes?"

"Right."

"If you don't want money for them, what do you want? I know people, and people who know people. My side of the family has connections."

I looked around the pizza joint. A lot of the kitchen staff smiled at me. I saw a lot of very dark hair and skin as olive as my own.

I didn't ask him about the connections. I made a deduction.

"Under other circumstances," I said, slowly, choosing my words carefully, "I might be interested in making use of your connections. As it is, I've, ah... persuaded? Persuaded a few rather *elderly* gentlemen how my problem is their problem, and they should deal with their problem."

Steve glanced at Rusty. Rusty shrugged.

"My son is not always as forthcoming as I wish," Steve replied. "Usually, he tells me everything. He told me of you, for example, and he told me of your friend, and of your meeting with Mark. He persuaded me it was for the best to let things lie, for several reasons. His mother, she was not so convinced about the man who shot her eldest son, but we left it alone because W—Rusty said he would be responsible. He is a big boy and I trust him, even if he is young.

"Now you tell me things I wish to know more of. I do not blame him for his closed mouth. It is a good thing, this knowing when to shut up. It has taken him a long time to learn it, if he has. But what he has said, I remember. Your father—he was one of these elderly gentlemen of which you speak?"

"This is your place, yes?"

"Yes."

"We can speak freely? Without worries about who is listening?"

"Yes."

"Then, yes. My Pop is a vampire. He's also a wizard—or a mage, or whatever you want to call it. He works magic and has done so for an awfully long time. I'm mortal, but I learned what he could teach me. And the vampires of New York are now aware of my problem—a fellow named Adam Alden."

Steve sipped at his wine and thought. Rusty looked back and forth between us as though wondering who was going to draw first.

"Has my son spoken to you about vampires?"

"He says you don't care for them."

"He is right." Steve sighed, slugged back the rest of his glass, poured another. "We do not trust them. They are wise and do not even trust each other. A long time ago, they tried to treat us like dogs, but we did not permit it. We still do not. We are wolves. As I say, we do not trust them."

"All things considered, you're probably right."

"Eh? I thought…?"

"Yes, Pop is a vampire. He's not like the local vampires. See, vampires come in different species. The most common sort is the sort you've encountered, I'm sure. There are a few other types. Pop's sort can go abroad by day, for example, even though it suppresses a lot of their powers. He doesn't have a permanent thirst that can never be satisfied, and he only really needs to… go out for a terminal drink once every few months."

"Ah! So there are better sorts than the vaff—ah, the common sort?"

"Yes, but there are also much worse."

"Your pardon, young lady, but I find believing this difficult."

So I had to describe to him the black-centered, truly evil sort of vampire.

"In short," I finished, "they're more like demons than vampires. They exist only to suck the life out of anything they touch, feeding it back to their dark patron in exchange for being immortal. Even then, they've been cheated. Their bodies continue to function as undead, their consciousness has a continuous chain of existence, but the souls involved are devoured." I paused for a moment. "I'm not sure if they know it or not. They're unrelentingly evil, that's certain, although they can fake goodness if it suits their purposes."

Steven drummed his fingers on the tabletop while the kitchen continued to work. While we spoke, a number of deliveries went out the back. I wondered if the "closed" sign was hurting business. Then again, nobody even came up to the door. I'm guessing we could have dispensed with the sign, but it was a nice safety measure against unexpected customers.

"And these blood-suckers… you send them against this priest? He is a problem for you, so you turn the vampires on him?"

"Ooo, no. I see where the confusion is. Adam Alden is not a priest. Well, maybe he is, technically, but he's doing very un-priestly things. He's a powerful psychic. He uses his powers to dominate the wills of others, to alter what they believe and what they think—and what they *can* think!—in order to enslave them and force them to obey him."

Steve shot a look at Rusty. Rusty nodded.

"This is not a good thing."

"I agree. Or do you mean the part about him being a priest?"

"Some of that, but mostly what he is doing. Men have free will, the gift of the Creator. It is not good that a priest should take away a gift of the Almighty. I do not like knowing a priest is being such a disgrace to the Church."

"If it matters, I'm not sure he's formally a priest, as such. He may have told people he was and forced them to accept it as a fact without checking."

"This is worse."

"I'm a little surprised," I admitted. "I thought the Church was against werewolves."

"Oh," Steve waved a hand. "We cannot help how we are born, can we? If it is a sin, then it is not ours. Someone ate a fruit they were told not to, long ago, and this is not our fault either. Many of us go to Mass and take confession. But we do not speak of what we are, only what we do. If I must hurt a man as a wolf, I confess the deed." He grinned again. "There may be surprises for the faithful in Heaven, no?"

"Could be," I allowed. Steve went back to sipping his wine and thinking.

"I am not sure what to say. I have not met with this may-be false priest."

"I wouldn't," Rusty added.

"Oh?"

"He reads minds. He'll know you know about him. And, after you meet him, you'll be *on his side*."

Steve stopped playing with his wineglass and set it carefully down.

"I do not call my son a liar. I do not call you a liar, Phoebe. But I must know, not only be told. How can I know?"

"You don't dare come near him, where he can grab you by the brain," I mused. "Tell me, do you ever venture into the subways and other underground tunnels?"

"There are those who favor them."

"Go down there. Meet the mindless minions. Alden has a horde of them, working in shifts. They beg for change, eat at soup kitchens, sleep on abandoned platforms, and spend the rest of their time doing whatever Alden wants. Spying, mostly, I think."

"Them, I will see. I, and others."

"Happy to help."

"If you want to help, I would not mind being in your debt."

"Something for the moonlight, something for the silver?" I asked.

"Only if it is not so much to ask. I am sure you like my son more than you like his father."

"Oh, I don't know. Older men can be quite appealing."

Steve laughed again and Rusty gave an obligatory chuckle.

"If I were not so happily married, you would not make such jokes, I know—but I thank you for the compliment." He nodded toward the kitchen and a man came out to unlock the front door. "This has been most pleasant. We will do this again."

"I look forward to it."

"And W—Rusty."

"Sir?"

"If you wish her to be with us when we are all upright, she is welcome."

"I'll bear it in mind, Dad."

"See you do. Good afternoon to you, Phoebe. It has been a pleasure."

Since I drove us there, I drove us back. Rusty didn't have anything to say.

"So," I began. "That's your Dad."

"Yeah."

"I didn't get a lot of Italian accent in your speech."

"What? Youse thinkin' I should-a talk-a like-a de Guido? Dis is how you a-speak-a to me, to say I don' sound like-a I should?"

"But you do the over-the-top impression really well."

"Thanks. Mom made me take voice lessons. Dad let her get away with most anything."

"The second son belongs to Mom, huh?"

"Yeah."

"He seems like a nice guy."

"He is. Mostly."

"Mostly? Was there a strap when you were a kid?"

"You have no idea. But I meant today. He's mostly a nice guy. He's jolly and happy and friendly until it's time to stop being jolly because something made him unhappy and then he gets unfriendly and someone else becomes unhappy."

"I take it you're not really related to any business-handling gentlemen in any formal organization?"

"It's more a long-standing friendship between families. We—werewolves—don't usually intermarry. Mom's right about that much. It's a bad idea. Dad agrees, but he also has a soft spot for 'twue wuv'."

"I thought your mother was the one who—"

"Yeah, but she's also more practical about it. Dad's the romantic. He told me, once, that even Grandma couldn't have made him marry if Mom didn't like him."

"What about him liking her?"

"He didn't mention anything about that. I guess he was willing to suffer, as long as she was happy."

"I like your Dad."

"So do I. Usually."

"Want to help me sort out a couple of experimental gadgets?" I asked, changing the subject.

"Why not. Maybe it'll take my mind off things."

"Excellent. Let's see if Pop is home. I want to use his workshop."

"Wait, what?"

Journal Entry #24

Rusty was a bit confused, at first, about the closets. It's one thing to talk about them, quite another to open and close the same door onto three different rooms. We had to go back and forth a few times to get it through his head he was teleporting.

Is it, technically, teleportation? I guess it is. I think of teleportation more as matter transmission things, but I suppose wormhole transitions count. It sure beats walking!

I heard Gus howl as we came through from the Madison Building to Iowa. As we stepped out of the Iowa closet, Gus came thundering down the hall and half-skidded on the carpet as he swung into the spare bedroom. He snarled at Rusty.

"Gus!"

He immediately shifted from guard dog to family pet. If I was here, Rusty was a guest, so it was okay. I was tempted to give Gus a stern talking-to, but he was doing exactly what he was supposed to. I haven't been so conflicted since Mister Stuffins tried to fillet a Chucklehead.

Gus is a huge, fluffy, supernaturally-enhanced attack dog, but my teddy bear is the killer.

"Why are we here?" Rusty asked. He was carefully using his body language to give Gus signals. It wasn't exactly an apology for being there. It was more like acknowledging he was entering Gus' territory—or my territory, or Pop's—and acknowledging Gus was responsible for it. "Is there something important in your Dad's workshop?"

"Not exactly. It's more a matter of where the workshop is."

"Is it built on top of an ancient center of power?"

"Ah... no. It's... well, it's set up so time goes by faster here."

"Huh?"

While I set up shop in Pop's workroom, I explained about alternate realities and time differentials. Not in detail, of course. It still took a while. Rusty sort-of followed, so I used the chalkboard—*of course* Pop has a blackboard and chalk in his workshop—to draw diagrams. He got the idea better with a visual aid. Rusty is more a nose person, I suspect, but when he's not a wolf, he's a visual person. Everybody has their own best way to learn new things.

"So, while we're here, every hour we spend here is a minute at your house? And everywhere else?"

"Kind of. It might not be a minute. It could be more or less. All I can say for sure is the clocks of everyone you know are running really slow compared to us. So, when an hour has gone by for them, we should be completely done with two healing gadgets—one for you, one for your Dad—and another moon-glass."

"Yay," he said, without enthusiasm. "I get to be a were-guinea pig."

"You also get free magical stuff. Don't knock it."

"Good point."

Rusty is a good sport. Now that I know he's the second son, I wonder if it has to do with never being the alpha in his family. His father was always in charge and Mark, as the older brother, was always expected to be the next in line. Did he learn to be an easygoing, go along to get along type? Or was it always his nature and his nurture had nothing to do with it?

I'll never know. And I'll never ask. He is who he is, and I like him. How he got that way isn't germane.

He held still for my poking and prodding, as well as a little stabbing and skewering. Werewolf regeneration is pretty fast. It's visible to the naked eye. Jab one with a needle and wipe away the drop of blood. It's healed. My healing amulet—a werewolf doesn't wear rings for obvious reasons—wasn't quite so fast, but it was still a great improvement. Normally, if you jab a werewolf with a silver needle they heal about as fast as a human does. With my amulet, in the time it would usually take to stop the bleeding, the wound is gone.

Not bad, if I do say so myself.

Adding a second spell to deal with burns, specifically, wasn't any harder. Pop developed a number of spells for stitching himself back together, but those tend to be a bit... what's the word? They remind me of "meatball" surgery. The objective is to save the patient's life—in the case of these spells, Pop's life—rather than deal with the ultimate reconstruction and rehabilitation of the patient. For that, Pop has all night to get better.

Used on merely mortal flesh and bone, the spells work, but they tend to be exhausting and not always a hundred percent correct. Oh, you'll live, but the wound might ache for the rest of your life. Yes, the bone will be intact, but it may let you know when the weather is about to change. Compared to bleeding to death, it's a small enough price to pay, but Pop didn't have a clue there might be long-term effects—by which I mean anything lasting longer than a day! How would he know? Until I came along, that is!

Once he knew they weren't working as perfectly as he thought, he finally got it into his head to refine them a bit further. He tested them on a bunch of normal creatures, first, of course, but he developed them for me. One of the revised spells was specifically for repairing fire damage.

Many forms of physical trauma involve putting things back together. Sure, your liver is now in six pieces and two of them are dangling next to your hip, but if you can glue it all back together, it'll recover. One arm-bone turns into eighty fragments, but it's a jigsaw puzzle and can be put back together. A sword-stroke may sever all sorts of nerves, muscles, and blood vessels, but it's not like you have any severed bits without a matching one. Tab A always has a Slot A, Tab B, Slot B.

This is a simplification, I know, but we're dealing with magic, not surgery. Or, no, we're dealing with magical surgery.

The problem with fire damage—or acid, or any of a number of other problems—is there are bits of you now *missing*. With a lopped-off limb, sticking it back on isn't out of the question, provided you do it quickly and don't have any other immediate plans. But when an eight-bladed mace carves a divot from your abdomen, you really can't gather up the missing pieces and stick them back in.

Well... I suppose you can, but the pieces are wiggly and gooey and doing that particular jigsaw is harder than you'd think. It hurts and there's a lot of blood coming out and a whole bunch of other things are working against you, but, *technically*, you could weld the pieces in place.

On the other hand, with fire the pieces are now ash. If your flesh gets cooked, the proteins are screwed. The cells are dead. The connective tissue is crispy. You don't stitch it back together. You don't glue it into place. You may stretch healthy bits across as a temporary covering, but you have to regenerate it wholesale. You need to make *new* pieces as replacements. You need cellular reproduction and a lot of it.

If I go to a butcher shop, I can assemble a pig from the pieces. All I need is thread, a kite, and a good thunderstorm to have Frankenpork. Assembling the sizzling pork chop, boiled trotters, and crispy bacon isn't going to work nearly so well. I might still get Frankenpork, but everything in the world is going to try and eat it.

Dealing with burns is *hard*. It's not complicated—oh, no! The simplest healing spell will deal with a burn—eventually! You body wants to fix burns anyway; the basic healing spell enhances your body's natural inclination and helps it along. This will repair the damage perfectly, but it will also take three things: Time, energy, and materials.

You can cut down on the time and, to a lesser extent, on the materials by using secondary spells. You need a spell to convert lots of stored magical energy into a much smaller amount of vital force. This keeps the cells dividing and growing. You also need something to balance out the drain on the rest of your body, since it's losing a lot of base materials.

Ideally, you have little bits of your body redistribute themselves, kind of like what Pop does with a stone-shaping or flesh-welding spell. You've got a lot of skin. Any of it loose? Let's tighten everything up and give you a facelift—and stretch threads of existing skin over and through the nasty burn you've got, interlacing it with a framework of healthy tissue. Got any muscle fibers in the vicinity? Maybe a few grams of it slide around, partially filling in the deficit from where the acid ate away at your hand—and, incidentally, forming a net along which to grow more. The tendons, ligaments, cartilage, bone? All doable.

And all risky. Don't lose a limb and expect to grow a new one by redistributing body mass. Not unless you're a vampire and don't care about things like shock, resource depletion, and so on. For us full-time living creatures, we have limits on those sorts of things.

Eat, drink, and be patient, because no practical amount of magic is going to get you on your feet again in time rejoin the fight. Plan to be laid up a while, recuperating and eating everything foolish enough to get near you.

Rusty wasn't too keen on the trial by fire test, but I promised him an anesthetic. When I demonstrated the nerve-deadening spell, he was amazed. I have to admit, Pop did a hell of a job on making things painless.

After we tested the fire-repair spell, Rusty flexed his now-unburned finger and shook his head.

"I don't want to see that ever again."

"I agree. It looks awesome, though."

"It's not your hand."

"True, but it's still amazing. How's it feel?"

"Stiff. A little sore. Like a sunburn, sort of, but all through the finger. It's weird."

"Does it hurt?"

"Not as such. It feels like it used to hurt, if that makes any sense."

"I'll add a lower-powered, longer-duration healing spell as a follow-up. It'll take over to handle any imbalances and leftovers from the main spell. Your regeneration doesn't do so well with fire, so a little touch-up work is for the best."

"Thanks," he said, still rubbing fingertips together.

A little later, he nodded appreciatively.

"I can feel it working. Everything is loosening up." He cocked his head, reminding me forcibly of a puzzled Gus. I will never, never, *ever* say so to him, but the expression was spot-on.

"I'm hungry," Rusty decided.

"Ah. That would be your metabolism trying to play catch-up. Let's go eat."

I took him into Cedar Rapids, driving Bronze's outfit. Sorry; the car she keeps in the Iowa garage. It's a big, two-toned steel monster, very much in keeping with the design aesthetic of the 1950s and with Bronze's love of high-speed bricks. She does appreciate aerodynamic things and all that stuff, but for day-to-day tooling around, she likes something solid and firmly planted on the road.

Rusty enjoyed touring what was, to him, the previous century. If they were parallel timelines, Pop's place was over a hundred years in the past. He especially liked the diner. It was the first one we came to, but the style was entirely on point. Chrome and steel and a lot of tile, with an aproned waitress and a big, clunky cash register at the end of the counter. We got a booth and I bought lunch, since I was the one with local money.

While he—again, ha ha—wolfed down his lunch, I managed to get through a sizable slice of calories, myself. It was a busy couple of days and I worked hard to get those enchantments hammered out. Even in Pop's overcharged magical environment—his house doesn't have a lot of demand—it wasn't a casual matter. It reminded me I needed to sit in an Ascension Sphere again, sometime, and see if it helped. The last two treatments certainly did. How many more could I take? Rather, how many more would be useful? I'm sure there's a maximum capacity for each individual, much the same as there's a maximum amount of muscle you can develop.

Is an Ascension Sphere like a workout, or like steroids? Will I gradually improve my capacity by working with high power? Or is the metaphor even valid? Does an Ascension Sphere accelerate your development, or does it actually enhance your potential? I'll have to ask Pop next time I see him.

Whenever that is.

Come to think of it, why would I have to ask him? I can find a pair of twins with moderate magical proficiency, have one work as a professional wizard and have the other stuffed in an Ascension Sphere. With comparison testing, I can answer the question.

Yeah. Pop might do that. I won't. I'll ask him and hope he already knows the answer. I don't want to accidentally cause him to go find out.

"I don't remember the last time I had a burger this good," Rusty observed, around a mouthful of lightly-carbonized cow.

"They use meat and nothing but meat."

"Big improvement over the veggie-fiber health substitutes."

"Hey, when the ecological impact of ranching is that big, you make sacrifices. Besides, most people can't tell the difference."

"Most people don't know what pure meat tastes like," he countered.

"You may have a point."

He slurped at his milkshake and rolled his eyes.

"This is so good. Can we come back here again?"

"Sure."

"And is it safe to talk about… stuff?"

"Not in public."

"Hmm?"

"I'll explain again, but not here."

"Oh. Okay." He fell back into chomping and I smirked a little. In this one way, he reminded me of Pop.

As I drove back toward Pop's house, Rusty asked if it was safe to talk. I told him to go ahead.

"I like this place. It's got flavor."

"It's a quiet little nowhere in the middle of nowhere, surrounded by nothing much."

"Aw, come on. You have to admit the food is good!"

"Granted. Nobody makes a good burger where you're from."

"New York?"

I sighed and explained again about multiple alternate realities. We made it back to Pop's place as I finished.

"Okay, so, we're presently in a world where it hasn't gotten past…"

"Nineteen-fifty-two."

"And I haven't traveled in time?"

"Nope."

"I'm in an alternate timeline where things haven't run quite as fast. So it only *looks* like I've gone back in time."

"Yep."

"I thought the universe was, what? Fourteen billion years old?"

"Something like that. The difference of a century amounts to an utterly tiny fraction of one percent. We could find a world a thousand years behind and it would still be a lot of zeroes in the 'point-zero-zero-zero whatever' percent."

"And you can find worlds where things have, uh, run faster? A thousand years ahead or more?"

"Want to find one where it's collapsing in on itself?"

"No, thanks. I don't like closed-in spaces."

"That's fair."

We went into the house and Rusty looked it over with more attention.

"So, this is where you grew up, huh?"

"No, not at all. Pop downsized to this place when I moved out to go live in New York in twenty-sixty…two? I think. I've been there a couple of years and the precise date isn't something I pay much attention to."

"Where did you grow up?"

"Good question. You're assuming I have."

"You'll always be a kid at heart?"

"That, too. I grew up in a bunch of places. We moved a lot to avoid awkward questions and the need to decapitate people. I'm a psychic witch, Pop's a vampire wizard from another dimension, and the locals are generally intolerant."

"I can imagine."

I recalled a time when a priest wanted to burn me at the stake. Then again, Rusty was a werewolf. How many people have wanted to murder him? Maybe he *can* imagine.

"How hard is it to get from one world to another?"

"Bloody damn tough. I can do it, but it takes a hell of a lot of effort. It takes even more effort to make a device to do the spell for you, but if you're going there more than a few times, it's probably better to make one. Pop made his closet so it would connect to my New York. Mostly so I could come home whenever I wanted and he could drop in to visit."

"I seem to recall you mentioning how Alden followed you here—I mean there," he mused. "It's been a while, so I don't remember exactly."

"A gate is different. It's a temporary doorway you step through. I, uh… well, I put a spell on a friend's closet door. I didn't think it would be an issue, but Alden did a lot of investigating after Pop and I left. He ripped information out of Cameron's mind and found out about it. It wasn't really a full gate, but Alden has at least a little magical training. He knew what it was supposed to do, from Cameron, and how Cameron used it. Alden figured out how to activate it." I shrugged.

"I don't know what he went through to get it to connect and open, but it wouldn't be impossible, especially with what Cameron knew about it. Power-intensive, yes. I guess it would be difficult in the sense of requiring great effort, rather than being overly complicated."

"The more I learn about this Alden guy, the more I worry about him. Are you sure he's someone you want to be kicking?"

"Only until his butt cheeks are keeping his ears warm."

"Ooo, ouch. Okay. If that's how you feel about him…"

"It is."

"…then I'm in. Let's do it. You've already got the vampires on his case, right?"

"I believe so."

"Good. So tell me all about him. Let's figure out how we're going to make his life miserable and short."

So I explained about Alden in all the detail I could. Psychic, priest, magic rosary, strong, regenerates, has magical abilities and stolen magic items, mind-controlling a lot a humans, and so on.

"Uh-huh," Rusty agreed, when I was done. "Okay, a lot of that I already knew, but it's good to have the whole picture. This is what we've got. What did there used to be?"

"I don't understand."

"Who is this guy? Where does he come from? Has he been in India, working on taking over? Has he been practicing his mind-control techniques as a psychiatrist? Did his parents know about his powers or did he make them forget? Did *they* have powers?"

"I don't know."

"Maybe we should find out?"

"Maybe we should. Are you busy today?"

"Nope!"

"Let me set up another time-ticker and we'll head back to my old house."

"How far is it?"

"Another world. Not this one. I told you about it, but it'll all sink in when I show you. We'll spend a week or two checking into Alden."

"A week? Hang on—"

"A week of local time," I corrected. "We'll still get back on the same day."

"Time travel confuses me."

"You're not alone."

We relocated to Shasta and took a few weeks to check up on Alden—who he was, where he came from, all that jazz. I had already done a little investigating when I came back to visit Cameron, but mostly it was about examining the people Alden had affected, not really digging into his background. Rusty and I were prepared to drive, sail, fly, or even take a gate to anywhere in the world.

I now have a deep and abiding sympathy for people who try to investigate Pop. Pop plants information he wants people to find, then simply doesn't generate anything else. He lives, if not off-grid, then at least off-radar. He doesn't draw attention to himself. He has a quiet little house in a quiet little neighborhood and he's the quiet neighbor who keeps mostly to himself, always has a friendly wave and smile, owns a wood chipper and a shovel, and never, ever bothers anybody.

You'd think more people would be suspicious.

As for Alden, he drew attention to himself. He was a preacher. He addressed whole congregations. He traveled. He made waves within the church hierarchy as he worked his way up to a position he liked.

And nobody remembered him.

Okay, I'm exaggerating, but Alden obviously did his nefarious work in my Shasta-world, too. People had their brains erased with greater or lesser degrees of obviousness.

There were a few exceptions. There were a bunch of locals who remembered him, but they remembered him as a visiting preacher. They were passerby, bystanders, tools, or pawns. They weren't deep in his councils. They didn't know anything about what he was doing.

Then there were people like Doctor Slade. The good doctor tried to investigate Alden and got his mind wiped. So did the private detective. So did everybody involved. It was as though someone simply lifted out wholesale chunks of information, like taking a file folder out of a cabinet. It left gaps, big ones, and he made no attempt to fill them in. Any memory problems you might have are your problems, not his.

How did we find all this out? Well, it helps when you have a nose for nervous people and a spell to detect psychic traces. I set up a spell to detect Alden's psychic signature and we drove around to find people. I asked questions. Sometimes they remembered seeing him, sometimes they had weird feelings about him, and sometimes they simply didn't remember—but they felt they were missing something. They knew something was wrong.

We started in Shasta, of course, but eventually backtrailed Alden to Sacramento. I did a lot more work on my psychic resonator detector, built a parabolic dish with a rhodium film, and vastly increased the sensitivity. It didn't help as much as I hoped, though. The range increased, but we started getting static. It was a background noise on a resonant sideband and it ate into our maximum range. Still, this let us find a lot more people Alden brain-drained, including Doctor Slade. At closer ranges, my detector could pick up the secondary psychic fingerprints Alden left behind.

I remembered Slade. He remembered me. He was not pleased to see me, but we managed to have a civil discussion. I don't think he wanted to be strapped to a table again. Alden left *that* memory intact, of course. Jerk.

Slade was as helpful as he could be, which wasn't very, considering what Alden did to his memory. What did Slade find out? I'll never know. Nor will Slade.

After much searching and many interviews, Rusty and I came to a few conclusions.

First off, Alden did a good job of hiding his existence in the Shasta world up until a few years ago. Farther back than that, he did a perfect job of it. I say it was perfect because we didn't find anything real or true. Not one thing. At all. It doesn't mean there weren't clues to be found, but they were too well-hidden for us.

Second, about five or six years ago, local time, he decided to become a priest.

Third, he didn't have a religious conversion. He didn't go through the usual process. He decided he wanted to be a priest and convinced a lot of people he was one. There were four people at Catholic University in Washington, D.C. who remembered him, or thought they did. These memories included his time at the university and what a wonderful candidate for the priesthood he was. They would swear he went to lots of classes and graduated with academic honors.

I checked. The memories were altered. I didn't bother to check the records. Any signatures on the paperwork would be genuine, not forgeries, although they might not remember signing anything.

In Rome, there were more people who had their thoughts rearranged so they would swear they were at Alden's ordainment, they worked with him, et cetera. These people were clearly there to be references if anyone asked. Again, I didn't bother to ask or check on paperwork.

So, five or six years ago, Alden decided to become a priest. Prior to that, he didn't exist. He was a shadow, a ghost—he stayed out of society and stayed quiet. Maybe he was a trust fund millionaire and enjoyed himself. Who knows? Then, one day, around the time Pop and I showed up in this world, *bam!* Time to be a priest.

Why? What was he after? And the question I keep coming back to: What changed?

My first and worst feeling was Pop was somehow responsible. The timing implied it, but it didn't prove anything, so I shoved the idea aside. Pop is powerful and has immense reach, but the universes don't revolve around him. There are lots of other things that could have happened.

"Name three," Rusty challenged. I had to think about it.

"Maybe he finally found a local magus—a real one, with ancient spells—and sucked up enough information to become a sort of low-grade wizard?"

"And so he joins the Church? He becomes a Catholic priest and then fakes his way through other denominations on his way to... what?"

"All right, maybe it doesn't make sense," I allowed. "I'm spitballing."

"Next shot?"

"He—" I broke off, because, related to the low-magic world, I had a thought. When Pop fired a brute-force shift-spell from another universe, it was like taking a hammer to Big Ben. Well, not quite. Maybe it would be more like a cannon firing, shorter, sharper, but still immensely loud. For those with the proper sensitivity, it would have been at least audible—if that's the word—halfway around the world. The local wizards probably didn't know what to make of it. I'm sure Alden didn't, either.

If you're a local wizard and you hear such a thunderclap, you check the weather. Are you about to have a problem? Is there something going on? Is there any sign of upcoming trouble? No? It all seems pretty normal? That's reassuring. After a day or two of continued nothing, you go back to normal routine.

On the other hand, if you're a powerful psychic with a burning desire to find another wizard and rip knowledge from his brain, you take it as a clue and go hunting for the source.

But this puts Pop back in the spotlight as the reason for Alden doing things. Alden didn't even know Pop existed! Why would he bother us, specifically?

And, in the back of my mind, I heard myself saying, *He didn't know what made the thunderclap, but he was looking for it in California.*

Dammit, Pop. I'm drawing a blank on other ideas!

So, as a working hypothesis, Pop rang the mystic gong by arriving. The base Earth-world split, branching off the Shasta universe. Alden noticed the...

Hmm. Did he notice the mystic gong of a brute-force gate opening, or did he notice the world splitting off? Pop said something relevant about looking for Alden to research him, but the exact thought escaped me. What was it?

Rusty kept an eye on things in our hotel room. We were in Rome, investigating the psychic traces and hadn't yet gone back to Shasta. Rusty likes flying and loved the planes of the era. In his world, even the dirigibles had cramped passenger space. They were mainly for use as cargo transports, skygoing versions of the seagoing cargo ships. The planes here were of an older type, designed when air travel was supposed to be glamorous and comfortable.

I decided I needed to hunt down the exact thought, which meant taking a trip into my memory. I lay down, went into my headspace, and went hunting for it.

What was it Pop said? It took a while to dig it out. My headspace library isn't as organized as his. Pop is ancient and brilliant and his mind is like the superalloy turbine of a high-power jet engine, sucking in everything and turning it to his use. I grew up with his influence, but he's got more native talent than I do, not to mention experience.

I remembered. Pop searched for Alden, looking for him with a gate search. This would find him in multiple realities, whether they be Earthlines or voidworlds. But Pop didn't find *any* others.

How the hell do we have an Alden in a branched timeline without an Alden in a base Earthline? The only way I could see for this to happen was for Alden to somehow discover the branched timeline—Shasta—and *leave* a base Earthline…

No! That won't work, either. When you branch a timeline, you copy everyone. Somewhere, there's a Cameron, still in his wheelchair, who never met me. The one *I* know is recovering in a funny farm. Therefore, in the same base Earthline, there should be an Alden who never met Pop, never met me, and has no idea we exist.

But there *isn't*.

So *how* do you get a unique being in a branched timeline? I don't see how it's possible! Where did he come from!?

I came out of my headspace in a foul temper. Rusty, wisely, didn't say much. He took me out to eat, instead.

I will say this: Dining outdoors in Rome on a lovely summer day makes it hard to stay grumpy. It didn't hurt that the wine was good and the alfredo sauce was almost exactly like the kind Pop used to make. Family loyalty demands I say his is better.

It's been a long time since Pop made a meal for me.

"Feeling better?" Rusty inquired.

"Yes, damn you."

"This is a bad thing?"

"I was enjoying being grumpy."

"Everyone has their little oddities. Want to tell me why you were grumpy? It might make you grumpy all over again."

"Good thought." So I explained about how timelines and branches work, and how this made it impossible for Alden to exist. I then braced myself for the inevitable stupid questions.

"I don't really understand everything, yet," Rusty began, and I nodded for him to continue. "If I get it wrong, tell me when I get to the wrong part, okay?"

"Okay."

"You have a basic timeline. Alden exists in it. Yes?"

"Sure."

"You tap it with a chaos gate thing and make it branch off."

"Yep."

"Afterward, you have two worlds, one where the original timeline still exists, and a temporary, unstable timeline. Sort of a 'what if?' timeline that only exists because 'what if you showed up through a chaos gate thing.' Am I following?"

"I think so."

"Alden only existed in the branch, not in the original timeline. Yes?"

"Yes."

"And he started doing stuff—making waves—after the branch was created."

"As far as we've seen? Yes."

"Is it possible he was created when the branch was created? Some sort of anomaly?"

"I don't think so. He'd have to be a chaos manifestation—I think. If he was, Pop would have recognized it in him instantly. I've been close enough to him; I would have recognized it, too. He's playing with celestial forces, so chaos entity is out."

"What else is there? Or, maybe a better question, is there anything that can exist in a basic timeline and in a branch, but doesn't get copied?"

"All material beings get copies. There are celestial entities on the associated energy planes, but those are energy planes, not material ones. I don't know how they relate. I don't think they get duplicated because they're not actually tied to the material planes. Alden, by contrast, is a physical being. He's rooted in... Hmm."

"Hmm?"

"I had a moment where I wondered if Alden somehow managed to gate from a base reality to the branch, but that doesn't figure, either. If he could gate between worlds, he wouldn't think Pop was a time traveler. Then again, there are weak places between worlds where you can wind up in an alternate reality by accident..."

"You said the first gate was a big signal to everyone with enough sensitivity. Could he have heard it and gone looking?"

"Maybe, but he would have still been stuck in the base Earthline. I'm not sure how it works, exactly, but the base Earthline goes on without being affected while the branch splits off, and Alden would *have* to at least start in the base Earthline."

"Maybe he found a weak place, later?"

"He found it pretty fast, then, and they're neither common nor easy to detect. And he would have shown up twice in this world—the original, from the baseline, comes through the thin place between world, and finds the copy created by the branching."

"So, whatever happened happened right around the time the world split in two?"

"I think so. It matches up with what we've found and the timetable of events here."

"Can you tell when a timeline is splitting?"

"I don't know. I'm not in a base timeline. We're in a branch."

"Oh."

"But you raise a good point. Maybe there are entities who sense when there's a timeline split. If so, they may also be able to pick which leg of the timeline trousers they slide down. It doesn't make a lot of sense to me, though, as the only things that should be able to detect shenanigans on such a level have a connection to a higher energy-state reality, giving them a bit more of an objective viewpoint. One not so limited by the material realm."

"And Alden doesn't?"

I thought about the celestial energies he used. As a priest, he might be able to do all of that, provided he had a close enough connection to a celestial energy-state entity. Or, come to think of it, if he was actively using such energies at the moment of the branching... If he was directly linked to a celestial plane, drawing on those powers, his perceptions would definitely be in an altered state.

"This line of questioning is starting to get above my pay grade," I confessed. "I'll have to call in a consultant."

"Oh? Who?"

"I have a crazy uncle who knows about this kind of thing."

"I look forward to meeting him."
"I'll get out a dustpan."
"Hmm?"
"You'll see."

Journal Entry #25

Once we were back in Rusty's world—my world—I got out a pie tin and a couple of spoons of flour. I've watched Pop use flour power to see god, but I never actually tried it myself. Still, I had the hard part handled; my mirror's frame has one of Pop's micro-gates on it. When I want to go places, the frame acts as a target for a gate transfer, but the micro-gate does the work. In this case, the micro-gate could open a brute-force hole to Uncle Dusty's energy plane so he could reach the pie tin and use it to communicate. The spell to form a dust-cloud face wasn't hard. Making the pie tin vibrate to produce sound was even easier.

After an hour and a half, I was ready to try it. I was pretty sure I duplicated the spells I saw on Pop's dustpan, but no doubt Uncle Dusty would figure it out. I should have done my spells before I came back, but I didn't think of it. I don't know how Pop keeps all the time differentials and whatnot straight. The man is a genius, that's all I can think.

I put a dynamo on either side of the Pie Tin of Revelation and invoked the Spirit of Whole-Wheat Organic Flour, sprinkling the powder liberally as I sent a thought out to him.

Oh, you have got to be kidding Me.

"What? I'm calling to ask if I can open a gate near you."

Never mind, I heard him sigh. *Concentrate. I'm sending you gate coordinates.*

He did so and I opened the micro-gate on the mirror. A blaze of white light shone through it, like being inside a giant pinhole camera. I felt the energies of a celestial plane as a needle-fine jet of power sprayed into the room. It was a warm, pleasant feeling of energy, like stepping out of a chilly hotel onto the sunny, tropical beach. I carefully waved a hand through the spray of energies, feeling the almost electric tingle as each finger slid through the brilliant light.

The flour on the pie tin heaved up, wriggled around, worked through all sorts of distortions, and settled into familiar features. It spoke, mouthing words amid a terrible buzzing and rattling. Gradually, the voice became more comprehensible.

"Testing. Testing. Alpha, Omega, Revelation, Damnation. Is this thing on? A-one, a-two, a-one-two-three-four, *bang!* Can you hear me now?"

"That seems to be doing it," I agreed. "Did I not get the spells right?"

"They work, but the... uh... hmm. The settings are a little weird? I'm playing a saxophone when I should be playing a clarinet, or something. It's not totally unrelated, but it's different enough I have to figure out how to use it."

"I'm sorry."

"No, you did a good job. Very simple to use, very well-crafted. It didn't take Me long to figure out how to interface with it."

"I'm glad."

"So, what merits the creation of a...?"

"Pie Tin of Revelation."

Uncle Dusty's eyes rolled like Las Vegas dice.

"Someday," he complained, "I would like something a little more formal."

"When I have a chance, I'll see what I can do."

"Promise?"

"I promise."

"Okay. What's on your mind?"

"First off, Uncle Dusty, meet my friend Rusty. Rusty, this is my Uncle Dusty. Rusty is a werewolf. Uncle Dusty is a demigod."

"Not there," Uncle Dusty corrected. "Where you are, I'm just a friendly spirit. Nice to meet you, Rusty."

"Likewise? I'm sure?"

"Relax. If you're going to hang around with My niece, you're going to have to get used to a whole lot of weird. Most of it isn't even her fault."

"He's not wrong," I agreed.

"I'm coping," Rusty said. "So far. Are you really a demigod, somewhere?"

"Depends on what world you're in. Here, I don't have much in the way of worshippers and it's hard to focus any real power."

"What about the micro-gate?" I asked.

"What leaks through isn't Me. It's bleed-through from an energy plane. If I tried to push power through it, rather than use it as a communications channel, it would rupture the connection. Kind of like trying to use old-fashioned telephone wire to connect to a wall socket."

"Oh."

"We're going to need to discuss ways to shield it, by the way. It's a bright spot on the map where celestial forces are in play. Minor ones, but the gate stands out right now."

"Pop never seemed to have a problem."

"He either builds the thing inside a device specifically for Me, or he casts additional shielding and grounding spells to minimize the celestial signature."

"Oh. I never knew that."

"I'm guessing he never anticipated you would try to build your own diviniphone."

"Yeah. Until I get new shielding spells, I should probably visit."

Rusty's ears perked up as he swiveled his head back and forth between the ghostly dust of my uncle's apparition and me.

"Good idea. You seem in good shape, so to what do I owe the pleasure of your call? Does Rusty have a problem?"

"Not me!" Rusty declared. "I'm fine. I'm great. Pretend I'm not here!"

"No, it's me," I added. "I've hit a wall with Alden and I'd like your help investigating him."

"This is the psychic priest trying to take over the world, right?"

"That's him. We've talked about him before."

"Yeah, and I promised to help if you needed it. What do you want done?"

So I explained about how Alden couldn't exist, not as far as I understood it, finishing with, "...but he uses celestial energies a lot, so I was wondering if he might be a unique being of an arcane or occult sort. If so, could he go sideways when Pop created a branch?"

"That's a good question." Uncle Dusty looked thoughtful. "Energy-state beings aren't copied in a branch; we exist outside the material universes, so we're not affected. Then again, if we're incarnate on a material plane, is that enough to duplicate us, or does the branch develop an unpossessed version, or what?" A hand came into view as he pulled at one cheek, thinking. "Where is this guy?"

"Zeno!"

A moment later, I had a map displayed on the monitor in my witchroom. A pulsing red dot marked Alden's location. He was somewhere downtown.

"I'm going to need directions," Uncle Dusty said.

"You can't just look for him?"

"He's wearing your Pop's devices, remember? He's cloaked. I couldn't find him with a flashlight. I'll need help zeroing in on him. Once I *find* him, I shouldn't have any trouble *looking* at him, but finding him is the hard part."

"Okay. What do we do?"

"I'll split My attention," he decided, sounding tired. "It's a good thing I've got freshly fueled reactors," he added.

"Isn't it, though?" I answered, smiling sweetly and batting my eyelashes.

"You sit down and believe in Me. Give Me the extra traction, okay?"

"Sure thing. Hey, Rusty," I asked, "can you believe in a god? A minor one, for a little while?"

"What do I have to do?"

"Concentrate on the fact I exist," Uncle Dusty said, "and think positive thoughts about having me around, on your side—that sort of thing."

"I can *definitely* think positive thoughts about you being on my side."

"Thanks. And can you get Zeno to shift from a street map to a satellite imagery map? One of Me is going high and heading down."

We sat quietly for a bit while Uncle Dusty did whatever pipsqueak demigods do when locating, observing, and analyzing strange psychic anomaly people. He flickered above the Pie Tin of Revelation for quite a while, frowning in concentration and occasionally asking for further directions. Finally, he relaxed and let out a well-milled sigh.

"Okay, I'm done."

"Fantastic! What's the sitch, Unc?"

"The situation is I'm having troubles with your father's gadgets," he grumped. "The sneaky thaumaturgical son of a— Um. I mean, the guy has upgraded his angel defenses. I can't find Alden, but we expected that. Turns out I can't *see* Alden, either, even when I'm looking right at him. I see a generic human being. The only clue I have is a discrepancy in size. Alden is physically bigger than the illusion says he is, but the illusion still overmasters my celestial vision."

"Can you probe it?" I asked.

"If I can get a target lock on him, yes, but I'll need eyeballs on the subject. Even then, it'll take more power than I have available in this universe to break it. On the other hand, I have an idea."

"Oh?"

"If you'll dial up your gate, I'll come visit. A physical avatar carries with it a better connection than I presently have, and it can also carry around a stored charge. Think of it as bringing along a power crystal and a couple of solar conversion spells. I'm guessing it's a valid comparison."

"Oo! Excellent! I know a fantastic pizza joint just off Harlem River Drive."

"Hey!" Rusty cried. "Is this safe?"

"For who?" Uncle Dusty asked. "For you or for Me?"

"For anybody."

"Looking at Alden is probably safe," he decided. "I won't be doing any active scanning, so any automated countermeasures shouldn't notice. You don't want them going off every time an angel-occupied body glances in your direction. As for the pizza, I think I'll be okay. I don't worry about cholesterol or garlic."

"Yeah, but... but... yeah, okay. Whatever."

"If you think it'll be a problem," I suggested, "maybe we could get a take-out order? They make a really good pie."

"She's right about that," Rusty agreed.

A few minutes later, I was introducing Uncle Dusty and Rusty again. Rusty gingerly shook hands with him.

"You don't look like your... dust?"

"The dust is a self-image," he explained. "I'm possessing this body."

"Oh. Well, that clears up everything."

"Good. Are you getting the pizza, or is it a delivery?"

"I'll go get it. The delivery fee this far south is pretty steep."

"Thank you. I appreciate it. Remind Me to do something nice for you."

"Uh... sure. Phoebe, I'm gonna go now, if that's all right."

"No problem. I think we'll do a little drive-by observation, maybe a walk-by, depending."

Rusty took a cab. Uncle Dusty and I went down to the basement garage and I used unladylike language. Janice's stuff was still jam-packed in my car.

"Problem?" he asked.

"Potentially, but not right now. Help me unload all this."

"Happy to." We opened all the doors and stacked everything against one wall, out of the way. It went quickly, thank goodness, so we weren't too far behind. I drove Uncle Dusty to the coordinates Zeno gave us. I noticed he reflexively held on to the grab handles in the car.

What can I say? I was in a hurry and Bronze taught me to drive. The first things I learned were how to operate the vehicle in a competent, efficient, precise manner. We went over the basic rules of the road after I learned to handle the machines.

You should see me drive a tank. Whee!

Alden was having a late lunch, or maybe a high tea. The restaurant was one of those enormously expensive places where they take your credit card information before they book the reservation, and then they charge you a cancellation fee if you change your mind. If you're the sort of clientele who cares, you're not the sort of clientele they cater to, and good riddance, peasant.

Rather than force our way in—I have no doubt I could convince the *maître d'hôtel* we had a reservation whether we did or not—it would be an exercise in power and we would be noticeable to Alden. On the other hand, ever since the robocabs took over, parking was much less of a problem in Manhattan. We found a spot with a view and waited. A little conversation with Zeno told me he'd been in there for quite a while, so he was due to exit the building.

Uncle Dusty and I chatted a bit about life in Manhattan, the local vampires, werewolves in general and Rusty in particular. Alden came out in less than half an hour and a car— driven by a human—pulled up next to the curb.

I watched Uncle Dusty as he glared at the priest. Alden, for his part, paused before getting in the car. He looked around with what I can only describe as unease. Alden turned away, suddenly and sharply, ducking into the car. He must have said something to the driver because the car pulled out into traffic and rushed away.

Uncle Dusty frowned.

"He felt My gaze," he noted.

"Is that bad?"

"I was going to say it was impossible, but I should qualify that. It's impossible for a human."

"Do you know what he is, then?"

"Let's go back to your place, pick up the pizza, and take it to My place. I'm starved and this discussion will go better over food. And I haven't had a pizza in forever."

"Do I bring wine or beer?"

"Yes, please."

"Oh, it's one of those."

We met Rusty at the house, sorted out our travel plans, and hustled through a home-made gate into a Reactor World.

"Put the pizza there," Uncle Dusty said, indicating the break-room table. "I'm starved."

"I hope so. This thing is meant to feed eight."

"We can get another one if we have to. We're a lot closer than you think. I have no doubt My niece can put the far end of a gate in the building."

I got out the dishes and Uncle Dusty scooted chairs into position.

In between mouthfuls, he answered my questions. I'm going to skip over the munching and slurping to hit the high points.

Alden wasn't fully human. He was human, yes, but one of his immediate ancestors was an energy-state being. Uncle Dusty theorized that, as a full-on avatar, if he sired a child and invested it with celestial forces, he might be able to produce something like Alden. The results might vary, depending on the exact methods, but it ought to result in something at least like a mythical hero—say, Perseus or Hercules.

It was obvious, once Uncle Dusty had physical eyes on him. Pop's cloaking gadgets didn't extend to hiding a celestial presence on the energy planes. Pop doesn't have one, so why hide what you don't have? Much like Alden's psychic forces shining through, his quasi-celestial nature did, as well.

However, Alden, being attuned to celestial forces, noticed Uncle Dusty's regard.

"The weird thing," Uncle Dusty said, wiping at his mouth after the last of the pizza disappeared, "was the way he seemed to have so much force behind him. In electrical terms, his amperage wasn't anything special, but his voltage was higher than I expected. He's practically crackling with celestial energy. As far as anyone on a physical plane is concerned, anyway."

"I think I can explain some of it. He has these bits of glass—tektites—and they resonate with his powers. Pop says they do something, amplify them somehow. Alden's been collecting them and adding them to his rosary as beads. He uses them for power points where he wants to produce a celestial effect, too."

"Tektites?" frowned Uncle Dusty. "That doesn't make sense. What does meteoric glass have to do with celestial energies?"

"I don't know they do. He's psychic and they hum along with him, like backup singers to his lead vocalist. Want to look at one?"

"A psychic tektite?"

"One that seems to have weird psychic resonance properties."

"You've got one?"

"Sure. I've been researching Alden preparatory to kicking him into an abandoned, empty world until he learns to play nice. The tektites might be a problem, so I wanted to know more about them. Still do."

"I'd love to see a tektite. At your convenience," he added, as I rose from the table. "No rush. I'm not in a hurry."

"So, is Alden a fair fight for you?"

"As an avatar? I'm going to say he isn't. In your world, if he somehow managed to sucker-punch Me as his opening move, I would be in for a bad time. Even so, if he doesn't drop Me with his opening shot, he doesn't have the endurance to go for long. Worst case, I'm still pretty sure I can take him."

"If you two do get into fight, is there anything I should do?"

"Shoot him. It will break his concentration."

"One in the leg?"

"I was thinking more along the lines of two in the chest, but My holy scriptures have specific things to say on the subject of kneecaps. Or they will, when I get around to writing them."

"You're as bad as Pop."

"I don't particularly like the guy, so kneecapping him doesn't seem unreasonable."

"I suppose it wouldn't be."

"Now, talk about these tektites."

"I don't know much about them, aside from the usual for tektites. Alden uses them as psychic amplifiers and as focus points for celestial energy effects."

"Yeah, you mentioned that. I thought you said they were psychic?"

"They have properties for both," I clarified.

"Do go on."

So I explained about the celestial-energy areas on bridges and in tunnels. Rusty paid close attention, too.

"I take it back. Go get it. I think I need to see this tektite of yours," Uncle Dusty decided.

"Sure. Mind if I power the gate from this end?"

"Help yourself."

I used the gate spell I built before to get back from a trip to Uncle Dusty's place. I stepped through, picked up the warded box with the tektite in question, and stepped right back into the Reactor World. Elapsed time, four seconds, tops. I unlocked the box and handed Uncle Dusty the black glass bead. It started glowing.

He held it in the palm of his hand and peered at it intently. It glowed brighter. A moment later, I shielded my eyes and turned away.

Rusty kept looking at it, at me, back at it.

"Do you not see that?" I asked, still shielding my eyes. As I spoke, I realized the light from the incandescent glass wasn't throwing shadows.

"See what? It's a rock. A shiny rock."

"It's radiating undifferentiated celestial energy," Uncle Dusty told me. "It's a side effect of being in a powerful field."

"It's not you doing it?"

"Only in the sense I'm concentrating the field around it."

"Oh. Would sunglasses help?"

"Probably not. You perceive it as a visual phenomenon but it's not really interacting with your eyes. You'll adapt to it."

"Okay. Figured anything out about it?"

"I think so." Uncle Dusty made a fist and masked the glow. "This isn't your regular meteoric glass."

"Well, duh. It's got psychic qualities."

"Yes, but that's not what I mean. It also interacts with celestial energies. It has to have been formed not only in a physical cataclysm, but in intense celestial energy fields."

"You're sure?"

"I'm sure. I may not know everything, but I know a lot."

"So these things are formed when… what? A fallen angel hits the ground?"

"That's one possibility, although I'm not sure how an angel can fall. They're not really free-willed, and this was made from physical matter, not an energy form."

"It would make them rare, at least."

"That's true," he admitted. "They would verge on nonexistent. No, what you're looking at is something like… oh… say a vampire tried to eat a saint. An angel might very well descend like a bolt of light to defend the saint, impacting the vampire and leaving a crater. Part of the superheated debris might, conceivably, form tektites. Of those, a few might become suitably aligned as they solidify in the intense field and become resonators, like this one."

"So, it's got to be a major, molten-gravel-producing incident, plus it has to involve a lot of angelic force?"

"Yep. Although it could be any celestial force. It doesn't have to be an angel, necessarily. The cataclysmic circumstances of formation probably wipe any sort of signature. It's like molten iron cooling in an intense magnetic field. Whatever it was before, the magnetic signature is completely different afterward."

I held out my hand and accepted the glowing little rock. It was warm to the touch and the glow diminished to something closer to a camping lantern.

"Okay, I can identify the things, but they don't seem to like me a whole lot. I'm human, so I don't have the proper celestial wavelength or whatever. Alden uses them, though. Is there a way to adjust the tuning on one of these things, or is he using rocks that only work for him?"

"I don't see any way to adjust the tektite to resonate with a specific pattern. I'd think anyone using celestial forces would be able to make it work. So, yeah, he's definitely like a mythological hero—a direct hybrid between a mortal and a celestial entity. That would class him as a Nephilim—a half-breed angel-human."

"Figures."

According to Uncle Dusty, the mechanism by which a possessed human body can sire a half-celestial being with a mortal is a straightforward one. I'm a little afraid of how he knows. Did he fall in love and have a kid? Or did he charm the pants off a lot of women? Or did he experiment with a thousand clones until he had a good data set? Or is it something much simpler—he asked another quasi-divine being and they told him? *How* he knows is not my first concern right now. *What* he knows is more important.

The angel doing the possessing—presumably a male, if only because of the time requirements—not only provides the genetic material of the host, but also a healthy dollop of celestial energy. Think of it as dipping the father's DNA in divine power before letting it bond with the mortal half. While this doesn't give the kid a battery of celestial energy, this does attune it to celestial forces.

"But what celestial forces? He's mortal, right? Nobody's worshipping him."

Well, sort of. He's a physical being, but not mortal. Instead, as a physical being, he acts as a sort of lightning rod, grounding out energy from the energy planes. While energy-state beings exist on the celestial planes, throwing energy at the material realms to create miraculous effects, this attuned mortal acts as a conduit for the ambient energy of the plane, itself.

"It's a different order of power," Uncle Dusty told me. "I work with my own energies, but he can draw on the energies of the plane."

"Why can't you? You're here and you're a physical being."

"It doesn't work that way."

"Why not?"

"You'll understand when you're older."

"First off, I'm capable of understanding now. Second, never say that to me again."

"Oh?" he asked, eyebrow rising. "Did your father never say that?"

"Never. He kept explaining until I got it, or I felt I understood it well enough."

"Did he? Really?"

"Really."

"Huh." He sounded surprised, not skeptical. "I wouldn't have thought he had the patience."

"Good. If you underestimate him, everyone will."

"I think I'll take it as a compliment. Sort of."

"In a backhanded way, maybe. So why can't you do what Alden does?"

"Okay, let me think a minute. I need to work out a metaphor."

"Take your time. Rusty? You have any questions?"

"*Tons* of them. None of which I care to ask because the answers will confuse me even more than I am now. I know when I'm ahead."

"I'm sorry. I promise, as soon as we have time, I'll sit down with you in a conjurer's circle and clear things up."

"I'm not even going to ask what you mean," he declared. "Why don't I clear the table? You two can get on with…" he trailed off, waving a hand at us.

"Thank you for all your help," Uncle Dusty said. "I appreciate it."

"Uh, you're welcome?"

"Phoebe," he went on, while Rusty did dishes. "There's no good way to describe this to someone tied to a flesh suit. What I'm about to tell you is wrong in many ways, but it's a good-enough working frame. Don't trust the details, but in general it should be close enough."

"Newton versus Einstein?"

"Closer to Aristotle versus Einstein. Look. The energy planes are a highly-charged environment. It's kind of like an oxygen-rich atmosphere. I can breathe here. Down there, in the material planes, I'm underwater. Fish may breathe oxygen, but there's so little of it, I suffocate."

"Alden's like a whale?"

"No… or not exactly. Let me start over. You know the various communication devices we use to talk from my energy plane to the material planes? They all have a key component. The itty-bitty gate. This direct connection allows the power of my highly-charged energy plane to ground out—somewhat—through the gate. It creates not only a conduit, but a charged area where I can manifest easily. The spells on the dust and whatnot make it even easier, which I appreciate."

"What if I opened a bigger gate?" I asked. "Could we funnel through a lot more power?"

"That's not relevant to the discussion, but no, it doesn't work like that. The… the material of the wormhole, if you'll forgive the imprecision, isn't really a conductor. It's an extremely thin-walled tube with chaos on the outside. The bigger it is, the less stable the tube—like blowing up a long balloon, sort of. If you put too much energy through this balloon-tube, it disrupts the unstable conduit and the whole thing collapses."

"All right, I get it, sort of. How does this relate to Alden?"

"The amount of energy coming through a gate is minimal, but it has its uses. Alden, with his celestial sensitivity, acts in much the same way. He's a type of grounding channel from a highly-charged energy plane to a relatively uncharged energy plane."

"Hold on," I interrupted. "If energy planes are charged and material planes aren't, why don't they discharge into material planes until they equalize?"

Uncle Dusty rubbed his temples and sighed.

"First off, this is a really bad metaphor, okay? Don't stretch it too far. Second, the chaos of the void acts as a dielectric medium in the energy ecology of the multiverses. Sort of. Again, it's not a great metaphor."

"Okay. Carry on."

"What I believe Alden is doing is acting kind of like a lightning rod. There's a lot of air between the clouds and the ground, but his celestial affinity allows him to act as though he's immensely tall. Celestial lightning pours into him when he reaches for it. He uses that energy to cause minor miracles."

"Setting vampires on fire is minor?"

"Igniting gasoline is difficult?"

"Ah."

"'Ah,' indeed. I will bet any money you care to name he doesn't cause earthquakes, meteor showers, part seas, walk on water, or any of a number of other, more material effects. He directs celestial energy into specific effects, or he metabolizes it to empower his psychic abilities, his physical strength, his body's ability to heal itself, and so on."

"Gotcha. He's a fire, like everyone else, but he has a pipe to bring in at least a little pure oxygen."

"Enough to burn very brightly, indeed. And his fire is bright enough and hot enough to do things mortals can't. Not much more, perhaps, in the greater scheme of things, but enough to be interesting."

"And the tektites?"

"I'm not a hundred percent sure, but if he can put his own celestial imprint on them, he might be able to set them to do something in particular. The vampire-roasting areas, for example. If they have a connection established to an energy plane, they may be used as transformers to achieve a specific effect. If they're not suitably tuned or imprinted or whatever, they may only act as amplifiers, resonating with celestial frequencies to increase Alden's conducting capacity."

"Does this do anything to you?"

"To me? No. As far as we celestial sorts are concerned, it's like a fish learning to breathe air. We have lots of air up here. We don't even notice it. But it matters a lot to you guys, down here, under the surface of the water. Now, if he learns to eat faith, then we're going to get interested in whose faith he's eating and how to keep him out of ours. He's a big fish in a small pond, but we don't live in ponds." He grinned. "We do, occasionally, go fishing."

"Okay. Any chance I can get your help shutting him up and shutting him down?"

"Sure. Always happy to help a relative."

"Me, too. I'll figure out how I need you to help when my plans get a little further along."

"I'll be here."

"Good." I pushed back from the table and stood. "It's been a good chat, Unc, but I've got to get back to my world. There's an angelic half-breed I'm planning to punish and I'm pretty sure I should tell the local vampires what they're getting into."

"No doubt. I'll keep an ear on you, so shout if you need me."

"Will do. Rusty?"

Rusty, by the break-room sink, turned off the water, dried his hands, and came over.

"All set," he said.

"All done?"

"I washed dishes in the restaurant since the time I could see over the sink."

"I thought you were surprisingly good at that. Let's go."

Rusty and I stepped into my witchroom and I closed down the gate. The power budget wasn't pleased with me, but it could have been a lot worse.

I'm starting to realize why Pop had a generator hooked up to the house's natural gas line. Forget the local power grid. Run the generator all the time and dedicate it to magical energy production. Sure, sure—connect it so it can switch over and power the house in the event of an outage. In the meantime, let it sit quietly in the basement, humming away, keeping the gate crystals charged. That man is more forward-thinking and practical than I ever realized.

"Phoebe?" Rusty asked.

"Yo."

"Um. I don't want to be pushy or anything, but are you going to explain about the conjurer's circle and everything else?"

"Oh. My conjurer's circle is a diagram on the floor. It'll help connect our brains telepathically so I can communicate what I know in a hurry."

"Connect our brains."

"It's the quickest way."

"I don't suppose you could, you know, *tell* me?"

"That could take days."

"I already had the briefing you gave Jason, right? I'm up to speed on magic and vampires and so on. But you did *not* explain to him about your Uncle Dusty—or about your father, or about multiple worlds, or a whole bunch of other things I can't even list because I don't know about them. Right?"

"Yes. Which is why I want to download it straight into your brain."

"Will you think less of me if I admit I'm not comfortable with this idea?"

"Oh." It hadn't even occurred to me Rusty might not be willing to have a telepathic conversation. We'd had moments of psychic connection before. Often, in fact, especially when Jason and I were inside a building and people were escaping. Rusty, in four-legged form, is *fast*. I didn't even consider he wouldn't want it all downloaded into his brain.

Just because I grew up with it doesn't mean it's normal for anyone else.

"All right," I agreed. I thought about the diagrams I drew on the blackboard while explaining multiverse theory. "Let's move to the media room. I want visual aids. And do you mind if we mind-talk, too? Like we have before. Nothing more."

"Can do."

"Thank you. It'll make this go a lot faster."

Journal Entry #26

It was late in the evening before Rusty was willing to call it quits. He had a pretty good grasp of the practicalities, but he was short on theory. Why did a gate connection cause a time differential? Don't care. It's magic. How does a shift-closet work? Don't care. More magic. Magic mirrors can see far away. How? Magic. If you really have to, you can open the mirror and step through. How? Magic.

I'm not sure I could stand not knowing. He understands what it all does and what it can do—the basics about how it works—so there's a big step up. He says he's fine with not understanding why it works, the theory behind it. I find that odd.

Maybe I shouldn't. I'm surrounded by people who use technology as if they understood it. They push buttons. They run fingertips over screens. They talk to invisible spirits—okay, voice-recognition programs—and make wishes. Later, the things they wish for are delivered right to their door.

Do they understand how it works? Do they know the theory behind a microchip? A supply chain? Digital banking systems? Anything at all about how it all comes together with machine precision to deliver wonders simply because you said you wanted them? No. Oh, the techno-wizards understand the technological spells, but the vast majority of people only use them.

I guess Rusty isn't too unusual in that respect.

While Rusty headed home to give his father the magic gadgets and go to bed, I called Jason. We had another virtual practice session scheduled for our cathedral raids, but I'd had a long day. Tomorrow night we would go through them again. I would work out a way to narrow down where the crystals were tomorrow. In the meantime, I was going to bed.

You know what annoys me most about growing up in the 1950s? Connectivity. Sure, we had a phone. I even had my own phone. It was mounted on the wall and had a long cord. If I didn't want to talk to anybody, I unplugged it.

Now the world is connected by invisible lines of electromagnetic force, constantly keeping everyone in touch, everywhere, at every instant. Instant messaging. Instant texts. Instant email. Instant phone call. Instant video call. Instant meetings. You can have as many different conversations going as your connection will handle—which is more than your brain will be able to process.

It was nearly midnight when my special phone rang. I was sleeping hard. Gus was curled up on his two-thirds of the bed and he licked me in the face when I didn't immediately answer. He's a smart dog, but I sometimes wish he wasn't quite so enthusiastic.

Since it was the phone linked to the relay in my old condo, I knew who it was. I didn't want to talk to Alden, but it was probably something important. The temptation to let it go to voicemail was a powerful one. I was still tired. Nevertheless...

"Hello, and make it worth it. Worth the boils and sores. Worth the permanent itching. Worth the incontinence and the hair loss. Make it *good*."

"Have I called at a bad time?" he asked, sounding amused.

"It's after midnight and I was asleep, so yes."

"My apologies. May I speak to your father, please?"

"He's unavailable."

"Still?"

"What do you mean?"

"I've left several messages."

I checked the phone. There were three voicemail messages. I knew I should have brought it with me.

"Yes, he's still unavailable."

"Wake him."

I counted to ten in Greek, French, and Japanese before answering.

"You've called me in the middle of the night, woken me up, and ordered me to do you a favor in a preemptory and demanding tone—and this is on top of constantly spying on me in a fashion more intense and worrisome than any celebrity's stalker. Did I miss anything, or is there something else to which I should take offense?"

Now it was Alden's turn to pause.

"If my tone was offensive, I apologize. It was not my intention. Urgency has demanded I attempt to reach your father. Perhaps I phrased my reply in a fashion not totally in line with my intent."

"That's a lousy apology and I don't accept it. You've got no goodwill here. What you do have is the opportunity for me to do Pop a favor. Tell me what you want and I'll relay a message in the morning, if I can. He goes where he will, when he will, and I'm not his keeper. I won't promise he'll get your message, only that I'll try to deliver it."

"That's not good enough."

"Then I won't bother." I hung up and plunked the phone on the nightstand. Gus, behind me, put his head in the angle of my neck and shoulder. I silently thanked Pop again for the anti-doggie-breath spell in his collar, then realized I was wasting the effort and thanked Uncle Dusty. He could actually *use* it. I'd thank Pop in person.

The phone rang again immediately. I let it ring four times before I answered it. I didn't bother to lift my head, just reached out, slid it between the pillow and my ear, and pushed the answer button.

"Molly Martin's Mutilated Meat Market. Special today: You guess it, you eat it free! This is Molly."

The silence on the other end was *deafening*. Could this be a wrong number? Was it even possible? Was it a deliberate transfer to another phone? Was it a joke, a trick, a prank?

"May I speak to Phoebe, please?"

"No. You had your chance." I hung up again. And, of course, he called back again. This time I answered in Italian.

"Vatican switchboard. How may I direct your call?"

"Phoebe!"

"One moment while I transfer you to the assistant manager."

"This isn't funny," he said, in English. I matched him.

"You think? It's past midnight and you keep calling a young lady after she's hung up on you. Twice. What are you going to do next? Breathe heavily and ask me what I'm wearing? Or have your minions take pictures of me so you can glue them to your bedroom ceiling?"

"That's not why I'm calling!"

"I don't know what else it would be. I already told you to stop bothering me. You cannot force me to do what you want, so I'm hanging up."

"I apologize."

"Eh?"

"I have called at an unreasonable hour because I have a matter of urgency. It is not a matter of urgency to *you*. I therefore request—politely—that you might be generous enough to deliver a message to your father at the first available opportunity."

"And why should I give any help at all to the thief who invades my home, assaults my Pop, and steals our property?"

"Because the fate of the world hangs in the balance."

"So you say. All right. I'll listen. If I disagree, I'll put the phone in a drawer and ignore it. Understand?"

"Perfectly," he replied. He had a trained voice. I couldn't tell a thing from his tone. My guess was he was plenty angry, but he needed something and was willing to go through the motions of being nice.

"Please tell your father," he went on, "that I would like to have a civil conversation."

"That's not going to get his attention," I argued. "He'll want to know why."

"I've already told you why."

"Oh, right. The fate of the world. Would you care to elaborate?"

"No."

"Even though he's probably not going to take your word for it?"

"I will only discuss the matter with him. I require his help and am prepared to make concessions to get it."

"Okay."

I hung up, turned off the phone, and rolled over.

One of the things bothering me was the way he said things. I get the impression he wants to talk to Pop because Pop is a peer. I'm merely an inconsequential apprentice and useless to his plans.

I don't want to be part of his plans. And, yes, I am just an apprentice—compared to Pop—but I am not inconsequential. I strongly doubt Alden is in Pop's league. I think he's in my league, although which of us is better remains to be seen.

It still rankles, being talked down to. Disregarded. Dismissed. You'd think I'd be more used to it, growing up an a patriarchal society where the little wifey was expected to stay home and take care of her man. And I am used to it. But being used to it and enjoying it are entirely different things.

I tried meditation, controlled breathing, even another pillow. Eventually, snuggling Gus, I finally managed to get back to sleep.

Journal Entry #27

I slept badly, woke up late, and had breakfast on my own. Almost. Gus sat beside me and was the very model of patience.

What did Alden want? What did he mean by "the fate of the world"? I didn't feel like phoning him up to ask. It was important to him, but did that make it important to me? Maybe. I keep my stuff here. I should find out what the problem was. I cannot imagine what could force Alden into asking Pop for a favor. They don't get along.

What would Alden want with Pop? They already had their arguments. Pop flat-out refuses to teach him magic and that's what Alden cares about.

On the other hand, I'm told Alden thinks Pop is a relative. The two of them had a conversation about how one had a mortal mother, the other a mortal father. Does Alden think Pop is an angelic half-breed? What does this say about Alden's ability to see inside people? It says he either never saw Pop at night or he never saw past Pop's angelic cloaking defenses. Or it says Alden can't see as clearly as Uncle Dusty. Maybe whatever sort of quasi-celestial he is can't automatically detect others.

Alden does want Pop's magic, that's certain. He might also want Pop to help him as a semi-celestial ally.

I chewed through breakfast, dumped entirely too much of it into Gus' bowl, and stormed into the computer room.

Zeno was no help. Intelligence analysis only showed Alden was still having regular talks with powerful figures on the city, state, and national level. He did, however, make a trip to the United Nations building to meet with an ambassador from Italy. I wasn't fooled. This meeting might be legitimate, but it was also a pretext to get him in the door and into proximity to a bunch of diplomats. Was this a stepping-stone to international leaders?

What annoyed me more than anything was the fact I could probably find out more by asking him.

Which was more important? Having an argument with a human-angel hybrid, or doing a drive-by on his favorite cathedrals to detect magical power sources? I considered it for a few minutes and decided I should probably have the argument.

I turned the phone back on, ignored a lot of missed call notifications, and waited. The phone rang once before he picked up.

"Mr. Kent?" he asked.

"No, it's Phoebe. Nice to hear from you, too."

"What do *you* want?"

"Is this a bad time?" I asked, sweetly.

"No, no. This is fine. Have you delivered my message?"

"Yes," I lied, "but Pop isn't interested."

"How can he not be interested? The fate of the world—"

"He really doesn't care," I told him. "He doesn't."

"How can he not care?"

"If the world ends, he'll go back to 1951 and live another hundred years before going back again."

"That's an extremely selfish attitude."

"What did the pot say to the kettle? Never mind. Look, I don't think he believes you. All he has is your say-so. If you want my advice, you'll tell him what the problem is. It's your only hope of getting him to take an interest. If you don't find a way to engage his interest, you won't hear from him. Trust me. I grew up with the man. I'm the expert. Listen to the expert!"

Alden did not reply, but I had the distinct impression his teeth were grinding together.

"Give me five minutes."

"Okay."

He hung up and I waited four minutes and eleven seconds. He called back.

"Are you somewhere private?" he asked, without so much as a greeting.

"Yes. I can talk freely."

"Now I can, as well. Listen closely. The undead are roaming the world in unprecedented numbers. I've never seen so many abroad at night. They've taken control of society and are exerting their collective will on the human herd. I've begun the process of liberating humanity from their dark enchantment, but they've realized what's happening."

"Oh? How do you know?"

"Last evening, I was on my way to a charity benefit. Someone shot me! They have been entirely too interested in my business of late, so I believe it was someone in their service."

I had a momentary flashback to a conversation about putting a hole in Alden's liver. Kudos to Jason for that one.

"Ooo, ouch. I take it you weren't seriously injured?"

"I do not wish to discuss it," he stated, flatly. Whatever else I could take from the conversation, he was not happy about being shot.

"Did the doctors at least recover the bullet?"

"It passed completely through."

"Oh. I guess it's a good thing. They stitched you up and released you awfully quickly."

"I said I would not discuss the matter," he reminded me.

"Ah. All right, vampires are stalking you at night. That's the problem?"

"It is *my* problem, not the larger one. The main issue is the control vampires have over mankind. It has become much more widespread in this era than in my own. I had hoped I might infiltrate my own influence, locate the puppets in key positions, and eradicate their hold. They have caught on much more quickly than I anticipated. While I have a few radical contingencies I can explore, I would rather unite the world against them. If I am to thus liberate the world from the forces of darkness, I now need help—real help—from someone with the power to fight these creatures."

"Hence Pop."

"Yes. I believe he and I share certain common traits. Surely, he will find my goal a worthy one."

"You do have a compelling argument. I'll relay it to him and try to make him see your side of it. I warn you, though, he doesn't like you at all."

"The feeling is entirely mutual. We have, however, an understanding."

"Oh? This is news to me. I thought he was trying to ignore you."

"He is. In fact, he has promised to do so as along as I fulfill my commitment. It is part of the arrangement. Now, will you please communicate to your father my information and my request?"

"You want his help... stopping? Eradicating? Overthrowing?"

"My ultimate goal is to eradicate all vampires. For now, I will settle for breaking their control over mortals."

"Okay. I'll see what I can do."

He hung up. Not even a word of thanks.

I called Jason and confirmed my suspicion. Yes, he followed Alden around, then posted himself at a good spot to watch and possibly shoot him. When the opportunity presented itself, he took the shot.

"He came out of the cathedral by a side door, late in the afternoon. It was still light enough out so the streetlights weren't on. He was a perfect target. One round, through the liver, as requested. Not bad for over two hundred meters."

"I agree. Well done."

"Thank you. I noticed he's out and about again today. He doesn't look happy, but he's moving. Do you want another round? Maybe through the shoulder? He's walking with a cane, so maybe the shoulder on the same side?"

"No, I think we've made our point. He'll be a lot less eager to go out at night. I'll also be interested in how long it takes him to recover. How big a hole did you put in him?"

"I used a high-power seven-six-two sabot round. I had the thing custom-made with a silver penetrator. The sabot was a semi-flammable plastic. They won't get ballistics off *that* in a hurry. The penetrator made a neat hole and buried itself somewhere in the pavement."

"How did he react?" I asked.

"He came to a halt. I think he was stunned for a second. He was a perfect target. Then he fled into the cathedral. Everyone around him did, too, but they didn't seem to be panicking. I didn't have another clear shot at him. He didn't scream when the silver went through him," he added.

"He might not care about silver. I suspect he doesn't. As for his companions-turned-bodyguards, either they were already under his control or he went to the effort of temporarily taking them over, at least to the extent of suppressing their fear and suggesting they should get inside. No doubt he then worked on their brains more extensively if he plans to keep his injury a secret. Assuming they weren't his to begin with."

"Good to know. Are we finishing our run-throughs tonight?" he inquired.

"Yes, but I hope to narrow down our targets today so we can focus on those buildings."

"Excellent. I hate not knowing which churches we'll have to remember."

"I'll take care of it," I promised. "Be aware, though: since Alden is nervous, his brain-drained minions may be in whichever building we target. In force."

"It's a semi-public building. A few dozen late-night attendees will be unusual, but not impossible. If there are enough of them to matter, there will be too many of them to hide."

"Maybe. We'll find out. I'm off to do my scans."

"Good plan. I think I'll take a nap."

While he had his nap, I showered, changed, and called an autocab. One advantage to the things is they let me concentrate on other tasks instead of worrying about traffic.

A review of our tracking showed us Alden favored four churches more than any others. While I couldn't put a scrying sensor in them and look around, I wasn't necessarily going to need to. I may not have the same hard-edged brilliance as Pop, but I'm brilliant in my own ways and I gave this specific problem quite a bit of thought.

In much the same way Alden emitted psychic radiation, powerful magical items radiate their own signature. Admittedly, Pop designed his stuff to be invisible in every sense but the visual, but my power crystals weren't. They were never meant to be hidden. Why bother? They were going to sit in my house, behind the house containment fields!

The static was still going to be a problem, but there wasn't much I could do about it besides punch through. My plan was to send out my most powerful detector pulse at the shortest possible range, get a bearing, and repeat the process at another angle. If the pulses were powerful enough, I should get a reading. Multiple readings would give me triangulation. Assuming I could slam a powerful-enough pulse through the static.

As the autocab drove me around Manhattan, past all the areas where Alden had a static field, I sent out my directional scan pulses, emptying a small power crystal with each one. I was careful not to aim any in a direction where Alden himself would be in the line of fire. I might or might not keep him from knowing about it, but I had to try.

I checked every site, not because I expected to find anything, but because Pop taught me to be thorough. I started with the four he favored. After the first three, I was thinking how disappointing it would be to get nothing. If I didn't get a detection ping, did it mean I couldn't penetrate the static, or mean my crystals were elsewhere? If I'd thought a bit farther ahead, I'd have run a control test with something on the street, outside a church, and tried to detect it from the street on the other side. Live and learn.

As it turns out, I didn't have to. Alden didn't have my crystals in the first three churches. I got a successful penetration and ping from cathedral #4!

The signal, however, had two things wrong with it. First, it wasn't a radar reflection from a power crystal. My scan pulse bounced off a *barrier*, not the target. I had a bad moment of wondering what that was all about until I recalled Alden had already found actual wizards. To a limited extent, he was a wizard—just not a very proficient one.

In the course of his life, Alden pried open wizard brains, taking from them what they knew about magic. It was an inefficient and wasteful process, losing the vast majority of the information he wanted. Worse for him, the wizards in question were hardly what I'd call professionals. Oh, they might have been professionals for their place and time, but Alden's source material was of poor quality compared to Pop.

I just had a chilling thought. Pop eats people. The inside, I mean; the spiritual portion. When he does, he gains part of what they know—thoughts, feelings, memories, skills. Are he and Alden more related than Uncle Dusty thinks?

Another horrible thought: Alden doesn't get much out of his mind-draining exercise. But Pop could train a whole class of beginning wizards and let Alden play catch-up by brain-draining the class, one by one. Pop would have issues with it, but Alden wouldn't. And I doubt Alden would be willing to sit at a desk and study like a good student. He strikes me as too proud.

Ick.

Anyway, horrible thoughts aside, I do know Alden knows at least a few spells. For one thing, he had a containment circle—needlessly complicated and known by rote, but a containment circle. No doubt there were other things, but he had a functional, unsophisticated barrier. It was a wall, a steel box, a vault. It had no other function.

It was a wall a scan pulse would bounce right off.

Okay, so I didn't get any reading from anywhere else. Here, I got a reading, but only because something in there was shielded. Something Alden went to the effort of deliberately trying to hide. I didn't have to ask myself what it might be. Alden had my crystals—and maybe other stolen goods?—stored down below.

Down below? Yes. Way below ground level. The scan pulses were like a square, headed away from me, and growing rapidly with distance. It defined a sort of pyramid shape, but it definitely covered belowground areas. I know old churches used to have catacombs and suchlike. The reflection came from considerably below street level, so I was glad I remembered to look deep down. I took careful readings—four separate sightings—and relayed everything to Zeno. I had a rough idea already of how far down the targets were, but Zeno ran the numbers.

Three hundred feet, give or take.

How in the holy hell did Alden get three hundred feet below ground level? I mean, it's Manhattan. Getting three hundred feet down isn't hard, just tedious. There are tunnels everywhere. But getting three hundred feet straight down under a church? Sure, they made catacombs, vaults, burial crypts, whatever. Did they dig them that deep when the church was being built? Or did Alden set his mindless minions to working on it, breaking through to other tunnels and working their way down?

I wish I could look inside. Well, I wish I could look down there. I could walk in and look around, no problem, but getting down into the basement was another matter.

On the other hand…

I stopped the cab, got out, and let it go. I put on my AR visor and went inside. Nobody gave me a second look—well, not for that—because people wear the things all the time. Tourists love them. They can wander around and record everything they see, sort of like taking your vacation video without having to lug around a camera.

Getting a good look at the place while Alden was elsewhere seemed a good idea. True, there was tourist video online already, but recent video? Detailed, high-resolution video? It seemed worth a quick look around to scope the place out.

The main doors were designed to look huge, but they were really part of the wall. The actual doors were standard fire doors, covered and decorated, one set of them in each of the three recessed faux doors. Inside was a narthex running the width of the building and three more sets of doors leading into the sanctuary.

I wandered around with a pamphlet I picked up out front, looking at everything, playing tourist. The perimeter of the narthex, its doors and windows. The nave, the transepts, all up and down the aisles, even—when no one seemed too interested in me—a quick swoop through the ambulatory behind the altar to check out the little chapels.

There were more doors than you might think. Some of them locked, some of them open, and one in particular—disguised as a section of wall in the ambulatory—with a brand-new, very modern lock.

I continued my wandering until I circled completely back to the front. I let myself out, grabbed an autocab, and went home.

The scruffier-looking people scattered around the pews never moved, which was a good thing. There were twenty-two of them.

At home, I went over everything Zeno could find about the place. He took my visor recordings and integrated them into builders' plans, other tourist photographs, official website information, the works. The result was an excellent render of the building, inside and out, suitable for doing an experimental walkthrough.

"But what can you tell me about the basement?"

The media room's holographic projector came up and the layout of the church appeared in blue.

"These are the church grounds and the known areas of crypts, catacombs, and other areas below ground level," Zeno chirped.

A red layout appeared and rotated, sliding into position relative to the church.

"These are the known city tunnels of all sorts. Maintenance, sewer, subway, and so on. I even included historical tunnels! These," icons blinked yellow, "are places where access is sealed off." Sections of tunnels turned orange, between yellow markers. "The orange areas are not accessible, but should have usable spaces if you want to go digging!"

Green icons appeared.

"By penetrating any of these points, a church-owned space could access extra spaces. Potentially," he added, brightly, as the green icons spread, filling areas of orange color, "these areas could be accessed covertly, without material risk of discovery by city employees."

"I don't think he's worried about them. How many places would he have to punch a hole to access the larger Manhattan underground?"

"There are many possibilities! Minimum is two. Any of these," little, colored stars appeared next to interface points, "and any of these," matching circles appeared.

"What have we got at the three-hundred-foot mark?"

"Six spaces, two of which are part of the crypts. Would you like to see footage from the virtual tours?"

"What's the latest footage? What date?"

"The last media uploaded from such a tour was eighteen months ago, Ma'am!"

"So, before Alden arrived."

"That's correct, Ma'am!"

"Can we narrow it down? The triangulated location, I mean."

"I regret the accuracy of the data does not permit further refinement, Ma'am!"

"Damn. I should have built another one of those telescope trackers and put it somewhere on the northwestern—" I broke off.

I'm an idiot. Pop raised an idiot. Pop would be so disappointed in me, he might even sigh. He would not be giving me a proud look, and I definitely wouldn't deserve one. I'm a complete and utter *moron!*

"Zeno."

"Yes, *Ma'am!*"

"How often does Alden go down below the church?"

"At least once a week. Every night he spends there, he is below street level."

"And how often does he go to the three hundred foot mark?"

"Every time!"

"Of *course* he does," I muttered, disgusted. "Show me."

Zeno obligingly added the thin, white line through the projected map to show all of Alden's routes up and down. He went through the same supposedly-sealed spaces to reach the city tunnels, so we marked those as open. He would spend an hour or two down in the city's underground, although what he was doing was impossible to tell; it was only a location fix. Usually, he would go back up to a sub-level of the church proper and spend the rest of the night there.

Priest quarters, maybe? Did they have a place where someone could stay? Or was it nothing more than a place with a bed and maybe running water? There was definitely a parsonage, or whatever you call it, on the grounds, but he didn't sleep there. He did remain within the walled border of the church building, itself, albeit lower down.

What really grabbed my attention, though, was the ten-minute detour. Every time he went down or came up—one or the other—he took a side trip, out of his way, to one of the crypts under the church. It was a moderate walk, maybe a minute and a half, so it wasn't an insignificant wander off the main path. Each time he went to a particular point and only emerged after several minutes. According to the time stamps, he sometimes stayed there all night.

"Mark that room," I told Zeno. "My crystals are there."

"Yes, Ma'am!"

"Hang on. What's with the time stamps?"

"Please elaborate, Ma'am!"

"This one doesn't say he stayed there from two in the morning to four. It says he was there at two in the morning *and* at four."

"That's correct, Ma'am!"

"So, where was he in between?"

"Those time stamp codes indicate when the system lost tracking on him and when it regained tracking."

"We *lost* him? He vanished from our sensors?"

"Yes, Ma'am!"

"Why didn't you tell me?"

"You didn't ask, Ma'am!"

I kicked myself a couple of times. It never occurred to me Alden might be able to hide from Pop's scanning system. I mean, Pop built it. Which, of course, raised the question of *how* he could drop off our radar. Maybe the barrier spell down in the dungeons was more extensive than I thought.

I planned to find out.

Journal Entry #28

Rusty came over, all excited.

"Dad loves your gadgets!" he gushed, without even a greeting. "He's never seen anything like them. Mom's impressed, too. I haven't seen her so shocked since Uncle Cosmo danced at cousin Luciana's wedding!"

"Is she, now? How nice. Not bad for a crystal-worshipping New Age vibration witch?"

"She didn't know any better," Rusty chided. "Now she does!"

"I should hope so."

"Oh, yes! Everyone does! The whole family thinks they're amazing! I can't tell you how many times I've been jabbed with a silver needle today. Dad, too. People were lined up to see."

"Lined up? How many people are we talking about?"

"Oh, about four dozen. Most of the family came around to see the silver-healing stuff. It'll be a little over a week before we can *really* show off the transformation gadget."

I did a quick check back through my mental calendar. I spent a lot of time in alternate worlds with different time streams. Yes, we were only a little past the full moon, now. It seemed longer. Rusty had dealt with the full and new moons in Shasta, so that's probably what messed with my thinking.

"I'm glad they like them."

"You have no idea. People are going to want to buy them. You're going to make a fortune."

I felt a moment of rising panic.

"Hold on! I didn't make these as advertising!"

"You're a professional witch, aren't you?"

"I'm a professional vigilante superhero. We knock over drug dealers."

"When's the last time we did that?"

I came to a sudden stop. He had a point. We hadn't gone on a midnight raid in… in… it felt like weeks. Not since the incident at JFK.

And it hit me, hit me hard, exactly what I did. And *why*. I was whacking criminals on the head, kicking them out of their nests, burning drugs, taking their money, and having a grand time doing it—all while not really making a dent in the whole operation. Fun, yes. Productive… purposeful… useful? No.

Jason was right. He was right about why I was doing it, at least at first. I was a kid on a lark, out to have fun. When did it change? When did I change? I used to look forward to finding a trap house and ruining their evening. Now it was all about aiming higher.

It's not fun anymore. It's all about plotting how to Make A Difference. Getting the whole "network," if I can call it that, in my sights. I shifted my focus and didn't even realize it. I no longer wanted to "waste" my time on petty criminals and dealers. I didn't want to micromanage a few blocks in Hell's Kitchen, or be a symbol of fear to a whole city's miscreants.

I've spent so much time wondering about Alden's motives and goals, I never stopped to ask myself what *I* wanted.

I wanted a supervillain, not street thugs. So, when Alden appeared, I wanted him as my adversary. Not as a problem for Pop to solve for me, but as *mine*. Batman has the Joker. Professor X has Magneto. Sherlock has Moriarty. I have Alden.

Which raises another question. If he's my supervillain, am I going to rehabilitate him? Am I going to lock him away for a year—or, if he's immortal, for a thousand—and hope he learns his lesson? If he doesn't, will I have to imprison him forever? Or will I have to kill him? How, exactly, is this going to end? Is he going to be in and out of an otherworldly Arkham? Or are we going to drop the polite and proper enemies thing and start going for the throat?

He doesn't want to kill me, obviously. He could have started a major conflict anytime. But he doesn't want me interfering, either, and he knows I'm capable of it. How is he going to take it when I swipe back my power crystals? Badly? Or can I spin this as me still not interfering—just taking back what's mine, and now we're even! Don't do it again!

As I thought about it, I realized something else. I didn't care if he took it badly.

All right, first things first. I'm the superhero. He's the supervillain, and he's winning. That needs to change.

"Well, I'm planning a raid on a supervillain's lair," I countered. "How's that?"

"I'm all ears, but I have to tell you—everybody in the know wants something to fix the silver issue. I told 'em the things are hand-crafted, but it doesn't seem to put 'em off."

"All right, all right. I'll make more," I promised, "but I'm not running a sweatshop."

"I'm glad. Wait until they get a load of the transformation thing, too!"

I had a future as a professional maker of magical charm collars, if I wanted it. I didn't, particularly. If there was such a high demand for these things, I'd have to figure out a way to make creating them easier. For now? Busy.

"We'll discuss it later. Come with me. I want you to wander around in a virtual environment and tell me what you think."

Rusty put on the headset, did the hand gestures for moving the point of view, all the usual stuff. He frowned a lot.

"Hey, are these people part of the Alden security force, or does this church have a soup kitchen attached to it?"

"I didn't find a soup kitchen. I'm pretty sure they're Alden's."

"Right. Still looking around."

"Carry on."

While he did his review of the site, I turned my attention to a magic mirror. I couldn't scry on the holy ground because Alden did something to his turf. I assume being part-angel was involved. Was it something he did consciously, or did it happen simply because he was there? No doubt Pop would study the phenomenon and figure out everything about it when he had a few minutes to spare.

My current question was less technical and more practical. How deep does "holy ground" go? Sure, if you map out the perimeter of the effect, it's got a shape. It's centered on the altar, generally, but the shape of the building also affects the geometry. It goes up into the structure, too, so landing on the roof is almost the same as stepping foot across the boundary line. No doubt the basement is also affected, as are crypts and catacombs. How far does this extend? To all the tunnels and rooms? Or does the effect go all the way to the center of the Earth? Or all the way through? Was there an antipode spot on the ocean floor to the southwest of Australia that counted as holy ground?

While I wondered about this, I sent a scrying sensor down into the more public tunnels of Manhattan and did more wandering around. Would it be easier to enter through the tunnels, or would it be easier to go in through the church?

I immediately came to two conclusions.

First, there were enough homeless down below to intimidate the entire police force of the Greater New York Area. Sure, there are a lot of cops, but these scruffians will run faster, hit harder, ignore injuries and tear gas, and swarm you. What are you going to do? Drive your urban pacification vehicle down there? It may work for the streets, but down in the tunnels you better be good at driving in reverse.

Second, the static-scrambling effect on scrying devices does go down that far. It does here, anyway. I tried mapping experiments, moving the sensor through solid rock until I could "see" darkness instead of glittery static. The effect did narrow somewhat from the ground-level perimeter and it petered out pretty quickly after reaching the lowest level of the catacombs.

I flew a few scrying sensors through the static and ran slap-bang into the barrier a couple of times. This caused the sensor to disintegrate and forced me to start again. The static was defense enough against scrying, so the barrier spell was overkill.

I admired his forethought and hated him for it. And for other reasons, but, at that moment, mostly for his forethought. Well, he knew he was dealing with a family of wizards, didn't he? I don't know why I'm surprised. Maybe I'm really upset because I already knew he had such spell! I should have seen it coming, anticipated it!

How hard would it be to bring down? Difficult, I decided. I couldn't see it to unravel it, and any containment spell is designed to be hard to break. I'd have to hammer on it until it cracked, which is power-intensive and possibly lengthy. Worse, at any distance, I'd be at a major disadvantage in any brute-force attack... plus, I couldn't see the thing, so I'd have to fire almost blind, hoping to hit. And if it held my power crystals, it could have enormous reserves...

I put the idea on hold and went to see how Rusty was faring. He was sitting on a stool and frowning as he turned his head, looking around.

"What's the verdict?" I asked.

"I don't like it."

"Not enough resolution?"

"The resolution is fine. It's the layout. I don't see how to get in and get out without blowing up half the place and setting fire to the other half."

I thought briefly about using a gate spell and my magic mirror to simply step in. I could get in—the gate wouldn't be stopped by the static—but getting out could be trickier. And the area with the barrier spell would still be off-limits...

"What problems do you see?"

"First off, going in through the subway means going through a lot of tunnels. Alden's got mind-controlled human zombies down there, right?"

"Yeah, and lots of them," I agreed.

"Which means we have to go through the top. Getting to the door behind the altar, in the ambulatory, isn't really an issue, I guess. They don't want to start anything in a public area. But it's not an insignificant door we have to go through. I know you can jigger it to open—you've done stuff to crackhouse doors, so I'm guessing this isn't much different?" At my nod, he went on.

"That means we go down into the basement. Do you know how many fanatical zombie guards he has down there?"

"Not a clue."

"And the ones on the pews may follow us through the access door?"

"Why follow? Wouldn't they try to keep us away from it?"

"Maybe, but I don't see how they can be effective while staying covert. Too many people wander in and out of the public areas. You can't have them jumping anybody who strolls along back there. I think they're tasked to let anyone through, but to keep anyone from coming back out. They can follow you through and make a scene in private, where no one can hear you screaming as they drag you down to the interrogation chamber."

"I hadn't considered that."

"Yeah. We don't know how many guys are waiting on the other side of the door, either. We don't know for sure the exact route to the target. We don't know how many more doors are involved. We don't know how anyone is armed. And we don't know how many people—how many crazed maniacs—are going to flood through the hallways as they try to kill us with everything from baseball bats to zombie teeth."

"Pretty much. It's liable to be one hell of a fight. Are you in?"

"Oh, *hell*, yes."

"Good, because I'm still not sure how we're going to pull this off."

"Want me to ask Dad?"

"Is he a tactical genius?"

"No, but he's a werewolf."

"How does this help?"

Rusty rolled his eyes.

"Wolves travel in *packs*, Phoebe."

I had a momentary vision of fifty or so half-human, half-wolf creatures tearing into an army of five hundred crazy homeless. How many of the crazies carried anything made of silver, much less a silver weapon?

"Do you think he'd go for it?"

"As long as we're not going in the front door of the church, I think I can talk him into it."

"You mean we'd have to go through the tunnels? Why?"

"We're Catholic."

"I—Oh. I see. But he wouldn't mind going up into the crypts?"

"There's a corrupt priest, or a fake one, or something, desecrating the crypts and using the church grounds for his own purposes, right?"

"I'll take that as an answer. And I'll consider the idea. I'm not sure I want to go that route."

"Why not?"

"Look, I just now demonstrated I can make magical items—two of them—which are of enormous value to lycanthrope-kind. It kind of looks as though I planned to use you for this. I don't want anyone to think I'm trying to manipulate werewolves."

"Ah." Rusty thought about it for a moment. "Yeah, I guess it does kind of look like that. I mean, *I* know you're not, but if it looks a certain way, there are always people who will assume."

"And I don't want to give you guys—excuse my racist stereotyping—any excuse to be angry at me."

"No offense taken. People think we have tempers. It's part and parcel of being a wild animal along with being human."

"You don't have tempers?"

"Same as with anyone else. We have more direct instincts than you do."

"So when you react to a threat by hitting it, people think it's your temper."

"Pretty much. We generally go along with saying we have anger management issues. It saves a lot of awkward explanations."

"Makes sense."

"But if you don't want a couple dozen killing machines howling down the tunnels, how do you plan on getting past the mind-controlled hordes? Blend in? Is it possible to disguise yourself as a homeless person and get ignored?"

"That's a really good question and I ought to find out. If you'll forgive the phrasing, how would you like to find a homeless person and fetch him here?"

"Got a spare toothbrush?"

"Huh? Sure. Why?"

"Because I'm going to want to brush my teeth. Those guys are *filthy*."

Rusty didn't rush out, grab one of the spies lurking outside, and drag him bodily back into my house. No, that would have been silly and stupid. We kidnapped one, knocked him unconscious, and dragged him into an abandoned building down by the waterfront.

Yeah, it was broad daylight. So what? We did it carefully and we weren't obvious about it. Besides, it's New York. In that neighborhood, anyone who noticed would try hard to pretend they didn't.

Could I have taken him home? Yes. I upgraded the psychic shielding to the point it would cut the subject off from the others. This presented me with a dilemma. Do I drag him into a shielded area and hope I can figure out how his brain works, or do I leave him in the network and risk discovery? We compromised by whacking him in the head and administering drugs.

Oddly enough, we knew where to get drugs. Handy coincidence, no?

Rusty handled the majority of the lifting and carrying. I handled the psychic shielding to cut the drone off from the homeless network. Rusty tied him down. I gave the drone something to help him sleep. Rusty went full-on wolf and started prowling around the place, watching for spies, invaders, and assaults. I went prowling around the drone's brain to figure out how it worked.

Pop was right. There wasn't enough of his mind left to make a decent vegetable soup. While the telepathic centers were in great shape, they were sensitized to a specific channel, making him even less psychic, overall, than an average human being. However, being so sensitized, all of his innate psychic ability was directed into one and only one thing: Being linked into the homeless collective.

Individually, they were almost as smart as a zombie. Collectively? Well, the more of them there are, the smarter they get. Distributed processing, you know.

How did I figure this out? Once I studied my victim and learned all I could with an individual, I opened the psychic shielding and watched as he reconnected to the network. He was still unconscious, so he wasn't telling anyone where he was or anything. He was like a computer with nothing but his operating system running. He wasn't doing anything, but he still connected to the network.

Which gave me, effectively, a terminal to access the network.

The nature of the network was, by necessity, a proximity-based function. He could connect directly to only those people within a short distance. Everyone in the network could communicate, however, because everyone acted as an echo, or a repeater, passing on what they heard from everyone else. My guy, being drugged into a coma, wasn't sending.

It was instructive to listen. I wasn't entirely sure what I was listening to, but I slowly started to puzzle out at least a little sense. Judging by nothing but echoes on the network, I couldn't get an accurate count of the total members. My best estimate was plus or minus a couple of thousand, but I pegged it at around twenty.

Twenty *thousand*.

That's... hang on, I know this. Companies form a battalion, then it's a regiment, brigade, division. A *division*'s worth of troops. Not well-armed, no, but infinitely motivated, perfectly—even mindlessly—obedient, and completely without regard for any wound short of a deathblow. Three or four brigades of homeless maniacs willing to throw themselves onto the guns of their enemies and, with their last breath, claw, kick, gouge, bite, grapple, stab, slash, and *spit*.

I think I know what Alden's been doing down in the tunnels.

No, there weren't twenty thousand people living in their own little community under the church's block. There were a few hundred in the immediate vicinity and, in the surrounding neighborhoods, maybe another thousand or two. But spread through all of Manhattan, it was an army.

It made me wonder what else he had on tap. If these were the spies and shock troops, how many people were merely modified? Not semi-erased, but altered slightly and told what to believe, what to think, what to do? I had no way to tell. I supposed it depended on how much effort it took. Was it harder to make a mindless zombie trooper? Or was it harder to lightly alter a person's thinking? It would take more power to semi-erase someone, but it wouldn't require much skill.

Maybe a better question was how much time it would take, rather than how much effort. If the homeless troops brought in a hundred or more recruits, could he summon up his powers, concentrate until the sweat dripped from his forehead, and be done in ten minutes? Whereas the careful, delicate procedure to operate on a living mind and leave it intact might take half an hour to do them, one by one?

Those are wild guesses, but they illustrate the idea. The homeless horde might be a horde because it's a simple operation. There might be materially fewer of the lightly-modified.

Or there might be even more. I only hope he has to abide by the same rules I do. Or the rules I believe I would have to abide by, if I were an evil, mind-controlling psychic priest instead of a cute, innocent psychic witch.

Watching the way the homeless troops operated made me think of ants. They were a social collective going about its collective business. They performed survival functions— ate, drank, begged for change, and so on. They slept, when necessary, as a biological need. And they went places to watch things. My house was one of the things. There were other houses, other buildings. I didn't recognize them, but the viewpoints were strange and the data being transferred wasn't the clearest.

Most of it was stripped to a mental shorthand. Instead of a clear picture of a building, it was a fuzzy picture of a *known* building—I didn't know it, but the network did—and the image of a person—again, a *known* person—going somewhere or doing something. It was the action they transmitted, passed along, distributed. That's what was important. They knew who they were watching, so they didn't have to pass along high-resolution information. They only reported what was going on.

What I did not expect to find was a smaller subset of the watchers. I thought of them in those terms. There were the Feeders, working on getting their own and others' food, the Sleepers, and the Watchers. I should think of them as Workers, I suppose. Most of them were watching things, true, but a few were doing recruitment work. I'm not sure of the particulars, but it seemed to me there were small groups, four to six members apiece, roaming around as though wandering aimlessly. They would close in on someone who wasn't sleeping in a city shelter and drag him or her down into the tunnels for conversion and assimilation.

Did the police not know? Did they know and not care? Did they know and they were told not to care? A combination of the three?

I was tempted to try and query the network, do a test run and ask it for information, but if I didn't do it right on the first try, there was a real risk someone would notice. Not the members of the network, but the owner. Once that happened, he would know I could tap into his network and, at minimum, he would start implementing network security. He might not know who did it, but if he recognized me it would be even worse. Things might escalate in our not-friends relationship.

Of course, I was risking an escalation by stealing back my stuff, but either he would accept it as a reasonable, proportional response, or he would have to devote time and effort to me—effort he might not want to spend, or maybe couldn't afford while vampires were hunting him. After all, didn't someone try to kill him one evening?

I also didn't want him knowing I could raise shields to block or jam their communications. I didn't know what sort of effect it would have on the individual members of the homeless horde. If there were enough of them, they might carry on with their last command. How many it might take would depend on the simplicity of their orders. It struck me as a good idea to keep the idea in reserve, though, in case I needed to stop of a lot of living zombies.

"Rusty?"

A moment later, he *woof*ed from the doorway.

"Do your friends at the waste processing plant charge by the pound?"

Journal Entry #29

Jason, Rusty, and I gathered in my media room to consider maps and holograms. They were best-guess maps, drawn from lots of historical and official sources, so they wouldn't be entirely accurate, but they gave us points of reference. We weighed the pros and cons, considering the best way in and the possible ways out.

I was glad I didn't have to explain a lot to Jason. Hunting monsters was what he wanted to do, and acknowledging there would be magic involved made the discussion much simpler.

"What it boils down to," Jason said, pointed at the hovering hologram, "is we go in through one of two main routes. If we go in at the top, we're probably going to be pursued by the zombies in the church. They lock the door behind them and cut off our escape even if they don't actively pursue us.

"If we go in from below, we have to get past even more zombies, but down there, both sides can attack openly. There's no need to keep quiet or avoid drawing attention. The tunnels can be a war zone and all anyone will notice is the subway train seems awfully loud.

"So far, so good. But here," he pointed again at the map, "is where I have questions. This area looks as though it touches another one. The orange on the map looks as though it could link this old tunnel and this unused space, which, in turn, either connects to or comes extremely close to one of the church's underground areas."

I obligingly expanded that section of the map, zooming in on it.

"It does," I agreed. "I don't see any icons indicating a connection, though."

"No, but if the wall there is as thin as it looks, we drill a couple of holes, pack them with plastique, and the wall opens up."

"Noisy," Rusty observed. "Look at the tunnel diagram. The echoes will easily reach the lower tunnels and might even be audible in the church. We can't count on having doors in the way to muffle the sound."

"True."

"How about we Kool-Aid Man our way through?" I suggested. "We build up a big charge in the armor and run through the wall."

"Maybe. It'll be quieter, I grant you, but if the wall is too thick, we'll expend our batteries and won't have anything left to operate the suit functions."

"Or," Rusty offered, "we could have a distraction."

"What sort of distraction?" Jason asked.

"Here's the thing. Most of the werewolves I know won't be happy about going into a church to do violence. It's not a monster thing. It's a Catholic thing, okay?"

"I'm not arguing. I wasn't even going to ask, but thank you for clearing it up. Please go on."

"Also, vampires won't go into a church because they can't. So the upstairs isn't a good way in for anyone except you two. Vampires could go in through the tunnels, but, when it comes right down to it, werewolves are the superior predators. No, hang on. I mean we're the better killers. Vampires are more subtle and sneaky and can be excellent predators, but werewolves have bigger claws, bigger jaws, and oh my what big teeth we have."

"I'll grant you that," Jason agreed. "They—you—are also much more frightening in appearance. Vampires look like people, at least until you get close enough to see the fangs. Werewolves can look like obvious monsters."

"Right. Doesn't help us here, not with living zombie types, but it can be useful. Now, I'm not sure we can get vampires to go down those holes and get into a fight with a horde of human zombies. Phoebe? You're the only one who's talked to the mosquito men. What do you think?"

"I'll have to ask. Carefully. Very carefully. But assume they're willing to go down there and claw their way through several hundred insane humans. What does this get us?"

"A diversion," Jason stated. "Right?"

"Right!" Rusty agreed. "But we have a force up top, too. One of you goes in there, lures in the guard force through the locked door, and either leads them on a chase or kills them all. Downstairs, the tunnel war draws in anyone else. And whichever of you two doesn't go in through the upstairs door can blow the wall and go in that way, driving straight for the prize."

Jason manipulated the map, turning it, looking it over. Rusty and I watched as he thought about it.

"It could work," he decided. "It might even be the best plan. I don't like the idea of someone going solo into the heart of the enemy camp, though, even with a diversion at both ends. Openly attacking might cause a reinforcement of the guards—assuming there are guards—and will definitely place everyone on high alert."

"How about you take the upstairs and I'll go with Phoebe? I'm not going to hang around in a dark tunnel with a bunch of zombies and vampires."

"Wise choice." He thought about it some more. "I think you've got a good idea. How about instead of me going in the top door, I pick a fight in the cathedral? *I* don't have any compunctions. It will give me room to move and it will still drag security from the lower levels up toward the door."

"Up to you," Rusty agreed. "We don't know what's waiting beyond the upstairs door."

"Phoebe? Do you have the visor layout for me? I'll head out to the village and do a walkthrough."

"Certainly. But what if the vampires aren't willing to help?"

"Then we come up with another plan. Either way, I still need to get used to the layout."

"You go ahead. I'll practice my necromancy."

"Necromancy?"

"Speaking with the dead."

After dark, I called Alicia and made an appointment. Dietrich decided he didn't really want to meet with me and would call me when he could get free.

The last time we met, I carried a suicide handbag. I guess I can't blame him for not wanting to talk in person. Zeno received a link to a phone application, vetted it, and approved it for me. I installed it and waited for Dietrich to call. When he did, I answered immediately.

"Hello."

What came out of the speaker was a meaningless garble. I looked at the phone, touched the prompt, and tried again.

"Hello?"

"Miss Kent? This is Dietrich. I am returning your call."

"Thank you. I take it this is a secured connection?"

"Insofar as is possible with a wireless connection. The encryption is, I am told, exceptional, but what can be encoded can be decoded, eventually. The app you are using is primarily for things with a very short half-life of usefulness, so I would appreciate it if discussion of anything more long-term was avoided."

"I see. Since it would be polite to accommodate you, I'll do my best."

"Thank you for your understanding. What can I do for you?"

"Just thought I'd update you on the latest discoveries in the video game."

"Oh? I am all attention."

"You know the main villain? The archbishop with the big smile?"

"I believe I do. The one with the army of minions with automatic morale success?"

"That's him. Turns out when you look at his code, there are a bunch of cheat flags. The game structure is set up so it favors him in several non-standard ways. In the game mythology, he's listed as only half-human. The other half is an angel. So, while he's not really a priest, he can access and use abilities from the priest list."

"I see. I haven't encountered an angel in the game. Are they real, or are they something listed in game mythos? Do I have to worry about encountering one?"

"They exist, but I don't know how you'd trigger one to spawn. They don't have fixed locations."

"Somewhat vexing and quite worrying. Can they spawn more hybrids if the game goes on long enough?"

"I'm sure they can. So far, though, I only know of the one."

"There goes any hope of using my preferred plan," he sighed. "The rest of my fellow gamers are going to take this badly, you know."

"I don't doubt it. For what it's worth, this has been the case since the game started. We're just now finding out about it."

"True, but they do tend to be somewhat reactionary."

"I can imagine."

"All right," he went on, "what else do these flags give to our mutual problem?"

"Oh, the usual stuff. He heals really fast, he has tons of minions, and he has an unbeatable charisma attack unless you have protection from mind-affecting powers. Most of his powers are especially good against necromancy-oriented characters—if you're developing your powers from the dark forces advancement tree, I mean. If you didn't select any of those attributes during character creation, he doesn't deal any bonus damage."

"Wonderful. Since I tend to favor those sorts, do you have any suggestions on how to deal with him?"

"Well, he's obviously a boss fight, but there are helpful tactics in the strategy guide. You don't have to face him directly until the end, so I'd suggest we whittle down his power base. You can grind minions for days, faster than he can make them, to keep the numbers manageable when the final battle happens."

"Is this what you plan to do?"

"Sort of. Underneath his fortress lair, he's got a spawning ground, down in the mines. If you can take out the spawn point, it'll reduce his power."

"How many minions does he have?"

"Where they spawn? Several hundred. Overall? I think he's in the ballpark of twenty thousand. I don't know how many spawn every day, but the longer it goes on, the more there are. I haven't seen anything to indicate an upper limit."

"I am becoming more disturbed by the moment. You're telling me this... this boss fight involves fighting through twenty thousand crazed berserkers to get to the final boss, and he has powers that will be particularly effective on, ah... characters based on dark magic?"

"Yeah. Sucks, doesn't it? But he can't have the whole crew with him all the time, obviously. If he's dealing with someone outside the main lair map, you can grind down the minions. He can spawn more, but it takes time.

"What I suggest," I continued, "is we all get online together for a raid. See, there's another strategy point. He also has magic crystals. According to the background material, he stole those from the good witch, the one who tells you all the stuff about the quest. He can't get more of those crystals, so breaking them or stealing them means his protective bonuses start to diminish.

"My thought is we do both. If someone will grind minions at the fortress gates, others can grind minions in the dungeon mines. This will empty most of the fortress and a sneaky sort can stealth their way to the vault and deal with the crystals. It's a win-win-win, all the way around."

Dietrich paused to think about it. I don't know how much he knew about video games or about the situation, but it was clear he wasn't totally unfamiliar. He still had to translate the gaming metaphor into the real world.

"I assume you will be playing one of these characters?" he asked.

"I'll go on the stealth run. I've got a couple of friends who can tackle the fortress gates as a diversion. I'm thinking we'll get most of your guild to go into the mines—the darksight special ability will be useful down there.

"It often proves to be an advantage. Send me a link to the reference materials and I'll consult with my guild."

"Awesome. I haven't been on a good raid in forever."

"I sympathize. I don't get to play too much, myself."

We said our goodbyes and Zeno—through devious and untraceable means—sent Dietrich a bunch of tunnel maps. Looked nice, too. Very much a fantasy map for an online multiplayer video game.

I wondered what Dietrich—and through him, the rest of the vampires—would make of it.

Jason reported back well after midnight. I anticipated he might, so I napped upstairs, in the media room. It has a nice couch.

"What did you think?" I asked. He took off his helmet and shrugged.

"It's a good render. I wish we had more to go on, but I feel comfortable with the layout. I know where all the little walkways are, where all the furniture is, and I won't be tripping over the little half-step at the start of the dais."

"Yeah, that one nearly got me," I admitted.

"It doesn't look tricky, but it's too broad for the height. I think it's a mistake in the original construction and nobody's had the guts to correct it in the renovations. It's 'historic,' or something."

"Probably."

"Any word on the vampires you want to use?"

"They're evaluating the idea. If they don't go for it, I'll ask Rusty to talk to his father. I'd rather not presume on their goodwill, though."

"Either way works for me."

"I also wanted to say I'm proud of you. You've been very polite to Rusty and made it easy for him to be polite to you."

"It's a professional relationship," Jason said. "I won't like him. I'm not sure I can. But I can work with anybody. He's not a werewolf. He's a member of my squad. His color, creed, or state of hairiness are immaterial."

"I like your attitude."

"Thank you. Now, I have to ask—do I get to use lethal ammunition?"

"In a church?"

"Against people who don't care if a beanbag round breaks a rib."

I had to admit his perspective was probably more practical.

"Well, if you're comfortable with bloodshed in a cathedral..."

"It's a fancy building to me."

"Suit yourself."

"I'll get my gear ready. Any idea on how long the vampires will take?"

"I'm guessing they'll send someone down to scout. Either they'll get a report on the tunnels back tonight or they won't get *anything* back, which means we could get a bunch of vampires going down tomorrow night."

"Yes, hot zones can be like that. I never expected to have to wait until the vampires got themselves sorted out." He shrugged. "Well, I'll be ready."

Journal Entry #30

I didn't hear back from Dietrich that night, so I slept in, figuring I'd earned it and would be up late tonight. If he called and said they could have a platoon ready to go down there in an hour, we would be ready, but I didn't think he'd spring it on me. He struck me as a very planned-out sort of person.

I checked in with Zeno, briefly, to see how things were progressing. He wanted to give me a full report on everything, but I nixed it.

"I'm working on too many things at once," I told him. "Right now, I'm concerned with the Alden problem. Gather information on all the projects and let me know if I need to switch mirrors for you. Other than that, I don't want to be distracted."

"Yes, *Ma'am!* I'll prepare reports for you and keep them updated! How else can I help, Ma'am?"

"For now, keep doing what you're doing. You're doing a great job, Zeno."

"Thank you, Ma'am!"

I have to admit, Pop gives the best presents. Zeno really was doing a great job on all fronts. I'd have to hire a whole think tank of specialists to replace him and I wouldn't trust them nearly as much.

On the subject of trust, though, I considered my latest werewolf acquaintances. Rusty knows I'm not a power-hungry lunatic trying to manipulate werewolves into being my personal guard and hit squad. Thing is, I don't want any of the rest to think it, either.

How do I handle this? They know—some of them know—I can help them regenerate silver wounds. It's not as fast or as effective as their own regeneration, but my spells work no matter what made the injury. Soon, they'll be aware they can control their shapeshifting more thoroughly. Between these two facts, I'm set to be either rich or immensely influential.

I could offer the things I make in exchange for specific help. You help me with this problem, I pay you with magic items. It's a straightforward transaction and there's no obligation either way.

On the other hand, I could give them the things as I make them, as a gesture of friendship. I don't want anything from them other than to be on good terms with them. True, I might need them to bury someone for me, someday, or something fitting their talents, but nothing specific. And I'd happily help them, too, in whatever ways I can. A two-way street, or something like that.

But the transaction path seems calculated and somewhat cold. It doesn't leave a lot of wiggle room, and I'd have to produce a lot of magic gadgets in a hurry. One doesn't buy anything from a werewolf on credit unless you're certain you can pay in a timely manner!

And the gifts-of-friendship path seems to be insincere, since I might actually need their help in the near future. It would be suspiciously convenient to come up with a wonderful magical item or two right when it turns out—oh-so-coincidentally—I need a bunch of big, vicious bruisers to rip people apart.

I finished breakfast, gave Gus a bite of bacon and the greasy plate, and went to my witchroom. Either way, I was going to need more of the gadgets.

And, of course, I realized about then how low my power budget was. Well, I've been running around, gating places, operating non-stop scrying devices, expending massive power bursts to punch through the sacred static, and had a new spell for psychically shielding a vast volume—the whole house!

I bit the bullet. Buying a generator or two wouldn't be a big issue. Rigging them so their output could be converted almost entirely to magical energy would be considerably more difficult. It was a lot of work, a lot of effort, and a lot of time to invest, but it was also kind of a requirement if I was going to be the Good Witch of the East Coast.

This still left me with immediate power problems if I wanted to enchant something for a werewolf.

All right. Step one: get more power. I placed an order online for a generator and was promised next-day delivery. Good start. Until then, I wasn't using all the electricity coming into the house because I didn't have enough transformers. It's kind of like saying I wasn't producing as much light as I could because I didn't have enough lamps.

Fortunately, the basics of an electromagical transformer spell are pretty simple. I needed wiring to put it on, but that was easy enough.

I took the shift-booth to the Madison Building closet and continued to Iowa. With a time differential running, I could charge up my expended crystals at Pop's house, no problem. And, if I wanted to be forward-thinking, I could make a few more transformers. All this would happen over the next day or two and I would still be back in time for lunch.

Journal Entry #31

I love it when a plan comes together.

I left the crystals alone to charge up, as they do in a high-magic field. I drove Bronze's spare suit into town, bought wire, light switches, and other materials for making "magic boxes," and arranged it all in Pop's workshop. I even got my werewolf-related crap in a stack so I would have it laid out and ready when it was time to do the werewolf enchantments!

I started with the transformers, of course. Nothing happens without power. I wasn't in any special hurry—Pop is the one who can sit down and happily tinker with things for decades on end, not me! But I did get started, at least.

Then I had my idea. As long as I was going to build things to produce power, why not build the physical devices, set up an Ascension Sphere, and do the work on them in there? I'm supposed to channel power as part of the exercise, aren't I? It would involve alterations so I could control the intensity of the field from inside, as well as let it ground out slowly, but I could make arrangements.

So, now I have three more electromagical transformers with multi-layered conversion spells inside them—they have about eighty percent efficiency, which involves forty— *forty!*—spells in each unit. That's a hundred and twenty times I had to cast the exact same spell to put together three transformers

Imagine writing out one of Shakespeare's sonnets. Write it slowly, write it carefully, with your best penmanship, so you get it right on the first try. Make it something you can frame and hang on a wall.

Now write it a hundred and nineteen more times.

They say repetition is the path to mastery. It's a long, boring trip.

That's how it feels. I think I did an excellent job and demonstrated amazing stick-to-itiveness.

Yes, yes, yes. I could have gone even longer, putting fifty spells in each unit. Nice number. But the diminishing returns meant the ten more spells (per unit, meaning *thirty* more!) would only get the units up to eighty-seven percent. Those seven percent were something I could chase at home, adding one to any given unit on Tuesdays and Thursdays and maybe once in a while on Saturdays.

As for the healing amulets and the lunar phase-spoofers, I got two of each made before I had to shut down the Ascension Sphere. I was sweating. Not perspiring. Sweating. As in the "dripping off my nose" kind. Doing this kind of enchantment work shouldn't be so hard, but I was working on myself, too, gathering and channeling as much force as I could. Think of it as a workout for the soul.

Then I remembered something else Pop said about Ascension Spheres. They can set fire to your soul. I don't know the exact mechanism, but having been inside the things, I presume it's like an oven. You can set fire to something inside the oven by turning it up too high, or you can turn batter into brownies.

Pop intended me to go through the baking process more than once. How do I know when I'm cake?

Where's the dividing line? Can I slowly work my way up to higher and higher intensities, or is there a maximum "safe" level? Is there any "safe" level, rather than a sliding scale of risk? I'm told Rethven magicians did an Ascension Sphere once, as a sort of initiation rite. Pop implied we could do it in stages. How far have I come? How much risk am I taking? Am I slowly burning away my soul, like a lit stick of incense? How do I *tell?*

Maybe I shouldn't be doing this. Certainly not on my own! I need someone qualified as an outside observer. Which, of course, means I have to figure out what it means to be qualified for this sort of thing…

During the cool-down, I added another spell iteration to the transformers. That makes forty-one, each, for about eighty-one percent conversion. I did it because A: it used up power inside the Ascension Sphere, and at a lower intensity than my main baking session, and B: because these are conversion spells, not enchantments. They take less power to build and are much more fragile. They're meant to sit at home and hum, not get dragged through the universes and exposed to various magical shenanigans. They belong in the lab, not in the field.

Besides, if they're a little fragile, magically speaking, this is a good thing. Pop made it very clear to me how leaving behind magical equipment is a Bad Thing. It messes with the locals and can, potentially, come back to bite. Electromagical transformers are a good example. Plug it in and even people with primitive magical skills—or a high talent and *no* skill—can sometimes produce magical effects!

I had a meal, slept for quite a while, had breakfast, went for a run, and did another set of werewolf talismans.

Funny thing. My regeneration spell is an established spell. It does a particular function and does it well. Fine and dandy for whoever is wearing it. But the lunar phase-spoofer isn't an established spell. It has a particular function, but it's not a firmly-established spell. It's a combination of established techniques with a fair amount of messy bits and wish-real-hard.

Thing is, as I work with it more, I keep seeing… not "shortcuts," exactly, but better ways to do it. In the last three times I've done it, I've figured out how to eliminate the wolf fur. Sure, it's easier with the fur on hand, but it's not required. Technically, neither is the human skin. If this keeps up, I may turn it into a Real Spell, rather than a cobbled-together ritual.

This isn't how Pop invents new spells. I would know. Is it how *normal* wizards do it? Do they stumble on a way to do what they want and slowly work out improvements? Some wizard finally figures out how to light a fire by chanting, waving his hands, drawing fire-symbols all around the wood, and dancing in a circle around it. Does his grandson do it with a quick gesture and a snap of the fingers?

Once I had my magical workout for the day, I pronounced myself fit. I didn't notice any improvement in my magical capacity from the latest Ascension Sphere treatment, but I wasn't doing anything overly strenuous. I was making sure I didn't strain anything. I cleaned everything up and headed home.

Yes. I was in time for lunch. So was Rusty. Gus, of course, followed me home.

Since I'd had quite a while to recover from my ordeal—and an Ascension Sphere is an ordeal in the most basic sense of the word—I felt up to cooking. Rusty and I talked about how things were going. I put sizzling meat in front of him and glanced significantly at Gus. Rusty nodded and made sure to share, once it had cooled enough.

And I had another great idea.

"I have a great idea," I told him.

"Oh?"

"I've been wondering how to lean on the subject of giving magical devices to werewolves. You know, making them feel like they're in my debt so they have to be my friends and so on. I don't like the way it looks, though."

"I was about to say it doesn't sound like a good idea to *me*."

"Instead, I think I have a solution."

"I'm all ears," he assured me, flipping a small bite of hamburger over his shoulder. There was a happy snapping sound somewhere below counter level but nowhere near the floor.

"How about I filter it through you?"

"How do you mean?"

"If I give these things to you, you can give them to whoever you want. You can spin it as saying you ask me for another one and I shrug and oblige. I wouldn't be making them at all if you didn't ask for them. Then you control who gets them and any favors they might be willing to trade—or even good old-fashioned cash—are entirely up to you. I never ask any of them for anything. Would it work? I mean, it has to look better if it's coming from you, right?"

Rusty chewed thoughtfully. There was a *woof* from behind him and he tossed something over his shoulder without even thinking about it.

"You know, it might work. It *might*. I'd want to talk to Dad about it. He's the guy who understands all the politics and stuff." He continued to eat with a pensive, thoughtful expression, so I didn't say anything. It gave me a chance to eat some of the cubed steak I had frying.

"It might be better," he said, finally, "if you were… I dunno. Friends? With my Mom, I mean. Dad likes you as much as he likes anyone who doesn't grow fur. If Mom liked you, too, then maybe Dad would be willing to… no, he would never ask for… hmm."

"Your Dad wouldn't ask me for gadgets for free?"

"Never. He's *lousy* at accepting gifts. He doesn't think 'Thank you' is adequate for anything. No, worse. He thinks 'Thank you' is a way to express resentment at having to come up with an equal gift in return."

"How very Japanese of him."

"Huh?"

"Nevermind. If this is going to work, it's got to be you. You're the only one who knows me at all well, and the only one I'd go to any effort for—for free, at least."

"Thank you."

"Is that resentment I hear?"

"No, I mean it. In a non-resentful way."

"Good to know. So, what do you think? Will it work?"

"Maybe. I'm willing to give it a try. Are you willing to make more of the things? I know people who will absolutely want to buy them."

"Sure. I don't know what's valuable to werewolves, though, aside from things in human culture. Money? Favors? I probably already owe someone for body disposal."

"I took care of it. It's a family thing."

"I'm not going to ask how you mean that."

"Probably for the best. Look, I have to ask, and I'm sorry I have to. Do you have a problem with crime, as crime, itself? Or certain types of crime?"

"Certain types."

"Uh-huh. Go on."

"Well, I'm not fond of taking advantage of the weak or the helpless. Don't tempt people to do drugs. Don't traffic in women or kids. I'm not overly fond of violent crime, but I'm not going out of my way to stamp it out. But there are types of criminal—let's say 'extralegal'—activities people are going to want no matter who provides it. Gambling, prostitution, drugs… yeah, these are all going to be with us no matter what we do. On the other hand, breaking people's arms because they can't pay a gambling debt means you let him gamble with money he didn't have. Who's fault is it? The gambler? How about prostitution? There's a big difference between a person who enjoys their work and someone who doesn't care what happens to their body if it means they get a fix. Drugs… drugs are even more slippery than the others. Who is a recreational user and who is an addict? Which drugs are too addictive? And who is to blame, the person who got hooked and can't wriggle free, or the person who provides a drug so addictive it creates a permanent market?" I sighed.

"Look, I haven't got all this worked out in my own head, okay? I haven't got hard rules about what is and is not okay. Well, mostly," I added. "I inherited a complete lack of sympathy for anyone harming children."

"What do you mean?" Rusty asked, curious.

"Harming children will get you killed. At least *I* will do it quickly."

"You will?"

"Yep."

"Who else would do it?"

"Pop. He will still kill you, but there's a better-than-even chance he'll make you suffer, first. He's the nicest ruthless monster you'll ever meet, but he completely loses his senses of fair play, humor, and mercy if you're nasty to children."

"Uh… Okay."

"So, let me ask this. Do you know of your father having anything to do with supplying children to whoever might want to buy them?"

"*No* way," Rusty stated, positively. "He might know people who loan out money at unreasonable rates, though. And there might be people who are liars, cheats, or otherwise unpleasant and who need to be removed from the world, but it's not his line of work. Sometimes people need money, but Dad is a wolf, not a loan shark. He'll still insist it gets paid back, but he's reasonable about being a part-owner of your business until it is. Most people think it's better than the alternatives, and so does Dad. Money also sometimes needs to mysteriously disappear in one place and reappear elsewhere, without anyone discovering the truth about how it got there. You know, typical stuff."

"Then I don't see any sort of problem. And to prove it, here." I fished out the devices I'd enchanted in Iowa. I laid them on the counter. Rusty picked up one and examined it.

"I thought you said you weren't going to sweat-shop a bunch of these?"

"I didn't. I was in Iowa."

"Ah. You took your time and then some?"

"Exactly. I've been gone a couple of days."

"That's…" he began, and shook his head. "This time-stretching business is going to take a lot of getting used to. Okay. I'll see if Mom wants to try them out. I'd like her to like you. It'll save a lot of family friction if she isn't frosty."

"Whatever works. You're in charge of werewolf relations."

"I've got lots of those."

Dietrich called me back shortly after dark. I was having an anticipatory nap, but woke up fast when Zeno told me who was calling.

"Hello?"

"Good evening. I trust I have not called at a bad time?"

"No, not at all. I was expecting it."

"I'm afraid I have bad news about the planned adventure."

"I'm sorry to hear it. I assume you and your friends won't be able to get online at any convenient time?"

"In a manner of speaking, yes. I'm afraid we've done more research on the main boss and the larger ramifications. Simply killing the main boss will be of limited utility in solving larger in-game issues. It is actually a trigger for a much larger quest."

"Is it? It's news to me. What sort of quest?"

"That has yet to be determined. The... the walkthrough isn't complete. There are flags in the code, however, to indicate certain factions within certain guilds will suddenly have quests at odds with other factions and guilds. Directly at odds."

"So, it might shift to a player-versus-player mode?"

"That's a possibility, but, as with any such shift, it depends on the player and their allegiances."

"I see. Are we likely to be at odds?"

"I certainly hope not. On a personal level, I'll do what I can to minimize your danger. You have my word."

"I accept your word as good."

"Thank you."

"Speaking of words, did you have any with the person responsible for getting me attacked in my home base?"

Dietrich parsed my deception for several seconds.

"I believe you're referring to the hacker in my guild? The one who corrupted the code on your followers?"

"Yep!"

"I spoke with an administrator about it. It violated the rules. Normally, one is banned for a year in such cases, and I'm happy to say this has been implemented. His account has been buried in the archives, despite all his screaming about it. No doubt he is still screaming, but no one is listening."

"I'm delighted to hear it."

"I'm glad. And I wish you luck with your current quest. While I agree weakening the boss prior to the fight is proper, my..." he trailed off and paused, hitting mute. He came back on with, "My guild feels it more reasonable to begin preparations for the resulting post-victory game-world changes. I trust you will still be having the major boss fight?"

"I certainly plan to, but not immediately. It's a process, whittling down his support before tackling him. To be clear, I don't intend to actually tackle him on this raid. I plan to do some grinding and make him more vulnerable for later. Assuming I can get enough people together for the raid."

"Ah, yes." Dietrich paused again, but he didn't mute. I heard, very faintly, what was probably drumming fingers. I wondered what it meant.

"Can you... Hmm. Do you mind if I offer unsolicited advice?"

"Not at all."

"The game world is an open world. It is not limited to the usual area maps. There are even features beyond mere terrain. Cabins in the mountains, deserted mineshafts, various other things in places far-distant from civilization. Hmm?" He covered the mouthpiece of his phone, but I heard a muffled murmur. "They might be called 'Easter eggs.' Do you follow?"

"Sure."

"I hear they can be immensely useful in certain situations. Have you ever gone out to look for one?"

"No, I can't say I have."

"Perhaps you should. You may find out why they are useful."

"I'll bear it in mind."

"Very good. And, again, I am sincerely sorry I couldn't talk my guild into participating in your raid."

"It's okay. Sometimes it comes together, sometimes it doesn't. No hard feelings. Anything else you especially want to know? I mean, I know you can't help me out on this, but it's not something we bargained on. Maybe there will be something later. With this thought in mind, what else can I tell you?"

"You've supplied me with enormous amounts of information. My guild is making good use of it, I assure you." He chuckled—"grimly," is how I would describe it. Maybe "mirthlessly." "Perhaps it would be better to say we are making *much* use of the information. It has certainly been the cause of a great deal of argument."

"I'm sorry."

"No, it is our own internal politics that have kept us shouting at each other rather than taking action. Now, I fear, our various factions are starting to polarize. We may even find our guild splitting into two if the arguments grow much more heated."

"Anything I can do to help?"

"Again, no. But remember two things. First, I believe you possess the capacity to be useful to me, personally, and, to a lesser extent, my guild—or my faction within it, if it comes down to cases. Second, remember what I said about finding those remote Easter egg sites off the usual area maps."

"I'll remember," I assured him. I tried to keep the puzzlement out of my voice.

"Then I will bid you good night and good luck."

"Thank you. Goodnight."

We hung up and I grumbled. I was going to need more muscle for the tunnels, but did I have to drag the werewolves into it?

I called Jason and asked him about the process for hiring mercenaries. As he explained, I discovered it was a painful, lengthy process for anyone not backed by a government. Worse, we would need a lot of them, they would need literally tons of equipment, and we would have to smuggle all of it into New York.

And, from Jason's point of view, it was throwing humans into the fight against zombies. Monsters were a much better option.

Well, fine. I should have expected that. So, reluctantly, I called Rusty. Maybe it was an omen to find he actually had his phone on him. He agreed to set up a meeting with his Dad—then he lowered the phone and shouted. "Hey, Dad! Can Phoebe come over? She wants to talk about a special job." I didn't hear the reply, but Rusty spoke into the phone again, telling me to come on over to the pizza place.

I wasn't sure if they were open at all hours or if I was a guest. Either way, I wouldn't miss it. They made me an offer I couldn't refuse.

Rusty held the door for me and closed it behind, rattling the blinds, and he locked it. The sign was already on the not-open side. Steve sat at a table with three other guys, all of them having a great time with beer, pizza, and cards. Since there were no in-store customers, they had dragged the other three tables closer to accommodate their food and drinks, leaving the center table free for the card game. I half-expected a smoky haze in the air to complete the scene, but nobody had so much as a cigarette.

"Come in, come in! Welcome!" Steve said, getting up and nearly knocking over the beer on one table. He held out his arms and I walked right up to him. He hugged me briefly before turning to his friends.

"Gentlemen! I am pleased to introduce to you the loveliest of witches. Phoebe Kent, may I present my younger brother, Carlos Giancomo, my youngest brother, Benito, and my eldest nephew, Roberto."

The three each rose for a moment, bowed slightly, and sat down again. Roberto, seated closest to me, bowed over my hand. All four of them bore a striking resemblance to each other, which was only to be expected, I suppose. Rusty was the only one with a hair color other than black.

"Do you play poker?" Carlos asked.

"No, I'm afraid I don't."

"Too bad."

"It offends people when I win all the time."

Steve burst out laughing and the rest joined in.

"Well, I *am* a witch," I pointed out. "I can't help it."

"You're serious?" Roberto asked.

"I'm afraid so. I can lose—the cards might not like me—but I can sense what everyone else's hand is like."

"Really!"

"Pick a card," I invited. He looked at the others as he reached for the deck. They shrugged or nodded. He took the top card, palmed it, glanced at it.

"Okay," he said. He was thinking it loud enough I had no trouble hearing him.

"Four of spades."

He flipped the four of spades onto the table. He reached for the deck, picked it up. He lifted the top card.

"Two of diamonds." Plop. "Jack of diamonds." Plop. "Ten of hearts." Plop. We went through the remainder of the deck as fast as he could pull the card up and look at it.

"We need to take her to Atlantic City!" Benito shouted.

"No, we don't," Steven answered, severely. "It is rude even to suggest it."

"I take it you have competitors in Atlantic City?" I guessed.

"In a manner of speaking," Steven agreed.

"How about I steal all the money from their vaults? It's faster than cheating them at cards. I need to ask a favor, anyway, and maybe this is a good trade."

The four of them stared at me for several seconds while they tried to decide if I was kidding. I could feel them thinking, *Well, she IS a witch...* Heads swiveled to look at Rusty. I didn't turn to look, but I knew he was nodding.

Chairs scooted around, squeezing aside to make room at the table. Roberto stood again and slid a chair into the gap for me. He held it and made a sweeping gesture as he bowed.

"Won't you please join us?"

Well, there went my career as a superhero. Apparently, I'm going to do a favor for the Italian Werewolf Mafia in exchange for their help in murdering a lot of subterranean zombies while I sneak onto holy ground to steal stuff.

Am I the bad guy, here? I could have sworn I was the *good* guy. I was *trying* to be! When I look at myself, I have to wonder. Not every time, but sometimes.

One thing that always bothered me was Pop's... I don't want to say "casual" attitude to killing. Maybe it's more fair to say he has a very matter-of-fact attitude toward it. Someone spills a drink on him, says, "Whoops! Sorry!" and staggers off to get a refill. The guy lives. He's tipsy and clumsy, not malicious. Pop ignores this sort of thing, usually. If someone deliberately dumps a milkshake over the back of a booth and all down Pop's neck, and laughs about it? It's malicious, but still not likely to get him killed. It's not impossible, but it's *highly* unlikely. But when you do something malicious and harmful, especially to people he likes, you're not toast, you're *ashes.*

I guess what I'm trying to say is Pop doesn't deal with every problem by killing someone. Don't assume you can be complacent about it. It's never completely off the table. But Pop has at least a moderate level of personal restraint.

Werewolves, by contrast, love a good fight. They regenerate. You cut one to the bone and he grabs the wound, applying direct pressure, howling in pain. I mean, that's what you do! He also keeps checking to see when the bleeding stops, because he knows it will. A minute or two later and he's flexing the affected area to see if it's still sore. You throw one through the window down at your local pub and he may be picking glass out of his hide for several minutes, but other than mild annoyance, a new shirt, and maybe a acknowledgement like, "Nice move," there's not much to show for it.

It's a species thing, I think, rather than a cultural one. Although it *is* a cultural thing, too. They settle individual disputes with fights! But they settle larger, group disputes by gathering around, having a discussion, and taking a vote. Even then, sometimes someone on one side will be so pissed off by the arguments of someone on the other side that everyone has to stand back and let them get it out of their systems.

Steve thought it was a foregone conclusion the Werewolf Mafia—"We're a family organization." His joke, not mine!—would go into the tunnels to dismember hordes of mind-controlled zombies. Not only to help me, although that was one reason. No, because it was a community-service, public-spirited thing to do.

"You take care of your neighborhood," he told me. "You take care of your people. If someone comes to your territory and he is being a prick, you cut it off as a warning to others. If they do not take the warning, you let them float downriver to whatever neighborhood will have them."

"I thought you weighted them down so they would 'sleep with the fishes'?"

"It is ecological, yes, but it is not a message to others."

So he got on the phone, made a few calls, and invited me upstairs to meet Rusty's mother. I couldn't turn that down.

Kathleen was an older woman, of course, but with a head of hair that belonged on Lucille Ball. It was a gorgeous, vivid red, and she had the green eyes to match. If I hadn't been told she was from Ireland, it would have been high on my list of guesses. I was surprised to find so many freckles, though. I haven't known many people with red hair. Is this a common thing? Do freckles go with red hair?

She was minding the residential level of the building, above the pizza shop, when Steve showed me up and introduced me. Kathleen was formally polite and apologized profusely for the state of the house, which, as far as I could see, was immaculate.

I asked her if she would like a cleaning spell on the house.

For the next two hours, we chatted like old friends. I showed her how a low-power cleaning spell worked by putting one on the sink. Dishwasher? What do you need a dishwasher for? Leave dishes in the sink overnight. Maybe rinse them first.

She showed me how to make cheesy Guinness bread. I'm not sure who got the better end of the conversation. Rusty, for his part, tried to stay out of our way, but the smell of the cheesy bread kept dragging him bodily back into the dining area adjacent to the kitchen.

By the time Steve came upstairs again, grinning madly, we had pints of Guinness and a lot of cheesy bread laid out and I felt confident I could make it.

Instead of talking, he went straight to the table, sat down, and Rusty immediately slid into a seat next to him. Kathleen insisted I take the fourth chair while she brought in the rest of the tableware.

We sat around, eating cheesy bread and drinking Guinness, chatting. Steve didn't bring up the subject of a werewolf raid, so I didn't. It was only after our snack, when we moved into the living room, that Steve mentioned the rule: No business at the family table.

"Seems like a good rule," I agreed. Kathleen smiled. Yep. Her rule. I could tell.

"It is," Steve agreed. "Now, we have business. Yes, we will do this thing you need, but we will not do it for you."

"Uh... I admit I don't understand."

"What you say makes clear many things we have seen. We did not know why certain... things... happened, and now we think we do. Things you do not know of, so do not fret. Things not of your concern, yes?"

"That, I understand."

"We think this is a good start, so we will do it. We will not stop with this one time, though. We will continue."

"You do know Alden will realize he's dealing with werewolves."

"And he will obtain silver, yes. This we know. There are ways and there are ways, but I have questions for you, mighty witch."

"I dunno about *mighty*."

"You make amulets to free us from moonlight and to make silver like it was only iron. I know of no other witch who can do more than chant over a cauldron and mutter about your future."

"They're a bit more than that, Dad," Rusty pointed out.

"Yes, yes," he agreed, waving a hand. "Perhaps one or two. None like *her*."

"Son," Kathleen said. "Mind your human manners. Do not interrupt."

"Yes, Mom." Rusty shut up.

I suddenly knew, absolutely knew, that Rusty went to Kathleen when I got mad at him and pitched him out of my house. She's the one who told him how to be polite. She's the one who gave him good advice. I know it, but I can't explain how I know it. I just do.

"What questions do you have?" I asked, looking at Steve. "O seeker of knowledge," I added, pretentiously. It got a chuckle.

"Silver is always a problem. Not always a big problem. It will become a big problem. How many of the amulets for silver do you have?"

"I gave them to Rusty. With the two I already made, those three... so, five, total."

"Those are not enough."

"I agree. However, I have a thought about how to hurry this up. I can make a wand. Rather than wear a thing, you could have someone with a wand. You get hurt with silver, you run over to him, and he applies the wand to the wound. Got a bullet hole? He sticks it in there and slowly pulls it out, sealing up the wound. Got a nasty cut? He draws the wand through it like he's making the cut and it closes up behind the wand."

"Hmm. Better. Many can use it?"

"You can keep using it on whoever shows up with a wound. Of course, the longer you spend fixing a wound, the better it will heal, but I'm told silver scars aren't necessarily bad things?"

"It can heal a wound enough to keep someone from dying and let them heal the rest naturally?"

"Yep. Don't use it for too long or it won't even leave a scar."

"I like it. You will teach Kathleen to use it?"

"Now, wait a minute!" she blazed. "If you think I'm not going to—"

"I do think it!" he snapped. They matched glares until she subsided with bad grace. "You may come with me when we go on the first raid. Then you will repair the hurts of whoever may need it, but especially—"

"I am not a *nurse!* I am a fighting—"

"—because I am taking Mark with me."

The statement shut her up. It shut everyone up. Conversation came to a sudden and unutterable halt.

I didn't understand why the three of them felt this was significant. Mark is a drug-addict moron, but he's still a werewolf.

"Are you sure?" Kathleen asked, finally.

"I am certain."

"Dad? Do you want me to come with you two?"

"You will go with her," Steve nodded toward me. "*I* will look after Mark."

I recognized the tone. Pop would have added, "I have spoken," but wouldn't have needed to. Dad was speaking *ex cathedra* and there would be no argument.

I wondered if Rusty would explain why, later. I wondered if I would ask. Maybe it was a werewolf thing. Maybe it was an Italian Werewolf Mafia thing. I decided the evening was probably over.

"Okay, well, it's been a lovely evening and I'm glad to have met you, Kathleen. Thank you all for having me over."

"It is our pleasure," Steve said. Kathleen smiled, a genuine smile, and agreed.

"So, the only thing left is the schedule. How quickly can we do this?"

"Tonight?" Steve suggested.

"Oh? Um. I've still got a wand to build. Tomorrow night?"

"You can have this magic wand ready by tomorrow night?"

"I'll have to figure out the exact method for it," I admitted. "Then I'll have to go through a couple of different versions until I've got it working the best way I can. And I'd like to rest afterward, to go in fresh."

"Sensible. We can do tomorrow. When?"

We discussed details and planned to go for it shortly after sunset—*provided* Alden was helpful enough to sleep in another rectory. If not, we would reschedule. Rusty stayed with his parents and I took a cab home.

Journal Entry #32

Either Alden has a super-sneaky plan, or he doesn't know what's about to hit him. I don't see how he *could* know, but he's a mind-reader. You can't be certain any secret is safe around us psychic types.

I spoke with Jason. He says he's ready to go in the front door. Considering Zeno notified me about his unusual ammunition expense report, I had no doubt he was.

Steven says he's got a whole pack of werewolves ready to get into a fight down in the tunnels of Manhattan.

Rusty says he's prepared to follow me through magic gateways, mystic portals, or teleportation closets—or through the old, forgotten tunnels on our way to the objective.

As for me, I spent two days at Pop's place, getting ready. Everything charged up and set to go? Yep! Got the wand for healing people? Yep! Did the R&D on it and included a big power crystal on the pommel, just in case.

While I was making it, I realized I was missing something important. Alden controls minds. I still don't know how fast he can do it. He might be able to grab a nearby mind and manipulate the person no matter how they squirm in his mental grip. I can't prove it, one way or the other. More relevant, werewolves might be as susceptible as humans.

So I did a little more R&D on one of my psychic shielding spells. This version has no finesse. It's neither a permanent nor subtle defense against anything a psychic might throw. It's meant as a temporary shield so when a psychic throws a lethal mind-bolt at you, you have a headache and know which way it came from.

I put it in another wand, included a brand-new, high-capacity power crystal, and gave Kathleen a couple of lessons on how to operate both of the wands.

Her estimation of me went up a couple of notches, then two more when Rusty volunteered to be the test subject for her healing-wand practice.

"She's done this sort of thing before," he said, reassuring his mother. "Phoebe does good work."

I'm proud of Pop, it's true. He taught me how to be a witch. But I'm also proud of *me*. I believe I have a right to be. There's a justifiable pride in achievement. I deserve it, as long as I can avoid vanity and overconfidence.

Once Rusty was intact again, we all took our places. Rather than risk communications, we scheduled an exact time to begin: Ten-twenty-two PM, Eastern Standard Time.

Everyone attacks at sunrise, or at midnight, or whatever. We picked a random, off-the-wall time and went with it. When your supervillain has a ritual that takes an hour to complete, don't show up at the last minute if you can possibly avoid it. Show up a half-hour early. They hate that!

Well before the start time, Rusty and I started through the secondary spaces underground. This involved going into a completely different building, sneaking down to a basement level, and accessing a forgotten sub-basement through a disused, rusted-shut door. Fortunately, I have a knife that cuts metal. It's not in the same league as Pop's Sword of Cut Anything, but it's also not as hard to keep safely stowed. I opened the door in about ten seconds and Rusty helped me put it back. He held it in place while I zapped little bits where it touched the doorframe, forming tiny spot-welds. If we came back this way, a good kick from this side would knock it flat.

Could I have opened a gate directly into the sub-basement crypts under the church? Sure! Why didn't I? Because I didn't want to discover there were a hundred angry zombies willing to charge through the hole. More important, I also didn't want to let them—and by extension, Alden—know I *could.* I held exiting via gate in reserve, in case we were trapped somewhere—say, with Rusty holding the door closed while maniacs tried to claw through it to get to us.

Once we were underground, we headed through a tunnel and kicked our way through a rotten wooden barrier and crumbling brickwork. Beyond was an old bootlegger hideaway. If we wanted to, we could dig out a now filled-in tunnel to an ancient speakeasy, but it was the wrong direction. We continued to the other end of the space and up to another section of ancient brickwork.

"This it?" Rusty asked.

"It should be the only real barrier between us and open spaces—places he's tapped, I mean. There may be doors, but there's a path to our target room."

Rusty made a thoughtful noise. He shoved the wall with his shoulder, as a test. This was a good, solid wall, not a mud-mortared pile of rocks.

"Looks like this is your problem," he told me.

"Looks like." I checked my watch. "Hang on a minute. The dance is about to begin. We want everyone to have a chance to choose partners."

"No problem."

He fished a small blowtorch out of his shoulder bag and a spark igniter. We waited and listened for any hint of alarms. We didn't hear anything, not even three minutes after the scheduled start time. Too far away? Too many walls and doors? Whatever the reason, we had to go on and hope everything was still according to plan. Rusty clicked the sparker and dialed it to a blue flame.

We came prepared.

I activated a spell I'd stored in one of my rings. It was a highly specialized spell, designed to do one thing: Isolate calcium. Calcium is the primary element in mortar, cement, and concrete. It bonds to silicon and it also forms an hydroxide. By forcing the calcium to "let go" of anything it bonded to, it drastically changed the structure of the mortar. The bricks weren't happy about it, either, but bricks can be made of so many different materials, I didn't even bother worrying about it. I focused on what held them together.

Rusty ran the flame along the lines of the mortar. White dust fluttered down as the mortar cracked and splintered. Way back when the mortar cured, the chemical reaction released a lot of heat over time. By putting heat back into the mortar, it made the spell much more quick and effective—and, most important, cheaper in energy costs. I didn't know if I'd need the power later, so we used mundane means to enhance my witchery. It was like casting a heating spell on a cauldron of water, but building a small fire under it, as well. Neither would boil water quickly, but together, they were much more effective. Same thing here.

After tracing the mortar lines in the wall, he gave it a shove. It crackled. He did a little more work with the blowtorch—two minutes, total, I'd say—and pushed a cluster of bricks through to the other side. He shut off the torch and set it aside.

We pulled bricks out of the way, dumping them to either side of our escape route, because beyond the former wall was an underground hallway. It was lit by electric lights—old ones—but according to our map, this tunnel was part of the catacombs or vaults.

We were in, and without any need for plastique. Yay, stealth!

We pitched out the few bricks we'd pushed in and I consulted the map on my visor. I pointed, for Rusty's benefit. He handed me his shoulder bag. I took it and slung it; his stuff might be damaged, but nothing in there would hurt me while I wore my armor. Rusty pulled off the loose shirt and sweatpants he wore and I stuffed them in the bag, too. A moment later, he rippled through all the stages of man-to-wolf transformation, stopping a little short of a normal wolf. He was bigger, more savage-looking. Maybe more primal, or primitive. Were wolves bigger and scarier back when humans were learning to chip flint for spears? Or are werewolves not concerned with regular wolves' evolutionary tree?

He sniffed the air and prowled ahead. It seemed wisest to let his nose lead. Rusty confirmed this when he sprang forward, raced around a corner, and immediately began to snarl.

I hurried after him to find six men, all dressed in dirty, ragged clothes, trying to deal with a big monster of a wolf. True, they had lengths of pipe suitable for baseball bats, but what they did not have was six working brains, all trying to do something different at the same time. They had the coordination of automatons.

Normally, I'd expect them to do better. Judging by the distant, barely-audible sounds of gunfire, I guessed the majority of their group processing power was being used elsewhere.

Rusty, looking a trifle larger than a moment ago, grabbed one by the knee, jerked him down and tossed him over one shoulder. I met the flying fellow halfway, grabbing him as he went by and swinging him face-first into a wall. On the rebound, I gave him an elbow in the back of the neck and moved on to the next zombie. He swung his length of pipe at me. I blocked it with a forearm guard. Without the spells, I'd have felt the impact. As it was, he started charging my momentum battery.

The pipe hit my forearm and stopped. I did a fast, circular disarm and now I had a pipe. I used it like a short staff. One-two-three broken bones, and a finishing shot to the head…

Rusty and I cleaned out all six in about twelve seconds. I did werewolf first aid. This consisted of making sure things were aligned properly so his regeneration had an easier time of it. Between his regeneration and the healing spell, he pulled himself together remarkably quickly.

The dead zombies were guards, of course, and they had guarded a door. The door was one of those bronze things you sometimes see on a tomb or mausoleum. It's not really meant to be opened on a regular basis, but the marks on it said someone did come down here fairly regularly. It was locked, but I had a lockpick. A knife, really. Because of the way it was inset in the wall, I couldn't cut the bolt. I had to cut a chunk out of the door to get to the bolt. So… thirty seconds?

Rusty stood guard, keeping an eye on the corridor behind us while I opened the crypt. When the door groaned open, he was right there with me.

The inside of the door had a diagram drawn on it. It looked familiar. The last time I saw it, it was under Pop, containing him and blocking attempts to locate him. So, yes, definitely an Alden-related area, as if I needed the confirmation.

The door fooled me. Beyond it was not a crypt, but a natural cavern. It wasn't large, no more than twenty feet wide at most. It was maybe ten or twelve feet across. It had no electric lights. From the look of it, I'd guess someone was digging to make spaces for crypts and struck water. There was a sizable trickle of water gushing from a crack in the rock face to my right. It ran across the chamber in a natural channel until it disappeared into the floor on the left.

Next to the door, there was a single, familiar-looking geode. I grabbed it and stuffed it in my shoulder bag. Rusty sniffed around the room and I went with him, senses peeled to detect any other power crystals. This was the only place where I detected anything unusual, so if they weren't in any of Alden's other lairs, they all ought to be here. If they weren't here, where were they?

Rusty and I didn't find them immediately.

What we did find, when we gave up the search for secret compartments or hidden doors, was much more interesting.

We left through the same opening we entered by—or we *thought* we did. As I started through it, I could see a brief stretch of rough-hewn cavern. The floor was irregular, the walls scarred where rock had been cut away, and there was not a single electric light to be seen.

Rusty looked at me. I looked at him. Since it was the only way out, we pressed on, following the curve of the rock. Ahead, I saw faint light. When we approached, it became clear we were seeing daylight. This bothered Rusty far more than it bothered me.

We emerged from a cave, taking it slowly and with great caution. Someone had used a pickaxe to cut the mouth of the cave into a more acceptable shape, rather than leave it as a giant crack in a rock face. A small log cabin stood not a hundred feet distant.

I saw something like this cave before, on a trip with Pop. No glass castles or faerie creatures, this time, but mountainside and forest restricted the view.

With a start, I realized my scrying and detection magic was working. The static Alden produced on holy ground was no longer around us. I detected my crystals.

The cabin was unoccupied. It wasn't finished, with a dirt floor and gaps between the logs. Most of the furniture was of the folding sort. Folding chairs, folding table, camping stove, a gas bottle, a full-sized collapsible cot—with an inflatable mattress—a camping shower, a couple of large water cans, several small crates with canned goods...

I collected my crystals. First things first. They were big and easily the most magical things in the room. The second-most magical thing was in a small jewelry box. Pop's Ring of Many Gates.

Why did Alden have it here? To keep it away from me? Did he not know what it did? Not that it actually did anything. It was really only a targeting point for gates—

If he did know, was he keeping it away from himself? Was he worried it might be used to find him? I don't know. I may never know. But, now that I have it back, I don't really care.

Rusty went outside and did a quick survey of the area. I switched to scrying and moved my viewpoint straight up, getting a bird's-eye view of the surroundings.

Temperate forest, rocky to the left, a river winding lazily along somewhat farther to the right. No sign of human habitation within a mile... two miles... five miles... ten miles...

I let my vision lapse back to the here and now while I looked around the tiny structure. Was there anything else of note? Tektites, perhaps?

Nope. Oh, well. They were small and easy to carry, not like a whole enchanted geode.

There was a cleared area around the cabin. There had to be. Where else would he get the material to build it? Judging from the state of the soil, it had rained in the past couple of days. The weather was cool and, from the way the clouds were massing, it was likely to rain again soon.

Rusty came in through the door and shifted, running through the process. Once he was man-shaped again, he could speak.

"Okay, I don't get it."

"Hold on. Do you want your clothes?"

"I'll shift back in a minute. What's going on, here? Are we still underground? Or what?"

"My initial guess is the church was built over a naturally-occurring weak place between two worlds. I'm thinking that's why nobody ever used that room for a crypt. People who went in to work on it sometimes didn't come back out."

"So, why put the crystals here?"

"They don't charge as quickly when they're in close proximity. It's kind of like putting three pumps in the same well. The well only fills up so fast, so more than one pump drains it. You want to put crystals in different locations—different wells—so you can charge them quickly."

"So, Alden found a doorway into…?"

"Another world, yes. He probably thinks this is still the same world, but at a different period in history. And he put these crystals here to charge so they would charge quickly. Relatively quickly," I amended. "The one back there, in the cave, was handy when he needed to recharge his stolen magic."

"How sure are you about this?"

"Some of it is certain. Most of it is what I'd call a logical necessity."

"So he built himself a cabin to live in?"

"It's not really to live in. Look around. Think of it as a wooden tent with a bunch of camping gear. It's stuff he could carry down by hand. But this is more important than a mere crystal-charging station. I would bet long odds this is his escape plan."

"Escape from what? Us?"

"Possibly, but I was thinking of the vampires. He worries about them. I'd even say he's scared of them. He thinks this is somewhere in the distant past of Earth—and it is, sort of—which makes it the perfect way to escape and start over if things go seriously wrong."

"Huh. Okay. Are we tearing it down?"

"I have plastique for blowing open walls," I pointed out. He nodded and went back through the various stages of becoming a big, prehistoric wolf.

Then again, as I thought about it, I realized blowing up the cabin would be nothing more than an inconvenience. Instead, I stacked the more flammable stuff on the cot, made sure the door was wedged open, lit the camp stove, and shoved it under the cot.

While the log cabin turned into a structure fire, we headed back into the cave, toward the crypt-cavern. I stopped outside it and quickly ran my knife through the stone, digging out a conical piece of rock. It cuts more than metal, but I wanted to test how fast I could dig away at the rock. Pretty quick, actually. Rock doesn't resist nearly as well as metal does. I dug several such holes, all in a row, and cut a narrow groove to connect them. I had Rusty switch back to human so he could pack plastique into the holes and press lines of it into the grooves, connecting them all.

I set a timer and we beat feet back into the cavern. This time, remembering how we got here, we walked around the cave in the opposite direction. It might not be necessary; simply entering the cavern might automatically mean you exit in whatever world your didn't come in by. I don't know how these things work!

"How long?" Rusty asked, as we emerged from the would-be crypt. I closed the door.

"Four minutes. That should be plenty of time, but I want to be as far away as possible. At minimum, we should have a cave-in on the other side. I don't know if it'll also destroy the interface between worlds, nor do I know what the side effects might be if it does."

"I love it when you risk the existence of the universe," he stated. He transformed again and galloped off ahead to make sure the way was clear. I chased after him, slowed by my bag of rocks.

As I ran, I wondered. Would the blast affect the ceiling here? Or only there? Would it ruin the interface, or would it be something Alden could eventually tunnel through? I did make sure to put the last hole for the plastique inside the cavern proper, above the entryway. I wanted it to destroy the point of congruence. Whatever Alden really wanted it for, I didn't want him to have it.

Regardless, being around if and when it quit was not a good idea. We hastened through the underground areas, back the way we came. Nothing intercepted us. I expected something, even if it was only a couple of scouts to find out what happened to the guards. As for why there wasn't anyone, my guess was that between Jason and the werewolves, there was too much going on to pay attention to six guard zombies who were no longer transmitting to the network. Their last transmission must have been very similar to what was going on elsewhere. Werewolves in the tunnels, armored person up top, and both in the middle? Their perceptions would have blended right in.

We made it down the corridor, through the broken wall, and down the abandoned tunnels before the timer on the explosives reached zero. We paused as the zero second approached, watching and listening for any signs.

Anything? No. All was quiet on this side of an inter-universal border zone. I wonder if I can look into that other world and see if it collapsed the cave. I probably can, but it wouldn't tell me if the border zone was still a border or if it was a cave, collapsed or not. Dang it, I'd have to go there and check—no, even then, if the outer cave has collapsed, I can't get to it... Grr. Well, at least Alden would have problems with it, too. I'll check on it later.

In the sub-basement, Rusty changed form and dressed. We exited the building, each in our own fashion, to avoid notice. Rusty made sure to call his father and let him know they could quit whenever they felt like it. I notified Jason and asked if he needed any help. He didn't, but he was quite content to quit chasing around the cathedral and simply fight his way out. The police were there, in force, but they were waiting for the SWAT team. The helicopter was going to be tricky, but he was tickled at the idea of evading it.

I left him to it and departed my building via the roof. I've missed leaping from rooftop to rooftop. It didn't hurt that I was feeling fantastic. A victory over the mind-controlling bastard! Hooray!

I made it home via the midnight rooftop route. Once inside, I checked in with everyone. Jason was fine, but he was out of ammunition and was almost out of charge in his suit. It was plugged in at his place and likely to stay plugged in for a while.

Rusty was okay, of course, and so were Steve and Kathy. There were no fatalities among the werewolves—not that we expected any—but the zombie hordes were considerably more dangerous than they counted on. I did try to warn them about the full, self-damaging strength and their relentless ability to ignore wounds. They had to encounter it to understand it. The techniques for fighting someone who ignores pain are very different from normal human beings!

Mark also survived. He fought well, which I gathered was important, somehow, as a step in regaining his honor, or whatever the cultural equivalent is.

I did a mirror-check on the other world, where Alden had his cabin. The cave in question had a collapse, so that was to the good. On the other hand, I couldn't tell if it sealed the gateway or not. Win some, lose some. At least the cabin fire didn't look as though it would spread anywhere.

With all this to the good, it was time to put some spin on it. I phoned up Alden. He answered on the third ring.

"Hello?"

"Good evening. I hope I'm not calling too late?"

"Not at all. Have you spoken to your father for me?"

"Actually, that's not what I wanted to talk about."

"I don't see what else there is," he admitted.

"Do you recall burglarizing my home? Do you recall the time you were a common thief, making off with whatever you could find to hand that seemed valuable to you?"

Alden was silent.

"Still there?" I asked.

"I'm listening." His tone was neutral. So neutral, it was like a manual gearshift with the engine racing. I'd bet he didn't like having his sins remembered. He didn't like the fact I was bringing this up right after something went sideways in one of his holy-ground hideaways. He *had* to be aware there was a major issue at the cathedral even if he wasn't watching the news. His zombies fought off a major assault! It *looked* like a victory—nobody got past them—but he was uncertain about the purpose of it, the motives behind it, and now he had to be wondering if he missed the point entirely.

"You stole several things from me. You stole several things from Pop, too, but that's your problem. My stuff is the issue at hand."

"How so?"

"I stole them back. You may have noticed a great deal of activity in your homeless network. When you get back to that church, you'll find a cavern has collapsed—not on this end, but the far end. You also have bodies to deal with, explanations to make, minds to modify—oh, dear! Something awful happened in a cathedral. It might have made the news. I do hope you've got a firm grip on anyone who works at the church. You *do*, don't you? And enough of a grip on the police to quash the investigation? Or manufacture a solution? Do you have enough influence with the media to cover it up? *All* of the news channels, I mean. Or the random passerby—few at that hour, I know—from uploading live footage to the Net? Or are you going to roll with it and use one of your slaves as a fall guy?"

I made a *tsk-tsk-tsk* sound.

"Now that I've taken back what you stole, I consider the matter closed. If you leave it closed. I will no longer hold your past thievery against you. I urge you not to reopen the matter. Are we clear?"

Alden was silent for several seconds.

"You... caused... a cave-in," he said, slowly, enunciating clearly and carefully. His statement told me where his priorities lay. Power crystals are nice. Control of mindless minions is important. But the time-portal cave was the big deal.

"Yep," I agreed, brightly. "Everything I did on the way to and from recovering the property you stole is kind of like interest. If I had made you a loan, you would have paid interest. Taking out a loan without my permission has simply made you pay more. Now, for the last time: Are we done?"

He hung up without a word. I think I made him mad. Yeah, I probably shouldn't have gloated at him, but it felt *so* good! I finally got something back!

I'm not entirely sure if I'm trying to punish him out of a sense of justice or for revenge, but my revenge tasted pretty sweet.

Journal Entry #33

I didn't hear from Alden for quite a while. I did check on the other world a few times, though. It was an Earth-world of some sort—Sun, Moon, constellations, all those checked out. There was nobody home, though. Maybe it was an Earth where people never evolved? Or maybe it was too early in the process for me to easily find hairless-ape hunter-gatherers? Still, I didn't find any signs of Alden clearing the rockfall or opening up the cavern. Go me!

But, damn it all, this completely shot down my plan to trick him into an otherwise-uninhabited world. If he knows about places where the worlds rub up against each other, where someone can wind up in one world or another depending on which way he's facing, then dumping him somewhere isn't necessarily going to keep him there. Inconvenience him, yes, but he'll eventually walk out to another world even if he thinks he's walking into another time.

These weak places aren't common, obviously. I'm not even sure how they work. Are they open only at certain times, during conjunctions, or something else? Can they be traversed by anyone, or does it require magical sensitivity—or require magical energy in close proximity, like a power crystal or other magic item? Or does it vary from border zone to border zone?

Hey! Is this why he wants Pop's supposed knowledge of time travel? Has Alden gone between different worlds, to different "times," but he has to take whatever happens to be available? He finds a portal in Mexico in 1441, another in Australia in 1600 BC, and another in Madagascar while it was still attached to Africa. None of these are where or when he wants to be, so he wants the time-travel spells to be able to choose, not be forced to take what he can find.

It's a theory. No, it's an hypothesis. What it means is I have to come up with a better way to imprison a half-angelic psychic sociopath with a fetish for killing vampires.

I hate it when a plan falls apart.

I did hear from Dietrich, though. Every night, in fact, for the next four nights, asking about updates on Alden's movements, who he was visiting, and always wanting more information on Alden's powers, abilities, and motives. He didn't insist on facts, either. He was perfectly happy with educated guesses.

Pop taught me a lot about intelligence analysis, but back then I was a silly girl! I never thought I'd actually use it! There are a lot of practical lessons parents teach us, whether we realize it or not.

Dietrich was a remarkably social creature. He didn't stick rigidly to the subject at hand, but also made casual conversation. He asked how I was doing, if I liked living in New York, if I had any plans for a vacation, and he told me about a lovely time he had on a long ocean cruise.

I doubted him instantly, what with the local vampires having water-crossing issues. I got the hint, though. A cabin in the remote woods. A long cruise. What next? A trip to London? Paris? Hong Kong? Or a pilgrimage to see the pyramids?

I was polite to Dietrich and helped him with all the information and analyses I could. I even agreed I should probably take a trip somewhere, but I wasn't sure when. He had a suggestion on that, too—"Soon!"

As much as I wanted to probe for more information, I restrained my curiosity. Dietrich wanted me out of New York. Why? Because I might not agree with his plans for dealing with Alden? Maybe. If they were planning to do something Pop-like—i.e., a bomb or something similarly destructive—I wouldn't be happy. I had no doubt they wanted to kill Alden outright, but were having problems.

After Jason's high-velocity message, Alden became a lot harder to kill with mundane things, like bullets. His movements involved more security. Of course, he also has regenerative abilities if he's only wounded, so you need a kill shot—preferably two or three, to make sure. Or enough explosives to puree the remains.

He's also socially hard to kill. What happens when he dies? Consider: Dietrich knows Alden has a thing about eliminating vampires. Also, Alden has control over an unknown but significant percentage of the city, county, and state officials. No doubt he has his fingers into national and international ones, too. If anything happens to him—if he's no longer around to give orders—what do these people do? It's not a case of a spell suddenly broken. This isn't an active effect he's generating, but a change he's made in the person. If you burn someone's hand with magical fire, the wound doesn't disappear when the magical flame goes out.

Zombies, at least, seem likely to keep going about their business because that's what they're programmed to do. More intelligent involuntary servants do their thing, too. The problem is the omega options—"If I die, do this!" Has Alden given them contingency instructions? Do they work together as a conspiracy to hunt down vampires on their own? Or do they come out to the public with whatever evidence they've accumulated and drag the hidden fact of vampire existence into the light?

I'm sure the vampires have ways to suppress or neutralize leaks, but something on this scale isn't a leak. It's a broken levee during a hurricane.

What would be the consequences of a worldwide revelation about vampire existence? I can't imagine a scenario where it would be to their benefit. It may not be good for human beings, either, but vampires legends are commonplace. Most people know how to kill one.

I'm not sure exactly what Dietrich is planning, nor why he wants me to be out of New York, but maybe it's time I looked into the matter more thoroughly.

Journal Entry #34

About a week after the geode recovery, I finally gave in to my curiosity and asked Rusty about the underground assault.

"Oh, that. Dad was over the moon about it."

"Was he?"

"He says he hasn't had such a good brawl since the Chinese Dholes tried to muscle in on his gambling operations."

"So, it was a good thing?"

"Well, no. It's bad for business and it attracts law enforcement. It's expensive in bribes and has a lot of risk. But sometimes you need to—as Dad put it, way back when, 'You needs ta make a fuckin' point.' Pardon my language."

"No, no. It's okay."

"It's your house, though."

"And you were answering my question with a direct quote. It's not like you're wandering around the house spouting profanity."

"Oh. Okay. Good. I'm never quite sure what I can say."

"Say anything. We're still working on finding those boundaries. I'll tell you if you've gone to far. But I do appreciate all the work you've done."

"Thanks. Anyway, Dad's happy, Mom's happy, and Mark is allowed in the house again."

"Is he clean?"

"I doubt it, but Dad isn't ready to beat him to death anymore."

I decided not to ask any of the questions this raised.

"Good. Now, can I ask for your help again?"

"What with?"

"I want to enchant your trousers."

Rusty looked down at the grey sweatpants he was wearing. They had seen better days. "Can I ask why?"

"I think I can get them to change shape and blend into you when you transform."

It took him a second to process the idea and maybe a tenth of a second to hand me his pants.

"Put those back on, doofus. You've got newer ones in the laundry. I'll need your help to enchant them."

"Just tell me what to do."

"You sound eager."

"You have no idea, do you?"

"It's a big issue?"

"In modern days, it's one of the most annoying things about being a werewolf!"

"Let's fix it, then."

He grabbed sweatpants from the laundry room and we met in my witchroom.

First, a cleaning spell. It wasn't strictly necessary for the test spell, but I wasn't about to skip it.

I'd been thinking about Rusty's clothing problem for quite a while. I thought I had a pretty good idea of how to fix it, but it was going to be "messy bits" magic—walking the line between a spell of directed will and a classical, formal spell. I didn't have any idea about how to do it until I worked with the spell for the voluntary change amulets. Once I started to get a better feel for the principles, the clothing spell wasn't such a monolith of impossibility.

Baby steps. Work all the parts of a problem, one by one. Look for connections. Work those connections, link them, and keep repeating until the whole problem is solved.

Rusty didn't actually have to do much. He had to participate and to contribute a bit, but I had to do the work. I was glad I had my geodes back.

I stitched symbols on the cuffs and around the waist. In silver thread, it basically said, *Wolf.* In black thread—like the dark phase of the Moon—it said *Man.* In both cases, I poked Rusty with the needle, in the correct form, before starting the symbols.

Then the sweatpants went into a cauldron of boiling water.

Yes, I have a cauldron. I'm a witch. If you think it's weird, take it up with my Pop.

The symbolism of mixing, of joining things into one thing, is a strong one. The boiling water was also symbolic for change; water was on the border between liquid and gas. Even if it isn't boiling, water has no form of its own. All valuable associations.

I had Rusty bleed into the cauldron, of course, just a few drops, to bind and attune the cloth to him. I snipped wolf-fur from him, too, sprinkling the hairs into the water. A modified repair spell used the clippings, adding them to the physical structure of the cloth, making it a hybrid of several types of fiber—but it included both of Rusty's forms, the fur of the wolf and the hair from the human! Those were the important bits. Then I sprinkled in actual, honest-to-goodness moon dust, stirred well, and made it an enchantment by binding it all together with a tight matrix of energy.

I'm glad Pop and I have done Ascension Sphere work. Between the house charge and my recovered geodes, it was a pretty big working. I was sweating. The spell would actually alter the state of matter, transmogrifying the cloth into fur, making it part of Rusty as he transformed. Later, if it worked, I could see about binding the spell into an actual enchantment.

Once the matrix was tight and the cauldron had cooled, I fished out his laundry and regarded it. It was the same rusty color as his hair and every thread was a pale line of magical light, invisible to normal eyes. I could see it when I looked for it, but it was bound into the fibers, part of them, as it should be. Excellent.

"Stick these in the dryer," I told him, "and don't try them until I'm awake to watch. I want to be sure they don't merge with you permanently."

Rusty handled the wet cloth gingerly.

"How likely is that?"

"Not very, but it's my first attempt at a transformation spell on clothes, aside from a resizing spell. I'd rather be cautious."

"I'll let you know when they're dry."

"Thanks."

Rusty nudged me, wearing his sweatpants. I woke up, we went to my witchroom, and he tried them.

They shifted with him, without a hitch, hiccup, or a tickle.

Could I have done better? Sure. Could I pare down the spell into a more classical version? Could I improve it for the next set of trousers? Of course. As a prototype, though, I was proud of it. I felt sure Pop would be proud of me, too.

Rusty went to show off the latest example of high-demand enchantment work—damn, I could be a rich witch. Why do I bother stealing drug-dealer money?—and I considered going back to bed. Focusing all that energy is tiring.

Instead, I had a talk with Zeno.

Long ago—it feels like long ago—I set Zeno up with scrying mirrors, cameras, and recording crystals. I sat down in the media room, scribbled a translation spell in my notebook—it's easier when you draw stuff instead of just visualize it—called up the recordings, and started going through them.

Yep. Translations came through beautifully! Whatever anyone said, I could understand it. Success!

However, this meant I had to sit and listen to hours—hours upon hours—days upon days—of vampire board meetings. Most of them were deathly dull. When you're running a secret society, there's a lot of protocol. There's also a lot of routine business that has to be handled face-to-face. Then there are discussions, debates, cost-benefit analyses, return on investment, questions of promotion and adoption…

To make matters worse, I had to listen to them *one at a time*. All the recording crystals could play back at the same time, sure, but it would be like having an eight-way split-screen of different conversations going at once. I could cast my translation spell eight times, but I don't think my brain is wired to handle that much input.

And the cherry on top of the sundae? Zeno couldn't hear them. They were psychic translations of the words. My mind got what the person was saying, not the words he said it with. Zeno heard whatever secret, ancient language they used but it was meaningless to him.

I could repeat what I heard for Zeno. He could then work out a translation program for the ancient language. It would only take a week or so, and it would still have vocabulary gaps, but it would be a start…

Rusty stuck his head into the media room. I was startled. He was back already? The clock said it had been several hours. Was it evening already? Where did the time go? Time flies when you're focused on a frustrating problem.

"Everything okay?"

"No!"

"Oh." He gently closed the door and left me alone. I was in a foul mood.

How do I set this up so Zeno can play back the recordings, translate them, and re-record them so I can listen to them? No, I can already listen to them. What I want him to do is "hear" the translation, somehow, so he can sort out what all the meetings were about, give me a list of subjects, and present me with a report! The fact he would then be able to also work out a translation program is a nice bonus, but not entirely necessary.

Now I know why Pop spent so much time with me in a workroom. Partly, it was because any magical widget we wanted was something we had to build. Later in my life, I would need to know it, down to my bones. And I do know it! I wanted a magical widget and I had to build it! The other reason was because he wanted me *able* to build it. And, dammit, if anyone besides Pop was going to be able to do this, it was *me!*

When I came out of my witchroom, late that night, Rusty and Gus were waiting. Rusty was in human form, playing Tug-of-War with Gus over Gus's latest chunk of rope. The ropes never last long.

The two of them quit their game when I came out and Gus put his front paws on my shoulders to lick my face. I needed that. I ruffled his fur and skritched his ears while he wagged his tail like he was keeping things at bay. Rusty grinned, relieved I was in a better mood.

"Bad news?" he asked.

"Annoying news," I countered, using one forearm to hold off Gus for a moment. "Dinner?"

Gus agreed wholeheartedly and dropped to the floor. He spun around to sit beside me and looked up at me expectantly.

"Dinner," Rusty agreed. "I can send out for a pizza."

"I thought I was too far south?"

"They'll deliver anywhere you are, I guarantee it. It might not be hot if you call from London, but they'd send it."

"You know what? It's tempting. I think, though... I've been working on things that don't want to work. I feel like cooking something because I *know* I can make it happen."

"Let me know if I can help."

Rusty did help. He stayed out of my way, ate what was set before him, and made appreciative noises. I made several things, including the old favorite of macaroni and cheese with tacos—very quick, and Gus appreciated bits of taco meat. I went on to my five spice chicken with a touch of cabbage. I also found I had salmon fillets and pork chops in the freezer. I glazed the pork chops in sauce and fried them, then added a different sauce for the second turn. The salmon went into aluminum foil for baking, along with salt, a bit of dill, a squeeze of lemon, a touch of olive oil, and a hint of fennel.

Everything turned out very well indeed. Food doesn't fight me nearly as hard as quasi-psychic spells. Gus and Rusty appreciated every bite, but they would have eaten anything this side of burnt. I, on the other hand, am a trifle more picky about the results. It made me feel a lot better to get things right on the first try.

Pop encouraged me to help him cook once I could see over the kitchen counter. That happened early on. He put in a slide-out step for me, below the kitchen drawers, so I could help. I think I started stirring things with Papa when I was three. And he ate a *lot*, so we spent a lot of time in the kitchen.

We pushed plates away—Gus pushed his into a corner and pinned it there during his cleaning cycle—and I breathed a sigh of relief. I can go on a temple raid with werewolves and super-suits and zombies, but eating something I cooked is at least as satisfying. They both give a feeling of accomplishment, although of different sorts.

"Want to tell me what you're working on?" Rusty asked, loosening the drawstrings on his new-ish sweatpants. "Or will it spoil a good after-dinner mood?"

"It's fine." I explained to him about the problems of getting a translation out of a recording and turning it into a digital format. He looked puzzled.

"You've got the recording, right?"

"Yes."

"You play back the sound and it's in a weird language, right?"

"Yes."

"You run it through your translator and it comes out as psychic stuff?"

"Yes."

"And the problem is getting the psychic stuff to be digital stuff?"

"Exactly. I have a lot of experience with psychic energies, but translating them into an electronic form Zeno can process is proving more difficult than I thought. And I knew it was going to be difficult, which means it may be impossible."

"Can you make the translator thing talk?"

"What do you mean?"

"I mean, can you make the thing talk? What if I want to hear it?"

"You don't exactly hear it. You get the translation in your head instead of the actual words."

"Yeah, so you said. I get the idea. But can you *make* it talk? Could you set it up so I could listen, too?"

"You could tap into the psychic portion and hear the words in your native language. Anyone could."

"No, that's not—" he broke off, frustrated. "If we were on the phone and you heard something about werewolves in the vampire conversation, could you do a magic trick to make the translation spell say things with sound? So you could hold out the phone and let me hear it without making me come over to stick my head in a psychic spell?"

"Probably," I agreed, thinking it over. "Yes. I'm certain I could. It would use something a lot like the audio portion of the Pie Tin of Revelation."

"There you go. Problem solved."

"How does this solve anything?"

"Doesn't Zeno have a microphone?"

Now I know how Pop felt when I asked a stupid question and changed everything he was thinking. I can only plead I was tired. My response was forceful and somewhat profane.

"Well," Rusty said, looking a little hurt, "I am a son of my mother, and Mom could be, technically, classified that way, but I'd think it's kind of rude to—"

I kissed him to shut him up. It worked beautifully. I then sprinted up to my witchroom.

My initial problem was skipping too many steps. I was trying to find a way to translate psychic impulses into a computer-compatible format. I wanted to plug something in to Zeno and let him download it, move on to the next crystal recording, and repeat.

Getting a crystal recording to play sounds, though… an old-fashioned speaker could be linked to it. The spell would vibrate the speaker cone. Zeno could listen to it and synchronize it with the video recording. He has days of conversation to use as a baseline for translation work, and it would take days to play it all back, but Zeno would listen and process day and night, non-stop, until he was all caught up!

Okay, it was harder than I thought to get the psychic imprint from a crystal to run through a translation spell and produce words. Duplicating the words spoken in the recording was easy. Putting a translation spell in the middle—that was hard. It doesn't give you translated words! It gives you the impression of words supplied by your own brain to match the *meaning*.

This caused a headache, but I got it to work eventually. I had a crystal talking in ancient vampire-ese to a translation spell, which talked to a speaker, which spoke aloud into Zeno's microphone, which Zeno then turned into digital media.

It was clunky and it worked. I'm overjoyed.

With the theory established, I could cast another seven translation spells tomorrow. Zeno has more than one microphone input, or would have when I finished a trip to ElectroShack. I went to bed. It had been a long day and a long night and I was *knackered*.

Journal Entry #35

Zeno didn't let the phone wake me, so the doorbell did. When I swam up through pillows I asked Zeno who it was.

"The person at the door is Brian Mesrole, Ma'am! Stacey Robinson has attempted to call you twice this morning. She called Brian immediately after failing to reach you. Brian is here at her behest."

"You listened to their conversation?"

"Stacey tried to call you, so I monitored her," he announced, cheerfully. Zeno can sometimes be a little unnerving. He doesn't think, really, just processes data according to rules. I sometimes wonder about the rules. *I* didn't tell him to monitor people's calls. Pop might have.

"Put him on the speaker." The light came on and the caption "Front Door Intercom" appeared at the top of my phone screen. My camera icon was barred, so I wasn't showing off my sleeping habits.

"Hello?" I called.

"Janice?"

"No, it's Phoebe. Brian?"

"Yes. Can I come in?"

"You woke me up. I'm still in bed. Long night. Is it important?"

"I need to ask you about Janice."

"She's not here."

"I didn't think so. Stacey's worried about her. We haven't heard from her or Oscar in over a week."

"Really? That's… concerning. Can you wait a couple of minutes while I pull myself together?"

"I didn't mean to get you out of bed," he apologized.

"I can sleep anytime. Two minutes?"

"I'll wait."

I took a brief trip through the bathroom, ran a hand through my hair to align it all, did a quick swish-and-spit to make up for not brushing before bed, and wrapped up in a bathrobe. It might have taken three minutes, total. Brian was still there.

I paused, hand on the inner door handle. Alden was pissed at me and had zombies watching the house.

"Zeno. Evaluate external security threats."

"High green."

Not even in the yellow. I was pleased. I didn't open the inner doors, though. I triggered the outer doors and let him into the vestibule. Once he was airlocked into the house—he didn't collapse in a pile of mouth-foaming madness—I showed him to the… living room? A social area for company. Is that a parlor? Have I been calling it the wrong thing all this time?

Those were my thoughts as I showed him in. I just woke up. Cut me some slack.

"Stacey's a worrier," he said, sitting on a chair. It's the chair I keep for Pop. Brian shifted uncomfortably. It's a very hard, sturdy chair. "She's been trying to reach Janice ever since she missed a test… last week? The week before? I'm not clear on the schedule. Now she's got me checking in with all her friends to see if they know where she is."

"Hasn't she filed a missing person report?"

"Sure, but do you know how long it takes before they actually *do* anything?"

"No, I don't. Is it a long time?"

"The police are always understaffed, or so I'm told. They blame funding issues and the two-year academy training requirements."

"I'm sure the politicians have their own viewpoint. I don't pay much attention."

"You really should. Voting is a fundamental—"

I cut him off before he could gain momentum. He's a political science major and he's one of those types who will talk theory until you run out of booze or patience or both.

"I know it's fundamental to democracy, but I don't feel I can give it enough attention to make informed decisions. Our issue at hand isn't the police, anyway. It's about Janice and Oscar. They're missing?"

"Yes."

"And Stacey has you hunting them down?"

"That's right. Calling around to all our friends hasn't been good enough for her," Brian went on, rolling his eyes. "I've got to come by and ask, like you've got her strapped to a bed or something."

"Not really my scene," I admitted. "Although Oscar is another story. If he wasn't such an asshole."

"Yeah, I figured as much. When's the last time you saw her?"

"A couple of weeks ago. She wanted help moving out—problems with Oscar. You know?"

"Yeah."

"So she crashed here a couple of nights while they processed her paperwork for an on-campus room."

"She applied for the dorms? I should check with administration, then. Do you know where?"

"No, sorry. I came home and her stuff was gone. Haven't seen her since. Oscar did come by looking for her. It was the same evening. I don't know where he went, either, but maybe he found out about the on-campus housing?"

"Could be. Or they went somewhere to be together for a while and patch things up. No," he corrected himself. "Not for this long. You think maybe Oscar could…"

"He can be a self-centered jerk, but I doubt he'd do anything, you know, *drastic.*"

"I'd say the same," he admitted, "but he does have a temper."

"When you put it that way…" I trailed off, looking troubled.

"Anyway, if you hear from them, will you call Stacey?"

"Not you?"

"Janice is a grown-up. So is Oscar. I don't want anything to have happened to either of them, but they're also not my responsibility. I'll help if I can, but I'm not going cruising through the city streets to look for them. I wouldn't even be here if Stacey hadn't told me I was visiting you today to ask."

"Stacey's really worried, huh?"

"More worried than she should be, maybe. She's a nicer person than I am."

"I know the feeling. Okay. You can check off your visit here. If I hear anything, I'll call her."

"Thanks."

Downstairs, I looked over the pile of Janice's things. Pop would be so disappointed in me. I left a ton of evidence in the basement and even more upstairs in a guest bathroom.

Who moves out and leaves everything behind? Not just books, but clothes, underwear, and toothbrush, too?

I missed Pop's cloak. It was my ultimate security blanket. I shamelessly stole it every night at bedtime. When I was older, it was my favorite article of clothing because it was anything I wanted it to be and it always fit. It seems I miss a lot of things, lately. Pop, Bronze, and my childhood leap to mind, too. This adulting thing is harder than I expected or like, dammit!

Pop's cloak is also the ultimate disposal unit. In addition to changing shape, it can open like a flexible hole into an endless nothingness. Dump something in there and you won't see it again, ever.

I had to content myself with stacking everything in the car-switching parking space. It's set for Iowa, but it wouldn't be hard to rig it to go elsewhere, if I wanted to go to the effort. Iowa would do, though. If I shoved all Janice's stuff into another universe, who was going to find it?

Dang. Toiletries. I went upstairs and cleaned out her bathroom. I also did a search through her room for luggage, clothes, and anything else she might have unpacked.

The bed was almost entirely repaired, at least. It had long cracks in it, but it was all in one piece. At least all the splintered areas were smoothed over.

Downstairs, I added the last bag to the pile and shifted it to Iowa.

Bronze's spare car appeared in the spot.

Cursing, I shifted everything back. I didn't think to go with it because I almost never use it; it's bigger, so it's more expensive to set off than the closets. I also forgot it would bring the car here.

I stepped into the area and shifted again. I appeared in the garage with Janice's stuff, moved it all out of the way, and took the shift-space back. Perfect!

The horse statue was still there, in my parking basement, along with my welding equipment. I had the new generator down there, too, but I hadn't yet had anyone come in to install the power transfer switch.

If you don't know, a power transfer switch is used to disconnect your house from the grid. You connect your generator to the power transfer box so you can select where your house gets power from. Switched over to the generator, you can plug appliances into the wall socket normally, rather than have to run a long cord down to the basement. That wasn't really the point of the generator, but it would be nice to have the ability to hook it into the house.

My plan was to do what Pop did. The generator would run off the natural gas line, pumping out electricity, which would then run through a high-efficiency converter to keep the house magically charged. I already had existing units plugged in upstairs, as well as the new ones. The idea was to have the generator's full output dedicated to nothing but magical energy. Which meant I had to build another electromagical transformer—a big one. Not one with forty or fifty conversion layers, but a hundred or more. Something with a conversion efficiency in the high nineties, at least. And, probably, a couple of conversion spells on the exhaust pipe, salvaging the waste heat and turning it into yet more magical energy.

Sometimes, it's tempting to start up a gas fireplace and keep adding conversion spells around it, turning heat directly into magic. Trouble is, it's not terribly portable. An electromagical transformer can be plugged in anywhere there's a power grid. Gas fireplace logs are large and heavy, but maybe if I enchanted one?

I could do all that, or I could do recreational work on the horse sculpture. It would be a day or three before Zeno had a report on the vampire councils. Alden was busy with his own plans, somewhat hampered by the vampires and a few recent magical setbacks. Rusty was doing his own thing, Gus was happily romping around in the Iowa woods...

Was I tired enough to go back to bed? Yes, but my sleep schedule would be all screwed up. I did get some good sleep before Brian showed up. If I stayed up the rest of the day, I could sleep all night and be back on a daytime schedule.

The welding flame was a pure blue color. I flipped down my protective mask and used tongs to pick up a gear.

I was happily humming along in the early evening when the lights suddenly quit. My music quit. Everything quit. About the only thing still working was the welding torch.

My first thought: bloody power companies. My second thought was about how I didn't hook up my generator, so *of course* the power went out. I should have expected it. When I was a little girl, I cast my very first rain-making weather spell. Bronze helped in the sense she occupied the car I washed. Even then I understood the principle. I washed the car to make it rain and it worked.

"Zeno!"

Nothing. Of course, nothing. Zeno was upstairs. The wiring connecting him to the rest of the house ran on house current, not on his laptop battery!

Muttering about low-budget power grids and the difficulties in scheduling an electrician, I was struck by an idea. Could this be a prelude to a zombie horde attack? Or a vampire invasion? Or a SWAT team assault? What if this *wasn't* a power company issue?

I flipped up my mask and moved to look out a window. In the basement parking area, they're set up rather high, so I had to kick a folding chair over and step up on it. The windows don't open; they're only for light. I put in a lot of security on the garage door. There would be no point to a secure door if a burglar could kick in a window.

Outside, it was dark. Eerily dark, in fact. The whole neighborhood was blacked out. There wasn't so much as a candle in a window.

Yep. Power company. What a relief.

I thought about it for a minute. What was there to do? Aside from cast a massive repair spell on the nearest power socket, was there anything I could do about it?

Although, now that I think about it, would it be practical to have a repair spell chasing through the power grid along any valid electrical connection? I wouldn't have to cast a repair spell on the whole power grid, just on a socket. It could spread to encompass the whole world-wide power grid, as well as anything and everything connected to it. Energizing it would be tricky, though. There would need to be either a huge, dedicated electromagical transformer turning grid power into magical energy, or the spell would need to have a parasitic function, drawing on power all through the grid to power itself.

Would it be worth it? If four percent of all electrical production was devoted to keeping the power grid intact, the only failures would be from outside damage. Nothing would wear out. Nothing would spontaneously fail. It would even cause electrical appliances of all sorts—refrigerator, heater, phones, computers, all of it—to never wear out again. Even broken things could eventually come back on-line as long as they were connected to the grid.

I had a really bad moment where I realized I could fundamentally alter the shape of the world. Imagine the ramifications if your wet phone only needed to be plugged in overnight to start working again. You only replace it when programming advances are too much for it. Batteries may run down, but they never wear out. Electric appliances, cars, transformers, wiring… No repairs again. Ever. For anything. Imagine a world were *nothing* electrical wears out. Ever. What does it do to the economy of the world when entropy isn't a factor?

I could even have a spell to upgrade the conductivity of heavy-gauge, long-run wire. The four percent the spell sucks up would be more than made up for by reducing how much is lost in power lines… Or would it? These days, they use superconductors for long-distance power transmission. In any older power grid, though, the spell would pay for itself by making the grid more efficient!

But all this was a flash of thought, an idea that came and went. I never seriously considered it, except maybe as something to try, one day, and see if I could make it work. More immediately, without a power grid and transformer power, what was I going to do about the power outage? Was there anything?

Seriously, when the power goes out, what can I do about it? If I knew exactly what was wrong, I suppose I could repair-spell the problem. I might be able to go there and get the repairs done before the repair crews did. I could help… if only I knew what the problem was. What blew up? A transformer? A substation? Was there a whole power plant in meltdown, or was it something local, in my neighborhood?

I suppose I could go up to the roof and do some stargazing. I could call someone and chatter about how the power was out. I could open the fridge and freezer and let out the cold air. I could go outside and take a walk in the city without street lighting of any sort.

Or I could stay off the streets, carry on with what I was doing, and wait to hear the sounds of someone trying to break in. If this power failure went on for long, there would be a lot of break-ins. If such was the case, I should be prepared.

I turned off the welding flame, went upstairs to put on a shoulder holster and a gun—my knife went on the other side, hilt-down, in proper style. I did my tour of the house to make sure everything was locked. I went back downstairs, leaving the door to the basement open. If anyone broke in, my alarm spells would notify me and I'd be up the stairs like a shot.

I sparked the welding flame again and went back to work. The power would come on again, sooner or later. Until then, my biggest concern was how much charge I had in my phone. If the mobile network still had power, it was probably jammed with callers. Later, though, someone might try to reach me.

Come to think of it, how much charge *did* I have? I pulled it out and checked, or at least I tried to check. Something was wrong with it.

I adjusted the welding flame so it was a flower of yellow instead of a tight cone of blue and propped it so I could use both hands. My phone was undamaged. The screen wasn't cracked, but it was unresponsive. On the theory the screen was the problem, I tried it with my AR visor. The visor wouldn't activate, either. Both of them were dead.

As I sat there, grumbling and getting ready to cast a repair spell, a white light blazed outside. It shone through the windows as though my house had just crushed the Wicked Witch in the village of the Sun Munchkins. The light slowly dimmed, fading from a stark white to a more yellow-orange.

I snatched up my dark goggles and held them over my eyes as I hopped up on the chair to look into the street again.

Everything was on fire. Everything that could burn, did. The Greenway, the cars on the street, trash, trees, everything in sight—

The light, which had blazed through the windows, finally found a counterpart in my head as the rumble through the ground reached my feet. I say "rumble," when what I mean is "shockwave." It threw me to the floor and sent cracks through every wall of the basement, brought down a shower of rubble and dust from the ceiling, and caused the reinforced concrete of the floor to buckle and shift like the fast version of a sidewalk along a tree-lined street.

What happened then is measured in fractions of a second, so let me walk you through it slowly. This is what happened in my now-active brain:

The power went out. Not only did the power lines quit, but the battery-powered electronic devices packed up. That's not a power company issue. That's the effect of an electromagnetic pulse. There was a long delay between the lights going out and a massive blast of light, so, presumably, they were two separate events.

The bright light was a characteristic of a nuclear detonation. Moreover, it wasn't far away. No, that's poorly phrased. It was *entirely too fucking close.* The thermal pulse hit first, setting fire to everything. Then the ground shock, traveling faster than the air-based shockwave, did nasty things to the structural integrity of my house. Given the brief delay between the light and the ground shock, there would be an even shorter delay between the ground shock and the air blast—but it was coming.

Okay, this is bad.

Can I escape through the closet? No. I *might* make it to the top of the basement stairs. The basement door was open, but the closet wasn't on the ground floor, so it might as well be in Peoria.

The car-shifter was the only shift-space close enough, but there were two problems with it. First, the lines of the diagram were broken by cracks in the floor. While I might be able to bridge the gap temporarily, setting off a space-frame shifter isn't the same as a dedicated closet. It takes concentration and an act of will—a few seconds, even if you're in a hurry. Add to this the trouble of brute-forcing a jump over a break in the diagram and the time required goes up even more. Ten seconds? Not much in the larger scheme of things, but significant when we're talking about the difference between the speed of sound in rock and in air.

Let's not talk about the risks associated with a panicked witch in a hurry doing interdimensional travel through a broken diagram. Screwing up a broken shifter spell can be worse than frying in a nuclear inferno. I've had precautionary lessons on this from a man who *knows.* Trust me.

Okay, there's a fraction of a second gone. Think, Phoebe. Think!

If I don't have time to shift out of here, what do I have time to do? Take cover? Under a car? Some large percentage of the house—or the building across the street!—is going to wind up in my basement. The car's suspension is good, but not *that* good. Should I be against the wall nearest the blast, so I can hide in the shadow and hope anything coming down is knocked far enough back to miss me? I can't count on it, and I'm not in my armor. How about I hide under the statue, so it can block falling masonry and maybe deflect half a house? It's not Bronze, but it's four metal pillars and a roof between them. It's better than anything else.

My decision took a half-second, maybe a little more.

My next house will be a hobbit-hole, I thought, *with concrete under the sod!*

I grabbed the welding rig, sent it skidding across the floor, away from the statue—I didn't want the soon-to-be-crushed gas bottles near me—and used the reaction to fling myself under the statue. I rolled onto my back, centering mys—

Journal Entry #36

I haven't been knocked unconscious many times. I can count them on one hand, in fact. If it didn't hurt so much to move, I might.

Okay. Situational inventory. Am I alive?

If I have to ask, things are not going well. Bonus points for being able to.

Therefore, tentatively, yes. When the neutrons hit the nuclei, I was below ground level so I was out of direct line for radiation effects. I was also out of direct line for blast effects. It's hot, though, so either I'm alive or my personal Hell is a really dark place. There's quite a bit of pain, so let's not rush to judgment.

I took a couple of breaths. I could breathe. No sulphur smell, so, tentatively, not Hell. The air was hot and stale, though.

The magical environment was still pretty charged, which I considered a good thing. The spells on the house used the structure to define their borders during the setup process, but they weren't *part* of the house. Once they were established, they were fixed in their location, not in the structure. Knocking down the building would only leave a house-shaped magical construct where it stood. Okay.

Carbon needs to be extracted from the carbon dioxide. It can form a layer on…

No, I'm doing this in the wrong order. I need to see. I conjured for a moment and breathed out a cloud of light. This spread like glowing mist through my little area, coating everything with a gentle glow. I looked up at the underside of a metal horse sculpture. It was dismayingly close to my face. Like, inches. Maybe eight. More likely six. Everything else was concrete and reinforcing rods.

Okay. Light. I can evaluate my situation better, now. Is there anything immediately lethal about to happen? No? Okay. Step one accomplished.

Step two: breathing. Carbon can form a layer over there. Separated from my own carbon dioxide, this leaves oxygen for me to breathe again. I'll sort out my airflow issues later and see if it's necessary to recycle. Right now, better safe than sorry.

Step three: temperature. I don't know if everything is on fire above me or if it's flash-heated from the blast. Either way, I don't want to be slow-roasted in the rubble of my own house. The rubble of my destroyed former house, I should say. Or, rather, I don't want to be cooked at all.

It's been a bad day.

All right, how about we start turning thermal energy into magical energy? It's not going to turn a profit on the magical front, but it's more efficient than shoving heat energy away.

As things slowly cooled down, I started taking stock of things I'd been actively avoiding thinking about.

Ow.

Left leg. There's the big issue. There's a slab of concrete lying on it. The near edge is about mid-thigh and I can't feel anything from there down. It hurts a lot at that point—the bone is obviously broken—but it's better than an entire leg full of screaming agony. Right now, I'll take it.

Right leg. Much better, in a way. It's only pinned by large chunks of rubble and the twisted reinforcing rods. It's not too damaged, but I'll have to chew it off to get it back. Or hire a forklift driver. No, as soon as I can reach it, I have a knife suitable for cutting myself free. Minor problem, really, compared to others.

Torso. Pretty good, actually. Covered in dust like everything else, but nothing broken or punctured. Bits are abraded, battered, bruised, displaced, lightly lacerated, or simply uncomfortable, but mostly okay. If there was internal bleeding, the healing spells on my ring already took care of it.

Right arm. Not bad. I can move it, but it hurts around the upper arm and shoulder. No blood, but a fracture high up on the humerus. No heavy lifting for me, but it's technically functional.

Left arm. Yeah, not so good. The forearm is broken, but there's no bone protruding. The upper arm might also be broken, but I won't try to move it until I get a better look at the damage. It hurts like blazes, though.

Head. It seems intact, but I did my best to center my head under the statue and covered with my arms. My arms took the brunt of it, so success, I guess. Chips of debris didn't do my face any good and I think I have a scalp laceration that's stopped bleeding, partly thanks to my hair. A quick fingertip check implied this, as well as reassured me about the quality of my skull. I'm very hard-headed.

Okay, where am I? I was surrounded by broken concrete and metal, buried in the ruins of—

What was left of the statue creaked. Dust filtered down. Something not far away cracked and made a momentary grinding noise. I made a squeaky sound.

Not good.

I could start a spell to gradually flow bits of concrete into a sort of arch, reinforcing the structure—or, more correctly, forming an actual structure—above me to support the weight of the debris pile. The drawback to this was how much harder it would make the job for the rescue crews. They would have to jackhammer me out, not lift away pieces of debris.

Hmm. Back up. Let's examine the assumptions.

Was anyone coming? Someone dropped a nuclear device on New York. Is this an isolated incident, or are there wider ramifications? Did the nation respond to an attack, or was it a nuclear terrorist? Was there a nuclear war going on, or was help actually going to get around to me, eventually? Did I want to be higher up, where I could get out, or farther down, to avoid radiation?

Damn. My family has more nuclear incidents than we do car crashes.

You know what? My injuries hurt like hell and I'm spending a lot of effort ignoring them. I should work on those as my immediate concerns. Then I can focus on the more long-term questions.

Dust dribbled down as something else above me shifted.

Okay, so, the *most* immediate thing is to continue to not get crushed to death. Support structure spell first. *Then* I can focus on injures. *Then* I can consider long-term plans for the distant future—like, later today.

Journal Entry #37

Much better. My little tomb is much less dusty. I had most of the dust crawl into cracks, filling empty places and forming bridges for the stone-merging spell. I can still hear settling noises, but nothing too close to me.

Once I was sure I wasn't about to be jam in a slab sandwich, I adjusted my position for maximum comfort—not much—and started fixing health issues. I'm not in pain anymore, so there's another bit of good news. My left arm is now lying in a straight line and the breaks in the bones are all welded together. It would ache from here to breakfast if I didn't have a nerve block on it. The fracture in my right arm is also welded, but the ache is minor enough I can mostly ignore it. My trapped leg is still trapped, but the concrete, at least, is slowly moving away. That material is flowing upward to join with more of the debris and give me a bit more open space in my tomb.

My other leg was in much worse shape. I started the process of removing the concrete slab on top of it. I say it's a process because the moment I started having the stone move away from my leg to give it space, my leg started bleeding.

Okay, so, pause the stone movement. Work on repairing blood vessels manually—a healing spell isn't going to do it in time. Stitch the ends together! Then let the stone move a little bit away, down my leg again. Any bleeding? Of course there is. Repeat the process. Burn as much power as it takes, because if I don't, I'm not going to be alive to care.

It's a long process because I have long legs. I also had to work on it a tiny bit at a time. On the other hand, I got pretty good at it.

Now the leg is no longer pinned and the bleeding is mostly stopped. It still hurts like hell. Or would, if I didn't have it almost totally numbed. What else is wrong with it? Shattered bones, crushed muscle… everything you'd expect when it's been stepped on by a *building*. There's only so much I can do at the moment, so I've had to settle for stabilizing it. Well, stabilizing it enough so the healing spell can handle all the capillaries and suchlike. There's also a fair amount of blood to reabsorb, but all the significant internal bleeding has stopped.

I wonder if I'm going to have to regrow a leg. I'm attached to this one. I'd like to keep it. If I have time to work on it, it'll get better. Assuming I get out of this hole, find food, and crawl to shelter so I can recover.

—like a cabin in the mountains? Like a nice little RV, out in the wilderness? Somewhere far away from civilization and especially Manhattan?

I took slow, careful breaths and performed my witchy calming exercises.

I had to remind myself I didn't know who was responsible. One can be aware of something without being responsible for it. Dietrich might have suspected what Alden was planning, or he might have known what his own people were planning. It could have been the vampires or Alden. Or even terrorists, although that seems less likely to me. There also existed the possibility of a bona fide nuclear war, too. I had my suspicions, but not enough information to be certain.

Would vampires go this far to deal with a half-angel? Would they need to? What have they already tried? Or have they simply stayed out of his way while planning this, their big move? Or was this Alden? Did he escape to Rome, hunker down on holy ground, and start a fire-from-the-heavens crusade against evil? If he arranged for the world to bomb itself back to the Stone Age, would the place be easier to control?

I hoped I would be able to ask Zeno what happened and who was responsible. Then I hoped Zeno survived. Then I settled for hoping I would survive.

I put fingertips on the emergency amulet Pop made for me. Did I want to call him? Was this worthy of his attention? He would certainly think so, but Pop would show up if I asked for help moving furniture! Yes, this was a major issue, but things weren't... what's the word? Immediate? As in, was this a problem I couldn't solve and it would kill me in the next few minutes?

This is definitely the sort of thing Pop had in mind. I, on the other hand, had a different primary criterion: Could I get myself out of this? If I had Pop show up, I'd be rescued—that was certain. It took a big load of worry off my mind! But, since rescue didn't worry me so much, I had room for other considerations. If Pop rescued me, there would be no way to stop him from hunting down whoever was responsible for me *needing* to be rescued.

I don't feel comfortable turning Pop loose on people. They had a lot of nukes. He has bigger ones, more of them, and things far worse than nukes. And a temper.

Maybe a more important issue was whether or not I should rely on the fact I could call on Pop for help. I'm a witch. He trained me in everything he could think of. For years, I didn't understand what I was being taught, or why. I thought my education was a normal one and everyone else was a little slow. Nope. Pop was preparing me to be my own person, to stand on my own feet as an independent, functional adult.

I don't think he ever understood that I didn't see it the same way. I didn't want to be fully independent. He's Pop. I love him. The most I ever wanted was to have my own place, really. Pop's big on free will and has always wanted me to exercise it. Maybe it's better to say he always wanted me to be prepared to be myself, in whatever way, shape, or form I decided on.

Am I summoning Pop to save me? No. No, I don't think I am. Not yet, anyway.

But, depending on how bad things are upstairs, I might have to summon him to save the world. World-saving is a little above my pay grade.

As I touched my emergency amulet and thought about whether or not to use it, it reacted. Buried inside it, there was an imprint. I focused on it, probing the crystal matrix, examining it without activating it.

In my mind's eye, a map of Manhattan took shape. Three areas of detail, or of attention, drew my focus. Tudor City, East Harlem, and Inwood. The mental map expanded, drawing my focus to two more places, one near Garden City, another to the west, somewhere south of Madison. The map expanded even more and revealed two more significant locations, one in rural, north-central Pennsylvania, and the last one in western Kentucky.

I didn't know any details, but I felt them. They were safe places. Prepared places. My crazy, paranoid, overprotective Pop went out of his way for me *again*, anticipating all sorts of potential problems. Because he didn't want to be bothered? No. Not at all. Because he wanted me to have the tools to be a self-rescuing princess, not the sort you find trapped up in a tower because she can't climb down a trellis in the stupid skirt.

I'd tear wide strips off the hem until my legs are free and use the material around my hands and feet so the thorny vines on the trellis don't draw blood. Obviously.

All right, I'm no longer dying in a hole in the ground. I'm still in the hole, but I've got the dying part under control. Things have stabilized. I'm not going to suffocate. I'm not going to bleed to death. I'm not going to die of thirst—I can draw moisture from the air.

Food is my main concern, but it's something to worry about over the next few days, not in the next twenty-four hours.

Let's take a look at what's going on outside. Do I work on surviving here until rescued, do I dig myself out, or do I start thinking about which world to retreat to? What's my goal?

I didn't have a magic mirror on me. I was at home and not expecting to need to be geared up for an adventure! Fortunately, there are less-sophisticated ways to look around. Normally, these involve a focus, but I have a talent for this sort of thing. In most cases, I use the safer methods, but you work with what you have.

I stepped out of my body and rose through tumbled concrete and broken brick.

The house had collapsed. It was easy to see which way the blast came from. If I hadn't had a multi-storey building across the street, I wouldn't have been buried very deep. As it was, there was quite a lot of debris, but most of it was shattered into small pieces. The larger slabs were from my front wall and formed the main barrier between me and a ton of bricks.

Yep, everything was either on fire or smoldering. Shocking.

I rose into the night sky to get a better view.

Although much of Manhattan was on fire, there were no obvious craters. Ergo, the detonations were airbursts, too high to carve out chunks of ground. Which is, of course, ideal if your objective is to do maximum destruction with minimum fallout. Nevertheless, ground zero was obvious. Buildings toppled or were blasted away from the center, while buildings farther away were scorched on the facing side. I could draw circles around the detonations and find each central point.

I said "detonations," didn't I? Yes, I did. One of them was in Manhattan, near the north end of Central Park. Others hit in the Bronx, northern Brooklyn, Yonkers, Fort Lee, Jackson Heights, Newark, and Jersey City. Several others were dotted around beyond those immediate ones, but the coverage was spotty. There wasn't usually much overlap. I'd have thought the Eastern Seaboard would be carpeted in blue-glowing craters. It made me wonder about missile defenses in this world. Anti-missile missiles? Laser weapons? What did they use?

Pop would know this stuff. Me, I wandered around, taking it for granted the locals weren't stupid enough to blow themselves up!

No, that's not fair. I had to remind myself I didn't know who was responsible. I had hope I might find out, eventually.

There's that word again. Hope. I've got a lot. At the moment, not a lot else, but when you're scraping the bottom of Pandora's box, you always find Hope. It's not something I'd suggest putting on a cracker. It's a flavor, not a food.

I wanted to find the safe spots in the amulet, marked on Pop's mental map, but I haven't practiced with astral projection a whole lot. Pop doesn't like it and we stuck mainly to the more complicated but safer forms of remote viewing.

One of the reasons I don't like it is the way Pop described it. There's supposed to be a line, string, or cord connecting me to my body. If my astral form goes places and gets lost, I twang the silvery rubber band and *spung!* I'm back in my body.

This is not the way it works for me. I step out and I'm out. There's no silvery cord, so I have to navigate by landmarks. Worse, I can get lost. How do I get back to my body if I can't find it? Sure, I can go to my address and find my room—whups! No streets. No addresses. Just piles of rubble. Is that my pile of rubble? Is there a coffin-sized spot in there? I'll have to search the whole pile. No? Maybe it's this other pile of collapsed brickwork. No? This could take a while! Given the situation, I didn't dare get too far from my tomb.

I also don't know how to home in on a target point. I wanted to go find people I knew and see how they were doing—Rusty leaped to mind—and I wanted to find Dietrich to see if he was presently cowering in a bunker or sipping type AB Negative from a champagne glass. At the moment, I was a free-floating spirit with navigational issues.

As I slid back into my body I realized it was in worse shape than I thought. Nothing hurt while I was outside, but coming back was like settling down on a bed of gravel despite the pain-blocking spells.

Fine. My ring is already running a couple of different healing spells. The first-aid spells activated automatically and helped keep me alive while I was unconscious, dealt with the initial symptoms of shock, and assisted with various other ills. One of them focused on enhancing what my body was already trying to do, namely, put things where they belong. Others overrode my body's natural responses, preventing swelling and other nastiness.

Everything still hurt. I'm not sure what it says about me that I stopped noticing after a while.

So let's decrease the pain sensors. I don't need to be notified constantly about the aches and ouches. I know they're there. I'm not trying to walk on a broken ankle. Doctor, I promise to lie still and avoid physical exertion. Can I please have more painkiller?

I'm already hungry, though, which is a bad thing when I'm trying to heal. Maybe I should put on more body fat to prepare for days like these.

There are a few meters of rubble above me. On top, it's on fire. As far as rescue is concerned, the most I can hope for is a cursory sweep for survivors and I doubt I'll even get that. No one is going to go digging on the off-chance someone is still alive in a basement. Not this close to a ground zero, anyway. Maybe, if it was one bomb, the emergency response would be extensive enough to be useful to me. As it is, I'm not sure there will *be* an emergency response.

I can get out of this. It'll take time, but I can do it. I'll have to wait until the fires go out, of course, but they should run out of fuel long before I reach the surface.

Magical math. The volume of space I occupy—how much force will it take to rise like a bubble through the stone? How does it compare to defining my personal space—roughly a half-cylinder—to shift it elsewhere? My estimates show it's much cheaper to drift slowly upward. The bonus is the surfacing is a gradual process, not a huge blast of energy. I can let it draw on ambient energy during the whole process rather than focus a massive amount of power into a single moment. I'm supposed to be taking things easy while I recover.

Can I afford to define a small space and steal someone's MRE? I need the calories and especially the protein. I've got a lot of damage to repair.

Let's see... volume of a half-cylinder a little short of six feet long versus a rectangular prism sufficient to grab an MRE... the difference in size is a ratio of over two hundred to one, with a corresponding decrease in power requirement. How about just the entrée? Those are much smaller. The ratio is then a little over a thousand to one. Yeah. I don't need most of the stuff in the pouch, just the major food item.

Someone isn't going to like this. It'll have to be a local snatch because reaching into another universe is drastically more expensive. It's not like I have great choices, though.

Damn. I need to enlarge my little nest a bit. I can't reach my notebook and pen. I'll get to it. In the meantime, I can scratch on the surface above me with my knife. It'll take a little longer, take a little more power, but I only need to do it the hard way one time.

I gathered power, told my ring's micro-gate to find me a packet of beef strips in sauce, and spent the power to force the spatial shift. The green box appeared directly above me and plopped onto my face.

Excellent start. Now I had something to eat and a box to use for next time.

Dream Journal #3

It's hard to remember my dream exactly. It wasn't one of those really lucid, clear dreams where you wake up remembering every little detail.

I was sitting on Pop's lap. It didn't matter that I was a grown woman. I felt like a little girl and Pop felt like a giant. He held me and he rocked me and he told me he was proud of me. I don't recall what he said, but I know what he meant.

The thing I do remember is this:

"Where are you, Pop?"

"As far away as hope in darkness, and no farther than the closing of your eyes."

I knew, then. I was dreaming.

I didn't wake up for quite some time. Rather, I *chose* not to wake up.

It was a good dream.

Journal Entry #38

I spent a lot of time sleeping, letting my body devote resources to pulling itself together, but I stepped out every so often to check on the surface. The fires died down in my area fairly quickly. Things still burned, but mostly it was a smoky smolder. Other places in the city were still burning quite well. A few new strikes appeared while I wasn't watching—I felt the rumbles in the ground, faint and distant—but none anywhere near me.

Great. People are still lobbing bombs and missiles at each other. Submarines? Bombers? Surely there were no normal launch facilities still intact by this point. Nuclear missile silos are primary targets. They go away in the first wave.

What is this world coming to when you can't expect things to settle down after a first strike? Is there someone stupid enough to think you can *win* a nuclear war?

Once I got my pen from my notebook, I carefully cut open the entrée box, folded it inside out, and drew on it with great care. With my power budget, I had to hit a fine balance between rising to the surface and eating regularly. I only had one power crystal on me and any others were likely to be about as useful as the Wicked Witch of the East after the house fell down.

The physical blast destroyed the house, but not the spells on it. The blast did destroy the geodes, though, which was more than bad enough. The resulting surge ruined quite a number of spells, from the repair spells to the psychic shield to the cleaning spells. About the only thing to survive was the power containment shield. Of course it would survive. The uncontrolled magical release—even one of a three-geode magnitude—was the kind of thing it was designed for This helped prevent spontaneous weirdness due to the magical surge, so there probably weren't too many glass flowers, hungry lipsticks, or razor-sharp spheres in the rubble.

Without constant replenishment from the wall-powered transformers, however, the field was slowly losing charge to the environment. I drew several diagrams on pages of my notebook, storing some of it, and made sure my personal gadgets were fully charged. It would be less of a strain on the containment spells if there was less it had to contain.

Eventually, though, with the electromagical transformers crushed and the solar conversion spells in the rooftop power-surged into oblivion, the inside and outside would equalize. The local magical field wasn't much, so the containment field couldn't be very strong. It's annoying how magical concentration spells work best in a high-magic environment where you don't need them as much.

On the other hand, it did motivate me to also summon a dozen meals immediately. High-cost spells were best cast up front, while the charge was high. With my immediate space occupied by snacks, I then assembled a magical conversion panel, connected it to my healing spells, and sent it up to the surface. I'd float to the surface eventually, but I also wanted to be in reasonably decent shape before I was exposed to the world again.

This left me with plenty of time to sleep, to rest and recover, and to think about what I wanted to do.

There wasn't much I could decide on. I didn't know enough. Which, of course, meant I decided to find out more. As soon as I got my scrying gear back in order. Right after I recovered from my injuries, which would be several days, at least. Which would be after I escaped from the crumbled ruins of the city. But, before that, I had to get out of this tomb...

Everything needs something else to happen first. Chronological order *sucks*.

I had another nap. Putting myself back into reasonably good shape was taking a toll, yes, but my leg was another story. It was going to be more of a project. It wasn't a simple break. It was shattered, pulped, mangled, ruined. I might have to pause and let it be ruined for a while. But then how would I get out of the neighborhood? Crawl over broken bricks and tumbled stone, dragging my leg behind me?

These are thoughts to keep you awake in your slowly-surfacing stone bubble.

Other thoughts haunting me involved the changes. All the changes.

Yesterday, I was wondering about how to imprison a psychic half-angel, what the vampires were discussing, when to drop a dime on all the major criminal activity in the world, what to get at the grocery store, whether the car needs an oil change, do I need a repair spell specifically for the things in the house rather than the house as a whole, do I have a good gambit to try on Sacha, is—

Blinding light, earthquake, fire, and everything is swept away.

Everyone I know in this world is *gone*. Everything about it I liked is history.

Oh, sure. There's a baseline Earth where I never went. Rusty lives there. Mark is probably still getting high on a regular basis. Jason is still whoever he was before Pop got hold of him. Pam might be doing okay in Hollywood. Sacha would still be solving chess problems over his black, bitter coffee. Janice and Oscar would still be having their troubles. Tim might not have met Orishi, yet. My little bonsai tree might still be okay—in someone else's house. Even my house would still be standing.

But it wouldn't be *my* house. It wouldn't have a parking garage. My apartment in the Madison Building might be rented by someone else. Nobody would recognize me. Nobody would know me. I wouldn't have Jason, Rusty, or Zeno.

This wasn't really my home. Not exactly. It was a nest. A place where I felt comfortable. I had connections, here. Maybe I didn't put down roots, but it was a place I liked. Now I'm not so sure. Everything I see around my little spot is a wasteland of fire, smoke, and rubble.

It hurts.

Journal Entry #39

I spent three days gradually rising toward the surface. Debris above me wasn't shoved aside. Rather, it joined with the roof of my stone bubble, flowed down as part of it, and formed a solid mass under me. I added a couple of alcoves, one to either side of my head. In one, I stacked stored rations. In the other was a depression where the condensation spell gathered water. These also provided a greater feeling of space.

Whenever I felt claustrophobic, I stepped out of my body and took a look around outside. This was depressing, but it was cheap.

More expensive were scrying spells. I polished a gear from the horse statue until it gleamed, then used it as a poor mirror. How was everything?

The fires were dying down all over the city and survivors were roaming around. Scavenging and salvaging seemed to be the main activities. There were quite a lot of burned bodies lying around. Most of them were killed by the flash from one or another detonation. Many of them were neatly laid out on streets adjacent to the surviving hospitals.

There were a few new fires. Not everything was peaceful and quiet. In three days, the survivors had managed to pull together, help each other, organize the wounded, arm themselves, scavenge supplies, steal them, fight for scraps, and start murdering each other. It was easy to see gangs were forming, territories developing. It wasn't anything as crude as a street gang and their turf. Citizen militia types marked off their buildings and shot at anyone who tried to cross the dead-car barricades.

Having a hospital in your area was quite a prize, I gathered. Maybe they were worried about running out of medicine. There were a lot of bullet holes in the bodies along the borders. Not that the mayhem was limited to gunfire. Quite a number of people were armed in less technologically sophisticated ways: baseball bats, lengths of pipe or rebar, lots of knives, and even a few swords.

I suspected the swords were mostly show pieces, unlikely to survive beyond the first couple of fights, but they looked nice.

In the larger sense, the whole East Coast was messy. As I first thought, the coverage was spotty. This led me to believe it wasn't a full exchange. Or it wasn't a fully-effective exchange. Maybe they shot down most of the missiles or bombers or whatever, despite the initial softening-up of the EMP bursts. I don't know who I'd ask.

Mechanized travel was almost out of the question. I didn't see any electric vehicles working and I doubt most of the gas-burners were operable, either. Maybe a few old-fashioned, antique diesels were running, or museum-piece tractors. I didn't see any, though. Part of the problem was the prevalence of dead vehicles on all the roads. Given you have something you can drive, how do you get anywhere? You need a bulldozer or a motorcycle, not something in between.

Farther west, there were several more incidents. Most of the major cities took at least one hit, sometimes as many as three. Things weren't good, but I found it odd there were so few ground-level hits. Almost all the detonations were airbursts. There were very few craters, only death from above and neat circles of ruin.

I also found it peculiar there were so few hits out in the middle of nowhere. Not exactly "nowhere." I mean out where there were no people. Say, for example, in the Dakotas, where there were nuclear missile silos galore. The lids were all off, the birds flown, but nothing to indicate they were ever even targeted.

Is this the modern way to win a nuclear war? Avoid fallout at all costs, since the radiation will be a problem for you, too? Damage populations centers, cut them off from each other, destroy the links supplying food and water, and let the population turn on itself?

And what's the military doing during all this? Good question. I looked at a couple of places I could locate just by geography. Edwards Air Force Base, for example, along with Fort Bragg, Fort Benning, and Cheyenne Mountain.

Multiple hits on each of them. In the case of Cheyenne Mountain, multiple *direct* hits. None of this airburst nonsense. Someone excavated the deeper bunkers under the original complex.

Was this part of the plan to keep things disorganized? Were there other backup command-and-control points? Did they get similar attention?

I didn't spent a lot of time on sightseeing. I figured it was important to know what was going on, but most of my waking moments were occupied in helping reconstruct a busted leg. Natural healing—enhanced—was taking care of the welded-together fractures and breaks everywhere else, so those little aches and pains were pretty much gone. But my leg! That wasn't something you heal. That was something you cut off and learn to live without. In Pop's case, it would be something to regenerate. I had hopes I could avoid anything as radical as amputation.

So I worked on reassembling bones. I had to build calcine lattices between each piece as I fitted them together. Muscles needed webworks of fibers to tell them where to grow and what to link. Ligaments, cartilage, nerve fibers, the works—all squished and splattered. They needed to be reshaped completely to match their original configuration.

Fortunately, I had a perfectly good leg as an example. And, after a couple of tries, I had a working template to overlay on my bad leg. It gave everything a much more detailed guide to follow and allowed me to start putting splinters of bone into place much more easily.

Ever done a ten-thousand-piece jigsaw? Or a mammoth Lego set—of a life-sized mammoth? Oof.

It was a long process, but it was something to do. I wasn't anywhere near done when I heard a noise. Early on the third morning—the fourth day?—as I chewed through my ration (lasagna), I heard something. It was a scrabbling, clunking sort of noise.

From *above*.

I've seen articles and read historical accounts of miners, trapped by cave-ins, who were successfully rescued. Pop and I once helped a bunch of silver miners, back in the 1800's, after a mine collapse. I think I am now qualified to say I have an idea how they felt.

The mangled statue clanked. Something hit it, hard. A second later, it happened again.

The polished brass gear I used as a scrying mirror gave me a view from above. I saw a shirtless man in sweatpants holding a claw hammer.

It's probably a good thing there was a lot of rock between us. I wanted to cry and hug him. He could have taken the crying, I think, but I might have hurt him with the hug.

Rusty was a bit burned, probably caught by the flash of a detonation, judging by the pattern of burns. The burns were healed up enough he didn't need to bandage them, at least, but they were far from fully healed. Werewolves don't like being set on fire.

The head of my sculpture, now badly battered and more than a little crunched down, projected above the remaining layer of debris. It developed a new dent as he hit it again.

I banged the hilt of my knife on the underside. He rapped twice. I rapped twice. He shouted, but it was a distant, tinny murmur. I shouted back.

The next sound was a scrabbling noise, not a clanking one. He tossed aside the remaining top cover of loose rubble fairly quickly, then hammered away at the stone and brick, perfectly willing to dig me out with nothing but a claw hammer and stubbornness.

I don't appreciate Rusty enough.

I did my part. I redirected the stone-flowing spell so it didn't try to float a bubble of stone up through the debris, but started developing grooves in the area Rusty hit. Instead of chipping away, he could more easily break loose whole chunks of rock—

Even as I started the new program, I changed my mind. Instead of helping him bring down heavy pieces of brick and concrete on me, maybe I should dig from my side, too. I reset the parameters. Stone flowed slowly away from a line I defined, trying to get out of the way of Rusty's mining work. It wouldn't be quick, but it would double or triple Rusty's efforts.

My original plan was to slowly rise through the mess until I could open the area behind my head, making it easy to crawl out. Now Rusty would be able to simply pull me up and out.

Three hours later, we had a hole the size of my fist through to the surface. I handed up my remaining ration packs to a very hungry werewolf, then handed up a used ration package, this one filled with condensation water. We kept handing up empty packs like cups of water until my supply was too shallow to dip out. He kept hammering away, chipping the opening wider, bit by bit, as I condensed more water for us. He appreciated the food, but he desperately needed the water.

"Phew," he said, waving a hand in front of his face. "I'm sorry I didn't get to you sooner."

"So am I, but I'll take it." I started a cleaning spell on me and started another one on him. "How are you alive?"

"I'm hard to kill."

"I meant about your location. One of the bombs went off or missiles hit or whatever up closer to where your Dad has a pizza shop."

"I wasn't in it. I was on the south side of Central Park, near Oak Bridge."

"You look burned."

"When the light went off, yeah. I went into the water faster than when the yacht caught fire. After the shockwave, all I had to do was get out of a forest fire. Your amulet has been a great help."

"I hope so. Have you heard anything about your...?"

"Let's talk about it later. We have to find someplace to hide before it gets dark."

"I agree. I'm in no shape to deal with a desperate survivor."

Rusty started to say something, stopped, started again, stopped.

"You've been in this hole."

"Yes. I didn't miss the big kaboom, but did I miss something afterward?"

"We'll talk about it after we get you out and get to shelter. Are you hurt?"

"Yes, but I've got the pain managed. Let's get me out of here and we'll work out the logistics."

"Deal."

It was still another three hours before we had a hole I could fit through. Rusty was exhausted, but he was also victorious. I held up both hands, he grasped my wrists, and he pulled, gently but firmly, sliding me up and out of my would-be tomb.

Is this how Pop feels every morning?

I stretched everything I could, enjoying my range of motion.

"Much better."

"I'm glad. Give me a minute and we'll get off this heap of rubble. We're exposed here and the hammering made a lot of noise."

"Okay. If you'll help me onto your back, I'll hang on."

"Do you need me to hold your legs?"

"Just one. The right one is okay, but the left one is still a mess. Let it hang and try not to jostle it too much, if you can manage."

"Got it."

"Hold on a minute."

"We're in a hurry."

"This will only take a minute."

I lay there on the broken rubble and looked around. I saw it all when I was an astral projection, but it's not the same. My house was flattened, knocked down and spread out to the southwest. Piles of brick and concrete were everywhere. I couldn't even see the street. The charred remains of Riverside Park was the only sign of ground.

I lived here for quite a while. I was comfortable. I was happy. I had everything the way I wanted it. Then, in one photoflash instant, it all went away. Snatched away. Blown away like a house of straw in front of a big, bad wolf. Only this time, the wolf rescues someone from the house of brick after someone else blew it down.

When I was little, Pop and I moved a lot, dodging awkward questions. I never liked moving into a new house. No, that's not right. I did like it. What I didn't like was moving away from an old house. We generally had a day or more while we prepared. It wasn't quite this sudden and we always had somewhere to go.

My house was gone, turned to broken pile of rocks with a suddenness that, days later, was still jarring and disturbing. The only thing familiar about this in any way was the map imprint in my pendant, assuring me there was, in fact, someplace to go. Because Pop loves me.

As for my house... it wasn't a home. It used to be. It was mine, and mine alone. Now it was tumbled stone and ashes. It was time to leave it behind and I was having trouble doing that. Why? Because it was *mine*. It wasn't Pop's house, the place where I lived. It was my house. I bought it. I managed it. I did the spells on it. I had contractors come in and fix it up exactly the way I wanted it, paying them with my money. It belonged to me. My castle. My kingdom. My domain.

And now it was my heap of broken images, living only in my memory. The memories I could take with me. The red, broken rocks of shattered brick would have to stay here.

I picked up one brick, chipped but intact, and scratched on it with my knife: *Look upon my works, ye mighty, and despair.* I placed it carefully next to the crushed, twisted head of a clockwork horsehead.

"I'm ready."

Rusty lay down so I could crawl onto his back. He stood up carefully. We adjusted ourselves and he put a hand on my forearms.

"Ready?"

"Ready. Where are we going?" I asked, as he picked his way through the tumbled stones.

"South, eventually. Farther from ground zero."

"Do we have a destination in mind?"

"Specifically? No. Right now, I'm looking for a building. One with structure left. A place we can hide out overnight."

"How are the subway tunnels?"

"Surprisingly awful. Don't go there. Avoid the entrances. Let me concentrate. It's not easy to carry you, cover ground, and conversate all at once."

"Sorry."

Tons of buildings were flattened, leaving broken terrain I wouldn't drive through in anything not track-laying. There were portions of walls still standing, usually corners, or a length aligned into the blast, minimizing surface area. Rusty had to pick his footing as he carried me through the ruins. Smoke still wreathed the place under a deeply overcast sky. I wondered if it had rained. I might not have noticed. Then again, I might also have drowned. If rain had started flooding my little cave, I'm not sure what I would have done.

"If we can get to the east side, near 40th, I think I know a place," I suggested.

"That's all the way across the island!"

"It can't be more than three or four miles."

"—carrying you through the smoking ruins of a major metropolis."

"You're tough."

He grumbled a bit and paused, going down to one knee. I put down my good leg to take some weight. Rusty carefully edged along his transformation track, getting bigger, hairier. His ears and face both lengthened somewhat, taking on wolf-like characteristics. His fingernails thickened. He couldn't be mistaken for a human being in this state, not without a hat, a high-collared coat, a big scarf, and maybe nightfall. Even then, people would think something was off about him. When he spoke again, his voice was thicker, harsher.

"Hard to talk," he growled.

"Doesn't it take a lot of concentration to hold that sort of in-between state? Won't it slow us down?"

He tapped the amulet on his chain necklace, the one I made to help with his involuntary transformations.

"Oh, right. Got it." I latched on firmly and he stood up. He was a few inches taller, too. We made good progress westward, which I disliked. Was he confused? No, he had a plan. There was next to no rubble in the park and he could make good progress there instead of trying to climb through the tumbled wreckage. One or two trees were still smoldering, but most of Riverside Park was a blackened, ash-covered wasteland.

Cars littered the Parkway. Autocabs had emergency brakes and came to a quick halt if their electronics failed. People driving on manual didn't, or not as fast. Several autocabs were burned out and there were quite a few older cars mixed in with them.

Everything in this world is computer-operated, chip-driven, and functions only because of micro-electronics. At least, that's how it used to be. Now? I think I'd be hard-pressed to find anything still working. Pretty much everything manufactured after 1980 was likely to be junk.

Rusty shifted to a jog, southward along the Parkway, but he did his best to move with a flowing gait rather than a bouncy one. It was painful, but I clamped my teeth together. We made excellent time.

The fires were mostly dead well before we reached 66th street. Buildings were starting to appear partly demolished instead of blasted. By 60th, it was even better. Windows were blown out, often on all sides, but the buildings were still standing. By 53rd, I would even be willing to take shelter in the buildings and trust they wouldn't fall down in a severe storm.

Rusty kept on going. I told him 40th street, but I wasn't sure how exact it was. We continued south, so probably we would turn on 42nd street and cross the whole island in one straight line. From what I remembered of my aerial view, there was another detonation in Brooklyn, but the Financial District, Lower East Side, Chinatown, Soho, Alphabet City… those were flaming ruins anyway. Anything as far north as 40th should be standing, or I hoped it would.

We turned on 50th, sooner than I expected. I didn't argue. Rusty roamed these streets all his life and had been out and about for the past three days. He knew more about it than I did.

He avoided, as best he could, long sight-lines. Crossing streets he handled at a brisk pace. He checked the corners before going around them. He moved from car to car, using them for cover. He kept changing streets, zig-zagging and sometimes taking alleys, but always working toward the goal.

We went down a stretch of 45th. I got a look at the massive police building near Times Square. A lot of the Times Square frontage in several different versions of New York doesn't have a fancy concrete-and-steel structure for the cops. Times Square is more of a tourist icon in those worlds. Here, though, the cops had a concrete cube with upper-floor windows and underground parking.

From what I could see along Broadway, there were a lot of bodies in the street. A lot of windows were broken out, mostly the lowest ones. Cars were all along that face of the building, a couple of them still burning fitfully. I think those were in front of the underground parking ramp. Someone might have rolled one or two down the ramp to pile up against the inner doors to the garage.

Bad design. I put my garage door at slightly above street level. I was thinking about rain and flooding. Still, you could park in front of it, but you couldn't roll something down the ramp to them. They should have fired the architect.

What was the problem with the police? Rioting? Civil disorders? A breakdown in social norms? All of the above? Maybe the police tried to organize the territorial gangs and the citizens in the territories didn't take kindly to it. Then again, how much food do the police keep on hand in their building? Guns, yes. Bullets, yes. Riot gear, tear gas, all sorts of munitions and equipment. But most of them go out for lunch, don't they?

We detoured down Madison Avenue, south, hit 40th, and headed east again. Rusty now kept up a brisk jog and stayed in the center of the street. He kept sniffing as he ran, turning his head one way and then the other. I didn't need to ask what he was alert for. I already scried on the roving gangs scavenging in the ruins. We didn't need to be loot for a larger group.

No one jumped out to argue with us as dusk gathered about the city. I saw very few figures, half-hidden as they watched us from upper floors, but they didn't want to be seen watching. They were laying low in the oncoming evening. Nobody even pointed a gun at us, as far as I could tell. Were they people simply hiding in their homes, hoping not to be noticed? Waiting for the Army to come in, guns blazing, to rescue them? Or restore order, at least? Or nomad scavengers, hiding out in their latest camp?

We reached the power substation on 40th and Rusty stopped. He sat me down on the front of a dead car and allowed himself to relax back into his human form, breathing hard and lying down.

"Okay," he gasped. "Lupus Taxi, when you absolutely, positively, have to run through hostile territory in a hurry. We'll settle up later. This it?" he asked, waving one hand at the building. It was no longer actively on fire, but the smell of smoke, melted metal, and scorched insulation was still strong.

"No, but we're near. Hang on. I have to find the exact spot."

"No rush, except I'm lying. We need to get a move on, pronto." Despite his words, he stretched out more comfortably and continued to rest, recovering his strength. I touched my amulet again and concentrated on a mental impression. This close to the destination, the information sprang into sharp relief in my mind. I looked up at a towering condo block.

"There," I said, pointing. "The Corinthian."

"Where?"

"Fourteenth floor."

"Isn't it really the thirteenth floor? Skyscrapers don't have thirteenth floors, or something?"

"I presume so, but I haven't checked. I've never been in the building before."

"You haven't?"

"Nope. I'm told there's a safehouse in it, though."

"In a luxury condo block?"

"I'm guessing it's Pop's sense of humor."

"Or his sense of irony. You ready? We have *got* to be off the street before dark."

"I'll want to know why—later. If it's important, let's go."

Rusty climbed to his feet and carried me again, but it was only a couple of blocks. We approached via the parklike area in front, getting out of sight and looking over the entrance rather than stomping directly up to it. The front doors were closed and locked. No one had shattered the vitril fronting, either. No point in looting an apartment complex? Or was something keeping looters and rioters at bay? I didn't see any defenses.

We knocked. Nobody answered. Either nobody was home or they weren't admitting it.

I didn't want to cut through the locking bolts and leave the place open to any random passerby, so I scribbled a spell in my notebook and directed it at the revolving door. There were metallic noises as the bolts drew back. Rusty carried me through and I allowed the bolts to snap back into place once we were inside.

The place was unlit. Power was still out all over the city. Despite the window-wall in the front, the lobby was heavily shadowed as the dusk deepened. Rusty sniffed the air, nodded in a satisfied manner, started for the elevators—and immediately looked woebegone.

"Fourteenth floor?" he asked.

"Yep," I agreed. His shoulders slumped.

"Where do they keep the stairwell?" he sighed.

Fourteen floors is a good stair-climb workout. It's a lot more exhausting when you've put in a full day hacking rock, your burns are bothering you, you already ran four miles through dangerous territory, and you're carrying someone up through the darkness. I know warriors in the Tassarian Empire who couldn't do it. I wonder if Rusty would like to be knighted? Maybe I'll ask. Pop would double-tap him with the flat of a sword, I felt sure.

We stopped a couple of times on landings. I insisted. I didn't want Rusty to be exhausted if we reached our floor and needed to hit a problem.

Getting out of the stairwell and into the condo was even easier than getting into the building. I visualized the pushbar on the other side of the fire door and concentrated. I can move small objects with my mind, but I generally don't. It takes mental effort. Rather than waste magical energy, I gave the bar a mighty shove and it clicked open. Rusty pulled as I pushed and the door swung wide.

We crept quietly along the corridor, found the condo door, and I was forced to fall back on my spells. I can pick a lock with telekinesis, but lurking in a hallway while I figured out all the ways the door was locked wasn't a good idea. Rusty pushed the door open, whispered about how he couldn't smell anyone, and we went inside.

"Don't make a light," he cautioned. "Those windows face the East River, but someone still might see."

"Got it. Put me down on the sofa. How's your night vision?"

"Really good, but nothing hides from The Nose."

He sniffed around. I rubbed my left leg, *really* glad to be able to lay it flat and straight for a while. I didn't do any work on the way over, but I was still sweating from the pain. I couldn't numb it while we were moving; I needed to keep track of how much damage we might be doing! Now, though, I put the pain-blocking spell back on and wished I had more power.

Blocking the pain was a minimal thing, but the healing spell was considerably more of a drain. Now I wasn't even in a charged environment. Fixing my leg might take a while, but I knew Pop. If this place was as safe as I expected it to be…

Rusty came back to the living room.

"A bedroom, a home office, one bathroom, really nice kitchen," he reported, quietly. "Nobody here but us, no running water, no power, but the furniture is all non-powered stuff. It's a lovely cave in the sky. It's also a bit stuffy."

"Yeah, the ventilation is also off. Can we open a window?"

"I'm not sure." We examined them. Two of them could open, sort of, as well as the door from the bedroom to the tiny balcony. The windows were designed to swing inward about an inch. It was enough for fresh air.

"What else did you find?" I asked, keeping my voice low because Rusty did.

"Filing cabinets. The home office is full of them. They're locked, though."

"I hate to have to get up."

"I'll carry you. Then you can go to bed. I need to find water and rest."

"Bring me a container from the kitchen. I'll get started on the water."

He didn't ask. He brought back a pitcher. I worked my magic on it, taking note of the power required. I set it by the window so it could start condensing water.

Rusty helped me up onto my good leg and I put an arm around his shoulders. The home office was as he described, although it was more of a filing room than an office. No desk, no computer, but plenty of filing cabinets all the way around. There was a small folding table in the center. There were boxes stacked on top of the cabinets and a few more under the table. I'd call it a storage room.

We went to the bedroom to look things over. A little light came through the windows—also facing southeast—so I could see immediately there was a balcony, two big wardrobes, and one of those beds designed with a storage area under it.

The wardrobes were locked, and not with a trivial, old-fashioned, decorative lock. These were serious. Most exterior doors don't have locks that good.

Locks are a way of saying, "Stay out." To get this far under normal circumstances, someone would have to get past building security, disable an alarm on the door, get through the door, and avoid the camera in the hallway. Now, after all that, they would have to be willing to either make a lot of noise busting open a wardrobe or take a lot of time picking complicated locks.

However, on the dressing table, there was a box of gaudy jewelry. None of it was enchanted, all of it looked valuable, and, at a guess, it was there to encourage anyone who got this far to grab it and go. The gems would be okay for spell crystals, but they were smallish, not really worth turning into power storage. They weren't there for me, of course, which I grasped immediately. It was a last line of defense to keep someone from looking too closely at the rest of the place. Here's the loot; take it and run!

I know how Pop thinks. I was mildly surprised there was nothing immediately lethal to eliminate intruders. Then I realized why not. Because the place was for me.

Was this place a hidden bunker? No. It was a safe house. They are two very different things. This was about as safe as one could expect.

Except I was forgetting something. What was it? Something about safety? Or danger? Oh, yes. Rusty was in such a hurry…

"Rusty? Why was it so important we get under cover before dark?"

"Vampires."

"Of *course*."

Journal Entry #40

I liked the condo. It would have been wonderful as a place to live. As a last-ditch safe house, it was positively luxurious. The bar is set a lot lower when all you want is to find shelter.

The big, metal filing cabinets weren't for files. They were mostly for ration storage. Who looks twice at a filing cabinet? Everything inside was neatly labeled and organized. Vacuum-packed, irradiated entrées were filed in alphabetical order. Rusty was perplexed to find a file slot for "Chili With Beans" and nothing in it, but I assured him it was only to be expected.

While the majority of the contents were food, there were a few other items. In a thick envelope, there were three sets of identification, including passports—one Canadian, one Swiss, one Australian—and credit cards to match. Knowing Pop and Zeno, they were entirely fictitious and could be utterly relied upon, assuming anyone was checking passports or taking credit cards.

These immediately told me the safe house was meant for a variety of disasters. If I was on the run but still unwilling to leave the world, I could comfortably change from Phoebe Kent to any of three other people and continue about my business. This would deal with most sorts of personal disasters. For a global disaster, there was food, water, and a place to hide until I could arrange to leave the globe.

I magically unlocked a drawer under the bed and found a lot of cash in American, British, and Swiss money, as well as gold and silver coins, several diamonds, two cartons of cigarettes, several lighters, pill bottles of what one might call recreational drugs, and a stack of dirty magazines. Depending on the situation and level of disaster, any of these might be considered currency.

The kitchen had all sorts of mundane things. There were different pots, most of which were built for camping, not for kitchens, as were the utensils. The cabinets held canned goods, bottled water, a survival water filter with a hand pump and a jerrycan, two manual can openers, a pair of church keys—all the stuff you might need for an extended stay under adverse conditions. There were even water purification tablets. Why? Because there was a tarp, a funnel, bungee cords, and a length of garden hose stored with the water. For collecting rainwater on the balcony? Probably.

The drawers under the bed held clothes. These were organized into grab-and-go outfits. One was a beautiful cocktail-party dress with matching shoes and jewelry—folded, yes, but made of a crease-free fabric. The rest were more practical, ranging sharply down the fashion spectrum into shirts, jeans, tactical trousers, sneakers, and field boots. In a separate section, there were all sorts of harness and gear-carrying belts, from shoulder holsters to load-bearing web harness.

When I finally got around to picking the locks, I found the wardrobes were equipment lockers in disguise. They didn't hold much in the way of clothes, but there was still a wide variety of gear. Guns and ammunition, yes, of course, but also compass, night vision goggles, ultrasonic motion detectors, mouthpiece breathing filters, an inflatable raft, binoculars, big stacks of laminated maps, and so on.

The keys to the lockers were taped to the inside of the doors. Pop is a thoughtful sort. I didn't say anything to Rusty about the silver ammunition. Rusty noticed it, but he didn't say anything to me about it, either.

The bedside alarm clock was much more than an alarm clock. It was a shortwave radio receiver, or it used to be. The electronics weren't working, naturally. I put a repair spell on it and hoped it would pull itself together.

In the bathroom, the cabinets were stocked with two towels, lots of toilet paper, and enough medical supplies for a trauma ward. We had everything from band-aids to antibiotics, scalpels to stitches, and a pressure can reminiscent of aerosol cheese dispensers. It was labeled in a language I didn't recognize. The icons on the label implied you sprayed it directly into burns, cuts, or other nastiness.

I found this pile of medical stuff ironic since there was a medical center about a block away. I guess you never know when a one-block walk will be a problem. Maybe more ironic is the fact I have spells that will do a better job than any of the medical gear. It told me Pop anticipated either a low power budget or a friend who could treat me until I recovered enough to treat myself.

I figured Rusty and I could sit quietly for about six months, if we needed to.

Overall, whatever disaster befell me, I had a good chance to refresh and recover here. All this says a lot about Pop. I'm not sure exactly what it says, but I think it's complimentary. I know I was grateful for it all.

While I sat with a loaded shotgun, covering the door, Rusty explored the rest of the building. There were several other tenants in residence. At least, there were four other floors with people on them, presumably tenants who couldn't leave on their own or who decided to stick it out where they were and hope for rescue.

The top floor was locked off, but several floors under it had all the apartments broken into and looted, raided for supplies. The residents at the top were working their way down in terms of salvage and scavenging. Judging by their progress, we had a while before they reached our floor, but there were other residents on nearer floors. We'd burn that bridge when someone got around to us.

Rusty insisted on putting cushions in front of our locked and bolted door. As a wolf, he curled up on them and slept there. I didn't argue. It beat keeping watches, and the door was *not* a regulation door. It was a steel plate with a pretty veneer covering it. The frame and the mounting in the wall was of similar construction. If someone started to monkey with the door, Rusty could bark. If anyone tried to fire through the door, they would only hurt themselves. A smart looter would go away for a week, until the dog starved. Meanwhile, Rusty would track them down by scent and make sure they didn't last a week.

I had a brief pang of worry about Gus. His feeder was only good for a month, even with the extra-large hopper. At least he wasn't in my house—I don't think he was in the house—when the bang went off. There wasn't a lot I could do about it, either way, but later, perhaps...

During two days in the new place—our first two days, I should say—we talked a lot. We stayed quiet, of course, so as not to attract attention, and accepted whatever light levels the windows provided. On a couple of occasions, we lay on the balcony and kept low, out of view. Every night, the city crackled and popped with the sound of gunfire. Mostly semi-automatic weapons, but lots of them. A few submachine guns. I didn't hear any heavy weapons, though.

"Sounds like the survivors are getting friskier about defending their turf," I observed.

"Oh, yes. Probably from the vampires. I doubt anyone is attacking another territory while the bloodsuckers are out in force."

"Tell me more."

While I was in the ground, a plague of vampires spread through the tunnels.

Is a group of vampires a plague? Or a coven? No, witches are covens. What's the group thing for vampires? I'm pretty sure a bunch of zombies is a "plague." So, vampires... a clutch? A brood? A nest? I've only ever dealt with *one!* What do you call a bunch of them? A family line of them might be a clan, I suppose, but what about a group that may or may not be part of a specific bloodline? A siege of vampires? A reflection? A vein? Actually, a "vein" of vampires sounds pretty good.

At any rate, Rusty wasn't much bothered by them, at first, since he stuck to his wolf form. In the underground darkness, his nose was more important than his eyes, and the vampires strongly preferred humans. After two days in the tunnels, there were enough of them to be a real problem, even for him. More and more people were in the process of becoming undead and humans were harder to come by. The new vampires' hunger for blood made them ravenous. Rats, cats, dogs, even wolves were now prey.

But those two days gave Rusty time to recuperate. His flash-burns were much better, so he felt confident enough to venture out and find a new den. He made his way around, seeing what was going on, trying to avoid getting shot, and scoping out the situation. It wasn't a good day, but it did mean he could at least scavenge for food instead of eating what he could find in the tunnels.

He didn't go into detail and I didn't ask.

Early the next morning, before he was really ready to wake up, an owl hooted at him. He came awake with a start and the owl, perched on the remains of a brick building corner, looked down at him. It flew off to a pile of tumbled concrete and watched him. A little more back-and-forth and Rusty finally went over to the broken concrete pile. The owl went on to another spot, leading him on. Eventually, it perched on the clockwork gear-head of my sculpture.

Rusty hunted around, found a hammer in the rubble, and whanged the horse-head. The rest I already knew.

"And this owl led you to me?"

"Yep. I thought you sent it to fetch me."

"Nope. Weird."

"I agree. Why would an owl do that?"

"Got me. I like owls, but I don't know any who would do me a favor. Maybe it was my Uncle Dusty."

Rusty shivered.

"Maybe. Ask him next time you see him."

"I might. So, vampires?"

"Yeah. They come out of the tunnels, roam the streets at night, bite anyone or anything they find, and most of them go underground again around sunrise."

"Most of them?"

"First morning out of the tunnels, I heard screaming and went to look. One stood in the middle of the street and screamed at the rising sun as he burst into flames."

"Interesting. Too stupid to go below? Or did he realize what was happening to him and decide to end it all?"

"Couldn't say. It was over pretty quick and the screams were kinda generic."

"I imagine."

"How's the leg?"

"Still pulling it together. I've got the bones mostly intact, at least. It doesn't hurt on its own anymore, but the spells forcing it to regrow the ruined tissues—that's a bit painful. I've still got the pain turned down, but that takes power, too."

"Weren't you doing a solar power spell thingy?"

"Yes. It takes a lot of work to gather up power to create such a spell, so I've had to start small. There are a dozen small spells on the windows, each providing a tiny trickle of power, mostly supplying the healing magic. Now I have enough of them I can, come morning, start making bigger ones. I'll build a line of them, north and south, tracking the Sun. I want to get to the point where I can build at least one more panel a day and still run the basic regeneration on my leg. Give me a week of clear skies and I should be far enough ahead to stop building panels and focus all the power on getting mobile again."

"Shouldn't you build up a power reserve?"

"I agree I need one, but my immediate concern is getting mobile. I'm pinned down here until I can run on my own. I'll try to keep adding to the array, but the important thing is to get on *both* feet again."

I didn't mention I'd been building the same damn spell over and over and over again for the past several days—small ones, only a few square inches at a time, mostly—and I was tired of it. Pop could make panels replicate on their own. I have to build the things by hand. Or almost by hand. I have the spell diagrams in my notebook, which saves time and effort, but I still have to do the mental weightlifting to energize it and place it.

"Running is overrated," he observed, "but you're a nicer person than I am."

"How do you figure?"

"I don't see a problem with killing someone when my life might depend on it."

"In general, I agree. Right now, I feel like a treed squirrel. If things go wrong, I don't have any choice about whether or not to run. I want the option."

"Suit yourself. Can I interest you in a game of Guess The Entrée?"

"Only if we follow it with Scrabble."

"You always win," he complained.

"Chess?"

"Ditto."

"Monopoly?"

"I want to stay friends."

"Gin rummy?"

"Okay. I haven't had a chance to lose at a card game, yet. But no mind reading!"

Journal Entry #41

My repair spell, once it got a decent amount of power, did get the radio operational again. I didn't like how much power it took. There's a peculiar sort of double curve when it comes to fixing things. Large, obvious rents in the structure require a lot of power simply because there's a large, obvious problem. But down on the scale where you need a microscope to see the damage, it takes a lot of power for those sorts of problems, too.

Pop says it's because mass and knowledge are both factors. If you know exactly what you want to do, it takes less power. If you're telling the spell, "Reverse entropy, please," it has to work one hell of a lot harder.

It's kind of like my leg. If I use a spell to look inside my leg, trace nerve lines by hand, and tell my body to put nerves back in order along those lines, it's not too power intensive. If I look at my leg and tell the spell, "Fix it!" it's going to be a horrible power hog.

This is why Pop has pattern-analysis and copying spells for healing magic. I gridded and copied an image of my good leg, mirrored it, and put it over my bad leg, locking it in place. This is the pattern the regeneration followed, so it's been going pretty quickly, all things considered.

If I'd had a working shortwave receiver, I might have been able to do the same thing. As it was, it took a while before we could listen to the airwaves. The battery was low, but Rusty and I took turns cranking a little survival generator. It was something Pop might have grabbed from the 1950s, made of steel, and tough enough to be dragged ashore at Normandy. Rusty figured out how to assemble the thing with its pedals and braces and whatnot. He pedaled. When he got tired, I hand-cranked it.

It worked fine, as did all the electronic stuff from the wardrobes. I'm guessing they were shielded, surrounded by the metal of the gun lockers. Why he didn't include a little shortwave receiver inside the lockers, I'm not sure. He could have crammed one in there. Probably. With a shoehorn, maybe. Or a crowbar.

Despite our efforts to listen to the world, there wasn't a lot on the radio. There were several coded things, bits of high-speed dit-dah-dit beeping, and three different mayday calls. One was in English and broadcasting from Nevada. Another was in French, calling for help from someplace called Le Villard. The third was in Hindi and needed help in Ukwa, wherever that is. If anybody else was talking, we weren't getting it. I'm not sure if nuclear weapons on such a scale do anything to the ionosphere, but I took comfort from the fact there wasn't an excessive amount of static—therefore, perhaps, not a huge amount of radiation in the upper atmosphere or anywhere near us.

I was sorely tempted to use magic to increase the effectiveness of the antenna, hoping to pick up weaker signals, but I resisted. I settled for experimenting with additional wire and getting Rusty to string it around the room. Either we did it wrong or it was an extremely taciturn planet.

"Shouldn't there be more, you know, talking and stuff?" Rusty asked.

"There absolutely should be, yes."

"Why aren't there?"

"Electromagnetic pulses are bad for electronics."

"What are those?"

I had a bad moment while I tried to wrap my head around the idea someone from a technological society could live their whole life and not know what an EMP is. I've had this disconnect before. Pop and I went on field trips to lots of places, some in the far past, some in the far future, and some so far to one side or the other they didn't even qualify to be on the same map. And, to be perfectly honest, a lot of the time *I* was the yokel from Hicksville who didn't understand anything.

"Okay," I began, "let me explain. EMP—Electro-Magnetic Pulse—is a side effect of putting a lot of energy into the atmosphere of a planet with a magnetic field. There are multiple stages to it, but the basic problem is it's a big magnetic burst inducing electricity in every conductor it encounters. The upshot of which is it acts a lot like a lightning strike inside the electronic gadget. Not a single lightning strike to the power grid, but an individual lightning strike on every single device in the area."

"It shorts stuff out."

"Yes. Now, one zap is bad, especially for electronics having really tiny, delicate components. Old stuff, like a vacuum tube, handles it a lot better than anything with a silicon chip. Anything on, with current already flowing, is especially vulnerable. Things turned off and unplugged are harder to hurt, but it can happen."

"So backup systems are probably okay? Like backup generators in a hospital?"

"Not so fast. Did you notice the power went out before the first fireball?"

"Uh… hmm. Yeah, the lights went out. The autocabs all came to a stop. But I thought this EMP thing was part of the warhead going off?"

"It depends on the warhead. I think the first blackout was from a chemically-fueled EMP. You can make an EMP bomb. With modern explosives and superconductors, I'm guessing you can make a really good one."

"So?"

"So the power goes out because you set off a normal-sized bomb. There's a boom, but a pickup truck full of bang doesn't register the same way as a nuke. This boom, however, is part of an EMP bomb. Done at altitude, electronics fry for miles around, but you don't know it's an attack. It's blackout. The power grid has done something unpleasant again and your neighborhood goes dark."

"I saw a dirigible on fire. Could that be part of it?"

"Was it on fire? Or did it have an explosion?"

"I'm not sure. It was a big fire, though, so I guess there could have been a bomb on board."

"There you go. Boom. Power surges, electronics fry, breakers pop—too late!—and everything goes dark. What do you turn on first?"

"I guess a flashlight. Maybe a camping radio?"

"And if you have a backup generator at home?"

"If I had one, yeah. I'd try to get news, probably, to find out how widespread the blackout is. Oh."

"Yeah. You spend fifteen, twenty minutes digging out what is, effectively, your survival equipment, whether you think of it that way or not. Then the big, bright light goes off and blasts out an even bigger, stronger EMP, fueled by atoms breaking up or getting cozy or both. This hits all those emergency things you've dusted off and turned on. It's kind of a worst-case scenario." Then I remembered the scattered additional strikes, the direct hits on military centers, and the lack of shortwave radio chatter. Something clicked.

"And if, after all this, you still have a working radio transmitter," I went on, slowly, "you eventually start to ask who might still be out there. Is there a government? Is there a military structure? Is there an emergency management plan in place? And those transmissions tell anyone who's interested exactly where to drop another real nuke, because a lot of military equipment is hardened against this sort of thing. I don't mean a military base; those are obvious. I mean a division out in the field on maneuvers, too far from their barracks to be destroyed with their base. You don't even have to worry about doing it yourself. Odds are, somewhere there's a submarine or a missile base or a bomber or a satellite with exactly those orders: kill centers of organization to prevent retaliation."

"But we're not all on fire," Rusty pointed out. "We didn't get killed in a massive wave of missiles. The Island is pretty banged up, but there are places you can stand, look around, and not realize there's a lot of city missing. Or is there more damage than I think?"

"Bring me the maps, please."

He did so. The bundle was a collection of laminated sheets connected in one corner by a ring. I flipped through the stack to a Manhattan street map. I drew circles for him, since he didn't get the astral-eye view I did. The rings of broken buildings defined circles centered on the Brooklyn Navy Yard to the south, Fort Lee to the north, and a point north of Central Park.

"There are a lot more elsewhere," I told him, "all across the country and the globe. It's not the carpet-bombing you'd expect from the Cold War propaganda, but it's plenty bad enough.

"I'm not sure what's going on," I continued. "I don't know if this was the planned opening move of a larger war. It might be major EMP strikes before a mild nuclear roasting, followed by picking off anyone indiscreet enough to chatter, then the ground invasion. I don't know what they would hope to gain. I can't think of a reason anyone would want to do it, aside from supernatural mind control powers."

"Alden?"

"Or the vampires. Those two sides are the ones running amok. Although," I added, "the spread of vampirism may be an accident. Vampires are bioweapons, of a sort. All it takes is one vampire going cuckoo and going on a biting spree—or even someone getting bit by a flash-burned vampire, fighting it off, and then going on his own blood-hungry rampage. It's not a case of doubling every few days. A vampire can bite over a thousand people in one night, if he really tries."

"Please don't say things like that."

"I'm sorry, but I've done this math. It's not good."

"So the vampires did this? Why? They need people to eat, don't they?"

"Yes, they do. I'm not sure they did it, though. As you say, they need people to eat. Spreading vampirism in an uncontrolled manner will be incredibly bad for them.

"But I'm not discounting Alden," I went on. "He was trying to isolate Manhattan from the undead, presumably to make it his own little kingdom. He might have had the idea to trigger an apocalypse and start over with his loyal hordes of minions. We did find he had an emergency escape route under one church. He went to the effort of setting up a line of retreat, so he was concerned it might be necessary."

"Good point. He'd be safe there?"

"Safe from any attacks here, yes. It's another world. The interface is kind of like a fixed gate. I don't know if they're always open, sometimes open, or if there's any sort of pattern to them or not. I've only seen a couple."

"But he can't escape that way. We made sure. He wouldn't still do this if he didn't have an out. Would he?"

"Thing is, the vampires were pushing him and may have screwed up his plans. This might not have been intentional, regardless of who did it." I frowned as a thought occurred. "Come to think of it, Alden and the vampires might have triggered it without meaning to."

"How? They give commands to their minions, don't they?"

"Yes, but what if someone discovered these two mind-controlling factions? It would look as though the choices were to either fall under the control of a psychic priest or under the control of blood-sucking monsters. 'No, thanks; I'll nuke us into oblivion so neither of you win.' Something like that could have happened, too."

"How likely is it?"

"The usual subtleties were fraying a bit in their conflict, I think. I don't think it's the most likely reason, but it can't be dismissed."

"So, it could have been humans. It could have been Alden. It could have been vampires. The reasons for it could range from accident to a moment of panic to a carefully-planned move for a larger purpose. I'm *so* glad we sorted everything out."

"I appreciate your sarcasm. Good job. Again, I don't know and don't see a good way to find out."

"Would Zeno know?" Rusty asked, suddenly.

"Zeno would probably have all the information, yes, but Zeno was EMP'd shortly before being crushed in a falling house. The best I can hope for is recovering his memory core, or at least the data from it."

"Why didn't he tell you someone was planning a nuclear attack?"

"I didn't tell him to find out," I explained, "and Zeno isn't a real intelligence. He acts like it, but he's only a complex of algorithms. He has no spells making him... what's the word? He's only an expert system, not a sapient, sentient being. He just runs programs. He only follows instructions. I had him spying on Alden, vampires, and criminal kingpins. Of the three, Alden was probably communicating with his minions psychically, the vampires were generally planning in a language he could record but not yet decipher, and the criminal kingpins were unlikely to be involved."

I rubbed my temples and wondered if I could spare the power to fix the developing headache. I decided on aspirin, instead.

"If I'd gotten around to translating a ton of vampire council meetings sooner, maybe it would have been something they mentioned, either as one of their own plans or their worries about who Alden was taking over—world leaders, military leaders, individual nuclear submarine commanders, whatever. If I'd thought to try and intercept any psychic impulses Alden sent out, maybe I could have monitored what he said to his minions. But there were problems, distractions. I had other things that seemed more important at the time. On top of everything, I would have to develop and deploy a lot of things I don't presently know how to do! I'm only one person!"

"It's not your fault," Rusty assured me. "Someone else did this."

"Yeah, but I didn't stop it."

"And you don't know you could have," he added.

"True. Some superhero I turned out to be."

"There's a learning curve."

"A sharp one. Sharp enough to draw blood."

"Hey, any one you walk away from, right? Or any one your sidekick carries you away from."

"Thanks, sidekick."

"Now do me a favor."

"Anything I can."

"Can you tell me how much radiation I got?"

"What? Why?"

"I'm a werewolf."

"…and?"

"We regenerate."

"Uh… yeah?"

"So I'm worried about radiation."

"Why? I'd think you'd be resistant to it, wouldn't you? You regenerate—or, no, would you? Your cells already replicate at a phenomenal rate…"

"I dunno. All I know is we can get cancer. If we don't get killed, we live a long time and age really well. But, these days, silver isn't what usually gets us. It's cancer. Old wolves get it and they die, usually pretty suddenly. It's a disease we know is deadly and we try like hell to avoid. It's the main reason you don't see a lot of us smoking. When we get lung cancer, it's fast and aggressive."

"Really?" I thought about it. A werewolf would regenerate from most things, but if his own cells started reproducing out of control, they might retain the regeneration of the original cells. Talk about a fast-growing tumor! And one immune or highly resistant to every sort of conventional treatment. Even surgery. Most surgeons don't use silver scalpels.

What happens if a werewolf's tumor is exposed to the full moon? I don't know and I *really* don't want to.

I had him lay on the couch and I looked him over. His burns were healed enough to be superficial scars. Even those would go away in another few days, thanks to my healing amulet. Physically, there was nothing wrong with him. Oddly enough, his sweatpants were also in good shape. I think they healed with him whenever they were part of him. I didn't anticipate that, but it made sense.

As for anything unusual, I was fairly confident the healing spell on his necklace would take care of it, at least while it was small and easily killed. Was there anything to indicate he had internal problems? He clearly didn't have radiation poisoning. We'd have seen symptoms by now. He had all his hair, had no problem eating, and certainly didn't have chronic fatigue. A close, fine scan didn't turn up any unusual growths, either.

"I'm not finding anything. We can check again in a month, but I don't think you actually got much radiation. You were far enough away to survive the heat pulse, so you were probably too far to get any real dose of ionizing radiation. Then you were underground for a couple of days, which means you avoided the worst of any fallout. I've checked for atmospheric radiation, but I'm not seeing much, if any, so we're probably okay on the fallout front. I would avoid any area directly under a detonation, but otherwise I think you'll be okay."

Rusty was greatly relieved. He helped me back to the bedroom. I did a scan of my own, just to be safe. I don't know if Pop thought about radiation resistance when he was helping me grow up. I'm ninety-nine percent sure he did, but that one percent meant I was doing a scan.

I was fine. My leg was still a problem, but it was coming along.

The only thing I wished was for more entertainment. The place didn't have enough books. I contented myself with knitting. I once knitted a scarf for Pop when I was learning how. I wanted to knit socks, but it sort of grew. He loved it, though. I wonder what became of it?

Journal Entry #42

I'm not sure how long it would take to completely regrow a leg, but I'm sure it would take longer than the six days it took to fix mine. Six days of high-powered work, I mean, not counting the three or so days of framework-building and healing spells I did in my temporary tomb.

The crush damage was extensive, but a fair amount of material was still there. Getting bone fragments to turn back into real bones was the easy part. Attaching ligaments, cartilage, and tendons wasn't much harder. Trouble was, a lot of muscle fiber was… well… ketchup. My body had to process the ruined stuff, which was not fun. At the same time, everything salvageable had to link into the framework and grow into new muscle.

For Pop, this is easy. For the rest of us, who actually have to be alive during the whole process, it's trickier.

Someone once compared a surgeon to a mechanic. It goes like this: A mechanic can take apart an engine, clean it, replace gaskets, replace worn parts, put it all back together, and make it run like new. A surgeon does the same thing, only he does his work while the engine is running. I couldn't shut down and rearrange things to suit myself, so it took a lot more time and attention.

Once I had the leg restored, I spent another day testing and exercising, making sure I had the proper muscle density, range of motion, and nerve response. It's one thing to put it back together. It's another thing to say it's in perfect condition. I wanted to be able to sprint like the wind if occasion called for it.

Rusty, of course, was in perfect shape before I was. His natural regeneration was enhanced by my magical additions, so the burns were the only things to annoy him for any length of time.

"Whatcha making?" he asked.

"I'm knitting."

"I can see that. What's it going to be?"

"I was thinking I could turn it into a magical transformer."

"How so?"

"If I can work it right—that is, if I can put enough energy-transforming spells in it—I should be able to wrap it around anything hot, or even leave it in the sunlight, and get magical energy out of it."

"Handy."

"Yep. But I'm done with it for now," I added, putting away my knitting. "I want to go through another yoga routine to make sure I'm back in top form, then I think I'm ready to go."

He looked up from the camp stove and watched, stirring idly to keep something from burning.

"You look good," he admitted. "Leg feeling back to normal?"

"Yep."

"You sure you don't want another day?"

"I'm fit and ready."

"Okay. What's the plan?"

"I want to find the remains of Zeno. He's got information I need."

"We're going to figure out who started this?"

"I want to know."

"I agree, if only for posterity, assuming there is one. I have other questions that might be more immediate."

"Such as?"

"You've got invisible solar panel spell things here. They're important for all the magic stuff. Right?"

"Sure."

"Can you bring them with us?"

I thought about it. It wouldn't be impossible. It would be a lot easier, in fact, than casting all new ones. It would certainly be easier than transporting actual solar panels for electricity. These were energy constructs—spells—not physical objects.

I had a "You idiot!" moment.

You know the moment when you've been doing something the hard way forever? And you suddenly realize how hard you've made it on yourself? And you see so clearly how you could have done it the easy way all this time, but you were too much of an idiot to realize it?

I have several decent gems in the jewelry box, plus the diamonds in the trade goods drawer. These aren't big enough to be much as power crystals, but I can permanently enchant one with a solar conversion spell, complete with enough power to cast the spell— some level of the spell, I mean. Whatever size panel it produces is still better than doing without. It'll only have enough power to work once, but then it can build up a charge until it's full, then I can activate it again to produce another panel.

If I'm clever—and I used to think I was—I might even rig up a temporary spell around such a gem to automatically set it off when it reached its power capacity. I'll still have to move them, place them, and connect them so they don't waste their produced power to the environment. It's a long, long way from self-replication, but it's a hell of a lot easier than what I was doing.

"I can either bring them with us or I can build more. I'll be prepared, after this. In fact, we can stay here for a while longer, getting ready."

"Good. I didn't want to ask while you were working so hard to get better, but now… You have a little power to spare?"

"Absolutely. What's on your mind?"

"Mom and Dad. I don't know where they were when the lights went out. If you're done with all the big stuff here, can you do something to find them? I mean, I don't know if they're alive or dead. If they're dead, there's not much I can do about it. If they're alive, then they might need our help—but if they've survived this long, the probably don't need help right now. So it's not really *urgent*, I guess, but I need to know."

"I can try. Tell you what. Let me enchant a gem and get it ready. Then we'll use the mirror in the bedroom as a scrying device and see what we can see."

"Thanks, Phoebe."

I selected the biggest gem in the box—a diamond. Pop likes diamonds. He says the carbon lattice is ideal for our purposes. I prefer rubies, myself, but emeralds are also nice. Sapphires are pretty, too. Diamonds always seem so cold to me, like ice that doesn't know when to quit.

Enchanting a solar panel spell into the gem wasn't as hard as I'd feared. I wanted a permanent emplacement in the gem because I anticipated it was going to see a lot of hard use. It would be much easier than casting the spell over and over. Right now, being able to hold a gem in my hand, point my finger, and produce a power panel was worth its weight in, well, diamonds.

With that set up, I put it on the chain I use for my own amulets. The diamond was built into a ring, but I didn't want to add something that big to my hands.

Time to find a couple of werewolves.

The first thing we did was get out the maps. I sent a scrying sensor up to get an overhead view of the northern Manhattan bombsite. There was no real crater to be found, but there was an obvious center to the devastation.

I did approximations from memory. Given the lack of crater, the blast damage, and the thermal damage, I worked backward to calculate an approximate yield and height of burst. I didn't have exact measurements so it wasn't terribly accurate, but an approximation can be useful.

Minimum values were three hundred kilotons at about two thousand meters, give or take.

The circles we drew gave us a detonation point near Malcolm X Boulevard and West 116th Street, almost exactly two miles away from my house. The pizza shop was only about three-quarters of a mile from ground zero.

I did the measurements before scrying because I wanted Rusty to be prepared for it. They were less than half my distance from the blast, if they were at home. I got lucky. I was in my basement and had a metal horse to hide under. They were werewolves, but what were they going to do? Jump into a pizza oven?

With trepidation and fear, I zoomed in, dropping the sensor down toward the approximate area. It helped to have the remains of the Third Avenue Bridge to navigate by. The bridge footings and the loop were still visible, mostly because they were surrounded by flash-burned parks. 129th wasn't visible at all, but the flattened, level-ish area of rubble implied a firm, flat surface underneath. I followed this westward and recognized the devastated area of Park Avenue as a cross street. About half a block farther...

"See anything?" I asked.

"No."

I circled the area, came back to criss-cross the wreckage.

"Can you fly the point of view down inside the rubble?" Rusty asked.

"Yes. Are you sure you want me to?"

"I have to know," he said, voice bleak.

"All right. Let me set up for darkness and ground-penetrating wavelengths."

"Whatever it takes."

I added a spectrum-shifter to the scrying spell, tuning it to amplify and shift all the x-rays and above into the visible spectrum. We wouldn't see well, but we would see shadows through the rocks.

This process went much more slowly, creeping through the rubble at the point Rusty indicated and spiraling out. We spent the rest of the day and part of the night doing a slow, thorough scan, moving slowly through the ruins. Our patience and thoroughness were rewarded, after a fashion.

Contrary to popular opinion, it does not take silver to kill a werewolf. You can do it with a wood chipper. You can do it with a sword and determination, or with enough ammunition for your machine gun. It's not easy, but there is no kill like overkill.

You can also do it by smearing them between tons of broken brick and concrete before cooking what's left in a firestorm.

Rusty recognized his father's ring. It wasn't a circle anymore, but it had a distinctive design. The carbonized stick inside it used to be bone.

"Do you want me to keep looking?" I asked, softly.

"No, but go ahead. We have to find Mom, now."

"If your Dad was downstairs, the blast would have toppled the building—"

"Just look, okay?"

I moved the scanner in an arc, back and forth, looking through the rubble at a higher level. It took less than an hour to find his mother. She was in better shape, if by "better" you mean she was less spread out.

Rusty turned away from the mirror.

"I'm going out for a while."

"Where to?"

"Out."

"There are vampires…?"

"Yeah. But sometimes you have to run with the wolves."

"I'll pretend I understand what you mean. I'll come with you and let you out."

And, I hope, let you back in, I thought. But I didn't say it.

I spent a long night in the lobby, keeping out of sight and wondering if Rusty would come back. He stripped out of his normal clothes and went wolf as soon as I had a side door unlocked and open.

Maybe it was a good night, or maybe nobody really thought an apartment block was a good place to scavenge. Maybe scavengers hadn't finished looting everything closer to their bases. Or, if there were tons of vampires out for blood, maybe nobody wanted to come out. How many people were left in Manhattan? There were almost two million in the last census, I think. Now? There was no way to tell.

Geographically, about seventy percent of the island was rubble, burned, or burned rubble. It's not really a valid comparison, but if I assume three-quarters of the population was also destroyed, it still leaves half a million people.

How many of those are vampires?

Nobody came near the doors, though I did hear the usual crackle of gunfire through most of the night.

Journal Entry #43

Rusty came back after dawn. He shook himself thoroughly outside the door, then shifted upward again, turning back into a man. I let him in and made sure the door locked behind him. No one was out and about that I could see.

"You alive?" I asked.

"I am."

"How do you feel?"

"Better. Not good. Better."

"Okay. Let's get upstairs."

"You're not going to yell at me for being stupid?" he asked.

"Nope. I do stupid things, too."

"Oh."

We climbed forty million stairs again. At least I was now certain my leg was in full working order. I unlocked the doors and let us in.

"Breakfast?"

"What have we got?"

"Green box, green box, green box, or the other green box. And water."

"I'll take what's in the box. No, wait! How about something in a box? Not that box; the other one."

I slid one over to him and he tore it open while I put a bottle of water in front of him. He didn't bother with the self-heating gimmick. He ate straight out of the package and gulped water. We had lots, but I put the condensation pitcher in front of him next. No sense in wasting the bottled stuff in our reserves.

"Anything new out there?" I asked.

"Not so I noticed. I wasn't really out to look. Just to run."

"Okay. I've been thinking it over and we should probably figure out what's going on."

"I thought you wanted to learn who was responsible?"

"I do. I'm starting to think it will wait. The ultimate responsibility for this isn't going to be easy to nail down, so I'll settle for who pushed the button. Even that can wait, though. I've been listening to gunfire every night, presumably as people in strong points hold off vampire hordes."

"Or hold off each other. If people are hunkered down, they might not realize the vampires have overrun the streets. And they won't, not until they, personally, get overrun."

"We should figure out what's going on right now and what we can do about it. Later, we can worry about punishing the wrongdoing."

"I thought you were big on punishing the wicked?"

"I am, but I'm not a fanatic about it. I'd never have time for anything else."

"Fair enough."

We used the mirrors on the vanity table to look all over the island. While I'd been hogging the power to heal, things had grown worse. Rusty, when he lived underground, noticed the spread of vampires. Now, a week later, things were looking ugly.

It's bad enough to have an urban area with no utilities—no power, no water, no nothing! A city becomes a collection of very comfortable caves, but not much more than that. The key, though, is food. Without supplies from outside, it turns into a deathtrap. You can salvage all sorts of tools and materials, but it's hard to grow food in a city park.

At least, grow and harvest it in time to keep from starving. Unless you've got a lot of lead time, it's futile. Even if you have supplies to last until the first harvest, the maximum number of people you can support this way is surprisingly low.

Fortunately, my earlier estimate of half a million living human beings was a bit high. Or maybe it wasn't. There was an ongoing decrease in living, breathing people. In the time between the blasts and now, the number continued to shrink. Now, after looking carefully around, my best guess was, at most, ten thousand.

The undead, on the other hand, more than made up the difference.

Rusty and I looked over everything. We started with the perimeter of the island, checking the bridges and tunnels as points of access. A few bridges were still in good shape. A small chunk of the island was relatively untouched, up by the 207th Street railyard. The Henry Hudson Bridge, along with Broadway and University Heights, were still standing. South of there, the only standing bridge was the Queensboro.

"Standing" doesn't necessarily mean "passable." When the EMP hit, electric cars came to a stop *en masse*. Zipping along a bridge didn't matter. It was a "safety feature." Anyone on manual, or driving a fuel-burner of any sort, also suffered a total loss of power, but human reaction times don't stop the car as quickly. There were chain-reaction accidents all up and down the bridges, coming and going.

They should have made the bridges autodrive-only, too. Oops.

One could walk across a bridge, threading between cars and wrecks, but there was no hope of driving. I'm not sure a motorcycle could get through the mess. It would involve unlocking the brakes on a lot of vehicles and pushing them to the side—sometimes pushing them *off*, to make room—by hand. It would take days to clear one lane.

The only other ways off the island, aside from water travel, were the tunnels. The Queens-Midtown tunnel looked okay. The Holland was buried in rubble at both ends and there was water slowly filling up the Lincoln. A strong swimmer could make it through the Lincoln, but it would take several yards of guts. A waterproof light would also be nice. The Midtown tunnel looked okay, but it was slowly flooding, too. At least the cars stayed on the bottom, so they weren't obstacles

Do the tunnels normally have pumps to keep them dry? Did these die when the power did, or did the preliminary kabooms fry their electronics? Or did they start out watertight and the real kabooms shook them hard enough to start leaks?

What we knew for sure was all the surviving bridges and the one functional tunnel each had a vampire trap in it, a place where they burst into flames. I wondered if that was by design. I doubted it. A vampire on foot had problems crossing running water, so all bridges and tunnels were impassable, now.

We then took a quick look around the blasted areas. The hit nearest my house flattened things pretty well in my neighborhood. South of 60th or thereabouts, most of the buildings were still standing. Another one went off somewhere around the Brooklyn Navy Yard. The blast made it well into Manhattan, of course. The curve of the destruction started on the east side, near the School of Medicine, and arced west and south until it hit the west side, roughly around 10th Street.

That still left a lot of area to cover with the magical equivalent of a camera drone—roughly five hundred city blocks.

Fortunately—sort of—there was a lot of focusing involved. Most buildings were abandoned. There might be someone living in there, hiding and hunkering down, like Rusty and I and our in-building neighbors, but the majority of the survivors were clustered in smaller areas, behind barricades and other makeshift fortifications.

Was the police building in Times Square such a fortification? Or did living people attack it to get weapons? On the other hand, did they need to? There were a lot of guns floating around the city, gun laws or no gun laws. I know I've been shot by drug dealers using everything from high-end, custom-made pistols to a North Korean copy of a Chinese knockoff of the Russian Kalashnikov.

I miss my armor. Recharging it in this environment would take a lot more time or a hell of a lot more panels, though, even if it survived the destruction.

Which reminded me of Jason. Where was he? He once mentioned he had a good view of Carnegie Hall, which would put him right on the border of broken buildings. If he wasn't in his armor, he might be dead. Even if he was in his armor, being too close to the blast would still kill him. Everything depended on where he was standing when the everything went to hell.

I tried a location spell. Could I find Jason? No, I could not. That didn't mean he was dead, of course. It only meant he was outside my range. If he wasn't standing somewhere unpleasant when the fireworks went off, he had over a week to escape the Manhattan Island deathtrap. If he did, he could be far, far away. He's a professional mercenary. No doubt he had resources.

On the other hand, he might be shuffling through the subway tunnels, looking for a rat to bite. My location spell was a high-efficiency thing, tuning in on his psychic emissions. I'm not sure it would register a proto-vampire version of him.

Did I want to know? Yes. On the other hand, did it matter? Either way, was there anything I could do for him? If he escaped Manhattan, maybe later. If he was a vampire, no, not really. I certainly couldn't do anything for him right now. Maybe next week. Next month. Next year.

He might also have died in the fighting. There were signs of human fortifications in several places. Most of them were gutted. Someone decided to barricade themselves into the meatpacking district. It did not end well, but it was a good idea. They focused on food stores, not on firepower. Another barricade was in the Hudson railyard. The train cars make good individual shelters and it's close to the Lincoln Tunnel, if you care to push your luck. It's also on the west side of the island, so you can easily signal any rescuers on the mainland. It's not a defensible position, though, and individual rail cars are like Twinkies with bloody filling as far as vampires are concerned.

Several groups took cover in various churches. This worked pretty well from the standpoint of keeping vampires from coming in, but it only forced the undead to get smarter. They lobbed simple firebombs in through windows.

Do these sorts of vampires get smarter because they encounter obstacles to their feeding? Someone gets bitten and they go bloody nuts. Will they stay a mindless, bloodthirsty monster forever if you keep them fed? Or do they gradually start to become… well, not more human, but more intelligent on their own? Is the process inevitable, but something you can accelerate? Or does it only happen when you force them to think?

The two remaining strongholds were a library and a bank.

The bank I understood. It was a masonry and concrete structure, solid as a brick, and when they locked up for the night, they didn't show themselves. They were avoiding notice by being completely hidden behind armored walls. Let the undead own the night! We won't come out until my wind-up alarm clock says daytime has been going on for half an hour!

If the vampires ever did find out they were there, though… yes, the walls would be a problem. Granted. But we're talking about full-on undead, here. They would *claw* their way in, given time. And time is one thing they have lots of.

The library was a bit more puzzling. The Fifth Avenue library wasn't a fort. I wouldn't even call it defensible. It had windows everywhere, all the way around the ground floor, in easy reach. Sure, it had good sight lines in front and back, where it had park-like areas, but the sides were limited to the width of the street.

Someone had improved it a little as a defensive position, anyway. Several of the upper windows were broken out for shooters to use. A lot of the usual greenery—the trees in front and Bryant Park in back—were cut down or burned away by hand. Cars were used as barricades, yes, but not near the building. They were overturned and burned in place at least a block away, out of sight of the building. Why?

No, forget the cars. Why the library? St. Peter's, sure. A police station. Even the Empire State Building. Those I could understand. But the *library*? How could you defend it from anything, let alone vampires? A human being could walk up to it and break in with a couple of swift kicks!

We figured it out when I swooped my viewpoint down toward it, trying to look inside. The scrying sensor fuzzed into glittering static.

"Shush!" Rusty cautioned me. "There are people in this building! People on the *street* could have heard you!"

I contained any further outburst and seethed inwardly.

A dozen nuclear detonations within a fifteen-mile radius of my house. Millions of people dead in the first few seconds, millions more succumb to their injuries in the next few days, and most of the rest die in the vampire-plague apocalypse. And *Alden* lives through it!

Why am I surprised? Pop might have, and Alden has Pop's old gear. Even so, it felt to me as though he somehow cheated death. Maybe I wanted him to die in a fireball and solve my own problem with him. If someone else vaporized him, I wouldn't still have the question of what to do about him. But that would be too damned *convenient*.

All right, Alden has the library. Normally, I have great respect for libraries. Today, though, I'm prepared to write it off. Other worlds have libraries exactly like it. Besides, the locals aren't exactly going to use it.

Does he have anyone in the library with him? It's daytime, so anyone else living there should be out and about. Are they? Yes, there are people roaming the streets. They're using those urban, public-access bicycles to get around quickly. They're breaking into everything they come across, opening every door, searching every room. Quite methodical. It doesn't look as if they're searching for anything in particular. They're gathering all the resources they can find in an orderly a manner. The methodical, thorough searching means if they've already searched a nearby building, they never need to search it again and can focus on the next one.

I couldn't do a full examination on them from here, but I could watch their behavior. They were more than merely methodical and orderly. They were robotic. They weren't using initiative, they weren't making judgments, they weren't thinking about what they were doing. They had a procedure and they followed it with perfect and inhuman thoroughness.

Conclusion?

Yeah, Alden is in the library. He's got his own little kingdom of mind-controlled zombies—survivors of an apocalypse. They're his, now.

To be certain, I returned my view to the library. A celestial effect was centered on the library and spread out quite a lot. It wasn't a circle, though. I had to weave around a lot, mapping out the edges of the effect. It wasn't a single point source. The outer edge was a wavy line, like… like…

Did you ever do the thing in art class—or maybe while doodling in geometry—where you draw a circle, then place six more identical circles around it? You center a new circle on the perimeter of the first one. Once you draw the second circle, where it crosses the first, you have points to center the next circles. And, when you complete the set, you have intersection points where you can place more circles, expanding the design.

The wavy external border indicated there were a lot of generation points, all of them overlapping. At a guess, he no longer had a use for all his extra tektites, so he set them up to defend himself. The zones covered at least a block in every direction, completely surrounding the library and Bryant Park.

Inside this safe zone of celestial forces, he could do whatever the pleased. At the moment, he pleased to have mindless minions collecting whatever might be useful to his survival and comfort.

Why wasn't he sounding a siren on the roof, summoning more survivors? Did he have enough? And why was he in the library, of all things? Was it where he happened to be when the lights went out? Or did the library have something he wanted? Was there another weak place between worlds in there, down underground?

Pop taught me a neat trick for spying at a distance. It's possible to create a sort of lens by altering the refractive index of the air in a specific volume in front of a scrying sensor. Multiple lenses can turn into what is effectively a telescope. I can do it, but as with so many of the spells I know, I usually cast them inside the house or in a high-magic world.

I shut down the scrying sensor and went out onto the balcony to sit and think and periodically set off my sun-stone.

Note to self: golden topaz. It seems more appropriate if I'm going to call the thing a "sun-stone." Next time I get a golden topaz, I'll use it.

"Phoebe?"

"Yeah, I'm in a foul mood."

"I had hints. It was something you saw. I didn't think it wise to interrupt while you were concentrating, but could you let me in on it now?"

So I explained, pausing every little while to add another panel to the array. The array's output was being used to charge the spell embedded in the gem, so it was fairly quick, but I needed to interrupt it after every new panel. I didn't want to overlap them—it cuts down on the efficiency—so I had to either move the whole array over one space or move the panel all the way to the end of the array.

Weirdly, it costs the same either way. They're linked in relation to each other, so moving one causes the others to adjust automatically, like a high school drill team squaring off by touching their neighbor's shoulder. It takes power to move them, though, so it delays the production of another panel.

I started a new row in the array. It would build up power more quickly and I could switch between the two, later. Or start a third row.

Rusty, bless him, ignored my occasional profanity and sat beside me. He listened as I explained what I knew.

"All right. He's a survivor and you hate him for that, too. I hate him a little, myself."

"Oh?"

"Why should he get to live when my parents didn't? He didn't deserve to live in the first place, but I didn't care a whole lot. I was against him because you were. I don't need another reason, but now I have one."

"Oh."

"I don't see how any of this changes anything. Sure, there are different problems. Big ones. Now there's a plague of vampires spreading through Manhattan. Alden may be opposing them. He's got the celestial force to do it, doesn't he? He could be obvious to them, sort of playing the bait, luring in all the bloodsuckers so they don't spread off the island."

"That's... a good point. If this is an isolated incident—one vampire got out of hand here—there may not be a spreading horde of them all over the world."

"Shouldn't you check?"

"Yes, I should. And I will. As soon as I finish adding more panels for the day. Now that I've got this new gem, it's a lot less of a pain in the brain to do."

Rusty regarded the gem as I fired it up and formed a new panel.

"Can you teach me how to do it? I mean, if it's easy. I could do whatever it is and you could get back to doing the lookie-lookie thing."

I had to wonder. Werewolves *are* magical. Can they learn spells? Somehow, it seemed odd, and it shouldn't. Pop's a vampire, a magical creature, isn't he? He can do spells. Do werewolves have varying talents for magic like humans do, or is all their magic tied up in what they are?

"I can try to teach you," I agreed, "but it'll wait until after dark. I don't want to waste daylight while I can add to our power reserves."

"Suits me. In the meantime, since we do have a lot of daylight, do you want me to go sniff around the library?"

"Is it safe?"

"It's only about six or seven blocks. As a wolf, it's nothing."

"I'll still have to magic the locks."

"The problem with this building," Rusty decided, "is it doesn't have a doggie door."

"I'll get you an enchanted lockpick, or something. Later. When we have the power budget for it."

"I can wait."

I spent the rest of the day with Rusty, explaining a bit about magic and how it worked, but formal lessons require a great deal of focus and uninterrupted attention. At shorter and shorter intervals, my attention was required to add to our array.

On the upside, tomorrow we would have enough power for most spells. Even small gates, if necessary. A person-sized shifter was still out of the question. It would require more power than the array produced, so it would have to be stored until there was enough charge to fire it. I'd need a much bigger crystal to do that, but I had plans.

Rusty, as it turns out, isn't a complete nosebleed when it comes to magic, but he's never going to be a wizard. He lacks the required sensitivity. He can "smell" the power on an object, now, because I've taught him how. That may be close to the limit of his skill. He doesn't see magic the way I do. He's more nose-oriented than eye-oriented and it's hard to bridge the gap during the lessons. There may come a day when he can sniff at an enchanted object and tell what it does, rather than say "It's magical," but that day is a long way off.

On the plus side, he can definitely use enchanted objects without much trouble. Turn them on, turn them off, even aim and operate them in simple ways. He's way better at it than Uncle Dusty's avatar.

We made a lot of progress in my headspace. Developing his own headspace is going to be… difficult. His thinking undergoes a radical shift whenever his physical form shifts, so I'm not sure we should monkey around with the werewolf's brain.

Rusty is getting quite a collection of little trinkets on his necklace. If this keeps up, it'll be a charm bracelet for his neck. The latest addition is a magical key. He has to actually touch the lock, but the spell is automated. It only works on pin-based locks, automatically adjusting the pins so the cylinder can turn. It's good enough for everything he wants to do.

I remembered to look around the world in more detail, now that it was dark on my half. The whole Western Hemisphere was on the night side, so any vampires should be out in force.

There were quite a number of fires visible from space. Africa and South America had a lot of area burning. Europe had several, too. A lot of the western United States was one big prairie fire, and a lot of California was ablaze. Several fires dotted the northwest, but the weather was being helpful. Wet forest will burn, but it tends to burn out unless someone keeps it going.

I doubted they were deliberately set. They were spreading from accidental sources. Fireballs probably started the majority, but survivors might be to blame for others. Humans wanted light and warmth, so they started fires, and fires aren't the usual method anymore. Almost nobody knows how to use an oil lamp safely, nor candles, nor even how to keep a campfire from spreading.

In the cities, the people were out and hungry. It was like a zombie apocalypse where the zombies want your blood instead of your brains and get smarter as time goes on.

I didn't like it. The world was gone in an hour, from the first EMP to the final fireball—not counting occasional aftershots—and now things were getting *worse*.

Did I want to fight Alden over *this*? The place was ruined. No one in their right mind would want to live here! Normal humans would be either food, vampire-ized, or turned into a mindless minion.

Come to think of it, which would be worse? Being a mindless minion or being a hungry immortal? Offhand, I'd say the former, but I don't know enough about how the local vampires work. Are they controlled by their creator? Is there a hierarchy? Or is it a purely competitive society where the best rise to the top?

I did not go to bed in a clear and definite frame of mind. Too many imponderables. All this left me uncertain about what I wanted to do.

Journal Entry #44

This morning, after a late breakfast, Rusty went off to test his lockpicking and do a little scouting. I locked a scrying sensor on him so a smaller mirror on the vanity table kept him in frame. The main mirror I used for more power-intensive scrying.

Last night, as I lay in bed and thought about it, I wondered if the places Alden zapped were still active. Was it something he had to maintain, or was it a permanent thing? In theory, with a special tektite for a focus, it might be permanent, but I didn't know for certain. So I checked the bridge and the tunnel and a couple of churches.

Yep. Still there, still going strong. No obvious diminishment, either, which indicated it was likely to last indefinitely. That jibed with Uncle Dusty's explanation.

It also made me realize something. The static wasn't only a defense. It was also a weakness. It was a marker, telling me what places Alden considered important. If there's a house on Bleeker Street with a static field around it to block scrying and fry vampires, it's more than a simple house. It has to be a place Alden wants protected.

I hadn't considered it before because I'd never considered it about my own house before. Pop put up containment fields around the house to keep us from being a shining beacon, but anyone who tried to probe the place would instantly realize it wasn't normal. How long has it been since Alden had to deal with anyone who could detect what he did? Has he ever? If so, did they care about keeping him—and themselves—a secret?

More to the point, was there any reason to keep things secret anymore? It's the end of the world. Why shouldn't there be vampires, wizards, half-angels, werewolves, and monsters of all sorts? What was anyone going to do? Call the cops? Alert the media? Complain to a congressman?

I sent a scrying sensor flying along, zipping rapidly at ground level through buildings. The flickering images of flying through walls were like a strobe light of images, broken only by the occasional fritz of static. Once I spotted the momentary sparkle, I knew approximately where it was, so I could go back and map it out.

I didn't see any pattern to it, at first. But I now had a telescope spell assembled so I could use it with a micro-gate and my scrying mirror. There was an urban rent-a-bike parked near the center of each of the outlying static zones. I didn't see the tektites, but those were probably in the cargo pockets. The bikes were always somewhere out of the way, in doorways or between parked cars, inconspicuous in themselves, and always damaged, unlikely to be scavenged nor moved very far.

It took me a while to figure it out. I never would have managed if I didn't have a laminated map and a marker. For most people, those broken bicycles were impossible to detect as the source of the celestial force. If zombies moved them every morning, they could make a labyrinth of power, forcing the vampires to lose a few—or a few hundred—of their number as they stumbled into a new hot zone.

Alden and his minions were holed up with him in the library. With power zones surrounding it, he was making it difficult for the vampires to get him out. Whatever his reason for fortifying the library, he was also using the vampires' own movements around his celestial island kill them off, a few more every night.

I started scanning around the library, looking in the windows. There were very few good lines of sight due to the static. There were too many buildings in the way. Probably by design. If the vampires had a straight line to the library, they would have burned it down by now. They weren't very smart, yet, so they hadn't considered going up a tall building outside the celestial zone and throwing firebombs over intervening structures. It would happen eventually, I felt sure, even if I had to draw someone a diagram.

Did Alden know his position couldn't be maintained? Was he aware the vampire spawn were being forced to learn, to adapt? While the vampires slept, he kept sending his zombies out to search and scavenge. To feed them? Or to stock up before making a break for somewhere safer?

If I had to guess, I'd say he didn't deliberately set off a nuclear war. He was too poorly prepared for it. On the other hand, if he set it in motion before we chopped off his escape route, he could easily have found himself grumbling in a library.

Did his presence in Midtown have anything to do with the lack of hits there? Was he capable of keeping people from launching missiles into his immediate vicinity? Or, rather, did he used to have the capability, back when people could launch missiles?

I spied as best I could on the library, peeping in the windows from long range. Most of the library seemed to be pretty much as you'd expect. Tables, chairs, shelves of books, all the usual stuff. No Alden, though. I did see a few of his zombies walking around, usually carrying books.

All right, if they're moving books around, they're doing it for a reason. He's looking for something. He wants to know something, and he's using the library to find out. Trouble is, it's a damned extensive library! The thing is huge. He could be researching anything.

I shut down my scrying mirror. The one tracking Rusty I left running. He was doing fine, gallivanting around, looking at things, sniffing other things, and avoiding people in much the same way a real wolf might. As far as I could tell, the zombies ignored him. As well they might, I suppose. How many stray dogs were loose in Manhattan? How many were locked in their apartments and eating their former owners? Or vice-versa?

Cats, now—there were a lot of stray cats. I was surprised. I would think the cats abandoned Manhattan as soon as the vampire population got past a hundred. Or is that only for Pop's sort?

Rusty went on doing his walkabout while I got a cardboard tube from inside a paper towel roll.

I took a break when Rusty made it to our floor. I let him into the apartment without him having to pick the locks or scratch at the door. He came in, dragging a mouthful of clothes, and shifted back to human form. He shook himself.

"Aren't you supposed to do that before you shift?"

"Only when wet. Good god, it felt fine to get out!"

"I can only imagine. What's with the… tactical gear?" He spread out the clothes. Black pants, black shirt, a vest with pockets, all the usual stuff.

"I went shopping. If I have to go somewhere as a human, I should be dressed for it. Your father left clothes for you, not for your guests."

"Fair point. Won't this stuff make shapeshifting kind of difficult?"

"Yes, but I'm hoping you can help me out. I need Velcro."

"So, instead of ripping, it parts along certain lines and off you go?"

"That's the idea."

"The belt is going to be tricky."

"Or, I suppose…" he trailed off, grinning at me.

"You want me to try and bind this stuff to you."

"If you think you can," he added. "I know you've got power problems."

I considered it. Each piece would need to be affected, but I had the basics of the spell down. If I spent a little time on it, I could refine it further, moving it along the spectrum from "wish real hard" to "actual spell." Even without the refinement, we already knew the technique worked.

"I'm pretty sure I can, but it'll take a while."

"No rush. It's only the end of the world."

"I noticed," I sighed, sitting down at my vanity table again.

"Can I ask what you're working on?"

"I conjured up a crystal today."

Rusty turned the paper towel tube over in his hands. He didn't recognize any of the writing on it, but we hadn't got far in his magical training.

"I presume you used this?"

"Yep."

"Doesn't smell magical."

"The symbols are part of a spell, not an enchantment. I have to power it to use it. It isn't an object of power on its own."

"Oh, yeah. Sorry. You told me."

"It's a lot to take in."

"No kidding. So, you summoned a crystal to fit in the tube." He nodded at the quartz crystal on the vanity. "Is it a power crystal, yet?"

"Nope. I'm running a spell through it to remove impurities and to homogenize its crystalline structure."

"Is that necessary?"

"Not at all. It helps to maximize the power capacity, though, and it decreases the rate at which it loses charge. It's like a battery. If you leave a battery alone, it slowly loses energy. This will, too."

"I thought crystals charged on their own?"

"Not exactly. You can make a power crystal that acts exactly like a battery, but..." I trailed off, trying to figure out where to start.

"Okay, short form. All magic crystals have spells in them. Small crystals usually have a spell and probably enough of a charge to fire the spell once. Power crystals are similar, but are built in a different way. They have a power-gathering component—or they *should!*—acting like an air compressor mounted on a giant pressure tank. Bigger crystal, bigger tank.

"The power-gathering function sucks in what it can, based on the local environment. Part of the power goes into running the spell and the rest gets compressed into the tank."

"Hang on. You've got a thing I've seen you do, a drawing—"

"A power diagram."

"Yeah. That's already doing the sucking in thing. How does it work with the sucking-in spell on an energy rock?"

"If a compressor is sucking in air on a mountaintop, where the air is thin, it takes a long time to fill the tank. If I take it into a survival shelter on the mountaintop, where another compressor has already pressurized the room to sea-level density, it works better."

"I'm sure this will all make sense, someday," he decided. "Is it supposed to make a crackling sound?"

"Not when it's ready and charging. What you're hearing is a different spell. It's removing impurities and defects. This will keep the storage losses down and maximize the power capacity of the battery. By removing impurities and imperfections, it also strengthens the physical crystal, itself. The crystals in the armor are all pre-treated, for example, to increase storage and strength. They're all lonsdaleite, not quartz, though. Quartz is silicon dioxide. Lonsdaleite is much harder."

"Lons...?"

"Lonsdaleite is hexagonal diamond. It's harder than regular diamonds. Pop thought it was a good idea to have something tough for power storage in the armor. I would be using it here, but I'd need to get a lot of diamonds together and turn them into one big crystal. It would take a lot longer because it would take much more power."

"Good to know. What's for dinner?"

I sighed. Sometimes, Rusty isn't as focused as he could be.

"Anything you like, as long as you can find it in a small green box. This is almost ready. Let me finish here and set it to charging, then we can break out the plastic-and-cardboard dinnerware."

Rusty, during his day out, went roaming around the library, both figuratively and literally. In the area surrounding the library, there were zombies galore, doing their usual search and salvage. Mostly, they were after food and water.

Inside the library, Rusty didn't have any trouble with doors. They were open. There was almost nobody in the library. What few zombies were present didn't seem to care about a wolf wandering around. Not part of their instruction set, perhaps.

"You shouldn't have gone in there!" I told him. "Alden controls minds!"

"Yeah?"

"What if he decided to try and control yours?"

"What? Why? I'm one more hairy quadruped. He doesn't care. You don't see a dozen guard dogs sitting out by the stone lions, do you?"

"What if he heard you thinking? You don't have wolf thoughts, do you?"

"I do, but not the same as a regular wolf. You think he could tell the difference?" Rusty asked, worried.

"Yes!"

"I guess you better read my mind, then. If he might have done things to my brain, he might have made me not remember it."

"Damn it!"

So I read Rusty's mind. No, I did not find signs of tampering. He really did wander around inside the library. He didn't find Alden, and maybe that's why he didn't get his brain run through a strainer.

"I'll get you something to prevent him from mind-controlling you," I promised. "I should have done it sooner, but it never occurred to me you might be anywhere near Alden. We were doing the superhero thing, so you didn't need it."

"And I couldn't carry it," he added. "Not until much later."

"I should have kept you up to date on the threats and got you more defenses. I'll get right on it."

"Fantabulous. I'm over the moon. I leap for joy, chasing the cow. But I have a much more pressing concern."

"More pressing? What?"

"If Alden isn't in the library, where did he go? Is he out and about, looking for *us*? Or for more people to add to his horde?"

"That's a good question. Did you look everywhere?"

"Everywhere I could get into as a wolf, and everywhere I could open a door without being observed. I didn't go down to the basement, though. I couldn't find a door that didn't have zombies tromping back and forth through it."

"I saw them roaming around. What were they doing?"

"Mostly taking books downstairs or back up. They don't file them properly, either. They put them on shelves any which way."

"Hang on. Did you see big piles of food lying around?"

"I saw some. There's a café of sorts attached to the library. Things that don't keep well are getting cooked and distributed to the troops in shifts. All that sort of stuff is piled up nearby. I don't know where all the canned things are, if that's what you're asking."

"Alden has a lair somewhere in there. I'm sure of it. It's too heavily fortified to be anything else. But where? If he and his food stores aren't in the rotunda or gallery or reading room, where are they?"

"Basement," Rusty said. "Obviously."

"How extensive is the basement under this library?"

"Got me. First time I've been in it."

"I thought you lived here all your life?"

"I have. Doesn't mean I've been up the Empire State, either, or out to the Statue of Freedom."

"Statue of Freedom?"

"The big statue in the harbor? Lady with a torch?"

"Oh. Right. Continue."

"While you were looking," Rusty went on, "did you happen to see what they did when they found people?"

"They found people?" I asked. "No, I didn't see such an incident."

"Yep. Family of five, hiding in an apartment. A lot like the other people in the building, I'd guess."

"Hang on. That reminds me."

I fired up the vanity and looked around on the top floor. The place was unlit, of course, either because they didn't have any candles or they didn't want to light up the penthouse and attract attention. There were two men, four women, and a lot of empty bottles. Every one of them was drunk. From the state of their clothes and the mess around the penthouse, I guessed they were following the "eat, drink, and be merry," philosophy.

"Looks like someone had a party," Rusty told me.

"Looks like. Do you know how far down their salvage efforts have gone?"

"No, but I'll find out tomorrow. I'll also check on the other residents. I smelled 'em on their floors, but the lower apartments are smaller. There are more of them per floor— meaning more kitchens—so they may not have looted very far."

"If they're smart, they should loot everything they can as quickly as they can. Get all the perishables eaten first, rather than wait to find them all gone bad in two weeks."

"Weird how the typical citizen isn't trained for post-apocalyptic survival, huh?"

"Good point," I agreed. "You were saying about the family Alden's zombies found?"

"I don't think it was their place. They had traveling gear. My guess is they knew enough to avoid the blasted areas and were hoping to find a way to the mainland. They took shelter overnight and didn't like the look of Alden's zombie squads, so they tried to hide."

"Didn't work, did it?" I asked.

"Nope. The zombies are thorough. Found 'em, grabbed 'em, dragged 'em to the library."

"Five more people in the zombie parade, then?"

"Four, more likely. Mom, Dad, and three kids."

"Why only four?"

"The youngest was about six. I'm not sure how useful a six-year-old zombie will be."

I had a cold feeling. I knew how Pop would feel about it. I definitely knew how I felt about it: The same, but not as strong. I may not have his knee-jerk reaction about abused children, but I also don't tear continents apart because of a knee-jerk reaction.

"In the morning, I'm calling Alden. We're going to ask what he's doing and see what he has to say for himself. If he's saving the world and this is the only way he knows how to do it, I might give him a pass. Otherwise, he's about to have his library card revoked."

"Are we killing him?"

"We'll see what he has to say for himself," I repeated.

Journal Entry #45

I slept like a brick. It was a long, exhausting day. Rusty and I had double rations for breakfast and I tested my new power crystal. It held a sizable charge and, as I zapped the various items of Rusty's latest clothing—I refined my binding spell a bit, first—the crystal discharged normally.

Success.

I placed it in a power diagram so the array could charge it directly.

Next on my list was a communications spell. My phone was in no shape to operate and the electronic relay to the gate connection was almost certainly shot. The whole radioactive-oxygen thing was certainly offline if not outright destroyed. The old phone wasn't going to help.

Okay, what did this leave? Did I want to try and establish psychic contact? No, I did not. But if I could find an antique phone of the same model, there might be another way to—

No, darn it. Even if I put a spell on a phone here to try and establish a temporary magical link to the phone Alden had, the phones would still need to be working. Or would they?

I experimented a little and scribbled a lot of notes, doing the thaumaturgical math. Two working phones could receive and transmit sound. Linking them magically would be possible. It would be easiest if I had both of them on hand to establish the link. Without that, I'd have to establish one end and reach out to the other. If they both could handle the sound part, it would be doable. But having the spell use the phones as foci relied on large chunks of a scrying spell and a locator spell. If Alden was inside the static zone—and he was—it would never connect.

If I could do this psychically, I was sure the static zone wouldn't interfere. Alden did most of his work in such a zone. But could I do anything psychically without Alden grabbing me by the brainstem?

Rusty went out for the afternoon while I growled at spell designs. I kept grumpily banging my head on how to build a psychic focusing spell for long-distance communication. The focusing element wasn't too hard. The hard part was figuring out how to include a filter. My existing psychic shields were designed to let me talk to people while still blocking out higher-powered psychic impulses. This was a long-distance shout, by definition a high-powered psychic impulse.

How do I communicate without giving Alden a free shot at my thinking machinery?

Then I had it. His zombies are part of a psychic network. If we grab one, we can use it as a remote terminal. Sure, Alden can direct whatever he wants to the zombie, but the brain of a zombie can't handle the wattage. Alden is stronger than I am, but if he's forced to reach through the bars of a cage, there's a limit to how much of his strength he can use. Or, think of it like calling a friend at a concert. The band may be ear-shattering loud, but the phone can't reproduce the volume.

I cast a couple of spells for the upcoming zombie communications, put a psychic shielding spell in a crystal—for capturing the zombie and isolating it temporarily from the network—and cast containment spells on the condo. We were starting to get a decent amount of power built up.

Then I went back to setting off the solar array gem, sorting out the new panels while I waited for Rusty to get back. It was boring and tedious and I was well on my way to hating it, but it might be necessary.

Rusty came back with a big, goofy grin.

"You look like you caught the cat."

"And ate it," he agreed, "although us not liking cats is a myth. They're delicious. Cats aren't terribly fond of us."

"You and Pop have that in common."

"Good to know. I brought you these!"

I accepted a pair of smartphones. They were thin, black bricks.

"You want me to fix them?"

"I don't know."

"What do you mean?"

"Do you have to fix them?"

"All the cellular services are down. Why would I *want* to fix them?"

"So you can use them. I figure you get them to do what you want to do, then we give one to a zombie and tell it to take it to Alden. You might even be able to track it, right? Or did I misunderstand the problem?"

How many times did I do this to Pop? He had a complicated, intricate, technically sophisticated idea and I asked one little question… Here I was, trying to get the old phones to work again and Rusty goes out and gets new ones.

"Rusty, you may be the smartest werewolf I know."

"I'm the only werewolf you know."

"A valid point, and I'm sorry I brought it up."

"It's okay. It's the end of the world." He shrugged. "I don't like it. I don't have to like it. But I'm alive and I have to deal with it."

"How are you dealing with it?"

"Not well. I'm trying to ignore it and mostly succeeding."

"Anything I can do to help?"

"I dunno if it'll help, but I'd like to kill someone."

"There are lots of zombies."

"Yeah, but if I kill one, all the others will shoot me on sight, right? I don't care for it. Then I won't be able to wander around, being ignored." He shrugged again. "What's a pack hunter to do?"

"I'm sorry about your world, Rusty. I really, truly am."

"Which reminds me. There are others, right?"

"Sure. Lots of them. I did explain."

"Yes, but I'm trying to make sure I understand. There's a world where all this never happened, right?"

"There's a base timeline, yes. We could poke it and create a new branch. I'm not sure how far along the original is, but it would be fundamentally the same."

"Would I still have Mom and Dad in it?"

"Most likely, barring an act of God or a weird quirk of fate. There would also be another you. One where you never met me."

Rusty sat down to think it over, no doubt considering how his mother would react to having retroactive twins.

As for me, I put down the phones, drew a diagram around each of them, and routed all the power I could spare into their repair.

Strangely, I found enough spare motivation lying around and used the leftover power to continue adding to the solar array.

The phones were working again by midnight, in the sense they were functional technological devices. I still had to magic the batteries into being charged, of course.

I did a couple of prototype drafts of the linking spell, using notebook paper. If I could make it work between two sheets of paper in different rooms, I was confident about two phones on the same planet. They were only tests, not the full-power versions, but we got them to work. I refined the design a few times, working by candlelight with the curtains drawn. I was confident the phones would work as advertised.

Unfortunately, I lost track of time and stayed up too late. No matter. It meant I had more time to perfect it—and to make sure everything was charged up for a real-world call instead of a laboratory test.

The next day, after I'd rested and looked at the spell with fresh eyes, I put the finishing touches on it. This final version I copied with great care, inscribing it directly onto the phone cases. If I'd had my druthers, I'd have inlaid the design with orichalcum foil. As it was, I did the best I could with what I had.

I was going to add a few more panels, but Rusty was already on the balcony. He had been using the gem to create panels, but he didn't really see them, didn't understand the arrangement.

We had another lesson in magical operations and I explained to him how it all got put together. With a psychic link in place, he helped me rearrange the scattered bunches of extra panels, incorporating them into the array. He may have made a mess, but it was only a problem of organization. We sorted it all out.

Then it was time for my nap. Tomorrow, early, we would package one phone, wrap it in a bright yellow ribbon, and he would leave it where the zombies were scheduled to loot next. Rusty suggested Roman candles, to make sure the zombies noticed.

Journal Entry #46

Rusty sat down next to me as I placed my phone on the vanity. The other package was already in the street, sparkling and shooting balls of fire into the air. I could see zombies moving toward it on the scrying mirror.

"No, don't sit by me. Sit over there," I directed. He moved to the chair.

"Why?"

"The phones have a magical correspondence connection, but there's also a strong psychic component. They need it to get through all the celestial static."

"So?"

"So? So, in addition to microphones and speakers, they have cameras. Whatever his phone sees, we'll see here. Rather, you will, in the mirror. I'll be talking to Alden, so I'll need all my concentration to make sure he isn't doing something devious and unpleasant. You need to be my eyes for everything else. Watch what happens, where the phone goes, everything you can. You're not part of the communications circuit, so there won't be any feedback into the loop for him to detect. With a little luck, he'll never know we slipped a camera into his lair and looked around."

"Won't he know it when he looks at the video call?"

"He's not too technology-savvy and the phone will only be displaying the lock screen—a picture of me and a 'call connected' display."

"Okay. I'll watch and keep quiet."

We waited. The zombies stood and stared at the fireworks for a bit, as though waiting. The Roman candles quit pretty quickly, but they did their job of attracting attention. One of the zombies picked up the phone and stared at it.

"Hello?" he asked.

"Hello. Please let me speak with Alden."

"Are you Phoebe?"

"Yes."

The zombie turned and headed for the library. The scrying mirror became ineffective, of course, but the phone still sent back camera images along the psychic link, so the mirror connected to the phone still worked.

I kept my attention on the call. I didn't want to see, didn't want to know, didn't want to have any inkling there even was a video connection. I wanted it to be nonexistent in my thoughts. It's not easy to do.

"Phoebe?"

"Alden. So good of you to take my call."

"I'm surprised to hear from you at all."

"The situation," I pointed out, "has changed."

"So it has. Might I suggest we speak to your father about going back a few weeks and making alterations? Perhaps he can help me with a few small issues in exchange for similar small services on my part."

"You know he doesn't like you."

"But, under the circumstances…?"

"I don't think he cares."

"About the end of the world?" Alden demanded.

"Doesn't affect him," I pointed out. "It doesn't matter to him. It isn't a problem. Not to him. So, if it isn't his problem…" I trailed off.

Alden was silent for several seconds, processing this.

"I suggest you find a way to make him see it as his problem. Or, rather see *you* have a problem. Does he not care about your situation?"

"My situation is stable and reasonably comfortable. It's a lot better than most people. How's yours?"

"I have suffered losses, but I feel confident I can recoup them. The destruction of civilization is an issue, of course, but I have weathered such difficulties before. The more pressing concern is the spread of the undead. I believe I can deal with it, given time, but avoiding the whole issue would be more practical. Do not trouble yourself about it. It is your father to whom I should talk. When can you put me in touch with him?"

Something inside me twanged angrily.

"I could arrange it in moments. I will not do so. He's made it clear he doesn't want to talk to you again. However, if you want me to explain to him what you want—in detail, because he despises being interrupted and I'll only do it once—I'll put it on his desk. He may not choose to answer. Nevertheless, *I* am the person you will speak with."

"I would much rather have the opportunity to tell *him* what needs to be done, in person. I can be very persuasive. A message simply doesn't have the same flair."

"Right now, your chances of getting him to help you are zero. If you persuade me to intercede on your behalf, your chances rise to something higher than zero. If you continue to dismiss me, the chance remains at zero. Now that we've done the math—you do understand math, don't you? Or do I need to dumb it down even more?"

"Your tone is less than polite."

"Your attitude is less than intelligent. Are you going to take your one in a hundred shot? Or are you going to take no shot at all?"

"Are you certain your father will be pleased with your obstructionism when he discovers I've been trying to reach him?"

"He knows. When we talk, he chuckles in amusement at your difficulties."

"What have you been telling him?" Alden demanded.

"Everything."

"You're spying for him," Alden spat. "All this… this *is* his doing! He said he wasn't going to interfere!"

"Which part?" I inquired, interested. It was possible Pop did interfere and didn't tell me.

"The wound! The wound that won't heal!"

"Oh. The one in your right side?" I guessed. It was a shot in the dark. Well, a shot in the evening, but close enough.

"Exactly! It healed rapidly until the bleeding stopped, but now it won't change! Nothing I do makes it any better, so there must be something—something he's done! What is it? —wait! Was it his gunman, too? Or did he take advantage of someone else's assassination attempt?"

"No idea," I lied. "As for the wound, I suppose I could fix it for you—oh, but no, I'm merely an under-appreciated apprentice. You don't want to talk to me. You want to talk to Pop, only Pop, always Pop, and I simply am not good enough."

"You are correct. Put me through to your father this instant!"

Whatever it was inside me that twanged before now twanged and snapped.

"Now you listen to me," I hissed. "You're an arrogant bastard with no real understanding of the forces you're using. You assume I don't know anything, but you're wrong. I'm a thousand times the wizard you will ever be. Even the devices you stole are beyond your comprehension, whereas I can *build* them! The phone you're using now is a product of my powers, allowing you to sneer at them!

"Right now, you keep asking to talk to Pop as though he's the only being in the universe who could possibly be your equal. You've repeatedly dismissed me as irrelevant, as nothing more than your personal messenger. What you've failed to understand is you cannot control me and you cannot order me around. You require my goodwill—and you, you fool, have not only treated me with no respect whatsoever, you have failed entirely to mollify my anger about your earlier actions!

"Therefore, you will *never* get to meet with Pop again unless you bow down, beg properly, and speak respectfully. If you fail in this, I will lose my temper. I haven't done it often, but who do you think I got it from? You don't want to see what happens. I don't want to see what happens. But you're a dipshit who doesn't know how much restraint I've already shown. Test me on this. I dare you. Go on. But be aware the next words you speak to me may well decide your fate."

"We shall see."

He hung up, or tried to. I hung up on my end and the connection quit.

"Well," Rusty said, "that sounded like a challenge."

"Shut up. I feel quite testy and you're in reach," I told him. He scooted his chair farther away before answering.

"How is being testy with the bad guy a bad thing?"

"Because it's leading me down the path of what Pop would do!" I stormed.

"And this is a bad thing...?" he asked, uncertainly.

"Pop always wanted me to be a better person than him! Everything, all my life, was about being something better! Not a better killer—that's impossible. Not a more dangerous monster—that's unlikely. About being a better *person.*

"Pop encounters a problem and kills things until the problem goes away!"

"Uh-huh?" Rusty encouraged. I took a breath.

"Okay, okay, that's not literally true, but it's a direction to think in, a point of departure, with all sorts of exceptions and qualifiers along the way."

"He starts on the Murder Highway and sometimes takes side roads?"

"Kinda. Thing is, he wants me to be a better person than he is."

"You keep saying that. What does it mean, exactly?"

"That's the trouble! I'm not entirely sure!"

"Oh, well, there's your problem."

"Will you *please* stop tempting me to hit you?"

"Sorry. Look, if you don't know what it means, shouldn't you ask?"

"Probably, but... now I'm... I'm independent. I'm grown up and on my own. I should be able to figure these things out for myself. As a grown-up, I'm *supposed* to figure this stuff out!"

"Okay, so, do it."

"Excuse me?"

"What does it mean to you? What makes someone a better person than your Dad?"

"That's the trouble. I don't have an objective view. I thought trying to avoid killing people would be a pretty easy way to be a better person."

"Avoiding casual murder is a good start," Rusty agreed.

"That's part of why I wanted to punish Alden. Yes, because he did terrible things, but also because I wanted to... I don't know. Prove myself? To do something like this without relying on the same tool as Pop."

"He uses the murder hammer a lot and you were hoping to use the retribution screwdriver?"

"Something like that." I brooded over the problem for a minute. Rusty sat silent, waiting patiently, watching me.

"Here's the thing," I decided. "I'm not my Pop. I'm a lot like him in a lot of ways, but we are not the same person."

"And I'm glad of it."

"Yeah. He raised me and I think he did a great job. He was always there for me, tried not to spoil me, gave me a good work ethic, made sure I had an education, looked out for my health to the best of his ability, all of it. He loved me and I loved him. I still do. It's hard to look at him objectively. So, when the question comes up of how to be a 'better person' than Pop, I have a hard time finding fault.

"That being said," I went on, "I can see a few a things. He does murder people, but he also looks through their flesh and into their spirits. When he sees someone, he sees who and what they are. There's none of this ethical or moral uncertainty crap. He's not a court of law, trying to pass the bar of reasonable doubt. He *knows* if you're a bastard who deserves death—and he delivers."

"Sounds handy."

"Yes. It's an ability I don't have, though, so I... hmm."

"Hmm?" Rusty echoed.

"I was going on about how I'm not Pop, and I don't have his ability to see inside people. There's something there. I feel I'm missing a point. It's there, but it isn't coming to the front of my mind. Give me a minute."

"Sure."

What was it? I had a hard time putting it into words. Pop isn't me. I'm not Pop. Pop has abilities I don't have. I can't make moral judgments like he can—

Or can he? He doesn't make a moral judgment. He observes a fact. No, he still makes a moral judgment. He sees the colors and patterns inside someone, but he chooses which ones he doesn't like. I don't know anyone who would disagree with his judgments—most cultures are against repeat rapists, aggressive pedophiles, serial murderers, and professional slavers. But they are still judgments based on his beliefs of right and wrong.

Whose morals am I following? Mine? Or Pop's morals, filtered through my understanding? I suppose I inherited his sense of morality, after a fashion, but I can't see inside people like he can. I can hear what they're thinking, sure, but thoughts aren't proof of what they are. Everyone has intrusive thoughts. Some people have terrible thoughts all the time and consciously refuse to act on them. To tell what someone is really like, I either have to dive into their minds and swim around in there to gauge them as people, or I have to stand back and judge them by their actions.

And, in judging them, I'm imposing my own morals on them.

"Rusty?"

"Yup."

"Am I a moral person?"

Rusty frowned and thought it over.

"I'm not sure what you mean."

"Am I a good person?"

"Oh. Yup."

"Are you sure?"

"Positive."

"How do you know?"

"You're nice to people. You're nice to me. You have a lot of powers and you're helpful with them. You work hard for your friends. You forgive me when I make you mad, and without hitting me with a newspaper." He grinned. "That last one is a real good indicator."

"I suppose it is."

"There's—" he began, and stopped.

"Go on."

"Well... there's a difference between being nice and being... I dunno. You know those motivational posters about how standing up for yourself isn't being arrogant or greedy? You can be assertive without being aggressive. Stuff like that, you know?"

"I'm familiar with the idea. I'm surprised to hear it from you."

"Anger management classes," he said, waving it away. "What I'm getting at is you tend to be real passive. You want to watch and know everything and plan it all out and make sure you're doing the right thing in the larger context and all the do-gooder bullshit. You sometimes miss what's right in front of you. Like the time in the alley behind the club. If there's a vampire trying to kill you, you stomp him."

"But what if—"

"No! That's exactly my point! You always have this 'but what if' mentality! You kill the vampire, period, end of discussion. Someone throws a grenade at you. You dive out of the way. 'But what if it's a dummy and they're trying to get me to move?' Then they succeed! And you *shoot* them!"

"What you're trying to say—correct me if I'm wrong—is I spend too much of my time trying to plan for every possible outcome, trying to pick the perfect choice."

"Nailed it. Exactly. That's exactly what you do. That's why Alden is still alive and mind-wiping people. How many thousands of people are currently drooling and doing the zombie shuffle because you *didn't* shoot him in the head?"

I didn't have a good answer. Rusty was entirely correct. Looking back, as soon as I knew what Alden was doing, I should have found a way to stop him. Not show him there were consequences to his actions. Not "punish" him for his evil ways. Not try to rehabilitate him. Not try to imprison him until he learned his lesson. Stop him, even if it meant splattering his head all over the nearest wall. His consequences should have been everything I could do to make sure he couldn't do it again.

Which left me with a question. Did I not do it because I wanted to be "better" than Pop? Or did I not want Pop to be right about what to do with evil men?

Maybe Pop *was* right. Maybe there are evil men who can't and shouldn't be reasoned with. I can't tell at a glance, but I can judge people on their actions. And sticking someone's brain in a meat grinder until you can squeeze it into the shape you want—that's evil. Evil I allowed to continue.

Pop always tried not to show it, but he had a lot of guilt on his conscience. Now I think I'm starting to understand, at least a little. With great power comes great responsibility, and the potential to do great harm.

Is feeling guilty part of being an adult? Knowing you could have done better and regretting you didn't? Knowing you wasted opportunities to be better, get better, or do better than you did?

"What this all comes down to," I said, slowly, "is what to do about Alden. If we leave him alone, he'll get into a fight with the vampire horde and he may or may not win. If he doesn't win, things will go very bad here. If he does win, he'll take over the world and the only person who will know it is him."

"Can't he take over other worlds, too?"

"Arguably, yes. He knows about the weak places between worlds. I think he believes them to be portals in time. He could find another one and escape even if he can't defeat the undead. If he keeps looking for them, he'll eventually figure out they lead to *alternate* worlds, not to different times in the same world. Then he could really start being a problem."

"Evil Overlord of a dozen universes, huh?"

"Worlds, anyway. He'd have to get off this planet to rule the universe—but there are worlds where he could."

"Great. So, what do we do?"

"I guess it depends on which is the greater threat, Alden or the vampires. Who would you rather won? The things drinking your blood, or the thing destroying your mind?"

"Tough choice."

"I agree." I got up and fetched a cardboard box.

"Whatcha doin'?"

"I'm angry, I'm tired, I have the weight of the world on my shoulders, and I want my teddy bear."

"Seems reasonable. But do you want to hear about the phone's walk through the library? I got to see a lot. The zombie was carrying it in front of him, like he was walking and talking on speakerphone."

I twiddled a marker in my fingers while I considered. The shift-box would wait another hour.

"Tell me."

"I have a better idea," Rusty suggested. "Come inside and see. If I tell you, I'll miss something. You can look at the memory."

"Most people aren't comfortable with that," I observed.

"I'm not comfortable with it, either, but I'm also not most people."

I had to agree, Rusty was entirely correct. So we sat down, I took his hands, and we both went into his memories.

The phone went on a long walk back to the library. The view wasn't the best, of course, since the zombie carrying it wasn't trying to film anything. Still, it was good enough. The zombie went up the front steps, into the building, and down into the basement. It passed between zombies standing guard at the basement door, down the steps to a guarded fire door, and continued through an underground hallway. An even heavier door, also open, had more guards.

Beyond was an archive. Shelves upon shelves of boxes, racks upon racks of media. The main library had books and more books, but this was where they kept the microfilm, the tapes, the digital media, the original maps, the rare volumes—all the things you want to preserve for posterity. Upstairs was the information; down here was the *archive*.

And Alden, like a spider, sat in the middle of all this. Everything came to him.

He looked awful.

Long ago, when I first saw him, he reminded me of those statues you see of the Greeks. Clean lines, angular features, classical design. Idealized figures. He was a big man to start with, but he was perfectly proportioned. Now, he was more than muscular. He was bulging. His clothing was loose and comfortable, but well into the extra-extra-extra sizes. His neck was almost too thick for a shirt. His wrists were too thick for me to put my hand around. Lets not even talk about the bulging forearms or the ridiculous biceps. He looked as though someone hooked him up to an air compressor and inflated him.

His breakfast tray was near at hand, set on a folding table away from the books he was studying. It was a surprisingly small breakfast. A grapefruit and toast. It didn't look as though it was enough to fuel him for an hour, much less start off the day.

There was a heavy cane hooked on the edge of the table. I wondered how badly Alden was wounded. Did he need a cane because of it? Or was it a convenience because his muscles were getting so big it was awkward to walk?

How much muscle can you put on a humanoid skeleton?

More to the point, why was this happening? Was this an effect of being poisoned by radioactive oxygen? He mentioned a wound that wouldn't heal. Was it healing very slowly because his body was constantly fighting off muscle cells as they grew more and more out of control? Were there any other cells growing tumors inside him?

Pop can be a vicious bastard. I wouldn't wish this sort of slow death on anyone.

On the other hand—thinking like Pop for a second—it wasn't unfair. If Alden wanted this to stop, all he had to do was apologize and give back what he stole. It would stop the process, at least, so it wouldn't get worse. Pop might even fix him, figuring the misery was a fair exchange.

And, at that moment, I realized what Pop had done. I said I wanted to punish Alden and Pop agreed to let me. He also took steps to back me up. He always has. He made *sure* there would be punishment. Not because he didn't think I could do it. Oh, no! He has absolute faith in me. When I tell him I can't do something, he has a hard time believing me because he believes *in* me. He did this so I would get what I wanted, no matter what. Alden would be punished as surely as if the skies opened up and a voice from above pronounced his doom.

Which, given how Uncle Dusty is a nuclear-powered demigod, was certainly a possibility.

Next time I see Pop, I'm going to squeeze him until he makes me stop.

I stepped out of Rusty's head and he grinned at me.

"See everything?"

"Yep! Your memory is pretty good."

"Thank you. I heard what you were thinking as you watched, kind of a running commentary. You saw his underground archive?"

"Yes. I'm not totally clear on where it is, though. My sense of direction got a little fuzzy in there."

"I wandered around the library, so I'm more oriented," Rusty assured me. "The tunnel goes out the back of the building, under Bryant Park. It's not long, so the archive must be buried under there."

"Good to know, if I want to launch penetrator shells. I doubt the archive is connected to sewers or subways."

"Probably not. No, I wouldn't think it is." Rusty considered the matter. "He's got himself a bunker."

"At least feels safe," I muttered, "and not without reason."

"In more ways than one. The library isn't much of a fort, but he's got those vampire-burning thingies, right? People aren't a problem, either. What's in a library? Books. Even if they're so desperate for something to read they break in, they have to find the right door, break through the steel door, then break the second door—and that one is even more serious; you saw—*and* they have to fight through a horde of mindless soldiers."

"It's almost," I mused, "as though he's worried about something more than vampires."

"I think you can take it as a compliment."

"Oh, it's not me he's worried about," I assured him. "It's Pop. And all the protection and precautions in the world won't save him if Pop decides to kill him."

"You have a lot of faith in your Dad," Rusty observed.

"You met my Uncle Dusty, right?"

"Yes." Rusty suppressed a shudder. Uncle Dusty can be a bit overwhelming, I suppose, especially in his place of power.

"Pop created him."

Rusty gulped.

"Now," I finished, "I have things to think about. But first, I still want my teddy bear."

"Go for it. I'm going to check on the other residents of the building. I think I heard someone in the hallway earlier. They may be out scavenging."

"Be careful."

"In a post-nuclear New York with vampires and mind-controlled zombie hordes? What do I need to be careful for?" He grinned at me and headed out.

I drew symbols on the box.

One of the most difficult things to do with a gate spell is to cut anything. You'd think by causing a spatial discontinuity midway through an object, you'd neatly sever it. Technically, you're correct. Unfortunately, it requires far more energy than you'd think. Never mind the chemical and mechanical bonds holding the object together. Folded space is—at least, as used in a gate spell—inappropriate as a cutting tool.

Think of it this way. You *can* cut a rope with a hammer, but you wouldn't.

Fortunately, Mister Stuffins was in surprisingly good shape. Being on an upper floor, there was less building to fall on him, but he was also buried well enough to not be immediately combustible. Even more helpful was the condition of the rubble. Instead of being tumbled among many different bricks, he was between two large, flat sections of what used to be walls of my house.

I observed his situation carefully, unfolded, re-folded, and duct-taped the box, and shifted him out of there. It cost a chunk of power since I couldn't get a perfect fit, but so what? I had my teddy bear. A bit distressed, true, but I gave him a thorough cleaning and wrapped him in a towel and another repair spell. Soon, the towel was in sorry shape, but Mister Stuffins was back to his old, fuzzy self.

Rusty took note of all this effort to recover my teddy bear and never said a word about it. Probably wise.

I repeated a lot of my efforts in recovering Zeno. Zeno was even higher up than Mister Stuffins, but closer to the fires on the surface. Much of his casing was a molten ruin and his internal components were, if not melted, then encased in now-cooled formerly-melted bits.

Zeno, as a computer, was dead. Data recovery, however, might not be out of the question. I wasn't going to plug his storage module into something and expect it to work, but I might be able to take it somewhere with a higher technology and let them do a forensic-level analysis and recovery.

Getting the module out remotely wasn't going to happen. Getting the whole former laptop might be, but, having been runny at one point, there was a sizable amount of rubble that had to either come along or be severed. Either way, it was going to cost.

It would almost be easier to go there with a pickaxe and a prybar.

I let the crystal charge up. I could at least give it a shot later.

The conversion panels never stop producing power. Even at night, there is still a little power production, even if it's only a trickle. Radio waves, cosmic rays, thermal energy radiating from buildings as they cool, whatever, all of it is grist for the mill. True, without the sun providing the lion's share, the amount they produce is minimal, but they never completely stop.

By the time the sun went down, my newest crystal was pretty much as charged as it was going to get. I could leave it all night, perhaps, but it wouldn't make a material difference.

I did more scouting on the Zeno module, working out how to get the smallest possible space versus the smallest possible shape. If I had to use a shifter to cut the module out, I wanted to fight with the least amount of material possible. Which would be more expensive? Cutting through a little material, or shifting a much larger volume of space?

I didn't get to finish the calculations. I was interrupted.

Rusty had just put his cushions in front of the door again and was about to change into his wolf form when we heard the sound of shattering glass from outside. It's amazing how well sound carries in the semi-abandoned ruins of a city. There wasn't even much gunfire. Certainly no traffic noises or loud music. Not even the hum of streetlights.

We both kept low as we went out on the balcony to look. Whatever caused the noise, it wasn't immediately visible from my balcony. Partly, this was because the sky was overcast and there was almost no light at all. Partly, because the front doors were due south and there was a larger-footprint base to the building, including an enormous carport. Whatever it was, it was coming from underneath.

On the other hand, scattered people sprinted toward us from the west.

"Looters?" I asked.

"Rioters?" Rusty countered. I held out my hand and pointed my arm down. My wristwatch was still set for vampires. It tingled.

"Vampires," I said. Rusty sighed. We went in and took a look at the mirror.

A hundred or more vampires were rampaging through the lobby. Perhaps a dozen figures were on the floor, mobbed by blood-crazed proto-vampires, all ravenously feeding. It looked as though a group of survivors got caught out after sunset, crashed through the glass wall at the front of the building, and died in the lobby.

Then one of the vampires, near the fire door at the bottom of one stairwell, kicked it in. I zoomed in on him and watched as he went to all fours, sniffing, licking at the floor.

I dialed up the light-amplifying mode and, yes, he was licking at what could only be blood.

How did it get there?

I sent the scrying sensor up through the stairwell, whirling up flights of stairs. About the ninth floor I found a man hustling rapidly up the steps. He carried an empty, plastic bottle from a water cooler in one hand and a plastic milk carton in the other. The carton was partly filled with blood and it burbled a bit as the blood leaked from a tiny hole in the bottom.

"I don't like this," Rusty said, glaring at the mirror.

"I don't, either. What's he doing? Leaving a trail for vampires to follow?"

"That's exactly what he's doing. He's luring them up the stairwell."

"Why? To get them away from someone? Everyone in the lobby is dead. Could the rest of his group be hiding in the basement?"

"I doubt it. Look, he's got a gallon jug of blood. That's not something you happen to have handy. It's something you bring when you're planning to lure vampires into your trap."

"You're right," I agreed. "He came here with it for a purpose. Turf war, maybe? Could someone in the building have pissed off a local gang? And is this their way of getting their competition eaten?"

"I doubt it. How's *he* going to get out without getting eaten? Which," Rusty added, "seems weird, now I think on it. You don't go to this level of planning only to get your buddies killed in the lobby."

"True."

"Maybe something went wrong."

"From our perspective, definitely."

The climber kept hustling along, ever upward, dribbling blood as he went. Below, two or three vampires were starting to take an interest in the stairwell, but most of them were still in the lobby, licking the floors and each other. Messy.

The climber reached the fourteenth floor and produced a key from his pocket. He unlocked the stairwell door, which I liked even less, due to the specialized planning it implied. True, they're generic fire-department keys, but he had one handy. He pulled the door wide open and kicked a wedge under it, then applied duct tape.

With the door fixed in place, he kicked the plastic water cooler bottle down the stairs, sending it bouncing. It boomed like a drum and echoed in the concrete-and-steel chamber of the stairwell, making a noise loud enough to wake the undead. It banged and boomed and echoed as it bounced its way down flight after flight.

It was disconcerting how I could hear it on the mirror and with my ears.

Vampires poured up the stairs like a reverse whirlpool. He picked up his jug of blood and poured it as he walked down the hallway, pausing only to splash the rest of it on a door.

My door.

Rusty left the bedroom, kicked his cushions out of the way, and flung open the door. Meanwhile, the man outside drew a gun. As Rusty opened the door, the man placed the barrel under his own chin and fired.

Rusty said a bad word about the same time I did. Same word, too. Rusty was upset about having blood splatter on him when vampires were closing in, as well as the shock of watching a man suicide at close range. I was upset about what it meant. You don't blow your own head off because someone opens a door. You do it to prevent interrogation.

Or to prevent mind-reading.

I couldn't prove Alden sent a baker's dozen zombies here to lure vampires into the building and, specifically, to my door. On the other hand, who else could it be? Alden had unknown powers. Could he have tracked the psychic link between phones? Could he have zombies parked in various structures, acting as observers? Or did Alden hear Rusty in the library and read his thoughts, wolfy though they might be, and forego altering anything so as not to alert me?

The possibilities were endless and annoying and made me want to kill him.

Rusty slammed the door, locked it, and started shoving furniture in front of it. I panned back into the stairwell.

I didn't like the stairwell. I had a bad feeling about it and a growing tingle in my wrist. They were close enough—vertically—to set off the proximity alarm.

Damn it. There were explosives in the wardrobe/arms locker. They included motion-sensing detonators. Now I know why. I should have put one in the stairwell!

I shut down the scrying sensor and started packing for departure. Rusty came in and grabbed a pair of machetes.

"What are you doing?" he asked.

"Getting set to leave," I replied. He lowered the machetes.

"Your plan is better than mine. How? Can we do the teleportation thing?"

"I might have enough power, if we had time for me to cast it carefully. I don't think we even have time for me to cast it hurriedly. Instead, I was thinking we use the rope," I hefted it out of the drawer at the bottom of a wardrobe, "and climb down."

"Is there enough?"

"I will bet you anything you like, sight unseen, this rope is within five meters of the exact length required."

"No bet. What if there are more undead on the ground?"

"We'll blow up that bridge after we cross it. Help me and we'll get out of here faster."

He handled the rope. I stuffed last-minute things in the bug-out bags and slung a bunch of guns—two rifles, two pistols, one submachine gun, extra magazines, and everything, wouldn't you know it, taking the same nine-millimeter ammunition. I felt certain these weapons were not initially designed to use identical ammunition, but someone either hunted down variants or had a word with a gunsmith.

Thanks, Pop.

Rusty, after kicking out a window, tied one end to the balcony door's frame. I handed him his equipment and he tied the other end around all the straps. He lowered the equipment down while I bought us more time.

I didn't know if the vampires included any smart ones or not, but I still cast a Nothing To See Here spell on the bedroom door before I locked it. If nothing else, they would have to force their way into the apartment, search it, overcome the spell, kick in the door, and eventually figure out the rope was significant...

...which *should* give us time to reach the ground.

I never thought I'd hope for a stupid vampire. As we half-slid, half-climbed down the rope in the overcast, lightless night, that's what I was hoping. Either they were, in fact, all stupid or my spell worked. Nothing came down the rope after us. Even better, nothing cut the rope while we were on our way down.

"You lose your bet," Rusty whispered, once we were both on our feet. He held up the leftover rope.

"We're not on the ground, yet," I replied. And we weren't. We reached the flat roof over the first two or three floors. I pulled the rope to the edge and took a quick look over the side. Nobody waited below, which suited me. I dropped the rest of the rope and we shinnied down it quickly.

There were about two extra feet of rope. Rusty rolled his eyes when I grinned at him. He handed me equipment and helped settle it all in place before he shifted into wolf form. I kept most things slung from one shoulder, ready to drop, and drew a machete. The blade would be more effective on a vampire than a gun. It also wouldn't finger my position for everyone in a half-mile. Rusty sniffed the air, growled a little, and led us eastward. I didn't argue with The Nose.

We headed alongside the Horizon building, along 38th, keeping out of sight as much as possible. We were almost to FDR Drive when the *whoosh* of a rocket and the heavy *whoomp* of an explosion lit the night behind us. A quarter of the way up the Corinthian building, half a floor was on fire. Screaming figures, also on fire, plummeted out the broken windows.

Rusty and I watched the spectacle for a moment. He shifted upward into human form. I was pleased to see my work paid off. He was still fully dressed.

"I'm gonna guess you pissed Alden off a *lot*," he whispered. "He wanted you to get eaten by vampires before you got blown up."

"Burned to death," I corrected.

"Huh?"

"That's an incendiary round. The blast might have killed me, but the flames are what would make sure."

"Damn," Rusty breathed. "What's got his goat?"

"He mentioned a wound that wouldn't heal. He seemed pretty angry about it. Just looking at him, he also has obvious health issues. As far as I know, Pop doesn't have anything in his gadgets to *stop* healing, but Alden can't be sure. I could probably figure out what the problem is, maybe even fix it, but he's an egomaniac with no respect for me, so I won't."

"Luring vampires to do his dirty work seems like he doesn't want to face you."

"Or it's a slap in the face. He could be saying he's aware of my attempt to use vampires against him."

"The rocket launcher doesn't exactly say he wants a showdown in the street, either."

"That's a fair point," I admitted, softly. "Let's talk about it elsewhere, shall we?"

"Okay." He slid down into wolf form again and padded ahead. I followed.

We crossed FDR and worked our way south, keeping low and making use of the East River Esplanade. It wasn't a big park, but it still had trees. Best of all, it was mostly blocked from view from the rest of the city by the off-ramp to 42nd. We crept down the length of it and Rusty stopped at the southern edge. He made unhappy, whimpering noises until he shifted back to human again.

"What's the matter?" I asked, as he changed.

"The thirty-fourth street ferry docks over there," he said, indicating the pier. "I was hoping for a boat. Vampires won't cross running water, remember?"

"Good thinking, but I'm more concerned about someone on shore seeing us, shooting us, or putting together a greeting party to meet us when we land. Out there on the water is a *bad* place to be. We're exposed to everyone, including angry people with rocket launchers."

"It doesn't matter," he answered. "There are no boats."

"I think you're mostly correct."

"Mostly?" he echoed.

"Look closer. Down there. Does it look like a boat?"

"Someone sank the ferry? Why?"

"Got me. It might not be deliberate. All it would take is a bilge pump failure. A couple of cars catching fire from an electrical surge could hurry it along. There's no telling how many things were indirectly destroyed when power failed."

"But where are the other boats?" he insisted.

"Some people thought their best strategy was to hunker down and wait. I bet others decided they wanted off the island at any cost. If the boats were functional, they might have taken them out to sea, down the coast, or anywhere. If not, maybe they rigged sails and sailed off into the sunrise. Point is, they're gone. What's next?"

Rusty's comment could have been misinterpreted as a suggestion, but this was neither the time nor the place.

"We need a place to hide," he said, finally.

"How about right here?"

"Here?"

"I can't gate us anywhere, but I can cast a Go Away spell. People and things will avoid this area. If we're quiet and still, we won't attract anyone."

"And if a thousand vampires come over the concrete barrier and pour down on us?"

"We swim. They don't."

"Curse you and your logic. Fine."

We hunkered down for the night. I had no problem settling in. I had Mister Stuffins.

Journal Entry #47

The East River Esplanade is a narrow strip along, unsurprisingly, the East River. It's easy to get to for a pedestrian, but if you don't know it's there, it's kind of hard to see. Add to this it has limited access, some of which is gated, and you've got an inconvenient place to get to. In an apocalypse, there's not a lot about it to recommend it to tourists. There's no *reason* to go there. Add in the fact I had spells diverting attention away from the access points and it was a good place to survive the night.

Watching the sun come up was a nice feeling. It meant we could move around without worrying so much. Attracting human problems was a better deal than attracting vampire problems. You can stop a vampire—most of them, and for a while—with a shot to the head. Humans might be reasoned with. Failing that, humans are also more fragile and don't recover nearly so well.

"What's next?" Rusty asked, yawning and stretching. We alternated naps through the night, so we were both tired, but we managed to keep a constant watch on our surroundings.

"We need a new hideout. Someplace where a hundred vampires aren't going to follow a blood trail."

"I guess we could scout around. Maybe we could hide in a building Alden's zombies have already searched. They don't search them again, do they?"

"I wouldn't think so. They have limited intelligence and tend to follow instructions rather blindly. I'm not comfortable being so close to Alden, though."

"That's fair."

"I need power," I sighed. "That's what it comes down to. I need time to gather energy, work out a plan of attack, prepare spells, and made the son of a bitch suffer."

"You mentioned you wanted to imprison him," Rusty half-asked.

"I did. Now I don't care. I want him to—" I broke off. "Oh, I know exactly what I want," I said, gleefully. Rusty looked at me with a peculiar expression. "What?" I asked. "What's the look for?"

"You know how a little girl looks when she has her perfect dress on for her birthday party and she gets the sparkly unicorn-decorated cake to go with her sparkly princess tiara?"

"Sure."

"You looked like that."

"That's bad?"

"You looked like that because you're about to do something awful to someone."

"I'll be getting what I want," I pointed out.

"Yeah, and what you want in this context worries me."

"Relax. It still requires planning and forethought and work, but I think it's doable. We still need someplace to hole up for a week, though."

"Pick a building."

"Let's go check out the Corinthian. There may be salvage. At the very least, I want to get at the panel spells and put more charge in my big crystal."

We crept out of the esplanade. There was a pedestrian tunnel under FDR Drive and we took it. It beat trying to cross the huge, flat, open space of the highway. We did our leapfrog advance, moving quietly, until I could see the garden area around the front of the Corinthian.

No vampires, obviously, but there were plenty of mind-controlled zombies. They were armed with everything you can imagine, including guns. A few of the weapons looked more than a little scorched and suspiciously familiar.

I pulled out a pocket mirror and sent a scrying spell up into the room. Yep, they looted the building. Were still looting it, in fact, taking water, food, and equipment. It put me in mind of a long line of ants, each one carrying a load back to the hive.

Rusty, peering cautiously from our cover, made a disgusted noise. Out front, the zombies put down their cargo, drew weapons, and spread out. They advanced in our direction.

"Did they spot us?" I asked.

"I don't see how. Not at this distance."

I looked around. Was there a scrying sensor? Did Alden know a scrying spell? Even if he did, would it work through his own static? I didn't see a sensor anywhere.

On the other hand, there was a pigeon perched on the Manhattan Place Building. This was hardly unusual, but it perched there, unmoving, one unwinking eye focused on us. What really got my attention was the aura of psychic energy surrounding it.

Okay, so Alden can control animals and look through their eyes. I mean, he can wipe a human mind and use them as zombie slaves, so I guess an animal isn't out of the question. I'd think it would be harder to maintain a connection, though, since the wattage on a bird-brain is so low. Then again, if it's anywhere near a human minion, it may be in range of the network.

"How many?" Rusty asked. I noticed his fingernails were longer than normal. Reflex, maybe.

"Thirty here, another thirty in the building?"

"Run or fight?"

"Run, then fight. Let's choose our ground."

"Suits me."

We fell back, sprinting along 37th for about half a block, until we reached the parking garage of the Horizon building. We cut left through the garage to 38th while the zombies were supposed to be focused on chasing us down 37th. Nope. Several of them were headed down 38th. Dang it. They're all in total communication with each other, instantly knowing what all the others know.

I paused as a shot went *wheet!* past us. A deflection spell wasn't out of order on Rusty, so I put one on him. He regenerates, sure, but bullets can still hurt him enough to slow him down, even put him down for a while. My own deflection spell isn't automatic, but I keep it on a bit of a hair trigger. It fired up normally.

Fine. Zombies, zombies everywhere and not a thought to think. Well, screw this. There's a whole block of empty space across 38th, on the far side of the fence. Rusty and I went over the chain-link fence like felons escaping. We sprinted toward the middle of the field.

"What's the plan?" he panted as we ran. "I thought we were supposed to avoid open spaces."

"We have more bullets than there are adversaries, at present. We can kill them all, but more will vector toward us. We have to break their line of sight to lose them, but they *all* instantly know where we are if *any* of them sees us. There's the problem. Long sight lines right now work to our advantage while I'm trying to figure out how to drop off the radar. You can shoot anyone you see while I work on breaking their link so we can bug out."

A few zombies thrust rifles through the fence and fired at us. At that range, I doubt they would have hit, anyway. We were perfectly safe, but they—and Alden—didn't know that. Rusty and I reached the middle of the area and crouched anyway. I pretended to hide behind him, but it was only to cut down on the power use. His deflection spell would handle any fire that was on-target. I handed him my spare magazines. He knelt and started picking off anyone climbing the fence.

"I wish we had a machine gun," he said, wistfully, between shots.

Rusty knew how to use a rifle. He took two sighting shots, getting the range, then started putting lethal hits into zombies. True, not all of these dropped zombies immediately. A fatal wound in a human is still a fatal wound in a zombie, but the zombie ignores it until he physically can't go on. Rusty ignored any zombie pumping out arterial blood—it's a bright, unmistakable red—and moved on to fresh ones as handgun- or blade-carrying zombies clambered over the fence.

I, for my part, did the math. Normally, open terrain is not defensible terrain. There are very few exceptions. In this case, we had an invisible fortification—deflection spells—and, for the moment, a limited number of adversaries in a big kill zone. If we both laid down fire, we might hold them off, but it was still unlikely. We would kill most, now or later, but in the meantime they wouldn't care. They would roll over us and bury us under them. Rusty, by himself, certainly couldn't hold them off, but putting a round through someone climbing a fence slows him down and *maybe* kills him. Head shots are easier when they're climbing. There's much less movement.

His shooting slowed them down and that was what I wanted, what I needed.

Alden's psychic link with his minions was usually an echo effect. Minion #1 shouted and Minion #2 repeated it, and so on, until a minion close enough to Alden echoed it to him. No doubt he was powerful enough to assume direct control of any minion he pleased, but for mass minion operations he had to rely on their collective link to each other. He gave them an order and their multiplex brain linkage carried it out. This is a very different thing than having a hundred independent people following an order. It's their biggest weakness, I think.

I, on the other hand, might be weaker than him, but I was also a lot closer to them.

I focused on a zombie on our side of the fence. He was one of three who already made it over, but he was the first one with a submachine gun. Rusty ignored him, focusing instead on the ones actually running toward us. As he should, since the ones with guns weren't really a threat at the moment.

I reached out to this zombie and grabbed him by what was left of his mind. He turned around and emptied his magazine into a group of five zombies still climbing the chain link. I dropped the connection immediately, before Alden could react to it. I wouldn't get away with it again, I felt sure, but it would certainly divert Alden's attention from directing zombies. They would be dumber, less quick to react to changing circumstances, and maybe less motivated without his constant psychic whipping.

It worked. The zombies moved less quickly. Alden was paying attention, urging them on, until I interfered. Now his attention was split, if not entirely diverted. He was watching for interference instead of pushing them. It still wouldn't end well for us, but it gave me more time.

My notebook isn't required for casting spells. I can gesture and speak and do all the usual stuff, but my notebook is very helpful to my focus. Pop always encouraged me to explore my interests and one of them was art. When I was little, he collected refrigerator art. We would set up a whole gallery of crayon drawings around a room and we would walk along while he critiqued each piece, using his thoughtful voice. "Here we see a prime example of the impressionist style, done in colored wax on purple paper. The surrealistic nature of the cow lends great significance to the tree, I feel, but the flowers are the key point of the piece. Look at the attention to detail!" I would giggle and feel good about my art and he would be pleased.

As a result, I draw things. Whether its lines on a floor or an archway on a wall or scribbles on a box or spells in a notebook, I draw. So I drew lines in my notebook.

The spell I wanted had to be timed very carefully. Preparing it wasn't much of a problem, but the range was limited. It would be effective all the way to the fence, I was certain, but perhaps only for a brief while. Alden had a powerful mind and would try to overcome it once he realized what was happening.

I pulled out both of our machetes. One I stuck point-down next to Rusty. The other I kept in hand.

The zombies without rifles had stopped charging individually and clustered together on our side of the fence. The outermost ones acted as shields for the others, soaking up Rusty's fire. It was easy to see what would happen. The wounded ones would charge if they could, still blocking bullets, or stand aside for the faster, fresher ones to clear the open space more quickly.

Rusty was not pleased. He preferred them to be scattered so he could pick off the ones in the lead. Instead, the whole group broke into a run, approaching as a group while the riflemen—riflezombies?—ceased fire to climb the fence. I restrained myself from a *squee* of delight.

I waited. I couldn't have asked for a better arrangement.

The leading group came within a dozen yards of us, handguns firing. The rifle-toting zombies landed inside the fence and sprinted after, trying to catch up. I slapped Rusty on the shoulder and pointed at the machete. He laid down the rifle and picked up the blade. Things were about to get personal and messy.

I tore out the notebook page and activated it. The page burst into flame from the energy surge as the spell went off. It was a psychic shout, a continuous scream to overwhelm any routine signals. It radiated from me, fading with distance, but I have no doubt it came as a complete surprise to Alden. It screamed a constant note, a single command, over and over: "*Stand still!*"

The zombies on hand, formerly under control of a psychic influence, linked together into a semi-intelligent hive-mind, suddenly found themselves to be individuals. Individual idiots with no real idea of what they were supposed to be doing. One might even regard them as drooling idiots, as soon as they had time to drool. The only thought in their heads—quite literally—was my command to stand still.

Rusty and I moved forward into the group.

A sharp, heavy blade is ideal for chopping meat. Go for the neck. You don't need to decapitate someone, just open up major blood vessels. When they've already been exerting themselves, the heart rate and blood pressure are up. Death isn't instantaneous, but it can be astonishingly quick.

Rusty knows how to chop, but he's in no sense a swordsman. I, on the other hand, have trained in so many forms of hand-to-hand combat I don't think I can name all of them. He lumbered in, hacking. I whirled in, slicing. His blows bit deep, often to the spine, before he yanked the blade free and swung at the next blank-faced zombie. I sliced, hitting, pressing, drawing the edge along in a cutting motion. The hit chopped deep, but the continued movement sliced deeper, drawing the blade free as I swung around at the next neck.

Score: Rusty, six. Me, sixteen. See the advantage of training?

We then moved on to the rifle zombies. One of them was kneeling, taking careful aim—probably under Alden's direct control, pushing hard through the spell. Since my psychic command spell was centered on me and radiating outward, it became harder for Alden to maintain contact. The zombie never actually fired, just aimed.

One-two, one-two! The machete blades went swish and splat! We left them dead to keep our heads and we went galumphing back. We collected the rifle and continued on across the open ground.

"That," Rusty said, once we'd cleared the fence and started northward, "was fantastic!"

"Yeah, don't let it go to your head. Alden may have a lot more where those came from."

"Maybe, but now they've got to find us and catch us!"

"And they can!"

"What? How?"

"Birds. I'm dead certain Alden was watching us through a bird, and I can't zap all the birds in Manhattan!"

Rusty's language was harsh, but understandable.

"What do we do?"

"I'm thinking! Right now, we're getting distance from his base so he has a harder time sending zombies after us! No doubt reinforcements were already sprinting our way when the fight started. They know where we are and which way we're going. I don't want them catching us or cutting us off!"

"We're faster than they are and they have a long way to go," Rusty reasoned.

"They have bicycles!"

"Damn!"

We kept up a jog for several blocks, past the Unification Building, all the way to the Queensboro Bridge. Buildings showed signs of damage from the Central Park blast. Windows, mostly, but several power lines were down, too. As always, there were dead cars, most of which had burned out. Shorted by the EMP? Maybe. We paused to rest a moment under the bridge.

"What do you think?" Rusty asked. "Do we cross the bridge? We can get farther away and the bridge makes a choke point."

"The bridge isn't a choke point," I countered. "It's too wide. They can climb over the dead cars and even use them as cover to get close. We couldn't lay down enough fire if there were a dozen of us. With the cars cleared, maybe, but we might as well wish for horses. Besides, I think I have an idea."

"I approve," he answered, instantly.

"Of the idea?"

"Yes. Whatever it is. It's better than anything I've got."

"I'd like to hear your idea."

"If I had one, I'd share it."

"Oh, it's like that, is it?"

I had let my psychic shout spell lapse since it wasn't going to do us any good. It's strictly a short-ranged thing for overriding zombies. Instead, I raised a psychic shield, a barrier around us. It was even shorter-ranged, but it was to prevent eavesdropping. I couldn't take the time to check every single rat, cat, bat, bird, and anything else that might be sheltering under the bridge with us.

I took his hand for physical linkage. Mentally, we talked.

Okay, Pop has another safe house. It's north of here and, judging by my maps of the blasts, probably intact.

Great! Rusty replied. *Let's go!*

There's a problem. It's on the north end of the island, a little east of Inwood Hill Park. We have to cross the blasted areas from the Central Park and the Fort Lee hits.

Radiation zones, you mean.

Yes.

I take it back. I'm not a fan of this idea.

Well, I have a solution.

Great!

You're not going to like it.

If it keeps me out of glow-in-the-dark places, I'll love it!

We take the tunnels. We'll be shielded by the rock above from any radiation, just like in a bunker.

Tunnels. You mean the underground, lightless tunnels? The lightless tunnels full of vampires? Those tunnels?

Yes.

I take it all back. I don't love it.

I don't like it, either, but it will also get us out of the line of sight of anything Alden is using to track us!

What about the tunnel rats and other vermin? he protested.

Didn't you say the vampires were hungry?

I felt him sigh.

Look, he went on, *I'm not a fan of being irradiated. I'm not a fan of tiptoeing through thousands of sleeping vampires, either!*

Are you a fan of being hunted by day and then being prey by night?

Can't you teleport us there? You've got a big power crystal!

It wasn't charged enough while we were at the first place and I've been using it since then to survive!

How long will it take to charge?

If we can reach a safe place where Alden isn't tracking us, you mean?

Rusty's verbal profanity is actually pretty mild. He doesn't say a tenth of what he thinks. His internal monologue isn't at all restrained. Sailors don't cuss like that. At least, their cussing isn't as filthy as Rusty's thinking. I refrained from any comments on his dirty mind. To be fair, it's harder to filter when you're not accustomed to telepathy.

*FINE! We'll go down in the tunnels. The **vampire-infested** tunnels! We'll go look and see what the situation is. But if we really do have to tiptoe through a carpet of vampires like we're sneaking through a daycare at naptime, we need a better plan!*

Agreed!

I let go of his hand and we started looking for a subway entrance.

We went down into the ground. Nothing flew in after us. I wasn't sure if that was because it would be too obvious or if it meant Alden felt we wouldn't be coming out again. Either way, we had a quiet moment where we had enough light to see by, but were far enough in to avoid zombies and watchful eyes.

"You know, I don't like this," Rusty said.

"I'm not fond of it, either. The only reason I think it's our best option is losing Alden. No zombies."

"No zombies, yeah, but instead we get vampires? How is this better?"

"Vampires sleep during the day. Most types, anyway, and these are no exception. I don't know how hard they are to wake up, or even if it's possible, but as long as we stay quiet, we can avoid the rush."

He slung the rifle he'd been carrying and drew the machete.

"Got it." He looked down the stairs. "It's going to be dark."

"Hang on. I've been thinking about this ever since we headed for the subway." I took the time to dig out a pair of shooter's safety glasses. I used my knifepoint to scratch along the frames. "There. Try this."

He put on the glasses and looked around.

"It's a spectrum-shifting spell," I told him, "kind of like a thermal camera. Usually, it keys off your pupils, but you can override it. Squint and the spell eases up. Open wide and it increases in power."

"Won't the vampires be room temperature?"

"It's a narrow band of temperatures. I calibrated it by aiming it at the stairs all the way at the bottom," I pointed. "Anything close to that temperature will show up as a color. A degree or two beyond it in either direction and it'll be white or black. Corpses will have enough differences to be seen. So will rails, walls, pillars, benches, and so on. They might be ghostly and hard to see, but they'll be visible."

"I'll believe it when I see it."

"Funny man."

"Why not use a light spell?"

"They can see a light spell from farther away than we can see."

"Couldn't you use some other kind of light? Infrared light, maybe, like with night vision goggles?"

"Oh, well, if you're going to be *intelligent* about it…" I grumped, and drew my knife again.

"You mean you can?"

"Sure. It didn't occur to me. If I run it on the local magic, it'll be weak. I'm not sure how far away it will illuminate. How about I put the thermal on one side and the infrared on the other?"

"Suits me. One more thing. If you're going to be casting preparatory spells, do you think we could get rid of the blood? I don't want to smell like food in a vampire lair."

I had to admit, Rusty's ideas were good ones. I ran the cleaning spell over us both and did it thoroughly, making sure to minimize our natural odors, too. Then I worked on our glasses again, modifying the existing spell and adding the infrared light source. One eye saw thermal; the other, a greyscale image. Thermal saw farther; infrared saw more detail. Between the two, it worked pretty well.

Would ultraviolet be better? Or would it hurt the vampires, make them wake up? No, it probably wouldn't. The nightclub had a lot of black lights and the vampires didn't seem to mind. Then again, ultraviolet light comes in a wide range of wavelengths. I didn't want to risk it.

We went down the stairs, into the dark. Before long, it really was dark, pitch dark, absolutely dark. Any emergency lights that might have survived had run out of power. I took a moment to adjust our thermal vision, re-centering the spectra on a wall. Things came into better contrast through the lens. The IR side stayed the same, of course, revealing everything within ten or fifteen feet.

A little further along and we reached the subway platform. We saw dozens of corpses scattered around. I wasn't surprised they were there; my wristwatch was constantly a-tingle with a proximity warning. I was surprised there were so *many*.

I found I needed to breathe, so I started again. My heart didn't slow down for several seconds, though. When it did, I realized I could hear Rusty's heartbeat. I wondered if the dead people could.

"This was a bad idea," I whispered, staring around at the bodies.

"Maybe," Rusty breathed. "See anyone moving?"

"No. Do you hear what I hear?"

"My heartbeat running fast?"

"I thought it was mine."

"As long as we both have one."

We stood there and regarded the dead people. It was more than a little freaky to me. Pop never did this. It was weird.

"Can they wake up?" Rusty asked, still whispering.

"I don't know."

"You're the expert."

"I was afraid you'd say that."

"Well?"

"All right. We'll test it before we get too far into the tunnels, while we still have daylight not far away."

"Okay."

We prepared to bring down machetes in heavy, two-handed blows. I carefully nudged a body. The body didn't react. Rusty covered me while I tugged firmly on one arm. The body still didn't react.

A quick check with my vampire detector didn't do me any good. The thing wasn't designed to pick out individuals from a sea of them. Still, it meant the intact-looking corpse was probably an undead. Legitimate corpses were likely to be a bit gnawed on.

I grabbed the guy by his collar and pulled, sliding him gently along the floor. He didn't protest. Up a few steps, up a few more, carefully and gently, and he didn't mind a bit.

As we got closer and closer to the surface, a faint, shadowy illumination started. The reflected sunlight, scattered from the walls and through the air, meant it wasn't totally black anymore. The dead guy twitched.

I stopped. Rusty stopped. Everything stopped, even the twitching.

After a moment, I resumed dragging him. He twitched again, but I kept going. The brighter it got, the worse the twitching got, until he was practically shivering. His heels drummed on the floor and I let go of him. He moaned, a low, ugly sound, and a gurgling rattle came from his throat. His eyes opened as he shuddered and shook.

He turned over onto his belly, still trembling, and hissed at us. He squinted in the near-darkness and scuttled backward, still hissing, smoking slightly, until he tumbled down the stairs.

We waited a few minutes. Things got quiet and stayed quiet.

"So, sunlight wakes them up?" Rusty asked.

"I'd guess so. It also looks like we can walk past them, no trouble. If I can drag one up a flight of stairs and he doesn't notice, they won't care if we walk past them."

"I'm so glad."

"You don't sound glad."

"I was lying."

We descended again, alert for our test subject. For all we knew, he might still be awake. But no, he was lying in a heap at the bottom of the stairs, once again an inert body. I nudged him with my toe. He reacted exactly as a full-time corpse would.

"I think we're good," I whispered.

"I'm glad someone does," Rusty muttered.

We headed north. It was about nine miles, give or take. On the surface, on streets, it might have been a brisk two- or three-hour walk. Over rubble and broken terrain? Probably an all-day, maybe all-night affair. The subway tunnels were straight and level, at least, so we wouldn't have terrain problems.

On the other hand, we still had to step carefully due to obstacle problems. Dragging a vampire up the stairs didn't hurt it any, but the low-intensity sunlight probably did. We didn't want to find out if squishing a finger had the same effect.

And there were so *many* of them! The dozens we saw on the platform were only the beginning. When sunrise started, they must have flooded down every opening into the underworld, running into the darkness as far as they could flee. Not to make room for others, no, but to get away from the light. It worked well for them, since it allowed more to crowd in behind the first ones rather than have to shove everyone forward. We climbed carefully down off the platform and stepped between the sprawled bodies even as we walked along the tunnel.

They were everywhere. We were surrounded.

I'm not claustrophobic. I spent three days in a personal tomb without much difficulty, after all. But this! This felt different. This wasn't a closed-in space. This was a feeling of being surrounded on all sides by things wanting to eat me. I didn't care for it.

We stepped carefully, walking northward. Nobody got up, nobody moved, nobody did anything unexpected. Everything was about as peachy-keen as jam on toast.

Of course, not everything went the way we hoped.

Rusty and I regarded the cave-in and suppressed our mutual urge to swear.

"What now?" Rusty asked, quietly. The vampires sleeping around us didn't answer.

"We go back, take a cross-tunnel, and try again."

"We're pretty far east of the central blast."

"So?"

"If we have a collapse here, won't there be collapses in tunnels closer to the center?"

"Not necessarily. This may have been a weak point."

"Or they may all be collapsed and impassable to the north."

"Or they may all be collapsed," I agreed. "What do you suggest?"

"We're going to have to go down."

"What do you mean?"

"The tunnels up here collapsed. Deeper tunnels may not have."

"You do know the pumping stations are off-line? The lowest tunnels are flooding. Flooded, I should say, by now."

"Maybe we can swim them?"

"How far can you go underwater? A hundred yards? A half-mile?"

"I knew I should have taken swimming lessons."

I refrained from another dog-paddling reference, but it was *not* easy.

"Look, I've got an idea. Let's go back to the subway train and see if there's an unoccupied car."

We did so and, yes, the train was unoccupied. The vampires didn't bother with opening doors and finding seats when the sunrise started. They ran as deep into the darkness as they could go before they fell down or lay down or whatever.

We closed up the car and sort-of hid in it. Rusty stood guard while I played with my pocket mirror.

Prior to the cave-in, I thought the idea was simple enough. Pick our way carefully north, through the now-unused tunnels. We would avoid any radioactive zones near ground zero. The vampires would be asleep. Alden shouldn't have anyone down here to spy on us. We would be concealed and safe—relatively safe. Safe-ish. Safer than on the surface while being hunted by a powerful psychic and his zombie minions, I mean.

Now the simple plan was complicated by not having reliable tunnels. Sure, this version of New York had a lot of tunnels and an almost grid-pattern subway system. But if the tunnels all had cave-ins, they were useless to us.

I sent out a scrying sensor. First, I checked the rockfall ahead of us. It wasn't extensive—only a hundred feet or so—but far too much for us to go through, even if I had Pop's old silver cloak. He left it with Leisel, but she showed it to me. I was fascinated with walking through walls for a while. Once I understood it, I kind of lost interest. I guess it was only a phase I went through.

Now I mapped the subway labyrinth. I followed the right-hand rule, sliding my sensor through the tunnels at high speed, always sticking to the right-side wall, drawing a rough map as I went. I found closed doors and hatches, but treated them as openings, instead. You never know when you're going to find a maintenance cross-connection going exactly where you need to. It was considerably faster than tromping down every tunnel and corridor.

I didn't like what my growing map showed.

All the subway trains ran at the same basic level. They didn't go uphill or downhill. This subway level stayed the same while the ground level above fluctuated. Subway stations had a few stairs or many, an escalator or an elevator, whatever was required for that location. So mapping all this out was relatively quick.

There wasn't a single clear passage from the south end of the island to the north end. There wasn't even a passage we could clear in any reasonable length of time. It didn't matter what tunnel or cross-connection we went through, there wasn't a way past the north end of Central Park. I might have missed a ventilation shaft, perhaps, but I don't think it would have mattered.

I dropped my sensor down a level, into older subway tunnels, wiring runs, sewer pipe tunnels—the unseen systems of the city. These were deeper, but they too were damaged. They were also more twisted and complicated, more extensive. Moving people around is simple. People know where they want to go and will figure it out. Everything else has to be laid down in wires and pipes. There's no simple grid plan for that. There are new systems piled on older systems, each with its own unique needs, and they twist and wind and overlay each other like vines in a jungle.

Mapping it all was a pain. What made it worse was the fact there were fewer cave-ins… but enough. Getting north of 110th looked impossible.

Still, Rusty was right. The collapses were fewer deeper down, farther from the blast.

I sent my sensor down even deeper.

Yep, the deep tunnels were partly flooded. Natural leakage? Cracks in the bedrock letting in the rivers? Or the inevitable consequence of not keeping them pumped out? I'll never know. Regardless, there were no vampires so deep down, so that was a bonus.

Counterpoint, there was water at least waist-deep everywhere. Vampires don't need to breathe. Would we see them coming if they chose to scramble along on all fours under the water?

Could they? Did standing water count? Could we sit in a raft in a swimming pool and be okay? Could we fill a jumbo kiddie pool and stand in the center, immune to these vampires? Or did it need to be natural water? Or flowing water? Or water that saw sunlight, rather than underground rivers? What are the rules on this?

After all my searching, I found two ways through the labyrinth. They were long and unpleasant, but ultimately possible. Go north, go down, go west, go north, down again, west again, up a level, a bit south, west again, down again, north, east, up, north, down, north... blah blah blah.

There was a lot of forward, around, back, and so on, following a line twisting like pig guts to avoid blocked areas, but it was possible to get from here to there without ever surfacing.

Rusty, meanwhile, unpacked lunch. He offered me cold pinto stew with ham while he opened a jalapeno beef curry for himself. We ate while I rested my eyes.

"Any luck?" he asked.

"Yes."

"Good or bad?"

"A bit of both."

"Typical."

"We can get there from here, but we're going to get wet. The lowest levels are entirely flooded. About two levels down, it's flood*ing*, but it's not fast. We probably have a couple of days before it's impassable."

"Yay," he said, without enthusiasm. We finished lunch. I made sure we were as clean and odor-free as possible again before we opened the door to slink out into the tunnels. Since I had the map in mind—literally—I led the way.

It was not a pleasant walk. There were, to be sure, long stretches of tunnels where there were practically no vampires. There were also places where they carpeted the ground like beggars in Bombay. Walking among them without stepping on anyone was... tricky.

Nevertheless, we made our way west and came to a maintenance hatchway. I suppressed the noise it would make while Rusty opened it. We went down the stairs, but we also closed the door behind us.

Once we were out of the subway level, the vampire density decreased sharply. It was easier to run deeper into the subway tunnels than to open a door, find a ladder, or hunt for other access to lower levels. We made much better progress, even though the tunnels were usually narrower. We even sprinted for a few stretches. The thermal vision gave us decent distance vision and the IR vision brought things into clear detail as we came up to them. It wasn't as good as actual sight—it was slightly headache-inducing, having a different view in each eye—but it worked.

We came to an access door and I did my thing to keep it quiet. Rusty looked puzzled.

"Shouldn't we keep going?" he asked.

"Everything from this point is a dead end, as far as we're concerned. A whole tree of potential routes either loop back or are blocked. The only way to make progress is to go down, wade east again, under a blocked area, and come up in another section we can't get to from this or the subway level."

"I feel like I'm in a Greek myth."

"The Labyrinth," I supplied, while he grunted at opening the hatch. "Theseus went in to slay the minotaur and used Ariadne's thread to find his way back out again."

"Does the mean—*hurrg!*—I'm Theseus?" He shoved one more time and the hatch, clearly seldom-used, gave up. Beyond was a ladderway.

"Sure. Ironic how I get to play Ariadne."

"Why ironic?"

"Ariadne was the granddaughter of Helios, the god of the sun. On the other hand, Pop and I always got along well with spiders."

We looked down the ladderway. Muddy water hid the bottom. At least, I hoped the brown color was from dirt.

"Was the minotaur aquatic?" Rusty asked.

"No."

"How deep, do you think?"

"Should be between three and four feet. Sometimes it's hard to gauge sizes in a scrying spell."

He went down and tested the water.

"It's cold."

"I'll call maintenance."

"Funny." He stepped down, down again, and stopped. "Yeah, about three feet. A little more."

I came down and stepped into the water. He was wrong about it being cold. It was incredibly cold. Frigid. Freezing. Icy Arctic. Horrible.

"Let's not dally," I suggested. "We need to get out of this, dry off, and warm up."

We waded as rapidly as we could. I kept my arm extended, scanning for vampires. Down here, we were far enough away from the main horde even one vampire should register.

Again, I wondered, did a flooded tunnel count as "running water?" Or did any water count? Could the local vampires use a swimming pool, but be unable to step across a gutter when it rained? How did it work? What were the specifics? I didn't know, and until someone proved to me a vampire couldn't be lying in wait under the surface, I was scanning. End of discussion.

We made it to the proper ladderway without incident, which made me feel ever so much better. I went up, did my sound dampening spell on the door, and applied my own Angrist to a particularly stubborn bolt.

Why are these hatches even down here if they never use them? They're watertight, so maybe they're a subterranean flood-control measure? But the ones I've seen are darn near rusted shut. Did they once have a real purpose, but time and history have moved on, making them forgotten leftovers? I'd like a word with the city planning office, assuming it doesn't glow in the dark.

The tunnels beyond were still mostly free of vampires. There was probably a better way down from the surface than the one we took. One that would lead almost directly to a simple path northward. But here we were, a hundred or more feet below sea level, and committed.

We stepped through and shut the door. I took a minute to clean us again, which also dried us off. I didn't dare spend power foolishly, though. We would warm up as we walked.

Up again, back to the subway level. This was a slidewalk area. It was a short-distance transport, kind of like a flat escalator or a conveyor belt, but it covered a block or so. I remember seeing them in airports before I came here. Nice idea. It kept pedestrians out of the rain and let people avoid waiting for a train if they had a medium-short distance to go. Now, of course, it was a metal sidewalk.

A metal sidewalk covered in vampires. But we had to get through.

We picked our way carefully down the tunnel, sometimes even resorting to the rubber-topped handrails to avoid stepping on anyone. It wasn't difficult, just delicate. They looked to me as though they ran into the tunnel from both ends, probably from different entrances. We made it past the thickest clump and out the other end. Sure enough, there was another platform. They were packed a bit more thickly than on other platforms, but I blamed the train. It was at the platform when the power went out, so the vampire flood only had pedestrian access, not an open tunnel in both directions to flee down.

Rusty tapped my shoulder to get my attention. When I looked at him, he touched his ear and pointed toward the train. I looked in the direction he indicated and listened. The train was unlit. I didn't see anything on thermal, at least not through the wall of the train. I did hear... something.

We moved to the gap between platform and train. There weren't a lot of vampires sprawled beside it. Quite a few clustered near the ends, presumably as they crowded through the choke points, trying to get farther into the tunnels.

As we drew closer, the sound became clearer. Someone sobbing? Yes. A captive? Someone crazy enough to go looking for a lost loved one? A would-be vampire hunter hiding because they didn't make it to daylight before the sun went down?

I checked my watch. It's a wind-up timepiece; Pop picked a fancy one. We still had at least three hours before this flophouse closed and the residents rose.

So, what do we do? Someone is down here and they're crying. It doesn't sound like a child. The vampires aren't stirring. So, sound isn't as major a concern as we feared. What *do* we do?

Yeah, we go look, because we're curious and stupid. I think I get it from Pop. I don't know what Rusty's excuse is.

One of the trickier things about looking at the world through different spectra— meaning things like ultraviolet, thermal radiation, radar, or anything else—is how different materials are opaque, translucent, or transparent. With sufficiently sensitive thermal gear, you can look right through a steel door or a concrete wall, but the radar is unlikely to see through the door. But, by the same token, glass may be nearly opaque to typical thermal images and to infrared light!

I peeked through a train-car window. Thermal gave me no joy and my IR lens showed me only my reflection. I ducked out of sight, but looked up through the glass, trying to see inside the car. As I did so, I started fiddling with my IR vision spell. Glass doesn't block all the non-visible wavelengths, so I slid the emissions and the reception in tandem until I found a wavelength that would go through the glass.

Then I looked inside.

A woman knelt in the middle of the car, curled in on herself, sobbing. Her hands clutched at the sides of her head. She looked like a survivor, all right—jeans, running shoes, leather jacket, an empty holster at her hip. There wasn't much else to see in her present position. I saw no one else in the train car, which struck me as odd. The doors on this side were open. Did the vampires not go into the car because it didn't allow them to keep running farther away? This would seem to match what I knew, but wouldn't they have smelled her? Or something? Or were they too preoccupied with fleeing the sunrise? Or did she come down in full daylight?

"What do you see?" Rusty whispered. I started to answer, but checked myself. The woman stopped sobbing and raised her head, tensely alert. I pressed a finger to Rusty's lips and waited. She eventually relaxed and curled up on her side, shivering.

Rusty couldn't see what I saw, so I adjusted his lens to match my wavelength. This had the additional bonus of letting us see what was around the other person, like two people illuminating areas with different flashlights.

I took his hand in mine.

I see one woman, I thought at him. *She seems distraught. I'm not sure why she's down here.*

Maybe we should ask her?

Quietly?

Calmly, for sure. If she runs and trips over a vampire, will it wake up?

I don't think so, but I also don't think it's a risk we want to run.

Rusty looked around us, as the scattered bodies of the undead.

I agree unreservedly.

Rusty drew his machete carefully, silently. I cleared my throat. The woman went tense again, listening intently.

"Miss?" I whispered. "Are you all right?"

She sprang to her feet and leaped out the door. I caught her as she barreled out, not wanting her to kick, stomp, or land on potentially unpleasant people.

She opened her mouth, hissed at me, and tried to sink fangs in my arm.

Aha!

This answered the question of what she was doing down here. She was in the middle stages of the transformation. Not human anymore, but not quite a total vampire. I suppose she was avoiding the sunlight, but wasn't quite to the point where she had to be comatose during the day. And, presumably, still retained enough of her usual thought processes to be confused and upset about the frightening changes still going on inside her.

Then she found sources of blood—us—and totally blew her cool.

She tried to bite me, but I twisted, rotating my arm down, under, and up again, putting her in a hammerlock. It wasn't easy. She resisted, and did a good job, too. She brute-forced her way out of it before I could break her shoulder. She turned, swiping fingernails at my midsection, and I danced back a step. She came on, still snarling, hands outstretched, and I grabbed her wrists. She didn't want me to, but wasn't fast enough. This confirmed to me she could see in the dark, at least somewhat.

Once I had her wrists, I turned them inward, keeping her arms in between us as I swung her to my right, putting the train to my back, giving me support and leverage while she pressed forward. She tried desperately to get her face closer to me, still snarling and chomping at me like a deranged Pac-Man.

With the leverage of the train to help, I kicked her, hard, breaking her leg. No, this isn't something you normally expect in a brawl. It's not something you usually see at a martial-arts tournament, either. She wasn't in a state to really counter it or defend against it, and the relative durability of these vampires was offset by my own strength.

She didn't care a whole lot, but she noticed. It didn't stop her from trying to push forward on one leg, though. I let her keep trying while I held on to her wrists and swung her off-balance, thumping her into the side of the subway car. This put her between me and a cocked, primed, and waiting Rusty.

Rusty rose magnificently to the occasion. With his machete in both hands, he took her head off in one epic chop. I have to say, decapitation is a tough thing to pull off with a single stroke, but he really put his back into it. The machete went through her neck, made a meaty cracking sound on the bones, and stopped when it cut into the side of the car! I suspect he also got her exactly right—a lucky hit—right between two of her neck vertebrae. It was *impressive*.

She dropped in two places, like a sack of potatoes and a leaky football. The head went crack-splat-roll, followed by the slithering thud of the body.

"Nice shot," I said, stepping back from the remains. I quickly made sure to get whatever was spattered on us *off* us. I don't know how infectious vampires are, but I didn't want to find out by watching Rusty—or me—growing fangs. Growing more fangs, in Rusty's case. Can werewolves even become vampires?

"Thanks," he replied, jerking the blade out of the side of the train.

A moaning sound echoed through the platform. We went back-to-back without thinking about it, trying to localize the source of the sound. It wasn't hard.

The nearest vampire twitched. His heels drummed on the ground as he twitched and trembled and shivered. Some of the others started doing the same thing. No, not some of the others. *All of them.*

I looked down at the decapitated vampire. A spreading pool of cold blood oozed from the severed neck. I said something unladylike. I don't think Pop would have minded, given the circumstances.

"I think I just did," Rusty whispered, staring around as the quivering crowd.

Starving vampires all around us sat up, hissing, eyes gleaming in the darkness.

"Rusty?" I breathed.

"Yeah?" he asked, whipping his machete through the air to make sure all the blood was off it.

"Run!"

Rusty, even in his human form, is a good runner. Nevertheless, he was hard put to keep up with me in the sprint down the length of the platform. In my sprint, I stepped on three separate vampires as they started to get up, putting them back on the floor. I hurdled a barrier-rail at the end of the platform, sailed into the tunnel, landed about eight feet lower down than the platform, and kept going. Rusty didn't hurdle it; he dove over, landed in a tumbling roll, regained his feet, and came sprinting after me.

From the sound of it, we were ahead of the pack, but they were still waking up.

I don't know how firmly dead the local vampires are. Does the smell of blood always wake them up? Does it only work on the really hungry ones? Do they get harder to wake up as they get older? Does it change at all? Are they easier to wake as the night wears on toward dawn? Would they still wake up, or take longer, if this had happened right after sunset? Or at midnight?

A more pressing line of inquiry was about their speed. Are they faster when they're hungry, driven by need? Or are the slower because they're running low on fuel? These are all excellent questions and deserve study in controlled environments. I would gather what data I could while in the field, though—and, with luck, survive to chart my observations.

I thought about it while I kept making distance. I was well ahead and pressing hard, but I wasn't deliberately leaving Rusty behind. I needed as much of a lead as possible. The next door we had to reach was down this way and it might or might not want to open for me. I wanted at least a couple of seconds to find out!

The door in question was another maintenance hatch. It led to a walking corridor running parallel to the subway line. If I remembered my map properly, we would go through the door, down the corridor, turn to a set of access stairs, go down, and continue from there.

The door, of course, was locked. I could have cast a spell to unlock it, but doing so would take more time than I felt I had. I already had my knife in hand in anticipation of this exact issue. The locking bolt and a sliver of door came away in one swipe and I banged through.

Rusty, somewhat behind me, sprinted madly for the door. I couldn't see the vampires in my infrared light, but their thermal images were ghostly figures, slightly off-color from the background, all pelting hard after him.

I readied a much simpler spell while Rusty came on. He didn't slow down as he approached and I didn't blame him a bit. Instead of a neat turn, he slammed into the doorframe, bounced off it to the inside of the secondary tunnel, and I tried to slam the door. Rusty, lying on the floor, stunned by the impact, blocked it with his feet. I screamed at him to move and he curled up into a ball. Good enough for this, at least. I slammed the door almost in the faces of the leading vampires.

My spell blazed around the perimeter of the door, fusing it shut. It wasn't welded in the traditional sense, but merged. Materials of whatever sort along the edges oozed together for a moment and solidified again. The door wasn't coming open.

A dent appeared in it. Another two followed it in quick succession. Several voices on the other side screamed about this, but what really chilled my marrow was the one screaming *words*.

"Open! *Open! Ooooooooopennnnnn!*"

Okay, the door couldn't open, but the vampires were perfectly content to go through the doorway once they destroyed the door. Worse, there was at least one intelligent vampire involved. Intelligent enough to give orders, at least. Was it also powerful enough to control the others? He could scream about tearing the door open, but would they listen?

The risk factor on this little trip just skyrocketed. Mindless bloodsucking monsters I can handle. Smart vampires scare me.

"Come on!" I demanded, helping Rusty to his feet. He had a nasty pressure cut on his forehead, from one eyebrow almost to his hairline. It was getting better rapidly, but I guessed he gave himself a concussion rather than slow down. Given what was happening in the corridor, he might have made the right choice. He wasn't going to be a hundred percent for a while. Nevertheless, he shook himself and staggered upright. I helped him move along the narrow, pipe-filled corridor while his regeneration uncracked things.

The sound of rending metal was not a welcome one. Instead of continuously beating on the door as they had been, someone was clawing it open and tearing pieces off.

I glanced back, evaluating the corridor. It was barely wide enough for Rusty and I to slide through it together. There were no doors, no handy gratings, only pipes and other conduits for, presumably, fluids and wiring. Nothing that would materially slow down a ravenous horde of berserk vampires.

More metal screamed.

"Stand here!" I commanded, leaning Rusty against one wall. He managed to focus both eyes on me while he pressed the palm of one hand against his forehead. He was responding better than a few moment ago, which was encouraging.

I reached into my pack and yanked out Mister Stuffins. I kissed him as something down the tunnel cracked. Probably a section of wall.

"I love you, Mister Stuffins, and I'm really sorry I have to do this."

Mister Stuffins understood. Mister Stuffins was, in a way, made for this. His job was to defend me from the monsters. Isn't that what all teddy bears are for? And Mister Stuffins was the best teddy bear ever made. If you don't believe me, go to hell.

I put him down in the narrow corridor, facing the way we came. All the way back at the door, a ghostly thermal image kicked through the doorway and entered the narrow maintenance tunnel, pushed by the pressure of the mob behind it.

"Mister Stuffins. *Kill*."

He stood up on his plushy little legs and walked slowly down the corridor. He looked about as threatening as you'd expect. He was *adorable*!

With deep regret, I turned away. I wanted to watch him and the upcoming vampire bloodbath. I couldn't. I grabbed Rusty and hustled us down the corridor. I wanted another door between us if at all possible. I also wanted to be far away, scent-wise, and out of line of sight. It was my hope the destroyed vampires would leak enough to distract the horde from chasing us.

Do starving vampires behave like sharks? Will they turn on each other if one is bloodied? Do they go in for feeding frenzies? Can they even drink from each other? Does it taste right? Does it "nourish" them? Or does the smell drive them crazy and they can only pursue the source?

It's hard keeping all the various species sorted out.

As we half-ran, I found a moment to hope Mister Stuffins would survive it, but didn't have much. He's a stuffed toy. He's lethal, but he's not tough. He wasn't meant to take being ripped apart by vampire claws.

Rusty and I made it to the next stairway on our route and went down to the real maintenance level. I sent a cleaning spell up the stairs to remove—hopefully—all our scent traces before we pressed on.

During all this, Rusty continued to regenerate. He stopped leaning on me and simply followed. He didn't ask questions because he still wasn't totally oriented—I could hear his confusion. He knew things were bad and trusted me, so he shut up and soldiered on.

For my part, I tried to ignore the wailing, shrieking, and howling echoing down to us. Mister Stuffins was holding his own.

Oh! I don't think I've explained. You may be wondering how a little girl's twenty-year-old teddy bear can hold off a horde of thirst-crazed vampires. Simple. Mister Stuffins held a choke point. It's a major tactical advantage. He's also an attack golem armed with monomolecular tentacles and a complete lack of fear. Pop has always been concerned about my safety. Nothing ever got past Mister Stuffins. Very few things every got *away* from Mister Stuffins, either.

We pressed on to another descending shaft and splashed down into the lower level. It was a long, long walk to the next upshaft—several hundred yards—and it was, again, a frigidly cold one. The only thing I liked about it was if the vampires succeeded in tracking us, somehow, they might be unable to follow at all. Even if they did, we would hear them splashing toward us. But if we could get to our upshaft and get out, I figured we would lose them completely.

Nothing chased us. Nothing splashed into the tunnel and swam after us. We slogged, soaking wet and shiveringly, teeth-chatteringly cold, to our next waypoint. We squished and sloshed up the ladderway and out of the water before I zapped us and the ladderway clean and dry. We weren't warm, not yet, but we would work on it when we had a chance.

Since Rusty was still a little unfocused, I decided to find a spot to camp out for a while. Sundown was only a couple of hours away and I didn't relish the level of risk involved.

Sneaking through a sleeping vampire horde during the day? Maybe. Wandering through their underground hive at night? No. And if they were getting easier to awaken the closer we got to sunset, the less I wanted to wander. Once the sun went down, they might all be topside, searching for their next meal and giving us free rein to move through the tunnels—but there was no way to guarantee it.

I found us a room. I don't know what it was supposed to be used for but someone turned it into their bedroom, bunker, or bomb shelter. At a guess, it was once home to someone who didn't have anywhere else.

Like us, come to think of it.

There was a folding cot and a toilet-chair with a bucket. Mercifully, the lid worked well. There were even a couple of candle stubs and a small collection of canned goods, none of which I wanted to use, although for different reasons.

I closed the hatch while Rusty settled down on the floor to rest. Two spells went up pretty quickly. One crawled down the corridor outside, eliminating our scent. The other wrapped itself around the door and tried to convince anyone nearby this was an insignificant door and not worth bothering about. I then fished out a passive audio sensor. It was a little gizmo with a green light and a red light. I fixed this to my side of the door so it could listen for anything out in the tunnel. It would blink red to warn us if it heard anything moving.

Then I looked Rusty over. He was sitting relatively comfortably, head leaned back against the wall. The pressure cut on his forehead was down to a scar. Even that would go away in time.

"How's the head?" I asked, softly.

"Ow."

I manually activated the healing spell on his amulet to speed things along. Normally, it only worries about fire and silver, but it functions by enhancing the normal healing ability of the user. Rusty might not need the help, but we also might have to fight our way out.

While he recuperated at one end of the room, I sat at the other and slowly pulled in power. My big crystal still had a pretty stiff charge in it, but I'd been using it as needed. Smaller spells, mostly, and I set them up to run themselves in the local magical environment whenever I could get away with it. My socks took considerably longer to dry than my shirt, for example. Now, though, I could temporarily turn off the spells on our glasses and leave only his healing spell and my vampire-detecting wristwatch running. This let me sit and gather power.

Gathering power is what wizards and witches do when they cast spells, especially in low-magic worlds. They do it a *lot*. When you see a witch going through an elaborate ritual with candles and a long walk around an intricate diagram, that's usually the purpose. There's not a lot of energy to be had on Earth, so you have to kind of scrape it up into a pile before you can cast your spell. If you don't, the spell fizzles.

What I did was the preliminary part of the spellcasting, but I stuffed it into my crystal. It wasn't a lot of power, but instead of spending two minutes gathering energy later to power a lockpicking spell, I would have those two minutes' worth of energy already stored and ready. It would actually take a bit longer than two minutes to store it, but I was willing to invest the time now to prevent the need for it later. And it was more than two minutes. It was closer to half an hour before Rusty stretched and cracked his neck.

"Feeling better?" I whispered. I probably didn't need to whisper; my wristwatch wasn't tingling.

"Much. I think I'm okay."

"Good." I deactivated his healing spell. I might want to stuff more power in my crystal and it would go faster if the local power wasn't being used.

"Tell me something."

"Sure."

"Did I hallucinate about you sending your teddy bear to kill vampires?"

"No."

"So, your teddy bear—"

"Mister Stuffins."

"—Mister Stuffins held off a vampire horde?"

"For a while," I agreed. "He's my teddy bear, and he's the *best*. I miss him already." I was proud of Mister Stuffins, but it also hurt to talk about it. I think Rusty could tell because he dropped the subject.

"Where are we?"

"Somewhere on the second sublevel. I'd guess we're near a building access of some sort. This used to be someone's squat."

"Okay. Why are we here?"

"Because sunset isn't far off and you needed someplace to pull your head together."

"True, but my chest was really hurt." He stretched, making popping sounds.

"Oh! I'm sorry. It didn't occur to me to check the rest of you."

"It's okay. The ribs are already better. Do we head on?"

"I'd rather wait until they all go back to sleep."

"You want to wait out the night in here?"

"You want to wander around while the vampires are definitely awake?"

"You make an excellent point and it bothers me a lot," he confessed. "What do you propose we do?"

"I'm thinking we take turns sleeping."

"Sleeping."

"Yep. The thing where you close your eyes and rest."

"With vampires roaming around?"

"We're as hidden as it's possible for us to be. They're going topside to hunt. Even when they come back, they don't come near this place. Besides—"

"Hang on. How do you know they don't come anywhere near here?"

"There weren't any when we came in. The corridor was empty."

"Oh. Carry on."

"Like I said, they're going to be hunting aboveground because that's where all the food is. They'll come back, lie down, and go all quiet again when it gets light up there. Then, rested and refreshed, we can finish our trip to the north end of the island."

Rusty thought it over for a bit as we sat there in the darkness. Our vision had adjusted as far as possible, so the tiny, green LED on the audio sensor was enough light to make out shapes and movement.

"We've got a little time, right?"

I checked my watch and made it glow ever so slightly.

"Sunset should be along in less than an hour," I agreed.

"We already lost Alden's tracking birds and whatnot. How about we go up topside and keep heading north? The vampires won't be looking for anyone in the rubble. They'll be after the living people, and those will be in the standing buildings, won't they?"

"We assume they will. Roaming, desperate vampires might enter the radioactive regions we would be tromping through, hoping for easy prey away from the others. And we still have to worry about being irradiated, at least a little. But, most telling of all, we've come far enough north to be in the destruction zones. Finding an open subway entrance, or a building with tunnel access, or anything else not covered over with collapsed ruins isn't likely. I don't feel comfortable tunneling upward for three days to reach daylight."

"So, we either press on or go back."

"Pretty much. Either way, I don't think we can make it out before sunset. And, to top it off, I'd like more lead time between leaving the tunnels and being pursued by vampires. I don't know how many there are north of the primary blast center. Fewer, probably, but the difference between three hundred versus thirty thousand doesn't matter much to us if we can't hide from them."

"Are you always this sensible?"

"No, but I have sense enough to look back and see I'm a idiot."

"I think it's called 'self-awareness'."

"I think it's called hindsight."

"I don't think you've been an idiot," Rusty offered.

"I do," I replied, sitting against a wall. I leaned my head back against the concrete and sighed. "I was preoccupied with too many things ever since I got here."

"I don't understand."

"It's hard to explain. My hobbies got the better of me. I started with the superhero stuff, then got a brand-new arch-villain as my very own nemesis. I should have dropped everything else and *focused.* I didn't." I clunked my head back against the concrete, kicking myself.

"I didn't pay enough attention to my supervillain. I wasted way too much time thinking about ways to *punish* Alden when I should have just… No, I take it back. I didn't waste the time. It was a learning experience for me. Pop was always big on those, so I recognize them after they slap me in the face. I'm not sure what I learned—it's hard to put it into words—but I do know I should have treated him as an immediate, serious threat."

"He doesn't seem too threatening now."

"True. Now I'm thinking I should try to use him to fight vampire hordes."

"Umm… Didn't you use vampires to fight him?"

"Yes. Now I'm thinking we push the two toward each other, harder, and then shoot at the winner. This world is going to hell in a handbasket and I don't want either of these groups in charge of the place. Things are going to be awful for humanity as it is. Whichever of these bastards wins will make it even worse."

"Unless the vampires eat everyone," he pointed out. "Then it'll be worse, but not for long."

"Thanks. So much. How about you get a nap? With the end of the world in mind I won't be able to sleep, anyway."

"Sorry."

"Yeah. So am I."

"What have you got to be sorry for?"

"I'm not sure, but I'm good at guilt. I learned it from Pop. Go to sleep. I'll wake you when it's your turn to keep watch."

Rusty got up, examined the cot, and carefully lay down on it. It creaked, but it held him. He settled down and I went back to stuffing power in a crystal, keeping an eye on the door-sensor, and anticipating a tingle in my wrist.

Around eight at night, I peeked out with my scrying mirror. Yes, the sun was down, the vampires were up, and going out in the corridors was far safer than being on the streets... but "safer" isn't the same thing as "safe." We probably wouldn't find any vampires in the tunnels. But if we found *one* vampire—just one—it would scream about finding prey. Then we would have *all* the vampires.

I took a brief look at the rest of the world, out of curiosity, by dropping my point of view into a few other metropolitan areas. Rather than hover over them, looking at the damage, I swooped my sensor through them, looking for anyone left alive. In the daylit places, there were definitely survivors. In the nighttime areas, there was a lot more movement, but no one I'd call a survivor. If there were any military forces abroad, I didn't see them, but I could easily have missed them. I didn't see any obvious signs of organization, of command and control, but it would take a lot more time and effort to do a proper survey of the *planet!*

I was tired of all my magical exercise, so I woke Rusty, took the cot for myself, and tried to have a nap. Tired as I was, I still had things on my mind.

As I observed to Rusty, the world was going to hell in a handbasket, provided the handbasket was properly weighted, aerodynamically shaped, and launched from a catapult.

How much of it was my fault? Quite a lot, actually. I'm the one who goofed badly enough to let Alden into the world. Whatever happened afterward was icing on the cake. First cause: Alden arrives. Everything followed from there.

Okay, enough with the blame. Forget it. What's done is done. Let's move on. There's a future to think about.

Which is worse? Alden or the vampires? Each of them has horrors galore, although different types of horror. If you had to pick, which would you prefer? A world full of bloodthirsty monsters, or a world where only one person has any ability to think for himself—and that person is *not* you. I suppose, in the second case, nobody would care, but that doesn't make it any less horrible!

This also raises a more material question. What am I going to do about it? Is there anything I *can* do about it?

That's what kept me awake.

Rusty nudged me and I took my watch while he napped. I hadn't slept, only dozed, but it was better than nothing.

My lying awake and thinking at least produced a few tiny ideas. There were a couple of things I could do. Things I could find out. First among them was to check on my teddy bear. I'd gathered power for quite a while, so I didn't feel bad about wasting a little on a personal issue.

The tunnel where Mister Stuffins made his stand was knee-deep in vampire dust for quite a distance. How many vampires was it? Ten? Twenty? Fifty? It was hard to tell through a scrying sensor. The sight of it filled me with a fierce pride in Mister Stuffins.

The dust, though, raised questions. The vampire Jason landed on crumbled to dust, but the one Rusty decapitated, next to the subway train, didn't. Because the transformation wasn't complete? Or did they ooze blood until something in them quit—kind of like brain death in a human?—and then crumble? Whatever, it was a lot of dust. Mister Stuffins gave good account of himself.

I *never* want Pop to design a war golem.

In all this dust, I saw no sign of Mister Stuffins. If they ripped him to shreds, the pieces might be buried. I checked down the length of the tunnel, both ways. He wasn't there. I went to the additional trouble of adding another spell, this one to show magical auras around anything I viewed. Still nothing.

Either Mister Stuffins was broken to the point where his enchantment was gone, or his remains were buried in the dust. If his remains were buried in the dust, it seemed like a good place. How many people get to have a grave defined by the heaps and piles of dead enemies? "With weeping and with laughter, still is the story told, how well Horatius kept the bridge in the brave days of old." Mister Stuffins didn't have a handy bridge and a river.

I know Mister Stuffins was never more than an enchanted, lifeless golem. Not really. Nevertheless, he was more than that *to me*. I'm going to miss him. There was no getting around it, and there was no way to keep from silently weeping over his loss, either.

I'm allowed to cry a little over the loss of a favorite childhood toy, aren't I? Well, aren't I?

When I decided I was done crying, I wiped my face and had something to eat. It's amazing how many calories you can burn by being upset. Besides, I always feel better after I eat something. I think it's a trait I learned from Pop.

Next up, the situation in the tunnels. I sent my scrying sensor whizzing out through the door and back along our route. I made sure to drive it under the surface of the water in the flooded tunnels, looking for any signs. As far as I could tell, we lost our pursuit when they had the Stuffins ripped out of them. To be fair, it's unlikely anything could ignore Mister Stuffins. I don't know how long they had to fight him. I don't know if they even recognized him as a problem; he was a lifeless, bloodless object and the monomolecular wires he used as weapons wouldn't even be visible.

Come to think of it, did they have a feeding frenzy? I wondered earlier, but I didn't have a way to tell. I suppose I still don't. I wouldn't think so, if they crumbled to dust instead of oozing. It would be very helpful to know, though. If Rusty rips an arm off a vampire, to the nearest ones turn on him and bite?

I sent my sensor up into the open air and slid it southward. Yes, the vampires were all over the place, searching, sniffing, prowling, looking for anyone still alive. I'm sure there were a lot of survivors—a low percentage, but a large number—still dwelling in the less-ruined areas, but the number kept creeping downward.

A sizable force of vampires, however, were investing the library. They surrounded the place in the sense there were vampires on every street. They weren't entering the charged areas, but many of them had burns on their hands or feet where they tested the borders. I wondered how many died by entering the charged areas and burning away, warning the others. I couldn't tell, not from the remains inside charged areas.

The rest stood there, making me wonder other things. If they're hungry, why aren't they out prowling? Sure, they probably know there are humans in there. They can smell them, or smell their trail, or something. But why do they stop at the edge and stay there? Shouldn't they give up and go after prey they can reach?

As I hovered my view over one street, watching their behavior, something unusual happened. Unusual in my experience with these vampires, anyway. One of them came up to the cordon, touched one of the watchers to get his attention, and led him away. This seemed too intelligent, too purposeful, so I followed.

They headed away from the library, found a looted deli, and the leader immediately attacked the follower. He grabbed the follower by the head and rammed it through the tile-and-brick wall. This stunned the victim and the leader sank fangs into his neck from behind. The feeding one didn't have the help of heart action to move the victim's blood out, but he had his technique down pretty well. He wrapped arms and legs around his victim and squeezed like emptying a tube of toothpaste, sucking for all he was worth. The victim struggled feebly, clearly still fuddled from the initial attack, and finally went limp.

—and crumbled to dust.

The attacker climbed to his feet and *wiped his mouth*. He didn't snarl animalistically. He didn't hiss or growl or bare his fangs in triumph. He wiped his mouth. It was the most civilized thing I'd seen these monsters do. He compounded his civilized gesture by brushing vampire dust off his clothes.

I still don't know if they go into a feeding frenzy, but they absolutely can feed on each other.

Is this unusual, this feeding on each other? It would seem so, since they aren't a lawless mob of cannibal monsters. Does feeding on other vampires accelerate the process of becoming an intelligent undead? Or was this one already well on his way to regaining self-awareness when he had the idea to feed on his fellow vampires?

I know how to find out. I need a dozen or so vampires, a holding facility, a blood supply, and time to conduct experiments. All I lack is the vampires, the facility, the blood supply, and the time.

There was so much going wrong in the world, with Alden and the vampires and whatever else. There's always a "whatever else," I think, somewhere. People are always having problems and don't need psychic overlords and blood-sucking monsters adding their nickel. At least people are always trying to solve their problems in one way or another.

Did the nuclear option provide any solutions? No, but it drastically changed the problems. Which brings me back to what I was wondering. What do I do about any of it? What *should* I do, and what *can* I do? I don't know. Maybe I'm too tired and not thinking clearly, but I know I feel as though something needs to be done.

I watched the predatory vampire lure away and kill another of his kind before I did another sweep through the nearby corridors. All was well, so I shut down my scrying and settled in to wait.

Journal Entry #48

Rusty and I traded off watches until dawn. I actually did manage to get a few naps. It wasn't enough, but it helped.

"Okay, sun's up," I told him, looking at the light in my mirror. "They should be down and out."

"Let's give them another half-hour," he suggested. "I don't like it when they wake up."

"I like the way you think."

"Thanks."

"So much, in fact, I want to ask your opinion."

"No, those pants are perfect on you."

"Smartass."

"Is that where you keep *your* brains?"

"Shut up and listen."

"Yes, Ma'am."

"Here's my problem. You met my Pop, right?"

"Sure. Seemed like a reasonable guy. A bit on the tempery side, maybe, but I think he was having a bad day."

"Tempery?"

"He didn't exactly threaten my life. He gave me fair warning about it being on the table. I didn't want to hurt him, so I left."

"You must have caught him on a bad day. It was a good idea to leave him alone."

"Since then, you've mentioned he can be dangerous."

"Some, yes, but I haven't really tried to get the true scope across to you. Now I have to. You need to understand before you can help me make a decision."

"I'm in no rush," Rusty told me, settling comfortably. "You've got something big on your mind, so take your time. I'm listening. Lay the groundwork, build on it, I'll ask silly questions, and we'll eventually get to what you need. Okay?"

"Okay. Let me think a minute."

"Take your time," he repeated. I thought it over, sorting out the situation, what I wanted to do with it, what I did to get it to this point, what I should have done, what I didn't do, where it was going, where it could go, all round and round and round again in my head until I had to stop it all and pick somewhere to start.

"At this point, I'm still trying to get a good grip on what's going on," I admitted. "The trouble, I think, is every time I start to make headway on the information gathering, something happens to change the situation and I have to... not start over, exactly, but it makes what I was learning less relevant. It *feels* like I have to start over, or that I've wasted a lot of time on something useless."

"I hate that."

"So do I. Now, as we stand, Alden has a lot of forces in his library, but he's fighting a defensive war. Everywhere else, people are being slaughtered out of hand. I've seen it in my mirror. I did random spot-checks around the globe. Manhattan's vampire problem is *not* an isolated incident. Vampires are spreading like the plague after a nuclear war. A limited nuclear war, I should say. I didn't see much in the way of organized resistance, but I could have missed pockets of it. I only checked on major cities. I didn't have time to make a full survey. That would take weeks—and something could change before I'm done with the survey, which will only make me madder."

"Do you mean 'angrier'?"

"I'm going a bit mad as it is."

"Can't argue with that. So, is this an extermination of humanity? By the vampires, I mean. I know Alden wants his zombies, but vampires may be out to kill everyone."

"I don't know. I doubt it, but maybe it's what we should hope for."

"*Hope* for?"

"If the vampires take over, the best case is they have nothing to feed on and turn on each other. Somewhat worse case? They win, shove humans into livestock pens, and enjoy a happy, decadent eternity. Absolute worst case… they eat everyone, there are no humans left, and they feed on each other until there's only one starving master vampire overlord ruling the lifeless husk of a world."

"What about Alden? He's putting up a fight."

"Good for him. As for us, we're dealing with vampires on one side, a mind-controlling monster on the other, and humanity—and lycanthropy, and everybody else—in the middle. I'm not sure which side to weigh in on. If I help the vampires get Alden, they'll take over the world. If I help Alden against the vampires, *he* will take over the world—and every living mind left in it."

Rusty was silent for several seconds.

"I'm torn," he admitted. "I don't like either side of this fight, but if there aren't any military units left on the board, it's really down to these two players, isn't it?"

"I'm sure there are at least a few human forces left in play, but as long as they're cut off from civilized support, they have severe limitations. They can't resupply. Their small arms need massed fire to be a problem to vampires. The soldiers are humans, who can be turned into vampires or be controlled by Alden. None of these bode well for human independence."

"I guess I'd have to go with Alden," Rusty said, slowly. "If we help him, maybe we can destroy the vampires. Then, if he's being an unreasonable prick, we assassinate him. It leaves us with a bunch of mindless zombie people, but they're still people."

"That's not what I'm asking about."

"Oh? Oh. Sorry. Could you repeat the question?"

I didn't answer immediately. I was thinking and holding on to the jewel Pop gave me. It had minor powers, such as the psychic map images, but it was built with one major function in mind. I was a little leery of using it.

"Rusty?"

"Yeah?"

"I'm thinking about calling for help. From Pop."

"You say that like it's a bad thing," he observed. I rubbed my temples, trying to figure out a way to explain something beyond his experience.

"Alden is one side of the major conflict, right?"

"Right."

"The vampire hordes spreading through the remains of the human population, that's another side, right?"

"Right!"

"One could argue the remnants of humanity constitute a third side, albeit one playing with serious disadvantages. Right?"

"I can see it, sure."

"If I call for help, Pop will be the fourth side, all by himself."

"Sounds like he'll be at a disadvantage, too. Unless he can swing some vampires to work for him?"

"Not a chance. He would despise what they're doing, whether it's enslavement or extinction. They're being wasteful and… and… *untidy*. Messy. He would be disgusted."

"You're worried he could get hurt?"

"Of all the things I could worry about, that one never crossed my mind."

"What is it, then? Exactly."

"Pop isn't like normal people. He's not even like normal vampires. He's unique. I've never met anyone like him. I'm not sure there is. He's powerful and unpredictable. If I call for help, he *absolutely* will help me, but he'll do it his way."

"So?"

"So? So, if I'm shooting at someone and I run out of ammunition, calling my Pop for a box of bullets won't work. He'd *bring* the bullets and enough backup to make sure I didn't need them—and don't even get me started on what sort of backup he can pack up and move into the field on a moment's notice! And if I didn't do something drastic to stop him, he'd turn whatever I was shooting at into screams."

"You mean he'd make the things scream?"

"There wouldn't be anything left but the screams."

"Still not seeing a downside," Rusty admitted, grinning.

"Damn it, my Pop doesn't understand the concept of *good enough*!" I clarified. "Or, no, it's the word *subtle* he doesn't fully grasp. He tries, I know he does, but the poor man does it about as well as Galileo trying to play dumb about heliocentrism!" I sighed and tried to marshal my thoughts.

"Maybe an example would help," Rusty suggested. "Tell me a Pop story."

"Hmm. Okay. Say there's a fortress somewhere. Big one, lots of masonry, thick walls, iron grating, drawbridge, the works. When you blow away the main gate, ruin the portcullis, and damage the wall around it so badly it'll have to be torn down and rebuilt, what do you call it?"

"I sense a trick question."

"Just answer me."

"Well, offhand, I'd probably call it a successful attack."

"Pop told me about the time he did exactly that. You know what he called it? A *warning shot!*"

"I like him."

I thumped the back of my head against the wall a couple of times in frustration.

"Either you're being deliberately thick," I told him, "or I'm not explaining it well enough. If I call him for help, it's like rubbing a lamp to let the genie out. And I'm not talking about the Disney versions. I'm talking about the unmodified originals, the thousand-and-one-nights type. This genie will grant my wish, sure, but it will do it in whatever way *it* thinks is best. I have almost no control over it, and it will probably overdo it. What am I saying? It will *definitely* overdo it. He's my Pop. I know him. And swatting a fly with a sledgehammer doesn't *begin* to cover it."

"Killing a wasp nest with a flamethrower, maybe?"

"Killing an ant with an orbital laser strike."

"He's got something against ants?" Rusty asked.

"Yes, but he doesn't like to talk about it."

"Is he always like that?"

"No, I wouldn't say so. He's like a fault line. If you can get him to move at all, things break. Thing is, we're talking about him showing up to help me. I don't think he'll be interested in a limited response. But it still might be better to call him and ask, rather than have him show up after I'm dead. If he finds out something killed me, or worse, can't figure out exactly who or what is responsible… I don't know for certain he can turn off a universe, but I have my suspicions."

"Hold on!" Rusty exclaimed. "A *universe?* You're saying he can end a universe?" The sensor on the door blinked back and forth from green to red in quick succession at the noise. I gestured for him to quiet down and the light returned to green.

"Yeah. I think so," I said, nearly whispering. "I'm not entirely sure, but I have my suspicions. Branch universes are inherently unstable and this is one of them. He tried to explain multiverse theory to me, but I can't wrap my head around the math."

"Now I think I get it."

"If you *think* you understand how far he will go, you don't. *I* don't. I only know what I've seen and the stories he's shared. I grew up with him, tried to learn everything he would teach me, and inferred things about the stuff he tried not to. What I suspect scares me."

"He didn't seem too scary when I met him."

"*I* think he's unpredictable and dangerous and not to be summoned lightly, and I'm his *daughter.* I'm also not sure we have any better option. He's the least bad of a lot of bad choices. Do we turn loose the genie and hope we can wish for something that won't blow up in our faces? *That's* the question I'm getting at. What do you think?"

Rusty looked thoughtful and drew his revolver, ticking it around one click at a time, thinking.

"Well?" I pressed.

"It'll either go really good or really bad, won't it?"

"There's not much of a middle ground unless you enjoy standing on a razor's edge," I agreed. "Therefore, knowing what you know, considering what he's capable of, looking at what we're up against… do we send out a summons? How bad does it have to be before we rub the lamp?"

"The world is either going to be eaten by vampires or owned by a power-mad monster. How bad does it *have* to get?"

"You raise a good point," I sighed. I hooked the chain with a thumb and drew the crystal pendant up out of my shirt. It glinted white, even in the dim, green LED light.

"What worries me is the phrase that goes with 'How bad could it be?'"

"What phrase?"

"You know how there's a superstition about never asking how things could possibly get worse?"

"Oh, that. Yeah? You're saying things could?"

"This was given to me for use in an emergency. Basically, if I don't think things could possibly get worse, it's time to use the pendant."

"That seems… ambivalent?"

"No. He'll really do his best for me, but according to his judgment. He's not cruel, not capricious, just… not like other people." *Not like people,* I thought, but quietly and to myself.

"I don't know enough to be sure about this," Rusty admitted. "What scares me is you aren't, either."

"I'm more *scared for,* not *scared of.* It's an important distinction. Pop loves me and that's more certain than the sun rising. My concern is how I'm trying to save the world and I don't know for sure if this will help or not. Either way, it won't be my problem anymore, and that bothers me dreadfully."

"Oh?"

"I wanted this to be mine. Not his. Something *I* did. And what I've done is screw it up! Not entirely, and it's not entirely my fault—I admit it. But I haven't been good enough to keep things from going into the handbasket. I can only hope it doesn't finish the trip, and try to do what I can to stop it, but I don't know how. I don't know what I need to do to fix anything! When I don't know the answers, I investigate, experiment, and determine—but I don't even know where to start fixing the world! So I need help. Big help."

"If you need the help—need it, not just want it—then is it really a question?"

"No," I sighed. "No, I suppose it isn't. Okay."

"Anything I should do?"

"Depends on his mood. Whatever you do, don't make any sudden moves and try to look as non-threatening as possible. This thing is a distress call. He may show up cocked and primed for a fight."

"I'll crawl under the cot," he chuckled.

"Good idea."

"I was kidding."

"I wasn't."

Rusty blinked at me for a moment to be certain I was serious.

"So... are we doing this?" he asked. He sounded worried.

"I think we are. Rather, I think I am. I don't want you to feel responsible for what happens. *I* will rub the lamp."

"Why does it bother me to hear you say that?"

"I don't know. Because you're concerned about me wanting to spare you the soul-crushing level of guilt that might possibly be about to fall on someone?"

"Probably," he agreed. "I'll be under the cot." He shifted into his wolf form and wormed his way underneath.

I cupped the crystal in both hands and whispered the activation words.

"I want my Papa."

The room filled with white light. It was a flare, a searchlight, a blaze like the heart of a star. I felt the power go out of the gem and I felt the attention, the searching, penetrating gaze. If the Eye of Sauron looked at me, it would feel like this, with one exception. This was benevolent. It was friendly. It was *on my side* and I knew it.

But it wasn't Pop.

The blaze of light dimmed to a single bright point, glowing inside the gem.

Okay, we have to talk fast. The spell on the amulet acts as a conduit, but I can't keep it open forever.

"Uncle Dusty!"

Yep! What's the trouble?

"I was calling for Pop!"

I know! He wasn't sure where he would be or what he would be doing. I have multiple attention points and can always respond. The gem notifies Me, I look over the problem, and I report to him on it. It wasn't meant for a long-term discussion, though, and it's been harder to reach your world ever since the dynamos went off-line. Talk faster!

Two emotions competed for space in my heart. One was a deep disappointment. I miss Pop and was, regardless of the circumstances, eager to see him again. The other was a profound relief, for obvious reasons.

"The dynamos were your major link, right. I hadn't considered that."

Bear in mind I need those things.

"Got it, Unc."

As far as I can tell, you've got a post-nuclear world. Did Alden survive all this?

"Yes. He's still around."

Oh, wonderful. Okay. First priority: get here, into one of My worlds, where we can talk without Me playing Atlas and shouldering half the sky. Does that work for you?

"I'm all for it! I don't have the necessary power to open a personal gate, though. This is an Earth, remember?"

Can you manage a micro-gate? I have a much higher power level here.

"Oo! Yes! Once I establish a connection to your world, it can draw power from your end!"

Exactly. You can switch the connection over to the same doorway we used last time.

"I'm on it, Unc. I'll see you in a little bit."

We'll talk more then!

The connection quit and I grinned. This was *much* better than turning Pop loose! The world's odds of surviving increased by at least an order of magnitude!

"*Woof?*" Rusty asked.

"Yes. It's safe."

"*Woof?*"

"Okay, it's safer than if Pop showed up. It was only my Uncle Dusty."

He wriggled out from under and shifted upward into his human form.

"I heard you talking, but I didn't hear anyone else. So, your Uncle Dusty is the demigod, right?"

"That's him."

"And he's safer to be around than your Dad?"

"Yes."

"O-kay… I never appreciated it when people made remarks about my family, so I guess I shouldn't make any about yours."

"Seems reasonable," I agreed. "Get the stuff together while I work on a spell. We're going to go back and visit Uncle Dusty again."

Rusty looked around the concrete chamber, visibly comparing it to the break room in a power plant.

"Suits me."

It seems weird I could move from one universe to another with relative ease, but going uptown was an epic quest. Why? Because both ends of uptown were low-magic zones. Any power I put into the gate I would have to already carry with me. On the other hand, I could open a tiny gate, not even the size of the eye of a needle, from here to Uncle Dusty's *extremely* high-magic zone. Then the spell could draw in ambient power at both ends, but draw a considerably larger amount from the destination. With a bit of a boost from my end—power crystal—we could transfer the micro-gate to a larger opening at both ends and keep it open long enough to step through safely.

We did so, stepping from near-total darkness into the white light of office space. It wasn't pleasant. The gate snapped shut behind us. While our eyes adjusted, I put on my sunglasses, adjusted the vision spells, and drew a power diagram on somebody's desk. I wanted it to help charge my big crystal.

"What do we do now?" Rusty asked, still blinking.

"We wait. He'll be here directly, I'm sure."

"Isn't he always here? I mean, in a sort of omnipresent sort of way?"

𝒴𝑒𝑠.

Rusty jumped higher than if he'd stepped on a Lego.

However, Uncle Dusty went on, more quietly, *it's a bit disconcerting for most people to have a direct revelation conversation. Which is—*

"—why I have an avatar," he continued, walking into the room. "People like it better when they hear with their ears. Not to say a direct communication doesn't have its place, especially when I'm trying to get a point across, but it's more polite to do things verbally. It doesn't disturb people nearly so much. Wouldn't you agree?"

"Absolutely!"

"Unc! Good to see you again!" I moved toward him and he held out his arms. I hugged him, since it was a clear invitation. "How's things here?"

"Oh, you know. Making progress by spinning in place." He let me go and gestured toward the facility break room. "I've added calabash to my gardening! I've also civilized wild chickens, so I can offer you eggs, if you like."

"I don't suppose you've got beehives for honey and a garden full of tea, do you?" I asked. We all walked together down the hall.

"No, I'm afraid not. I can send a robot for some wild honey, though."

"I'll pass."

"Suit yourself. So, I've been trying to keep up with what's going on. It's been difficult, what with the loss of all the dynamos in your world. I haven't been able to keep an all-seeing eye on things as I'd like to. You want to fill Me in on how you wound up in a subway-level storage closet?"

"Vampires," Rusty said. Uncle Dusty shot him a startled look.

"Vampires? I thought the half-angel guy was the issue? Him and the nuclear apocalypse, I mean."

"He is," I told him. "He's part of it, anyway. One of several related issues."

"This should be good."

"So, let me see if I have it all," he began, munching on fried potato slices. He leaned back in the chair and put his feet on another one. "You've got an apocalyptic planet in the rapidly-strengthening grip of a vampire plague. There's a half-angel grabbing anyone he can, whittling them down to the brainstem, and using them as his personal army. Somewhere on the planet, there may be humans who are up to speed on the vampire problem, but humans aren't expecting the Manhattan Inquisition because they don't know he exists. Those are the major players?"

"Pretty much."

"Things are now so bad," he went on, "that you're willing to call My former avatar in, but you don't really want to because he'll flip the board, have Firebrand set it on fire, and put it out by letting Bronze stomp it, assuming he doesn't throw his cloak over it and make the problem disappear. Am I still with you?"

"Mostly. I'm kind of hoping he can help me, rather than take over completely."

"I'm not sanguine about your chances. I mean, maybe. He might do it your way, since it's you who's asking, but I'm not feeling a little flutter urging me to bet, either way."

"Me, either."

Dusty thought it over. I sliced more potatoes and added them to the little pan on the hot plate. Microwaving them didn't cook them properly. Rusty opened another high-calorie nutrition bar and handed one to Dusty. He was entirely pleased with it. I get the impression his diet has been a bit mundane. Maybe he needs an angel of his own. Sometimes Pop needed a keeper, or at least someone to keep him grounded in whatever reality we were in.

It used to be my job. I felt a rush of longing and missed him fiercely, wondering where he was, what he was doing, and especially how things were going for him.

"What bothers me," Dusty said, finally, "is the weak place between worlds."

"Huh?"

"The cave. Under the church."

"It's busted. It's out of play. I don't see how it has anything to do with anything else."

"I agree, but I don't mean that particular one is important. The point is, there are places where the universes overlap. They're hard to see. You have to look at them at just the right angle to catch the glint."

"How does one do that?"

"Uh… I'm not sure you can. I should have said they're hard for Me to see. I don't know how you would detect them. My point is, where the universes have a sort of congruence as well as proximity, they can be weak places where you can step through."

"Yay!" I declared, clapping my hands together. "That's wonderful! I've learned something about cosmology!" I dropped the false delight. "Aaaand? What of it?"

"Sarcasm. How did he ever cope?"

"He did it better."

"Oh, so *that's* how you got so good at it."

"I learned from the best. Now answer my question."

"These weak places are a way out of one world and into another. If I were Alden, looking around the planet and seeing a carpet of vampires spreading like mold on cold pizza, I'd want a new planet."

"But he doesn't know these… what do we call them? Thin places? Weak points? Overlap zones?… go to other worlds! He thinks they're portals for time travel!"

"So what? He winds up in a world where Columbus is still dickering with the King of Spain and flirting with Isabella, or maybe the other way around. What does he care? Or, no, he cares a lot—he can keep the world from going all undead. Maybe. He can try to change history, or thinks he can."

"Won't his interference provoke them into a worldwide uprising?"

"There's a lot to unpack in that question," he sighed.

"I'm in no rush. Not here, anyway. What's our time differential?"

"I think it averages to around twelve to one, here, but that's an approximation."

"Good enough. Start talking."

"Phoebe, I can, off the top of My head, think of at least three things to act as major handicaps to vampires—as a society, not as individuals—in the Medieval or Renaissance eras.

"First, communications. Some of them may be able to psychically project over long distances, but by no means all of them. Putting together a global conspiracy takes time and planning. By the time they have the conspiracy all set up, someone has done something to change the equation and a new balance of power has to be hammered out.

"Second, architecture. Do you know how few buildings are truly light-tight in those eras? How hard it is to have a vampire army on the move? Especially when they're a bunch of mindless brutes such as you describe?

"Which leads me to the third: Control. It's one thing to take out major population centers in an interconnected, industrialized world, but back then? People were less dependent on globalized industry, electricity, and other big, social constructs that altered the nature of civilization. Take out Rome and you still have lots of little towns and villages. Your mindless brutes will swarm, and swarm like army ants or zombie hordes, killing everyone they come across. You can't control the hordes and you can't control the fabric of society.

"Fourth, people still believed in vampires. The first time someone screamed and people came a-running, they'd know what they were dealing with. Out come the crosses and wooden stakes and the shovels, the price of garlic skyrockets, and where's the nearest crossroads? I have no doubt there are plenty of worlds where the undead are extinct, or nearly so, just as there are worlds where they exist only as furtive little families.

"Fifth, the vampires, by their nature, are not social hunters. They work independently, with occasional exceptions working in pairs. They don't much care, as a group, or as a species, what's going on. So they aren't incentivized to react when someone is dumb enough to be caught and staked or quick-fried in the sunlight. They might even encourage, as a policy, executing any fresh creations to keep from spreading too much or too quickly.

"Sixth, the smart ones don't feel threatened. Even Renaissance technology can stake them, sure, and a pot of oil can ignite them, but they don't have to worry about machine guns, flamethrowers, and easy-to-use explosives. They're still predators and humans are still prey. Humans aren't dangerous individuals until they develop much more powerful weapons. And it takes even longer before vampires will start to recognize it, longer still before they'll admit it to themselves.

"Seventh—"

"You said there were three!" I interrupted.

"I thought of more once I started!"

"Okay! Okay! I bow before the all-knowing wisdom of the nuclear demigod. I give. All right?"

"I'm just saying," he went on, reasonably, "if Alden goes back in time—or thinks he does; same difference to him—he might use what he already knows about the future to prevent it from happening, to control the direction of development, to steer it. And, since his *modus operandi* so far is to grab a forebrain, strip it down, and use it for his own purposes, he's likely to continue it in another world."

"He didn't do it in Shasta," I pointed out.

"Didn't he?"

I thought about it. I didn't find evidence he even existed in Shasta until Pop and I showed up, so he was keeping a low profile. Then, once he got nearer to us, he started gathering more people under his psychic control. Not as directly as the ready-made army of Manhattan's homeless, but just as certainly.

"So, what do I do?" I asked. "If I can find a place to stay, I can set up, gather survivors, and try to hold off the vampires. They don't reproduce like humans do. They have limited numbers and, as you pointed out, we can get weapons even vampires can't stand up to.

"The way I see it," I went on, "is I can either do this on my own and hope Alden gets his psychic head ripped off by a mob of the things, or I can invite him to help. Hopefully, we defeat the vampire hordes and find a way to disable him afterward."

"Shotgun to the head," Rusty piped up. "It disables everything I know of even if it doesn't kill it outright. Make sure to do it when he's not looking."

"You'd shoot a man in the back?" Dusty asked.

"Well, it's the safest way, isn't it?" Rusty pointed out. "And it's the back of the head. It's not like he's going to suffer."

"Which reminds me," I interrupted. "Something weird is going on with him."

"Oh?"

So I described the way he was developing a huge, hyper-muscular physique, but still walked with a cane.

"He's clearly becoming more physically powerful," I finished, "but he doesn't seem to be healing the wound in his side. I find it incredibly weird. He's wearing Pop's old gear, so he ought to be fully healed by now even if he'd lost an entire limb."

"Weird," Dusty agreed. "Very weird. There's no telling what My former avatar put in his amulet and ring. Something might be interacting with a human or near-human physiology in an unexpected way. His gear is designed to work for him, not a full-time human. Living being, I mean."

"Can we ask him?"

Dusty munched another fried potato slice and looked at the ceiling.

"That could be a little tricky."

"Don't tell me. He's still fighting the whole Tassarian Empire."

"No. No, it's not that. We dealt with that problem a while ago. —and don't ask Me how long ago. Time differentials confuse Me. I live in more than one at once."

"Pop understands them better than I do," I admitted. "I lose track of the daisy-chains and circles and whatever other configurations he may have set up. But why is asking him tricky?"

"I can't find him."

If you spend enough time in the pool, there will eventually come a day when you're splashing about in the deep end, having a great time, and, eyes shut against the chlorination, you'll paddle blindly to the edge, reach out—and it won't be there. You'll flounder in the water, suddenly lost in something the size of a swimming pool. It'll feel as though the whole ocean snuck up on you, slid underneath, and now you're alone in a vast emptiness with no hope and no chance. Maybe it's only a fleeting instant, but it's an intense, terrible instant, and one that can put you off from ever stepping away from the shore again.

I can't imagine why it leaped to mind.

"What do you mean, you can't find him?"

"*Sit down.*"

I sat. Rusty lowered his hands from his ears. Dusty sighed.

"Sorry. You were shouting."

"I guess I was," I admitted, gripping the seat's sides. "I apologize. Now answer the question!" I demanded, and got a grip on my tone again. "Please," I added.

"It's his anti-angel stuff. He upgraded his spells after Alden took everything. Well," he corrected, "I guess he upgraded the things before, but Alden's thievery motivated him to build new stuff, so he used the upgraded spells."

"But you're not an angel!"

"No, but I'm a celestial being. The principles are strikingly similar."

The universe was a big place, full of heaving waves, up and down, with currents unpredictable and strange. It's not at all like the shallow end of the pool.

"When did you last see him?"

"In Tauta. He took off to do his angelic dissection research." Dusty shrugged. "I didn't think much of it. He's been planning to do it and he finally got around to it."

"Didn't he tell anyone where he was going?"

"Why would he? Nobody knows what he's up to. Not even Me! He keeps his own counsel and makes his own plans." He paused, thoughtfully, and added, "Velina."

"Velina? What's she got to do with this?"

"He took her with him. Maybe I can find her."

"He took *Velina?*" I thought for a long minute. Velina and I talked a lot during my visits. She's quite the chatty sort. Very friendly. She's been in love with Pop almost from the day she met him. I'd say she had a crush on him and it grew into something more. She signed on into his service the moment opportunity presented itself and she's been all about that noble-service-cheerfully-rendered life ever since. No emperor ever had a more loyal samurai.

"Yeah, I know," Dusty said. "I wouldn't have called it, but she asked to go with him and he let her. I don't know what he was thinking. Her, either."

"Okay. If that's how we find him, go find Velina."

"Hang on. Don't we have more important things to worry about?"

"What's more important than finding Pop?"

"A half-angel brain-eater who wants to take over the world with his zombie hordes? A vampire apocalypse? You know, the things that kind of brought you here in the first place?"

"Nothing is more important than finding Pop."

Dusty sighed and ran a hand over his face, as though brushing cobwebs away.

"Look, wherever he is, *he went there*. Whatever he's doing, he's been planning it for ages. Can we assume he's a big boy and can take care of himself?"

I wanted to argue. I really wanted to argue. I desperately wanted to argue. What held me back? Maybe it was the fact I wanted to be recognized as a big girl who could take care of herself.

"Fine," I snapped. "Which means *you* get the job as stand-in for Pop. How do we fix the world, Not-Pop?" I asked. I saw him wince, either from my tone or from the deliberate use of the "Not-Pop" nickname.

"The first thing we do is deal with Alden."

"Alden? Why? Shouldn't we use him against the vampires then shoot at the winner?"

"I'm for that," Rusty agreed.

"*Silence*," Uncle Dusty snapped. Rusty moved his mouth to say something but nothing came out. He felt his throat, brows drawing together.

"Uncle!"

"All right, all right. You may speak. But keep quiet while I talk to My niece."

"Understood, *sir!*"

"The reason," Uncle Dusty went on, "has to do with my earlier observation vis-à-vis the universe overlap points. Alden knows about holes from one world to another. If he's fortified himself in a major library, he may be doing research on locations where strange things happen, people go missing, ships disappear, cryptids wander about, and all those sorts of things. If he is, he's looking for a way out of what he thinks is a major catastrophe—a portal in time so he can escape, as he believes, to an earlier age. We need him to stop being."

"You mean we need to kill him."

Uncle Dusty leaned across the table and glared at me.

"Since I'm standing in for your father, allow Me to put this bluntly:

"I do mean that. I do *not* mean we need to capture him. I do *not* mean we need to spank him. He is not going to accept punishment, learn his lesson, nor change his ways. He is exactly who he is and, short of brain surgery, he's not going to become a better person. If you have any other ideas, put them on the table right now. If not, accept the inevitability of removing his head and heart to burn them separately from his body."

"Will that kill him?"

"I certainly hope so! But *you* need to get this into *your* head and heart. We're not going after him halfway. We're not going to 'get even.' We're not shooting for 'justice'— whatever definition you slap on it. We're not even going to shoot for an armed détente where he restricts his activities lest he risk incurring heavy penalties. On the mortal planes, he is a serious threat and we're going to eliminate that threat."

"But there are bigger—"

"No, there are not bigger threats on the material planes," he shot back. "Vampires are a horde of problems, but they're not actively trying to roam through the multiverse. Your vampires have one world. Alden is actively trying to break out of his world and we're going to make sure he doesn't, which will involve *murdering* him.

"Now, look Me in the eye and tell Me you understand and agree."

I thought about it. He didn't insist on an instant answer, so I thought about it for a while. Not more than a century, I'm sure.

If I agreed, did it make me a conscienceless killer? I know Pop isn't actually like that, but he often seems like it, and I know he worries about whether or not he's become one. If I'm honest, he doesn't view life and death the same way we mere mortals do. It has to matter more to us. Doesn't it? And, sometimes, we have to admit it's appropriate to kill the other guy. Not only when he's trying to kill you, but sometimes we have to *decide* to kill. There are times when you look at someone and consider everything you know—and acknowledge the many things you may not know—and still decide he needs to die. Then you plan it, organize it, and carry it out.

I recognize there are schools of thought saying it is never acceptable to kill someone. I never went to those schools. I don't see how they can possibly apply to the real world. Being a pacifist means you lose a war of attrition. I mean, it's all well and good to have the Aristotelean conceptualization of good and virtue, but it's hard to make it work when you start factoring in things like, you know, *people*.

Sometimes, the other guy has to die. No, more accurately, sometimes you have to make the choice instead of act in the heat of the moment. Pop can look inside someone and see more than mortal eyes ever will, so his decisions are quicker, which makes him seem careless. I can't see people the way Pop does, with their hearts writ large to read at a glance, so I must decide with less-than-perfect data.

I didn't have to like it, but I did have to accept it. Okay, so, I accept it. I still don't like it.

"Fine. Alden first, then the vampires."

"I'm glad we agree."

"How do we do this?"

"How?" he echoed. "I have no idea. You're the one who's been hunting him for the past however long. You figure it out."

Journal Entry #49

I will reluctantly admit Uncle Dusty has an effective leadership style. Once we established I didn't want to do it and agreed I would do it anyway, he put me in charge of it. Now it's my responsibility, regardless of how reluctant I am. I'm free to ignore it entirely, procrastinate forever, do a shoddy job of it, or shut up and soldier. He knows me from our occasional visits, calls on the various dustpans, a couple of psychic contacts, and he knows how Pop raised me.

I am not amused.

Rusty helped. While Uncle Dusty was physically elsewhere, tending to his various reactor worlds, Rusty offered to spar with me.

"It'll be good for you," he suggested. "You can work out your frustration."

"I don't want to hurt you."

"I regenerate, remember?"

"You talked me into it. Turn into the half-man, half-wolf thing. It's harder to break those bones, right?"

"Yeah. And I regenerate faster when I'm—hang on. We're just working out frustrations, right?"

"You offered."

"So I did."

I'll say this for him. Rusty is a good sport and a good friend. I had a lot of frustration and anger to use up. Getting it out had to hurt. It also took a lot longer than he expected, I think. Partly because I don't tire easily, but partly because I wasn't entirely happy about hitting Rusty. Two steps forward, one step back sort of thing. There was progress, but it wasn't as much as we hoped.

When he went to clean up and find something to eat, I wondered... How does Pop manage? Does he go on murder sprees? Does he find a Gomorrah somewhere, and turn it into a bloodless wasteland?

And the thought struck me: Does he have any friends who would step up and spar with him? Warriors, sure, but does he have any real friends? How many people does he know, and how many of them actually *like* him? Not owe him allegiance or something, but enjoy his company? How many does *he* like? Aside from Bronze, Firebrand, Uncle Dusty, and me, does Pop actually have any friends?

It was a terrible, terrible thought. And it was made worse by the realization I didn't have much in the way of friends, either. We moved a lot when I was younger, so those are all distant memories. Now everyone I knew in New York—my New York—was diffused through the atmosphere or hunting for blood.

Like father, like daughter?

Ever since I insisted on being out there, in the worlds, and on my own, I've been thinking about how I was brought up. While I lived under Pop's roof, I thought he was the perfect father. Now, I'm not so sure. I can see a couple of ways where he fell short. Not things to blame him for, necessarily. He did his best and it was a prodigious best. He taught me how to meet people and make friends, but he never got around to how to *be* friends. I had to figure it out on my own.

Another thing—and maybe a key one—is my education. Pop gave me knowledge you don't find in schools and practical experience in everything from gardening to blacksmithing, jewelry-making to cooking. He wanted me to know how to do almost anything, and I'd say he did a good job of it. But, by making me capable of anything, he didn't prepare me to actually *do* anything.

I can pilot a starship or dig coal. What I can't do is hold down a job. I'm a wanderer, an itinerant, with no real home unless I make it. For a career, I tried being a superhero! I'm not going to get a job running a cash register or a marketing campaign. I can't sit in a cubicle for eight hours a day. Not without going quietly insane, at least.

I did try being a professional witch, once. It didn't end well, so I'm reluctant to try it again.

I'm coming to realize there is a lot about my life I don't like, and even more of it I don't understand.

Oh, *damn*. I'm in the middle of some sort of coming-of-age crap for the genetically-enhanced daughter of a trans-dimensional vampire. My life is a *soap opera!*

No, no, no. I need to calm down. Just because soap operas sometimes mimic real life doesn't mean I need to panic. Unless there's an entity, somewhere, watching me as I go about my life. If it changes the channel, do I vanish?

I'm tired and my ideas get weird when I'm tired. I'm going to bed.

Journal Entry #50

One of the weirdest things about living with Uncle Dusty is the way everything has a sort of make-do quality about it. There's nothing skimpy or half-assed about the reactor, the generators, the dynamo farms, or the cloning facility, but that's all Pop's work.

The rest of it, though! This was a reactor plant, not a hotel. Bed space is either a couch in the break room or in the director's office. Makeshift flops can be built of cushions salvaged from office furniture. Kitchen space was minimal—a microwave and a sink, with a salvaged hot plate from somewhere. Showers? Yes, if you like them cold. They're emergency decontamination showers. Not fun. Food? Most of it is fresh from the garden or hunted from the surrounding land.

I sometimes wonder why this world is what Pop classed as an "NLA" world—a Nobody Left Alive world. Clearly, it wasn't irradiated into oblivion, didn't suffer a climate catastrophe, and wasn't abandoned by humanity for a better planet. Biowarfare, maybe? Maybe a super-plague killed off all the people?

I'm a little afraid to ask.

The worst part, though, is Uncle Dusty doesn't take coffee. I'm not sure his physical form sleeps, so why would he need coffee in the morning? You'd think he could grow coffee beans, or at least some decent tea leaves.

This isn't visiting a relative. This is camping. No, it's squatting in someone else's building. If I want soap for my shower, I need to bring it. If I want coffee in the morning, I need to bring it. If I want—

Never mind. It's early, I'm cranky, and I have a lot of work to do while I figure out how to kill Alden.

I'm going to murder someone, and I use the word advisedly. "Kill" can be ambiguous. "He came at me with a gun and I killed him," is a whole different animal from "I went looking for him and I put a bullet through his heart." See the difference? *I* sure do. Sometimes I wonder if I'm the only one who does.

I need to focus on how to do it. Not why. Not the fact of it. I've decided to do this. All that's left is the how.

Right this minute, though, I'm going to build a shift-box for getting stuff.

The principle is simple. It's a box. It's divided into two equal-sized parts. You put a sample of something in the side marked "sample." The micro-gate searches for a close match. When it finds one, it locks on and shifts the thing it found into the other side of the box. You take out your new whatever-it-is and can trigger the box to find you another one.

This means you have to have one already, of course. If you don't have an original sample, you have to manually search for one. This is harder, especially if you're trying to search in other worlds. Even in the same world, it requires a lot of attention on the process, visualizing what you're looking for. Searching other universes is worse. I'm not sure why. Maybe there's a lot of interference from the inter-universal void, or maybe it's a lot farther to reach. Whatever the reason, searching other universes requires intense focus, a single-minded concentration on your goal, and it has to be maintained, without wavering, until the micro-gate finds what you envision. It's not impossible, but it's a brain-bending exercise and that degree of focusing effort causes headaches, nosebleeds, and, after a long enough, fainting.

I like the idea of putting an example in the box. Let the spells do the work.

From His Shadow

I built the spells on the thing and settled in to summon stuff. The local stuff I could manually locate and summon pretty easily. Soap, for example, still in the shrink-wrapped plastic. Freeze-dried, vacuum-sealed coffee, too—not great coffee, but it wasn't half bad. The towel was harder. I got one, but it wasn't in great shape. After I had two, I put them together, used a repair spell to draw material from one to the other, and had a decent towel. Then I used the decent towel to summon an equally-decent towel. All it took was a little in-the-box thinking.

I should have made the box bigger. See next year's model.

My procrastination isn't really procrastination. I can justify this by saying I've set myself up in a comfortable environment where I can concentrate on the problem without worrying about distractions and discomforts. Hot shower? Not exactly, but I know a spell to heat up water. We'll work on rerouting water from an electric water heater another day. Adequate food? Yes, we're covered. Comfy place to sleep? Gotcha. Everything vital is checked off my list. Now I can focus!

See? I'm rational. Rationalizing, more likely, but it's all logical if not sensible.

It's also given me time for non-logical things, like my emotional difficulty in becoming an assassin.

I'm going to plot someone's murder. There are a lot of qualifiers along the lines of, "Yeah, but…" You can finish the statement however you like. It still boils down to killing someone because he needs to be dead. No, I'm wrong. It boils down to killing someone because you *decided* he needs to be dead, whether he really does or not!

I haven't come up with a better choice. Oh, I suppose I could go ahead and build a prison for him, here in a reactor world, and ask Uncle Dusty to be his jailer. But Uncle Dusty *clearly* doesn't want to do it, so it isn't really an option. I don't have a solution that doesn't involve killing Alden. This bothers me. I don't want to be a murderer.

Am I being a hypocrite? I get into situations—used to get into situations—where criminals wanted to kill me, knowing it would put *them* in a situation where their lives would be at risk. I tried to subdue whenever possible, but they didn't always survive the encounter. Since I went in knowing that, I knowingly risked other people's lives. Doesn't that make me a murderer?

Yes, I suppose it does. But, again, that's logic. Emotionally, it doesn't feel the same. I go punch drug dealers in the face, some of them shoot at me, and some of them get punched through a wall and into traffic. I always felt bad about it, but not enough to stop.

Does this make me a bad person? More to the point, am I the bad guy? Or am I a good guy? Or am I a bad guy who isn't as bad as the really bad guys?

Damn it! Pop tried to teach me about ethics, but the blood-drinking monster might not have been the best choice as a tutor.

Regardless, all this woolgathering isn't helping. I have an Alden to hunt down and kill. I've wasted a lot of time—here—on making life a shade less than dreadful. This has not only improved the local living conditions, it let me gradually get used to the emotional realities of being promoted from "vigilante" to "assassin."

I still don't like it, but I don't have to like it. I only have to do it.

So, how do I hunt him down and kill him?

First option: Bomb him. There are nuclear devices on my Earth. There are plenty of them left, if I want to take the trouble to go look for them. Swipe one, drop it on the library, and check that box as "problem solved."

362

Uncle Dusty doesn't think this is a good idea. Nothing good ever comes of nuking the planet. *I* don't see the problem. Sometimes, you nuke it from orbit if it's the only way to be sure. He says this isn't one of those times. He can't explain why to my satisfaction, but he insists we don't use more nukes on an already-nuked world. I think he has an aversion to atomic weapons, but okay, I'll humor him.

Second option: I don't really have one. I need to know more about the situation before I can make any sort of plans.

All right. I need an idea. Time to get thinking.

Good thing I've got a comfortable living arrangements, isn't it?

Journal Entry #51

Since I'm in a reactor-powered magical environment with no ideas, I've been wandering around the powerplant grounds, periodically setting off my solar power converter gem and adding to the existing array. It's something to do while I'm thinking. It also raises the efficiency of the dynamos by increasing the level of magical force in which they spin. It's kind of like upping the magnetic intensity in an electrical generator.

I've built a stick with three gems mounted on it. Two of them are for targeting and linking, while the third is the power panel spell. It's as idiot-proof as I can make it, and I've gotten good at making things user-friendly. Even Uncle Dusty can wander around and put more panels in his power farms.

As for me, I was helping him out, yes, but going for a walk is sometimes the most important part of the thinking process. If you're not finding an idea in your study or your bedroom, take a shower. Is there an idea there? No? How about in the kitchen? The garden? The woods out back? Go look. Sometimes ideas are hard to find.

Finally, after a couple of days of tromping around the property, I decided to look for an idea somewhere closer to the problem. One mobile micro-gate and a complicated scrying spell later, I was using a wraparound headset as a virtual flying viewpoint, complete with telescopic, thermal, and low-light vision.

I spent a day and a night watching the library and the vampires roaming around its borders. Several of the vampires tested the barriers. They didn't burst into flames, but sizzled or even shriveled when they edged into the energy-dense areas. It was less of a sharp demarcation than it was a fuzzy area. The intensity fell below ignition point and declined from there over the space of a couple of feet.

A campfire isn't an all-or-nothing proposition. There's no line with zero heat on one side and burning on the other. You can feel the heat before you burn your hand. In the case of a vampire zipping along in a taxi, it may feel like a sudden immolation, but standing there and regarding the effect, they clearly felt it before it became dangerous.

I found it interesting how more of them were testing the borders, rather than roaming mindlessly alongside. The process of recovering or evolving their intelligence was ongoing. Eating others of their kind might accelerate the process for a few, but having an obstacle to overcome was driving all of them to think.

On the upside, if something happened to the celestial energies permeating the library and the surrounding area, vampires would pour in by the thousands almost immediately. There was nothing to prevent me from walking into such an area, finding the tektite, and walking away with it. Nothing but quasi-mindless human zombies. Lots of quasi-mindless human zombies. Lots of heavily armed quasi-mindless human zombies. All right, maybe there were a few things to prevent me from walking in and taking the tektites.

Dang. The charge on the area was a problem, too. The tektites kept providing power, kind of like the fuel in a wood-burning stove. If you suddenly removed the fire, the stove would still be hot enough to burn you. Not only did I need to remove the source of the energy, I needed a way to cool the area down quickly. What could I use to spray down the metaphorical stove?

Or do I need another metaphor? Who says I have to cool it down? Maybe I can think of it as electricity, instead, and ground out the charge.

"Uncle Dusty!"

"Yes? Hello. What?"

"I want your help with an experiment."

"Sure. What do you need?"

"The dynamos are made of osmium, right?"

"The primary rotors spin cylinders of osmium, yes."

"They're three-dee printed?"

"Most of them."

"Then you should have a lot of osmium wire."

Uncle Dusty did not enjoy the experimentation, but he was a good sport about it. Not as good a sport as Rusty was when I tested his regeneration, but good enough. The theory was sound, but the spell was strictly a "wish real hard" sort. It didn't have any basis to start from, much less work with, for attuning the wire in the way I wanted. We got the wire to act as a conductor for celestial energies, but it was a painful process and made Uncle Dusty more than a little uncomfortable.

When we were done, his avatar rubbed his hand. Energies flowed out of his hand and into the wire, grounding out into the floor.

"That hurts," he repeated, for something like the thousandth time.

"And I'm still sorry," I replied, again. "The good news is it's grounding out pretty well, but it's not a big charge differential."

"How do you mean?"

"We're on your holy ground, right?"

"Right."

"So there's a charge in the ground. It's not as much as there is in your physical form, but it's not draining away into a vacuum, so the... voltage? I think? It's not drawing energy from you as hard and fast as it could."

"Yeah, I figured that out on My own," he agreed. "If you don't mind, I'm going to go figure out a way to keep from being damaged by this."

"Knock yourself out, Unc. Rusty and I can handle the rest."

So we did.

Late one evening, we returned to my Manhattan. Not much time had passed on my Earth, so things were still largely as we left them.

We were kitted out in tactical gear. In addition to a few weapons, I carried a pair of gate spells set up in hula hoops. One was a dedicated link to the hoop Rusty carried, but the other one was much more complex and thorough, linked specifically to a matching hoop in one of Uncle Dusty's reactor worlds. I also brought along a pair of large, fully-charged power crystals and a pre-made micro-gate—just in case. I wasn't getting stuck again!

My notebook was stuffed with prepared spells. Most paper drawings can't hold much power; the containment isn't perfect and the leakage causes the paper to burn. This leads to a runaway power discharge and is Bad. However, with a power containment diagram on one side and a spell on the other, it's still a pretty good way to have a spell handy without going to all the effort of embedding it in a gem. It's faster to make and, when you need to use it, faster than casting it on the spot. You may still have to add outside energy to the spell, and it still burns up the paper, but for a one-shot spell, who cares?

It's cheap, it's weak, and it's relatively quick. But it has its uses. Pop agreed it could have good points, but I don't recall he ever bothered. He usually visualizes his spells and deals in much higher voltage. I can do only a few minor spells his way.

Rusty was much more heavily armed and encumbered. The backpack had a rocket launcher, sure, but it also had quite a lot of freshly-magicked osmium wire. He would handle the majority of the penetration. I would start the process, then start overwatching for anything going wrong.

I wished, not for the first time, for my armor. The armor might be relatively intact—it was damn tough—but the defensive systems weren't active when a building and a half fell on it. Between the magical discharge in the house and the impact, the crystals inside were probably blown to smithereens.

Eat that, Wicked Witch of the East! I had a house fall on *me* and *I* got out!

In broad daylight, Rusty headed up 42nd, between Grand Central and the library. A veritable flood of vampires came out at night from the main terminal, so we wanted to open up a hole in the defenses straight through to Alden's lair. Rusty wasn't worried about vampires during the day, but Alden's zombies were another matter. Not all of them were in the library by dark. I assume Alden left some out as scouts. I had to cover Rusty in a Somebody Else's Problem spell. He couldn't turn into a wolf and still carry all the equipment he needed, and I wasn't going to open a full-sized gate anywhere within ten blocks of Alden, lest he notice the power surge. Not until it was time to leave, anyway.

I posted up in a corner office of the Vanderbilt building. I needed the view and time to prepare.

"McQuade to Glinda. McQuade to Glinda. Come in, Glinda. Over."

I made a mental note to talk to Rusty about his choice of code names. Next time, we work them out in advance.

"Go ahead. Over."

"The wolf is in the strip joint. I say again, the wolf is in the strip joint. We have eyes on the henhouse. Over."

"Rusty, if you mean you're in position and ready, say so!"

"Aww."

"Did you lay out the wire?"

"Yep."

"Okay. When we spot the first vampire, we go."

"I know. I'm watching now."

I went back to drawing on the marble floor. It was a really nice penthouse, but nobody was going to care, so I didn't feel bad about it. With my diagram set up, I kept gathering power into the containment subsections. I'd already narrowed down the targeting and brought a big power reserve, but every little bit helps.

"I've got a vampire," Rusty said. I keyed my radio and answered.

"Where away?"

"Grand Central, or near enough. It's moving with purpose, though. There might be a human about to get eaten."

"Open fire."

While Rusty did his job, I did mine.

Somewhere near the center of each celestial-energy area, there was—in theory—a tektite. Since they're small things, about the size of a fingernail, finding one could be difficult, especially if there was any sort of zombie guard. So I cheated.

Finding the center of a circle when you only have one arc of it is a matter for geometry. Draw a line anywhere through the arc. Find the midpoint and draw a perpendicular line through it. Draw two more lines in the same circle, anywhere else, and you'll see two lines cross in the center of the circle.

Pop taught me that. There's a lot of geometry involved in magical diagrams. Euclid would recognize a little of it, but most of it is logical only if you know about the extra dimensions.

Okay, so, I have targeting points on my map. I have someplace to aim for, rather than "somewhere over there." I still don't know exactly where these celestial tektites are, but I've narrowed it down by a factor of thousands. This is not enough to target the tektite specifically, though. For that, I'd need to be able to scry on it, and that wasn't going to happen in a static field.

Fortunately, I have a few things working for me. Alden is a lousy wizard. He can hide them, but he doesn't know how to shield them from magical attack. Also, I have a hammer and a small anvil I've scratched spells onto. I also have plain tektites I've prepared for my voodoo correspondence magic. And, best of all, tektites are made of glass.

I put on my safety glasses.

The little anvil—it's only about six inches, overall—went in the diagram. I put my first tektite on it. I started my spell and aimed it at the designated coordinates. I couldn't aim at the tektite I wanted, but I could aim for where it had to be. So, instead of shooting it, I dropped my spell-like grenade on the GPS coordinates. Go that way, this far, and land there.

My hammer came down with all the strength of my arm behind it, slamming my tektite here into the anvil. The glass disintegrated in a most satisfying manner. Hopefully, the tektite I was targeting also disintegrated.

I repeated the process, shifting my aim to another circle's center area, the place where each celestial-energy tektite had to be. Crunch! Crunch! Crunch! Crunch! Again and again.

Okay, the power sources for these holy ground areas is now gone. Fine. What now? Wait until it slowly leaches away into the environment? Wait until it's expended in frying, scorching, and sizzling vampires?

Nope.

Osmium, as it turns out, isn't, in its base state, a good conductor of celestial energies. It interacts with it pretty well, though. By attuning the wire to the pattern of a celestial entity, you can move the osmium through an intense magical field and produce power that entity can use. It works even if you don't attune it, but the output is undifferentiated energy. The first is like producing the exact sort of light your plants love. The second is like producing all sorts of light, some for growing plants, some for attracting bugs. These principles are well-established and understanding them was vital to the building of the dynamo farms.

Lay down an untreated osmium wire along the street. You put one end in a charged area and the other in an uncharged area. The energies flow along it, trickling away like water leaking out of a bucket. But if you find a way—like I did, with Uncle Dusty's help—to *attune* the wire to celestial energies, the leak is considerable. Kind of like how raw iron isn't a great conductor, but if you cool it down to cryogenic temperatures, it starts to work really well.

Earlier, during the day, Rusty laid out wire into three of the outermost circles, taking care to avoid zombie patrols. This didn't matter much while there were tektites in the center, constantly powering them up again, but when I anviled them into fragments, there was nothing to replace the power leaking away.

The inner layers, on the other hand, were harder to get to.

No, that's not quite correct. They were harder to *go* to. Zombies, again, were the problem. Getting to them was easy. Getting out again without tipping Alden to the fact we were up to something—and without being chased by a zombie horde—was more difficult.

Rusty's idea was simple, effective, and involved shooting things. From his vantage point on… on… crap, I can't remember the name of the building. Big thing, across the street and southwest of me… Three hundred Madison Avenue, whatever that one is!

Rusty was on the roof with a line-throwing gun. It wasn't loaded with rope. The spear it threw was connected to a long strand of coated osmium wire! With his height advantage, he launched a shot that darn near went into the front of the library. Then he connected the end of the wire to another coil, reloaded, and fired another shot the opposite direction, giving the area a good, long grounding run. He repeated the process about fifteen degrees to the left and right of his first shot, then again to the left and right for the grounding shots.

I watched the glow through the window. Other places were still shining with a celestial aura. Where we did our work, the glow was visibly shrinking. It would still be a while before any vampire wanted to enter the area, but they were pressing closer already. The fires were dying down, so to speak, so they felt comfortable moving forward, feeling for the hot zone.

Some got too close, pushed by the ones behind. They scorched and sizzled and screamed, but this, too, hastened the dying of the light. Without a source to resupply the areas, they fizzled away.

"Any problems?" Rusty asked.

"Not on my end. How about you?"

"Not yet. I'm still inside a holy ground field, but the vampire mob is getting closer. I take it this is working?"

"Yes."

"Wonderful! I'm being surrounded by starving vampire hordes. Success!"

"Looks like."

"I'm glad you're pleased. Maybe we should think about getting me out of here?" he suggested. "I mean, I locked doors and stuff as I came up, but once they reach the building, the doors won't be enough."

"I'm on it. Come around to the north side so I can see you."

"On my way."

A moment later, I saw him waving. I don't think he could see me. He was on the roof. I was behind glass.

"Got you. Got your hula hoop?"

"Yes, I do."

"Put it down and prepare to jump down through the hole."

"Ready when you are."

I sent my one-shot, local-gate hoop up to the ceiling and held it there with nothing but concentration. A moment later, Rusty dropped through it, hit the floor, and rolled. The gate snapped shut behind him. On the rooftop across the street, there was a small, brief fire. At this end, the hoop destroyed itself by pulsing a magical disruption around its length. This eradicated traces of the spell and shredded the plastic into confetti.

"How's it looking?" he asked. We went to the window to watch. Vampires were still pushing forward.

"Give it another twenty minutes and they should break through. Less, if they keep pushing each other into contact with the area."

As I spoke, two vampires seized a third, lifted him, and threw him bodily into a still-charged area. He wailed as the energies coursed through him, igniting him. He thrashed and screamed as he burned away to ash.

The rest surged forward when their comfort zone did. A few in front didn't stop, couldn't stop in time. A dozen more were badly burned, but they shared the hurt as the energies dissipated further. The process of collapse accelerated as the mob forced itself onward.

"Okay, not twenty minutes," I observed. "Make it two."

"They don't care, do they?" Rusty asked, softly. "They really don't mind sacrificing each other as long as it gets them closer to the blood."

"They don't. What concerns me, though, is those first two pitching a third. They deliberately grabbed a guy and flung him. It was more than an intelligent thing to do. It was a knowledgeable thing. They had to have a reason to think it would help, which means some of them are getting *smart*. They've been testing the barriers, learning about them. Someone made an educated guess and tested his hypothesis. And he got a friend—an ally, anyway—to help him."

"Aren't smart vampires always the problem?"

"Only when there are a few of them. Hordes of mindless blood-drinking monsters are a different sort of problem."

"Yeah, I guess. Look! They're on the lawn."

"So I see. Zombies are shooting at them, but they're not doing any good."

"Nope. There went the front doors."

"It cost the vamps thirty or forty of their number to get through the residual celestial zones, but I expected more."

"Maybe having a lot of them crossing the danger line at once spread the damage out?"

"No doubt. I don't think it matters much when they have thousands—"

"What's that?" he asked, pointing.

It was an explosion. It came from beyond the library, near the fountain at the far end of Bryant Park. Another followed.

"Vampires?" Rusty asked.

"Can't be. We only opened up one side of the defenses. The explosions are inside a tektite-powered area. They can't be back that far."

A third explosion went off. A cloud of dust puffed into the sky.

"There's a library archive under Bryant Park, right?" I asked.

"Yeah. It's part of the library, where they keep old stuff. Kind of like an attic, or a museum basement, or something. It's where Alden is holed up."

"How far does it run?"

"How do you mean?"

"How long does it stretch? Under the park? From the library to the middle of the park? All the way across?"

"I have no idea."

I turned to the nearest mirror and chanted at it, waving my hands in a hurry. A minute or two later, I looked down on the site. The explosions had blown a sizable hole down into—or, rather, up out of—an underground chamber.

Alden, covered in dust, was being helped out of the hole by a dozen of his zombies. The zombies were all damaged to one degree or another, mostly bleeding from the hands. There were even more in the hole, acting as a human stairway for him to climb out and for those following after.

Rusty made a disgusted sound.

"He's not getting eaten by vampires tonight," he complained.

"He still might. He's not moving with any great speed."

"He'll go fort up in a place with a vampire-frying aura."

"No," I said, thinking. "He can't."

"Why not?"

"He's not an idiot, more's the pity. He doesn't know what dropped his other barriers— or maybe he does. Zombie spies might have seen it. Either way, he can't assume it won't happen wherever he goes. He can't depend on that particular form of defense and his zombies can't hold off a vampire horde. He needs to escape. Besides, with bleeding people around, the vampires might be crazy enough to soak up all the existing charge from a tektite area faster than it can replenish it."

"This ought to be good, then."

"Just in case, get the rocket launcher. Wherever he decides to stop running, I want him to be at a severe disadvantage when we go in."

"Most people don't think of a rocket launcher as a 'softening-up' tactic."

"Most people aren't hunting half-angels, either."

"Fair point." He hefted the tube and held it respectfully, examining the handgrip. "Is this safety on or off?"

"Off."

He clicked it to "safe" and slung it. Alden, meanwhile, entered a building west of Bryant Park. He came out again with a tektite in hand. Bringing along the holy ground, perhaps? I would, if I had to be out at night in a vampire-infested city. He walked south along 6th Avenue, hurrying but not running, surrounded by twenty or so minions. More minions trailed behind, but they were damaged to one degree or another. Were they unable to keep up? No, they were keeping up, but they were spaced out. Decoys and delaying tactics probably.

"Okay, I'm ready," Rusty announced. "How do we get out of this building to chase him? There are vampires all over the place."

"I'm still not convinced the vampires won't get him. Hang on."

"Sure. Whatcha doing?"

"I brought a lot of tektites. Keep tight in on him, keep him in frame. I can't lock on to him. If we don't keep track of him, we'll might not find him again."

"I'm not sure I know how."

"You've played enough video games. Keep moving the point of view so we're looking down at him. Don't try to zoom in. All I need is for him to be on the screen."

"Gotcha."

Five minutes later, I hammered another tektite, centering the effect on Alden's location. Rusty, still monitoring the mirror, whooped with delight.

"What is it?" I asked, wiping my brow.

"He stopped!"

"Stopped?"

"He and his zombies aren't moving."

"Let me see."

I maneuvered the viewpoint around and zoomed in.

"Whoa," Rusty said. "Looks like half his rosary exploded! And his hand is as bloody as if he put it in a blender. What was he doing? Holding on to it?"

"Could be. Bloody poetic justice, I'd say. I've no sympathy at all. But the whole rosary should have shattered. It was all in the target area."

"Why didn't it?"

"Pick a reason. He's sensitive to magical operations. Pop's spells may be partly shielding him. The glass may be tougher to break when they're inside his aura, or when he's using them. Hell if I know. Hang on."

I drew heavily on my power crystals, building up my spell again while Rusty kept tracking Alden. I cycled up the biggest, most destructive piece of unsympathetic magic I could muster. There was no point in pecking away at him with little shots, not now. With a suitable power source, it would be practical to wear him down, but he was carrying around a scrambled, static-y zone. If he so much as went into a building, I wouldn't be able to target him precisely enough.

Alden and his minions really began to hustle. Now he was in a hurry. I didn't mind, since he was sticking to a street rather than taking shortcuts through buildings. I took aim several feet ahead of him, watching carefully on the mirror. I set the detonation point at chest-level for him, to maximize the proximity to his necklace. He advanced down the street with his zombies and, while he didn't squarely hit my target-locked point, he came so close I wanted to squeal in glee.

I drove the hammer down on my sample tektite with both hands. My spell translated the impact and destruction across space, bursting it outward from the target point, affecting nothing at all—unless it was made of meteoric glass. Every tektite in his rosary popped like a gunshot.

Rusty laughed in delight. I let myself collapse to the floor, breathing heavily. I mopped sweat from my face while Rusty settled into evil chuckles.

"What happened?" I asked. Rusty helped me into a comfy chair. I wiped sweat from the back of my neck and pulled out my canteen. I put an awful lot into my spell. It's all right for Pop to channel massive amounts of power, but either I need to be an immortal or I need more time in an Ascension Sphere. On second thought, maybe I don't. I'm still concerned about the potential slow-roasting of my soul.

"The rest of his rosary blew up," Rusty told me, "and blew up big."

"I saw that part. Then what?"

"Some of the metal links broke! It's like he was wearing a chain of firecrackers around his neck. He's bleeding everywhere there was a bead. Not bad, but there are vampires out on the street. They can probably smell him."

"Good. I was only aiming to destroy his amplifiers and the scrying-fuzzing effect around them, but if he smells appetizing, so much the better." I drank deeply, leaned back and poured water over my face.

"Now he's *really* in a hurry," Rusty told me. "He and his zombies are running."

"Running? He can run?"

"He's carrying his cane," Rusty answered, concentrating hard on the mirror to keep Alden centered. "I think it hurts him to walk, but if he's willing to grunt and tough it out, he doesn't actually need it."

"Mmm. Probably." I shoved the chair over to sit in front of the mirror with him. "Look at the expression on his face. Running is painful."

"And he's scared," Rusty pointed out. "I know what someone looks like when they're running scared."

I decided not to ask.

"I know why he's scared," I said, instead. "He's bleeding and there are vampire hordes around. Plus, someone is actively targeting him, weakening him, taking away his power. And he just lost all his holy aura vampire defenses."

"That'll do it. Thing is, he's got minions with him. Are they guards or decoys, do you think?"

"I have no doubt they're both," I decided, "at least until he chooses to sacrifice one."

"He's an entity, not a human. Does he need to be scared? I mean, can he sit somewhere and pray and surround himself with a three-foot aura of vampire incineration?"

"Maybe. I wouldn't want to try it. He might be able to do it, but they might throw bricks. I don't know what he can do, but *he* does. At a guess, I'd say this is the most dangerous thing he's done in a while."

Like a flash of lightning, a lot of things leaped into brilliant relief. Why didn't Alden try to take over Cameron's world, back in the 1950s? Because the world was bigger, then. It wasn't tied together so tightly, so interdependent. It was a bunch of independent nations, most of whom were willing to go to war again if they needed to.

Here? In this world? Hopping a jet for a weekend in Europe wasn't much more unusual than a trip across town. Breakfast in Rome, lunch in Paris, tea in London, and a late dinner in Washington. The global interdependence of the world made it more unified, less likely to be split into smaller groups. He could create a world state much more easily…

…if he was unopposed.

Did Alden make a mistake and cause this world's nuclear war? No. He did not. Watching him as he ran for his life, it was clear he wanted to live. It was his chief aim: stay alive. Everything else revolved around it. Power? Nice to have, since it helped him defend himself and stay alive. Money? Handy for buying things he would enjoy while he was alive. All that sort of thing.

His own life was far too precious a thing for him to risk being in New York, of all places, when bombs fell. The moment Rusty and I shot down his escape route under the church, he would have worked as hard as possible to stop any sort of global holocaust. What am I saying? He would work against such a thing, regardless, but when it was his head on the chopping block, he would go all-out.

Which doesn't mean he succeeded. Who benefited from the nuclear exchange? Alden? No. But humans were now involved in open war against creatures wanting to feed on them. The wholesale destruction of technological society went a long way toward reducing humans to prey animals and, suitably infected, as shock troops.

But vampires need humans. How were they going to survive if all the humans were killed off by the freshly-transformed hordes? This could still be a mistake on someone's part, but I felt certain—given Dietrich's comments—at least one vampire faction was, at the very least, taking advantage of it.

Regardless, it was something I could think about later. Alden was running through the night, bleeding and frightened, limping slightly as he slapped shoe leather.

"Schadenfreude" is defined as pleasure derived from another's misfortune. I'm no saint. You better believe I derived pleasure from it.

It was, in a small way, painful to watch. Here was this huge, muscled hulk, now thundering along at his best speed, trying to ignore his wounds. He panted and puffed, clearly not used to sprinting. He was much more the steroid-jacked weightlifter type than a runner. Serves him right for skipping his cardio workouts.

One of his fingers was somewhat purplish, probably due to the exertion. At a guess, Pop's rings weren't set to resize automatically—and, come to think of it, why should they? It's not like his fingers ever change size. Alden's whole body was constantly building muscles, so whatever finger he originally put it on was thicker, now. It wasn't coming off. I suppose the finger could. It might be safer than cutting the ring.

On the other hand, if he can't heal a gunshot wound through the liver, losing a finger might be permanent.

He and his minions beat feet down 6th, veered left down Broadway, and kept going. The snarling hiss of a vampire warned him of his danger, but a minion intercepted it, struggling violently and hopelessly. The minion succeeded, though, in diverting the vampire from Alden. The two fell down in their struggle, but the vampire fastened fangs in the flesh of the throat, voraciously sucking while Alden and the others kept right on sprinting.

I was impressed. Most people can't run at a full-on sprint for a hundred yards, much less several blocks. I expected the zombies to because they didn't care about little things like shortness of breath, chest pains, or dizziness. Alden, even wounded, kept up this surprising pace. I had to remind myself he wasn't fully human.

"Where's he think he's going?" Rusty asked.

"No idea. I'm guessing he's not running *to* so much as he's running *away*. There's a vampire mob invading his library. He wants to be far away from that. Once he finds a place to ride out the night—a church, maybe—then he can worry about where he wants to go *to*. It's what I would do, anyway. We'll sort out where he is when he comes to rest."

"I'm getting the hang of this," Rusty assured me.

"Once the static isn't an issue, scrying becomes a lot easier," I agreed. "You don't have to concentrate on the zoom controls, just on the point of view. Height helps, though, if you're trying to get a big picture."

"It's okay. I recognize the area. He's coming up on the twenty-eighth street station. It's not sealed by anything, so there ought to be a lot of vampires around."

"Does he know?" I wondered. We watched as he continued.

If he knew it, it didn't slow him down any. He and his guards kept right on going at full speed. Vampires did show up, but they weren't specifically after him. When minions threw themselves into the fray, the vampires were only too happy to take whatever presented itself. Alden passed the station with his guard reduced to about half a dozen and kept right on going.

It was a constant war of attrition, all on the zombie minions. Over the whole distance, a vampire would show up, a minion would be sacrificed to it, and the rest would keep running. One here, another there, a dozen in one big lump, then another along the way…

When he ran low on minions, he switched tactics. Instead of sprinting, he turned left, into a park. This one wasn't flash-burned by a nuke. Using cover, they proceeded more cautiously, more quietly, trying to avoid attention instead of accepting the risks of gaining distance at speed. He'd gone the better part of a mile in one long sprint. Maybe he felt the risk factors had shifted. The horde might not follow him this far, so the major threats were now the free-roaming individuals and small packs.

Or maybe he was just tired. His side was definitely bothering him.

They stopped in the greenery of the park, off the paths, hiding while they caught their collective breath. I watched gleefully as Alden lay flat, clutched at his side, and gasped out a string of very bad words. His evening was ruined, but as soon as he found a spot to hide out overnight, Rusty and I were going to ruin far more than that!

I took the opportunity to examine him more thoroughly. His shirt was shredded by the destruction of the rosary, but his chest already stopped bleeding. Pity the shattering glass wasn't more forceful. The injuries were only skin deep. His hand had stopped bleeding, too, but it still had bits of broken glass in it. His ring finger was much darker due to the physical exertion. The wound in his side never did bleed, but from the way he clutched at it with his good hand, it hurt him something fierce.

Once he recovered his breath, he and his decoys worked through the park, keeping out of sight. They exited along the south side and worked east, using doorways, dead cars, and other cover. They moved carefully. There was a lot of broken glass on the street and a small amount of rubble. Judging from the damage, they were near the northern curve of the Brooklyn Navy Yard blast. Windows and glass doors were mostly broken, especially if they faced south. I didn't even want to think what it would be like on the street when the glass came raining down.

They moved through the remains of broken doors and into a building, navigating through the near-darkness to keep pressing on, farther in, away from the street. Alden led the way through the shadowy darkness, picking through looted shops and tumbled wreckage, hunting for something.

When he came to the fire stairs, he sighed in relief. Whatever building he was in, he wasn't stopping on the ground floor. He headed up, probably hoping to avoid notice until dawn.

If all he had to worry about was vampires, it was a good tactic, but risky. Without a solid reason, they didn't usually bash open fire doors. They didn't methodically search. They sniffed, hoping to catch a scent. Twenty floors above ground, it's hard to be detected via nasal appraisal. But if they detected anything up there and chose to investigate, there was no good way to escape. It was an all-or-nothing proposition.

In the absolute darkness of the stairwell, Alden rubbed his hands over his face, which began to glow, illuminating the stairs well enough to climb. It was good for us, too. We didn't have to adjust the light-amplifying mode.

He kept going up even though his limp grew more pronounced. From the look on his radiant countenance, he was in considerable pain. He was forcing himself upward another floor, then another one. I wondered if he'd make it to the top or give up along the way, somewhere.

He called it quits well short of the top. He was high enough for it to be reasonably safe. He laid a hand on the fire door, concentrated, and it opened. It's not meant to open from the stairwell side, but a simple telekinetic push on the bar from the hallway side is all it takes. He swung it open and headed down the hallway.

Something about the hallway bothered me. There were no signs of anything amiss, aside from the power being out. No bodies, no debris, nothing to indicate anything unusual happened. The outside of the building had cosmetic damage from the blast, but there were no windows in the hallway. While apartments and offices certainly had windows blasted out, much like the ground floor's glass doors were, the inner hallway should, in fact, look exactly as it did: pretty much untouched.

What was it? The weird lighting? The way I saw it in a magic mirror?

Alden picked an apartment. He struck it twice with his fist, speaking magical phrases. That's when I realized what was wrong.

My locking spell failed under his magical assault. The door went in when he kicked it with an over-muscled, powerful leg. The alarm spell on the door sent me an alert, letting me know someone entered my old apartment.

I grabbed control of the spell from Rusty and shot the viewpoint out of the building, going up a bit, getting a big-picture view. Madison Square Park, to the west, was where he started being stealthy instead of sprinty…

Rusty jerked away from me in surprise as I shouted.

"What?" he asked. "What? What's the matter?"

"He's in my old apartment! He's getting *away!*"

"What do you mean? He's a bunch of floors up. He's taking shelter for the night."

"My old apartment has my old witchroom! If he can figure out how to operate the micro-gate and the mirror's gate spell, he could go *anywhere!*"

"Anywhere?"

"Any universe!"

"And that's a problem? I mean, if he's gone, he's gone, right?"

"Weren't you listening? There's nothing to prevent him from solving all his personal problems, enslaving a planet or ten, and coming *back!* That's why we're *here*, to stop him before he becomes a much bigger problem!"

"Oh. Right. Um… I hate to bring this up, but we're between the library and Grand Central, right in the heart of vampire horde headquarters. How do we get to your old place? A hula hoop?"

"This one is tuned, dedicated to the other one. Yours was to get you to me. Mine is to get us back to Uncle Dusty's place."

"But you can use it as a doorway even if you don't use the spell, right? Or have I misunderstood?"

"Yes, but I can't take it with me through itself. Besides, I didn't want to leave them behind, so they self-destruct after I use them!"

"That's a problem. Think we can get out of the building and sneak south?"

"It'll take too long!"

"Look, I'm trying to think of a way to get from here to there. You don't have to snap at me."

"I'm trying to think, too!"

"Go ahead!"

I glared at Rusty, then at the mirror. I focused in again and ran into a problem. My old apartment was still warded against magical spying. The building didn't collapse and there were no geodes to break. The spells on the place were still there, even though they were running down ever since the power went off. I could look from the hallway through the front door and see most of the living room, but there was no one visible. Even the zombies were gone. There wasn't a blood trail—nobody was bleeding badly enough—but a lot of dirty footprints disappeared into the hallway.

My comment was, shall we say, unladylike.

How do I get from here to there in a hurry? I can draw a gate on the wall, but I don't have the power to open it. I burned most of my power reserves in shattering Alden's tektites. Even if I did have the energy for it, I didn't think I had time for it. True, I had a magic mirror to target—wait. Did it have enough charge in the crystals to open on its own? Probably! But if Alden used it, maybe not. Damn it, it would take too long to build a gate spell on this end!

Could I open a micro-gate from here to the mirror's micro-gate? It wouldn't take much power. I could activate the micro-gate from here and transfer the gate to the mirror frame, using the power crystals mounted on the back. I'd still need to draw a gateway here, though, and empower it a bit to take this end of the gate. That would be faster. Although, here in this apartment, I had several open doorways that would be even better…

Palm. Forehead. Hard.

"Follow me!" I shouted, and threw down the Hula Hoop of Escape. Rusty didn't argue. I activated the highly-charged hoop, stepped into it, and promptly fell through the linked gate in Uncle Dusty's reactor world. I hit the floor, rolled aside, and wound up on my back, hands already rising to take aim at the gate. Rusty followed without a word, tumbled easily to the floor, and rolled to his feet. I gestured and spoke a word to slam the gate shut as quickly as I could. The hula-hoop glued to the hallway ceiling stayed intact. The one on Earth was the only one set to disintegrate.

Rusty helped me to my feet.

"Okay, we're here again."

"In a world where there's a time differential," I said, "and a vastly higher level of energy available."

"Ah. So we're farther way, but in a much better position to do stuff?"

"Think of it as backing up to get a running start."

"Got it. What's the plan?"

"Plan?"

"Oh, it's like *that*. Okay. What do we do next?"

"Next, I spend a few minutes on another gate spell."

"How long does that work out to on Earth?"

"How should I know? Temporal differentials confuse me! Take these crystals and put them in the charging diagram. I've got to get busy."

I immediately turned my attention to the doorframe we normally used as a gate target in this reactor world. It already had a basic spell on it to make it a good lock-on point.

I didn't know if Alden had already found my mirror and used it. He managed to reestablish a pilot connection between my mirror and Cameron's closet, once, so it shouldn't take him long to find wherever he wanted to go.

No, not wherever. Whenever. It wasn't a doorway between universes. He thought of it as time travel. If he pictured a scene in ancient Egypt, or the building of a pyramid in Central America, or even a herd of woolly mammoths, he would have what he thought of as the era he wanted. With his powers, settling in and making himself at home would be simple enough. He might not need to spend hours with the mirror, searching for exactly what he wanted. He might not need minutes!

"How are those crystals?" I asked, preparing the gate. Rusty sounded baffled.

"They're in the circle thingies?"

"Right. Right. Sorry. Are you still armed?"

He hefted the rocket launcher.

"Good. This is a straight-up assault—" I began, happy with the setup of the gate. I'd connect the micro-gate to the mirror's micro-gate, but once I did, the time differential would lock. Rusty dropped his backpack as I spoke.

"—but is likely to be indoors. Maybe something a bit less explosive?" He slung the launcher and readied an assault carbine. "Much better. I'm opening a gate in a few more seconds."

"Go for it."

I stepped back from the doorway. The micro-gate locked on to the one on my old mirror. Good. At least Alden wasn't using it at the moment. On the other hand, our time advantage disappeared when it connected. I immediately switched it to the framework and mirror. Everything spun away, snapped back, and showed me a floor. I recognized the carpet. The mirror was face-down on the floor. We both stared at the rug for a moment.

"Uh, I hate to ask…"

"I don't know!"

"That's two of us, then. I don't suppose your uncle can tell us anything?"

Yes.

Rusty jumped as though jabbed with a hot poker.

"I *hate* it when you do that!"

Sorry. My avatar is shifting over and headed your way, but it's a considerable physical distance. In the meantime, what do you need from Me?

"Unc, my mirror is on the floor of my witchroom, so it's not terribly useful as a gate. I could turn it off, put this one on the ground, and open it again, I suppose, so we could stand inside and lift the other one… I think. But we don't know how many times we'll get shot or clubbed or whatever in the process."

Since the gate is open, I can take a look. Hmm. Looks like a half-dozen of Alden's zombies are guarding it. They all have something. A bat, a stick, a length of pipe. No guns in evidence, though.

"Where's Alden?"

Remember, I can't scan for him. But I looked everywhere in the apartment. He's not there.

I said another unladylike word and switched back to the micro-gates. I retargeted the link. Instead of switching the micro-gate at the far end to the mirror frame, I switched it to the doorway into the witchroom. It wasn't prepared to take the spell, so it was difficult and expensive, but I was prepared to go to considerable expense in exchange for getting it done quickly.

The gate flushed away, snapped back, and Rusty didn't hesitate. He saw the zombies surrounding the face-down mirror. They turned toward the doorway. He squeezed the trigger and held it, controlling the carbine with both hands. He anticipated and prepared for the muzzle rise, braced the weapon against the recoil, and walked the stream of fire in a controlled, careful manner across them at mid-torso level.

Rusty has fired automatic weapons before. How did I not know this? We should talk more.

While he fired, I drew my knife and put on my sunglasses—the same glasses I used in the subway. The room wasn't illuminated and the muzzle flashes strobed brightly, ruining night vision for everyone.

The carbine clicked empty and I went through the gate. Human zombies—living ones—can be killed by bullets. You blow holes in the chest and they die, but they don't die immediately. They don't go into shock. They don't scream and clutch at the wounds. They ignore them until they physically cannot continue.

On the other hand, you put six to eight hollow-point rounds into someone's upper chest and they're not going to be at their best.

On the left, I kicked the closest one in the abdomen, sending him into two of his friends. The one on the right I killed immediately by sticking my knife up under his chin and into his brain. Another swung a length of pipe in my direction and I stepped inside his swing, turning as I did. I grabbed his pipe-wielding arm as I pressed my back to his chest, turned him, felt the impacts of two other zombies with various clubs—they hit him, not me—and I stabbed over my shoulder, putting my knife into what was left of my shield's brain.

Rusty came through about then, a half-man, half-wolf, full-on monster. I wasn't sure if his night vision was up to this or not, but he didn't seem to have any misgivings about it. I dropped my backpack zombie and ducked, rolling between blind or semi-blind zombies. A spray of blood and brains splattered across them and half the room as something very large made very large wounds in a zombie or two.

The spray didn't bother the rest of them, but I think that's more of a weakness than a strength. They don't operate as a team. They operate as a mob. Unless they're being controlled and guided, they're a bunch of lurching individuals, not a unit.

I parried a swing with my knife, parting someone's forearm about halfway. I broke someone else's knee and grabbed his arm as he flailed for balance. A moment later, I had him face-first in a wall an instant before I thrust my knife up the back of his neck. My knife cuts metal; flesh and bone are like tofu.

The severed-arm guy grabbed with his remaining hand. I ducked under his grip, holding his hand and turning to place his arm in a lock. It didn't bother him; he continued to struggle. It gave me a good way to hold him and make my next shot with the knife perfect, up behind his ear. He shuddered and quit.

Meanwhile, Rusty was as busy as a fox in a henhouse, or a werewolf in a witchroom. Bloody bits came out of zombies, some of whom fell down temporarily. Rusty hadn't quite got the hang of dealing with these things. Sever the spine. Crush the head. Destroy the brain. These are the quick-acting, instant-kill sorts of things. Flinging someone's kidney into someone else's face may momentarily blind him, but it's not instantly fatal to either one.

If we'd had to lift the mirror-gate, standing inside a ring of these guys, it would have been ugly. As it was, I wasn't hurt and Rusty would be fully recovered in minutes.

He slid down the spectrum into human form again. I observed the process of his clothing shapeshifting with him.

I want to say, as an aside, that I am *extremely* proud of my spell.

The mirror's stand was broken. We lifted the mirror and propped it against a table. I fired up the micro-gate instantly and was very careful not to specify any sort of destination. It wouldn't necessarily reconnect to wherever it went before, but if we were fast enough, the wormhole connection might still have the equivalent of an ionized track, like a path of least resistance for an electrical discharge.

My scrying through the micro-gate connection showed me Cameron's old bedroom. I didn't like it. This connection was a regular one, often made, almost routine. It might not be where Alden went. It might be nothing more than an affinity between here and there caused by all the former use.

Did Alden go through to Cameron's house? There was no sign of anyone. No muddy footprints, nothing. I couldn't look at much of the house because the scrying sensor blurred as it got away from the gate, but I could dial up the sound and listen. No slamming doors, no screams, no tires squealing as someone drove away. With a trifle of amplification, I heard something. It took me a moment to identify it as snoring. If Alden came through, fleeing from pursuit, vampires, and me, he was courteous enough to close doors behind him and gentle enough to not wake anyone.

I considered this unlikely.

I slapped the micro-gate shut and turned my attention to the frame.

"What's up?"

"Wherever Alden is, we can't find him using most methods. Uncle Dusty says he's nowhere around here, so he must have gone through the mirror. I'm trying to pick up any sort of leftover after-image, sort of, from where he went." I wished silently for my real witchroom, before it got blown to bits.

"Thing is, I've used the micro-gate on this mirror several times, so it's not going to be helpful at all. I've used the frame, too, but not as many times. It won't be easy to pick up a latent image from a gate spell in the first place, but the frame is my best chance. It's kind of like an old-fashioned magnetic data medium. The gate was used, then closed—closing it is like erasing the media. It would be a pain to recover the coordinates, but it's at least possible. Now, though, the media has been written over by a new gate connection and erased again—when we looked through and saw carpet, remember?"

"And you can't search for him because he's invisible to general searching stuff?"

"That's right."

"Anything I can do to help?"

"No."

Rusty recognized the frustration in my tone. He opened the curtains a bit to let in moonlight, dragged bodies out of my witchroom, and generally stayed out of my way.

As for me, I spent half an hour struggling with ever-more-sensitive spells, trying to get any inkling of where the mirror's frame connected. Not last time. The time before that. At least I proved my theory was sound. I could get a latent afterimage of Uncle Dusty's reception frame in his reactor world. Prior to that, I couldn't find anything. Simply turning a gate off doesn't purge the faint impression it leaves, but overwriting it with another gate apparently does.

I sat back and ground the heels of my hands into my eyes. Rusty handed me his canteen and I drank half of it.

"No dice?"

"Not even craps," I replied. "The recent usage has scrubbed anything beforehand."

"And the mirror can go anywhere?"

"Yes."

"So, Alden could pick anyplace he could imagine and step through?"

"Yes."

"But if it's local—and correct me if I'm wrong—it costs a lot less power?"

"Yes."

"Is there any way to check how much power the mirror used? It's got crystals mounted on the back, and I know you use crystals as batteries. If really long jumps to other universes cost more, maybe really distant universes are especially pricey? I don't know enough about how it works, but if he used a certain amount of fuel, wouldn't it give you an idea of how *far* he could have gone?"

I grabbed Rusty, kissed him, and flipped the mirror around. He wasn't entirely wrong. The difference between going across town or across the galaxy was negligible when you factored in unknowns like the duration of the gate. But going from one universe to another was a major expenditure no matter what. At the very least, I could determine if he left the world or went elsewhere within it.

I didn't expect him to be on this Earth, not after the mess, but you never know. He might have someplace he desperately wanted to be. My money was on him fleeing into "the past" to undo everything. It's what one does when one time travels.

After careful figuring, accounting for the times I connected to it, which parts connected—the micro-gate or the frame—the amount of energy from the other end, the local magical field in my old apartment and how much of it was likely used, as well as everything else I could think of, I had my answer.

He didn't use the mirror.

"Are you sure?" Rusty asked.

"Of course I'm sure!" I snapped. "Not totally sure, but mostly sure. There would have to be major differences in the initial conditions to account for what we have now, and there isn't any way to do that. There's not enough energy difference to account for another full-size gate."

"But there are discrepancies?"

"Not discrepancies. Differences. Inaccuracies. If I don't know how much cereal was in the container, I can still account for how many bowls I poured in one morning. I may not know exactly how much was in each bowl, but it's close enough to figure out roughly where the level was when we started."

"There's too much energy in the mirror for there to have been another bowl poured out?"

"Yes."

"Could he have provided it, somehow?"

"Doubtful. I stole back my geodes and I don't think he can reroute the dedicated power crystals in Pop's old amulet. Even if he could, it doesn't have *that* much power. Gate spells are *awful*."

"So what does that tell us? He's not here. How did he leave?"

"I don't know."

"Could this all be a setup to throw us off his trail?" Rusty asked.

"It seems too elaborate—no, on second thought… It wouldn't have to be elaborate. He could come here, go into my witchroom, and leave minions to intercept me when I came to investigate. Meanwhile, he could simply walk away on his own. He might go down a floor or two and lay low. He very well could be throwing us off his scent!"

"Boy, is he in for a shock," Rusty said, grinning.

"What do you mean?"

In answer, his face lengthened and he dropped to all fours. In a moment, there was a black-furred wolf sniffing at the floor.

Note to self. Get Rusty more of a wardrobe. The tactical clothes were black, but his fur would take on whatever color we picked out. What would he look like as a camo-colored wolf?

Rusty sniffed around the apartment, checking the front door, the hallway, the witchroom. He shifted back into a biped and shook himself.

"He left through there," he stated, positively. "There" was the witchroom closet.

"That goes to Iowa!"

As I said it, I realized a key point in my problem tracing the mirror. It wasn't an erased and overwritten signature. It simply wasn't there! The micro-gate? Of course it connected to Cameron's bedroom. It had an affinity for it because of all the times we used it! No sign of Alden in the house? Naturally, because he went to Iowa, not California!

"There's a smell of forest, river mud, and Gus in it, too," Rusty went on. "This is the other closet?"

"My closet connected to here, halfway across town. Mine's destroyed. This closet was connected to two closets, but now the only place it's linked to is Pop's place in Iowa."

"Does he have a witchroom, too?"

"You've seen it. I've used it a couple of times."

"Now I get it. The house in the woods with the porch?"

I admit, teleportation closets can be confusing, at first. I had to remind myself they were still new to Rusty.

"Yes, that's the place."

"Then let's go!"

"No! Alden may be waiting for us, or he may have set up an ambush, or rigged a trap, or whatever. Let's look, first."

I fired up the mirror again, this time linking it to the mirror in Pop's Iowa workroom. The micro-gates connected normally and the image on the mirror swam into focus. The workroom looked pretty normal. Nothing was out of the ordinary. The closet door was open, though, which was unusual. I couldn't look through the rest of the house because of the scrying sensor's distortion through the gate.

"Okay. We can go. We'll have to go through the mirror, though. The closet is open."

"I don't understand."

"Look, it's really simple. Or," I corrected myself. "No. Wait. I think I see part of the reason this is confusing. Whenever we left my house to go to Iowa, it didn't really feel as though we had a midway stop. We never opened the door when we switched, did we?"

"No. Not until it was time to go in or out. We went into the closet. You did a thing. You did the thing again. Then we stepped out into the smaller house."

"There's a reason I left the doors closed. It's built into the enchantment. It's a safety thing to be certain no one is stepping into the closet when it shifts. I'm told it hurts a lot to have your body divided between two universes."

"I'll take your word for it."

I opened the mirror and we stepped through. Instantly, Rusty sniffed.

"He was here. And I smell blood."

"He was wounded."

Rusty checked the chamber on his carbine and aimed at the workroom door. I nodded, readied my own, and moved to one side. I held up two fingers, one finger, and yanked the door open.

There was blood spattered all over the hallway. Rusty went through the door first. He regenerates. I don't. I came through slightly behind him and checked the opposite direction in the hallway before following him.

We found Gus.

He was in the living room amid broken furniture and more than a few holes in the walls. The scene was one of carnage and destruction. It was one *hell* of a fight. But Gus lost. Someone had killed him, then gone to great lengths to make absolutely sure he was dead. There were caved-in portions where his chest was crushed. Something sharp had sawn halfway through his neck, slightly above the collar. His fur was soaked, matted with blood, but there was a lot in his mouth and on his muzzle, so it wasn't all his own.

Rusty moved on, searching, while I threw myself on Gus. He was cold. The blood was partly dried and tacky to the touch. I didn't care if it made a mess. I didn't care about anything. This was *Gus*!

This *was* Gus.

The damage to the house was considerable. The cleaning and repair spells had a lot of work ahead of them. Given time, it would all be fine—except there was no magic capable of bringing back my friend. Even *Pop* couldn't do it, and I don't put much of anything past Pop. It would take a—

I picked Gus up. It's not easy, hefting so much limp weight, but I managed, trying not to think about how Gus' shape felt wrong. I shouted for Rusty and he came inside, gun held ready.

"We're leaving!"

"Suits me. He's not here. I didn't find any trace of him outside."

"He did come here," I snapped.

"Then maybe he left through the mirror?"

"Shut up and get the door!"

We filed through the mirror into Uncle Dusty's reactor world. His avatar wasn't on hand, but it didn't need to be. I let out a psychic scream that echoed around the world. I felt his attention snap to me.

WHAT!?

"Fix him," I stated, laying Gus down on the tile floor. Attention shifted, examining the body. I felt what he was about to say before he said it.

He's dead.

"Listen to me," I hissed, addressing the nearest light fixture. "I don't ask you for much, but when I do, it's important. I need a miracle. You're either a god or a megalomaniac liar. Which is it? —And don't give me any crap about proof versus faith. Either you can do this or you can't. If you are unable to do it, say so! If you *can* do it, then *do it!*"

There was a long silence, but I felt the movement of forces in the room. Uncle Dusty did something, so I held my tongue and let him work.

There are many sorts of miracles, he began, *many of which are presently beyond My power. Or, rather, say they are beyond My skill. Here, in this place of power, I believe I have the strength to do this, but I am still a young god. I have not yet mastered the techniques required. I regret, My niece, that I cannot—not **will** not, but **can** not—give you the miracle you want.*

I was about to snap something hurtful at him, but he went on.

Although I cannot give you the miracle you require of Me, I can give you another. Not what you have asked for, but perhaps enough of one to soothe your pain somewhat and diminish your loss.

"I'm listening."

This body is, by and large, dead. The major systems have shut down. The spirit has departed to the bourn from which there is no returning—and even I cannot undo it, not after so long a time. The only life within this flesh consists of individual cells and tissues, and not many of those.

There are also still patterns within the brain. Not all of them, of course, but there are fragments of who he was. There are more, I am sure, I can recover or reconstruct.

The full restoration of your friend is beyond My skill. The full restoration, I say. Whatever I might return to you would be... not the same. It would look the same, but it would not think the same, act the same. Despite My best efforts, I am very much afraid it would be a "Monkey's Paw" sort of resurrection, which would be worse than nothing. I fear to give you this miracle, for I would not have you grow to hate what once you loved.

What I can do, what I freely offer to you, is to give you his son. I can nurture a sample of Gus until it becomes another dog, as much alike to his sire as any child has ever been. I can give this young pup... let us say I can give him knowledge of a past life. He will have memories of a former existence as Gus, but he will be his own self, rather than an incomplete copy, a faulty reconstruction.

If you do not wish those memories to be preserved, of course, I can also give you a second Gus, once again a puppy, to grow naturally into whatever sort of dog you are willing to help him become.

These things are all I can offer. I am sorry I am inadequate to the miracle you desire.

"How much time do I have to decide?"

I have already placed the memory fragments in stasis—don't ask me to explain; it's a celestial thing—and we need to take samples of what cells are still alive. The samples should be taken immediately. Once this is done, you may take ten seconds, ten years, or as long as your wounded heart requires.

I didn't have to decide instantly. There were other things that had to be done instantly, but this decision would wait. Okay. I could do the things and think about it later.

"Where do we take the body?"

At Uncle Dusty's instruction, Rusty and I took Gus to the cloning laboratory. His avatar met us there.

"The human body I wear was grown here," he told us, preparing instruments while we placed the corpse on a table. "It's designed for growing human clones. There's no reason we can't grow a dog—even one as special as Gus."

"I'm not sure Gus is special on a genetic level," I warned him. "Pop did a lot of experimentation on him. A *lot*."

"I'll monitor his progress," Dusty assured me. "If it seems he's not developing into the spitting image of his father, I feel confident there are *some* miracles I can work on your behalf." Dusty grinned at me and lowered a medical face shield. "Your father did his part. Here, in this place of My power, I will do My part. If you want another dog, I promise you, you shall have a worthy successor to the Gus."

"*'The* Gus'?" Rusty asked.

"There was only one," Dusty answered, sliding a long needle through the bloody fur. "There has never been a dog like him, ever, in any history of the Earth. I can, with a bit of effort, find ten thousand or ten million of *you,* but of Gus, there was only one."

Rusty looked at me. I nodded.

"He's not wrong."

"I believe you," Rusty decided.

"Got everything you need, Unc?" I asked. He lifted a tray of little containers.

"Yes, I think so. I'll put these away so you can have them when you want them."

"Thank you. Where can we... that is, do you have a shovel?"

"You plan to bury Gus?"

"Yes."

"Not here, surely."

"Why not?"

"Is this where you think he would be happiest? I mean, don't people usually pick a nice place for a grave? Or do you think he'd prefer to be cremated?"

"No. You're right. Thank you for pointing it out. I wasn't thinking. Now that I consider it, I know just the place. Rusty, will you help me?"

"Yes."

I like that about Rusty. He knew I was still upset even if I was now clamping down hard on it, controlling it. He didn't say, "Sure, but where are we going?" The answer was, "Yes." Period.

"We should get non-spark shovels for gravedigging."

"Uh... why?"

"Those sorts are made of an alloy, not steel. It's important."

"If you say so. Shouldn't we be tracing Alden?"

"It'll wait. We do this first. But, before we go—Unc?"

"Yes?"

"You say there are remnants of Gus' memories."

"Yes."

"Can you tell me what his last memories were? What happened when he was killed?"

"Are you sure you want to know?"

I bit back a sharp response.

"Uncle Dusty. I am not in a good mood. Tell me. Please. Without making it any harder by asking questions."

Uncle Dusty has to have things pointed out to him, but once he understands the problem, he's a good sort.

"Gus remembered Alden. When Alden came through without you or your father, he attacked. Alden was surprised—or I judge him to have been so. I think Alden tried to stop Gus with his mind and failed. I think this panicked him. Gus tore up his arm pretty well and got knocked around. Gus was one tough son of a bitch and immensely strong, to boot. Judging by what I could get of Alden's expression, Alden was *terrified*. Gus kept fighting, tore up one of Alden's legs, got Alden on the ground, and went for the throat. Alden blocked with his damaged arm and managed to get a grip in the fur. Alden held him and kicked him, hit him, methodically and repeatedly, until Gus died."

"There's a lot more to it than that, isn't there?"

"There are more details. The events as outlined are what happened."

"Thank you. Now I can be angry all at once instead of getting angry again, later."

Journal Entry #52

I buried my dog today.

If anybody ever asks me what the saddest statement in the world is, I'll have to give that one due consideration. There must be something sadder, but I'm having a hard time thinking of one at the moment.

If you're not a dog person, you won't understand.

I rescued him when he was a puppy. I played with him when I was a child. He was my friend, my loyal comrade, and my protector. He was the one person—and don't get me started on what qualifies as a "person"—my Pop ever unconditionally approved of.

Pop sees inside people. Gus was someone he *trusted.*

No, I take it back. Pop didn't trust, because trust means you can't prove it, but you're willing to take the chance. Pop *knew.* Gus was absolutely my dog and both of them knew it. I didn't know it, not like Pop knew it, but I believed it with all the might of a child's heart. If there was someone I loved as much as my Pop, it was Gus.

I buried Gus in the Brightwood, in a clearing where I used to play with Argestes, the unicorn. I cleaned Gus thoroughly and wrapped him in a white shroud. Rusty helped me dig. It takes a while to dig a grave, and the perpetual summer's day in that place advanced to afternoon before we were done.

I glimpsed a unicorn among the trees, but Argestes wouldn't come out. I think it was because of Rusty. He'll still show himself and run around, but he won't let me touch him anymore. I have some regrets about that.

Come to think of it, Argestes might have been avoiding the grave. Unicorns—like most faerie beings—don't really understand death. They get the general idea, but it's not something they understand. When someone stops moving forever, it puzzles them. I think it has to do with being a unilateral entity. They don't have bodies and souls. Their existence is a single thing, not divided into parts. You kill one and they're gone, I think. They stop being. For them, that's the only death they understand. Having a corpse is strange because if the body is present, the person is. Sometimes faerie creatures explode in light, or crumble to dust, or whatever, but you don't get an intact corpse.

I laid Gus down in his hole. I scooped loose, black earth in on top of him. I patted it down, leveled it, and put back lumps of sod on top. It wasn't perfect, but in a year the clearing would be exactly as it was.

"No marker?" Rusty asked.

"The only person who will ever visit this grave knows where it is."

Rusty started to speak, stopped, decided against it. We stood there while the afternoon turned to evening. Rusty put his arm around my shoulders, carefully, in case I objected in a non-verbal way.

"I'm sorry."

"It's not your fault."

"I mean, I'm sorry he's dead. I liked him."

"You did?"

"I learned to. When he started to like me. We worked out most of our differences."

"Did you ever sort out who was the alpha?"

"Nope. I maintained I was. He maintained he was. We agreed to disagree."

"I'm glad you worked something out, at least."

"By the way… uh… is a unicorn lurking in the trees?"

"Yes. Whatever you do, don't chase him."

"I'm stupid, not a fool. It's a nice place," he added.

"I always liked it here. Gus did, too. He thought it smelled better than anywhere else."

"He was right."

"Pop says it's because there are no humans."

"Could be."

"He's a cynic."

"Doesn't mean he's wrong."

"Don't you start."

"Sorry."

We fell silent for a time. The shades of night drew close and the forest noises changed.

"I'm sorry about Uncle Dusty," I said.

"For what?"

"When he said he could find lots of you, but Gus was unique."

"Eh. He's a demigod. I never know what to think about anything he says. I'm hoping I can stay on his good side."

"It was still kind of insulting. And he didn't mention the important parts."

"What important parts?"

"He could find other copies of you, but not *you*. You're the one I know. You're my friend. That makes you unique. All the other variations of you may be the same to *him*, but they wouldn't be the same to *me*."

Rusty was silent for a bit. Stars came out and a laughing breeze murmured through the trees.

"Need a shoulder to cry on?" Rusty asked.

"I have no tears."

"Oh?"

"They'll turn to steam."

"Is this a metaphor for how you've got a fiery hatred?"

"Yes."

"Ah. So, what do you want to do?"

"Beat Alden nearly to death and burn him the rest of the way."

Rusty bit his lip, started to speak, bit his lip again.

"Comment?" I asked, as sweetly as I knew how.

"This seems… I mean… Is this because of Gus?"

"Partly."

"I don't understand. First you want to punish Alden. Then you wand to imprison Alden—"

"It was always all about the consequences. He needed to know he was opposed so he would back off on his psychic rampage."

"Okay, so it's even simpler. You wanted to punish him. Your Uncle Dusty convinced you he had to die. Now you're eager to kill him. Over Gus?"

I rubbed my temples and restrained myself. I was feeling ready to explode and Rusty was provoking me. Not really and not intentionally, but I wasn't in the most stable of emotional places. I held up a finger for silence while I took a moment. I marshalled my thoughts and considered what I wanted to say and how to say it.

"Listen. Alden beats up my Pop and steals his stuff. None of that is permanent. None of that—in the greater scheme of things—is more than an inconvenience. Pop gets better in a matter of hours, at most. It's offensive, but it's like banging your funny bone. It hurts, but it goes away. The stuff? Pop replaced it so fast it's like it never happened. The theft, itself, was offensive, but it was temporary, ephemeral. A passing annoyance. Getting slapped in the face and or spat on in public is temporary, too. It still makes one angry and possibly vindictive. For what he did to Pop, Alden deserved a beating, at the very least. Maybe not an outright murder, but he deserved to get his ass handed to him, deeply tenderized and fire-grilled.

"That's the sort of mental geography I was in when we had our come-to-Dusty moment. Alden is a power, one who would try to dominate the world and spread out to other worlds. Being a hybrid of angel and human, he might someday be a power among the universes. Uncle Dusty knows this stuff better than I do. He says Alden has to be stopped. My plans to stop him involved trapping him, imprisoning him, but doing so seemed impractical. Reluctantly, I had to agree with Uncle Dusty. This guy is a bad person and he has to die. I didn't like it—I'm not Farashan the Assassin, in the service of the Lord of Nuclear Fire—but I agreed it had to be done.

"Now this son of celestial has killed one of the best friends I've ever had. And the key word here is 'killed.' *Killed.* Dead. No last-minute resuscitation, no resurrection, no miracle, no getting him back. It's not temporary. It's not something he can take back. It's not something he can replace. This is final, eternal, forever.

"He's carved a piece of my heart out of my chest and beaten it to a pulp on the living room floor. I've buried it because I can never get it back. Even if I go with Uncle Dusty's offer to give me Gus's descendant, it won't be Gus. *The* Gus.

"So, yeah. I was on board with killing him because Uncle Dusty convinced me. He talked me into it, proved it was necessary, and I did not make the decision lightly. Now this happened. I don't care what anybody has to say, what reasons are given, what arguments are made, what persuasion is used. All Uncle Dusty got was my agreement. Now Alden's got my *enthusiasm.*"

"I understand," Rusty said. "I can't understand perfectly, since I'm not in your shoes, but I think I can imagine something close. Let's go kill the bastard."

Journal Entry #53

It's not impossible to track a gate connection. You have to have the physical gate, of course, and it helps a lot if it hasn't been used and if the signature is recent. I know how to do it, although I'm not sure how good I am at it.

Rather than go immediately to Iowa and start fiddling with the mirror, though, I had a sneaking suspicion about where Alden might be. Rusty reported there were no signs of Alden leaving Pop's house. I trusted The Nose. What did that leave? The closet? It only went one place. The mirror? Yes, that seemed most likely. But the mirror could take him anywhere—or, from his perspective, any*when* he wanted. Where and when? What would he be looking for?

He had a long-term injury from being shot. It was a constant problem, but he was coping with it. Now Gus tore him up fairly well, too. Add to his wounds the problems of exhaustion, thirst, and maybe hunger. Factor in the emotional impact of the recent loss of his tektite amplification and the feeling of vulnerability that had to come with it. He had to be feeling puny, hurt, and tired—maybe even afraid. He would be looking for someplace safe, someplace to rest, lick his wounds, and build up his power. He would want someplace familiar, someplace where he had all the advantages.

Using Uncle Dusty's powerplant, I brute-forced a micro-gate into a very specific Earth. To wit: Cameron's room. It was perfectly intact, but *this* time there were dried bloodstains everywhere.

Of course.

Alden knows that closet door. He knows that world. He still has some level of influence in it from when he was there before. When seeking the familiar, where else would he go? He went to Iowa and got into a fight with Gus. Meanwhile, I checked the mirror and didn't find him in Cameron's house. Then I set about carefully picking over the signatures in the mirror and the micro-gate while he used Pop's mirror to go to Cameron's house.

I retargeted the gate, parking it in the kitchen. There was a bit of a mess. Someone's dinner was partially eaten, right off the kitchen counter. The rest was cold and dry. There were also kitchen knives lying around. These were marked by heat and gunked with burned blood and skin. Gus might have got him better than Uncle Dusty realized if Alden resorted to cauterization to stop the bleeding.

Good.

"That's where he went," Rusty agreed, watching over my shoulder in the mirror. "You were right."

"Yes."

"So, we go there and do nasty things to him?"

"Yes, but we go back to my Midtown apartment and then to Iowa on the way."

"What did we forget?"

"Nothing. I want to cut off any easy escape. He knows about those closets and those mirrors. I don't want to find out he's learned enough about them to go back whenever he pleases. Plus, my plans require the psychic telescope and other things Pop built."

"Ah."

So we detoured on our way back to Shasta. If Alden tried to access either mirror, he was going to have a hard time. I disconnected the enchantment—well, routed around portions of it, much the same way I did with my werewolf detector—so it didn't help with a connection. The mirrors were still frames, but any energy costs were paid entirely from the other end.

I brought them back to a reactor world. I cleared out an office and mounted them on the ceiling. Below, I laid out a dense arrangement of pointy things called caltrops. I hoped he was in a hurry and diving through the gate if he decided to use them. As for breaking out of the room, I was sure he could do it, but it would take a moment. If he was lucky, he would encounter Uncle Dusty's avatar. If he hung around for too long, picking spikes out of his flesh, he would encounter Uncle Dusty and *me*.

The telescope, on the other hand, wasn't something Alden knew about or understood. He wasn't going to make use of it, but he would regret the fact I did. It was the only thing I had capable of getting a line on him. Only one survived, so I couldn't triangulate his position, but I could get a definite direction. It wasn't the best way to target him, but I didn't need to know his exact location. This wasn't going to be subtle. It was going to be *brutal*.

Rusty and I appeared in what used to be the ash-coated basement of my old house in Shasta. I knew there was no one around, but I also wasn't taking chances. We were out of line-of-sight for anyone not actually standing beside the hole. This let us arrive, sort ourselves out, and confirm with eyeballs there was no one around.

"Okay. Now we're here, what's the plan?"

"We set up shop."

"What, here?"

"Exactly here."

Rusty looked around at the muddy basement floor and up at the open sky.

"And what, pray, are we going to do here?"

"We're going to hunt Alden down like a rabbit."

"That's one dangerous rabbit."

"Fine. We hunt him down like a vorpal rabbit. I can be a necromancer if I have to. You can be Arthur. I have hand grenades."

"That's not how you hunt a rabbit. You chase them down and dig them out."

"As a wolf, maybe you do. So we hunt him like a tiger and dig a trap for him. But we don't stop. We push him and we keep pushing him, hard. We don't let up on him, ever, until he stops being a person and starts being a pile."

"A pile of what?"

"Meat will do. Ashes are preferred. If you eat him and crap him on the lawn, I'm okay with it. It all depends on what gets him."

"Got it. What do we do first?"

"Fortify our position."

"Is there a particular reason we need to fortify a... a hole in the ground? Instead of, I dunno, finding someplace with a roof?"

"Yes."

"Can I ask what it is?"

"There are several reasons. The main reason is because Alden knows where this place is."

"And he knows it's a ruin, so it's the last place he'll look. Got it."

I didn't correct him.

I checked over the property while Rusty prowled the woods. We didn't have anybody near enough to bother us. As far as we could tell, the last person who came out here was me, setting up to grab a partial statue. The place was badly neglected and growing wild. Even the flowerbeds had gone mostly to grass.

Uncle Dusty was very helpful from his end. I used the gates in a reactor world to find and grab all the equipment we needed. We shuttled everything through his reactor world on the way to Shasta. We took quite a chunk out of his magical power field, which cut down on the efficiency of all the dynamos. On the upside, I also made sure he was deploying the power conversion panels correctly. As he kept adding them, he would replace all the power we used and more. Raising the intensity of the magical field without drawing on the reactor would increase the dynamos' efficiency.

It was a good investment, especially since he could repeat the process on all his reactor worlds. He could also juggle which of his worlds were ticking faster than others, making the upgrade happen more quickly.

It was a good thing we had his support. We would have had a terrible time trying to work with the power available at the Shasta end. Just getting to and from would have been difficult. And as for a solar power farm in Shasta, Pop's array was gone, *poof*, when we left. I had to start from scratch. I couldn't even use the power line and an electromagical transformer. The power to the property wasn't connected.

Nevertheless, we did set up pretty quickly. I had batteries—both magical and electrical—I could shuttle back and forth, for one thing. We also discovered how to move magical power through a gate. It's tricky.

Zapping magical force through the wormhole tends to feed the wormhole spells rather than transmit anything. If you exceed that threshold, however, you start destabilizing the wormhole. This collapses the gate connection, so it costs you a ton of power to send a few metaphorical ounces. Using a magically-generated spatial instability as a pipe through which to pour raw magic is a lot like using toilet paper to transport water. It soaks up a lot, then comes apart.

"Story of My life," Uncle Dusty told me. "I have a similar problem all the time."

"Yeah, but I was taught to cheat."

"Oh? What do you have in mind?"

"You have access to orichalcum wire, do you not?"

"Of course. I have to have it to build replacement dynamos."

"I'll need a spool, please, of a fairly heavy gauge."

I set up a couple of mini-gates, threaded the wire through it, and used the wire as a conductor. The gate spells ran normally, the wormhole stayed stable, and power came out the Shasta end without much fuss at all. Then we ramped up the power and the whole thing collapsed on us.

Something sticking through a wormhole when it collapses normally gets shoved out one end or the other. The collapse of one gate causes a wave effect from it down the extradimensional length of the wormhole. This means it tries to shove things out rather than sever them. If you've got the thing in question mounted firmly and are prepared to force the issue, yes, a collapsing wormhole gate can cut something in two, but usually it spits it out.

Not so when you're collapsing the wormhole from the inside—such as when you overload the gate by feeding too much power through it. It spaghetti-sucks instead. Wire slurped into both gates until the collapse was complete.

Where did it go? Dunno. Some random world? Into the great Void of Chaos? Not a clue.

"Needs insulation," Dusty suggested, once we opened the gate again.

"That's a problem for another day. It worked pretty well in low-voltage mode. It's not a high-power connection, but it is like a normal power outlet. It'll do to run the equivalent of power tools while I get set up here."

"All right. Go ahead. Set it up again."

Once I had a steady supply, I started chucking out power panels as fast as I could fire the spell-gem. They would only be useful during the day, but I needed a bigger power source. I made doubly sure, though, of the destruct sequence in the panels. I wanted them on a hair trigger.

And, thinking about it, I realized I'd forgotten the panels back on my Earth, in Manhattan. I opened a small gate above the Corinthian, kicked the self-destruct on the panels, and watched them disintegrate. Good. The last thing I needed was to find a bunch of magically-sensitive vampires were using them.

Rusty, meanwhile, did the majority of the work in assembling an inflatable dome over the basement. I swiped it for him from another Earth. The instructions said it could be set up by one man, but I think the instructions were written by a man at a desk. Still, Rusty did get it mostly sorted before he called me in to help.

The dome had two layers. Once it inflated, the gap between them was filled with a two-component foam. This hardened into a structure tough enough to last a hundred years and stand up to thunderstorms, blizzards, hailstones, hurricanes, tornadoes, small meteorites, and other minor weather disturbances.

There would definitely be bad weather. If necessary, I would arrange it. I didn't need it, but it was my first choice.

For less environmental, more bullet-type threats, Rusty and I are also painting a sticky resin over the outside of the dome, then applying a ballistic fabric to it, gluing it in place. The dome isn't rated against bullets, so I'm uncertain about the ballistic qualities, but adding a dozen layers of ballistic cloth around the ground floor won't hurt. We'll spray the whole thing with a layer of epoxy afterward. It won't be pretty, but it will work.

The basement is now covered over. We've done the shoveling and propping and put in a few beams and so forth, so we've got good flooring. We have a home base! As for the rest of the place, we've already cleared away the remains of the former house—what was left of the portico, mostly—and cleaned up. However, I specifically forbade any mowing of the yard. Judging from the look on Rusty's face, he wanted to ask but manfully suppressed the impulse. I smiled at him and winked.

There is method to my madness. There better be. I get it from Pop.

Only after setting up the shelter and sorting out the property did we set up the insides. Shasta was in an era before cable television, so a television antenna was necessary. I wanted the news, all of it. I got us a radio receiver and a television, one with a split-screen, multi-monitor for all the available video. I wasn't concerned about anachronistic equipment, so I probably got a better picture than the guys in the studio.

Nothing in the news screamed "Alden" to me, but I didn't worry. If he was recuperating, it meant we could be more prepared. I was hurrying, though, because I wanted to be ahead and stay ahead, or to catch up and get ahead.

Fortress? Check. Monitoring? Check. Attack spell? Coming right up...

The spell I set up used the telescope as an aiming device, much like a rifle uses a scope.

Before, when I was considering how to wear down Alden's defenses, I was hesitant to try hammering on them until they collapsed. The process would take time and tons of power, but the real issue was how obvious it would be. It would give him a clear line on where the trouble came from. He might not notice the micro-gate in the phone he stole—

it's a magical device, so he expects to sense magic there—but frequent, regular, magical attacks, all coming from the same direction? He couldn't miss them.

Just like, with a telescope to target him, *I* couldn't miss.

Imagine, if you will, a circle saw, one of those electrical hand-held things. It spins a saw-toothed wheel at great speed so you can push the whole gadget over a piece of wood and leave behind a long, straight cut.

Now take away the motor and handle. Leave only the blade, hovering there, spinning madly. Spin it faster. Now make it intangible and invisible. It will pass harmlessly through anything and everything. No one will even know it went whizzing through them because it's harmless.

The telescope, because of its enchantments, always aims itself directly at Alden. So we fire this metaphysical circle saw blade down the line defined by the telescope at ludicrous speed. It goes hurtling away like a runaway truck tire with teeth, screaming through the ether as it carves through space and time on its way down the line we've defined.

Until, that is, it hits a magical field. Not just any magic—the world has magic in it, and this spell will have the equivalent of ram scoops on either side in order to have the maximum possible range and force. Let's target *intense* magical fields. That sounds like a good choice, doesn't it? We may not be able to detect magical radiations from Pop's devices, but when we run into the Invisible Man, we know where he is.

Then the voracious truck-tire of saw-bladed teeth explodes on a magical level, trying to blow anything magical into frittering little fragments. It won't hurt the physical object, of course. It can't hurt anything physical; it's not built for that. It's meant to attack other spells, to shatter them, and to force whatever generated them to go to greater efforts in rebuilding them.

I'm not sure I can design a spell to attack the physical structure of a magical object. I don't know if it's possible. I think the usual method is to drastically overload the spell and destroy the object as a side effect. I know there's no hope in hell I can pull that off against one of Pop's gadgets. What I can do is wear the batteries down until it's out of power. No power in the universe can prevent it.

Unless…

Well, there is one way. Alden will have to come out here and stop me.

See? I *said* there was method to my madness.

I set the wheels in motion, if you'll forgive the pun, one about every hour. As I added more power panels, we could fire more frequently. The power panels were fine for daylight assaults, but they also had to save enough power in crystal energy banks to keep firing through the night, as well.

Even if Alden sat down on a magical reactor, at least I'd ruin his sleep. When these things went off, it was like a feeling you get when… when…

Have you ever blasted out of a sound sleep, nearly sitting up, wide awake in an instant and wondering what it was that woke you? Maybe you heard a gunshot, or a car backfiring, or a transformer blew up two blocks over, or something. Boom! Instantly awake and wondering what did it. Imagine this sort of thing happening every hour. All day. All night. Non-stop.

And, as time goes on, the assaults come more quickly. After a while, it's every fifty-nine minutes. As I produce more panels and charge more crystals, it's every fifty-eight minutes. Then fifty-seven…

How long would you let this go on?

I had Rusty go into the front yard and start digging post-holes around the circle drive. I kept working on expanding the solar panel arrays, monitoring the power storage inside the fortress, and still found time for the most powerful weather-working I'd ever done in my life.

I was proud of my weather spell. I'm not sure Pop would be proud of it, but he would be proud of me. I put a lot of effort into it. It was a real beast of a spell, built to grab the local weather and get immediate results. It also had unique bits for control I didn't learn from Pop. I had a backup plan, but I really wanted the weather to do the work.

Journal Entry #54

The very next day, we got results. Alden did *not* like what was happening, so we had a visitor. Technically, the visitor is still here, but as soon as I can open a gate to dump the body through...

I don't enjoy killing people, but sometimes I agree it's necessary. Any brain-drained zombie spy Alden sends is already a dead man walking. They're animated shells, not people.

Rusty came inside, still dripping blood. At least he shook outside.

"I shouldn't enjoy that as much as I do," he admitted.

"What?"

"The fighting. The killing."

"Something I meant to ask. You once mentioned how being a wolf has an effect on your thought processes. Care to elaborate?"

"There are a lot of older wolves who talk about the spirit of the wolf, as though you can only be a wolf through some mystical inner journey. I don't agree. Things are different when I'm in another form. I'm seeing differently, smelling differently. All my senses have changed, so how I react to the world changes. I don't feel any different—I'm still me—but I do feel a more... instinctive?" He shook his head. "There's an impulsive feeling. I react quicker, but I don't think about it as much. It might be different if I was a country wolf and spent most of my time on paws.

"Now, about the zombie. Is this why I've been patrolling the property line?"

"I suspected there would be someone of the sort coming to visit," I admitted.

"A scout? But how would he know to send someone here?"

"It's pretty easy to figure out if you're the one being bombarded. The telescope automatically tracks Alden and points directly at him, but the line works both ways. Anyone with a feel for the forces would know which way the blow came from, much the same as if I hit you with a baseball. At noon he gets hit from *this* direction. Make a line on the map. Around dinnertime, he gets hit from *that* direction. Make another line on the map. Where they intersect should be roughly the origin of the assault. And, once he looks at the map, he'll recognize *exactly* where he needs to look. This is where he lost a fistfight with Pop."

"So there's history here. Got it. What's next for the mind-controlling half-angel?"

"Well, under normal circumstances, I imagine Alden would wander around, gather followers, build up a sizable force, and attack. The only trouble with this plan is the near-constant bombardment. We're down to a headache-inducing forty-three-minute interval between shots. I don't know about anyone else, but *I* would consider this to be an *intensely* urgent matter."

"I thought you were planning to reduce the time by a minute per day?"

"I forgot to factor in the power outlet from the reactor world. I'm making a lot more progress than I anticipated."

"Makes sense. Another question. Why should Alden care so much? Aside from a headache, I mean. It's not actually hurting him. Or have I misunderstood?"

"The headache is a side effect. He won't be sleeping more than forty minutes at a time—less, as I add more panels. Which reminds me. I need to prepare another big crystal."

"Do I get to help?"

"Sure."

"Fantastic. Now, get back to why Alden will be insane with eagerness to get you to stop bouncing your basketball off the wall of his mental bedroom."

"It's a little worse than that, but the personal issues aren't the main ones. What makes it doubly—possibly quadruply or octuply urgent—is the way the magical protection devices keep failing after every hit. It takes a little time to fire off the low-level cloaking magic, to say nothing of the higher-order healing spells.

"I'm surprised they can manage as well as they do on an Earth world," I added. "I should have expected it. Pop is the most powerful wizard I've ever met."

"And you're his apprentice. He impresses you as much as you impress normal people. And by 'normal' I mean 'werewolves.' Think about that while I try not to think about your father. So, Alden's stolen gadgets stop working when you hit them? This is important?"

"Extremely important. I do a location spell, now and again, but I'm keeping most of our reserves for the assault. The cloaking spells keep starting up again, but maybe Alden is wizard enough to manually gather energies, feed them into the enchanted devices, and sort of kick-start them into motion. If he does, it's something he has to do every forty minutes or so. It takes him time to do it, and he knows it. During that window, I could be targeting him with anything! He doesn't know we're burning our power as fast as we can to keep up a constant assault."

"But... holy ground?"

"Yes, yes, yes. Scrying spells still give only glittering static. Big deal. Let him hide in there. He doesn't know I can't see him. All he knows is I can *find* him." I checked the charge on the Astral Tire of Terror spell.

"Hang on a second. I want to get a shout ready."

"A shout?"

"A mental projection pulse—sort of a psychic shout, amplified and focused."

"Sure."

Rusty waited while I imprinted a mental projection into a crystal, tuned it to Alden's channel, and waited. The latest magical flaming tire of doom spun invisibly out of the launcher, shot away into the distance, and detonated.

Approximately a mile away, straight-line distance. Not bad. It roughed in well with the location of the church. It wasn't exact enough for hand grenades, not even for a cruise missile, but it would work as an artillery grid square.

Once the magic-disrupting kaboom did its thing, I fired the new spell, sending out a powerful psychic pulse:

"*There you are!*"

It was clearly my thought, quite powerfully sent, and deliberately focused on him. It drove home the point like hammering a railroad spike. I knew there was no way I could target him with any accuracy, but *he* didn't know it.

I couldn't see his reaction, nor did I include a return-message function. I don't know if he crapped himself, or if he tried to send back a sizzling-hot bolt of pure psychic force, or what. I like to think he needed a change of underwear.

"Okay, what just happened?" Rusty asked.

"I poked the bear."

"Is that wise?"

"I *want* him to react. I want him to come here and make me stop doing it. His plans have been shot down. His escape into another time has not proven fully successful. And now someone he thought not worth his attention is *actively hunting him.*

"I can imagine many different ways he might feel, but I'm hoping really hard he's both frightened and angry. I want to provoke him into doing something stupid and he hasn't. Not yet."

"And if he shows up with the cavalry and a couple of Marine divisions?"

"It'll take him a long time to influence people into doing that on American soil. He can't afford to take his time and do it right. I'm pushing him hard, so he *has* to do something *now*, which means he'll have to show up with whoever he can scrape up, and he might have to show up personally. He knows I can cut off his control to his minions—remember in the vacant lot? He'll need to supervise, to counter any control I might gain over them. I want him here to do exactly that. That's the goal. That's the plan."

"I guess I'll finish putting up the barbed wire."

"No, work on planting the posts along the edges, around the circle drive. I'll help tomorrow. I'll also handle the barbed wire. I don't want the fences finished, just well started."

"Huh?"

"Trust me."

"Can do. Care to remove bloodstains for me?"

"Sure."

Journal Entry #55

Alden was hesitant to drop by with a bundt cake and welcome me back to the neighborhood. A man in a Bell Telephone truck came down the driveway, halted at the gate, and got out. He scratched his head, examined the clipboard, and finally opened the gate. He left the truck where it was and walked up to me.

I was driving another metal reinforcement post for the barbed-wire fence. It would be more than one fence, really. The posts ran around the inside edge of the circle driveway, then the outside edge. If completed, the fence would act as a choke, forcing anyone coming in the gate to travel only on the gravel drive.

I laid down the sledgehammer and wiped my forehead. The man politely touched the brim of his cap and turned it into a wave. He eyed the rough dome of the field structure where the house used to be. It wasn't architecture he'd seen before and likely wouldn't, not for at least a century.

"Good morning, Ma'am. I'm from the phone company."

"Good morning to you," I returned. "How can I help you?"

"Sorry to bother you, but I got a work order to connect a phone line?"

"Oh? So soon?" I asked. I was surprised, but I rolled with it. *I* didn't ask for a phone line, but someone did.

"Yes, Ma'am. I was wondering if I had the right place. I didn't see an address on the mailbox, just a route number."

"May I see the work order?"

He handed me the clipboard. His movements, intonation, and demeanor suggested he was a Perfectly Normal Person who got orders from his boss. I double-checked, anyway. A cursory examination said he wasn't tampered with. A pawn, not a zombie.

"Yes, this is the place. We've always had a problem with people finding it. The postal codes are a bit odd out here. I think the original phone lines came up along over there," I pointed. "Anything I can do to help?"

"I'll go look."

He went to examine the situation and I went back to driving posts. Rusty did most of them for me, so I figured to be done with post-work today. Tomorrow, there would be barbed wire. Not a lot, but a good beginning, especially up near the entry gate.

"Ma'am?"

"Yes?"

"I've got phone wire almost all the way up to the... the... the big dome thing, no problem. I'm gonna need to drill a hole, run a line in through it, that sort of thing, but it don't have no overhang I can get under. First time it rains, it's gonna leak."

"But the telephone service is turned on?"

"Oh, the switchboard has your number, yeah." He scribbled it down and handed it to me. "I don't see a good way to run you a line. A line, yeah, can do. But not a *good* way."

"I'll take care of it. My Pop is an electrical engineer and handyman. I'm sure there's a way to make a watertight opening and run the wire through. It's a simple parallel pair, joined up there on the pole, right?"

"Uh?" he asked, surprised. "Yes, Ma'am."

"Then you've done your job. I'll tell Pop and he'll sort it out for me."

"If you say so, Ma'am. Sorry I couldn't be more help."

"You've been wonderfully helpful, sir. Do have a nice day."

Once he was gone, I ran the line myself. We still had more ballistic cloth, resin, and epoxy sealant. Not only was the tiny hole I drilled barely big enough for the wire, sealing the hole pretty much set the line in permanently.

Rusty and I sat down next to a speakerphone. I wanted him to hear this, in case I missed anything. I wished, right then, that I'd found a replacement for Zeno. An analysis of Alden's voice inflections and any background chatter might be useful, too.

"Hello? Operator?"

"This is the operator. How may I direct your call?"

I asked for the number to the church Alden used to use—and now used again—as his base of operations. Three rings, one request, and less than a minute of waiting.

"Hello."

"Ah, Reverend Alden. And how are we feeling today? I assume you wanted to talk to me?"

I sounded perky and cheerful, bordering on chirpy. He sounded tired. How long since he got more than a short nap? Four days, now? Five?

"You do not know what you are doing, child."

"Really? I put a lot of thought into it. More than you have, at this point. I've got you over a barrel and I'm shooting the fish in it."

"You listen to me," he hissed, and I felt the waves of psychic force wash against my shields like storm-surf on a rocky shore—and with about as much effect. I thought he had to be fairly close to do that, but maybe the fact I could hear him gave his powers the necessary focus to reach farther. Even so, it wasn't his full force, not at this range. Or was it? Was this the best he could do without a necklace full of special tektites?

"I'm listening," I agreed, on my mental guard.

"Your father made a threat," Alden told me. "He made it clear to me the price I would pay if I harmed you. If I left you alone, he would not go back in time to end my existence before I began. I have kept my end of the bargain even when it would have been far, far easier to murder you out of hand. And do not be such a fool as to say I could not have done so!"

So *that* was why Alden kept spying on me, but avoided contact! My Pop. Always looking out for me. Even when he knew he was going to be out of town on business, he made sure to give me every advantage.

"Goodness," I exclaimed. "You do sound upset. Am I to take it, then, you are altering the deal? Or should I pray you don't alter it any further?"

"Your father will have a hard time, I believe, determining your fate if he does not know when you are. Since I now intend to kill you—and I am still here—I believe this is evidence of his inability to keep close track. Or…" he trailed off.

"Or?" I prompted.

"Or I will not find it necessary to kill—" he broke off, grunting, as my latest Wheel of Smacking went spinning down the line to explode around his head. My psychic message projection also went off, this time sending, "*I see you!*"

"It's nice that you might not need to kill me," I said, while he struggled to recover from the momentary assault. "I'd much rather survive our conflict."

"You childish bitch," he snarled. "Cease this assault or I *will* kill you. If you are lucky, I will kill you *quickly!*"

"Hmm. That's an interesting offer. Stop doing something you can't stop me from doing. In exchange for giving up all the work I've done to set it in motion, you promise not to do something you can't do. You think I need you to allow me to live."

"Yes! Stop it! Now!"

"You know, I can feel you trying to command me. You don't have your magic rocks to help, so you can't do it at this range. You're too weak. And you look kind of sick and injured to me. Is the curse on Pop's amulet and ring starting to take its toll?"

"What do you mean?" he asked, guardedly.

"Oh, nothing. It's just they aren't meant for a being like you. You're more resistant to the negative effects than a human, I'm sure, but long-term? I'm surprised you can still breathe, much less walk around. You're even tougher than I thought."

I shifted forward and spoke into the microphone, conspiratorially, seductively.

"But you're slowly dying, Alden. Your stolen powers are killing you. Your magic rocks keep shattering and will continue to shatter as long as I live. You'll never get another three together before I break them. And you'll *bleed*, Alden. I'll *make* you bleed. And you won't sleep again, ever. The spells seeking you out and blasting your brain are fully automatic. They don't need me to operate them. They'll run for a thousand years! You'll slowly go mad. Already your sleep-deprived brain is weakening. Soon, your mind will be so feeble you won't be *able* to change my mind. *That* is why Pop won't have to unmake you. *I* will drive you insane and watch you waste away, drooling and gibbering, as my mind cuts yours to pieces, before I kill you."

There was a long pause on the line, a silence broken only by heavy breathing.

"Why?" he asked. "I've offended your father, obviously. You, though. What have I done to you? A debt of honor for mistreating your father?"

"Does it matter?"

"If I am to die," he suggested, persuasively—damn, but he could switch gears in an instant!—"would it not be better, from your perspective, to make sure I know exactly why I am being murdered?"

I gritted my teeth, but I was resolved. I did not waver, despite his language.

"Very well. Hurting Pop was one thing. He got better. You made powerful enemies by that action, but I interceded, claiming the right to punish you. You were also a thief. That, too, made us enemies. My things I have recovered from your underground lair and punished you for your theft in the process. The curses Pop prepared for thieves are obviously affecting you, so I do not need to steal back Pop's items—they are their own punishment, more potent and destructive than the curses on the tombs of Egypt!

"The way you live your life is also offensive to me. You take the free will of people away. You destroy minds. You don't simply steal material things; you strip people of their identities, of their *selves*, and purely to serve your own selfish interests. This, alone, would make us enemies.

"All these things that have offended me are things I wanted to punish you for. There are others who wanted to kill you, but I—perhaps foolishly—resisted this idea. I do not like to kill. I get no pleasure from killing. But this time, I will *take* pleasure in watching you die, in knowing I am the one responsible for your madness and death, because you took from me something you cannot give back. You took the life of my dog."

"Your *dog?*"

"The big, floofy guy at the house in the woods."

"It attacked me!"

"You invaded the house!" I snapped back. "That's what a guard dog *does!*"

Rusty put a hand on my forearm to remind me to be calm. From the way my throat felt raw, I realized I had screamed.

"I apologize for that," Alden said, smoothly. Cool, sincere, slick, greasy.

"I will never accept your apology," I replied, just as smooth and cool. "Listen and understand. It is now a simple case of who dies first. There is no other goal in my life, no other purpose to it. I am going to drive you mad and then kill you—unless you kill yourself, of course, to escape the madness you can already feel creeping in at the edges of your mind. Goodbye, Reverend. Give my regards to whoever claims you."

"Wait!"

"Wait? For what?"

"There is one other option."

"You can't buy your way out of this, Alden."

"No, I was thinking of what I said before."

"Something about Pop?" I asked, doing my best to sound puzzled. I knew what he meant, but you've got to let them deliver their lines. It kind of cements the idea in their heads, unconsciously commits them to the course of action.

"No. The other option is I kill you."

"Ha. Good one. You're already dying. Killing me won't stop the assault. You'd have to literally alter my brain to make it stop—and I don't believe you can. Not anymore. Not after I destroyed your rosary. Not now, after days of sleeplessness and mental fatigue. You're too weak, and growing weaker. Give up and die with whatever dignity you can muster."

I hung up on him without another word. He didn't bother to call back.

"Think he'll go for it?" I asked.

"You mean, do I think he'll rush out here to get into a fight? No."

"It would be nice, though."

"Yeah," Rusty agreed.

"What would you do, in his shoes?"

"I'm thinking I'd forcibly tell the local law there's an armed serial killer out here and send them to get slaughtered. Then, with a bloodbath as an excuse, call in all the neighboring cops, then keep escalating until they send in the National Guard. We can't hold off the military, can we?"

"No, but mobilizing a force takes time, and Alden doesn't have a lot of it. Also, I wasn't kidding about pummeling his brain. I lied to him a lot, I admit, but my psychic powers aren't at their sharpest after a long day and I'm certain he's had the better part of a week to be sleepless, fatigued, and exhausted. Unless he already has all the local constabulary under his thumb, it'll take him quite a while to convince them to go on a frontal assault. Plus, he's got injuries that may or may not be healing, and I have no doubt those are distracting him somewhat."

"So, what do we do?"

"I string barbed wire as a bluff and diversion. Then I think I'll dial back the power on my assault spell launcher. I've knocked down the targets' battery charge, so I can hit him less hard but more often, make sure he can't catch even a decent nap. I'll need another detonation condition, though, now that the cloaking spells are sometimes deactivated. What I should have done is tune it to Alden's psychic signature in the first place..."

"Why bother? Won't the widgets keep re-upping the shields?"

"Yeah, but now he thinks they might be cursed. He might put them away somewhere. He might do it anyway, thinking I'm targeting those instead of him."

"Ah. And your spells aren't targeting them?"

"Not exactly. The telescope is tracking him, acting like sights on a rifle. The warheads I'm firing only go off, though, in proximity to something magical. The spells will currently keep heading straight at him, but if he loses the amulet and ring, the warheads go right through and off into nowhere, uselessly. I need to re-target so they detonate on either the shields or when they detect his psychic signature."

"Makes sense," Rusty agreed. "I still have a lot to learn about this magic stuff."

"So do I."

"You want to work on that while I string wire? Even if he hops in a car and burns rubber immediately, how fast can he be here?" Rusty asked.

"On these twisty roads? It'll be a while. You'd get there faster than a car by running in a straight line. Okay. I'll watch the telescope and keep a scrying spell on the highway. I might have convinced him he doesn't have a second to spare, but I'm reasonably sure he'll want to collect as much help as his current powers will permit. We definitely have fifteen minutes. We probably have until tomorrow. But he could show up anytime between."

"I'll try not to wear myself out," he assured me.

"Good. And don't string much wire. Put some along the inside edge, maybe, between the house and the outer gate."

"Shouldn't I get as far as I can?"

"No. Trust me. I want it to be an inconvenience, not a barrier."

"I don't understand."

"Good. Then Alden won't even suspect."

The telescope kept swinging, but nobody showed up. Judging by the rate of swing and the distance of the spell-detonations, Alden was out and about. I would have tried to keep track of him in the intervals between cloaking spell restarts, but I had more pressing matters. Besides, I had his approximate distance. He wasn't anywhere close by and Rusty was on guard, which meant I could work without fear of interruption.

I worked out the psychic sensor on my bombardment spell and placed it in the matrix. I also scaled back the power buildup before firing. I got the launches down to fifteen minutes, but I wanted them to keep getting faster. Once I got them down to five minutes, I would start raising the power again. I wasn't sure this whole plan would take so long, but it's good to plan ahead.

The panels charged the battery crystals and the spell. I used the power line from Uncle Dusty's world with my panel-making spell-gem and built more panels. Progress wasn't too quick, though. I took a break, checked on Alden with a scrying spell, and discovered he wasn't on holy ground. I actually got a good look at him. He was in the back of a car, riding somewhere. He almost had to be in the back. He was a big, over-muscled brute. His whole body was swollen, making me wonder if all those muscles were tumor tissue, growing out of control. If things kept going the way they were, there would come a day when he would need people to push him around in a wheelchair. How long would it be before he couldn't breathe?

He also had injuries. His face was okay, but his left hand was savaged. Something big, strong, loyal, and brave sank teeth into it and tried to rip it off. Against a human, it would have succeeded. The injury looked fresh, too. Scabs everywhere. I'd have thought they would have at least healed to scar tissue by now, but maybe he wasn't healing properly at all. Pop's radiation poisoning might have really screwed him up.

About then he slapped his right hand through my scrying sensor and the image disappeared.

Oh, well. I could still track him if I chose. I decided to make his life more difficult.

I popped into Uncle Dusty's reactor world and shifted through his linked teleport booths to the fastest. Six large crystals later, I took a nap. When I woke up, I had quite a lot of power to bring home. I did so—having wasted very little time in Shasta—and added them to the battery array.

Dusty sent me a thought through the gate, so I put a scrying spell at both ends. He appeared on a mirror in his avatar form.

"Any idea how much longer this is going to take?"

"I shouldn't think it will be more than a week. Likely it will be much less. He can't keep this up."

"Do you want Me to come over and rough him up?"

"No. This is mine to do. You convinced me it had to be done, so I'm doing it."

"I didn't engage your enthusiasm."

"No, Alden did. And he'll regret it."

"Just be careful. You're making him angry so he'll make a mistake. He's already made you angry. Are you making mistakes?"

"I hope not. I don't think I am."

"Be careful, anyway."

"Yes, Mother."

Uncle Dusty rolled his eyes and waved a hand at the mirror. He frowned.

"How do you shut this thing off?"

I closed the connection, chuckling to myself.

Journal Entry #56

Clouds darkened the sky prematurely, but I have a pretty good feel for when the sun comes up or goes down. It's part of my upbringing. There would have been a bloody glow in the west when Alden arrived, if not for the churning stormclouds. Alden didn't arrive alone. I knew he was coming. The distance my Tires of Terror traveled before detonating kept decreasing. When the spell alarm went off at the head of the dirt road of our driveway, Rusty and I got our guns.

Three farm trucks turned off the public road and rumbled slowly down the long track through the woods. A single car followed them. They all stopped when the first truck reached the gate. They parked where they were and sixty or so men climbed out, all carrying weapons. A few had hunting guns—rifles or shotguns—a few more had farm tools of the vicious-looking sort, and the rest had lengths of wood or pipe.

Rusty and I stood on the brickwork of the front porch as we checked our weapons. It was almost totally black outside, but the truck headlights silhouetted the attackers. We couldn't see them well, but the road to the gate didn't let the trucks aim their headlights at the porch, so they didn't see us too clearly, either. The occasional bit of lightning gave everyone photo-flashes of the larger scene. It didn't matter much to Rusty and I. We were wearing light enhancement sunglasses.

Ha. Sunglasses. In this lighting, they made everything look as bright as day.

"Phoebe?"

"They're controlled. Alden did a lot of spadework on the people in this area the first time he was here. Even in his reduced state, throwing together suicide troops wouldn't be hard. I am surprised he could get so many, though. I was guessing about half of this."

"Why have they stopped? Shouldn't they ram through the gate and drive right up?"

"They probably heard about the pit trap."

"What pit trap?"

"Local legend. And, let me tell you, it was *legen*—wait for it—*dary*. Don't worry about it."

"How about I worry about what they're going to do?"

"How about we start shooting?"

Rusty worked the bolt on his weapon, shifted forward on the brick steps, and braced. I did much the same.

Our shooting styles are very different. I took careful aim at one guy and put a highly-specialized, extremely expensive round through not only his head but also everything in a line behind it. Blood and brains followed the projectile and the shockwaves inside the skull did the owner no good whatsoever. He might not be dead, technically, but his brain was in no shape to consider alternatives.

For the technically-minded, it was a high-power, discarding-sabot round with a tungsten-iridium long-rod penetrator. After the sabot fell away, my .223 rounds were reduced to something more like a single flechette. It didn't make large holes, but it made holes all the way through everything. There was no practical way to "take cover." You might not be visible behind the truck, but you could still be shot!

Rusty, by contrast, is bigger than I am, bulkier, and heavier. His school of shooting states there is no kill like overkill. He took my shot as the signal, squeezed his trigger, and held it. In seconds, he emptied an extended magazine of .338 into the oncoming horde. I put one down. He staggered half a dozen. A couple of them fell, but I could feel the psychic whip of Alden's mind forcing them on. So what if it's a fatal injury? You're not dead, yet! Get up and get moving!

Rusty flicked his weapon with a twist, tossing out the empty magazine even as he drew a fresh one. He slapped it in and repeated the process, chewing gobbets out of more zombies with his automatic fire. I didn't mind. It slowed them down immediately and would kill them rapidly, maybe rapidly enough. He loves to hand out massive amounts of damage with heavy, expanding rounds, inflicting so much trauma that the biological machines shut down. The only way he could be happier was with a belt-fed weapon.

As for me, I could go full-auto, but I preferred not to. Semi-auto means the gun fires as fast as I can pull the trigger and the smaller caliber kept the recoil in my comfort zone. So I kept pulling the trigger whenever my sights slid between eyebrows. An armor-piercing round through the heart will kill a living zombie, but it has to bleed to death. This takes a while. Worse, until they actually notice they're dead, they provide cover for the ones behind. Hence my targeting the brain. Alive or dead, it didn't matter. There was nothing left for Alden to command. And, once in a while, a shot would go through one head and score a kill on one farther back.

As a whole, they came for us. The ones in the lead clambered over the property-line fence. It's only a glorified split-rail fence near the gate, for the aesthetic. It's chain link everywhere else. Going over it gave them no trouble at all, but it did keep them from sprinting as a mob. If someone had been thinking, they would have parked farther back. The lead truck wouldn't let them move through the gate easily.

Once over the outer fence, they encountered the beginnings of the barbed wire fence along the inside edge of the circle drive. Under Alden's control, they went around it rather than risk getting tangled up in it. It was faster. They came straight for us through the ankle-high grass inside the circle drive.

If we hadn't started the preemptive fire, they would have massed just inside the gate and advanced as a horde. That would have been a problem. One could argue it still was a problem, but I felt this was closer to manageable. By being strung out, it was a matter of dropping them faster than they could approach, and it wasn't going to happen if all those living zombies charged us as a cohesive unit.

It was still touch and go. Fortunately, it was pretty dark—it didn't matter to Rusty and I—so the ones we dropped were hazards the others had to negotiate. A few tripped, and occasionally tripped others. The rest ran toward us, but we kept knocking down the ones in the lead. Rather, I kept knocking down the ones in the lead. Rusty blew holes in the leaders coming around his end of the barbed wire and took chunks out of anything farther back, too. Automatic fire isn't terribly accurate. Either way, anyone on the ground was a problem for later; it was the mobile ones that concerned us.

I was also pleased about the dozen or so zombies with guns. They spread to either side and used the fence as a shooting rest. I didn't have time to shake my head. I suppose he didn't know any better. Most of Pop's physical defenses don't automatically engage, so how was he to know about deflection spells? And I was dumping a lot of power into the spell launcher. Maybe he thought I didn't have any to spare.

But I did. The deflection spells on Rusty and myself worked, literally, like a charm.

So we ignored their gunfire and kept pumping out rounds. Rusty sprayed, using both hands to ruthlessly control the recoil, even using it to help sweep his arc of fire along the right-hand stream of attackers. I handled the left side and kept dropping them as they came. Pow! Pow! Pow! Once, I even got three with a single shot—a lucky shot, as they lined up perfectly as I fired. Hooray for penetration and neat holes!

Rusty's method was more fun, maybe, but it was also much more ammo-intensive. He killed or wounded a lot of them before he ran out of rounds. When the remaining zombies were almost on us, he set his weapon aside and shifted, going into his hybrid form. Then it was claws and teeth and a lot of snarling.

I stood up, backed up a step, and continued firing. I switched to targeting the zombies farthest away, now, to cut down on the reinforcements while he defended my position. They kept trying to get around him, but I was on the porch—a fairly narrow area—and I was backed up against a wall. In his hybrid form, Rusty was much taller and had more reach. They only struck at him in trying to get away, get around, get past. They wanted—Alden wanted—to get to me.

If Alden had brought a dozen more zombies—or if he'd forgone the guns and used those guys as infantry—I might have had to deal with a melee attack. As it was, I shot a zombie in the head by stabbing him with the barrel and pulling the trigger.

Note to self: this is why they make bayonets.

Rusty grabbed the one behind my guy, dragged it back down to the ground and ripped out the left side of its ribcage. Rusty spat blood and brain fluid, shook himself, and crouched.

I, meanwhile, picked off the gunmen. It was like knocking down ducks in a shooting gallery.

When it was all over, there was nothing but the grumbling thunder, the rumbling engines idling, and the ringing in the ears that comes with firing serious weapons.

"Want to try again tomorrow?" I screamed. I put two rounds into the engine compartment of the car, at the back of the line. I know I didn't get the radiator—I couldn't see it from where I was—but steam started to rise from under the hood. I fired my last two rounds into the wheels I could see, dropped the empty magazine, and loaded my last one.

"Go on, run! I want to see your cute little panicked waddle again! I'll let you go waddle away while I get bigger guns ready! Throw all the zombies you want, Alden! You're losing and you know it!"

The lightning flashed, the thunder growled, and the sky started to spit at us.

Car doors went *ka-chunk!* Gritty footsteps and silhouetted figures moved in front of headlights. I really need an anti-glare function in my night-vision spell. Alden and his two remaining zombies came to the front of their little convoy and stood before the lead truck. I knelt and took aim.

"I have something you want," he called. "Do anything to me, and it will cost you."

I looked up from my sights, wondering what he meant.

"Why don't you come up here and we'll discuss it?" I shouted back.

He looked left and right, along the circle drive. The fenceposts. The bits of fencing already strung. The coils of barbed wire not yet up. The strewn zombies all over the lawn. Clearly, he got here before we could finish with the fencing. The incomplete fencing laid out and designed to force him and his zombies to walk along the gravel drive. If we were planning to force him along the road, the road was the one place he didn't want to go. Whether it was because it would expose them to gunfire for longer or because the road had landmines didn't really matter. The yard was, clearly, the safer option from his point of view.

One of his zombies climbed over the fence and worked the manual latch on the gate. I let him. The trio advanced to the partial fence and went around it, crossing the grass, avoiding the suspiciously-inviting curve of the drive. They stepped carefully over dead zombies. The footing was more treacherous than Alden knew.

About halfway across the lawn, I shouted again.

"That's close enough!"

I didn't want him too close, and by then I could see what he meant about having something I wanted.

Following him, there were two zombies—or, rather, two figures. Their zombification status was uncertain, but one of them was the Reverend Culson. He had a sizable knife. The other figure also had a knife.

It was Cameron.

Alden, standing between them, smiled. *Smiled.* It was a smarmy, self-satisfied, unbearably smug smile.

"I suspected I might have insufficient force to actually take your house, especially after what my spy saw." He gestured with his cane, pointing at Rusty. "That thing is more of a nuisance than I care to dwell on. Oh, do stop looking at me that way, you smelly pile of wet fur. You don't dare try to bite my head off. And you, young lady, don't dare try to blow it off."

"And just why not?" I asked, looking at him through my sights.

"Because I've already programmed these two. It doesn't matter what happens to me. Cameron will—" he broke off, grunting in obvious pain as the spell launcher in the house reached full power and automatically fired again. Rusty and I were close enough to the point of impact that our spells took a bit of a hit. I consciously acted to reinforce them, keep our defenses up. The last thing I wanted was to have our psychic defenses go down. I doubt Alden noticed anything I was doing. He was dealing with a direct hit.

He straightened again after a moment, glaring, but contained it quickly. He really did have something on his mind. Worse, he was right. I wanted Cameron and was prepared to consider negotiating. He settled into his smug smile again.

"I don't suppose I can convince you to shut that off while we talk?"

"Think of it as my way of telling you to not waste my time."

Alden's grip on his cane tightened until I thought he might leave finger marks in the metal handle. But, to give him his due, he never showed it in his face.

"Cameron, as I was saying, will kill himself. He has absolutely no choice in the matter. The good Culson will, of course, assist him in this. Suspenders and belt, if you follow."

"And I presume you'll hand over Cameron in exchange for me turning off the attacking spell?"

"No, no. That would be worse than useless. You would take your beloved boyfriend with the damaged mind and become even more enraged. I could never feel secure again."

"Then what do you *want?*"

"First, put down the gun. You, of all people should be cognizant of the dangers of an accident at this juncture."

He was right, although I hated to admit it. As I stared at him through my sights, I knew it would be very easy to end him. There were a few little problems with that. A Cameron zombie and a Culson zombie. I couldn't deal with both brains, not with Alden right there. Even if Alden wasn't part of it, keeping both zombies from carrying out their programming, at the same time, would be almost impossible. If I were Alden, I would have built powerful structures in their minds to resist just such any tampering. If there was only Cameron as a hostage, maybe…

Without taking the time to overthink it, I switched my aim slightly and blew a neat hole completely through Culson's head. He dropped instantly and started twitching.

"And maybe," I shouted, "I don't want to put it down. How's that grab you?"

Alden pursed his lips, clearly trying to decide if he wanted to make an issue of it and not certain how to do so. He could kill Cameron to show me he meant business, but Cameron was his bargaining chip, his hostage, and his shield. And, almost as obviously, he dismissed the notion of fussing over the loss of Culson. Culson was only another meat puppet, a tool. Not important. If I wanted to blow him away to demonstrate defiance, did it fundamentally change the situation?

"I suppose you feel better now?"

"Much."

"I'm so glad. I assure you I have done nothing to your dear young man's mind that will not wear off in the course of time. It's only a compulsion and a mild suppression of the will. If he lives, it will all fade in a matter of weeks. He will not even require your services in restoring his rather mundane thought processes.

"But before then, you and I will have finished our business. You will undo your father's curse so I can heal my injuries. Then you will surrender yourself to me, utterly and without reservation. In exchange, I will allow your boyfriend to live a normal life. Perhaps even a happy one. Fail me in this and he will die in a very bloody fashion by his own hand."

"You expect me to give up my own life to save his?"

"Yes."

I thought to myself what an arrogant, presumptuous prick Alden was. Then I realized he might not be wrong. That only made it worse. On the other hand, I had the beginnings of an idea. It was a risky idea. A very risky idea. I didn't *like* the idea, but it seemed to be the best of the last of my options.

"How do I know Cameron will really recover?"

"You have my word."

"And?"

"And what?"

"How do I know Cameron will really recover?"

"If you're angling for the opportunity to probe his mind and block the compulsion, the answer is no. I will not permit you to circumvent my offer in such a fashion."

I stayed where I was, crouched behind a rifle, thinking. I'm tempted to say I was thinking furiously, but that's a bit too on the nose.

"I don't have any assurance you're telling anything like the truth. You might keep me and Cameron."

"You have my assurance."

"Which is worthless. Tell you what: Give him to Rusty. Rusty can take him away from here. Then it will be me and you."

"While you are armed? —And do not, please, attempt to assure me I can trust your word. Your mutt takes your boyfriend away, immobilizes him, and then you shoot me. No, I think not."

"All right. Compromise offer. You send Cameron back to your car. He can watch from there. Rusty can back off, too. You've already determined you can't read his mind. I know you have. Admit it."

"I admit it."

"Thanks. With them out of the way, you can take whatever I know—you can try to, anyway. No matter what happens to anyone, I'm not going down without a fight."

"If you win, Cameron dies," he reminded me.

"And? I'm willing to risk my life for him. I'm not willing to put my head down on the block and let you take it. If I can beat you, you won't be able to stop me from blasting Cameron hard enough to stun him. While you're able to block me, I can't stop him from killing himself. It's a risk I'm willing to take."

"I see your point." He considered it for several seconds as raindrops pattered gently down. He brushed water from his face and nodded. "All right. I agree."

"Just to be clear, if you win, you'll have your hands full dealing with what you find in my head before it gets away. True?"

"Yes."

"Which means Rusty can grab Cameron and leave. Rusty has a powerful ward on him, so you can't control him psychically. He can subdue Cameron if he has to and you'll be too busy and too far away to stop him physically. If you win, there's my assurance your word is good. Yes?"

"Agreed."

"Rusty?" I asked, quietly, still not taking my sights off Alden.

"Don't like it," he snarled. His hybrid form can talk, but it sounds like something from the dark forest, thick-voiced and guttural.

"I'm not asking you to like it. I'm asking you to do whatever it takes to care for Cameron. I'll take care of Alden. You *stay away* from him, as far away as you possibly can. Trust me?"

"Yes."

"Then sit down and be ready to move aside *fast*. You don't want to be between us when the riot starts."

Rusty shifted into his wolf form. He padded down to the driveway and crouched, as though ready to spring at Alden. He was also low enough to not be in danger if I chose to shoot, and could easily go left or right to get out of the line of fire.

Alden, seeing Rusty shift out of his overgrown combat-monster form, took it as a gesture of good faith. In a manner of speaking, it was de-escalating the situation. Cameron picked up the knife from the dead Culson. With a knife in either hand, he crossed his arms and walked back toward the gate. I kept Alden covered, watching his smug face in the scope while I tracked Cameron with my naked eye.

When Cameron almost reached the gate, I thumbed the magnification up on my scope, shifted my aim, and held my breath. He stepped around the gatepost, as he had to do, moving exactly through the space I knew he would. He put himself perfectly in my sight picture.

The cervical vertebrae are numbered one through seven. Number four is generally right under the edge of the jaw. The placement makes it possible to punch a neat hole into the back of the neck, through the throat, and out the front without taking off someone's face in the process. It helps if you have a little elevation, too, for the angle, which was another good reason to be up a couple of steps on the porch.

I had to hit him high. I couldn't remember which spinal nerves controlled his arms and hands. If I could put a bullet cleanly through the exact center of his neck, he'd simply be paralyzed. More paralyzed than before he met me, in fact, but alive. I've had a lot of experience in fixing neurological problems in the upper spine and brainstem. I made a special study of it. If I didn't kill him, I could fix him.

My aim was dead on. Cameron dropped like a puppet with his strings cut. It was a good, clean puncture, straight through the back of his neck and out the front. The hole in his throat meant he could still drown in his own blood, but it would take quite a while.

There were a lot of things suddenly wrong with him and most of them life-threatening, but not necessarily as immediate and irrevocable as drawing two razor-sharp knives across either side of his neck! It was a compromise. Not a great compromise, I grant you, but it was the best I could do!

Rusty sprang up, hung a sharp right, and kept going, paws still digging in as he accelerated into the darkness. He would circle around to do what he could for Cameron, but I was the one who had to save his life. Rusty might keep him alive long enough for me to do it.

Alden was dumbfounded for all of a tenth of a second. I shot his hostage. I *shot* his *hostage*! What kind of maniac shoots the hostage!? Then he switched mental tracks. If the hostage was down, he was in mortal danger of being the next person shot. He raised his hands, crossing his forearms, making fists. Forces swirled around him, but nothing came at me.

I centered my sights on his chest and tried to shoot him. I put four rounds into his chest—or I would have. I missed every single time.

Alden laughed, glaring at me between his fists.

"Did you think I never examined these artifacts?" he mocked. "I am not fully their master, but did you think I failed to divine *any* of the functions? I am not so much a fool as to trust to your sentiment—and rightly so, since you slew your precious human."

To myself, I admitted I might have made a mistake. Sure, I knew he had stolen magical knowledge from lesser practitioners, but I never really got a bead on how much of a wizard he was. I didn't even think about what he might have learned from Pop's gear. In truth, I doubted he learned much. How to turn different functions on and off, perhaps. What some of the functions did—although some were surely beyond his comprehension. He knew enough.

I put my rifle down and moved forward, down one step. The lightning flashed in the sky again and the rain picked up. The wind lashed cold drops against us.

"All right. It really has come down to you and me, hasn't it?"

"It has. Even now, you have no hope of victory." He pushed both hands at me and I felt the psychic forces mounting, pressing on my shields. He wasn't as strong as I remembered, but the last time he tried anything on me, he had tektites amplifying his power. He was stronger than I was, but I had magical devices shielding my mind. What if I devoted all my energies to the attack until my shields started to fail? Could I wear him down enough, pummel him enough, while he wasted his efforts burning through my spells? He couldn't be any more certain about the outcome than I could. We were both risking everything on this one encounter.

Of course, Alden always had faith in his own powers. I wondered if they had ever failed him. Aside from with Pop, of course. Since he had encountered my mind before, he certainly had cause to believe he could defeat me.

Dang it, Pop's devices have psychic shielding, too. If he knows how to turn it on, it's not a fight between us. My psychic powers and my magic against his psychic powers and magic. He might have Pop's unwilling help!

Could I hold him off until the next magical disruption shot went off? Possibly. Then I might shoot him—which raised the question of how he still had a deflection spell at all. Did he manually direct energies into the amulet's deflection function? Probably. Occam's Razor. But, with my proximity to the next detonation, it would affect my own spells, as well. Not as much, but the previous shot had weakened them and they were presently under Alden's powerful assault. At least my weather spell wasn't local. All I had on me of the weather control was the settings, and I built those to take a pounding. They weren't fundamental to my plan, but, for sentimental reasons, they were my first option.

Pop's the weather control guru. He can put a tornado where he wants it and tell it to stay. I have to put in the work to get the weather I want—so I put in the work.

I decided not to have this fight. Alden was handicapped, but still older and stronger in the psychic department. I didn't need to prove anything. I didn't lure him onto my home turf to play games by his rules. I didn't want to play by rules at all. When it came right down to it, I didn't even come here to play fair.

I clapped my hands and reached upward, letting him assault my shields. They would hold for a while—probably long enough. I already used Pop's paranoia and lack of compunctions to prepare a two-stage surprise.

Alden saw me doing something magical. When all the hair on his body stood up, he knew what was about to happen. His psychic assault vanished instantly as he changed his focus, raised his hands, and redirected all his forces. A dome of power flickered into being, forming a nearly-visible barrier.

The whole sky lit up as though Zeus didn't like him. The bolt descended like, well, lightning, jagged and crackling and bright.

Alden wasn't some primitive. He understood at least the basics about electricity. The lightning should have hit him in the head and fused the ground he stood on into glassy footprints, cooking everything in between. Instead, it splashed, shattering into a dozen smaller rivulets of light, conducted along the outside of his sphere of forces, passing harmlessly around him. The broken lightning grounded out in the yard.

The explosive net Pop wove into the front lawn went off with one hell of a bang. About eight thousand meters per second of fiery kaboom, give or take. I don't know how much det cord Pop ultimately put underground, but his intent was to eliminate a mob of pitchfork-wielding villagers.

I'll say this for Pop. He's a top-notch do-it-yourselfer. When he sets up defenses, he doesn't fool around. He's the one who taught me how to set up a claymore mine.

The lawn blasted skyward, taking dirt, grass, and chunky zombie salsa mix. The explosive flash and blast merged with the storm, almost indistinguishable from the lightning and thunder. If Alden screamed, I didn't hear it.

Hot damn. It worked.

Wet earth settled, steaming and splattering and smoking. What little dust there was washed out of the air quickly. Now that I wouldn't need it, I tossed aside the radio detonator. I drew my knife and squelched out through the muddy, bloody dirt to examine the remains.

Alden was still alive. His feet were gone and he was bleeding badly from what remained of his legs. Pink foam flecked his lips and his eyes were bloodshot. The rest of him was untouched—deflection spells work on shrapnel, too—but the shockwave threw him into the air and hammered him like a truck. He landed hard. Deflection spells don't work against concussion effects and falls.

I kicked him in the head to keep him stunned. I probably didn't need to, but I was through taking chances. I grabbed one of his hands. My knife made short work of mere flesh and bone. I cut the ring from his hand and claimed it as an heirloom of my house, for it was precious to me, even if it was only for sentimental value. Considering he took a chisel to Pop's fingers to steal stuff in the first place, it seemed fair. Then I pulled the amulet off, yanking it up over his head. That, too, belonged to my family.

"Dead, yet?" I asked. Alden's eyes rolled in their sockets and he coughed up more pink foam. "I guess not. Working on it, though."

He mouthed something, but no sound came out.

"You know," I told him, kneeling beside him in the chewed-up earth, "I've never killed anyone in cold blood before. I've never set out to murder someone, had them at my mercy, and followed through on it. But you! Someone convinced me I had to kill you—that I should kill you and needed to. I probably still do." I laid my knife on his chest, point touching the soft place under his chin, and leaned down to whisper in his ear.

"But now I *want* to."

Alden's mouth worked. He tried to speak, coughed again. I sat up and put my knife through the shoulder of his less-damaged arm, making sure he wasn't about to do anything surprising. He screamed and hacked up blood rather than pinkish foam.

"What..." he rasped, pawing at my shirt with his four-fingered hand, trying to grasp it, leaving bloody smears.

"Go on. I'm listening," I told him, holding his wrist.

"What power... is this? That you can... do this... to me?" he gasped, trailing off.

I looked down at him as he bled, dying in the mud, speckled by blood and rain, and the answer came to me like a bolt of lightning.

"I am my father's daughter."

I did my best to nail his head to the ground.

Bright fire sprang up from the wound, blazing white and gold, racing up my arm, tracing lines of heat and light like a nervous system aflame all through me. My body was strangely untouched. My hand didn't hurt. My skin didn't blister. Yet there was a part of me, deep inside, that felt the power escaping as I sundered his flesh. Once freed, it could not remain, and like lightning it grounded out into everything, everywhere, including me. I reveled in his death as his spirit faded into nothing, dissolved into the earth and air, water and fire, gone, gone, gone.

With that release, I let go of my restraint. He was dead and I wanted him dead. More dead, as if it was possible. I hit him again, stabbing through his heart. And again, because something inside me still needed to kill him. And again and again, as I finally let myself punish him as he deserved, for everything he ever did to Pop, to Gus, to Cameron, to me...

The rain kept coming down, washing away the mud and the blood, and I didn't care. I knelt in the sodden earth next to the ruined body and nobody could tell if I wept, not even me.

Distantly, I heard Rusty shouting my name. Alden was dead. If I didn't want Cameron to die, I couldn't let go, I couldn't relax. Not yet. I didn't want to get up. I didn't want to move. There was too much to do and I was so tired... but, damn it all, there *was* so much to do...

I heaved myself to my feet to slog and stagger through the swampy remains of what was once the lawn.

"He's alive," Rusty reported. "I didn't know what to do for him, so I put my necklace on him. I figured the healing spells couldn't hurt."

"Very clever. Smart. Good work, Rusty."

"Thanks. What do we do for him now?"

"Help me lay him in the bed of the truck. You drive. Roll slowly and carefully around the disaster area while I work on stabilizing him. Then we'll get him inside."

Rusty and I picked him up. Rusty did the heavy lifting and I kept Cameron's head straight and level, immobilizing his neck. While Rusty fired up the truck and rolled slowly, gently around to the porch, I worked a couple of auxiliary spells. Cameron needed the blood leaking into his lungs to be inside his veins. He needed the cerebrospinal fluid to get back inside his brain and spine and, most important, to stop leaking out. He needed other stuff to stay out of the cerebrospinal fluid. There are so many different fluids in a person and they all need to stick pretty strictly to their own areas! He also needed to have something to make sure his breathing was regular and his heartbeat steady. A lot of neurological wiring went to hell and none of it could be trusted.

I realized, belatedly, that I could have hit him substantially lower down. The shockwave through the fluid in the spinal column was like being kicked in the head. Paralyzed or not, he would have been out like a candle in a river.

Live and learn. Hopefully, I was learning fast enough to let Cameron live.

Rusty stopped the truck, parked it, set the brake, and killed the engine. He went inside and fetched out a blanket. We carefully slid it under Cameron and used it as a stretcher, shuffling slowly along so as to disturb him as little as possible.

Inside, I laid him out and did more bone-welding. The nerve fibers would take spells of considerably more sophistication, but you fix what you can reach, so to speak.

At least I remembered to shut down the Alden-bombardment launcher. It didn't matter if it fired or not; there was nothing for it to hit anymore. The shots would rocket away into the distance and eventually waste away to nothing. The power, however, could be much more profitably used in Cameron's restorative spells.

As a precaution, I worked a mild sleep spell on him. He was in no condition to wake up, but I didn't want him to wake up and start trying to move. Besides, there was a compulsion in there, somewhere, and I wanted to find it before he could act on it.

"How's he doing?"

"I'm busy."

"Sorry."

"Don't go far. I'll need your help for the vitality portion of the spell."

"I don't like the sound of that."

"It's tiring, but not complicated."

"Tiring?"

"Yes. Go eat something. A lot of something. And bring me a lot of it, whatever it is."

"You got it, bossy lady."

Journal Entry #57

I worked on Cameron for sixteen hours.

After all my magical surgery, intense healing spell work, and the wiring of both Rusty and myself into a vitality-sharing spell, there was good news. Cameron breathed on his own. His heart regained a regular sinus rhythm. He had no blood in his lungs and had enough in his veins to live on. Best of all, his body had reclaimed—via spell—or produced enough cerebrospinal fluid to be useful.

He rested comfortably. I was glad. I was also bloody damn tired. I took a nap. When I woke up from my too-brief nap, I checked my patient. Cameron was still unconscious, held there by my sleep spell. Rusty had strapped him down to the bed, just in case. Not a bad idea. I should have thought of it.

Rusty was still asleep, curled up in wolf form. Cameron was on Rusty's bed, so that made sense. I opened and nuked several things for breakfast while the coffee boiled. I should have brought in an espresso machine.

Rusty had the good sense to shift back into human form before asking about breakfast. I don't think I could have taken it if he'd sat there and looked at me expectantly.

I miss Gus and it hurts. A lot of things hurt right now.

We ate, not well but a lot. Cameron was still tied in to us, drawing on our vitality to help repair things I'd welded together. We were supplementing his own vitality, as well as the artificial stuff. Pop taught me a spell for converting magical energy into vitality, but it's not a good conversion ratio. I had most of the panels doing what they could for him. The rest were keeping the most subtle and thorough of the healing spells I knew running at full tilt.

"How's the patient?" Rusty asked, still chewing.

"Better. I'm going to have to wake him up soon, though."

"Oh?"

"He needs to eat."

"Ah. Want me to get more duct tape?"

"No, he's restrained enough. I have to rest for a while, out of the vitality loop, then I'll go inside his head and see if I can find whatever Alden did to him. If nothing else, I should be able to lock him down inside his head. I ought to be able to drive him like a car and use his body well enough to eat. Or maybe I'll put everything through a sausage grinder and stuff the paste down his throat." I rubbed my face with both hands and sighed. "Or I'll get out of the vitality circuit and have a better idea when I'm not so damn tired."

"Yeah. Okay. Anything special I should know or do?"

"Don't let him hurt himself."

"I'll do my best. Want me to put my necklace back on him?"

"I've got much more specific spells running, but thanks for offering."

"Anytime."

I disconnected from the vitality-sharing and used a spell to sleep. I needed to be rested for the psychic work.

Journal Entry #58

I swam through the shifting vistas of Cameron's mind. There were signs of the original damage Alden inflicted, like thin scars. There were still signs of Pop's stitching, too, where Cameron needed torn places held together. A thousand memories flashed by like a school of bright fish, changing color as they whirled. Thoughts flowed, slow and sluggish, like gentle currents in his sleeping mind.

It was all wrong.

I dove deeper, exploring, trying to find what it was that didn't ring true. All of this was Cameron, but it wasn't all of Cameron. There were memories I recognized and memories I didn't. There was more to him than what I could find. Things were missing.

Down deep, in the darker places, where the light of consciousness seldom touched, there were the bombs. The mines. The traps and the triggers and the charges. That's where the missing pieces would be hidden—the bits of Cameron that had to be put away, put aside, so there would be a clear path from trigger to action.

Alden had planted a compulsion. I had no doubts. It was the sort of thing he would do. I can't find it without digging through a pile of unstable subconscious munitions, but, logically and emotionally, I know it's there.

If he told the truth, it would decay over time into an impulse, then an intrusive thought, then finally dissolve entirely. But the most effective way of lying is to conceal a lie between truths. Would the buried, booby-trapped compulsion fade? Or would it lurk, waiting for a stimulus? Was there also a long-term compulsion, sort of an insurance policy of vengeance beyond the grave? Maybe a suicidal impulse, but maybe something more subtle—a seed of something to flower into antagonism, even hatred? Or maybe an erasure of a piece of personality to make him boring, possibly even repulsive?

If I tell Cameron Alden is dead, will it trigger the compulsion to suicide? Once I see it operating, I'm fairly sure I can remove the trigger. It has to be visible when it's engaged. Which raises the question of how many triggers it has. Does it go off every time someone new tells him Alden is dead? Does it happen after a fixed amount of time? Does he get random thoughts about Alden and ask where he is?

Worse than the compulsion, the subconscious bombs. Their exact contents were impossible to determine. I was afraid to even examine them closely. Their triggering mechanisms were thoughts, types of thoughts, maybe even things he could see or hear or simply know. Buried down here in the mud at the lower depths, they might never affect him, like the munitions of a sunken ship might never go off. But if they did, it would be like bombs in a basement. The structure above would be destroyed. Or, if not quite enough to destroy the structure, it would still be badly damaged as its foundations were pummeled.

I wished Alden was still alive to interrogate. Or alive so I could kill him again.

When I released Cameron's head and sat back, Rusty handed me the water bottle. I drank half of it and pressed the cold bottle to my neck.

"What's the word?"

"The word is 'dammit'."

"I think that's two words."

"When *I* use a word, it means what I choose it to mean. And the word is still 'dammit.' Get over it."

"Got. Is he gonna live?"

"For a while. Alden didn't lie, exactly. He left out a lot of details."

"Complicated ones?"

"Yes."

"Then don't bother telling me. Kid's got a condition. Okay. How do we fix it?"

"I'm not sure I can. The physical damage, yes. I can fix that. He'll be back in shape in a week—two weeks, tops. But I'm not a bomb-disposal expert, and that's what I'm dealing with in the basement of Cameron's mind. If I go poking around in there, I *know* Alden has set it up with booby-traps. It's like reaching into a box, blindfolded, trying not to trigger any of the mousetraps, electric eyes, or the bobcat."

Rusty thought about it for a minute while I drank the rest of my water.

"Did Alden have any reason to want Cameron?" Rusty asked.

"How do you mean?"

"Was Cameron going to be useful to him? Or was Cameron completely expendable as long as he got you?"

"I'm pretty sure Alden thought of him as expendable. Why?"

"Crap. I thought everything you can arm, you can disarm, provided you do it right. Then I thought about exceptions. It's possible to make a bomb that arms when you close the door, or the drawer, or whatever, and goes off when you open it. This is great as a trap, but it's not good if you ever want to get into the box again."

"Maybe there is a way," I sighed. "I've barely begun to map out what's lying in wait down there. What little I've seen so far doesn't fill me with hope. Alden was stronger than me and obviously more skilled."

"Do you know anybody who's a better expert than you?"

"Yes. Pop. He's unavailable, though."

"So we take him to your uncle?"

"Yes. I'm not so proud I won't ask for help, even if I don't need an actual miracle."

"Good to know."

"There is one thing I need to finish, though."

"What's that?"

"Bring what's left of Alden. I don't care what Uncle Dusty says. We're burning what's left of him. I want to be sure."

"I'll get the wheelbarrow."

I wheeled Cameron's gurney along the hallway. Rusty, gallant soul that he is, opened doors for me. The office areas of a powerplant are not hospital halls with swinging doors. Some of them also have the pneumatic auto-closing thing. They're all narrower, too, so you have to maneuver.

We set Cameron up in the break room. Seemed logical. There we had running water, tile floors, nothing vital to the powerplant, and—once the tables were scooted aside—plenty of room.

Uncle Dusty, of course, knew it the moment we arrived. I knew he knew it, and he knew I wanted him. Rather than discuss it mentally, he sent his avatar after us.

What does he do with his body all day long? Farm? Dynamo maintenance? Work with the new power-panel wand? Or does it stand around, staring blankly, like a game avatar when no one is holding the controller?

I think the last option is kind of creepy. Maybe I don't want to know.

Rusty double-checked the straps holding Cameron to the gurney. I didn't think he was going anywhere, but Rusty doesn't trust potential zombies. He's been in enough close combat with them to respect their strength.

Uncle Dusty let himself into the break room.

"I heard you calling for Me even before you arrived. Cameron?"

"Cameron," I agreed. "Here's the poop." I explained the circumstances and what I found planted in Cameron's mind. Uncle Dusty nodded as I spoke, listening with his avatar. I think he was also looking inside Cameron's head, but I couldn't be sure. The whole place was alive with his energies, so multiple attention streams wouldn't be obvious.

"And you say you killed Alden. He's dead, no question, and unavailable for comment?"

"He's so dead even Pop wouldn't be interested."

"That's pretty dead," he agreed. "Cameron's got a lot of interesting architecture wired in there. Taking it out isn't going to be easy."

"But... but we're *here*," I protested. "We're in your place of power. There's no cross-universe power transmission difficulty!"

"Perhaps I was inexact. The power requirements won't be exceptional—although, if you don't mind, I'd like your help in stepping up the production in this particular reactor world. I've been elsewhere while you've been mooching off this one. Linked to Shasta, it's had to be at the head of the line for time differential purposes."

"Of course."

"Like I said, it won't take more power than I can afford. It's a complicated piece of psychic engineering and will require considerable thought. It will require something more precious than power. It will require focus and attention."

He grinned at me, flashing perfect teeth.

"Don't look so glum!" he told me. "It's not as bad as all that."

"So, you can fix him?"

"I don't know. It depends on what you mean by 'fix,' and it depends on exactly what Alden did to him. It may be possible to restore him perfectly. On the other hand, it may not. We won't know until I disarm the mess in there."

"But you can disarm the mess?"

"Probably. It'll take time. I can't go in and rip it all out without ripping out large chunks of Cameron, too. I presume that's unacceptable."

"I should think so!"

"So do I. So I have to carefully probe the psychic structures and figure out how to remove, short, or bypass each of the ways it connects to his mind. At first blush, it appears Alden used a sort of organic algorithm to *grow* these problems—excuse me, 'security features'—in Cameron's mind, rather than go in and install them all by hand, as it were. My first priority will be to make sure it isn't still spreading."

"Could it be?"

"Yes, but only slowly. I didn't see it growing, but it might know to hold still while under observation."

"I didn't know such a thing could be done."

"There's a lot you learn by the time you're My age. I've been around the block more times than I can count."

"All right. What do you need from me?"

"Funny you should ask," he grinned. "Most people don't get miracles on demand. You're family, so I'll make an exception. Since you ask, though, I definitely could use your help with a few things."

"Name it."

"We need to set up a better infirmary—a hospital room for Cameron. He's not going anywhere for a while. I'll need you to enchant hospital equipment, too. I'm not going to change his diaper or the sheets. That sort of thing."

"Consider it done."

"Once we have Cameron set up for his convalescence, I'll need you to go out and do other things, too. To achieve the focus and delicacy I want, I'll need my avatar here, focused on Cameron. This means I need you to do the traveling."

"Where do I go? What do I do?"

"There are any number of things needing doing," he said. "One of them is finding your father."

"I thought he didn't want to be found."

"True," Uncle Dusty agreed, "but there's more to it. I'm supposed to alert him when certain things happen—and I can't. Not without knowing how to reach him. For that, I need help. Can I count on you?"

"Absolutely. Now, where can I burn Alden's body?"

"I'll send some robots to gather wood."

Journal Entry #59

It looks as though I'm now in the family business. Gods, avatars, prophets, religion, magic, and all the infinite worlds of If.

I get the feeling I've been suckered, somehow, but I'm at a loss to explain.

Maybe it's part of growing up. I was a child, with childish notions, when I first started my superhero career. I was still a child when I took on the challenge of Alden. Have I grown up? Have I matured? Have I changed?

Now I'm playing in the big leagues. I worry about this. Am I still a child? Am I grown-up enough for this? Or am I just young? I'm the new kid on the block, as it were— but am I no longer a child?

Am I up to this? Am I ready to… what's the word?

I don't know. I just don't know.

On the upside, Uncle Dusty is working on Cameron, sorting out the problems Alden buried in his mind. That's good. He's also letting me use this reactor world as a base of operations for conducting a thorough, methodical search for Pop.

Why am I searching for Pop? Well, there are the Uncle Dusty reasons, and there are my reasons.

Uncle Dusty is afraid of time differentials. Pop has things to do in the world of Rethven. Or, rather, will have things to do. If Uncle Dusty can't shout for him and get him to come back from wherever he went, I gather this will be a Bad Thing.

My reasons are a little less world-shattering. I miss him. I also worry about him. I want to know he's all right and things are going well for him. A postcard would do.

He never did get around to replacing my inter-universal phone. Pop isn't exactly absent-minded, but he does sometimes forget things.

I'm going to have to give this a lot of thought. How do I find a multi-universal vampire wizard when he doesn't want to be found? According to Uncle Dusty, Pop is capturing angels, interrogating, dissecting, and analyzing them. It's an intelligence-gathering process so he can figure out a way to defeat a powerful celestial entity in his favorite world. That was the plan, at any rate. The only trouble is, he didn't remember to tell Uncle Dusty exactly where he was going to do all this.

I love my Pop. The doofus.

It makes sense, though, that he doesn't want to be found. He's got to not only hide himself, but hide his angelic victim, too. If other angels hear one screaming, he's going to have problems. So he has to have a bunker buried somewhere.

We'll find him. Sooner or later.

So we're going to search. Uncle Dusty's non-corporeal manifestations can sniff around for traces of Pop's activities. I can use gates to search for more physical signs of Pop's presence. Between us, we'll eventually pick up enough clues to find him.

"Eventually" could be a long time.

I miss him.